The Glassblower
of Murano

Marina Fiorato

St. Martin's Griffin   New York

THE GLASSBLOWER OF MURANO. Copyright © 2008 by Marina Fiorato. All rights reserved. Printed in the United States of America. For information, address St. Martin's Press, 175 Fifth Avenue, New York, N.Y. 10010.

www.stmartins.com

The Library of Congress has cataloged the first trade paperback edition as follows:

Fiorato, Marina.
    The glassblower of Murano / Marina Fiorato. – 1st U.S. ed.
        p.cm.
    ISBN 978-0-312-38698-6
    1. Glassworkers–Italy–Fiction.   2. Glass blowing and working–
Fiction.   3. Trade secrets–Fiction.   4. Venice (Italy)–Fiction.   I. Title.
    PR6106.I67G63 2009
    823'.92–dc22

                                                                2009002564

First published in Great Britain by Beautiful Books Limited

ISBN 978-1-250-00050-7 (trade paperback)

Second St. Martin's Griffin Edition: May 2011

10 9 8 7 6 5 4 3 2 1

For Conrad, Ruby and, most of all, Sacha;
you are all in this book somewhere.

CHAPTER 1

The Book

As Corradino Manin looked on the lights of San Marco for the last time, Venice from the lagoon seemed to him a golden constellation in the dark blue velvet dusk. How many of those windowpanes, that adorned his city like costly gems, had he made with his own hands? Now they were stars lit to guide him at the end of the journey of his life. Guide him home at last.

As the boat drew into San Zaccaria he thought not – for once – of how he would interpret the vista in glass with a *pulegoso* of leaf gold and hot lapis, but instead that he would never see this beloved sight again. He stood in the prow of the boat, a brine-flecked figurehead, and looked left to Santa Maria della Salute, straining to see the white-domed bulk looming in its newness from the dark. The foundations of the great church had been laid in 1631, the year of Corradino's birth, to thank the Virgin for delivering the city from the Plague. His childhood and adulthood had kept pace with the growing edifice. Now it was complete, in 1681, the year of his death. He had never seen its full splendour in daylight, and now never would. He heard a *traghetto* man mournfully calling for passenger trade as he traversed the Canal Grande. His black boat recalled a funeral gondola. Corradino shivered.

He considered whether he should remove his white *bauta* mask as soon as his feet touched the shore; a poetic moment – a grand gesture on his return to the *Serenissima*.

No, there is one more thing I must do before they find me.

He closed his black cloak over his shoulders against the darkling mists and made his way across the Piazzetta under cover of his tricorn and *bauta*. The traditional *tabarro* costume, black from head to foot save the white mask, should make him anonymous enough to buy the time he needed. The *bauta* itself, a spectral slab of a mask shaped like a gravedigger's shovel, had the short nose and long chin which would eerily alter his voice if he should speak. Little wonder, he thought, that the mask borrowed its name from the '*baubau*', the 'bad beast' which parents invoked to terrify their errant children.

From habit borne of superstition Corradino moved swiftly through the two columns of San Marco and the San Teodoro that rose, white and symmetrical, into the dark. The Saint and the chimera that topped their pediments were lost in the blackness. It was bad luck to linger there, as criminals were executed between the pillars – hung from above or buried alive below. Corradino made the sign of the cross, caught himself, and smiled. What more bad luck could befall him? And yet his step still quickened.

There is one misfortune that could yet undo me: to be prevented from completing my final task.

As he entered the Piazza San Marco he noted that all that was familiar and beloved had taken on an evil and threatening cast. In the bright moon the shadow of the Campanile was a dark knife slashing across the square. Roosting pigeons flew like malevolent phantoms in his face. Regiments of dark arches had the square surrounded – who lurked in their shadows? The great doors of the Basilica were open; Corradino saw the gleam of candles from the golden belly of the church. He was briefly cheered – an island of brightness in this threatening landscape.

Perhaps it is not too late to enter this house of God, throw myself on the mercy of the priests and seek sanctuary?

But those who sought him also paid for this jewelled shrine that housed the bones of Venice's shrivelled Saint, and tiled the walls with the priceless glittering mosaics that now sent the candlelight out into the night. There could be no sanctuary within for Corradino. No mercy.

Past the Basilica then and under the arch of the Torre

dell'Orologio he hurried, allowing himself one more glance at the face of the huge clock, where tonight it seemed the fantastical beasts of the zodiac revolved in a more solemn measure. A dance of death. Thereafter Corradino tortured himself no more with final glances, but fixed his eyes on the paving underfoot. Even this gave him no respite, for all he could think of was the beautiful *tessere* glasswork he used to make; fusing hot nuggets of irregular glass together, all shapes and hues, before blowing the whole into a wondrous vessel delicate and colourful as a butterfly's wing.

I know I will never touch the glass again.

As he entered the Merceria dell'Orologio the market traders were packing away their pitches for the night. Corradino passed a glass-seller, with his wares ranked jewel-like on his stall. In his mind's eye the goblets and trinkets began to glow rosily and their shapes began to shift – he could almost feel the heat of the furnace again, and smell the sulphur and silica. Since childhood such sights and smells had always reassured him. Now the memory seemed a premonition of hellfires. For was hell not where traitors were placed? The Florentine, Dante, was clear on the subject. Would Corradino – like Brutus and Cassius and Judas – be devoured by Lucifer, the Devil's tears mingling with his blood as he was ripped asunder? Or perhaps, like the traitors that had betrayed their families, he would be encased for all eternity in '... *un lago che per gelo avea di vetro e non d'acqua sembiante* ... a lake that, frozen fast, had lost the look of water and seemed glass.' Corradino recalled the words of the poet and almost smiled. Yes, a fitting punishment – glass had been his life, why not his death also?

Not if I do this last thing. Not if I am granted absolution.

With a new urgency he doubled back as he had planned and took the narrow bridges and winding alleys or *calles* that led back to the Riva degli Schiavoni. Here and there shrines were set into the corners of the houses – welltended flames burned and illumined the face of the Virgin.

I dare not look in her eyes, not yet.

At last the lights of the Orphanage at the Ospedale della Pietà drew near and as he saw the candlelight warmth he heard too the music of the viols.

Perhaps it is she that plays – I wish it were so – but I will never know.

He passed the grille without a glance inside and banged on the door. As the maid approached with a candle he did not wait for her inquisition before hissing: 'Padre Tommaso – *subito!*' He knew the maid – a surly, taciturn wench who delighted in being obstructive, but tonight his voice carried such urgency that even she turned at once and soon the priest came.

'*Signore?*'

Corradino opened his cloak and found the leather gourd of French gold. Into the bag he tucked the vellum note-book, so she would know how it had been and one day, perhaps, forgive him. He took a swift glance around the dim alley – no, no-one could have drawn close enough to see him.

They must not know she has the book.

In a voice too low for any but the priest to hear he said: '*Padre*, I give you this money for the care of the orphans of the Pietà.' The mask changed Corradino's voice as he had intended. The priest made as if to take the bag with the usual formula of thanks, but Corradino held it back until the father was forced to meet his eyes. Father Tommaso alone must know him for who he was. 'For the orphans,' said Corradino again, with emphasis.

Recognition reached the priest at last. He turned over the hand that held the bag and looked closely at the fin-gertips – smooth with no prints. He began to speak but the eyes in the mask flashed a warning. Changing his mind the father said, 'I will make sure they receive it,' and then, as if he knew; 'may God bless you.' A warm hand and a cold one clasped for an instant and the door was closed.

Corradino continued on, he knew not where, until he was well away from the Orphanage.

Then, finally, he removed his mask.

Shall I walk on till they find me? How will it be done?

At once, he knew where he should go. The night darkened as he passed through the streets, the canals whispering goodbye as they splashed the *calli*, and now at last Corradino could hear footsteps behind keeping pace. At last he reached the Calle della Morte – the street of death – and stopped. The footsteps stopped too. Corradino faced the water and, without turning, said 'Will Leonora be safe?'

The pause seemed interminable – splash, splash – then a voice as dry as dust replied.

'Yes. You have the word of The Ten.'

Corradino breathed relief and waited for the final act.

As the knife entered his back he felt the pain a moment after the recognition had already made him smile. The subtlety, the clarity with which the blade insinuated itself between his ribs could only mean one thing. He started to laugh. Here was the poetry, the irony he had searched for on the dock. What an idiot, romanticizing himself, supposing himself a hero in the drama and pathos of his final sacrifice. All the time it was *they* who had planned the final act with such a sense of theatre, of what was fitting, an amusing *Carnevale* exit. A Venetian exit. They had used a glass dagger – Murano glass.

Most likely one of my own making.

He laughed harder with the last of his breath. He felt the assassin's final twist of the blade to snap handle from haft, felt his skin close behind the blade to leave no more than an innocent graze at the point of entry. Corradino pitched forward into the water and just before he broke the surface he met his own eyes in his reflection for the first and last time in his life. He saw a fool laughing at his own death. As he submerged in the freezing depths, the water closed behind his body to leave no more than an innocent graze at the point of entry.

CHAPTER 2

Belmont

Nora Manin woke at 4am exactly. She was not surprised, but blinked sleepily as the digital numbers of her bedside clock blinked back. She had woken at this time every night since Stephen left.

Sometimes she read, sometimes she made a drink and watched TV, numbing her mind with the inane programming for insomniacs. But tonight was different – tonight she knew there was no point even trying to get back to sleep. Because tomorrow – today – she was leaving for Venice and a new life, as the old one was over.

The digital clock and the bed were all that remained in the room that didn't wait in a box or a bag. Nora's life had been neatly packed and was destined for storage or ... or what? She rose with a groan and padded to the bathroom. Clicked on the fluorescent strip that blinked into life over the basin mirror. She splashed her face and then studied it in the glass, looking for resolve in her reflection, finding only fear. Nora pressed both hands to the place on her front between her ribs and stomach where her sadness seemed to reside. Stephen would no doubt have some medical term for it – something long and Latin. 'It wearies me,' she said aloud to her reflection.

It did. She was tired of being sad. Tired of being bright and breezy to those friends that knew Stephen's defection had left her shattered. Tired of the mundane workload of dividing what they had bought together. She remembered the excitement with which they had found and bought this house, in the first days of marriage, when Stephen had got his post at the Royal Free Hospital. She thought that Hampstead seemed impossibly grand for a teacher of glass and ceramics. 'Not when they marry surgeons,' her mother had dryly said. The house even had a name – Belmont. Nora was not accustomed to houses so grand that they deserved their own names. This one sat, appropriately, on the beautiful hill that led to Hampstead village. A model of pleasing Georgian architecture, square, white and symmetrical. They had loved the place instantly, made an offer and had, for a time, been happy. Nora supposed she should be glad. At least the money from Belmont had provided her with security. Security – she smiled wryly at the word.

I have never felt less secure. I am vulnerable now. It is cold outside of a marriage.

For the thousandth time she began to take an inventory of her reflection, looking for clues as to why Stephen had left. 'Item – two eyes, wide and indifferent green. Item – hair; blonde, long, straw-coloured. Item – skin; olive. Item – two lips; chapped with the perpetual chewing of self doubt.' She stopped. For one thing she was no Shakespearean widow, despite the fact that she felt bereaved. And for another, it gave her no comfort to know that she was younger and blonder and, yes, prettier than Stephen's mistress. He had fallen for a forty-year-old brunette hospital administrator who wore severe suits. Carol. Her antithesis. She knew that Carol wouldn't sleep in an ancient Brooklyn Dodgers t-shirt and a scruffy plait.

'He used to call me his Primavera,' Nora told her reflection. She remembered when she and Stephen had seen the Botticelli painting in Florence on their honeymoon. They were both taken by the figure of Spring in her flowing white gown sprigged with flowers, smiling her slight, hermetic smile, beautiful and full of promise. With her burnished blonde ropes of hair and her leaf-green hooded eyes she bore a startling resemblance to Nora. Stephen had stood her by the painting and taken down her hair while she blushed and squirmed. She remembered the Italians calling '*bellissima*', while the Japanese took photographs. Stephen had kissed her and put a hand on her stomach. 'You'll look even more like her when . . .'

It had been the first year they had been trying for a baby. They were full of optimism. They were both in their early thirties, both healthy – she was a runner and Stephen a gym fanatic – and their only vice was quantities of red wine, which they virtuously reduced. But a year went by and eventually they visited a colleague of Stephen's at the Royal Free, a round and cheerful aristocrat with a bow tie. Interminable tests later, nothing was found. 'Unspecific infertility'.

'You may as well try blue smarties, they'll work as well as anything,' said the colleague, flippantly. Nora had cried. She had not fulfilled the fruitful promise of the *Primavera*.

I wanted something to be found – something that could be fixed.

They put themselves through a number of invasive, intrusive and unsuccessful procedures. Procedures denoted by acronyms that had nothing to do with love or nature, or the miracles that Nora associated with conception. HSG, FSH, IVF. They became obsessed. They took their eyes off their marriage, and when they looked back, it was gone. By the time Nora entered her third cycle of IVF both knew, but neither admitted, that there was not enough love left between them to spare for a third party.

It was around this time that a well-meaning friend had begun to drop hints that she had seen Stephen in a Hampstead bar with a woman. Jane had been very nonchalant about the information – she had not been damning, as if to say; 'I'm just telling you this in case you don't know. It may be innocent. I will say nothing which you cannot ignore with impunity, if you choose to. Nothing from which you cannot draw back. Nothing is lost. Only be aware.'

But Nora was consumed by the insecurity of her infertility and challenged Stephen. She expected denial, or admission of guilt and pleas for forgiveness. She got neither. The situation backfired on her horribly. Stephen admitted full culpability and, in his misplaced conceit of honourable behavior, offered to move out and then did. Six months later she learned from him that Carol was pregnant. And that was when Nora decided to move to Venice.

I *am the cliché after all. Stephen is not. He left a young blonde woman for an older brunette. A jeans-wearing artist for a bean-counter in a suit. I on the other hand, instantly enter a mid-life crisis and decide on a whim to leave for the city of my ancestors and start again, like some bad TV drama.*

She turned away from the mirror and looked at her packing, wondering for the millionth time if she was doing the right thing.

But I can't stay here. I can't be always running into Stephen, or her, or the child.

It had happened, with astonishing bad luck, on a fairly

regular basis, despite Nora's attempts to scrupulously avoid the environs of the hospital. Once she met them on the Heath, of all places – all that square mileage and she had met them while running. It occurred to her to keep going, and had she not been attempting civility with Stephen over the division of Belmont, she would have. Stephen and Carol were hand in hand, wearing similar leisure clothes, looking happy and rested. Carol's pregnancy was clearly evident. Nora was bathed in sweat and confusion. After a stilted exchange about the weather and the house contracts, Nora ran on and cried all the way home, tears streaming into her ears. Yet Stephen had been more than generous – he had all but given her the house. He has acted well throughout, thought Nora.

He is no pantomime villain. I can't demonize him, I can't even hate him. Damn him.

The house sale had given her freedom. She could now embark on her adventure, or her mistake. She had told no-one what she planned, not even her mother Elinor. Especially not her mother. Her mother had no love for Venice.

Elinor Manin was an academic who specialized in Renaissance Art. In the seventies she had gone on a tutor exchange from King's College London with her opposite number in Ca' Foscari at the University of Venice. While there she had rejected the advances of the earnest baby professors from Oxford and Cambridge and fallen instead for Bruno Manin, simply because he looked like he had stepped from a painting.

Elinor had seen him every day on the Linea 52 *vaporetto* which took her from the Lido where she lived to the university. He worked on the boat – opening and closing the gate, tying and untying the boat at each *fermata* stop. Bruno twisted the heavy ropes between his long fingers and leapt from the boat to shore and back again with a curious catlike grace and skill. She studied his face, his aquiline nose, his trim beard, his curling black hair, and tried to identify the painting he had come from. Was it a Titian or a Tiepolo? A Bellini? Which Bellini? As Elinor looked from his profile to the impossibly beautiful *palazzi* of the Canal Grande, she was suddenly on fire with enthusiasm for this culture where the houses and the people kept their genetic essence so pure for millennia that they looked the same now as in the Renaissance. This fire that she felt, this continuity and rightness, did not leave her when Bruno noticed her glances and asked her for a drink. It did not leave her when he took her back to his shared house in Dorsoduro and bedded her. It did not even leave her when she found that she was pregnant.

They married in haste and decided to call the baby Corrado if it was a boy and Leonora if it was a girl, after Bruno's parents. As they lay in bed with the waters of the canal casting an undulating crystal mesh onto the ceiling,

Bruno told her of his ancestor, the famous *maestro* of glass-blowers, Corrado Manin, known as Corradino. Bruno told Elinor that Corradino was the best glass-maker in the world, and gave her a glass heart made by the *maestro's* own hand. It was all incredibly romantic. They were happy. Elinor made the heart reflect the light on to the ceiling, while Bruno lay with his hand on her belly. Here inside her, thought Elinor, was that fire, that continuity, that eternal flame of the Venetian genome. But the feeling faded as the modern world broke into theirs. Elinor's parents, not sur-prisingly, felt none of the respect for Bruno's profession that the Venetians feel for their boatmen. Nor were they impressed by his refusal to leave Venice and move to London.

For Elinor too, this was a shock. Her reverie ended abruptly, she was back in London in the seventies with a small daughter, and a promise from Bruno to write and visit. Baby Leonora spent her first months with her grand-parents or at the University crèche. When Bruno did not write Elinor was hurt but not surprised. Her pride stopped her from getting in touch with him. She made a gesture of retaliation by anglicizing her daughter's name to Nora. She began to appreciate feminist ideas and spent a great deal of time at single mother's groups rubbishing Bruno and men in general. At the Christmas of Nora's first year, Elinor received a Christmas card from an Italian friend from Ca' Foscari. *Dottore* Padovani had been a colleague in her department, a middle-aged man of intelligence and biting humour, not one given to patronage or sympathy. But Elinor detected a note of sympathy in his Christmas greetings. She rang as soon as the Christmas vacation was over to demand why he thought that just because a woman was a single parent she deserved to be pitied. He told her gently that Bruno had died of a heart attack not long after she had left – he assumed that she had heard. Bruno had died at work, and Elinor pictured him as she had first seen him, but now clutching his chest and pitching forward into the canal, the city claiming its own. The fire was out. For Elinor her love affair with Venice was over. She continued in her studies but moved her sphere of interest south to Florence, and in the Botticellis and Giottos felt safe that she would not keep seeing Bruno's face.

Nora grew up amongst women. Her mother and grandmother, the women of Elinor's discussion groups; they were her family. She grew up to be taught to develop her own mind and her creativity. She was perpetually warned of the ways of men. Nora was sent to an all-girl school in Islington and showed an aptitude for arts. She was encouraged in her sculpture by Elinor who had dreams of her daughter following in the footsteps of Michelangelo. But Elinor had reckoned without the workings of fate and the call of Nora's ancestors.

For whilst studying sculpture and ceramics at Wimbledon School of Art Nora met a visiting tutor who had her own glass foundry in Snowdonia. Gaenor Davis was in her sixties and made glass *objets* to sell in London, and she encouraged Nora's interest in glass, and the blower's art. Nora's fascination for the medium grew with the amber-rose bubbles of glass that she blew and her expertise developed during a summer month spent at Gaenor's foundry. With the fanciful, pretentious nature of the naïve student she saw her own self in the glass. This strange material was at once liquid and solid, and had moods and a finite nature, a narrow window in which she would allow herself to be malleable before her nature cooled and her designs were set, until the heat freed her again. Elinor, watching her daughter's specialism become apparent, began to have the uneasy feeling that that continuity, that enduring genome that she had identified in Venice, would not be so easily dismissed and was rising to the surface in her daughter.

But Nora had distractions – she was discovering men. Having been largely ignorant of the male sex for the whole of her childhood and adolescence, she found that she adored them. None of her mother's bitterness had passed to her – she surrounded herself with male friends and cheerfully slept with most of them. After three years of sex and sculpture Nora embarked on a Masters degree in ceramics and glass at Central St Martin's and there began to tire of artistic men. They seemed to her without direction, without conviction, without responsibility. She was ripe for a man like Stephen Carey, and when they met in a Charing Cross bar, her attraction was immediate.

He came from not the arts but the sciences – he was

doctor. He wore a suit. He had a high-powered, well paid job at Charing Cross Hospital. He was handsome, but in a clean-shaven way – no stubble, no ironic seventies t-shirts, no skater clothes. Their courtship was accelerated by similar feeling on Stephen's side – here was a beautiful, free-thinking, artistic girl dressed in a slightly funky fashion, charming him with a world he knew nothing of.

When Nora brought Stephen home to Islington Elinor sighed inwardly. She liked Stephen – with his old-world manners and Cambridge education – but could see what was happening. In her womens' group her friends agreed. Nora was seeking out her father, but what could Elinor do?

Elinor gave her daughter the glass heart that Bruno had given her. She told Nora what she knew of her father's family, of the famous Corradino Manin, in an attempt to give her daughter a sense of paternal identity. But at that time Nora was no more than momentarily interested – her heart was full of Stephen. Nora finished her Masters and was offered a teaching post, Stephen got a surgical residency at the Royal Free, and there was nothing left to do but get married. They did so in a solid conventional fashion in Norfolk, with Stephen's wealthy family running the day. Elinor sat through the ceremony in her new hat and sighed again.

The couple went to Florence for their honeymoon at Elinor's suggestion. Nora was enchanted by Italy, Stephen less so.

Perhaps I should have sensed something wasn't right, even then.

She now remembered that Stephen detested the traffic and tourism of Florence. He resented her speaking to the locals in her hard-learnt but fluent Italian. It was as if he resented her heritage – felt threatened. In the Uffizi he himself braided her hair again after his brief, uncharacteristic moment of romance in front of the Botticelli. He said that her blondeness attracted too much unwanted attention in the street. Yet even with her hair bound she collected admiring glances from the immaculately dressed young men who hunted in designer-suited packs of five or ten, raising their sunglasses and whistling.

It was Stephen, too, who had resisted her suggestion to call herself Leonora again – too fancy, he said, too Mills and Boon. She had kept the name Manin for her work, as she exhibited her glassware in a small way in some London Galleries. Her chequebook and cashcards, however, said Carey.

Nora wondered if Stephen had only accepted Nora Manin because it sounded as if it could be English. Few people identified Manin as an Italian name, with no giveaway vowel at the end.

Is it because Stephen resented my 'Italian-ness' that I am anxious to embrace it so wholeheartedly, now he is gone?

Nora turned from the luggage and searched in her makeup bag for her talisman. Among the mascara wands and bright palettes of colour she found what she was looking for. She held the glass heart in her hand, marvelling at its iridescence. It seemed to capture the light of the bathroom's fluorescent tube and hold it within itself. She threaded a blue hair ribbon through the hole in its crease and tied it round her neck. Over the last horrible months it had become her rosary, her touchstone for all the hopes of the future. She would hold it tight as she cried at those 4am wakings and tell herself if she could only get to Venice, everything would be alright.

The second part of her plan she did not want to think about yet – she had told no-one, and could barely even say it to herself as it sounded such a ridiculous, fanciful notion. 'I am going to Venice to work as a glassblower. It is my birthright.' She spoke to her reflection, aloud, clearly and defiantly. She heard the words, unnaturally loud in the quiet of the small hours, and cringed. But in determination, she clasped the heart tighter and looked again at her reflection. She thought she looked a little more courageous and felt cheered.

CHAPTER 3

Corradino's Heart

There were letters cut into the stone.

The words on the plaque which adorned the Orphanage of the Pietà were thrown into sharp relief by the midday sun. Corradino's fingers scored the grooves of the inscription. He knew well what it said;

'*Fulmine il Signor Iddio maledetione e scomuniche* ... May the Lord God strike with curses and excommunications all those who send or permit their sons and daughters – whether legitimate or natural – to be sent to this hospital of the Pietà, having the means and ability to bring them up.'

Did you read these words, Nunzio dei Vescovi, you old bastard? Seven years ago to this day, when you abandoned your only grandchild here? Did you feel the guilt pressing on your heart?

22

Did you look over your shoulder in fear of the Lord God and the Pope as you slunk home to your palazzo *and your coffers of gold?*

Corradino looked down at the worn step and pictured the newborn girl swaddled there, still slick with birthblood. Birthblood and deathblood, for her mother had died on her childbed. Corradino clenched his fists till the nails bit.

I do not want to think of Angelina.

He turned instead to find peace in the view across the lagoon. He liked to study the water and gauge its mood – today in sunshine the waves resembled his *ghiaccio* work – blown blue glass, several different hues, melted together and plunged in ice to give a finely crackled surface. Corradino had refined the art of *ghiaccio* by floating sulfate of silver on the surface of the iced water. This way the hot glass would accept the metal as it cracked and seal it within when it cooled, giving the impression of sunlit water. The sight of the *laguna* looking exactly thus gave him confidence.

I am a master. No-one can make the glass sing like I do. I am the best glassblower in the world. I hear the water reply; yes, but that is why the French want you *and no-one else.*

He looked across the lagoon to San Giorgio Maggiore, and watched the spice boats pass the unfinished church of Santa Maria della Salute. The rich reds and yellows of the spices and the dark hues of the merchants' skins were framed by the clean white stones of the vast structure. These were all sights that he relished. Gondolas sliced the water and courtesans rode bare-breasted and wanton in their *Carnevale* finery. Corradino admired not their flesh but the silk of their gowns. The colour and form of the falling material as it caught the sun. The rainbow of hues like the inside of an oyster. He watched for a while, enjoying one of his rare moments of freedom from the foundry, from the *fornace*, from Murano. He admired the axe shaped prow of the gondola, with the six branches to denote the six *sestiere* or regions of the city. The city he loved. The city he was leaving tomorrow. He said the names over to himself, rolling the words on his tongue like a poem or a prayer.

Cannaregio, Dorsoduro, Castello, Santa Croce, San Polo and San Marco.

In time the wash of the gondola reached him, slapping gently against the mossy marble of the dock, and brought him to himself. He must not tarry too long.

I have a present for her.

Corradino ducked down the *calle* at the side of the church of Santa Maria della Pietà which adjoined the Orphanage. He peered through the ornamental grille that allowed passersby to see through to the cool darkness within. He could see a group of the orphan girls with their viols and violoncellos, with their sheet music. Seated at the edge he could see her blonde head bobbing as she talked to her friends. He saw, too, the head of Father Tommaso at the front, tonsured by nature, instructing a group that stood ready to sing. Now was his moment.

With his indifferent voice echoing in the *calle*, Corradino began to sing a well known tune used by meat traders or pastry sellers to attract buyers to their wares. The words, however, were changed, so that only one person would know him for who he was, and she, alone, would come to him:

'Leonora *mia*, bo bo bo,

Leonora *mia*, bo bo bo.'

Soon she was there at the grille, her little fingers curled through the ornamental panel to touch his. '*Buon giorno* Leonora.'

'*Buon giorno Signore.*'

'Leonora, I told you that you can call me Papà.'

'*Sì Signore.*'

But she smiled. He loved her sense of humour and the way she had become familiar enough with him to take liberties. He supposed she was growing up – soon she would be a practised *coquette* of marriageable age.

'Did you bring me a present?'

'Well, now, let's see. Perhaps you can tell me how old you are today?'

More little digits pushed through the grille. Five, six, seven. 'Seven.'

'That's right. And haven't I always given you presents on your name day?'

'Always.'

'Well, let's hope I haven't forgotten it.' He made a pantomime of searching through his smock and all his jerkin pockets. At last he reached behind his ear and pulled out the glass heart. With relief he saw his measurements were correct as he pushed the gem easily through the grille and heard Leonora gasp as it fell into her hand. She turned it over on her little palm to admire the captured light.

'Is it magic?' she asked.

'Yes. A special sort. Come closer and I'll explain.'

Leonora pressed her face to the grille. The sun caught the gold motes in her green eyes and Corradino's heart failed him.

There's some beauty in this world I could never recreate.

'*Ascolta*, Leonora. I have to go away for a while. But that heart will tell you that I will always be with you, and when you look at that heart and hold it in your hand you will know how much I love you. Try it now.'

Her fingers closed round the heart, putting out the light.

She closed her eyes. 'Can you feel it?' Corradino asked.

Leonora opened her eyes again and smiled 'Yes,' she said.

'See, I told you it was magic. Now do you have that ribbon I gave you on your last name-day?'

She nodded.

'Well push it through the special hole I made and hang it round your neck. Don't let the Prioress see it, or Father Tommaso, or lend it to the other girls.' She clasped the heart and nodded again.

'Are you going to come back?'

He knew he could not. 'Someday.'

She thought for a moment. 'I'll miss you.'

He suddenly felt that his insides had been gutted, like the fish in the *Pescheria* market. He wished he could tell her of what he had planned – that he would send for her a soon as it was safe. But he dare not trust himself. The less she knew the better.

What she does not know, she cannot not tell; what she cannot tell, cannot not hurt her. And I know too well the poison that is hope, the waiting and the wanting. What if I can never send for her?

So he only said; 'I'll miss you too, Leonora *mia*.'

She pushed her fingers through the grille again in their acknowledged sign. He caught the message and placed each of his printless pads on her tiny finger tips, little finger to little finger, thumb to thumb.

Suddenly the door to the *calle* opened and the tonsured head appeared. 'Corradino, how many times do I have to tell you not to come sniffing round my girls? Is that not how this sorry mess came to pass in the first place? Leonora, return to the orchestra, we are ready to begin.'

With a last glance, Leonora was gone, and Corradino muttered an apology and made as if to leave. But when the priest had gone back inside the church, he stole back down the *calle* and listened as the music began. The sweetness of the harmony, and the soaring counterpoint, bled into his soul. Corradino knew what would happen, but he gave in to it.

For when she holds the glass heart in her hand she holds my own heart there too.

He knew he may never see Leonora again, so this time he leant against the church wall and let the tears flow, as if they would never stop.

CHAPTER 4

Through the Looking Glass

Still the music played.

Nora sat in the church of Santa Maria della Pietà and tried
to think of a word for what she was feeling. Enchanted?
Too reminiscent of old-world courtesies. Bewitched? No;
the word seemed to imply an entrapment by a malign
force.

But no-one has done this to me. I came here of my own voli-
tion.

She glanced left and right, at her unknown companions.
The church was packed – her neighbour, an elegant Italian
matron, sat so close that her red sleeve lay across Nora's
forearm. But Nora did not mind. They were all here for
the same reason, bound together, all – that was it; enrap-
tured – by the music.

Antonio Vivaldi. Nora knew the soundbite version of his life – a red-headed priest, had asthma, taught orphans, wrote the Four Seasons. But he had never really troubled her musical radar until now. She had found him too clichéd for her art-student trendiness – music for lifts and supermarkets, done to death. But here, in the warmth of candlelight, she heard Vivaldi played by live musicians, in the very church where he had written these pieces, first rehearsed them with his orphan girls. The musicians were all young, studious looking Italians, all extremely accomplished, who played with passion as well as technical excellence. They had not pandered to tourist sensibilities by donning period dress – they let the music speak. And here, Nora heard the Four Seasons as if for the first time.

Oh, she knew that the church itself had changed – she knew from her pamphlet guide that the Palladian façade was late eighteenth century, added after the *maestro's* death, but she felt as if the priest were here. She peered into the candling shadows beyond the pillars, where keen locals stood to hear the music, and looked fancifully for his red head amongst them.

When Nora had arrived in Venice she felt unmoored – as if she drifted, loosed from harbour, flowing here and there on the relentless arteries of tourism. Carried by crowds, lost in babel of foreign tongues she was caught in a glut of guttural Germans, or a juvenile crocodile of fluorescent French. Wandering, dazed, through San Marco she had reached the famous frontage of the Libreria Sansoviniana in the *Broglio*. Nora fell through its portals in the manner of one stumbling into Casualty in search of much needed medical attention. She did not want to act like a tourist, and felt a strong resistance to their number. The beauty that she saw everywhere almost made her believe in God; it certainly made her believe in Venice. But the city had physically shocked her to such an extent that she began to feel afraid of it – she needed to find an anchor, to feel that she could belong here as a native. Here in the library she would search for Corradino. Kindly, tangible words, factual lines of prose scattered with dates would be the longitudes and latitudes to bring her into safe harbour. Here he would meet her like a relative at an airport. Let me show you around, he would say. You belong here. You are family.

The concierge at her hotel, a kindly, avuncular man, had recognized her mental state in the manner of one used to the effect of his city. It was he who had suggested the Libreria as a good place to learn of her ancestor, and of where she could view his work around the city. The short answer *Signorina*, he said, was 'almost anywhere'. Nora was cheered by his familiarity with the name of Corradino Manin; he spoke of him as a familiar drinking acquaintance. But as to what to see in the city itself his advice was simple. He waved his hand expansively. '*Faccia soltanto una passeggiata, Signorina. Soltanto una passeggiata.*' Just walk, only walk.

He was right of course. From her pleasant hotel in Castello, she had wandered the *calli*, losing track of time and direction, and caring not at all. Everything here was beautiful, even the decay. Rotting houses stood next to glorious palaces, squeezed on either side by grandeur, their lower floors showing tidemarks of erosion where the lagoon was eating them alive. The stained masonry crumbled into the canal like *biscotti* dipped in Marsala but this seemed only to add to their charms. It was as if they submitted with pleasure to the tides – a consummation, one devoutly to be wished. Nora wandered the bridges, as enchanted by a string of washing hanging from window to window across a narrow canal, or by a handful of scruffy boys kicking a football in a deserted square, as she was by the delicate Moorish traceries of the fenestrations.

Nora resisted the notion of planning her direction. In London her life had been mapped out for her, signposted and marked down. She had not been lost, properly lost, for many years. She knew exactly how to get around her capital, aided, if need be, by the regimented, colour coded tube map or the A–Z. Stephen, always a mine of information, had told her that when the tube map was designed, the artist deliberately kept the distances between the stations constant, even though in fact they were widely different. This was an attempt to make the citizens of the metropolis feel safe, to accept this weird, subterranean mode of transport; to feel that they could move through exceptionally well-marked out quadrants of the city with ease and security.

But here in Venice Nora's desire for spontaneity was aided by the city itself. She had a map in the back of her hotel guide – it was useless. Only two directions were posted on the walls of the *calli* in ancient yellow signage – San Marco, and Rialto. But, as the S-shape of the Grand Canal dictated, these were often in the same direction. She actually arrived in one *piazza* where a wall bore two yellow signs for San Marco, each one with an arrow, each one pointing in the opposite direction.

I am Alice. These are directions designed by the Cheshire Cat.

Her image of life through the Looking Glass became even stronger, when, as the sun began to set, she decided she really had better try to reach San Marco. But as she attempted to follow the signs, they enticed her farther and farther away, leaving her at last at the white arch of the Rialto.

Nora stopped for a restorative coffee under the bridge. She watched the tourists swarm across, anxious for news like the merchants of old, clutching guidebooks and copies of Shakespeare. She mentally removed herself from these crowds.

I am no tourist. I am here to stay, to live.

Her life was packed up and held in storage crates in the unlovely shipyards of nearby Mestre, waiting on the mainland, paid up for a month – the time she had given herself to get an apartment and a work permit.

She watched the *vaporetti* chug by, and thought of her father. As a crowded boat stopped at the Rialto *fermata* she watched a young man in the customary blue overalls leap to the dock, coil the tow rope and pull the boat into its mooring with the ease of long practice.

My father.

The idea was alien to her. The idea of her mother doing anything so free as coming here and falling both in love and pregnant, was also alien to her. She turned her thoughts from her mother. She did not want to acknowledge that she had been there first. She wanted this to be *her* odyssey. 'I'm not my mother,' she said aloud. Instantly, the waiter was at her elbow, with a friendly questioning air. She shook her head, smiling; paid, tipped, and left.

This time, she borrowed her strategy from the Red Queen of the Looking Glass. She went the *opposite* way from that instructed by the San Marco signs, and soon, sure enough, found herself entering what Napoleon had termed, inadequately, 'the finest drawing room in Europe'.

The sun was lowering, the shadows enormous. The Campanile loomed over the square like the giant gnomon of a sundial; the loggias housed elongated arcs of light. Nora gazed aghast at the opulent bronzed domes of the Basilica – such decoration, such grandeur, a trove of treasure looted from the east. Here Rome and Constantinople had mated to bring forth this strange and wondrous humped-backed beast, an entirely new creature, a dragon of coils and spurs to guard her city. And, in contrast, the exquisite wedding cake of the Doge's Palace, serene and homogenous, iced with a filigree of white stone. Only here would the Orologio, a clock made for giants, where golden beasts of the zodiac roamed across its face instead of numbers, seem fitting and in keeping. Nora felt as if she needed to sit down. Her head was spinning. She opened her guidebook, but the words made no sense – they swam before her eyes, the black and white facts an irrelevance when faced with this technicolour splendour. Besides, she had set herself apart from the tourists at the Rialto and had no wish to return to their number, guidebook glued to hand, eyes flicking from page to monument like an inept newscaster struggling between script and camera.

Why did no one warn me about this?

She had been told for years to come here by friends, art tutors, even by her mother. No one could believe she had never been before, as an artist, as a half-Venetian. But her coffee by the Rialto had given her a moment of clarity. She knew she had not been before *because* of her mother. Elinor had had the Venetian adventure, and been cruelly hurt. The *Serenissima* had thrown her back, found her wanting. Nora had not wanted to come here and make comparisons, find echoes of that story, stand in her mother's shoes. She had wanted to make her own discoveries of Italy – Florence, Ravenna, Urbino. All those champions of Venice amongst her friends had told her that it was the one place in the world that lived up to the hype. *They had all told her.*

But those she charged with her ill-preparedness were the artists, the writers.

Canaletto, why did you not adequately depict this place? Why were you, in all your mastery, not able to describe this to me? Why did you merely sketch, not capture the details of this beauty? Turner, why couldn't you capture the sun bleeding into the lagoon as I see it now? Henry James, why did you not prepare me for this? Evelyn Waugh, your passages of praise were faint insults when faced with the real thing. Thomas Mann, why leave so much out? Nicholas Roeg, even with your cameras and your celluloid, why could you not tell me either?

The young woman in the great reception chambers of the Library explained to Nora in her precise and perfect English that unfortunately she may not enter the inner sanctum of the building. Visitors without reader's cards were, however, welcome to use the reference section. Nora produced her passport and watched the girl write out a day-pass in her neat round hand, and followed her, tingling, through double doors to the left of the main doors, which whispered a greeting as they closed behind her. The books waited in the still and stuffy air, dust and warm leather welcoming Nora with the familiarity of her student days. An elderly man was her only companion. He looked up, nodded, then dropped his bright eyes to his texts. The girl offered a brief explanation of the catalogues and melted away.

Nora began her search among the yellowing cards of the catalogues. 'Manin' offered a bewildering number of entries, but she quickly realized that most of them pertained to a Doge – Lodovico; or Daniele, a revolutionary lawyer who had resisted the Austrian occupation of 1848. The sun moved across the great windows before she found the numerous references to Corrado Manin, and from a distant shelf hauled down a huge tome of the kind that adorns the coffee tables of the world, its photographs unloved and un-looked at from years end to years end. Seated at a leather covered table she leafed through its pages and was dazzled – even the faded 1960s photography did little to diminish what she saw there. Page after page of beauty, intricacy and sheer majesty, the work made her drop her head to her hands and prompted the old man to glance at her with concern.

I came here to find a city cousin to give me an entrée into Venice, and I find instead a Master – a Leonardo, a Michelangelo.

Nora felt humility, inadequacy and pride in equal measure. Her eyes rested at last on a chandelier of surpassing beauty and read the legend beneath. '*Candelabro – La Chiesa di Santa Maria della Pietà, Venezia.*' Memory prompted her – she had seen, pasted on the warm walls of the city, a bill which proclaimed that tonight saw the beginning of a series of concerts of Venetian music in their original settings. The church of the Pietà had been listed. Nora quickly replaced the book and headed out into the light, turning right to the Tourist Information Office in the Casino da Caffè. She bought her concert ticket and headed for San Zaccaria, stopping for a plate of pasta which she ate watching the sun dissolve into the lagoon.

Now, in the church of the Pietà, she knew she had made a good choice for her first night. The day had been such a revelation, such an assault on her senses, that she needed this time to just sit, to be forced into inertia for a couple of hours. She sat, let the music creep in her ears, and tried to collect her thoughts.

From the moment she arrived at Marco Polo airport she had felt a loss of control – as the motor launch whisked herself and her suitcase across the lagoon towards Venice she felt buffeted, physically by the wind, and mentally by her experience.

Since her waking in the small hours she had been in a kind of trance, automatically going through the well rehearsed motions of going abroad – taxi to the airport, checking in luggage. The feeling of lightness and of no return, as, unencumbered by bags, she wandered through the airport shops, all full of things she didn't need. In the bookshop she picked up a novel with a reproduction of Canaletto on the cover, and thought it strange that, by noon, she would be walking in the very precincts that he had painted. She put the book down – she had no need for fantasy. She was entering her own reality of Venice.

On the flight, she still felt in control. She accepted with thanks her food and drinks, her courtesy magazine, listened carefully to the safety instructions. But the moment she landed Nora began to feel this new, but not unpleasant, helplessness. She realized that, in her futile, ludicrous day-dreams, she had pictured the plane landing in Saint Mark's Square, on some futuristic runway. But the reality was almost as strange – Marco Polo seemed to be actually *on* the water, an island airport, surrounded by sea. She had not thought through the next stage either, but now realized that she would be taking a boat to Venice. Of course. As the driver handed her on board the rocking water taxi she contrasted the experience with the black cab and cheerful cockney driver that had taken her to Heathrow at six.

Something else she had not realized. The boat soon reached a landmass and began to chug along a narrow canal. Nora knew at once this was not Venice itself, but heard a strange distant chime, like the fading resonance of a bell, calling to her. As if he read her thoughts the driver jerked a thumb at the ancient buildings and shouted briefly above the wind '*Murano.*'

Murano. The home of Glass. The workplace of her ancestors. She felt a jolt as she passed the *fondamente* crowded
with glass factories. The same *fornaci*, in the same places,
housing the same skills that they had for centuries. She
knew that the next day she would be back, to enquire
about work. Instead of feeling afraid of her mad scheme,
she felt suddenly sure. This was real, and she was going to
make it work. The word destiny came into her mind. A
silly, romantic word, but once there it would not leave. She
clasped the glass heart around her neck and felt suddenly
theatrical. She wanted to make some sort of gesture. She
began to unplait her hair, and let the mass of it blow in
the wind. She meant to salute Murano, but knew that, in
truth, the gesture was for Stephen.

She regretted the impulse when she had checked into
her hotel, trying to comb the tangled mess into some sort
of order in the mock rococo mirror in her bathroom. She
looked so different to the way she had looked in her own
mirror at four in the morning. She looked at her Venetian
self in the Venetian glass. Her hair was wild, her cheeks
ruddy from the sea breeze, her eyes shining with a zealot's
light. The glass heart was the only constant, as it still hung
from her neck. She thought she looked a mess – even a
little crazy, but at the same time, rather beautiful.

Someone else thought so too.

He sat across the aisle from her in the church. Probably

thirty or so, extremely well groomed like most Italian men, tall as his legs tucked uncomfortably behind the pew. And his face – before she realized, the thought had formed in her head.

He looks like he has stepped from a painting.

At once, she remembered her mother's story, was horrified that their thoughts had chimed in the same way thirty years apart. She turned away. But having thought it, she couldn't take it back. She looked again, and he was still looking at her. Her cheeks burned and she turned determinedly away once again.

The music sweetened her thoughts and Nora focused her eyes on what she had come to see; the great, decorative glass chandelier that was suspended high above her head, looming out of the dark of the roofspace like an inverted crystal tree. Numerous droplets hung from decorative branches which seemed so impossibly delicate that they could hardly support their diamond fruits. Nora tried to follow each arm of the glass with her eyes, to see how it curved and turned, but each time she lost her place as the design bested her. Each crystal teardrop seemed to capture the candle flames and hold them within the perfection of the prism. She could hear, ringing in her head, the resonant note she had heard earlier as she passed Murano, but in another instant realized that this note was real, tangible. The glass itself was sweetly singing, the timbre of the strings and their vibrations caused every branch and pendant crystal to sound their own, almost imperceptible counterpoint. Nora looked at her pamphlet for information on this miracle her own ancestor had wrought. There was nothing, but Nora smiled to herself with what she knew.

It was here when you were alive, Antonio Vivaldi.

Then, as now, you heard your own compositions echoing back to you in this crystalline harmony. In point of fact, it was here before you were even born. And it was made by Corradino Manin.

CHAPTER 5

The Camelopard

The great chandelier crossed the lagoon, hanging in the dark barrel. Submerged in water, swinging in complement to the waves, muffled from all sound and sense. The water that surrounded it was ink dark, but tiny motes of moonlight hit the prisms here and there, like single diamonds in pitch. The fluid was cushioning, safe, amniotic. Tomorrow the chandelier would be born into its purpose. Last night it had been completed. Tonight it waited. The barrel was lashed upright in the boat by so many ropes that the great dark mass looked to have been captured in a fisherman's net. The boatmen splashed and heaved their oars, singing an old song of the *Piemontese*. From inside the barrel, the chandelier began to sing too.

Corradino ached, but he would not stop. The chandelier hung before him on an iron chain in a near-finished state, shining gold in the flamelight from the furnace. Its crystal arms reached out to him in supplication, as if begging for completion. One of its five delicate limbs was missing, so for the final time Corradino reached in the fire. Pushing his *canna da soffio* rod into the heart of the melt he rolled it expertly, drawing out a gather of molten glass, which clung to the end of his blowpipe. He began rolling the glass against a hardwood paddle, marvering it into the correct shape to begin its transformation. Corradino thought of the glass as living, always living. He had made a cocoon from which something beautiful could now grow.

He took a breath and blew. The glass miraculously arched from his lips into a long, delicate balloon. Corradino always held the breath out of his lungs until he had made sure that the bubble, or parison, he had created was perfect in all dimensions. His fellows joked that he was such a perfectionist that, were the parison not perfect, Manin would never take another breath in, and expire on the spot. In truth, Corradino knew that the slightest winds of his breath at the crucial heat meant the difference between perfection and imperfection, between the divine and the merely beautiful.

He watched the glass changing, chameleon-like, through all shades of red, rose, orange, amber, yellow and finally white as it began to grow cool. Corradino knew he must work fast. He thrust the parison into the *forno* to reheat it briefly, then began to manipulate it with his hands.

Not for him the protective wads of cotton or paper that

others used to save their skin from shriveling and blistering with the heat. He had long since sacrificed his fingertips to his art. They had burned, scarred and eventually healed smooth with no prints. Corradino recalled the tales of Marco Polo who had said that the ancient T'ang dynasty of China used fingerprints as a means of identification, and the practice had endured in the Orient ever since.

My identity has become one with the glass. Somewhere in Venice, or far overseas, my own skin lies embedded in the hard silica of a goblet or candlestick.

Corradino knew that his glass was the best because he held her in his hands, touching her skin with his, feeling her breathe. He took up his *tagianti* shears and began to pull a delicate filigree of curlicues from the main cylinder, until a forest of crystalline branches sprang from the tube. Corradino swiftly broke the blowpipe free, and transferring the piece to a solid iron rod – the *pontello* – he began to work with the open end. Finally running out of time as the unforgiving glass hardened, he took it to the mother structure and wound the new arm round the main trunk, in a decorative spiral. There was no rough spot – no *pontello* mark – to remain, like an umbilicus, to betray the origins of the limb.

He stood holding the arm while the final hardening took place, admiring his work, then finally stood back and wiped his brow. Although shirtless, as the *maestri* always worked, he still felt the burning of the furnace fires on his skin from dawn till dusk. He wondered, looking at the diligent workers around him, whether this profession were a good preparation for hellfires. What was it that Dante wrote?

'. . . tall flames flowed fierce,
Heating them so white hot as ever burned
Iron in the forge of any artificers.'

Corradino knew the work of the Florentine well. His father had allowed all the family to bring one possession – one most precious thing – with them from the Palazzo Manin on the night they escaped. His father had brought a precious vellum copy of Dante's *Divina Commedia* from his library.

That was my father's choice. It's the only book I own. It's the only thing that remains of my father.

Corradino banished the thought of him and turned back to the punishing flames.

No wonder that, back in 1291, the Grand Council of Venice had decreed that all glass-making should take place on the island of Murano, because of the constant threat of fire to the city. A blaze begun by the furnaces had more than once threatened to engulf Venice. It had been a wise idea to move the centre of production, for just a few years back the English city of London had been all but destroyed by fire. Not, mind you, that it had been started by anything as artistic as a glass foundry. The latest rumour among the merchants on the Rialto had spoken of the blaze beginning in a pie-shop. Corradino snorted.

'Tis an English trait – always thinking of the stomach.

The London fire had meant good business here on Murano. The English King Charles seemed to want to create London anew, and fill his grand modern buildings with mirrors and glasswork. There was, therefore, much demand from that chilly capital for the work of Corradino and his comrades.

Although Corradino had finished the main frame of his chandelier there was still much to do. It was growing dark, and one by one, the fire-breathing mouths of the furnaces were extinguished, doors closed, and his fellows left. He called to one of the *garzoni* to a last errand, and as the boy ran through the *fornace*, jumping over iron pipes and dodging around buckets as the men worked, Corradino smiled and thought the apprentices' nickname '*scimmia di vetro*' – glass monkeys – seemed particularly apt.

The boy was soon back with the box. '*Eccolo Maestro.*'

Corradino opened the long rosewood box. Inside were 100 small square partitions, all numbered, all lined with a wad of flock wool. Corradino got to work. He took a small *pontello*, much smaller than his trusty blowpipe, and dipped it into the glass that lay, molten and unformed, waiting, at the bottom of his furnace. He pulled out the rod which now resembled a lit candle. Waiting a moment, he then plucked the glowing orb from the rod and began to roll the glass in his palms, and then more delicately in his fingers. When satisfied, he pulled out a string of the glass to form a teardrop, and fashioned a delicate hook on its end. He dropped the jewel he had made into the bucket of water that rested between his knees. After a long moment, he plunged his hand into the bucket and rescued the gem.

His action brought to his mind the stories of the pearl fishers of the East, stories that were brought back in the days of Venice's mastery over Constantinople, way back in the thirteenth century.

Do those boys who dive for pearls in the deep, striving for the oysters while their lungs burst, feel the same satisfaction I do? Surely, no: when they find a pearl, it is mere luck – a beneficence of nature. When their brothers in the Hartz mountains in Germany who mine for silver in the heat and dark of the hills, find a pure seam of silver, do they feel as if they have created this treasure? And you diamond miners of the Africas, as you prise a perfect gem from the rocks, can you feel the pride that I do? No, for I have made these things of beauty. God made the others. And now in this world of men, in our seventeenth century, glass is more precious than any of your treasures; more than gold, more than saffron.

Dry instantly in the heat of the flames, the droplet

Corradino had made was placed delicately in the compartment marked '*uno*' in the rosewood box. Even nestling in the wool flock its diamond-like purity was not dulled. Corradino sent up a silent prayer of thanks to Angelo Barovier, the *Maestro* who had, two centuries ago, invented this '*cristallo*' glass of hard silica with which Corradino now worked. Before then, all glass was coloured, even white glass had an impurity or dullness, the hue of sand or milk or smoke. *Cristallo* meant that, for the first time, full transparency and crystal clarity could be achieved, and Corradino blessed the day.

Corradino turned back to the making of his droplets. He still had ninety-nine to make before he would allow himself to return to his quarters for his wine and polenta supper. He could not entrust this work to one of the *servente* apprentices, because each one of the hundred droplets was different. In a move that had astounded his fellows, Corradino insisted that each droplet, because of its position on the chandelier, its distance from each candle, had to be a slightly different shape in order to transmit the same luminescence from every angle when suspended from the ceiling of a church or *palazzo*. The other glassmakers in the *fornace* and the boys used to gaze for hours on end at the contents of Corradino's droplet boxes, shaking their heads. They all looked exactly the same. Corradino saw them looking and smiled. He knew he had no need to hide his work – they could look all day long and would not know how he did it. Even he did not really understand what his fingers did as he thought of where this particular droplet would hang on the finished piece.

Corradino always went to look at the place where his chandeliers would hang. He asked his customers endless questions about how the room would be lit, he looked at the windows and shutters, he even considered the movement of the sunlight and the impact of the reflections from the water of the canal. And each time he noted down his calculations in a little vellum notebook, recording everything. This precious volume was now, at the height of Corradino's mastery, crammed with his ugly handwriting and his beautiful drawings. Numbers, forming intricate measurements and equations, also jostled for room on the page as Corradino believed in the power of the ancient science of mathematics. Thus, each piece that he made and each advancement in technique was documented so that he could develop his art by making reference to his previous pieces. Now, having finished the last unique glass drop, he took out his book. He found the calculations he had taken from Santa Maria della Pietà and made a quick quill sketch of his finished piece. Even on the page the chandelier seemed to stand out in a crystal relief.

Corradino guarded the book well, wearing it next to his skin at all times, but knew that even if his fellows could see it, they would not be able to decipher its secrets. He also knew that the other *maestri* laughed at him, and passed around the jest that Manin even wore his book when he pleasured a woman. He was truly an unusual man. But a genius, oh yes, truly a genius.

The testament to his genius was in every *palazzo* in Venice, every church, every grand eating house. It was in every shining chalice he made, every mirror smooth as the lagoon in summer, even every glass bubble or bonbon he made as *Carnevale* favours. They all had the same glow of an expensive gem. And now he knew that his newest work would illuminate the dark, vaulted ceilings of the Santa Maria della Pietà like no light they had ever seen. And it would sing, as many of his pieces spoke or sang. At the flick of a fingernail one of his cups would ring out the tale of the gold that painted its rim – of Samarkand and the Bosporus and the white hot days of eastern summer. This chandelier would echo the music of the girls that played in the Pietà. The girls that were orphaned, and had no one to love or love them, so poured their love into their music. His glass would sing back. It would tell them that at least one among them was loved.

The Pietà. Corradino smiled. Tomorrow he himself would go to the Pietà with the chandelier droplets. The chandelier itself would travel ahead of him in a special, flat-bottomed boat. Corradino had himself designed the packing system for his precious *candelabri* – they were suspended from the lid of a huge barrel filled with filtered lagoon water. This meant that the fragile design was cushioned from all knocks, and could survive all but a capsizement.

Then to arrive in Santa Maria della Pietà, to be winched from the barrel, water streaming from it in the godlight of the windows, like an extension of the exquisite glasswork. To fulfill its destiny, to light the church for perhaps centuries, to enable the girls to see the dark insects of the music notes as they raced across the pages of their scores, to enable the sublime noise that they made to the ultimate glory of God. And Corradino would complete the process as he painstakingly hung each drop in its proper place before the final piece was winched to the ceiling.

I myself will finish it, as is fitting.

It was the second greatest pleasure of this life of his. And tomorrow it would be married to the first – seeing Leonora. He began to make his final glass jewel, not heeding that all the slots in his rosewood box were already full. This was not to be a droplet for the chandelier – it was a gift for her.

Corradino knew that, when the glassmakers had been moved from Venice to Murano there had been another motive than that of civic safety. Venetian glass was the best in the world, and had been since eastern glassmaking techniques had been brought back from the fall of Constantinople. Such methods were honed and developed, techniques were passed from *maestro* to apprentice and a powerful monopoly grew for the Republic on the back of these secrets. One the Grand Council was reluctant to relinquish. Almost at once, for the glassmakers of Murano, the island became not just their living and working quarters, but something of a prison. The *Consiglio Maggiore* understood well the saying; 'He who hath a secret to keep must first keep it secret.' Isolation was the key to the keeping of these secrets. Even now, permission to go to the mainland was rarely given. And more often than not, the *maestri* would be followed by agents of the Council. Corradino, because of his talent, and his practice of taking careful measurements, and the necessity of placing final touches himself, was given more latitude than most. But he had, once before this time, abused this trust. For on such a mainland trip he had met Angelina.

She was beautiful. Corradino was no celibate, but he was used to seeing beauty only in the things that he had made. In her he saw something divine, something that he could not make. He met her in her father's *palazzo* on the Grand Canal. Principe Nunzio dei Vescovi wished to discuss a set of two hundred goblets that were needed for his daughter's wedding celebration. They were to match his daughter's wedding gown and mask. Corradino brought, as instructed, an inlaid box full of pigments and gems that he might use to achieve the colour.

All the great houses of Venice had two entrances, denoting their own unmistakable dichotomy of class. The water entrance was always fantastically grand, an imposing, decorative portal, with great double doors and part-submerged boat-poles striped in the colours of the household. The water door opened to invite the honoured guest into an enclosed pool, marble-walled, with a landing stage leading to the exalted reception rooms of the *palazzo*. The trade doors, opening into the *calle* at the side of the house, were more modest, for tradesmen and messengers and servants, opening directly onto the pavement. This distinction, this difference of doors, revealed much about the city – Venice owed everything to the water. The Lagoon was all. It was on the water, those shifting but faithful tides, that Venice had built her supremacy and her empire – how fitting, therefore, that the waterways of Venice were given precedence in this way. Corradino's gondola, on that fateful day, was waved to the water entrance. The great silver palace enveloped him and he was shown to the main apartments by a deferential liveried servant. As Corradino, in the humble leathers of a *soffiature di vetro* entered the beautiful salons looking out onto the water he realized that all had been done for him in deference to his rare talent. The Prince, a man with the long features and silver hair of nobility, received him as he would a kinsman. Corradino's place in the world seemed assured.

A servant was sent to fetch the Principessa Angelina, and the dress. The Prince discussed the pigments and their prices with Corradino over a fine Valpolicella, then as the old man looked up and said 'there you are my dear,' Corradino heard no more.

She was a revelation.

Blonde hair like filaments of gold. Green eyes like leaves in spring rain. And the countenance of a goddess. She was a vision in blue – the silks of her wedding dress seemed to have a hundred hues in the morning light and the dappled reflections of the canal.

As for the *Principessa*, she knew of Corradino by repute, and had longed to see the artist that all spoke of. She was surprised to find him so young – not more than twenty, she guessed. She was pleased to find him handsome, although not unusually so, with the dark eyes and curls of the region. His face – perpetually tanned by the furnaces – recalled the stern, dark, eastern icons that looked down from their jewel encrusted frames in the Basilica at Mass. In his person, he looked quite commonplace. But he was not. He was as priceless, she knew, as those icons themselves with all their jewels.

Angelina remembered being among the privileged company that had gone, the year before, to see an exhibition of a fabled creature at the Doge's Palace, the Palazzo Ducale. They called the creature a Camelopard, the fabled *Giraffa camelopardalis*, and it had been loaned by a King of the Africas. The name meant nothing to the *Principessa*. But when she saw the animal she felt an almost feral excitement as she watched from behind her mask. Enormously tall, chequered like a Harlequin, and with an impossibly long neck, the creature strode slowly around; its form slicing through the sunlight shafts that flooded in through the *palazzo's* windows. The great chamber of the *Sala del Maggior Consiglio*, cavernous, gorgeously painted in red and gold frescoes and with the highest ceilings in Venice, seemed the only room fitting for the display of this fantastical beast. From the ceiling, seventy-six past Doges of Venice, rendered by the great Veronese, looked down unmoved at the sight. Their living successor looked on in wonder from his throne, crowned with his *corno* hat, whispering to his consort from behind his beringed hand. Meanwhile, the alien silent creature paused to examine a high scarlet drapery with a snake-like black tongue, eliciting delighted gasps from the audience. It lifted its tail and expelled a pile of neat droppings onto the priceless floors, treading in its own excrement. The ladies giggled and squealed while the men guffawed, and Angelina pressed a floral posy to her nose. But her excitement remained. She felt herself in the presence of something truly unusual, something unique. She did not ask herself if the Camelopard were beautiful or not. That question was an irrelevance. If the beast had been for sale she would have had her father buy it.

She looked now at Corradino and felt the same sensations. It mattered not if he was young and handsome, only that he was truly unusual, something unique. She felt the need to possess him. When Angelina dei Vescovi smiled at him all thought of the pigments went out of Corradino's head.

He soon remembered them though, oh yes. In fact, he found it necessary to make many trips to the Palazzo Vescovo in the months before the wedding, to discuss those all-important pigments. Sometimes he saw the Prince as well as his daughter. But mostly he saw the *Principessa* alone. These were very important matters, you understand. It was crucial to get such things absolutely right.

A week before her wedding it was discovered that the Principessa Angelina dei Vescovi was with child. The *Principessa's* tiring maid, a tool and spy of the Prince, observed her mistresses' linens, which remained a blanched white throughout the time of her monthly courses. The wench reported the *Principessa's* pregnancy to the Prince almost before Angelina knew of it herself. The betrothal was broken on grounds of ill health, and Angelina was spirited away, in the utmost secrecy, to her father's estates in Vicenza for her confinement. In an effort to salvage his daughter's reputation, the Prince threatened his servants with death if any word were breathed back in Venice of Angelina's disgrace. Corradino, in a clandestine visit to the palace to see Angelina, found himself met by two of the Prince's gentlemen and carted upstairs to the Prince's study. There he had a brief and bitter interview with Nunzio dei Vescovi in which he was told in no uncertain terms that it was more than his life was worth either to attempt to contact Angelina again or to remain in the city. So harsh were the Prince's words, so belittling of Corradino's status, that he instantly lost all semblance of the nobility he had regained when he had first been received at the palace. He felt, now, that his talents were no match for the riches and the standing of the Prince, which he had once had and now lost. In years to come his mind would not let him remember many of the Prince's bitter words, but one exchange would not leave his memory.

After Nunzio had spent his rage he turned his back on Corradino and looked out over the lagoon. In a soft, defeated voice, he had said; 'Sometimes, Signor Manin, even by *touching* something beautiful, we ruin it for ever. Did you know that a butterfly, that most wondrous of insects, can never again fly once her wings have been touched by the fingers of man? The scales of her wings fall away, and they are useless. This you have done to my daughter.'

This sentiment, and the notion that Corradino was capable of destroying the beauty he had always striven to create, somehow frightened him more than anything else the Prince had said. For the second time in his life, Corradino fled in real fear back to Murano.

Corradino blamed the *Libro D'oro*, The Book of Gold. In 1376, in recognition of the skill of glassblowers and their value to the Republic, it had been decreed that the daughter of a glassblower could marry the son of a noble. But no such dispensation was given for the daughter of a noble to marry a humble glassblower, even one that came from noble stock. There was no future for Corradino and Angelina. Corradino returned to Murano with no idea of how the affair had been discovered, or of the child that he had fathered. He confided only in his dearest friend and mentor, who advised him to stay on Murano lest the Prince should make good his threat to seek revenge.

For two years Corradino heard nothing of his lover and worked as if a demon rode his back. Then he was given a dispensation to go into Venice to make a reliquary for the Basilica of San Marco and deemed it safe to return at last. On his first day in the city for two years he contrived to see Nunzio dei Vescovi.

His entry into the Palazzo dei Vescovi was quite different this time. The grand doors to the water stood open as Corradino's gondola drew near – one partly unhinged and hacked for firewood. The great salons stood empty; looted of all their riches, the rich draperies rat-nibbled or torn down. No servants remained, and as Corradino mounted the rotting stairs he began to guess why.

The stench of the sickroom brought bile rising to Corradino's throat. Twisted on the bed lay Nunzio dei Vescovi, cocooned in his vile coverlet, half his face eaten by the '*male francese*' – the 'French Disease'. Syphilis. The man was dying. But the thing on the bed – once a Prince – began to gasp at Corradino and it was long moments before Corradino understood. Nunzio's face was twisted meat, the disease had eaten large portions of his lips, and the sibilants and plosives of speech were denied to him.

'. . . *ino*.' A claw-like hand extended to the table by the bed. On it sat a flask of wine and a goblet, dusty with the syrup of an ancient draught slick in the bottom. God only knew how long it had been since the man had been tended by another human soul.

Corradino crossed himself and poured the wine. A dead wasp fell into the glass, but it did not seem to matter. The Prince eased himself onto his shoulder with palpable agony, and drank, the wine dribbling like blood from his roofless mouth. Corradino knew he did not have long – he asked the only question he had. 'Angelina?'

'... ead.'

Corradino turned to go. He had expected as much. He would send a priest for Nunzio, but he could do no more.

'In ... hildbirth.'

The hideous whisper halted him. Corradino turned.

'There's a child?'

'In ... ietà. ... ell o-ne ... onour of family. ... o-one.'

Very well. He could grant this last thing. He nodded, in an unspoken agreement to keep the secret.

'And her name?'

'... eonora. ... anin.'

The supreme irony.

She has my *name.*

Corradino watched Nunzio die, the moment after the wretch had unburdened his heart. He shed no tears for the Prince and was no more than momentarily saddened about Angelina – he had done his mourning for her in his two years on Murano. And he had not loved her. Corradino had never been in love. But he went to see the two-year-old Leonora Manin at Santa Maria della Pietà and fell in love for the first time in his life.

On the dock of San Zaccaria, at the entrance to the Piazzetta di San Marco, there stand two tall white pillars. They hold aloft the statue of Saint Theodosius of Constantinople, and the chimera of the winged lion, adopted and bastardized by the city as the Lion of St Mark. The Lion's paw rests on a book, the pages of which read '*Pax Marce in Tibia*' 'Peace be with you Mark' – the fabled greeting of the Angels as they dubbed Mark the Saint of Venice. Three pillars were looted from distant Tyre to stand here, but the third toppled into the sea while being unloaded, and still lies at the bottom of the lagoon. At the instant that Corradino first laid eyes on his daughter, the Camelopard – thin and weary from its three year progress around the great courts of Milan, Genoa and Turin – was being loaded onto a ship bound for home. A mass of ropes encircling its long neck, it was but two short steps from the vessel that would carry it back to the African potentate who had lent it to the north. But the planks that ramped to the ship were glassy with rain; the creature reluctant to walk into the heaving sea. Like the pillar centuries before, the Camelopard pitched forward into the lagoon as its handlers leapt clear. Its enormous height meant that the noble head could be seen above the water, liquid brown eyes rolling, black tongue lashing, as it swallowed salt water. A gathering crowd pulled at the slippery ropes, but the creature's gawky limbs were too ungainly for rescue and, within an hour, the Camelopard died. It sank to the bottom of the lagoon, in silent peace, and in a last motion of grace the long neck and heavy head sank to rest over the lost pillar of Tyre.

CHAPTER 6

The Mirror

Nora looked at her reflection and knew she had made a horrible mistake. She should never have come. There was none of the resolve in her eyes that had been there earlier.

I see the portrait of a blinking idiot.

It was her second day in Venice and she was on a trip to Murano, organized by her hotel. Thousands of tourists every year were shuttled over to Murano by the boatload, cameras in hand. Ostensibly they had come to have a trip around the glass factories and marvel at the glassblowers' skill. In actuality, such trips were little more than a shopping expedition for wealthy Americans and Japanese. The highlight of Nora's trip had come earlier – a five minute tour around the factory floor. She watched the men at work, blowing and shaping the glass, some with serious intent, some with crowd-pleasing theatricals. She looked at the building and the furnaces, and knew they had hardly changed in four hundred years. She wanted very much to be a part of it, knew she could do a little of what these men did. She stood, rapt, and was jostled by a crowd of impatient Germans eager to get to the point of sale.

So that they could buy a conversation piece for their Hamburg dinner table, and say to the Helpmanns over coffee; 'Yes, we picked this up in Venice, genuine blown Murano glass, you know.'

This was *their* endpoint – this large shopping area, well lit, whitewashed, and bright with glass of every sort. Goblets stood in regimental ranks on the shelves, their orderly lines belied by the spectra of coloured helixes that twisted through their stems. Chandeliers and *candelabri* of astonishing baroque detail hung from the ceilings, crowding each other like the branches of some fantastical forest. Beasts and birds seemed moulded from volcanic larva of all hues of orange and red. Subtle pieces with the clarity and texture of cracked ice jostled with hideously ugly nineteenth century work; fat birds trapped in perpetual song by trellised cages. And the walls were crowded with mirrors, of all sizes, like a collection of portraits which featured only their admirers. I will frame your face, was their fickle promise. You are my subject. I will make you beautiful. Until you pass me by and the next face stares

into my depths. Then only that visage will be my concern.

Nora looked now into one such.

*Little wonder that a mirror is known as a looking glass. We're
all looking for something when we gaze into one. But I am not
looking at myself today, but the glass itself. The glass, the glass
is what matters.*

A mantra which was meant to make her brave again. She
looked to the mirror's frame for reassurance. Weaving around
it were glass flowers of such delicacy, such colour, that she
felt she could pluck one and smell its scents. Such artistry
convinced her – not to go on, but to go back.

*I am crazy. I will look round a little more and then go home,
all the way home, to London. I must have been mad to think
that I could come here and expect an entrée into one of the oldest
and most skilled Venetian professions. Just on the basis of my
name and my own small talents.*

She clutched the A4 black portfolio which she had brought
with her. It contained glossy photographs of the glasswork
she had exhibited in Cork Street. She had been proud of
it, until she saw this room.

Mad. I will go.

'*È molto bello, questo specchio; vetro* Fiorato. *Vuole guardare la lista dei prezzi?*'

The voice came close to her ear, shocking her out of her dismal reverie. It belonged to one of the smooth, well dressed gentlemen that helped the customers with their purchases. He looked elderly, proprietorial, kind. He could see that he had surprised her, and looked regretful.

'*Mi scusi, Signorina. Lei, è italiana?*'

Nora smiled, in apology for her reaction.

'No, not Italian.' Now was not the time to explain her pedigree. '*Sono inglese.*'

'I apologize,' said the gentleman in perfect English. 'But truly, you have the look of an Italian. A Botticelli,' he smiled with great charm. 'Would you like to see our catalogue, our price list?'

Nora screwed up the last of her resolve. His recognizing her for an Italian seemed an invitation into the last chance saloon. 'Actually, I wanted to enquire about a job.'

Instantly the man's demeanour changed. Nora had slipped, in his eyes, from wealthy customer to worthless backpacker. He had such enquiries for shopwork daily. Why couldn't they all go to Tuscany and pick grapes? '*Signorina*, I regret that we don't take foreign nationals to work in the shop.'

He made as if to leave her. She said, with desperation, 'I don't mean in the shop. I want to work in the *fornace*. As a glassblower. *Una soffiatrice di vetro.*'

She wasn't sure if the request sounded more ridiculous

in English or Italian.

The man laughed with derision. 'What you suggest is impossible. Such work takes years of training. It is a highly skilled profession. A Venetian's profession. And,' this to her blonde tresses, 'a man's profession.' He turned from her to a German couple arguing loudly over a goblet set.

'Wait,' Nora said in Italian. She knew she had to leave, but not like this. Not with this man thinking her an idiot, a nuisance. She could not be dismissed this way. 'I wish to buy this mirror.' She wanted the mirror of flowers to take back to London. She had gazed into it while her dream died, and the flowers would serve to remind her of what a beautiful dream it once was.

Seamlessly, the man altered his manner again. With smooth charm he gave orders for the mirror to be packed, and took Nora downstairs to the shipping desk. He asked for an address in England and Nora, on an impulse, gave her mother's. The mirror could stay with Elinor until Nora sorted herself out. She despondently wrote out her own details and signed the Amex slip, while the man checked her signature with a cursory glance.

She was actually walking down the staircase before he called her back.

'*Signorina?*'

She returned to the desk, now weary of the trip. All she wanted now was to be able to leave, to get back on the boat with all the rest of the tourists, for that was where she now belonged.

'Is there some problem?' she asked.

The man was looking at her mother's address, and back to her Amex slip.

'Manin?' he said. 'Your name is Manin?'

'*Sì.*'

He took off his half-moon glasses as if dazed. In Italian, as if unable to compute his English anymore, he said, 'Are you – do you know ... have you heard of Corrado Manin, known as Corradino?'

'Yes, he is my direct ancestor. He is the reason I wanted to come here, and learn the glass.' She suddenly felt tears pricking her eyes. She was an abject failure, failed mother, failed wife, failed adventurer on a fool's enterprise. She wanted to go, before she cried in front of this man. But, surprisingly, he stayed her by holding out his hand. 'I am Adelino della Vigna. Come with me for a moment, I'd just like to check something.'

Nora let him steer her by the elbow, not down the main staircase but through a side door marked, forbiddingly, '*Privato.*' The Germans looked on with interest, sure that the *fraulein* had been caught shoplifting.

Nora followed Adelino down an iron staircase, until the smell and heat told her they were approaching the factory floor. He led her through a heavy sliding door, its materials warm from the temperatures within. She felt the full blast of the *forno* for the first time.

Like the fifth of November when your front is toasted by the bonfire but your back stays cold.

Adelino led her to the flames, answering in swift Italian the whistles and teases of the *maestri* who made predictable comments on old Adelino entering with a young blonde. The old man stripped off his jacket and reached for a blowpipe. Nora began to proffer her portfolio, but Adelino waved it away. 'You may as well throw that on the fire. Here we begin all things new.' He pushed the blowpipe into the fire, raddling the coals till they spat. 'I run this place. All I deal with now is point of sale and shipping, but I used to work the glass, before my lungs went. Show me what you can do with this.'

Nora took off her coat and slung it behind a pile of buckets. She took the rod gingerly, knowing she had only one chance.

Help me, Corradino.

Nora collected the gather from the *forno* and began, gently, to blow the glass. She rolled it, reheated, shaped and blew, holding her breath out until the parison had formed. Only when satisfied did she breathe in again. Corradino had heard her. It was perfect.

Nora drank the evil, dark espresso Adelino had poured her while he hunted round his chaotic desk for a pen.

'I'm taking you on as an apprentice, for one month, on trial. The pay is low, and you'll just be a *servente* helping the *maestri*. No finished pieces. You understand?'

Nora nodded, incredulous. He handed her a form, covered in his inky scrawl.

'Take this to the *Questura* – the Police Station – in Castello. It's on the Fondamenta San Lorenzo. You need to get a residency permit and a work permit. This will take a while, but it should help that your father is from the city, and that you were born here.' For now Nora had recounted her history to Adelino. 'Meantime get this form franked by them and you can work here while the paperwork is being processed.' He shrugged expressively. 'This is *Venezia*, and she takes her sweet time.'

Nora put down her cup gently on the desk, afraid that any sudden moves would break the spell; that she would wake and find herself back though the Looking Glass again, staring at her reflection in the shop. Adelino caught her eye.

'Understand this. You have a small talent for this work, which may grow. But I'm hiring you solely on your name, and my respect for Corradino's art. Try to live up to him.' He rose dismissively. 'Be here on Monday at 6am sharp. No lateness, or you'll be fired before you are hired.' He allowed himself a smile at his small witticism, which lightened the asperity of his speech. 'Now I must get back to the shop.'

Nora stumbled into the daylight, dizzy with disbelief. She looked at the long low red building that was her new workplace, at the small ranks of red houses by the canal, and the faded street sign on the wall. She stared.

The Fondamenta Manin. Manin Street. The main street of Murano is named for Corradino. For Daniele. For me.

The spires of San Marco spiked in the distance, a tiara of piercing beauty crowning the lagoon. Nora had never seen Venice from such an aspect before. She jumped as high as she could and screamed with joy, and went to join the baffled Germans on the waiting boat.

From his office window, Adelino watched her, and narrowed his eyes meditatively in an unfathomable expression which his late wife would have recognized as a danger sign. His gaze lighted on the same street sign that Nora had just seen. The Fondamenta Manin. The whole place was named for her. Her family *is* glassblowing, time out of mind. She had talent – talent that would quickly grow. She had the great Corradino on her team. And she was certainly beautiful.

He turned his back on the vista and faced his office and reality. This was not the seventeenth century. No longer did this foundry, or this city, hold the monopoly on glassmaking. Murano and San Marco were crammed with glass factories and gift shops selling gew-gaws and bon-bons of glass, confections for the tourists to take home. Competition for the patronage of the wealthier tourists, those Americans or Japanese who would invest in a larger piece, was fierce. Adelino was forced to make ruinous deals with the more exclusive hotels to run glass tours, and more often than not in these times the tourists would take photos and get back in their boats having ordered nothing from his shop.

He sat down heavily at his desk. His business was in trouble, so why had he just hired a green girl, whom he would have to pay a wage? Why were his fingertips damp with perspiration? Why did his heart quicken? Adelino began to tingle, as the age-old mercantile tides ebbed and flowed in his veins. A lovely girl, a famous genius of an ancestor, and his own struggling glass factory. They all added up to one word; Opportunity. It was one of his favourites.

Four days later, Elinor Manin received a well-wrapped parcel at her Islington home. It was a Venetian glass mirror of great beauty, sprigged with glass flowers so delicate it seemed as if they lived. There was no note. Elinor sat at the kitchen table, looking in the mirror resting on the debris of its wrappings, at her sixty-year-old face. She began to cry, her hot tears splashing the cool glass.

She felt as if somehow, from beyond the grave, the mirror was from Bruno.

CHAPTER 7

The Lion and the Book

The *Questura* in Castello was an attractive building. Like many municipal offices in Venice, the Police Station had a past life as a *palazzo* and its former existence was betrayed by the Moorish mullions of its windows. Even so, Nora would have been happy to visit it just the once.

This was not to be. The slow workings of Venetian administration meant that this was her sixth visit in four weeks. She had filled in form after form, all with incomprehensible names or numbers. She had produced every single paper or certificate that had documented her life, from birth certificate to driving licence. And each time she had dealt with a different policeman, recounting her tale from the beginning, dealing with reactions that ran the gamut from frank incredulity to plain indifference. This English *Signorina* had somehow been given an apprenticeship with the *maestri* on Murano, and now needed a living permit and a work permit. Each official had a different take on her plight.

The *Signorina* must have a rental address in Venice, then after she had attained her living permit, or *permesso di soggiorno*, she would then apply for the *permesso di lavoro*, or work permit. No, said another, she must be given her *permesso di lavoro* first, then have it ratified by her employer, then she would qualify to take rental quarters in the *sestiere*, then she could apply for a *permesso di sogiorno*.

I want to scream.

Nora's manner had metamorphosed over these visits from the friendly, slightly ignorant blonde demeanour that she had found all her life to work well with officialdom, to the hard-nosed, demanding manner of a harridan. The progress of her application, however, had stayed exactly the same, retaining its state of complete inertia.

I have a recurring dream where I'm floating underwater in the lagoon, gasping for breath, but unable to swim to the surface because I'm bound with reams and reams of red tape.

Today, a peerless autumn day, she entered the door of the police station with steely determination, her features brittle with counterfeit smiles.

I have been in Venice for a full month. I need to get this sorted.

The last month had passed with that strange elasticity which characterizes significant periods of life. On the one hand, the time had slipped by with a rapidity which surprised Nora. On the other, she could not believe that it was only four weeks ago that she had been living at Belmont, amid the detritus of her dead marriage. She had worked hard at the furnaces from that first Monday, when she had entered the *fornace* with an air of one going to school for the first time. She had bound her hair in a scarf and worn her oldest jeans in an effort to blend in as much as possible. It had not worked. The heat was such that in the space of half an hour she had shed the scarf and was working in jeans, bare feet and a vest top, to predictable comments from the others.

But all in all, Nora's first day at the *fornace* was both exhausting and exhilarating. Most of the men were guardedly friendly, in a manner which made her suspect that they had been given instruction by Adelino. Two of the younger glassblowers, a goodlooking pair who seemed to be somewhat of a double act, were friendly and helpful and watched her progress with dark, appraising eyes. She left when the others did, congratulating herself on having made no major mistakes that day, and was gratified when her two young colleagues asked her to come for a drink with the others. Adelino was not with them, but thinking herself safe in numbers Nora followed gratefully along the Fondamenta Manin to a warmly-lit welcoming bar. The *maestri* were clearly regulars, as their 'usual' ten Peroni beers sat ready on the bar like the green bottles of the song. Nora collapsed on the bar stool chivalrously proffered by Roberto and rolled her head around on her aching neck. She heard some of the gathered men joking about offering her a massage and she smiled along.

I must get used to barracking and locker-room jokes; I must not be phased by it all. This is a man's world – always has been – and I have to learn to fit in. No princess behaviour.

She pressed the cold bottle of Peroni to a forehead still hot and flushed from the furnace's kiss, and felt the welcome chill of condensation dripping to her cheek. She took a long cool slug of the beer and, as her lips touched the bottle and her teeth chinked the glass she thought of the continuity of the glassmakers' art. Here in her hand was the equivalent of the wares produced by Corradino and his colleagues, but now mass-produced, recycled, soulless and utilitarian. Above the bar MTV blared, interrupting her thoughts, and Roberto beckoned her to a small corner table which Luca had already secured. Nora sat, smiled, and answered their questions about London, Chelsea FC and Robbie Williams in that order. In turn, she discovered that both men were the sons of glassblowers.

'In fact,' said Luca, 'Roberto here has the longest glassblowing history of all of us here, even though he's the youngest.'

'But the most talented,' put in Roberto, his white grin mitigating the boast.

'Actually, that's annoyingly true,' countered Luca. 'Old Adelino is always blowing smoke up your arse.'

'He says I've inherited the family "breath",' Roberto explained modestly to Nora.

'Yeah,' said Luca holding his nose, 'I think I know what he means. You stink.'

Roberto cuffed Luca and they both roared with laughter. Nora shifted in her seat and suddenly felt very old. These boys were charming, but a bit ... immature? She dragged the conversation back to her point of interest and addressed Roberto. 'Your family? They've always been in the trade?'

'For ever. Right back to the seventeenth century, in fact. My ancestor, Giacomo del Piero, was the foreman of our very *fornace* back then.'

The seventeenth century! Corradino would have been here too! Could the two men have known each other?

'I suppose,' Nora began nonchalantly, suppressing her excitement, 'that there were many different *fornaci* here then?'

'No,' said Luca, who seemed slightly more intellectual than his colleague, 'in those days, there was only one glass foundry on Murano. Venice was still a Republic so it was easier to control the monopoly that way. All the glassmakers in Venice lived and died here after the foundry was moved in 1291; actually they were threatened with death if they tried to leave, and if anyone escaped their families were imprisoned or murdered to force the fugitives to return.' Luca paused to emphasise this ghoulish fact and took a swig of beer. 'After the city state fell many more factories grew up here; there were about three hundred factories in the city then. But then Murano declined once the glass monopoly was lost and other nations learned how to make good glass. In 1805 the glass guild was abolished, the furnaces shuttered and the artists scattered throughout Europe.'

'It's a very different trade now,' put in Roberto. 'In Giacomo's time, all kinds of glass were made here, from the humblest bottle,' he waved his Peroni in an echo of Nora's own thoughts, 'to the finest mirrors. Now, everyday glassware is made in huge bottle plants in Germany, or at Dulux in France or Palaks in Turkey. Our only lifeline is the quality market – the "art" if you like. Tourists are our only buyers, and our foundry only gets a small part of that market. Competition is fierce now. In fact,' here he looked speculatively at Nora, 'you were lucky to be taken on.'

Nora lowered her eyes as Roberto took a slug at his beer. She felt uncomfortable, almost slighted, but Roberto carried on.

'So you could say Giacomo was the best back then,' he concluded, 'as he was the foreman of the only factory.'

She noticed how Roberto talked of ancient history as if it were no more than a heartbeat ago. 'You speak of him as if you knew him,' she said, recognizing something of her own sentiments.

'All Venetians do that,' said Roberto smiling. 'Here the past is all around. It happened only yesterday.'

Nora recognized the connection to his ancestor that she felt for Corradino, and this decided her; she would share her history. 'This is all really strange, because *my* ancestor worked here too, around the same time. He must have known Giacomo. His name was Corrado Manin, known as Corradino. Have you heard of him?'

Roberto's face went suddenly still. He exchanged a look with Luca. 'No,' he said abruptly. 'Sorry. Another Peroni?' He rose at once and headed to the bar without waiting for a reply.

Nora sat stunned, her face tingling as if from a slap. What was bothering the man? She turned to Luca who bathed her in a charming smile. 'Don't mind Roberto. He's a bit funny about his ancestor. Thinks he owns the *fornace*. He's always trying to get Adelino to raise his profile, and sell the glass on the del Piero name. Probably thought you were trying to muscle in.'

'But ... I wasn't ... I didn't ...'

'Really, it's cool. Forget it. Here he comes.'

As Roberto returned with three more Peroni Nora did her best to be particularly charming, flattering him with questions about glassblowing in an effort to atone for her gaffe, although she was still not entirely clear what she had done wrong. Roberto unbent and showed some signs of being mollified, but there was something else there too – as time passed he was getting heavily drunk. The hour was becoming late and Nora began to fret about her boat back to Venice, when it suddenly occurred to her that Luca had gone to the toilet about twenty minutes ago and not come back. She glanced around the bar but he was nowhere to be seen, and moreover, all the other *maestri* had gone too. She recognized no one.

Oh Christ.

Nora sighed gustily. She was suddenly transported back ten years to St Martin's, when it had been her unhappy duty to shepherd maudlin friends home when they had had a skinful. Surely she did not have to do that now, at her age, for this drunken boy? She swore under her breath and took Roberto's arm, helping him to stagger outside. He swayed gently at the canalside, and she wondered if he was going to be sick, but then he smiled unsteadily and lunged towards her, planting his mouth roughly on hers.

Nora's response was so Victorian it surprised her. She pushed him roughly away and fetched him a stinging slap which nearly sent him into the canal. That sobered Roberto up. His good looks disappeared as the handsome mouth curled into a sneer, and Nora suddenly felt afraid. 'Come on,' he said, moving in once more. 'You owe me something, you Manin slut.'

Nora turned and ran.

She didn't stop until she came to the *Faro vaporetto* stop, but the thought occurred that Roberto too would make his way here, as it was the nearest *fermata* on the island. Shaken and edgy, aware that she was the only one waiting, she hailed a passing water taxi and spent far too much money getting back to her hotel.

The next day and for many others she reaped her reward. Roberto had done his work — none of the men talked to her at all now. She wondered what he had told them all about her that was so bad that even the affable Luca barely acknowledged her. Roberto either ignored her, or attempted to make her life difficult with little shows of petulance or spite. Her tools would go missing, her own small experiments in glass would be found broken. With growing incredulity Nora realized that she was being bullied. She began to feel the same dread that she had felt at school when she encountered the sixth form girls with too much eyeliner who called her 'hippy' because of her long hair. She had never dreamed that a man could be so vindictive to a woman who had turned down his charms — she had assumed that after the incident she would merely drop off Roberto's radar. Sometimes she would feel a chill on her neck and turn to find him staring at her with such freezing hatred that she felt sure that there must be something wrong with him

– something that drove him to hate her over and above sexual rejection.

But what could it possibly be? I hardly know the man. Is he unbalanced?

Now she had no-one, except a gentle soul called Francesco who would occasionally, unsmilingly, show her the proper way to do her work and then respond to her thanks with a shy nod. She knew they were all waiting for her to give up and go home. She saw Adelino occasionally when he came down to the factory floor, and welcomed his presence as she used to welcome the appearance of a teacher in those long breaktimes at school – she knew that, in his presence, the bullying would stop. She knew he checked up on her progress, but so far he had had no cause to speak to her about it.

But in her lonely bubble, her own hermetically sealed vessel of silence, she knew her work was improving. In the absence of company or conversation the glass became her friend. She began to understand its ways in a manner she would not have done if she had been distracted with banter and conversation. Her duties at this stage were no more than to melt the gather, clear any impurities, and blow the occasional parison. She had no shaping or moulding duties beyond the most rudimentary, but did some cooling and reheating. Yet she began to see this compound of silica and sand as something living and organic. She understood that it breathed — taking in oxygen as hungrily as any living thing. It had moods — from the hot red, to the honeyed gold, to the crystal white. It had textures, sometimes as flowing as sweet syrup, sometimes as hard as tempered steel. She could well believe that in Corradino's time they made knives of glass — deadly, silent, clean.

Corradino. She thought of him often. She felt as if the glass connected them, that it was drawn out between them until the connection were as thin and stretched as a cello string, yet it still resonated with a low, long note across the centuries.

He is my companion while the others talk around me. I talk to him.

By osmosis, Nora's Italian, already good, quickly became excellent. When her month's trial was complete she went to Adelino, who expressed pleasure at her progress and her wish to remain. But he was concerned that she had not yet obtained her work permit, and seemed particularly insistent that she get one, as if he himself was working to some undisclosed timetable.

So back to the Police Station Nora went. As she entered the lobby she determined not to leave without her permit. She waited patiently in the designated area reading endless leaflets and posters about the dangers of drugs, guidelines for motorized boats and street crime. When she was finally shown through to an inner office Nora sighed as she noted that the smart young officer that came to attend her was unfamiliar to her, and she prepared to repeat her entire saga again.

This young man, however, despite his abrupt manner, seemed to have more of a clue than those that had gone before. He seemed fairly well acquainted with her case. She was so taken aback by this that it was fully half an hour before she realized that she had seen him before.

Years later she could remember exactly the moment when she realized this. He was looking through her documentation and seemed to spot a discrepancy. He looked from her birth certificate to her application for a work permit and frowned slightly.

'*Signorina*.' He shuffled the papers again. 'Here on your application you have named yourself Nora Manin.' He stumbled a little over the foreign name. 'But on your certificate of birth from the Ospedali Civili Riuniti here in Venice you are named as Leonora Angelina Manin. Can you explain this to me?'

'It's an abbreviation. Because I was brought up in England my mother gave me the English version of my Italian name.'

The officer nodded, his eyes on the forms. 'I see. But you understand, I will need you to fill in this form again with your given name.' He stood and pulled a fresh buff form efficiently from a nearby filing cabinet.

Nora attempted to keep her rage in check. 'Can't I just correct *this* form?'

In answer the young officer located his pen, unscrewed the cap and laid it definitely in front of her.

Nora seethed as she filled in the form yet again, calculating that it must be the fourth time she had done so, each time because of a trifling error such as this. Even worse, this form had already been signed by Adelino, so now she must ask him to do it again, which meant at least one more trip back here. Nora silently cursed the form, cursed the city, cursed the officer with the clean fingernails who was such a jobsworth that he had made her jump through this hoop. Finally done, she watched him check it through meticulously, hating him.

'*Bene*,' he said finally. He handed the form back. As he did so he said, with his first hint of friendliness, 'You know, Leonora is a much better name than Nora. And it is the right name for a Venetian. See,' he pointed to the Lion of Saint Mark, which adorned the top of Nora's form. 'The Lion. *Il Leone*. Leonora.' He raised his eyes to hers for the first time, and she placed him at last – he was the man from the Pietà, the one that had glanced at her in the Vivaldi concert.

She wondered if he had recognized her too, before she registered what he had said about her name. It struck her that it was the exact opposite of what Stephen had said to her – that Leonora was pretentious and affected. Here it was not. Here it fitted. Here Nora was the strange name, an English name, a cause for comment. She was becoming a Venetian. She looked at the man who had invited this epiphany, and smiled.

He returned the smile, then instantly the professionalism was back. He looked down at the forms again. 'You are still living at the Hotel Santo Stefano?'

'Yes.'

The officer took a sharp intake of breath, making that peculiar sound that, in any language, denotes great expense.

'I know. I'm looking for a flat at the moment.' Nora felt the urgency better than anyone. The money from the sale of Belmont was fast disappearing, and a month in a hotel hadn't helped.

The officer looked thoughtful. 'I know someone who could help you. My cousin is an agent for a number of apartments in San Marco. If you want, I could show you some. Maybe at the weekend? I'm off on Saturday?'

Nora felt doubtful, memories of the evening with Roberto and Luca fresh in her mind. But this man was a public official. And she did need a flat. She was determined however, to plan future meetings in the safety of daytime.

'What about 3 o'clock?'

He nodded.

'Where?' she asked.

He got up to open the door for her. 'How about the Cantina Do Mori? The Two Moors? In San Polo?'

Where else. A little known, ancient, steadfastly Venetian drinking place. To a tourist, he would have suggested Florian's. She felt flattered. 'Perfect.'

He held out his hand as she made to leave, and as she shook it he said, 'I'm Officer Alessandro Bardolino.'

She smiled again. 'At the Do Mori, then, Officer Bardolino.'

And Leonora Manin walked out of the *Questura*, once again without her *permesso di lavoro*.

CHAPTER 8

La Bocca del Leone

The first time Corradino fled for his life to Murano went like this.

The Manins were a powerful and wealthy family. They accrued a significant fortune from their mercantile interests along the Black Sea to the Levant and Constantinople. By the mid-seventeenth century they had attained considerable political power to match.

The head of the family, Corrado Manin, lived with his twin younger brothers Azolo and Ugolino, in a grand *palazzo* in the Campo Manin, a square named in the family's honour. Corrado took a wife, Maria Bovolo, a woman of good character and even better connections. They had a son, also called Corrado, but known as Corradino, the diminutive form which distinguished him from his father. The family adored each other and the house ran like the well appointed merchant ships that had made the Manin fortune. There were many servants, a French tutor for little Corradino, and the Manin men were free to pursue their interests in the political sphere.

One summer, when Corradino was ten, and becoming a well-formed intelligent boy, the Manin fortunes changed.

Corrado was elected to the Council of Ten, the close-knit junta that ran the Republic of Venice. Azolo was also elected in the same year. Ugolino was excluded from office by an ancient edict that stated that no more than two members of any one family could serve at the same time. This stricture was designed to avoid familial corruption, but merely fostered it. Embittered by his exclusion, for Ugolino was actually a half-hour older than his twin, he continued to assist his brothers in their clandestine objective – to secretly win friends among others of The Ten in order to depose the Doge and replace him with Corrado. Corrado and his brothers loved their *palazzo*, but how much better to live in the Doge's Palace, and protect the family interests with the Dukedom of Venice? In this Corrado took his great love for his family to its natural conclusion. He wanted everything for them.

But Venice was ever a place of duplicity. Like its revellers the city also wore a mask. Beneath the beauty and artifice of its surface ran the deep waters of deceit and treachery. This ever present threat was embodied in the *Bocca del Leone* – the Lion's mouth.

In deepest precincts of the Doge's Palace a stone Lion's head waited, carved into the wall in sharp relief. As the inscription below the dark slit invited, those who had information on another citizen of the Republic were to write down their suspicions and feed the document through the Lion's mouth: '*Denontie secrete contro chi occvltera gratie et officii o collvdera per nasconder der la vera rendita d'essi.*' The *Maggior Consiglio* would deal with the matter, swiftly and thoroughly. Many such letterboxes adorned the walls of the city, their inscriptions specifying the type of denunciation with which they dealt – tax evasion, usury, bad trading practice. But here in the Doge's Palace the Lion dealt with the highest of crimes – political treachery against the State. And on the day of *La Festa del Redentore* in high summer, when the cool chambers were empty and quiet as the crowds shouted and cheered far away, a hand fed a letter through the Lion's mouth into the infinite blackness within. The letter bore Corrado Manin's name. The Lion consumed him. And the hand belonged to Ugolino Manin.

The second Ugolino's hand let go of the paper he wanted it back. He actually contemplated reaching into the dark to try to retrieve it, but the baleful stone eyes of the Lion warned him. He felt that his hand would be bitten by unseen teeth. He could ask for it back, but from whom? The denunciations were secret – he knew not where the slit led, or to whom. Admission into that inner sanctum might mean his own death. He knew only that every name swallowed by the Lion soon reached the ears of The Ten, and, as all Europe knew, a word to The Ten was a death sentence. Ugolino stumbled out of the palace, down the Giants' staircase, feeling sick at heart. Mars and Neptune, great stone sentinels of the steps, judged him with their blank white eyes. As his own sight was blasted by the daylight Ugolino ran, blinded, through the Piazza San Marco. The great square was empty this day as he had known it must be. He had calculated that this was the only day on which his crime would go unseen, as all citizens of Venice crowded the banks of the Giudecca canal on the other side of the city. He knew that the crowds would be watching the spectacle of the bridge of boats, built over the width of the canal to the door of the church of the Redentore. Ugolino pictured the faithful walking to church over the water as Our Lord had done, to give thanks for their redemption from the Plague.

Redemption. He needed it now.

He felt his knees give way in an involuntary genuflection, his knees cracked on the hard stone, and he knelt for a moment. But he could not pray until he had made all things right. He rose and began to race through the sunlit square, and even in the dark narrow *calli* he still could not see, this time because his eyes were flooded with tears. He thought of his brothers and sister Maria, and most of all of little Corradino. He had now bought their deaths. Unless .... He knew what he must do.

★ ★ ★

Corradino felt cold lips pressing his warm cheek. He woke to see his father's face illumined by a single candle. All else was blackness. His father was smiling but looked strained. 'Wake up, Corradino *mio*. We are going on an adventure.'

Corradino rubbed his eyes. 'Where to, Papà?' he asked, his ten year old mind consumed with his characteristic curiosity.

'To the *Pescheria*.'

The Fishmarket? Corradino rolled out of bed and began to dress. He had been to the Fishmarket on the Rialto before, but always with Rafealla, the maid. Never with his father.

But 'tis true that you must visit early – the catch comes in at dawn.

'Quickly, my little monkey. *Presto, piccola scimmia.*'

As they were about to leave the chamber Corrado said: 'Wait, *scimmia*. You can choose one thing from your room to take with you. It should be the thing you like the best, Corradino.'

Corradino was puzzled. 'Why?'

'Because we may be away for a little while. Look – I have my choice.' Corrado opened his coat and Corradino saw the shadowy shape of a book.

It must be that book by the Dante fellow. The one about comedy.

Father loves it. Perhaps it makes him laugh?

Corradino began to search his chamber in the lowlight. Corrado stood waiting, not wishing to alarm the boy, but knowing they must hurry. Ugolino had come to him at sunset with the worst news – he had been watching the Redentore and had got wind of a plot to denounce Corrado to the Doge. Their scheme was undone and they must flee at once.

'Found it!' Corradino clasped his favourite possession in his hand. It was a glass horse, a delicate replica of the bronze horses on the Basilica di San Marco.

Corrado nodded and led his son quickly out of the room and down the staircase. Corradino noticed the eerie shapes the candle cast on the walls – strange dark phantoms chasing him and his father. The portraits of his ancestors, usually friendly with their Manin features, looked down now with the malevolent envy that the long dead reserved for the living. Corradino shivered, and fixed his eyes on the new painting hanging in pride of place at the foot of the stair. It was a family group, painted on his tenth name-day, picturing himself at the centre of his father and uncles. Behind the family was an allegorical seascape, in which the richly appointed Manin fleet avoided stormy clouds and fantastical sea snakes to come safely home to harbour. He remembered that his costume had itched and his ruff scratched at his ear – he had fidgeted and been reprimanded by his father. 'Be as a statue.' Corrado had said. 'Like the

Gods in the courtyards of the Doge.' But Corradino had not – in his mind he had become one of the horses on the top of the Basilica. He and his father and uncles formed the great bronze quartet in his head – noble, all-seeing and so so still. Now, below the painting as if they had stepped from the frame, he saw his mother and uncles waiting at the foot of the stairs, masked, cloaked and booted – ready for travel also. Corradino's fear grew and he flung himself into his mother's arms, something he usually thought he was too old to do. Maria held him tight and kissed his hair.

Her bosom smells of vanilla, as it always does. The spice merchant comes to her once a twelvemonth and sells her the pods for the essence that she makes. They look like long black shriveled slugs with seeds inside. How can something so ugly smell so beautiful?

Quite different smells awaited them at the *Pescheria*. Corradino sniffed the saltiness in the grey dawnlight as they left their covered gondola at the Rialto. The white bridge loomed out of the morning mists – a ghostly sentinel that bid them halt and go no further. Corradino followed held his mother's hand tight as they wove through the mass of maids and merchants to the vaulted arches of the market. His father disappeared at once behind a pillar and, by craning round the edifice, Corradino saw that he was speaking to a hooded figure. As the figure turned its head as if hunted, Corradino could see it was Monsieur Loisy, his French tutor.

Monsieur Loisy? What does he here?

The conference went on for some time, and Corradino distracted himself by looking at the mass of fish spread on the wooden trestles before him. There seemed an infinite variety, smooth silvered shoals and spiky, danger-ous-looking crustaceans. Some tiny as a glass sliver, some so huge and weighty it seemed a miracle they could ever swim the seas. Usually Corradino loved to look at the alien fish on these outings, ducking under the trestles and losing himself in the fabulous strangeness of the market. Raffealla always lost her patience and the maid allowed herself to use some of the words that were familiar enough to the fish-vendors, but with which the mistress didn't wish Corradino to become acquainted. Today though, the eyes of the fishes seemed to hold a threat, and Corradino went back to be close to his mother. He knew of the Venetian saying 'healthy as a fish', but these fish weren't healthy. They were dead.

His father and Monsieur Loisy were now joined by a third man. He was not masked and cloaked, and by his dress and scaly hands Corradino knew him for a fisherman. The three men began to nod and a leather purse changed hands. Corrado beckoned and led the family to the dark recesses of the covered market. There lay a large fishcrate, and, incredulously, Corradino watched his mother lie in the bloodied straw.

'Go on Corradino,' urged his father. 'I told you we were going on an adventure.'

Corradino lay down in his mother's arms, and soon felt the heavy press of his uncles and father by his side. He thought of the fishes that he had seen packed into their boxes, their silver shapes straightened and compressed.

We are fishes too.

Corradino saw his tutor's face through the wooden slats as the lid closed. '*Au revoir petit.*'

Corradino was cheered by the form of words. He loved his tutor and his French was excellent for his years. Surely if Monsieur Loisy meant never to see him again, he would have used the more final form '*adieu*', rather than, 'I'll see you again?'

Corradino settled into his mother's arms and smelt the essence of vanilla again. He felt a lifting and a rocking as if on water. Then he slept.

He woke with a sharp pain in his side and shifted with discomfort. Soon a heavy jolt told of their landing and the lid of the crate was prised loose. Disheveled and stinking, Corradino clambered out, blinking in the early morning light. He looked about him at the small ranks of red houses by a canal, and behind him, the spires of San Marco from what seemed a great distance. He had never seen Venice from such an aspect before. The water on the lagoon was dappled silver like the skin of a fish, the smell of which remained in his nostrils. He watched as his uncles Azolo and Ugolino paid the boatman. Uncle Ugolino looked ill. Perhaps the odour of fish, thought Corradino. But now there was a new smell − a sharp, astringent, *burning* smell. 'Where are we?' he asked his mother.

'Murano,' she said. 'Where they make the glass.'

Then he remembered. Corradino reached into his jerkin to find the place where he had felt the pain. He drew out his glass horse − it was in pieces.

I am sick of this house.

It seemed to Corradino that he had been inside for years, though he knew it had only been two days. The house was a tiny, whitewashed shack, with only two floors and four chambers, not what a little princeling was used to. Corradino was wiser than he had been two days ago. He had learned much. Some he had been told, some he had worked out.

I know that this house belongs to the fisherman father met in the Pescheria and he was paid to bring us here in the crate and keep us hidden and my father is in trouble with the Doge and uncle Ugolino found out in time and warned him we must escape. Also Monsieur Loisy has helped us — he made the contact at the Fishmarket and suggested that we come to Murano because glass deliveries go from here to France and Monsieur Loisy has friends in France that could help us and we must hide on Murano for a time until we can be smuggled out. To France.

Corradino knew little of France, despite Monsieur Loisy's enthusiasm for his homeland. He had even less desire to go there.

My father and uncles have told me that I must not leave the house where we hide, even for a moment.

But as the days went by they all began to feel a little safer, and Corradino felt his legendary curiosity begin to surface.

I want to explore.

So, on the third day, Corradino waited till his mother was at her toilet and unbolted the rickety wooden door. He found himself in an alleyway and made his way down to the canal, which he could see at the end. He wandered by the waterway, meaning only to look at the boats and throw stones at the gulls. But soon he began to smell the aroma that he had detected when he arrived, and followed his nose until he came upon a large, red building on the waterfront, facing into the lagoon.

There were sluicegates leading into the building, smoking with steam. Doorways opened into the fresh air and in one such, a man stood. The man was about the age of his father. He wore a pair of breeches and no shirt and had a thick bracelet of hide on each arm. In one hand he held a long pole on the end of which there seemed to be a burning coal. He winked at Corradino. '*Buon giorno.*'

Corradino was not sure that he should be speaking to the man – he was clearly a tradesman. But he liked the man's twinkly eyes.

Corradino bowed as he had been taught, '*Piacere.*'

The man laughed. 'Ah, *un Signorino.*'

Corradino knew he was being mocked, and felt that he should walk away, head high. But his curiosity won – he badly wanted to know what the man was doing. He pointed to the coal. 'What's that?'

'It's glass, Your Majesty.'

Corradino heard the tease, but the voice was kind.

'But glass is hard.'

'When it is grown up, yes. When it has just been born, it looks like this.'

The man dunked his coal in the water of the canal, where it hissed viciously. When he pulled it out it was white and clear. Corradino looked on with great interest. Then, remembering, 'I used to have a glass horse.'

The man looked up. 'But you don't any more?'

Corradino felt suddenly as if he were going to cry. The glass horse, and its loss, felt all of a piece with the loss of his house, of Venice, of his old life. 'It broke,' he said, and his voice did too.

The man's eyes softened. 'Come with me.' He held out his hand. Corradino hesitated. The glass-maker bowed formally, and said, 'My name is Giacomo del Piero.'

Corradino felt reassured by the formality. 'Corrado Manin. They call me Corradino.'

Corradino put his small soft hand in the man's big rough one and was led inside the building. He was astonished by what he saw.

There were fires everywhere, banked in iron holes with doors. At each doorway at least one man worked, shirtless, with rods and coals like his new friend. They put the rods to their mouths as if drinking, but seemed to blow.

I remember a painting I saw when me and my father were guests of the Doge in his palace. It showed the four winds of the earth with their cheeks puffed out as they blew a fleet of Venetian ships into safe harbour at the Arsenale. These men look like that.

As they blew the glowing coals of glass grew, and changed, into shapes Corradino recognized – vases, *candelabri*, dishes. Some worked with shears, some with wooden paddles. Everywhere there was steam as the shapes were cooled in water. Everywhere small boys ran, fetching and carrying, boys not much older than he. They were shirtless too. Corradino began to feel hot.

Giacomo noted this. 'You should take off your coat. It looks expensive. Your Mamma will be angry if you burn it.'

Corradino's coat was the worse for his journey. It was dirty, it had lost more than one of its opal buttons and it smelt of fish. But it would be a stupid man who did not see at once that it was highly valuable. And Giacomo del Piero was not a stupid man.

Corradino took off the coat, and his silk undershirt and cravat too. Feeling much better as he slung them behind a pile of buckets, he turned to face the glare of the fire and felt for the first time in his life the bone-bending heat of a glass *forno*. Giacomo pulled a blob of orange glass from the fire with his rod. He rolled it on a wooden paddle and Corradino could already see its colour change to a dark red. Giacomo waited for a moment. Then took up a small pair of iron shears and pinched and worked at the glowing material. Before Corradino's eyes his horse was born again – with arched neck like the horses of Araby, delicate hooves and flouncing mane. Amazed, he watched as Giacomo set the little creature down, and it gradually cooled to a clear, crystal white. 'Pick it up. It's yours.'

Corradino picked up the horse. 'Thank you. I love it.'

He looked regretfully to the doorway, at the midday sunlight. 'I should go.'

'As you wish,' said Giacomo. 'Perhaps you will visit again.'

I may not get a chance. I am going to France, any day now.

'Perhaps I could stay a bit longer? Just to watch you work?'

Giacomo smiled. 'You can. But only if you keep out of the way.'

Corradino promised.

For the rest of the day Corradino watched as Giacomo worked what seemed to be miracles in glass. To take an unformed lump of matter and change it, like a conjuror or alchemist, into such works of art seemed to Corradino almost magical. He watched carefully each heating and reheating, each spin of the rod, each tender breath filling the belly of the red glass. He broke his promise many times as he crowded Giacomo, until the kindly man began to give him errands, and soon Corradino was as dirty as the other boys. Soon, too soon, the shadows began to lengthen in the doorway, and regretfully, Corradino supposed that he must go. But just as he was about to voice his thought a terrifying shape filled the doorframe.

It was a tall figure, black-cloaked and hooded, wearing a black mask. But the figure held none of the jollity of the *Carnevale* festivities. And when it spoke, its chilling tones seemed able to freeze the furnaces themselves.

'I seek a noble boy. Corrado Manin. Is he here?'

Giacomo alone stopped his work, as the nearest to the door. Glass-work was too precious, too easily ruined, to stop and stare. Even at this man, who was clearly someone of importance. And so it proved.

'I am an emissary of the *Consiglio Maggiore*. I have a writ to search for the boy.'

Giacomo subtly put his bulk between Corradino and the figure. He scratched his head and spoke, to belie his intelligence, in the wheedling tones of a peasant. 'Gracious *Signore*, the only boys we have are the *garzoni*. The *scimmia di vetro*. There are no nobles here.' From the corner of his eye Giacomo could see the opal buttons of Corradino's coat winking in the furnace light, as if to betray their young master to the dark phantom. Giacomo turned away from the coat, hoping to draw the dark eyes of the mask with him.

Sure enough, the chilling orbs held his gaze. 'If you see him, you have a duty to the State to inform the Council. Is that clear?'

'*Sì Signore.*'

'Just the boy, you understand. We have the rest of the family.'

They have my family?

Giacomo heard the boy gasp and step from his shadow. Instantly he turned and cuffed Corradino to the ground, a stinging blow that burst his lip and gave him reason for his tears. 'Franco, for the last time, go and draw some water! *Che stronzo!*' Giacomo turned back to the figure. 'These boys, I tell you. I wish The Ten *would* send us some nobles to work here. More brains, less thickheaded.'

The eyes in the masked face looked from Giacomo to the boy on the floor. Filthy, shirtless, bleeding, snivelling. A mere glass monkey. With a flounce of the black cloak, the agent was gone.

Giacomo picked up the tear-sodden boy and cradled him in his arms while he wept. Not just now, but for years later, as his apprentice, living in his house, when Corradino woke at night screaming.

In my dream my mother smells of vanilla and blood.

Giacomo never told the other *maestri* where his new *garzon* was from. And he never told Corradino what his neighbour told him of the fisherman's house where the Manin family had been found. It was left as a warning – empty, no bodies, but its white walls slick with blood from floor to ceiling, like the scene of a butchery.

Of course, they found Corradino eventually. But it took five years, and by that time Giacomo, now foreman of the *fornace*, was able to plead for his apprentice's life in front of the Council, in the *Sala del Maggior Consiglio* of the Doge's Palace. He stood, tiny in the cavernous rooms, beneath the riotous frescoes of red and gold, and argued Corradino's case before The Ten. For the boy, at the age of fifteen, was almost preternaturally talented.

He could already work with glass like no-one Giacomo had seen.

The Council was disposed to keep Corradino alive. The Manin family was no threat any more, it was practically wiped out, and Corradino would be kept, like all other *maestri*, a prisoner on Murano.

How were any of those gathered on that day, when Giacomo pled for Corradino's life, to know that they were wrong about the fortunes of the Manin family? How was poor dead Corrado Manin to know that his family would rise at last to greatness, and that one of his descendants *would* occupy the throne of the Doge? And how were any of them to know that Lodovico Manin would be the last Doge of Venice who would, in that very chamber, sign the death warrant of the Republic? That when he put his hand to the Treaty of Campo Formio in 1797 the city would be sold to Austria, and Manin's signature would sit below that of Venice's new ruler, Napoleon Bonaparte?

If the Council had known, they would not have spared Corradino Manin. But they did not know, and they did spare him.

Not through the quality of mercy, but because of the mirrors that he made.

CHAPTER 9

Paradiso Perduto

Leonora got to the Cantina Do Mori at a quarter to three on Saturday. As she looked at the frontage of the café with its distinctive bottle-glass doors she wondered if she had been the victim of an elaborate joke. Perhaps Officer Bardolino was laughing at her with his workmates. Leonora gave herself a little shake – this wasn't primary school. She had been so affected by her situation at work that the shoots of her paranoia were taking hold. The man seemed to be in earnest – no doubt he would like to find a tenant for his cousin. She would just go in and wait.

It was raining so the café was quite busy. But despite the crowds Leonora found a quiet table at the back under a huge double mirror. She admired the workmanship, and the slightly greeny-gold look of old glass in its gilded baroque frame. The bevel seemed perfect to her although she knew the work must be centuries old. She ordered an *espresso* and looked around at her leisure. The clientele today were clearly Venetian – the waiter had addressed her in Veneziano, and she had surprised herself with the force with which she replied in her fluent Italian, echoing his local accent with her own. Once again she felt pleased that Officer Bardolino had suggested this place. It was still a secret well kept from the tourist hordes. Then it occurred to her that he was, in a courteous way, attempting to give her a treat.

If he shows up.

But she need not have worried. On the dot of three, with the characteristic efficiency he had shown in her interview, he walked through the doors. She was taken aback by the fact that he was now in jeans and a smart jacket – more as she had first seen him in Santa Maria della Pietà. Leonora had somehow, ridiculously, pictured him turning up in uniform. But he still recalled the painting – what was it? – and turned the heads of a group of lunching ladies. With a sort of shock, as he brushed the raindrops from his black curls, Leonora faced the facts.

He's a very good-looking man. They all see it too.

She felt a whisper of fear.

He greeted her, sat, and summoned the waiter with practised ease. He shed his jacket, and settled back on the bench comfortably. He seemed to have a certain elegance coupled with an ability to be instantly comfortable, like a cat. Leonora smiled and waited for their discourse to begin. She felt suddenly confident. Would he enter straight into the business of the day or engage in pleasantries first?

'Why are you drinking coffee?'

Leonora laughed. His question seemed so incongruous that it caught her by surprise.

'You are laughing at me,' he said, caught between amusement and annoyance.

'A little. Why shouldn't I drink coffee? Have I made some sort of social *faux pas*?'

'No, no. I just wondered if you were . . .' he searched for the word, 'teetotal. Such a strange English word. I always thought it meant one totally drank tea.'

Leonora smiled. 'No, no, I drink. A lot. Well, not a *lot*. But I do like my wine.'

'Good.' He grinned. '*Due ombre, per favore.*' This to the waiter who hovered at his shoulder.

'What's an *ombra*?'

Officer Bardolino grinned again. 'A shadow.'

'I know what it *means*. But what is it when it's a drink?'

'Don't worry. It's just a little cup of house wine. The name is centuries old. There used to be wine carts in San Marco in medieval days, and the wine merchants would slowly move the carts all day to stay in the shadow of the Campanile. To keep the wine cool.'

The waiter set down the cups on the dark wood board. Leonora tasted the wine and felt that its flavours were enhanced by the story. 'I love tales like that. But I've not been able to read a guidebook since I got here. It's almost like I'm too busy seeing, and living, to read.'

Her companion nodded. 'You are right. Better to find these things out as you go, from those that live here. Guidebooks are full of soundbites.'

She smiled to hear his opinions chiming with her own. 'Tell me more about this place.'

He returned the smile. 'In a soundbite? Casanova used to drink here.'

'Is that why you brought me here?'

I shouldn't have said that. How presumptuous and . . . clumsy. I'm behaving like a schoolgirl.

'You thought that was a line,' he said, with a perception which surprised her. 'I actually brought you here because of the glass.' He indicated the mirror. 'It is unique. This double-looking glass is famous because it was the largest mirror made of its time in which the panes are perfect twins. I thought it might interest you, as you work on Murano.'

I've misjudged him. Have I ruined the day by being flippant? Should I tell him about Corradino?

'Officer . . .'

'Please, for God's sake, call me Alessandro.' The humour was back, thankfully.

'I love it here, thank you.'

He smiled again, then resumed his businesslike mask. 'Did your *fornace* fill in the counterfoil of your form for you?'

'Yes.' Adelino had obliged again.

'Then bring it by next week and we should be able to wrap up this work permit. Then if you get a flat too, you can get your *permesso di soggiorno.*' He waved away her thanks.

After a pause, Leonora spoke. 'Can I ask you a question?'

He nodded.

'It seemed to take you less time than the others. How come?'

Alessandro stretched. 'I detest paperwork, so my only solution is to cut through it as quickly as possible. My colleagues – they hate paperwork too, but their solution is to bury it with more paper, to hope that it goes away. See,' he dug out some papers from his pocket; 'more efficiency.' He spread the papers on the table for her. She could see they had photocopied pictures of houses and details below, much like the information from an estate agent. 'My cousin, Marta, has given me the keys to these four. We'll go and see, and if you like any, you can move in tonight.'

'Tonight?'

'You are surprised?'

Leonora shook her head, bemused.

'It's just that I've been trying to see apartments for a month and there have always been delays, or problems, or paperwork ...' This extraordinary man seemed to cut through all of Venice's sedentary rhythms.

'Ah, that's what comes of knowing a local.' Alessandro smiled. 'Here's the one I think you should see first. It's quite close to here.' He pointed to one of the four, two rooms in a beautiful three storey house. She followed Alessandro's finger. The address was printed clearly – Campo Manin.

It was a top floor flat in a large, shabby, once-grand house. Though modern in all other respects, she was intrigued on entry by the original staircase that formed the axis for all the apartments, now with ugly modern fire doors. It was grand and beautifully worked. Leonora put out a hand and touched the flaking, turquoise paint. When it and the gilt was new, did family portraits stare down from these walls, to watch the servants and masters mount and descend? As if catching an echo she said, 'Corradino?'

Alessandro was struggling with the latch of apartment 3C. 'What?'

'Nothing.' It was too early to confess that her best friend in all of Venice was a ghost. 'I just wondered if any other Manins had lived here.'

Alessandro shrugged, his mind on the door. 'It's possible.

Very possible. Ah . . .' This as the door gave way and Leonora followed him into the flat. It was plain, sparsely furnished, but with two enormous windows which looked out onto the campo, and best of all, a rickety spiral stair of wrought iron which led onto a flat terrace, and the crazy rooftops of Venice all around. Leonora leant on the crumbling balustrade and gazed at the Campanile in the distance. She could hear bells.

I want to live here. I knew as soon as I walked in the door.

Alessandro's no-nonsense approach to practicalities continued to astonish Leonora for the rest of the day. She presumed her choice would result in a further couple of weeks of negotiations, followed by a protracted moving-in period. But Alessandro was on his mobile phone to his cousin at once, speaking in rapid tones. They had barely completed the tour of the rudimentary bathroom ('don't expect hot water all the time; not in Venice,') when the cousin – Marta – appeared. She was a businesslike, friendly woman with glasses, short hair and none of the physical beauties of her cousin. She sat with Leonora at the well scrubbed table, on one of the odd chairs. By the time Leonora had signed the twelvemonth lease, Alessandro had contacted the storage company on Mestre and arranged for an unheard-of Sunday delivery of Leonora's belongings for the next day. Both cousins offered to be present to help with the furniture, Leonora was given the key, and she and Alessandro went to her hotel to pack and check out.

He seemed in no hurry to be elsewhere, nor did he seem overly friendly in the odious way she had detected in her colleagues – the friendship of men who want more. They talked constantly as they walked and worked, mostly of that holy Italian trinity – art, food and football. Once her luggage was installed in her new flat, together with some essential supplies for morning, she began to feel, incredibly, that he was enjoying her company. Her pleasure and confusion grew, as with the arrival of dusk he said, with the brusque, no-nonsense manner she now recognized as characteristic: 'Shall we get a drink? We should celebrate. I know a good place.'

Leonora raised a brow. 'As good as the Do Mori?'

He laughed. 'You can't get better than this place I'm thinking of. It is, quite literally, Paradise.'

She looked carefully at him. His eyes did not look calculating, or lustful. They looked frankly back at her. He looked thirsty.

I know I shouldn't go. I know that I'm going to.

Paradise on a Saturday night was a noisy place. Leonora, crushed against Alessandro at the bar, had to scream her order for a Peroni directly into his ear. He emerged from the crush with four bottles ('to save time') and led her to the end of one of the long refectory-like tables crowded with flamboyant young bohemians. Alessandro secured them two seats opposite each other in a dark alcove illuminated by the inevitable candle stuffed in a wine bottle. Gouts of multicoloured wax masked the bottle completely and told the story of the candles that had gone before. As was her habit, Leonora began to pick at the solid mass. By her side, sitting close, a youth with multiple piercings rattled rapid Veneto to his equally punctured girlfriend opposite. Alessandro took a long drink and Leonora looked at him. The noise had abated a little, but she still had to bellow. 'What *is* this place?'

He smiled. 'I wasn't wholly truthful with you. This isn't Paradise, it's *Paradiso Perduto* – Paradise Lost. It's just about the only late bar in Venice – always full of students. It's a bit of a crush, but at least you can get a drink past midnight.'

Leonora smiled wryly into her beer. Paradise Lost.

Have I lost my Paradise? Was Stephen, and Belmont and St Martin's my Paradise? Or have I come to find a new one here?

As if reading her mind Alessandro asked, quite suddenly: 'Why did your husband leave you?'

Leonora nearly choked on her Peroni. She was daily surprised by the forthrightness of the Venetians. She expected them to be as winding and circumspect as the secret alleyways of their city, or as circuitous as their bureaucracy. But they were neither. Only this morning the lady serving her in the café where she took breakfast had asked her whether she had a special *amore* back home. The receptionist at her hotel, that avuncular, kindly gentleman, had already identified her marital status and her lack of children. And now, here was this unfathomable man asking her the most personal of questions. It seemed that Venetians had an ability to cleave to the point as cleanly as the prow of a boat slicing the waters of the canal. She played for time, holding the glass heart at her throat to steady herself.

'How do you know he left me?'

Alessandro sat back in his chair. 'You have a tan line where your wedding band once was. And your finger has changed shape somewhat, receding towards the knuckle, which means you were wearing the ring for some years, not just a short engagement. And you are sad. And you are *here* – I think if *you* had left *him* you would have stayed at home?'

Leonora looked up from her hand and saw a sympathy in the intelligent dark eyes which twisted her gut. Stung to a crushing retort, her own reply surprised her.

'He chose a golden casket.'

'How come?'

'*Merchant of Venice*? Portia's suitors had to choose between three caskets of silver lead and gold. Happiness lay in the lead casket, not the gold.'

Alessandro smiled, 'I know. I *live* here. D'you think you

can grow up in this city without knowing the story? What I meant was, in what sense did he choose gold?'

'I think he fell for the packaging. Such as it was.'

'Don't do that.'

'What?'

'"Such as it was." You're very beautiful.' He stated it baldly, not as a compliment but as a matter of empirical fact.

She twisted a golden rope of hair around her hand. 'Once, perhaps. But misery and loss seem to drain it all. I feel black and white now, not colour.' She dropped the skein of hair. 'I was an artist then, a creative, a bundle of emotions, rather than the ...' she searched for a phrase, 'synaptic circuit of chemical reactions which made Stephen. I think he fell for the opposites in us. But once he opened the casket he realized that what he really wanted was something practical and scientific, exactly like himself.'

'And did he find it?'

'Yes. It's called Carol.'

'Ah.'

Leonora took another slug of beer, and it began to warm her. At that moment she knew that she wouldn't mention her infertility to Alessandro. Some small primal voice prevented her – she didn't want this man to know that she was not complete.

At length he spoke, but not of her. From now on it was clearly *quid pro quo*. 'But you know, it's possible to be *too* alike. I had a girlfriend till last year who was pretty much my twin. We grew up together, we liked all the same things, we were both ambitious, we even supported the same football team. But then she was offered a promotion based in Rome. She took it. Left. *Finito*. Her ambition separated us in the end.' He drank.

Leonora was stumped. She didn't see this man as vulnerable – but he too had been left. She said gently, 'Was she in the police too?'

'No. A journalist.' He seemed reluctant to say more, and Leonora let their personal silence fall amid the universal chatter. At length, though, he continued.

'Until then we were happy. There didn't seem to be any problems. No ... bones of contention.'

Leonora was struck at once by both the story and his articulation, and saw a way to divert the course of their conversation.

'Where did you learn such good English?'

'London. I went there for two years after my military service, while I was deciding what to do with my life. I worked in a restaurant – with Niccolò, another cousin. I spent my time between a Soho kitchen and the London Hippodrome, picking up terrible women.' He grinned. 'I learned the swearwords first.'

'Where?'

'Both places. Then I came back to the Police Academy in Milan, and then home to Venice when I qualified.'

Alessandro expertly tapped out a cigarette, and offered

her one with that international symbol of the raised eye-brows and questioning grunt. When she waved it away, he lit his own and took a long draw. She thought of what he had said. Home. Venice.

My home too now.

'So you made your decisions, then, in London?' she asked.

'Not really. There was never really a choice. My parents were indulging me with those two years, giving me a false sense of autonomy. But I was always going to be a policeman. They knew it and I did too.'

'Why?'

Alessandro shrugged expressively. 'Bardolino tradition. Father, uncles, grandfather . . . .'

'But you're happy?'

'I will be, if I pass for Detective. That's what I'm training for now.'

'Well. The Mystery of the Missing Wedding Ring was all pretty convincing.'

He laughed, not displeased. 'Sherlock Holmes, eh? We'll see. It depends if I pass the exams. But being a beat cop in Venice is not much fun, unless you can take your nourish-ment from the views alone. It's all stolen cameras and lost luggage – tourist teething troubles. And we have a terrible reputation for stupidity – have you heard the one about why Venetian policemen always go around in twos?'

Leonora shook her head.

'One can read and one can write.'

She smiled.

'You think that's bad. The fire service have it even worse – they say the fire station in Venice has an answerphone for their emergency number, and a recorded message tells you that they'll attend to your fire in the morning.'

Leonora laughed. 'Is that how you lost the Fenice?' Venice's jewel of a theatre had burned to the ground ten years before.

'No, that was the city's fault. The canal to the Fenice was so silted up that the *pompieri* boats could not get through in time to stop the blaze. Civic irresponsibility, I'm afraid. This place is falling apart.'

'And sinking?'

Alessandro shook his head. 'None of the locals really believe that the city is sinking. But one thing they do believe is that lots of people are making money out of perpetuating the fear that it is. There are plenty of so-called funds collecting to save the city, but most of the money just lines the pockets of the officials. No, the tourists are more of a problem than the water.'

Leonora was at once surprised at this statement and gratified that Alessandro did not seem to include her in his definition. 'The tourists?' she queried. 'Aren't they the lifeblood of the city?'

Alessandro shrugged expressively. 'Yes. But if blood pressure gets too high it can kill, you know. There are about a hundred tourists for each native Venetian now. That's why all the locals know each other. We stick together. And the city will survive. Venice has been here for centuries, and she'll be here for centuries more. There's a certain ... continuity.'

Leonora nodded, while her fingers plucked at the wax. 'I know what you mean.' Then, as if taking a step towards intimacy, she admitted, 'When I first saw you, I thought you looked like a painting. I don't know which one though.'

'I do.' He smiled, but did not elaborate. 'It's common here. You see the same features walking around that have been here for hundreds of years. The same faces. The only face you never see is that of Venice. She always goes masked, and beneath the mask she's always been corrupt.'

'Plenty to do for a Detective then, with such widespread corruption.'

Alessandro gave a wry smile. 'Yes, actually. High Crime in Venice is as interesting as the petty crime is tedious. Art theft, property fraud, smuggling. Boys' own stuff.'

She could sense that he wasn't entirely joking. 'And when are the exams?'

'In two month's time. If I pass those, I'll be happy.' He finished his beer and regarded her over the empty bottle. 'And you? What will make you happy? Are you looking for a lead casket? A new Paradise?'

Leonora dropped her eyes. Again his thoughts had chimed with hers – plucked out the heart of her mystery. She looked at the candle between them and realized that she had picked off every vestige of wax from the bottle that held it. The glass stood as green and smooth as when it had first held wine, freed from its wax prison. As she watched, fresh clear wax spilled from the pool below the wick and assumed a milk-white solidity as it fell on the virgin glass. She answered at last. 'No. I'm not looking.'

I believed what I said . . . then. I went on believing it right up until the moment that he leaned over and kissed me. Hard stubble, soft mouth, and a fire I had forgotten about.

They walked in silence through the empty streets. San Marco was deserted, a yawning space like a roofless cathedral. Only the crystal stars formed the crossribs and bosses overhead. The night was chill but Leonora burned. The pigeons now roosted but her thoughts flew.

With an impulse she could not explain she turned perfect cartwheels across the square, stars wheeling over her feet, hair sweeping the stones. She could hear Alessandro laughing as she span. She did not know the meaning of the kiss, but she knew what she was feeling.

It feels too much like joy, senseless joy.

CHAPTER 10

Rendezvous

Corradino stared into his double mirror with satisfaction. It hung, in pride of place, on the back wall of the Cantina Do Mori. He knew he had done good work – the surface was smooth as the lagoon on a spring day and the bevel was perfect – even his eye could see no flaw. He averted his gaze before it could meet itself and sat at the couch beneath his mirror to wait. Corradino had never met his own eyes in a mirror. He barely knew his own image. He always looked at the glass – his vision stopped at the surface and looked no deeper to peruse his own visage. Perhaps he feared what he may find there, or perhaps he had no interest in his own features, but only those of the glass. He never asked himself these questions.

He only knew that Signor Baccia, the *proprietario* of the Do Mori, would be pleased with this mirror. He wondered though, why he had been summoned again – the walls of the Cantina were now completely clothed in paintings or mirrors. Such opulence reflected the prosperity of the place, a thriving watering hole for two centuries now. Baccia no doubt had more money to spend, and was about to overdo it. Corradino winced – more mirror work would throw off the beautiful lucent balance of his unique double mirror, shining in its twin loveliness – like Castor and Pollux – a constellation of perfection. Part of Corradino's disgust was reserved for this new brew, coffee, that he was sampling as he waited. He had never really formed a taste for it.

It rots my guts. Give me a good goblet of Valpolicella any day.

At length Signor Baccia emerged from the back of the busy café. Rotund and richly dressed in the latest French-style chemise, he stopped to talk to a group of gaudy Venetian matrons who were participating – a little self consciously – in this latest of fashions.

Baccia looks a little strange today.

Normally the *proprietario* was affable, avuncular, jolly. Today he was all of those things, but seemed nervous, as if today his demeanor was little more than an act. A heavy man, he nonetheless sweated too copiously for the cool of the day, and cast darting glances from side to side, as if followed. Corradino wondered if he had got himself into some kind of trouble with The Ten, and was under the eyes of an agent. Corradino had no such doubts about himself. He had the relaxed air of someone who *knew* he was constantly being followed.

He had seen eyes staring at him from masked darkness for years now. The man leaning at the *traghetto* stop. The bonbon trader in the street who looked a little too hard at him. The courtesan on the Ponte delle Tette with a warm smile but eyes of flint. A thousand different guises in a thousand different places. Always discreet, but over the years Corradino had learned to identify them in a moment. Each time his eyes fleetingly met those of these spies, whether tall or short, male or female, he had a sick fancy that each pair belonged to the same agent – the dark phantom that had followed him to the *fornace* all those years ago.

The man that murdered my family.

But surely Baccia had nothing to fear? He was a man of the State through and through. Corradino knew that the Council subsidized the rents of this plot, and that much of the Republic's business was conducted at the Do Mori under the mask of sociability. And yet Baccia did look – yes, definitely, he looked ill at ease. The *proprietario* made his way at last to Corradino and, at the greeting kisses, Corradino could feel the film of perspiration on Baccia's cheeks.

'Antonio?' said Corradino interrogatively as Baccia sat heavily on the brocade couch opposite. 'What's the purpose of this meeting? Not more mirrors to tip your *caffè* into the realms of a brothel?'

Baccia looked positively ill as he leaned in to Corradino, his breath heavy and laced with wine. 'Corradino. Listen well. Lean back in your seat for me.'

'What? . . .' Corradino was perplexed, but at a fervent nod from his friend he did as he was bid. He pushed his shoulders back, further, further, until at last they met other shoulders – of the patron sitting back to back with him on the other side of the settle. At once Corradino made as if to address the man, to excuse himself, but a voice stopped him which was not Baccia's.

'No. Don't turn around. Eyes are upon us.'

The Italian was perfect, but had the Frankish accent that took Corradino back twenty years to his French tutor. His childhood flooded into his head like a blush as the blood thrummed in his ears.

'Monsieur Loisy?' It was all he could do not to turn and throw himself into the man's arms.

'No. My name is Duparcmieur. Gaston Duparcmieur. We have never met. But in time you shall know me better.' The voice had an authority, but was warmed with a touch of amusement.

Corradino felt irritated at his mistake – as if he had given himself away. He clothed his discomfort in anger but something, still, kept him from turning round. With his eyes on the discomfited Baccia he said sharply, 'What's this about? I will not place myself in danger.'

He felt the shoulders shift, and again, the amusement and authority married in the voice of the Frenchman. 'Corradino, you have always been in danger. Since the day that your uncle Ugolino betrayed you to The Ten and you and your family flew for your lives. Did you know too that it was your uncle who betrayed your family's whereabouts to the agents of the Republic? He sold the death of your mother for his own safety, but in this he was deceived – they took him too and left only you, my little glassblower.'

Corradino leapt from his seat, and was immediately encircled firmly in the bearlike arms of Baccia. The *proprietario* clasped him and kissed him again on both cheeks. Loudly he bellowed; 'That's settled then. Two more mirrors for the salon. And they shall be works of art, just as you have made before.' He drew Corradino close and Corradino felt warm breath on his ear as Baccia hissed; 'Corradino, you must listen to this man, do not rise or turn, do not give in to your passions. This man can help you, but we are watched. Be still. Sit and talk to him, as if you talk to me.'

Corradino sat slowly and tried to collect himself. What did this mean? Could it be true of his uncle Ugolino, who had loved him so well? That he was a traitor? A thousand questions crowded his brain. The only one he could articulate was; 'Who are you?'

'If you would know me, you may gaze into your own mirror. But be swift, and secret.'

Corradino slid his eyes left and met those of the man

who sat behind him. He was dressed in wine velvet, in the style of a doctor of Padua, and a long nosed, white, *medico* mask lay in his lap. But the pointed beard and curled moustaches were those of a French dandy. His eyes, as they steadily held Corradino's, were of the grey slate that he powdered and added to his marver for the semblance of pewter. The Frenchman looked young, not much beyond his middle years. Perhaps thirty like Corradino himself.

'You see, you and I are of an age,' said the Frenchman, as if reading thought. 'But our differences are more marked. I love my country, as you have ceased to love yours. And you can work the glass like an Alchemist trained by Angels. And that is why I am here.'

'How do you know of my family?'

'You mentioned a man of my country that you loved well. He is known to me also.'

'Monsieur Loisy? He lives?'

'He does not.' The voice was brief. 'He was betrayed and the assassins found him. But not before he could tell us of his extraordinary pupil. You see, he never lost his concern for you and your well-being. He made enquiries and found that you lived, and were working on Murano. He followed your progress, as did we. But those who seek can also be found. His tracing of you led to the tracing of him. He was found, and poisoned by The Ten as he visited these shores hoping for sight of you.'

Corradino's head throbbed with his pulses and he could barely draw breath. Sadness for Loisy, and love for his loyalty, could not be given space here as the questions succeeded one upon the other. 'How do you know this?'

'Because I was one of those that aided him.'

'And stood by as he was murdered?'

'Loisy was warned not to return here. He did not heed my advice. You should not emulate him.'

Corradino held the eyes of the silent Baccia as his stomach lurched. The treacherous coffee beans ground the humours in his stomach and left a residue in his mouth – he tasted them and this evil news together. His searching brain at last found the needful question. 'What do you want of me?'

'We want your skills. What else?'

'And who is We?'

'Myself, of course. But more importantly, His Majesty King Louis XIV of France.'

Corradino choked. He stared into Baccia's bloodshot orbs, traced the map of capillaries he saw there as if perusing the royal bloodlines of France.

'What can you mean?'

'All will be told to you in time. But know this. We can help you; give you the life you deserve, in Paris. You will be feted as an artist, celebrated as a genius, not treated as a menial slave as you are here. We can give you riches, and nobility. Think of it – your country of Venice has used you for her ends, to augment her beauty, but has given you nothing. She has enslaved you – you, of the noble line of Manin. Not only that, but she has taken your family from you,' the voice paused, 'nearly all your family.'

Corradino's head snapped left and again he met the pewter eyes. What followed was little more than a whisper from the Frenchman.

'You could bring her too.'

Leonora. He knows of Leonora.

'Don't decide now,' said the voice as Corradino turned away in sick turmoil. 'You must not tarry here or we will be discovered. Stay and talk with Signor Baccia. He will make all seem as usual – he will order somewhat of you, and you must take the measurements and write them in your vellum notebook as you always do. Then leave, go back to Murano, and do nothing. Presently your foreman will tell you of a commission at the Old Theatre, and that you are to come to Venice to meet with a Maestro Domenico about a candlebra. If you come to this meeting you will see me again – I will be Maestro Domenico, and I will tell you of the King's desires. If you decide you want no more of this, plead of sickness and send another in your place. We will not trouble you again.'

Corradino felt the shoulders shift as the Frenchman rose. As Duparcmieur adjusted his cloak and mask he said, in a final undertone, 'Think on this, Corradino. What do you owe your Republic of Venice? Why not begin again, in France, with your daughter?'

Then, with a flourish, he was gone.

Corradino sat, as if stunned, as the *proprietario* went mechanically through his instructions for a mirror that would never be made. Then he made his way through the crowds of San Marco as if sleepwalking, while his ever-present shadow followed him. In his stupor he almost wandered towards San Zaccaria, to the Pietà, to tell Leonora. But he checked himself. He must not risk it, not when the footsteps were following. He must not spoil it now.

Not now that there is a way for us to be together.

CHAPTER 11

The Merchant of Venice

As soon as Leonora entered Adelino's office, and took the proffered seat, she could tell that something was afoot. For one thing, there was a large white flip chart obscuring the beloved view across the lagoon. For another, two extra chairs held a pair of fairly unusual and wholly unfamiliar individuals. Adelino introduced them as 'Chiara Londesa and Semi, from the Attenzione! Agency in Milan.' On hearing the word 'agency', Leonora knew she had not imagined that exclamation mark. They were in advertising.

Warily, she eyed the strangers, as they eyed her back in the manner of a couple examining a cut of meat before purchase. Chiara Londesa sported a cropped t-shirt featuring a near-pornographic manga design. Her swarthy colouring and calculating sloe eyes were offset by a shock of brutally short peroxide hair. Her colleague Semi, who seemed to boast no surname, was even odder. From top to toe he was dressed as the perfect English gentleman – Norfolk jacket, severely knotted tie, and polished Lobb shoes. As he leant forward Leonora could see – surely not? – the glint of a fob watch and chain peeping from his pocket. She fought the urge to laugh.

In the prolonged silence Semi rose and circled Leonora's chair, stroking his chin in an affected gesture straight from a James Mason movie. With the air of one selling his daughter to white slavers Adelino said, 'see? Didn't I tell you?'

Semi, still circling, nodded. Expecting cut-glass Brideshead tones, Leonora found his perfect Italian an audible shock. '*Sì. Perfetto.*'

Perfect for what?

Semi and Chiara, now ignoring Leonora, began to converse passionately in urbane Milanese. Through the frantic hand-gestures and rattled speech Leonora picked out a number of ominous words. Press ads. Interviews. Local, then national. Flyers to hotels for their hospitality packs. Photoshoot. Storyboard. At this last Chiara crossed to the flip chart and revealed an image which seemed to depict a blonde Botticelli Angel blowing a trumpet at heaven's gates. Leonora rose and looked closer. She had been mistaken. The angel was wearing jeans and a tight fitting vest. The trumpet was no trumpet but a blowpipe. The bell of the trumpet was an exquisite vase. The angel was blowing glass. The image was beautiful and terrible, and now at last Leonora did laugh. She turned back to three totally serious faces.

'Let me be clear about this. You're proposing to run some sort of . . . advertising campaign . . . on the back of, well, *me*?'

'Not just you, Signorina Manin, but your exalted ancestor.' With a practised flourish, Chiara turned the page. 'May I introduce: The Manin range.'

Oh no.

Visuals and slogans shouted at Leonora. Photos, mock-ups for packaging.

More pages with copy lines writ large: 'The Glass that built the Republic.' 'See the real Venice through our Glass.' 'Manin Glass, made by true Venetians for 400 years.' 'Manin Glass, the original Venetian Glass.' Over and again there were images of the blonde Botticelli (presumably herself) and a dark child in a frock coat and ruff.

'Unfortunately, there is no adult portrait of Corrado Manin. He fled his family home aged ten, so there is just this which we took from a family group.' Chiara's shrug expressed regret for this personal tragedy – not for the little boy's loss, but that she herself was inconvenienced by the lack of an adult image. Leonora studied the closed, serious face of the little boy who had grown into greatness.

The designers had excised him from the painting, separated him from his family once again to stand alone. She had not known of this portrait, or even this part of his history, and felt ashamed.

How is it that these grotesques straight from the Commedia dell'Arte know more of Corradino than I do myself? Because they bothered to find out. I must know more about him.

Chiara's pitch continued apace. 'Our campaign depends on two major elements – Corrado Manin, the Mozart of glassmaking, gives this foundry's output the continuity of long history – the solid, antique image with an impeccable *Venetian* pedigree. And you *Signorina*, are his ancestor – and the only female glassblower on the islands. We can sell the *modernity* of the latest designs on your image – the contemporary, the avant-garde, but always with the weight of your family history at your back.'

I feel sick.

Leonora turned to Adelino and spoke urgently in *sotto voce* Veneziano. 'This is obscene!'

Adelino rose and took her to the window. '*Scusi,*' – this to the Milanese who had gone into a huddle over a layout pad, clearly planning their next assault on the Manin name.

Adelino weighed in with a pitch of his own. 'Leonora

mia, calm down. It has always been like this. The Rialto tradesmen of the Renaissance, and Corradino himself, would have done anything to rise above the competition. They had no artistic sensibilities. They were businessmen – just as I am.' Seeing her resistance he took her hand in a final appeal. 'Leonora, I am overstretched. I have offshore interests; have borrowed widely to prop up the business. The *fornace* is struggling.'

Leonora looked across at the spires of San Marco; the view that had delighted her just a few short weeks ago when she had been given this job. Now the beloved towers seemed a bed of nails, a nest of swords where she would be impaled as a public spectacle. The lagoon was still and serene today, but her mind felt buffeted by tidal winds.

My mind is tossing on the ocean.

'What will the *maestri* think? I am a newcomer, a novice.' Leonora thought of Roberto's chilling antagonism, and the dislike of her that he had spread like a virus through the *fornace*. 'I can't put myself forward in this way. It's unthinkable.'

'On the contrary,' countered Adelino. 'Your family have been here longer than any. Corrado Manin built this industry. And you yourself have a talent, a precocious talent. Don't worry about the *maestri*, they will be grateful. If you improve business, they will do well, and keep their jobs. Maybe even receive bonuses. Their families will thank you too.'

It was the irresistible argument. If she could do anything to help the *maestri*, she knew she would do it. If the prosperity of the *fornace* turned around, would not even Roberto, in time, be forced to acknowledge her uses and forget their unfortunate start? Moreover, Leonora knew the unsaid truth: if she did not do this for Adelino, what good was she? Why did he need an extra worker, a beginner at that?

I am to be the pound of flesh.

'Do I have a choice?'

In answer Adelino turned back to the Milanese. 'She agrees. Set it all up.'

Chiara and Semi looked up from their pad with expressions of faint amazement. They had never felt that Leonora's compliance would be in any doubt.

Adelino was alone at last. His head ached after a protracted discussion in which the advertising team had been forced to make several concessions to Leonora in the battle for good taste. He glanced at the screen of his ancient computer, where the portrait of a ten-year-old Corradino sat, still and silent under glass. He addressed the long dead boy.

'What can you do for me, Corradino?'

Catching himself, he turned to the window. The flipchart had gone back to Milan, so he could gaze out to sea unobstructed, like a merchant of old waiting for his argosies to richly come to harbour.

CHAPTER 12

The Dream of a King

Corradino clutched at the heavy velvet curtains, feeling the sweat from his printless fingertips soak into the nap of the fabric. For a moment he felt a fear that was so palpable it sent a chill through his stomach and bowels, and muddled his senses so that he could barely remember what he must say.

'Maestro Domenico?' At last the name that he had repeated in his head like a catechism for the last month returned to him.

He had gone back to work after meeting Duparcmieur and tried to live as normal. But normality had left him now, seemingly forever. He recalled the conversation constantly in his head, remembering every word, every look, every nuance. For days he lived in the dread and excitement of hearing the summons of Maestro Domenico. In his dreams this alias had assumed an identity of its own, a ghostly, terrifying shade who removed his mask to reveal the rotting countenance of his uncle Ugolino. Ever present, too was the mortal fear that The Ten would discover that he had attended a clandestine meeting and at last seek his life. Corradino even considered denouncing the Frenchman to the Council – he could take an agent to the next meeting and have Duparcmieur put to death, and prove himself a loyal member of the Republic. Three things stayed him from this course.

Firstly, he felt a natural resistance to taking the path of his uncle and denouncing another man through the Lion's mouth. He had long thought it odd that in Dante's *Divina Commedia* – the book he read now as his bible – the lisping, hapless traitor that suffered the torments of the Inferno was called Ugolino, like his beloved dead uncle. Now he knew how fitting it was that his uncle shared a name with this unfortunate Florentine.

For my uncle was the worst kind of traitor; one who betrayed his family.

Betrayal of the State was but a small sin next to this. Which brought Corradino to the second reason.

Duparcmieur's words rang in his head: 'What do you owe the Republic, Corradino? She has enslaved you.'

It was true. He loved his work – lived it even, but he knew that only his skills kept him alive. If for any reason he ceased to be able to do his work, he would be lost. And they had done worse, much worse . . . 'Taken your family from you . . . nearly all . . .' Aye, that 'nearly' was what stopped him betraying Duparcmieur. The third reason.

Leonora.

As the days turned to weeks of waiting – to the point where Corradino asked himself if he had dreamt all – he had the overriding desire to find out more of the Frenchman's plan. Was there a way he could begin a life overseas with Leonora? She whom he loved as he had loved no one else since his own mother?

Over the weeks his fears receded and were replaced. He now felt a hunger, an impatience to be contacted. Would the summons ever come? Had the Frenchman been denounced by another – perhaps Baccia – and even now lay tortured, dying, dead?

Yesternight, though, the summons had come at last. Giacomo, with the air of one who knew nothing beyond his words, had passed on a message that Corradino was to meet Maestro Domenico of the Old Theatre at noon of the next day. Corradino had given a disinterested nod while his stomach lurched. He excused himself, went outside, and vomited into the canal.

Here, now, at the Teatro Vecchio, the maze of stairs and corridors had brought him to this curtain. He knew not where it led, only that once he drew its folds aside, there could be no return.

Or I could leave now.

In tones hoarse as a crow, he spoke the name, and there was silence. With a mixture of disappointment and relief he wondered if there were no one there. But those accents he remembered so well spoke from beyond the arras.

'*Sì. Entrate.*'

With a shaking hand, Corradino drew the heavy drape aside and entered into he knew not what. Like the Dante of his book – of his father's book – he entered on a new path, with a new guide, midway through the journey of his life. He knew naught of where the road would lead, or the one who would lead him.

'So, you have come, Corradino.'

Corradino's ready reply died on his lips. He could not see the one who spoke, only the spectacle below.

He was standing in a box-like extrusion above a dark and cavernous space. But at the fore of the space was a shining arc of gold, a baroque riot of giltwork crowning a stage that was brilliant with the light of a thousand candles. On the stage were characters – such characters! Not the pantomime costumes of the *Commedia dell'Arte*, or the gaudy garb of the *Carnevale*, but players dressed in cloth of gold, jewels, and tissue of silver. One such princess stood with the company grouped around her in the attitude of an antique painting, and she sang with such passing beauty that Corradino all but forgot his fear and trouble. But this was not the holy beauty of the Pietà choir, but a secular, joyful song in a language he did not know.

'Monteverdi,' said Duparcmieur's voice. 'This is an aria from *L'incoronazione di Poppea*. Claudio was considered to be somewhat of a genius, but, as with most of that type, a deeply irritating man. You have not been to the opera before?'

Corradino shook his head, dazed.

'These and other delights await you when you enter Paris, an even greater city of culture. Close the drapes behind us, and we may have our conference while we enjoy the song. It is, of course, vital that we are not seen. This is why we meet as these players rehearse.'

Corradino did as he was bid, and as his eyes adjusted to the darkness of the box he could at last make out the figure of his conspirator.

'Do sit down, my dear fellow. There is a chair behind you.'

As Corradino sat, he peered at Duparcmieur through the gloom. Gone were the doctor's weeds, and in their place the flamboyant garb of a theatrical impresario. The hair and whiskers were unstyled today, and silvered to give an aged artistic look.

'Well. And to our business. I think our best approach is for me to put our proposal to you, and then you may question me. Agreed?'

Corradino nodded faintly in the dark, but the movement was caught by the Frenchman.

'Good. Then I will begin, for our time here is short. You have heard, I suppose, of His most illustrious Majesty, King Louis XIV of France.'

Another nod.

'Indeed. Who has not. In reflection of his glorious reign and great wisdom, the finest architects are even now building what will be the most magnificent royal palace in the known world, in the lands of Versailles near Paris. Greater than those of the ancient Roman or Egyptian peoples, than those of the Nabobs and Maharjees of the Indies, than the antique and noble Greeks. Greater even than those strange and wonderful mansions of the Chinois in the Orient that your own countryman, Marco Polo, lately found. And yet, in order to do this, and set such a place apart, His Majesty has himself had a notion which will have men wondering for centuries.'

Corradino found his voice. 'And what is his notion?'

'He wishes to construct a great chamber entirely out of mirrors.'

Corradino was silent. The song from below drifted through his brain as he imagined such an audacious thing.

'How interesting.' The amusement that he remembered well returned to the Frenchman's voice.

'What interests you?' asked Corradino.

'That you did not say at once that it could not be done.

This convinces me even more that you are the man for the task.'

'Why must the King build such a thing? The expense will be very great, the work difficult and long.'

In the gloom Corradino could see the expansive wave of the Frenchman's hand.

'These things matter not to His Majesty. What matters is the show and pomp of royalty. Such a palace, with such a hall, will make other great men esteem him greatly. Politics hang upon magnificence, Corradino. We are esteemed by our person, and our possessions. Such a place could become a centre of policy for centuries to come. Great councils will be held there, and great deeds done.'

'I see. And you want me to help you.'

Now was Duparcmieur's turn to nod.

'We wish you to come to Paris. We will quarter you in comfort and luxury in the lands around the Palace, and you will superintend the mirror and glasswork. After a time, when all is safe and the work progresses well, we will send for your daughter.'

Corradino started 'She cannot travel with me?'

A shake of the perfumed head. 'Not at once. The danger is great for one, much greater for two. It is much safer that she stays here for now. You must tell her nothing of this, for her own sake, even when you take your leave.'

'But Monsieur, there is no possibility of my being able to leave the city alive. I am watched at every turn and under great suspicion for reasons of my family.'

Then Duparcmieur leaned close, so close that Corradino could smell the pomade of his hair, and feel the warmth of his breath. 'Corradino, you will *not* leave the city alive.'

CHAPTER 13

The Cardinal's Nephew

The house at least, is mine. I am the tenant. I will make it a home.

Discomfited by the developments at the *fornace*, dreading the photoshoots and interviews she knew would come, Leonora had two comforts: her work, as the glass began to answer to her hand and breath, and the little flat in the Campo Manin. When she returned home in the amber light of the evening – for there were to be no more invitations from her colleagues to keep her out after dark – she felt her heart lift as she got her first glimpse of the old building, sleeping in the evening sun, bricks the colour of a lion's pelt. Her eyes raised automatically to the two uppermost windows – *her* windows.

This was the first home that was truly hers. Here she was answerable to no-one, not her mother with her academic books and fine prints, not her student housemates with their hippy artschool chic, and not Stephen with his solid, unoriginal antiques and magnolia walls. She would create the home that *she* wanted – surround herself with the colours and textures and *things* that she wanted to see every day, to offset her own new self.

She began to spend her weekends wandering the markets of the city – alone but not lonely, picking up fabrics and objects that spoke to her of Venice. She rooted through the little dark and secret shops of the Accademia on her own private treasure hunt. She returned home triumphant with her booty like a latter-day Marco Polo. The darkwood bowl she had found in the Campo San Vio was placed on the kitchen table and filled with a pyramid of fragrant lemons from the San Barnaba fruit boats. The enormous stone toe, hewn from some statue (where? And when?) which was so hefty she had had to have it delivered, now propped open the kitchen door. She poured over paint charts and spent long hours covering the walls – her living-room-bedroom she painted the sea-turquoise she had seen in the stairway, a colour she hoped had bled through time from Corradino's age, which she garnished with gilt edging and gold sconces. She found an enormous old mahogany box bed, which had to be hoisted through the window with the help of her enthusiastic and voluble neighbours. She made it up with soft pillows and bedspreads of creamy Burano lace, tatted by the old women who sat in the doorways of their coloured houses, warmed by the sun as their fingers flew in their laps. The kitchen she painted a glowing blood red, and collected little tiles the colour of stained glass, to mosaic above the sink. She found a block of ancient wood at a house clearance – huge and dark, it had the vestiges of carving which suggested it had been hewn from a palace door. It served perfectly for a chopping board.

The roof terrace she swept and tiled with terracotta slabs from Florence. She wired the balustrade for safety and bought numerous pots to fill with plants to give day-colour and night-scent – dotted around the terrace like portly little men. Many were filled with herbs to pinch for cooking – the basil she took downstairs to the kitchen windowsill, as the herb she knew she would use the most.

Leonora and the pot of basil. I remember from school that ridiculous poem about Isabella – she hid her lover's head in her pot, under the herb. Perhaps Keats' mad bad and dangerous pal had more of a clue about love – Byron lived here, loved here. Mind you, he threw his mistresses into the grand canal when he tired of them. Have I been discarded too? Will I see him again?

Leonora's Cork Street glassware languished, carefully packed, stowed in the kitchen cupboard. It seemed to her now too sterile, clever and over-worked. Instead she chose some of the more amateur, earthy pieces she had blown on Murano

– squat, shallow hurricane lamps in primary colours – and ranged them along the balustrade. Tealights flickered inside, warming the glass as the dusk fell. She decided against any patio furniture – she had no expectation of guests – but bought luxurious, fat cushions in jewel coloured silk, on which she lounged on sunny evenings with a glass of *prosecco*. Sometimes she sat on until the night chilled and the stars came. They seemed larger here. In London, even on the Heath, the stars seemed distant; refracted through a dusky prism of smog and dust. Here the stars stooped close – she felt she could reach up her hand and pluck one of the burning orbs like a celestial fruit. The sky was the dusky blue of the Virgin's cloak.

Marta, her landlady, came round now and again, on little matters to do with the house, and had begun to stay for a glass of wine. She had become a tentative friend, and once brought round a fragrant Venetian stew of fish and beans in a warm stone pot. As the two women shared the feast and a bottle of wine, it was Marta who told Leonora the secret to Venetian cooking. 'Simplicity,' she said briefly. 'Here we have a saying: *"non più di cinque"*. Never more than five. Venetians say that you should not use more ingredients than you have fingers of one hand.'

Leonora nodded but her thoughts were elsewhere. She steeled herself not to ask about Alessandro.

Alessandro.

She told herself, as the flat took shape, and as her work improved at the *fornace*, that she was happy. She was a glass-blower. She lived in this gem of a flat in this jewel of a city. But on the Saturday that she found the final piece to complete her home, she was brought face to face with the truth.

She had gone to a shop she knew, behind the Chiesa San Giorgio by the Accademia Bridge, to find something to hang in the empty space above her bed. It was there, hanging on the back wall, behind the armoires and busts and lampshades – an icon of Our Lady of the Sacred Heart. The Virgin held the burning heart in her hands, her face serene, the heart a visceral beating red against the cerulean cloak. Leonora bought it at once, took it home and hung it. Perfect. Then she understood.

My *heart burns too.*

It was one kiss, and he had never called her, never come round in four weeks. On subsequent, necessary trips to the Police Station she had, as before, seen a new officer each time. Yet she yearned for Alessandro, even to catch a glimpse of him. Leonora had never read Dante but recalled one of his lines (from – of all things – *Hannibal*) 'He ate that burning heart out of her hand.' Another Beatrice, namesake of Dante's great love, had spoken of eating a man's heart in the marketplace. Leonora felt the description to be apt – she felt, in a muddle of Dante and Shakespeare, that those poets had spoken of exactly how she felt – that she had eaten a burning heart which was now lodged in her chest. She felt none of the serenity of the Blessed Virgin. She wanted Alessandro, pure and simple. She thought her heart had cooled and set for ever after Stephen, hard and cold like the glass heart she wore.

But no, for even this heart that I wear, after four hundred years, would be melted again if I placed it in the fire.

And then, into her completed house, he came. That same Saturday, in the evening, an unfamiliar rasping brought her out of her reverie. She realized it was her own doorbell, and opened her door to Alessandro, smiling, brandishing her work permit, her residence permit and a bottle of Valpolicella. He made no reference to his absence, but came characteristically straight to the point.

'Shall we get some dinner? I know somewhere you'd like.'

Leonora felt shocked, and breathless. Vanity made her grateful that she was at least in the right clothes – she had put on a white crochet dress for the heat of the day. Determined not to be won over immediately she raised a brow. 'Another cousin?'

He laughed. 'Actually, yes.'

She looked carefully at him. He proffered her white permits like a flag of peace.

They walked abreast through the narrow *calli* to the trattoria, neither one ahead or behind. Their knuckles grazed one another's and before Leonora could register the pleasurable shock of the touch she felt her fingers clasped firmly in his warm hand. Since childhood, when her hand had been held, whether by her mother or later Stephen, Leonora had felt awkward – always waiting for the moment when she could comfortably let go without giving offence. Now, for the first time, she let this virtual stranger hold her hand in comfort, only breaking away as they arrived at the trattoria and began to weave through the crowded diners.

Alessandro was greeted by the *proprietario* like a long-lost and much missed brother. 'Niccolò, my cousin,' explained Alessandro from the corner of his mouth, as Leonora found herself on the receiving end of two effusive kisses – not the air-kisses of the English vicarage tea-party, but well-planted, warm salutes. Niccolò, a similar age but twice the girth of Alessandro, led them to the best table, with a peerless view of the twilit Campo San Barnaba, with the fat, full moon rising.

'The moon shines bright . . . On such a night as this . . .' No, I must not get ahead of myself. Take everything as it comes.

As they settled themselves at the red-chequered cloth Niccolò appeared unbidden with two menus, a pair of glasses and a bottle of wine. He plonked the bottle in front of Alessandro, gave him a wink and a clap on the shoulder, then melted away.

As Leonora studied the menu she felt suddenly shy and discomfited. Their conversations had always been so direct and easy before that the silence troubled her. Her eyes scanned the Italian type, looking for comfort. She seized on two familiar words in her panic. 'Minestrone and lasagne.'

Alessandro shook his head. 'No.'

'What!' she was briefly incensed.

'That stuff is for tourists. You *live* here. You should have this.' He rattled off two dishes in Veneziano so rapid that even her attuned ear didn't catch the words. 'Polenta with calves liver and risotto *d'oro*. Both delicious, both Venetian specialities. You'll love the risotto, it's made with tiny flecks of gold leaf. Truly a dish of the *gran signori*.' He dropped his voice 'You're not . . . vegetarian are you?' as if enquiring after a delicate medical condition.

She shook her head emphatically.

'Thank God. All the English are. Niccolò!' Alessandro's cousin appeared from nowhere and took their order before Leonora could protest. She sat back, befuddled, and began to munch on a breadstick to buy some time. She had been furious when, in the past, Stephen had overruled her choices with his superior culinary knowledge. Why wasn't she angry now?

Because, you little fool, you're being introduced to Venice by a

Venetian; you're being included, treated like a local, just as you wanted.

As if to reflect her thought, Alessandro spoke again. 'You know, there's a story that breadsticks come from Venetian ship's biscuits, the food that built our trading empire. The recipe was handed down by mouth over the generations until the end of the eighteenth century, when it was lost forever. But then in 1821 someone found a whole batch of them in a bricked-up Venetian outpost in Crete, and reconstructed the formula from there.'

Leonora smiled, relaxed, and took another. 'It's strange to think of my ancestors munching on these very same biscuits, tasting what I taste, feeling them crumble in the mouth like I do. The Manins had quite a shipping empire at one time. And my ... father ... he worked on the *vaporetti*. So I guess the sea is in the blood.'

'It's in everyone's blood here. Your father ... is he still alive?'

'No. He died when I was very little. My mother took me back to England. So though I was born here you are right to call me English – it's what I am really.'

Alessandro shook his head. 'No, you are a Venetian. Do you have any other family here?'

'I remember my mother saying my Italian grandparents are dead. And I think my father was an only child.' It was on the tip of Leonora's tongue to tell Alessandro about Corradino, but something stopped her. It was he, and not

Bruno, to whom she felt the connection of family, but didn't know how to adequately explain that she felt far more curiosity about the long-dead glassblower than she did about her own father, the man who broke her mother's heart.

'It would be interesting to find out more about him – now you're here. Give you some history. I could … help … if you let me? I've got contacts through the *Questura*.'

Leonora smiled. 'Perhaps.'

But it's Corradino who calls to me.

When the food arrived, it was indeed delicious. She ate heartily, but with nothing of the relish and concentration that Alessandro afforded to his meal, head down, spooning up his dishes. She watched him indulgently, and he caught her at it.

'What?'

'You eat with such … not appetite, not hunger, not lust, but a bit of all three.'

'*Gusto?*'

'Yes, exactly! It means all those things and more. I guess we don't have an equivalent word in English.'

'The English don't need one,' he said, including her again. And then he smiled.

And that was that.

Gusto. The word stayed in her head for the rest of the night.

Gusto, she thought, as he kissed her hungrily on the Ponte San Barnaba.

Gusto, she thought as they drank Valpolicella straight from the bottle on the balustrade of her roof garden, their feet dangling perilously over the canal far below.

Gusto, she thought as he took her by the wrist and led her, unprotesting, to her bed.

Gusto, she thought, as he took her loudly in the darkness.

In her dream they were in bed; Leonora's blonde hair tumbled on Alessandro's chest. But when she woke he was gone. Light from the canal played on the ceiling of her apartment, and illuminated the icon above her bed, with the heart burning still. Brighter today.

Leonora smelled coffee and padded through to the kitchen. The pot was on the stove, still warm, with plenty left. She poured herself a cup, concentrating hard on not feeling hurt.

He owes me nothing, has promised me nothing, why should he stay?

When she went to the fridge for milk she saw it. A postcard stuck under her fridge magnet. She recognized the style of Titian; a picture of a cardinal flanked by two young men. The man on the right, also in priests' robes, was the image of Alessandro. Leonora read the back; Tiziano Vecelli, portrait of Pope Clement X with his nephews, Niccolò and – surely not! – Alessandro. 1546. Beside the legend there was something else too. A hasty scrawl which read: '*Ciao bella.*'

Leonora sat heavily at the table, heart thumping. What did it mean? Was the postcard something he carried around with him, a device for susceptible foreign girls? What did '*Ciao bella*' mean? It had a terrible ring to it, the tacky sign-off of a lothario from a hundred movies. Even '*bella*' in this context held no weight. It was all of a piece with the offhand phrase – it did not denote beauty. She tortured herself over the semantics of the phrase. She knew that *Ciao* came from '*ci vediamo*'. The same meaning as the French '*Au revoir*' – I'll see you again. She did not know the Italian for '*Adieu*'.

Leonora shook her head. She did not want to plan, or flagellate herself with these thoughts. She did not know what Alessandro wanted from her, if anything. She watched the water on the ceiling, listened to the cries of children playing outside and two old men having a shouted conversation with each other across the *campo*. Sunday stretched ahead, yawning empty. She must busy herself; find something to do, something to think about, before it was too late.

It's already too late. I'm in love.

CHAPTER 14

A Rival

It was Monday. Leonora was on the roof, leaning on the balustrade, looking over to the lagoon and wishing she were on the boat to Murano. But today Adelino had insisted that she stay at home, to be interviewed by a journalist from *Il Gazzettino*, the foremost newspaper of the Veneto region. She had dressed carefully in a white linen dress she had found on the Rialto, and bound her abundant hair with lace ribbons. She knew that today there was to be no photographer, but she was under instruction from the Milanese advertisers to appear as feminine as possible at all times. They didn't want to sell their campaign on the back of a tomboy – the whole point of Leonora's appeal, apparently, was that she was a girl in a man's job. Oh well. If she could project an image of womanly vulnerability she might appeal to the journalist's better instincts.

If he has any.

What she really wanted to do was don her usual uniform of old jeans, vest and ancient army jacket, put up her hair and take the number 41 to work. She was sick of being primped and posed – the last few weeks had been a test of her endurance as she had been photographed at work, at home and even in period costume. She had to grudgingly admit that the resulting print adverts and posters did make her look … well … pretty, and they were certainly more tasteful than what had first been proposed. They had centred on placing Corradino in modern environments and Leonora in ancient ones. Leonora had balked at the idea of sharing a frame with her dead ancestor, but the results had been interesting, even intelligent. One featured a modern café with a couple enjoying wine from a pair of exquisitely modern goblets from the newly launched 'Manin' range.

The scene was determinedly contemporary, but a careful look in the 'Manin' mirror beside their table showed a reflection of the interior of the Do Mori, circa 1640, with patrons in period costume and a composite of the young Corradino standing at one of the tables. Leonora found it quite ghostly, but intriguing in the manner of The Marriage of Arnolfini: the image in the mirror was the point of the piece. Her role was to bring modernity to the Antique end of Adelino's business. In modern day dress she was placed in classic Venetian paintings which featured glasswork and mirrors. In the main image she was computer manipulated to match the colour and style of paint and brushwork. She was dressed in seventeenth century costume of golds and greens, her hair flowing in the golden ripples of the most desired courtesans, her ivory skin given the craquelure of ancient tempera. Once again, in the image in a mirror – antique Manin this time – she was reflected in her work clothes, holding the tools of her trade instead of a fan or flower. But however tasteful the ads, Leonora felt increasingly uncomfortable as the huge machine of the campaign swung into motion. She knew that Adelino had poured all the money he had into the enterprise, borrowing against collateral he no longer owned, plunging deeper into debt on this one desperate chance. She felt too, the growing contempt of her colleagues – her face burned as she posed in front of the furnace – not from the heat but from the glances of her colleagues who, watching, worked around her. At the centre of the antagonism Roberto was ever present, his resentment and growing hatred palpable on his face. It was clear that, at the same time that he thought Leonora unworthy of such attention, he thought himself very much worthy of it. She knew that he had approached the Milanese with his own family history; by chance she had heard Semi and Chiara laughing about him. Roberto did not enjoy being laughed at.

Leonora felt a chill as a breeze reached the balcony. Autumn was coming, and the tourists would soon be gone. She looked down into the *campo* and noticed that already the steady stream of tourist traffic had abated as, swallow-like, they prepared to move south to warmer climes. Firenze, Napoli, Amalfi, Roma.

Not me. This is my home.

She looked fondly down at the square, her square, which shared her name and Corradino's too. It occurred to her for the first time that this place she had chosen was the architectural embodiment of past and present, of herself and Corradino, of Adelino's cross-centuries campaign. Along one side, Luigi Nervi's vast modern bank, the Cassa di Risparmio di Venezia. On the other, the beauteous historical houses where she now lived. And in the middle (she had been delighted to learn) a statue of another Manin: Daniele, the revolutionary whose past she had glimpsed in the library that day. An unknown kinsman who came between herself and Corradino on the timeline of centuries. An upstanding lawyer who had resisted the occupation of the Austrians with as much conviction as Doge Lodovico Manin had sold the city to them. Rewarded for his loyalty he stood upon his plinth, the winged lion of Saint Mark crouching at his feet, one hand tucked Napoleon-style into his waistcoat with unconscious irony. But his sacrifice and struggle had been corroded to comedy by the passing years, as the dignified copper of his likeness had oxidized to bright jester's green.

As she watched, her attention was caught by a sharply

dressed woman crossing the square with purpose, her stiletto heels clicking on the stone.

No tourist she: clearly a local.

She wore a navy suit which screamed designer tailoring, with a nipped-in waist and a skirt with a length just the right side of trashiness. Her hair, razor cut to skim her shoulders, flashed blue-black in the sunlight. She wore the inevitable sunglasses, which only gave greater emphasis to her glossy red lips. Her sexy confidence allowed her to acknowledge but at the same time ignore the vocal admiration of a handful of masons working on the bridge. She was clearly accustomed to such tributes.

A woman like that would tell Semi and Chiara to go to hell.

She watched the woman with admiration until she disappeared from sight, and seconds later heard the now familiar rasp of her own doorbell. Leonora ran down her spiral steps, heart thumping. She would not admit that each time the doorbell rang she hoped for Alessandro.

But it was not Alessandro. It was the woman from the square. She held out her hand.

'Signorina Manin? I'm Vittoria Minotto.' Such was the force of her personality that Leonora reached out to shake her hand, and moved aside to give passage to the apartment. She clearly looked as confused as she felt, for in explanation the woman said, 'From *Il Gazzettino*.' She flashed a press card in the manner of a member of the FBI.

Leonora attempted to pull herself together and offered a chair, but the journalist was off, stalking around the house, peering at the furnishings, picking up objects and putting them down again. With a practised gesture she pushed her shades into her raven hair and peered at the view as if making mental notes. Her one word *'bello'* at once praised the décor and condemned it. 'This will do for *you*,' it seemed to say, 'but it is not in *my* taste.' At close proximity her confidence and sexuality were almost tangible. Her style and poise, her sharpness of dress, made Leonora feel blowsy and badly put together. Her dress and the twisted locks of her loose hair, with which she had been pleased as she looked in the mirror that morning, now seemed messy and amateur.

I'm behaving like a sixth-former with a crush. If she's having this effect on me, *what must she do to a man?*

With an effort that she was afraid was visible to her guest, Leonora pulled herself together, trying to regain her composure, and with it, the ascendancy. 'Can I offer you a drink? Coffee?'

Vittoria turned and favoured Leonora with a smile of immense charm and startling whiteness. 'Please.'

The journalist sat, this time unbidden, at the kitchen

table and snapped open her briefcase with the sound of a cocked gun. She took out an innocuous notebook and pen, and something else – small, silver and threatening, it squatted on the table. A tape recorder. Vittoria took out a third item, a pack of cigarettes, shook one out and lit it. Both the brand and the way she lit the thing reminded Leonora sharply of Alessandro, with a brief stab of pain. Vittoria made a waving gesture, and the smoke wreathed around her blood-red nails. 'You don't mind?'

Leonora was unsure whether the journalist was referring to the tape recorder or the cigarette. She minded both, but shook her head.

Click. Vittoria's thumbnail depressed the button and the tiny spools began to cycle. Leonora brought the coffee from the stove and sat opposite the journalist, feeling the air of contest. The recorder whirred like the timer of a chess match.

'Can you tell me a bit about yourself?'

'What do you want to know?'

'Perhaps a little background for our readers?'

'Starting in England? Or here? I'm sorry ... I'm not used to this. Perhaps ... could you ... I think I'd find it easier if you asked me direct questions.'

A sip of coffee. 'Fine. What made you come to Venice?'

'Well, I was born here, even though I was brought up in England. My father was Venetian. And I trained as an artist, was always interested in glassblowing. My mother told me the story of Corradino, when she gave me this heart which he made.'

Vittoria's eyes narrowed and she reached out to grasp the trinket. Her fingers were cold, and smelled of nicotine. '*Bello,*' she said, with exactly the same inflection as before.

She released the heart as Leonora went on, 'and I was intrigued. I wanted to come and see if I could carry on the family trade.'

Family trade. That was good. Chiara and Semi will be pleased with me. Now please let's get away from England, I don't want to talk about Stephen.

'Just like that? Wasn't it hard to leave family and friends? Boyfriend? Husband?'

Damn.

'I ... was married. He ... we divorced.'

A drag of cigarette. A nod of the head. 'Ah I *see.*'

Leonora felt that somehow Vittoria had divined her whole sorry history.

This woman has never been left by anyone. She has always been the leaver, and pities women who have been abandoned. Women like me. Even Alessandro didn't come back for more.

'And once here, you went to Signor della Vigna for work?'

'Adelino. Yes. I was very lucky.'

A raise of the eyebrow. 'Indeed. When you got the job, how much d'you think was down to your talent, and how much was down to your famous ancestor, Corrado Manin?'

Leonora would not rise. 'If I'm honest, I don't think I would have gotten the chance that I got if it weren't for Corradino. But then again, Adelino would never have employed me if I couldn't actually blow glass. He'd be a fool to, and he's no fool.'

She was reminded of all those interviews with budding young actors from theatrical dynasties, who always protested that being a Redgrave, or a Fox, was actually a hindrance to their careers. She and Stephen always used to scoff at the TV. She was no more convinced by her own answers than she was by theirs.

Vittoria nodded, in retreat, but the next attack was close. 'And your colleagues? The *maestri* that have been blowing glass for years? What do they think of you?'

Leonora shifted, thinking of Roberto. 'They were very welcoming, on my very first day.'

That at least, was true. It wasn't till we all went to the bar that it went sour.

'I think they had … reservations … when the whole Manin line and the ad campaign was first mooted. But, after all, if it does well, things will improve for them …

for all of us.'

'But what do they think of you personally?' persisted Vittoria. 'Are they your friends?'

'You'd have to ask them.'

Vittoria's lips curled into a sleepy smile. 'Perhaps I will.'

A mistake.

The journalist began to tap her biro against her perfect teeth. It was a technique she employed to good effect in her interviews with male officials. She did it to draw attention to her mouth – white even teeth parted slightly over her pink tongue between a slick of red lipstick. Her subjects usually forgot what they were about to say, and were led to commit some indiscretion. Leonora wondered what was coming.

'And how about the personal angle? Have you found any romance here in the city of love?'

Leonora could hear the heavy cynicism which underlay Vittoria's question. She was not about to admit her feelings to this woman – this woman who clearly did not believe in love – at least, not the romantic kind.

'No, there's no-one.'

Vittoria lowered her eyes and made as if to pack up her paraphernalia. It was another favourite trick of hers – they always started to relax. She shot Leonora a look of pity. 'It sounds very lonely. No friends, no boyfriend, just a long dead ancestor.'

Leonora was stung. Vittoria had already made her feel inadequate – she could not handle pity too. She rose to the bait. 'Actually there is someone. But it's all very new, so I'd rather not say anything more till I see how things pan out.'

This time both dark brows shot up. 'Could you give us anything? A tiny hint?'

Leonora smiled to herself in a private joke. 'He looks like he has stepped from a painting.'

Vittoria shrugged and snapped off the recorder with finality. 'Who doesn't?'

But as Vittoria passed the fridge on the way out she caught sight of him, staring out of the Titian postcard. The Cardinal's Nephew. Alessandro Bardolino. She'd seen the painting before, of course, in his house. His mother had bought a Titian print for him as part of a family joke. It had hung in his kitchen, and Vittoria had passed it a hundred times a day, before, of course, she had been promoted to Rome. And then, last month, been promoted back to Venice. She had seen the picture every day for the three years they had lived together.

Vittoria turned to Leonora and took her leave with such warmth and good manners that Leonora began to think she had imagined the needling of the interview. She was amazed that Vittoria seemed so upbeat – she had been careful to give little away, and the interview had been ...

well, quite boring?

But Vittoria Minotto crossed the Campo Manin with a spring in her step. The interview had been an undoubted success. She had several promising leads. Not least that the little *vetraia* was dating Alessandro. How amusing to take him off her.

How *interesting* life was.

CHAPTER 15

Treachery

It was late, and Leonora was alone at the *fornace*. She had stoked and stacked all of the furnaces and left them sleeping for nighttime, except the one solitary firehole at which she worked.

She had seen little of Alessandro, but he had, at least, telephoned her only last night. He was in Vicenza, on a course to complete his promotion to Detective, provided that he passed the stringent exam paper that he would sit at the end of it. For the duration of the course Leonora had vowed to stay on at the *fornace* late into the evening to work on her glassblowing skills, so that she would not yearn for the chimes of doorbell or telephone. In this new bubble of love in which she lived, she was afraid that she would lose her motivation, and that the glass, like a neglected friend, would turn upon her. She knew also that she needed to keep this strand of her life going as there was no knowing when the vessel that held her happiness would crack or burst under the intensity of her new passion.

For her fire for Alessandro still burned bright. She had been in her new apartment for just over a month, and there were just a handful of days when they had seen one another, and yet she thought of him constantly. His concentration on his promotion, his absence in Vicenza, all absolved him from any charges of neglect in her eyes. She made excuses for him. She comforted herself with the intimacy of the moments which they did spend together, and lived on daydreams of those times. She learned more about him, in snatches of conversation. He told her of his parents – his father a retired policeman, his mother a retired nurse, who had moved to the Umbrian hills to escape the relentlessness of Venice's tourism. She clung to these details, hoping that they brought him close, and tried to ignore the fact that she had never once been inside his house.

But now his physical distance gave her the chance she needed to clear her head and justify her position at the centre of the Manin advertising campaign. She tirelessly worked on her glass, while the moon rose outside over the lagoon. Her aim tonight was simple, and, at the same time, difficult. She wanted to learn to make a glass heart, such as the one she had been given that Corradino made. She still wore it, always, around her neck. Now, she undid the blue ribbon from which it hung and laid the heart tenderly on her *banco* – near enough to see for her comparisons, but far enough away from the blistering heat that would damage it. She recalled, in her first week here, attempting to make one, expecting it to be fairly easy compared to the wonders that the *maestri* wrung from their hands daily. But the kindly Francesco, her one ally, gently laughed at her – the heart of glass, he said, was one of the hardest things to make. Particularly one of such absolute symmetry, with a perfect, spherical bubble trapped at its centre, such as the one she wore.

Resolutely, she began. She took a small blob of gather from the fire, spun it for a second then transferred it deftly to a smaller blowpipe than she normally used. She took a short breath and exhaled, gently, as the parison grew like a water drop. Quickly she twisted off the bulb and began to marver it with her *borselle* tongs, making the creased depression between the two ears of the heart. But it was too late – the interior bubble had collapsed and separated, the lugs were different sizes. Leonora cooled the heart, and dropped it into a bucket at her feet, to be re-melted later. She began again. This time, she breathed the parison quickly, like a gasp, and had better success, but still this second heart joined the first in the bucket. She worked on, for perhaps an hour, oblivious to the sounds of the staff leaving the showroom, to sounds of cashing up, locking up. She was genuinely startled at a tap on her shoulder.

It was Adelino. 'Leonora *mia*, it is time for *me* to go home, therefore I'm damned sure it's time for *you* to go home.' He spoke in his usual, half-gruff, half-affectionate tones.

But his voice warmed as he saw the task she had set herself. 'Ah, the elusive glass heart. *Molto difficile, vero?*'

Leonora nodded ruefully. Adelino crouched and began to sort through her bucket of rejects – now full. 'Yes, as you see, very difficult. But these are not bad. What did you find wanting about this one?' He held up her last attempt. It seemed to him perfect, but Leonora had seen some anomaly in it. It was strange – with Alessandro, she wanted to believe that all was right; endlessly she made excuses and allowances to preserve her hopes. At the *fornace* she sought perfection and accepted no less. Even if everything looked in order, but her eyes were seeking hidden fissures, imperfect reflections, skewed illumination.

'It's not right,' she said stubbornly.

Adelino smiled, and stood. 'Always the perfectionist, eh? Actually, I'm glad you're here. I wanted to show you this.' He proffered a glossy photo. 'It's the first press ad. It's due to run on Monday.' Leonora, with studied nonchalance, closed the *forno* door and turned off the gas feed. Mentally she was preparing herself for the image – the picture that would launch her on the public. She took the print and perused it carefully. It wasn't bad. Ironically, they had gone with a Titian image first – a mock-up of herself dressed as Titian's famous Woman with a Mirror. One hand clasped a bundle of her flowing hair and the other held a glass orb. The image in the mirror showed the busy *fornace*, with her modern self stooping over the furnace. She looked at the picture for a long moment. Adelino took her silence for disapproval.

'Leonora,' he seemed to hesitate. 'I'm not a bad man. This is a tasteful, classy, campaign. It will benefit all of us. And besides,' she met his eyes at last 'I think you are ready to be a *maestra*. I think you are ready to make the pieces that we sell.'

Leonora felt numb, searching his eyes to detect a joke. She had been here a mere four months. Surely that was too soon to metamorphose from apprentice to *maestra*.

'Adelino, how much of this is to do with the Manin campaign? I want to earn promotion on my merits, not on the back of these ads.'

Adelino took back the picture. 'Look. Obviously it helps the campaign if you are a *maestra* here and not just a *servente*. But I wouldn't be offering you the chance unless I thought you were worthy. If these past few weeks have taught you anything about me, you'll know that I prize the reputation of my business above anything. I wouldn't let substandard glass be sold from this foundry.' Adelino bent to pick from the bucket the last heart she had made. 'This is true, and clear. It's good. Don't be so grudging. It's an excellent chance for you.'

Leonora relented. 'I am grateful. Thank you. I won't let you down.' As she turned to pick up her jacket Adelino surreptitiously put the heart she had made in his pocket.

'Now, please, clean up this God-awful mess. And clear off, so I can lock up.' They shared a smile at his affected gruffness.

His secret rescue had come just in time. For Leonora, before she shut the last firehole door, threw the bucket of imperfect hearts onto the dying heat of the coals, to melt down for gather the next day. She grabbed her bag, said a last 'thank you' to Adelino, and ran for her boat, tying Corradino's heart around her neck as she went.

Adelino felt the solid shape of the heart in his jacket pocket. Then without knowing why, he opened the door of the firehole to watch the crystal hearts bleeding and dying on the red coals, melting down into one mass. He had spoken the truth. He knew the girl *was* good enough to be the first *maestra* on Murano, but he hoped the men would accept this. He closed the door and shivered. Like Leonora before him, he had stared into the flames and looked for trouble.

It soon came, and from a not entirely unexpected quarter.

'What?' Roberto del Piero's shout sounded unnaturally high. The glassblower snatched up his latest piece — a beautiful *pasta vitrea* vase, clear glass with bright beads of colour trapped inside — and threw it against the furnace where it smashed into a million gems. Adelino had gathered the *maestri* together in the morning and made a short announcement of Leonora's promotion. There had been a stony silence from all the men — save one.

'You can't do this. You can't make this *puttana* a *maestra*. First those ridiculous adverts and now this. We'll be a laughing stock,' spluttered Roberto.

Leonora reacted instantly to the insult, and, as the whole the room froze following the smash of the vase – even as Adelino's white eyebrows drew down into a frown – she crossed the floor and landed a stinging slap on Roberto's face for the second time in their short acquaintance. 'Not so much of a *puttana* that I would sleep with a man like you. *That's* what's bothering you – you got turned down.'

Adelino intervened at last, grabbing the two of them like brawling cats. 'In my office, both of you.' With a strength that belied his years, he carted them off to his inner sanctum, an iron grip on their upper arms. Once inside and released, Leonora and Roberto eyed each other, she with anger, he with a malice that chilled her bones. She could hardly believe that such hatred had been engendered by a brush-off outside a Murano bar.

Adelino sat behind his desk, with a deep sigh. The trouble he had foreseen had come to pass. He knew of their altercation in the bar – staff gossip always reached him – but he sensed too that Roberto's hatred ran much deeper, and hoped to God he could be silenced before the truth, whatever it was, emerged. 'Roberto,' Adelino began, 'that vase would have fetched three hundred euros. That amount will be taken from your wages.'

'Take what you like,' the man sneered. 'But I will not work with this, this ...'

'Don't say it again,' Leonora interjected, deadly serious.

Adelino broke in. 'Leonora. *Silenzio.* Now, Roberto, am

I to understand that you are giving me an ultimatum? That if I make Leonora a *maestra* you will go?'

Roberto, cooling, nodded. Adelino sighed again, refusing to meet Leonora's questioning eyes. She couldn't believe what was about to happen. Last night she had thought hard on the boat home and concluded that, whatever the state of play with Alessandro, she had achieved a great thing – she was the first female glassblower on Murano, a *maestra*. She had what she came to Venice for. She at last had the job that she wanted – an outlet for her creative and artistic passions.

And after one short night it is to be taken away, I'm to be pushed back down to servente*, through the malice of a man I hardly know. For Adelino will never get rid of Roberto. He is the best glassblower on the island.*

At length Adelino spoke. 'This is very difficult for me.' He raised his eyes, but met those of the man not the girl before him. 'Roberto, you are the best *maestro* here, but your head is as hot as the furnace. You can collect your money from accounts and go. The vase was on me.'

Leonora gasped, and turned to Roberto, almost expecting him to strike Adelino. But the *maestro* turned on her instead. Before Adelino could stop him, Roberto had Leonora against the wall, his hand cruelly twisted at her throat, holding the glass heart in his palm, the blue ribbon twined round his hard fingers. Their pose held a cruel echo of his amorous advances outside the bar, but his words were very different.

'Yes, you have wormed your way in here, *puttana*, but I bet they haven't told you that you are the spawn of a traitor? That your precious ancestor betrayed mine, and sold the secrets of the glass to France, where he died a rich man? Your grand ad campaign is a joke, based on a lie.'

'It's you who lies!' Leonora spat in the leering visage. 'Corradino lived here, worked here, and died here.'

'Little idiot. He died in France.'

Adelino, galvanized at last, hissed, 'Roberto, let her go, and get out of my sight.'

Roberto, as if spent by his revelations, released Leonora, and slammed out of the room.

The girl sank into a chair, as if dazed. Adelino fussed around her, appalled by the scene he had allowed to take place. He gave her water, and, as she waved his attentions away, sat down again, shaken himself. At last she looked up. 'What did he mean, about Corradino? How could he be a traitor? And how did he harm Roberto's family?

Adelino shook his head, bemused. 'Roberto is a del Piero. All those centuries ago, his ancestor Giacomo was a great *maestro*, and the mentor of Corradino. As far as I know they were the best of friends.'

'Then why would Roberto say what he said? Why would he hate Corradino and me? And what did he mean about treachery – and about France? I thought Corradino died here?'

Adelino nodded. 'Certainly he died here, of mercury poisoning, so the history books say.'

Leonora tried to absorb this, the threads of a hundred half-remembered tales of Corradino spinning webs in her addled brain. She soon realized that she was nodding her head repeatedly. 'Yes,' she said, 'that must be right . . .'

Adelino crossed the room and took her by the shoulder. 'Look. Why don't you take the rest of the day off? I'll smooth things over here. Come in tomorrow as normal and this will all blow over. Big day tomorrow, the first press ads go out. Get some rest.'

Leonora registered his kind tone but her stomach shrivelled at the thought of the ordeal to come. She stumbled thankfully out into the sunlight and turned to walk to the boat along the Fondamenta Manin. This time the familiar street name gave her no comfort. Instead she looked up at it and addressed the faded sign. 'Corradino, what did you do?'

CHAPTER 16

A Knife of Obsidian

And now, to make a knife.

The glass blades that Corradino made for The Ten's assassins, those deadly points which entered the skin with barely a whisper, they would not do for his purpose. Such knives hung, glittering, on racks on the walls of the *fornace* – ranked like so many chilling icicles that brought the cold winter of death. They were made here in great number for good reason. They could be used but once. Each knife was designed to snap at the haft after the fatal wound had been delivered. The wound would close and heal in death, concealing the manner of the victim's leavetaking. But for those friends or families that sought a *post-mortem* for their dead beloved, the glass blade served as the ultimate warning from the Council. Corradino knew that his blades were the most favoured by the dark shades that reaped for The Ten. When he honed their deadly points he sometimes thought of the men that would meet their ends as these blades entered their flesh, separating muscle and sinew, rending artery and vein. He felt haunted by the cries of their women and children; keening, bereft of their men and fathers, as he himself had wept for his dead parents. But he dismissed the thought with another:

If I refused to make these knives, my own life would be forfeit.

Corradino mitigated his guilt by making the blades as thin, strong and clean as his skill allowed. Like a surgeon, if he had to assist such butchery, he would make the passing as painless as possible.

The *fornace* was empty – all the *maestri* had gone, even Giacomo, whose age was beginning to tell. Corradino was alone with the glittering blades, the half-finished *candelabri* standing like amputees waiting for their missing limbs, and the shining goblets singing almost imperceptibly as they cooled. He looked around the cavernous space that had been his home for twenty years, cool now that the fires were dead. He checked that every last soul had gone and then lit a single candle. He turned to the door of a disused furnace that was set back into the wall. He opened the door and entered the gaping maw, his feet crunching on the detritus of old goblets and candlesticks that had been littered in here like damaged treasure, since the furnace had been stopped up many years ago. Corradino felt for the blackened brickwork at the back of the firehole, felt expertly for the metal hook and pulled. An inner door silently sprang open and he stepped inside.

Instantly he was at home. He lit from memory the candles on the many branched stick inside the door and the room that warmed into light resembled not a place of work but an attractive Venetian salon. A velvet chaise lounged in the corner. A firehole, dominating one wall, burned as merrily as a nobleman's hearth. And on the walls, reflecting heat and light, hung some of Corradino's most treasured pieces; the pieces that he knew would have to be released for sale one day, but not yet – not quite yet. Great mirrors spanned from floor to ceiling, making the room twice as large. Sconces, reaching out from the walls in a heartbreaking arabesque, rivalled the beauty of the flames they carried. Picture frames that held no image, but that would diminish any portrait in the world, no matter how celebrated the beauty of the subject. Only the centre of the room belied the appearance of a luxurious *palazzo* for here stood the tools of Corradino's trade – long water vats and silvering tanks, vials of multicoloured pigments and limbecs of evil-smelling chemicals.

This chamber is mine. Secret, safe, and the right place for the office which I carry tonight.

Corradino knew what was needed – a knife of his own design, called a *dente*, or tooth. It was well named; not slim and deadly like the assassin's knives that he was charged to make, and not designed to break off at the haft like them. Short but sturdy, made of dense dark glass and with a wicked point, the *dente* would do well for cutting and digging alike. He was still for a moment, surveying his benchful of powders and unguents, thinking of the type of glass that was needed. Then he knew.

Obsidian. The oldest glass in the world.

He stripped off his jerkin and went to work. The heat of his chamber was intense, as the firehole was large and the room – though sizeable enough for its purpose – heated quickly. Corradino thrust a handful of ash-like pumice from Stromboli into the fire instead of the customary sand. Then followed a handful of sulphur which burned his nose and made him tie a kerchief about his face. His task tonight was to recreate the hard black natural glass that spewed forth, time out of mind, from the volcanoes of the south. The kind of glass which set like stone. The kind of glass which had entombed the poor dead souls of Pompeii and Herculaneum, trapped like flies in amber – first liquid, then diamond hard. With a firehardened paddle he mixed the powders with a fiery blob of gather which had been heating in the fire all day like a sleeping salamander. He mixed and reheated the glowing orb, adding more pumice and a little pitch, until the glass was as dark and sluggish as treacle. Only then did he take his *pontello* and shape the knife, rolling the handle on the wood and leather *scagno* saddle which stood by the fire. When he was happy – for there must be no error tonight – he took the handle to the fire again and flamed the blade end for a long moment. When the dark handle glowed at the haft he brought it out and set it in a vice, blade end down, and watched as the rosy tip of the handle grew downwards with the force of gravity, and the molten glass dripped like a fiery stalactite into a wicked point. Corradino had invented this drip method, finding that it yielded a more perfect point than any amount of grinding or polishing after the fact. This way, the glass made its own edge. The glass must best decide how its enemies were to be dispatched. He counted his heartbeats and, at exactly the right moment and not before, he turned the vice so that the cooling blade turned, curving and hardening into the fang of the beast. Small and stubby, black and pin-sharp, the evil point glinted in the fire-light

Yes – this should serve. The blade and handle are made all of a piece, so there is no weakness in the knife.

As Corradino sat and watched his black knife cool, he looked his last around the chamber. Known to no other save Giacomo, the room had been made for Corradino the day after he had discovered the secret of how to make his mirrors. All his most private work was done here. This salon kept the secret.

The secret, which lay buried in the art of glassblowing.

The secret that he merely stumbled upon when a vase that he was making went wrong. The secret which saved him from death at the hands of his greedy masters, The Ten. The secret which had freed him from the prison of Murano and given him the status to walk about Venice almost as other men, and thus give life to his greatest creation, Leonora. The secret which was not written anywhere, even in his vellum notebook, and was known to no man but he. The secret that was coveted by the foreign king who had brought him to this pass.

The secret which I swore to take to my grave. I did not know how true I spoke.

CHAPTER 17

Dead Letter Drop

Vittoria Minotto was intrigued. It was not a state of mind she experienced often, and in order to revel in the sensation fully she had suggested Florian's as a meeting place. If one was to put in for expenses, one might as well enjoy the experience.

The day was fine but there was a breath of Autumn in the breeze, so Vittoria chose a table just inside the famous green and gold salon, where he would easily be able to find her. There were no strains of string quartet or piano today. Many of the tourists were now gone – Venice was preparing to enter her period of hibernation before Carnevale. It was interesting to note – and as a local she had become aware of it over the years – that the thronging school parties and coach trips of summer gave way, in the winter months, to quiet weeks with the 'city break' couples dotting the *piazza* for the four days from Thursday to Monday.

Vittoria ordered her ruinously expensive *caffè americano* and lit her cigarette. She looked out into the square, to see if she could spot her date arriving. Ah, there he was. Young, good-looking, walking with a purposeful stride which scattered the pigeons. Better and better.

He found her at once. 'Signorina Minotto?' It was the voice from the phone call. Low, driven and agitated.

She inclined her head and blew out smoke. '*Sì.*'

He sat and, unbidden, took a cigarette and lit it. She liked him at once.

'I think I might know something which might interest you. About Leonora Manin. Actually no, it goes further back than that. About Corrado Manin. It might make quite a good story.'

That was it. He had said it. The word that she loved, that she lived for. The word that had captured her attention from being a little girl at her father's knee, holding her breathless from the words; 'Once Upon a Time'. How she had begged to stay up, to hear more!

A Story.

'Go on.'

CHAPTER 18

Non Omnis Moriar

Giacomo del Piero looked from his window over the Murano canal. He was sure he heard something stir without and carried his candle high, peering through the narrow quarrels of his window. He saw nothing, but the flame of his candle illuminated only his own reflection, fractured by the leadings of the panes. He saw an old man.

Giacomo turned from his image and thought of what he would do now. He supposed he must eat – there was some fine Bolognese sausage in the pantry, and a jug of wine to go with it, but somehow he had no appetite. He felt he needed to eat less as his age advanced – other things nourished him now. His books, his work, and his friendships. He thought of Corradino in particular, and that the boy had become as a son to him over the years. Perhaps he should go down the path to Corradino's lodgings, and share the wine with him? No, the boy was exhausted with this commission for that mysterious client, Maestro

Domenico of the Teatro Vecchio. Giacomo had never met the man, but he knew that the work kept Corradino at the *fornace* at all hours. Perhaps Corradino was even yet not at home to receive a visit.

Giacomo took up his ancient viol instead and his bow and fingers, unbidden, found a melancholy folk song of the Veneto which matched his mood. He felt a foreboding, a heaviness of heart which he could not explain. It was this feeling that had made him go to the window repeatedly since he had returned from the *fornace*.

So the muffled knock at the door when it came did not surprise him, as he had felt expectant all evening. As he set down his viol carefully on the trestle, he had a horrid fancy that he would be opening the door to Death itself, come at last to claim him. But the figure who stood there was not Death. It was Corradino.

They kissed each other heartily, although Giacomo thought at once that his friend looked agitated. Once inside he could not seem to sit or stand, and waved away the offer of wine, before accepting and downing the cup in one swallow.

'Corradino, what ails you? Have you a fever? Is it the mercury?' For Corradino had suffered much from a hacking cough of late – a sign which could indicate a corruption of the lungs from the mercury used to silver the mirrors. Only last week Giacomo had insisted that his friend place four peppercorns under his tongue to ward off the lung sickness – like all Venetians Giacomo had an enormous respect for the mysterious spices of the east. But even spices could not prevent mercury poisoning. The silver devil brought most of the glassblowers to their deaths – their art consumed them in the end. Corradino shook his head fervently at Giacomo's diagnosis, but his eyes burned in his head. 'I came to . . .' he began, and stopped abruptly.

Giacomo grabbed Corradino's arm and pulled him down on the trestle beside him. 'Compose yourself, Corradino *mio*. What is it you would say? Are you in trouble?'

Corradino laughed, but shook his head again. 'I came to say . . . I know not what . . . I want you to know . . . there is so much I cannot tell you!' He took a breath. 'I wanted to tell you that I owe you everything, that you are a father to me, that you saved my life over and again, that I can't ever repay you, and that, whatever may befall me, I wish you to try to think well of me.' He clasped the old man's hands fervently. 'Promise me this – that you will try to think well of me.'

'Corradino, I will always think well of you. What *is* this coil?'

'One more thing. If you should see Leonora, if you should ever see her, tell her that I have always loved her, and love her still.'

'Corradino . . .'

'Promise!'

'I promise, but you must tell me what you mean by all this. What has become of you tonight? What are you planning?'

Corradino reacted instantly. 'I am planning nothing. Nothing. I ...' he laughed and dropped his head into his hands, his fingers parting the dark curls. Then, in more normal tones he said, 'Forgive me. It is some mood, some fancy. Dark humours come from the gibbous moon, which shines tonight.'

He motioned toward the window, and Giacomo saw, sure enough, that the moon was almost full, and had a strange hue. Perhaps that accounted for his own melancholy. 'Aye, I felt somewhat of the same mind myself. Come, let's drink this folly away.'

Corradino waved away the wine jug. 'I must go. But remember all I said.'

Giacomo shrugged. 'I will. But I'll see you at the *fornace* tomorrow.'

'Aye, tomorrow. I'll see you then.'

The hug was fervent and prolonged. Then Corradino was gone, and Giacomo was once again alone. As he stared out into the night, he wondered if he had really seen tears shining in his friend's eyes as he turned away. Despite the talk of tomorrow, the whole interview had the manner of a leavetaking.

A leavetaking indeed. When Corradino did not arrive at the *fornace* in the morning, Giacomo's foreboding reached its peak, awful voices clamouring in his head. He went at once to Corradino's lodgings, running as fast as his old limbs would carry him. He entered the little cot without knocking and headed to the second room – the bedchamber. There, he saw the worst. His friend lay on the truckle bed, fully dressed, and still. He thought at first that Corradino had taken his own life, that this had been the meaning of the farewell yestereve. But then, through new tears, he saw a telltale streak of black running from the corner of the open mouth to the coverlet. He turned over one of Corradino's cold hands – the fingertips were also black. Giacomo had seen such signals more times in his life than he wished to. Mercury. The plague of the glassblower had taken Corradino at last. Giacomo sat at the foot of the bed and wept.

He had known.

Corradino had known that he was dying, last night when he had visited. He *had* been saying goodbye. Giacomo stood at last and pulled the coverlet over the face that was so dear to him. As he did so he lamented, as fathers have always lamented as they beheld their dead sons: 'Lord, why did you not take me?'

That night, Giacomo returned at last to his house. It had been the most painful day of his long life, and he felt he would gladly go to sleep and never wake. He had reported Corradino's death to the mayor of Murano, and a *medico* had been sent to verify cause. The doctor had prodded Corradino with great care, snipping hair and letting blood, a thoroughness which Giacomo knew had been ordered by The Ten. In his dark robes and white mask with its long, beaked nose stuffed with herbs to prevent infection, the doctor looked for all the world like a vulture come to feed on the carrion of Corradino. But, if one of their great assets died, the Council always wished to make sure there was no misadventure. Only the knowledge of this prevented Giacomo from intervening to plead for his dead friend's dignity. He kept his peace. But when the *medico* at last released the body he seemed surprised that Giacomo requested permission to fulfill the proper rites for his friend. As the post-mortem was complete however, the doctor saw no reason not to grant this whim and Corradino was carried to Giacomo's house to be laid out.

Giacomo attended while the women he had paid made Corradino ready. They cleaned his face, arranged his hair and tied his feet together and his jaw closed. As candles burned around them they sewed the dead man into sack cloth, and Giacomo watched the face he loved disappear into darkness as the stitches closed the shroud. With his last glance of Corradino he thought how comely his son had been, that his curls shone in the candlelight, the cheeks held a faint flush and the lashes that lay across them were still lustrous. It was almost as if he slept. He chided himself; and, in a last act of leave-taking, Giacomo tenderly placed a golden ducat over each closed eye. He gave away a twelvemonth's wages without a thought. He had given the boy everything: his home, his skills with the glass, and all the love his old heart could hold. Corradino had been his heir in all things, so in place of an inheritance Giacomo paid the fare for Corradino's final journey. He turned away, his heart breaking.

At last two constables came to carry the body to the boat which would take it to Sant'Ariano, the burial island. Giacomo asked to come to the quay, but was prevented.

'*Signore,*' said the taller constable, his eyes shining with sympathy behind their mask, 'we have two cases of plague to carry too. We could not vouch for your safety.'

So Corradino had gone, the constables had gone and the women had gone, gratefully biting the coins that Giacomo had given them for their trouble.

He was once again alone, as he had been the night before, before all this sorry business had come to pass. He could cry now for the friend – the son – who had gone. But his tears had left him, and he felt nothing but a dry grief for his loss. Once again he took up his viol, exactly as he had done before his world changed. But all was not exactly as before – there was a piece of vellum twisted in the strings. Vellum that Giacomo would know anywhere – it was the fine Florentine vellum of Corradino's notebook. Giacomo remembered now, as his heart beat fast in his throat, how he had pulled Corradino to sit down right next to the instrument the night before. With shaking fingers Giacomo slipped the note out from under the strings. Corradino was not one for penmanship, as he had been untimely ripped from Monsieur Loisy's tutelage at the age of ten, but these letters were clear enough. He had carefully spelt out, in the middle of the page, the Latin tag:

NON OMNIS MORIAR

Corradino was no great reader – in fact the only volume he knew well was the Dante from his father. But Giacomo was a learned man, and had no need to search through the volumes in his chamber for the meaning of the phrase. It all fitted – the bloom on Corradino's cheeks, the shine of his hair, the loving leavetaking of the night before.

NON OMNIS MORIAR
I SHALL NOT ALTOGETHER DIE

Giacomo clasped the vellum to his heart before pressing it gently between the pages of his own copy of Dante. As he closed the book he smiled for the first time that day.

Corradino was still alive.

CHAPTER 19

The Fourth Estate

'Read this.'

The newspaper slapped down onto Adelino's desk in front of Leonora. She could smell the acrid printer's ink under her nose. Adelino turned his back and went to the window, struggling with some emotion she could not yet divine. Could it be anger? She supposed that the press had bungled the ads, or misspelled something. Warning bells only began to ring when she saw Vittoria Minotto's byline and photo on the folded page.

My interview? No, worse.

"Hapless *vetraio* Adelino della Vigna has spectacularly backed the wrong horse for his splashy advertising campaign. In an effort to flog the glass of his ailing Vetreria Della Vigna on Murano, he recently introduced the Manin range, an exclusive line of antique and modern glass. The range was to be sold on the back of famous *maestro* Corrado Manin, known as Corradino, and his decorative ancestor Leonora Manin, who lately became the first *maestra* on the island. Our readers will remember, just days ago, the glossy ads in these and other publications featuring the two Manins, and our eyes have been assailed by the posters adorning the walls of our fair city. But little did we know then what this paper has been able to discover, with the help of one of the master glassblowers of the *fornace,* Roberto del Piero."

Leonora went cold.

Roberto.

Shaking, her sweating fingertips blurring the print, she read on.

"'The whole thing is a joke,' says Signor del Piero. 'Corrado Manin was indeed a master glassblower, but he was a traitor to the Republic and his craft. He was solicited by French spies and went to Paris to sell our secrets to the French, who were then our greatest trade rivals. Corradino single-handedly smashed the Venetian glass monopoly. It would be laughable except for the fact that the affair holds a sinister history for my own family. My own ancestor Giacomo del Piero was Corradino's lifelong friend and mentor, and yet Corradino betrayed him and caused his death. He's a Murderer, not a Maestro.'"

This catchy piece of alliteration had obviously drawn

the editor's eye, as the words 'Murderer not Maestro' formed the subheading of the paragraph. Leonora swallowed and read below.

"Signor del Piero's grievances are modern as well as ancient. 'I approached the advertisers with my own story. Giacomo was Corradino's mentor – he taught him everything he knew. Moreover, there have been del Pieros working at the *fornace* ever since his day. I offered them the opportunity to introduce a line of glass in *my* family name, and they threw it back in my face. Clearly they preferred this bimbo who's only been in Venice a few months.' Signor del Piero is dismissive of Signorina Manin's talents. 'She can blow the glass a little, but really she's just an English girl with no talent and a yard of blonde hair.' Particularly hard, then, is the fact that after hundreds of years of service to the glassblowing industry, the family's run now seems to be over. 'I tried to alert Adelino to the truth, and his answer was to fire me. He'd rather keep his precious bimbo because he needs her for his ad campaign.'

"We should stress at this point that this paper is not in the habit of printing the vengeful vitriol of the wrongly dismissed. We have been shown documentary evidence of the treachery of Corrado Manin from what historians would term a 'Primary Source'.

"These revelations will be an undoubted embarrassment to Signor della Vigna, who has been touting for business with the aid of such copylines as 'The Glass that built the

Republic'. Such phrases must be ringing in his ears this morning, and may explain why he has so far refused to comment. Readers can expect to see the campaign withdrawn."

'Is this true? You're withdrawing the campaign?'

Adelino turned, his face bleak. 'What else can I do?' He took the paper from her hands and flipped over the folded page. The black headline bawled out at her. 'TREACHERY ON MURANO.' There flanking the type was the portrait of ten-year-old, innocent Corradino, and herself, in her vest and jeans by the furnace.

Then, all at once, of the sea of her thoughts one alone surfaced and consumed her body:

I'm going to be sick.

She rushed from the room and through the *fornace*, to the canalside where she vomited helplessly. How could she know that Corradino had done the same, four centuries before, the night before he became a traitor?

CHAPTER 20

The Eyes of the Old

Leonora stood outside the University of Ca' Foscari in Dorsoduro. She had come to meet Professor Padovani, the only link in the city to her family, to her past.

She had come home the previous night, from the scene at the *fornace*, distraught and upset, her nausea remaining with her as she left Murano. Even the welcoming sight of the night lights of San Marco did little to soothe her mood. She left the island boat at Ferrovia and waited, as she rarely did, for the number 82 *vaporetto* to take her up the Grand Canal to the Rialto. As the *vaporetto* roared to a stop, and the gateman expertly tied the boat, she thought of her father for the first time in weeks. His presence here, his very existence, seemed ephemeral when compared to the relationship she had with Corradino, dead for many centuries longer. She felt clearly now how much she had relied on Corradino, felt pride in him and even love for him. She could not have been more devastated by such accusations of treachery had they been directed at her own father. She felt her father to have been someone belonging to her mother alone – Leonora had never seen him and Bruno had never seen her. Their link was purely biological.

My connection to Corradino, paradoxically, seems much more real to me.

And yet Roberto del Piero had struck at the very roots of that cross-centuries bond. She felt vulnerable, exposed. Even the sight of the silver palaces roosting in the twilight along the canal did not give her the usual comfort. Autumn was here, and the friendly frontages of the buildings had assumed a shuttered look as the lifeblood of the tourist trade ebbed away from their faces like a fading blush. The decorative windows looked back, blank-eyed and uninviting now. She wondered if Corradino had betrayed all this, of what secret conferences he had had, what meetings he had held in these very buildings. As she disembarked at Rialto and ducked down the darkening *calli* to the Campo Manin her feelings of unease multiplied – she began to feel hunted, followed, to listen out for soft footfalls in the shadows. She felt tainted by the slur on Corradino.

If he has done this thing, the city remembers and condemns me too.

Leonora felt rejected by the stones that had lately welcomed her. Even when she walked at last into the Campo Manin she felt pursued. The beautiful shadows could hold ugliness too.

Don't Look Now . . .

She chided herself. For it wasn't a dwarfish red figure that she feared, but Roberto del Piero. She had ended his career at the *fornace*, and his family profession. He could, of course, work elsewhere, but it was she who had cuckooed him out of his nest.

She ran across the still-warm stones of the *campo* and fumbled for her keys. In a childish game she felt she was outrunning the unseen assassins.

If I can just reach my door . . .

As she fitted the key in her lock she expected a hand to pluck at her sleeve, or even clutch at her throat . . . struggling with the latch she wrenched the door open and fell inside. She backed the door closed and leaned in the dark, breathing hard. Seconds later she left her skin as the phone began to ring. Shaking, she moved into the kitchen and picked up the receiver. But it was not the rasping tones of a horror film cliché. It was him.

'Alessandro!'

She sank into a chair and switched on the lamp. As the

pool of light spread and she listened to the longed-for voice, the shades of her daymares fled.

He laughed at the fervour of her greeting.

'Detective Bardolino to you.'

'You passed!'

'Yes.' Pride in the voice. 'I have a week of orientation here and then I start at division, back in Venice.'

She could not dampen his enthusiasm with her own troubles. *Il Gazzettino* was a local paper, and news of her humiliation or Corradino's reputation would not yet have reached Vicenza. Plenty of time to talk of that face to face. She suddenly felt terribly tired, and besides, a small sense of shame lodged just below her heart would not let her tell this man of her tarnished ancestor. While Alessandro talked about his weeks away and the exam, Leonora felt the fear and panic abate. She felt confident in the circle of his conversation as if protected by his nativity. Of course Corradino was no traitor. It was not true. It was an ugly rumour perpetrated by his rival. And what did it matter anyway? Corradino was long dead, and his work lived on to testify for him.

But it does *matter. I want to know for myself, to find out for certain.*

Something Alessandro had said floated back from memory. 'When we first met, you told me that you might be able to help me find out more about my family ... my father. Well, I'd like to, if you can make any suggestions?'

Alessandro considered. 'When your mother and father were together in Venice, did they have any friends or colleagues that may still be here?'

'There was someone. A lecturer at Ca' Foscari. I met him when I was very little.'

'Can you remember his name?'

'It was Padovani. I remember because my mother explained to me that his name meant "comes from Padua". She taught me an old rhyme ...'

'Ah yes, *Veneziani gran signori, Padovani gran dottori ...*'

'*Vicentini mangia gatti, Veronesi tutti matti.*' Leonora finished. 'I always wondered why the Vicenzans ate cats in the rhyme. But I suppose it's better than being mad, like the Veronese.'

'Ah yes, but the best thing to be of all is a great lord, like the Venetians.' Alessandro interjected proudly.

'Anyway, Professore Padovani still sends Christmas cards to my mother. But I don't know if he's still at Ca' Foscari.'

She could hear him stretching on the other end of the line. He was clearly tired, but his voice was alert and she was encouraged that he was treating her enquiry in earnest. 'Then I think the thing to do is to talk to this man, if he is still there. He will certainly know something of your father, which seems a good place to start. Go tomorrow,' he said with his customary dispatch, 'because on Sunday I'm back for the day and we'll do something, if you're free.'

She clutched the receiver with joy, feeling like a teenager. But with a desperate effort for detachment, she stayed with her theme. 'D'you really think I can find out about him, after all these years?' And it was Corradino she meant.

'Sure. He only died in, what was it? 1972? And, you know, if you want to find something out, you should really have a Detective on your team.' She could hear him grinning down the phone as he signed off with promises to see her on Sunday.

Leonora felt a sudden resolve to unravel the mystery of Corradino, and felt that the *Professore* would be a good start. She couldn't wait for tomorrow. She couldn't explain to herself why she had not been entirely honest with Alessandro, had let him think that she wished to find out principally about her father.

She slept badly, and in the morning was sick again. Nerves, she thought.

But I know it isn't nerves.

Leonora entered the modest side gate leading into the University precincts from the Calle della Foscari. Once inside, Leonora was deafened by the antics going on around her. Though it was Saturday morning, a study day for most students, there seemed to be some sort of Rag taking place – Leonora recognized the same misrule, the same anarchic spirit, which had moved her to dress as a nurse and help push a hospital bed down the Charing Cross Road during Rag week at St Martin's.

Eggs and flour were flying everywhere, and she had to duck more than once as she crossed the desecrated lawn.

They must be graduating. I read somewhere that Italian students think that making cakes of themselves is a fitting way to mark their transition to Dottore. *Soon they'll all be gone, like the tourists.*

She perused the faculty lists on a noticeboard cloistered behind glass, with fading hope, but at last Leonora spotted; 'Professore Ermanno Padovani.'

He's head of the faculty for 'Storia del Rinascimento'. Renaissance History. I might just be in luck. 'Padovani gran dottori' *indeed.*

She mounted the ancient stairs and trawled the empty corridors reading the names on the history department doors. From here the screams and merriment from outside were muffled. It felt like there was no one in these upper floors at all, so when she reached the *Professore's* door at last, Leonora felt little hope of him being inside. But when she knocked and heard a faint '*Entrate,*' muffled by the oak, her insides fluttered with the knowledge that the man inside this room may have some of the answers that she sought. As Leonora entered the sight she beheld almost made her forget why she had come. Ahead was a wide, ornate window, made up of a quartet of the most perfect, intricate, Moorish frames of which Venice was so proud. And beyond – the most incredible vista of the San Marco bank of the Canal Grande, water shimmering at the foot of the splendid palaces, as if in supplication to their grandeur. Leonora was so lost in the view that the voice that addressed her was an audible shock.

'One of the privileges of having taught here for thirty years is that I get the best room in the faculty. One of the drawbacks is, sometimes I find it very hard to get any work done. You must have come in the back way, through the gate? A pity. It is not the best aspect of the place.'

Leonora turned to the old man, who had emerged from behind his book and desk with the aid of a stick. Kindly, white-bearded, beautifully dressed and with penetrating eyes, he looked faintly amused. She apologized. 'But it's so beautiful, for a ...'

'You were going to say for a University? But it has not always been one. Ca' Foscari was formerly a palace built for the Bishops of Venice, and you know how prelates like their creature comforts. And surely, *Signorina*, you have beautiful seats of learning in your own country do you not? Oxford and Cambridge?'

Leonora started. She had flattered herself that her English accent was gone. But she was not chastened – it seemed that this was a man with a formidable intelligence, from whom nothing could be hidden. It seemed all the more likely that he could help her. She took a deep breath. '*Professore*, I apologize for disturbing you. I'd like to ask you a few ... historical questions, if you have a moment.'

The old man smiled, his bright eyes crinkling at the corners. 'Of course,' he said. 'I can spare more than that for the daughter of my old friend Elinor Manin. How are you, my dear Nora? Or,' the old eyes twinkled immoderately, 'is it *Leonora* now that you have become ... *assimilated*.'

Leonora marvelled at the quickness of the *Professore's* mind. Not only had he remembered her instantly, but he had divined, in a few short seconds, that she had changed her life and her name. She smiled.

'You're right. I am Leonora. And I'm amazed you remember me. I must have been ... what ... five years old?'

'Six,' countered Padovani. 'It was at a University drinks party in London. You proudly showed me your brand new shoes. They were nicer than the ones you have on today.' His eyes travelled to Leonora's battered converse trainers, which she shifted sheepishly on the wooden floor. 'And, you know, you mustn't give me too much credit for my perspicacity. You have become somewhat ... notorious ... since you arrived here, have you not?'

Il Gazzettino. Of course. The paper was taken by just about every household in Venice.

'But the rest of you has grown up so well, I suppose we must not be so exacting. The *Primavera*, yes? Botticelli is much more you than those Titian poses they put you in. But I suppose you have been told this many times, by younger men than me.'

Encouraged by his old-world charm, Leonora got to the point. 'I wanted to ask you some questions about my family ... if you have a little time.'

The *Professore* smiled. 'Time is plentiful at my age.' He motioned to the window, where four easy chairs were placed for tutorials. 'Sit down then. I'm going to, so you might as well.'

They sat in front of the peerless view, the chairs comfortable, but not cosy enough to induce sleep in the drowsy scholar. Settling himself, the *Professore* began, 'At the risk of sounding like the villain of a bad movie – they always seem to be English, don't they, my dear? I wonder why – I've been expecting you. I take it Elinor doesn't know that you are here.'

Leonora shook her head. 'No. I mean, she knows that I'm in Venice, but she doesn't know that I've come to talk to you.'

The *Professore* nodded, and his gnarled hands tapped the head of his cane. 'I see. Then I must tell you, first of all, that I will not divulge anything which she has shared with me in confidence, but other than that, I will be as helpful as I can be.' The *Professore* looked frankly at Leonora, waiting. Her fingers were twisting the glass heart she wore on its ribbon – a sign, surely, of stress. He thought the trinket was a clue to which relative she would ask about first. And so it proved.

'What do you know of Corradino Manin?'

'Corrado Manin was the finest glassmaker of his time, and of any other. He escaped the murder of his family and hid on Murano, where he was taught the ways of the glass and became a *maestro*. He was particularly proficient at making mirrors, and became famous for it. It is said that the mercury of the mirrors finally killed him, as it killed many.'

'So he died on Murano?'

'I don't know for certain. But it seems likely.'

Leonora exhaled with relief, but persisted.

'Do you know anything about the story that he may have gone to France?'

For the first time in the interview, the Professor looked discomfited. 'Yes, I read that exposé. Your colleague seems to be harbouring quite a grievance. I'd like to know what the 'Primary Source' is that he thinks he has. I imagine that you would not feel comfortable approaching him yourself?'

'There's absolutely no way that Roberto would tell me anything, least of all help me to exonerate Corradino. He's so angry with me that I'm afraid of him. I keep expecting him to ambush me from the shadows.' She tried to laugh, but could see the *Professore* was not convinced. He did not probe further into her fears, but moved on.

'And the young lady at the paper? Might she be approached?'

Leonora shook her head. She had put in a call to *Il Gazzettino* as soon as she had read Roberto's revelations. She was eventually put through to a frosty sounding Vittoria, who had abandoned all pretence of friendliness. She was sorry, Signorina Manin, but the supporting documents of her sources were strictly confidential, particularly in this case as Signor Roberto del Piero had asked that they remain so. There was a chance that they'd be doing a follow-up story in which the source would be reproduced, and Signorina Manin could look forward to that.

'Hmm.' Padovani shrugged expressively 'Ah well. One of the wonderful things about the study of history is that there is never just *one* definitive source, but many. If facts are diamonds, then our sources are the facets, each set at a discrete angle to make up the whole gem. We can do some detective work of our own, and find those other facets.'

Leonora was encouraged by his use of the word 'we' while his reference to detection warmed her with the thought of Alessandro.

'It's possible that Corrado went abroad. But highly unlikely. It's true that French mirror-making took an enormous leap forward in the late seventeenth century, evidenced by the *Palais de Versailles*, which became the flagship for the enlightened century. Some say they had foreign intelligence, others say that they arrived at these methods through convergent evolution.'

'Convergent evolution?' queried Leonora.

The Professor explained. 'In Africa, from the primeval mulch of single-celled soup, there evolved an enormous mastodon with large ears which we now call the African elephant. In India, there evolved, by the same method, a creature the same in all respects save the size of its ears. Both creatures evolved independently, separated by seas and landmasses, by tectonics, to arrive at the same place. Neither 'copied' the other. They merely share a distant ancestor, as all glassware shares its mother; sand. They underwent convergent evolution.'

Leonora pressed the point. '*Professore*, why would you say that it was highly unlikely that Corradino went to France?'

'Because The Ten, the ruling body of the *Consiglio Maggiore*, took great exception to the defection of their artisans. They threatened their families with death if craftsmen took their secrets to foreign powers. Murano itself was something of a prison, although perhaps less so for a man like Corrado, who was possessed of a prodigious talent and was given dispensation to visit the city for his work.'

Leonora broke in with the question that seemed obvious to her. 'But *Professore*, why would The Ten hold any threat for Corradino, if all his family were dead?'

'Because, my dear young lady, not *all* his family were dead. I have but a rudimentary grasp of the Biological Sciences but I do know that, if they were all dead, there would be no descendants such as yourself, my dear. Corradino had a daughter.'

★ ★ ★

Leonora pressed her face into the towel, not caring how many grubby student hands had dried there before. She felt a fool – running out of the *Professore's* room like that, and skidding into the nearest bathroom to heave into the nearest toilet bowl. Why was this revelation such a shock to her? If she had even thought it through logically, there must have been someone else, some lineage, or else how was she here? How did she have the glass heart that Corradino passed down all the way to her? She held the heart for courage as she walked shakily back down the hall and timidly re-entered the *Professore's* room. Padovani courteously stood, with concern in his eyes. She sat again and apologized.

'Forgive me, I've been … unwell … for a couple of days now.'

The *Professore* nodded and took up his story. 'Corrado's daughter was also called Leonora. She was the product of an illegitimate union between Corrado and a noblewoman, Angelina dei Vescovi, who died in childbirth. Leonora was taken in to the Pietà orphanage and trained in music. She was given the name of Manin, but surnames were never used at the orphanage. The girls in the Pietà were always known by the instrument they played – *'cello, violino* – to maintain the anonymity of the bastard children of some very highly born families. She was always Leonora *della viola*, and was a very accomplished player. None would have known of her connection to Corradino, or even of

213

her existence unless he himself told of it. Even The Ten had to respect the secrets of the Pietà, as the foundation had the weight of the church and its laws of sanctuary behind it. After Corradino's death Leonora was found by a distant cousin – a Milanese called Lorenzo Visconti-Manin – who was attempting to trace the disparate fragments of his family. The two fell in love and married, and she once again came into her rightful name. The Manins became a powerful force in Venice once again, and their descendant Lodovico Manin became a Doge, the last of Venice before the Republic fell.'

Leonora's head spun, but her nausea was gone in the hope that now consumed her. 'So Corradino would not have left, for fear of his daughter's safety.'

'No,' said the *Professore*. 'That is not what I meant. The Ten knew nothing of the child, for she was secreted in the Pietà by her grandfather and no one knew who had fathered her. Angelina never told the name of her seducer, and took the secret to her grave. I merely meant that I thought it unlikely that Corradino would have left Venice while Leonora lived. Visits to a secret daughter in the Pietà would be risky, but not impossible. And I imagine the temptation would be very hard to resist.'

Leonora was silent, digesting this.

So the treachery story could still be true, if unlikely. And what of this new character, the lost girl with my name that had no family but the Pietà and only music for her friend. At least she found love in the end.

She asked, 'how would we find out more? Can we ever know for sure if Corradino left Venice?'

'You could try the large library in San Marco – the Sansoviniana – they have guild records and also records of births and death, going back centuries. But I have told you all I know of Corradino's history, and this is the account that I gave Elinor.' The *Professore* stood to stretch his bad leg. 'My only other suggestion would be to try to find something out from the French end. I have some contacts at the Sorbonne who could help you.'

Leonora took his cue and stood. 'May I see you again? And will you contact me if you think of anything more?'

'Of course. And you may mention my name for a reference in the rare book collections of the Sansoviniana.'

I remember my first day here, when they would barely let me through the front door of the Sansoviniana. Now I am to be admitted to the inner sanctum.

The *Professore* moved to his desk to write down numbers and the names of various document collections that might be helpful. Leonora scribbled down her phone numbers and as the papers were exchanged Padovani wondered if Leonora was actually going to leave without asking of that other Manin, but at last she said: 'And my father? Did you know him?'

The *Professore* shook his head, with sympathy in his eyes. 'As is the manner of young women in love, Elinor saw little of her friends and kept Bruno to herself. I only heard of his death through the local news.'

At the mention of her father's name in this context, Leonora felt a wave of shame that she had not bothered to enquire after him before, so consumed was she with Corradino.

'Is there any family still in Venice?'

'I don't know. Elinor mentioned that Bruno's parents lived in Verona, but they died long since.'

Leonora knew of this but had not contemplated the loss before – of that immediate family that most take for granted; Grandparents. They had gone – without any of the usual meetings, knitted jumpers, chocolate bars, holiday outings. She collected herself – she knew that she must leave the *Professore*, and was anxious to begin her researches of the documents he had suggested, but felt she had a thousand more questions.

As she moved to the door, with murmurs of thanks and promises to return, the *Professore* embraced Leonora warmly. Holding her arms he said, 'one more thing. Tomorrow is the feast of All Souls, the *Festa dei Morte,* when the people of Venice honour their dead. If you would see your father, he is buried on San Michele. Perhaps you will visit him. He too should be mourned.'

Leonora felt reproach, but also affection.

I know I should go and see his grave. We should meet at last.

I'll ask Alessandro to come too.

She moved into the corridor and made to walk towards the stairs. The *Professore* called, 'Leonora!'

She turned. The old man looked directly at her, and said softly, 'There are some things an old man can see that a young man can't. Look after yourself.'

'I will,' she replied.

The oak door closed and she headed down the stairs.

I wonder how he knew?

CHAPTER 21

The Island of the Dead (part 1)

The number 41 *vaporetto* to the Isola San Michele resembled a flower garden. On this day, the festival of All Souls, Venetians all honoured their dead with floral tributes, and headed for the cemetery on the island of San Michele. Leonora was pressed close to Alessandro, but equally close on her other side was a sizeable matron carrying an immense bunch of chrysanthemums. Leonora stared at the huge ugly blooms, and breathed their pungent antiseptic scent. She had never liked the flower — not just for aesthetic sensibilities, but because she associated them with death. Looking around the boat, she could see that, as in France also, chrysanthemums were indeed the flower of choice for mourners.

Leonora and Alessandro had caught the boat from the Fondamenta Nuove. It was a short crossing — indeed the cemetery with its red walls and cloistered gates could be clearly seen from the city islands. Leonora was thankful for the brevity of the trip. With the crush of people and the smell of boat fuel, her nausea had returned. She moved closer to Alessandro and he dropped a reassuring kiss on her head – as he would to a child, she thought. She had told him that he needn't come with her, but he had pro-tested that he wished to visit his grandmother's grave anyway. She knew this was only partly true – that he was there in support of her and her meeting with her father. She felt a warm thankfulness replace the sickness in her solar plexus. When he was with her she believed in him. She almost began to feel secure, that they had something like a relationship.

They disembarked with the crowds, and entered the iron gates of the cemetery. Alessandro steered Leonora to a booth where one could purchase a map of the grave-sites.

'There are three cemeteries here,' said Alessandro 'all tended by Fransiscan monks as they always have been. Although as you'll see, a little more care is taken of the Catholic plots than those of the other two – the Protestants and the Greek orthodox,' he smiled wryly, 'so your father and my *nonna* are fortunate.'

Leonora registered his flippant ghoulishness and consid-ered that it was his way of dealing with death. She was curious about this strange island where only the dead dwelt. She had the feeling that she would not like to live along the Fondamenta Nuove, where fancy would lead one to the window of an evening to watch for phosphorescent spirits rising over the sea. She gave herself a little shake and asked, 'When did this island become a cemetery?'

'In the days of Napoleon. Before that, the dead were taken to Sant'Ariano, which is just an ossuary now.'

'A what?'

'An island of bones.' Alessandro seemed to taste the words, as if contemplating the title for a sensational novel. 'When the time runs out for the bodies here, they get shifted away to make way for new ones.'

'What *can* you mean?'

Alessandro led her up the tended pathway to the Catholic quarter. 'I mean that Venetians are only allowed to be buried here for a certain length of time, after which they are dug up and moved.' He caught the look on Leonora's face. 'It has to be so. Because of room – it's limited.' He shrugged, callously.

'I didn't mean that ...'

'Oh, I see. You mean you think he might not still be here? He will. You get forty years I think. And if your relatives pay, you can stay longer.'

Leonora suddenly felt angry as she followed Alessandro through the quiet courts. She felt that there was no permanence, no rest for these people. But as she watched the mourners walking quietly between the graves, like flowing water that would always find its way between and round its obstacles, she relented. This end, this rest that was not rest, was a fitting end for the shifting, itinerant seafaring people. Venetians lived their lives crossing from island to island, from Rialto to San Marco, Giudecca to Lido, Torcello to Murano. Why not continue after death, this relentless flux, with the sea as your steed? What could be better for those merchants and crusaders who had boarded the boats at Zattere and left them at Constantinople? And for her father too, who had jumped from shore to boat, from boat to shore, to earn his living all his adult life. Leonora realized that tears were sliding down her cheeks.

Idiot. You didn't even know him.

But when it came to it, as Alessandro led her through the ranks of almost military-style graves, and she was brought face to face with her father's name etched neatly in stone, she felt nothing but a dry emptiness. She felt no urge for tears. Alessandro murmured that he would find his grandmother, and melted away, but Leonora hardly noticed.

BRUNO GIOVANNI BATTISTA MANIN 1949-1972

He was only twenty-three when he died.

She didn't know what to do. She was visiting the bones of a twenty-three year old man – a man she had never met, a man who was still ten years younger than her living self.

And forever shall be . . .

The words – half remembered from school and Sunday church, rang their solemn refrain in her head. She was lost. At length, she lay down her tribute on the headstone – simple white daisies. Buy your favourite, don't try to guess his, Alessandro had said, and he had been right. Then she sat on the grass, looked at the stark letters and numerals again, and simply said: 'Hello, I'm Leonora.'

Alessandro found his grandmother in a matter of moments, and placed his roses at her headstone. He could scarcely remember her now, but though the complete memory eluded him, specifics remained. He remembered her black clothes, worn daily since the death of his grandfather. He remembered her *tagliatelle con burro e salvia*, which had never, in his opinion, been bettered by any trattoria. He remembered her wholly unexpected love for Vicenza Calcio, a love which had begun his own lifelong obsession with the team, and the game of football itself. He felt no grief, just fondness, as he crouched to flick dried twigs away from her plot and ran his thumbnail under a frill of lichen. He straightened up to look for Leonora, and quickly identified her bright head, bowed, her face hidden under her mass of hair. Discomfited, he thought she might be crying, then, as he saw her lips move, that she was praying. He crossed himself, but Leonora's eyes were open, and her demeanour more casual, more comfortable than one at prayer. He realized that, for the first time, she was having a conversation with her father.

She did not know how long she had been talking. She had begun at the beginning, and told her father all about her life: her childhood, her art, Stephen, the childlessness, the divorce, the move to Venice, Murano, the house in the Campo Manin, and Alessandro. She talked of Corradino, of her extraordinary fondness for her – for their – ancestor. She spoke of the stain of treachery of which she had just learned, of Roberto, Vittoria and *Professore* Padovani. She even spoke of Elinor, of their difficult relationship, and asked about the Elinor that Bruno knew – that different Elinor of long ago, the romantic and reckless Elinor, so different from the buttoned and bitter woman that Leonora knew. She talked herself to a standstill, and felt better. She looked up at last, stretched her aching legs, and beckoned to a hovering Alessandro that they could go. As he started towards her she turned for one private farewell. She laid her hand on the warm stone with affection. 'Goodbye. I'll come again.'

And I will.

Alessandro and she walked to the *vaporetto* stop and prepared to cross the Styx again – but this time the water would take them from the province of the dead back to the land of the living. She had found some peace here. She still needed to find the truth about Corradino but it had done her good to connect with her father – her immediate family – first. And he had been so easy to talk to. She had told him everything. Everything save one thing.

I didn't tell him I was pregnant.

CHAPTER 22

The Island of the Dead (part 2)

The feeling of grit in my mouth, grating between my teeth.

In his dream Corradino was on the Lido di Venezia, with his mother. The household were on a summer trip and the servants had roasted oysters on the beach while *piccolo* Corradino ran hither and thither in the surf, soaking his breeches with the whispering salt water. He was called to eat, and reclined on the blood-coloured velvet cushions with his mother's arm around him, her bosom smelling of vanilla. He tried an oyster for the first time, his eight-year-old palate first rejecting, then accepting the gelatinous creature as it slid down his throat. He tasted the oyster once it had left his mouth, and so began a lifelong partiality for this peasant food. The taste remained in the grittiness of the sand, left as a residue on his tongue, like sand washed up by a high tide; the *acqua alta*. In his dream he tasted the sand, the flesh of the oyster and the vanilla scent of his mother all at once, but when he woke at last, he knew he was far from the happiness of that day.

He felt the coarse sackcloth pressing on his face, planting a rough kiss on his lips like the greeting of his uncle Ugolino. Always bearded, it was ever a scratchy embrace – a traitor's kiss. Corradino struggled to breathe and turned his head slightly – it was better, but the stifling dark was hot and crushing and he was afraid. As his head turned he heard a metallic chink and felt two cold objects fall to the back of his head – the two ducat coins that Giacomo had pressed on his eyes after death, to pay the ferryman. He felt them move in his hair, cold metal for the dead sliding among the warm hair of the living. Perspiration soaked him in an instant as panic swelled in his throat and he fought the desperate urge to struggle and scream. They had not bound him, as they had promised not to, but they had no need – he could not feel his legs. A muffled scream escaped him once, then with a supreme effort he calmed himself. To keep the black panic at bay he began, for the next long moments, to remember with exactitude, with perfect detail, what the Frenchman had said.

'Corradino, have you heard of *Romeo e Giulietta*?'

Corradino was sitting in the confessional of his church, Santi Maria e Donato on the island of Murano. All the *maestri* worshipped here on Sundays. Religious observance was not required by the State, as the civic attitude was summed up in the phrase; '*Veneziani prima, poi cristiani*'

– 'Venetians first, then Christians'. But the glassblowers
were more devout than most, as they appreciated the gifts
which elevated them above the common man. Corradino,
in the arrogance of a great artisan, often had the blas-
phemous notion that he and God shared the same satisfaction in the creation of beauty. In his humbler moods
he felt himself a tool or instrument of the Creator.
Sometimes he listened to the words of the mass, but on
other days he spent long moments marvelling at the
Byzantine splendour of the mosaic that adorned the nave
floor. He felt a respect and a brotherhood for the long-
dead-craftsmen who knew how to combine such abstract
patterns with realistic beasts. In the universe of the mosaic
nature was strange and sometimes inverted; here an eagle
carried off a deer in his talons, there two roosters carried
a helpless fox slung from a pole.

The mosaic is allegorickal – it describes my own existence to me.
It is made of thousands of nuggets of glass just as my life is, and
it depicts nature as it is and nature as it is not. Some of my
daily life has remained the same, some is greatly changed.

Today he had come to confession as usual, but he did not
confess to his usual priest. He realized as soon as the voice
spoke in the warm dark that it was Duparcmieur.

They had never met in the same place twice, and no
longer in Venice. The Frenchman had been a merchant on
Burano where Corradino had gone to buy gold leaf,

Duparcmieur's costume flamboyant enough to make him disappear in the spectrum of the multicoloured fishing houses. He had been a boatman who murmured to Corradino in low tones as he rowed the ferry between Venice and Giudecca. And now, he was a Catholic priest.

He changes every time so completely, like the fabled lizards of the Indies who can dissemble as a leaf or a rock. I feel that I live in a dream, or a commedia *played out by actors in San Marco.*

But Duparcmieur was no comic muse – he dealt in Death. Today they were here to plan Corradino's demise, although the Frenchman's opening gambit seemed to belie the seriousness of their business.

'*Romeo e Giulietta*?' Corradino was bemused. But he had learned in their conversations that it were best to answer the Frenchman literally – apart from anything else, it saved time.

Although Corradino's formal education was halted at ten when Monsieur Loisy was wrested from him, Giacomo had done right by him and continued the boy's tutelage as best he could. So Corradino was able to reply with some confidence. 'It's an old tale, supposedly true, from Verona during the Italian wars, about two tragic lovers from opposing families. It was written up into a story, and embellished, by a monk; Matteo Bandello.'

'Very good.' Duparcmieur's voice passed clearly through

the grille, dry as sand, and low enough not to be overheard through the thick frontal drapes of the confessional.

'You may be interested to know that it was lately made into a play in England by one Master William Shakespeare. It was written in the time of *La Reine* Elizabeth, but I believe its popularity continues at court even now. It is the final act of the tragedy that concerns us; or, more specifically, you.'

Corradino waited. He had learned, too, that interruptions were fruitless.

'In the play, Giulietta takes a Mantuan poison in order to avoid an unwelcome marriage. The draught makes the body mimic death in every particular – the countenance grows paler, the pulses slow to an imperceptible rate, the fires of the humours are damped – but not extinguished. Pain is never felt – even attempts to bleed the victim yield no flow of blood, and give no pain. In the drama, Giulietta wakes, some days later, unharmed as if from a deep sleep. Of course by then, her beau has taken his own life and all is for nought. But this is not the burden of our tale.' Duparcmieur dismissed the fates of the long-dead lovers in a manner Corradino found chilling. 'The point is, my dear Corradino, that one thing your little city states make rather well – for it certainly isn't the food or wine,' he sniffed fastidiously, 'is poison.' He took a breath. 'I suppose that in all those years of internecine strife, your Guelfs and Ghibbelines, your Borgias and Medicis, the art became somewhat,' he searched for a phrase, 'more *developed* than in my own more civilized nation.'

This Corradino would not have. 'Perhaps you are forgetting the wonderful artistic heritage of our states, sponsored by those very warring families? Is art not civilization? Does France boast a Leonardo, or a Michelangelo? And perhaps you also forget that you have come to *me* to ask for *my* expertise to help *your* King?'

He heard the impossible man chuckling through the grille. 'You have fire in your belly, Corradino. That's good. But you must learn to love France, you know, it will be your country too soon enough, with the will of God. Now, to business.' The Frenchman's voice changed abruptly. 'When we leave this confessional, kneel and kiss my hand. In it I hold the draught I have procured for you. Not, it is true, from Mantua, but from somewhere in your own fair Republic. Take it tonight, and but three hours later you will fall into a deep state of sleep, and never wake in the morning. Instead you will sleep the day through. That night, you will wake one day exactly, almost to the moment, from the time you fell asleep.'

'And where will I be then?'

'Well, here you must inform me, Corradino. Who is it that will find your body?'

Corradino shivered at the term – Duparcmieur spoke as if he were already dead. He thought for a moment but needed no longer – he knew that if he did not appear at the *fornace* for the first time in ten years save for the time he had the water sickness, Giacomo would come to his house as he had that day too. The old man had brought him an eel from the market, and an orange, bright as a tiny sun, which was reputed to clear the sickness, and did.

'Giacomo – my ... friend will find me.'

'Very well. And does he love you well enough to provide the proper rites for you? Or will you be put in the pauper's pit on Sant'Ariano? It matters not, we can plan for each eventuality.'

Corradino found that the only way to contemplate the plan was to adopt the impersonal tone of Duparcmieur. If he thought closely about the actuality he would drive himself distracted.

'He will pay for a burial.'

Corradino felt, rather than saw, Duparcmieur nod on the other side of the grille. 'Then he will send for the constables. But they will not be those of The Ten, they will be working for me. You will be taken to Sant'Ariano, and when you wake you will be buried under soil.'

Corradino choked, as if in anticipation of this fate. 'What?'

'My dear man,' said the Frenchman smoothly, 'consider that you may well be followed even after death by those that watch you now.' Duparcmieur, after some reflection, thought that he would not trouble Corradino with the possibility that The Ten may send their own *medico* to check that Corradino was truly dead, and that the doctor might, as had been known, plunge a surgical blade deep into the corpse's chest just to be sure. He merely continued; 'everything must appear true. My men will not bind you, and they will not bury you deep. You will easily be able to escape once your strength returns.'

'And when will that be?'

'Ah yes. Now listen well, Corradino. Your limbs will take some little time to regain their feeling. Your head and neck will wake first, as they reign supreme in the corporeal order. Then your heart and chestspoon and arms. Then as your humours heat in your stomach again your legs will gradually regain their feeling, with your feet waking last of all. Be not afraid as this process happens, for giving way to your fears will rob the vapours around you of their nourishing gases. Instead you must think of this conversation, remain calm, and wait to make your escape. Do you have a good knife?'

I will take no chances – I will make one myself. I will trust no other man's blade with an office such as this.

'Yes.'

'Then secrete it in your hose before you take the draught. You'll need it to cut the sacking and dig.' Again, the Frenchman thought that the possibility that The Ten's doctor would find and confiscate the knife was best kept from Corradino. The thought brought him to a more important concealment; 'and, Corradino, that book that you carry,

which details your methods,' he met the glassblower's surprised gaze candidly, 'of course we know of it. You must
hide that on your person too, and we must hope it is not
discovered ... ahem ... *post mortem*. We are buying yourself
and your secrets, Corradino, and if France is to steal a
march on Venice in the matter of glassware, we cannot
afford for your notebook to remain in the city. Unless, of
course,' here the veiled eyes lifted, 'you wish to entrust the
book to me now? No? I thought not.'

Corradino swallowed. His voice nearly failed as he asked,
'and if I get out, what next?'

'When, my dear fellow, when,' said Duparcmieur airily.
'Then you do exactly as I'm about to tell you.'

Corradino sat in his house on Murano as the sky darkened
outside. He looked around the simple but homely room
with affection, but soon his eyes were inexorably pulled
back to the vial in his hands. He knew not how long he
had been staring at the little bottle – roughly made green
glass with a sedimentary liquid gleaming dully inside. It
looked like canal water – had the Frenchman been duped?
Or worse, had Corradino been given a deadly poison instead
– had Duparcmieur realized that he had made a mistake
in recruiting him but that Corradino now knew too much
to live? Corradino chased such thoughts away by perusing
the glasswork with a professional eye – unevenly made,
but the ground glass stopper fit snugly, and there was quite
a pleasing luminance to the bottle.

'Tis passing strange that my destiny is now held inside a vial of glass.

He thought suddenly of Giacomo, and felt sorry for what was to come. He felt like he was losing his father all over again, and experienced the crushing remorse that Giacomo was about to feel the pain of losing a son. He would visit him tonight, one last time.

Giacomo.

Could Corradino let him suffer, when he would still be alive, perhaps prospering in France with Leonora? Duparcmieur had warned him sternly to tell no one of the plan, or all would be discovered. But Giacomo? Surely it would be safe to tell him ... no ... to *hint* to him? Before he could change his mind, Corradino unstoppered the vial and drank back the draught. Fear almost made him vomit, but he swallowed back the bitter bile, for if he spat the poison all would be lost. His mouth tasted faintly of almonds, and he began to feel a strange sense of euphoria. Giddy, he reached for his quill and inkpot and sand, and scratched some words on a page of his book which he tore from its parent. As he sanded the words he fervently hoped they were true. Then he left the house for Giacomo's, tossing the bottle discreetly into the canal as he had been told, the poison already coursing through his veins.

★ ★ ★

If he reached down, his numb fingers crawling down his leg, a pale subterranean spider, he could feel the outline of the black *dente* inside his breeches. Wrapped beside it was the vellum book. His relief that his secrets had been buried with him was almost as great as finding that the knife had not been found. After three tries he pulled the blade from his stocking, ripping through the fabric. Slowly, so slowly, he fought the weight of the soil as he ponderously drew the knife up to his chest.

At least I have the means to end my life if I cannot free myself.

Once he was sure that his legs were awake, and that every toe could be moved in turn, Corradino began to cut the sacking over his trunk.

Night earth everywhere, dark and damp and heavy, in my eyes and in my mouth.

Corradino spat and coughed and heaved, his chest bursting as he dug ever upwards. *Giulietta* he thought, *Giulietta*. The name came incongruously to his mind in his panicked state, he repeated it in his head like an *Ave Maria*, then he said the *Ave Maria*, then he muddled the two in his head, the Blessed Virgin and the tragic heroine becoming one in his addled head, together with his mother Maria and *piccola* Leonora, whom all this was for. He dug and choked for what seemed hours, ever fearful that they had buried him too deep, that they had packed the earth down, that they never meant him to get out, that he was digging sideways and not upwards and would therefore dig forever until he drowned in soil. Then a coolness and a wetness on his fingertips. Blood? No − rain and a night breeze. He dug frantically, his lungs on fire, and gasped the night air in the most beautiful moment of his life. He staggered from his grave, weak, vomiting, and sat for a moment digging the earth out of his eyes. Rain pelted down and turned him to a man of mud. He thought he would never be afraid again.

But soon fear returned. He remembered the Frenchman's warning; 'Keep yourself low, and invisible. They may still be looking out for you. Get to the north side of the island, look for the lights of San Marco in the distance and follow them. Then look for me.'

Once again Corradino pressed into the ground. He crawled over the cemetery, face to face with numberless corpses, separated only by a stratus of earth. His hands clawed divots of soil and strange plants that bloomed on the flesh of the dead. He thought he heard ghastly whispers, and his memory did not spare him the details of Dante's *Inferno* and the dreadful inmates, mutilated sinners, traitors like his uncle, traitors like himself. He seemed to crawl for ever, every moment expecting to grasp a rotten limb or to feel the crunch of bones below. As his hands reached out to grasp the turf ahead of him, he felt a hundred spidery forms crawl over his arm. He stifled a scream and remembered that these were no insects of hell but the *mazzenette*, the soft-shell crabs that were fished in these islands. Tonight was full moon so the catch was larger, as the crabs responded eerily to the pull of the lunar tides. He shook the creatures from his sleeve and kept onward, but the creatures were on his face and in his hair. He kept his terror at bay by remembering that one of his favourite dishes as a child had been made from these very crabs. Graziella, their elderly cook at the Palazzo Manin, had taken him to the kitchens and shown him how she dropped the living creatures into her pancake mix to gorge themselves to death, whereupon the crabs were cooked, with an eggy softness both inside and outside the shell. Corradino crawled forever, crablike himself, his stomach turning with the thought that the crabs that he had enjoyed must have fed on the flesh of the dead. Never more would one pass his lips. Then at last he saw San Marco, the lights from a thousand windows shining like votive candles. His eyes made out a cloaked figure and a fishing bark in the quarterlight. Instantly his treacherous memory recalled the phantom at the *fornace* when he was ten. Had that angel of death come to claim him at last? Sweat mingled with the rain as he croaked out the agreed greeting: '*Vicentini mangia gatti.*'

The answer came back: '*Veronesi tutti matti.*'

Corradino had never thought he would be glad to see Gaston Duparcmieur. But he could have wept with joy as he went to board the boat, and grasped the proffered hand with real warmth.

As he hunched, chilled, in the bottom of the bark as it shot silently into the lagoon with no more than the faint plash of the oars, Corradino considered the truth of the passwords. The Veronese were mad indeed – Giulietta was a Veronese, and she must have been mad to put herself through what he had just experienced. But then he checked himself.

She was not mad, for she did what she did for love. And so did I.

CHAPTER 23

The Vessel

To have wanted something for so long, to have hoped against hope, until hope itself dies, and resignation sets in. To have almost forgotten what it was that you wanted so much. And then, at last, to be given the thing that you desired, and be filled with joy and terror in equal measure. Venice is a prism. Light enters white and leaves in a rainbow of colours. Everything is changed here. I am changed.

Leonora lay beside Alessandro with her hands on her bare stomach, holding the child within.

The cacophony of bells that rang through Venice always woke her, while the native Alessandro slept solidly through the city's song.

Be not afeared. The isle is full of noises,
Sounds, and sweet airs, that give delight and hurt not . . .

She never minded this waking – it was a delight to her to be pulled from her dreams by the bells, to lie in the gold morning light watching the curve of Alessandro's back, perhaps gently touching his warm hair, and to think idly of the day ahead. But today her thoughts were muddled as she attempted to absorb what had happened to her and the implications for her life. Her mind raced from the practical – what would she tell Adelino? What of her job? Did she still have one? – to the fantastical; she and Alessandro dandling a golden-headed child as their gondola swooped beneath the Bridge of Sighs. Her thoughts were ordered in one aspect – like a flock of gulls at a trawler they wheeled away singly but returned always to mass at the straining nets. All her thoughts came back to the child within her, and above all, how to tell Alessandro.

She had thought for so long that she was 'barren'. The old fashioned word stuck in her head. It seemed so expressive of everything in her life then – not just the childlessness but the sensation of being alone, left. 'Barren' described an empty, dark, Brontë moorland where nothing grew and no one ever trod. Her 'barrenness' had become a part of her, the label that she applied to herself. She carried it like a burden. So entrenched was her psyche that after the 'safe sex' of their first encounter, she had never used contraception with Alessandro. He, in the Italian way, had assumed that Leonora was 'taking care of it'. She said that she was.

I believed it myself.

So convinced was she that nothing could happen that even the classic sign that a schoolgirl would recognize with dread – morning nausea – had passed her by unnoticed. Even the absence of her periods she had attributed to the stress of the row at work and the press revelations, but in the end, she could ignore the signs no more that signalled that her barren body was actually bearing fruit. She did not understand the science of it – that what would not work with one man would work with another.

Perhaps fate or nature (for that goddess has many names) has a way of divining when one has found the right person. After all Stephen was the wrong person, and he had had no difficulty in getting Carol pregnant.

Stephen. She had not thought of him for weeks. He ... they ... must have had their child by now. What kind of father had he made? Leonora imagined he was somewhat of an absentee – there for school reports and hothousing but not for midnight feeds. He seemed a long way away. But Alessandro was here.

And he could be *the right man, I know it.*

But how would he take the news? Leonora had read enough literature and seen enough movies to know that the classic response of the foreign lothario was to disappear without trace at the first mention of a child. It was not lost on her that her situation uncannily reflected her mother's, and that Elinor and Bruno had had anything but a happy ending.

And yet, yesterday had been a day of almost perfect happiness. Though the wind was cold, the low orange November sun shone constantly, burnishing the city, making her friendly once more. When she was with Alessandro she felt the city loved her again. Only when she was alone did the palaces wear a different mask, and the shadows threaten her with figures and footfalls. After they returned from the cemetery Alessandro took her to the water-borne vegetable market at the Ponte dei Pugni, where the vendors sold their wares from *bragozzo* boats strung out under the bridge. As they wandered at the canalside, smelling the fragrant orange zucchini blossoms and the wizened porcini mushrooms, or handling the heavy bruise-black eggs that were the aubergines, Leonora felt a heady sensation of contentment. If only he were always here. If only they could bridge the distance that he had imposed between them, not the geographical distance necessitated by his training, but the psychological sense of removal that she felt at almost every moment they spent together.

There is something holding him back, I know it.

And now, she was aware that her news would change everything. It may cost her any semblance of togetherness they had. To stay the thought she pressed her belly harder.

At least I have you.

Her child. With her hands on her stomach, she imagined it growing, distending as it must over the next few months. She saw her stomach as a parison, growing to a perfect roundness as the breath of life filled it. She herself was now a vessel – the host for the child within. Venice had breathed a new life into her. She was an hourglass, swelling to mark the months before her burden would be delivered. The running sands, the baby, the glass, all seemed connected in an enormous, fateful plan. She felt as strong and as brittle as glass itself. All her old hopes sprang alive again – those long forgotten excitements that she remembered from back when she and Stephen were first trying. Names, nursery colours, imagining the face of the child by mentally combining her features with his. And now, even if Alessandro left, she had his child. Her features would be combined with his now. 'Our child,' she said aloud to her belly.

Alessandro rolled over sleepily. 'What did you say?'

The moment had come.

She turned to him so they faced each other. Her swollen breasts fell sideways on the coverlet and a skein of gold hair fell across her face. As he brushed it away Alessandro thought she had never looked more beautiful, as if lit from within. He reached for her but she stopped him with the words. She had never liked the bald clinical statement "I'm pregnant," so instead she said, 'I'm going to have your child.'

Shock registered on his face, and after a dazed moment his hands searched for her belly and rested there with hers. Then he lowered his head and she felt his soft curls as he laid his rough cheek on her stomach. She felt a wetness, and when he raised his face it was running with tears. From that moment she knew that it would be alright.

It was alright. Alessandro was delighted and called everyone he knew with the news that he was going to have a son. 'How do you know?' laughed Leonora as he refused to consider the alternative. 'I just do,' he said. She teased him with being a 'typical Italian', but he did not rise, saying, 'No, no, *cara*, if we had a girl I would love her just as much. But I *know* this is a boy.' And he refused to be moved.

For the rest of the morning he treated her like the glass of her metaphor, bringing water, getting her chairs, and lifting even the lightest burdens for her. She teased him, but her teasing came of sheer relief and gladness.

And yet . . .

All too soon, he was gone. Today was a public holiday, the day after All Souls Sunday, but tomorrow his course began again. He must return this afternoon, to complete his reading before tomorrow morning. As he left the house he kissed her with extra tenderness, but in all the sweetness Leonora thought of the week ahead without him. And after that, when he took up his post in Venice, what then?

I dare not ask.

Leonora fidgeted around the house, fruitlessly beginning tasks she could not finish, and then decided to go to the Sansoviniana Library and do some digging about Corradino. For tomorrow she must go back to the *fornace*, to face Adelino's wrath over the shattered ad campaign and now this news.

And then what?

She had to be honest with herself. In all his excitement Alessandro had never once mentioned future plans. All talk had been of the child, and while Leonora did not expect a Victorian proposal of marriage, she now thought it strange that he had never once mentioned the possibility of moving in.

As she walked across the *campo*, Leonora felt the city begin to retreat from her again. She felt her lover and her profession slipping away and the cold, empty Venice of winter closing in. She thought of the tourists and trippers, the pleasure-seekers and lotus-eaters who had now gone.

They never saw the city like this. This was the facet of the place that was for residents only. The dark days, the old stones, and the emptiness. She held her head high and thought only of her child.

I must find out about Corradino before the baby is born. I must reconcile my past before I turn to the future. For Corradino is the baby's past too.

CHAPTER 24

Banished

'I'm sorry, Leonora.'

To be fair, he did look sorry. Adelino also looked old and ill.

'I've had to cancel the campaign. They're calling in my debts. I can't possibly keep you on just now.' He walked to the window of his office, as he always did, searching for comfort in the peerless view.

Leonora felt a lurch in her stomach.

Was that the baby? Or the realization that I've just lost the job that I came here for?

She put a hand down there and he turned in time to catch the gesture. He waved at her stomach.

'And now with your ... wonderful news, there are not just financial considerations but implications for your health. All the chemicals and pigments that we use here, to say nothing of the heat. You'd have to leave soon anyway. When are you due? February?'

She nodded.

'Well.' He sat heavily at his desk. 'Let's just call this maternity leave. I'll have to see how things go here. I must re-trench.'

Leonora found her voice, 'And afterwards?'

Adelino shook his head. 'I really don't know. It depends on business. We always have a slump in between Christmas and *Carnevale*. It could be the end of me.' He took off his glasses and rubbed his eyes. 'To be honest Leonora, I can't afford to pay you anything, apart from your money to the end of the month. You could sue me, I suppose, for maternity pay, or whatever you call it. It would certainly be a first on this island. But there's nothing to give you.'

'I never asked.' She felt absurdly like crying – as if she had done this to him. Although she never wanted a part of the ad campaign, and although it was *his* greed that had sunk his ships, she felt responsible.

'I'd love to say that you could come back. But the truth is, I just don't know. And certainly for the moment, in the light of all the press your presence here is somewhat . . .'

She finished for him, 'Embarrassing?'

Adelino's eyes, small and unfamiliar without his glasses, dropped to the desk.

There was one more thing she must know. 'And Roberto? Will you reinstate him?'

'Leonora, you're not listening. I can't employ *anyone* else at present, however accomplished. Even if . . .'

'Even if what? You've tried, haven't you?'

Adelino let out a long sigh. 'I went to see him, yes. But his neighbours said he'd gone away.'

'Gone? Where?'

'They don't know. They think abroad.'

Leonora looked at him. She wanted to feel anger but felt instead only pity. Her sadness at the inevitable course of the interview was only tempered by relief that Roberto had gone from the city.

She got up. She walked down the stairs, through the hot door, and onto the factory floor. The men stopped to stare, but without Roberto's malign presence she felt animosity but no sense of danger. She felt the heat of the furnaces, so well-loved, so final. The *maestri* swung their blowpipe *canne* in cooling arcs like so many pendulums. Tick, tock. Time is up. She looked at the pieces of glass, a rainbow of colours, ranged around the workshop in various states of evolution. She smelled the silica and sulphur and turned for the door before the flames blurred in her tears. It felt so odd, this muddle of emotions. In one sense, she was happier than she had ever been. She was going to have a child, a child that grew inside her every day. She held the heart at her throat. The baby was *this* size now – the size of the heart she wore. But at the same time, she had lost what she came here for. Her creative outlet, her livelihood. Outside she took her leave of the street sign.

The Fondamenta Manin. If I could just find out that Corradino was innocent, if he could become a hero again, could he save this place that I have helped to ruin?

CHAPTER 25

The King

Corradino felt sick. He didn't know whether the stench was worse inside or outside of the carriage – outside the bewildering sounds and rotten smells of Paris, and inside the overpowering perfume of the powdered and pomaded Duparcmieur, all dressed up for their audience with the King. Corradino, too, was richly dressed in fine brocade; his transition from the mud-covered-risen-dead to aristo-crat-amongst-craftsmen had been accomplished on the voyage. He felt even sicker now than he had then, when he was shuttled from bark to boat, from boat to ship, from ship to carriage.

I could vomit on my fine new breeches.

Paris seemed to him a bewildering and hellish place. Against all sense it was the *space* that oppressed him – the tight canals and *calli* of Venice and Murano had made him feel secure, but here the streets were wide and he felt vulnerable.

And the stench.

The smell of human ordure was everywhere – no wonder Duparcmieur constantly held a small perfumed kerchief to his nose. At least in Venice there was an efficient and healthy disposal of wastes; with a canal on every doorstep, you could merely throw your filth into the water, or shit directly into the canal. Here it seemed that the sluggish brown Seine was a central artery of human waste that infected the whole city with its stench and miasma of pests.

And the noise! In Venice there was barely a sound to be heard beyond the gentle splashing waters as gondolas cleaved through the canal's surface. The only cacophonies were the pleasing sounds of *Carnevale* merriment or play-making. Here Corradino's head rang to the sound of horses' hooves, and the rumble of carriage wheels. Before today the greatest number of horses that Corradino had seen together were the four bronze statues standing silent sentinel over Venice from the top of the Basilica di San Marco. Here there were thousands of the creatures – big, ugly and unpredictable. The foul sweet aroma of their leavings was everywhere in the streets, steaming piles which the well dressed citizens stepped delicately over.

The buildings, while tall and grand, had none of the delicate traceries of the Venetian palaces on the Canal

Grande. But they were certainly imposing. One great white church reached high into the sky, with twin towers and spires of jagged teeth.

'Observe,' said Duparcmieur, 'the magnificent gargoyles watching over us.'

A comical word. What can the fellow mean?

As Corradino craned out of the carriage he saw, high up, malevolent demons crouched in the masonry, gazing down on him with ill intent. He drew back in, suddenly afraid, and as the carriage drew up at a particularly impressive edifice Corradino felt a wholly unwanted pang for the city he had left behind.

'We're here,' said Duparcmieur, as a powdered and liveried footman sprang to open the carriage door.

The King's presence chamber was gilded and grand, but, to Corradino's mind, not a patch on the Palazzo Ducale where he had been with his father for an audience with the Doge.

And the *King* himself – wholly unexpected.

Slumped in a beautifully carved chair elevated on a dais, the monarch's face was all but obscured by the curls of his wig as he leaned to the floor where a small dog played around his ringed hand. The dog slavered for a treat concealed in the King's chubby palm. Ever a student of detail,

Corradino noted the richness of the rings on the plump fingers, and the white powder clogged in the creases between the royal digits. Although they had been announced, the King spoke as if to himself.

'A gift from the English King. *Epagneul de Roi Charles.* A "King Charles spaniel".' A strange fit seemed to come over him as he began to snuffle like a truffling pig.

Corradino waited for the Royal aides to step forward with a draught of medicine, or to burn a feather under the King's nose to bring him out of his malady, when he realized the King was *laughing*.

'The English King is a dog! The English King is a dog! And a little one too!' Louis enjoyed his own wit for some further moments, before returning to the game. 'I shall call you Minou. A good French name. *Yes* I will. *Yes* I will.'

The spaniel circled the hand, impatient now, and was rewarded for her persistence as the King relinquished the comfit. The dog gobbled the bon-bon, and then squatted, shivering and straining, to shit on the rug. There was silence as the court regarded the perfect turd glistening on the priceless Persian weave. Corradino looked to the King, anticipating anger, but the fit had overtaken him again – the King threw back his head in mirth and Corradino at last saw his face. Contorted like the gargoyle he had seen earlier, eyes closed and streaming, with a slick of mucus from nose to mouth. Corradino felt nothing but contempt for this man who was said to be the greatest monarch in Christendom. He glanced to Duparcmieur, who bowed low and made as if to leave, clearly acknowledging that the planned audience would not take place today. Corradino followed suit and they had all but reached the door when a voice stayed them.

'Duparcmieur!'

Both men turned to meet the sight of a different man sitting on the throne. The face was composed, the wig arranged, the eyes flint.

'So you have brought me the Venetian to complete my vision, yes?'

Duparcmieur's smooth mask slipped for an instant in the face of such a startling transition, but soon the practised urbanity was back.

'Yes, Majesty. Allow me to present Signor Corrado Manin of the fair city of Venice. I believe and trust that you will not be disappointed in his artistry.'

'Hmmmm.' The King tapped his teeth with a nail, both teeth and nail yellow against the powdered white cheeks. And then, abruptly, 'Have you seen the Sainte Chapelle?'

Corradino realized he was being addressed. He bowed low. 'No, Your Majesty.'

'You should. It is really quite beautiful. It is considered a marvellous example of stained glasswork.' For a moment the King's face seemed to shine with pride at his city's finest jewel. 'But of course, it is in fact, no more beautiful to me than Minou's little tribute there.' To underline his startling *volte face*, he indicated the dog's waste, still sitting on the rug. 'Little nuggets of glass, multicoloured fancies, tiny bon-bons, minute panes all muddled together. Good enough for a child. Good enough for God.' He rose from his chair. 'But I am King. I want glorious, clean glass, huge pieces, mirrors of white and gold to reflect my Majesty. Can you do that for me, *Signore*?'

Corradino was afraid, but he knew his capabilities. 'Yes,' he said in ringing tones. 'I can.'

The King smiled pleasantly. 'Good.' He came close – Duparcmieur lowered his head but Corradino met the royal eyes. 'If you please me, we will reward you greatly. Fail me, and you will find me no more merciful than your own Venetian overlords, with their embarrassingly *thorough* methods of justice.' The King turned and walked back to his throne, deliberately stepping in the dog turd on the way. As the great doors closed on Duparcmieur and himself, Corradino could see the underside of the King's satin slipper, smeared with shit.

Duparcmieur was surprisingly cheerful in the carriage. 'Good. You've met the King, and he seems pleased with you. I thought that went terribly well.'

Corradino was amazed and silent.

'Do you not think he is indeed the most glorious of monarchs?'

'My experience of monarchs is limited to that one audience, Duparcmieur, but I'll admit he had an ... interesting ... manner.'

In truth your King is a disgusting child, but to speak my thought would show little diplomacy, and may even be dangerous.

'You find him charming? I do. He seemed in a very good mood today.'

I hope that I am never witness to his bad mood.

Duparcmieur leaned forward in a businesslike fashion. 'Now, we'll take you to your lodgings in Trianon – quite well appointed, I think you'll find. We have provided work clothes for you there. When you are properly attired for work I'll take you to the site of the palace at Versailles. I think you will be impressed by the building work – it looks marvellous already. Although, you have seen many marvels today, to be sure.'

Corradino grimly agreed. He had seen a King who was not a King. Thinking of the monarch's double nature he voiced a concern which had grown in his chestspoon over the last hours. 'Duparcmieur. How can I know that I can trust you and your – the King? How do I know that you will bring Leonora to me as you promised, and that you will not kill me when I have told my secrets?'

Duparcmieur met his troubled eyes with a candid gaze. Either the eyes of a man telling the truth or the eyes of a practised liar.

'My dear fellow, you have my word. I don't know how you run things in Venice, but in France a man's word is his bond.'

'Oh in Venice too. Even The Ten keep their word once given, for good or ill.'

'Then you understand me. I propose that you teach our foreman your ways with the mirror for one month, to show good faith. Then we bring Leonora to you. Then you remain for the next eleven months to oversee the work in the palace. At the end of the year you are free, to live with your daughter, and you can work with the glass or not, just as you choose.'

It sounds too wonderful to be true.

'Your foreman of the glassworks, what kind of man is he?'

'His name is Guillaume Seve. He is very experienced, a man of mature years, a good craftsman.'

Corradino shook his head. 'No good. I need a young man, someone with natural aptitude, a willingness to learn, but who has not already learned all the wrong methods. Someone who will learn from me, a *servente*, not someone older than me.'

'Very well.' Duparcmieur thought for a moment. 'Then that would probably be Jacques Chauvire, just an apprentice, but talented. He is but one and twenty.'

Corradino nodded. 'Perfect. It will take time, and dedication. Such things cannot be taught in a short span.'

Duparcmieur sat back. 'All will be well,' he said airily.

'You'll have everything you need – time, materials, men. The palace will be magnificent, you'll see.'

★ ★ ★

The palace already was. Sitting in new work clothes, the leather of his apron and wrist bands smelling sweetly, Corradino sat with his back to the half built palace facing the gardens. His back rested on newly-hewn masonry warmed by the setting sun, he watched the gardeners shaping the gorgeous green lawns for as far as the eye could see, while waterworkers diverted natural sources into the huge ornamental lakes which began to fill before his eyes – great mirrors themselves. Despite the distant chink of the mason's hammer and the banging of carpentry Corradino felt at peace for the first time since he arrived in France. A shadow cut his sun and he looked up – a gangly youth with tousled hair and dark eyes held a hand to him.

'I'm Jacques Chauvire.'

Corradino took the hand and pulled himself to his feet. The boy, expecting a handshake, smiled at the unexpectedness of the action. Corradino's eyes were level with his. The boy had good eyes, dark and true. He had no need to search for their meaning like he did with Duparcmieur. Nor was it lost on him that the name Jacques was the French version of Giacomo, the family he had left behind.

'Let's get to work, Jacques,' said Corradino. He threw a friendly arm around the boy's shoulders, turned his back on the vista and they walked together to the foundry.

The boy will do.

CHAPTER 26

Purgatorio

When I entered the fornace at Versailles I was at home at last.

As Jacques opened the secret chamber to which only he and his new master had the key, Corradino saw that all that he had asked for had been given to him. There were the water vats, the silvering tanks. There was the furnace, with the coals stoked and ready, and a glowing red gather of *cristallo* glass at its heart. There were his *pontelli*, his blowpipes, his paddles. There were his *scagno* saddles and *borselle* pliers. There were his pigments; lapis blue, scarab red and leaf gold among them. There were his bottles and flasks of nitrates and sulfates and mercuries. Here then, at home, he could work once again.

His printless fingers itched to touch the rods and pigments, to make something again after his long month at sea and on road. The presence of Jacques at his shoulder felt incongruous, so used was he to working alone. But

261

today was the day he must at last share his methods, and he felt a sick reluctance in his chestspoon. Not because he thought the boy's skills would ever exceed his, but because he alone had made mirrors in this way for ten years now, and he felt he was giving away a precious possession; a part of himself, a skill which had defined him for so long.

A skill which has saved my life, for 'twas for this that The Ten spared me. Once this has gone from my grasp what do I have to protect me from the King?

Would Louis decide, once Corradino had told his secret, that he would be better out of the way? And yet what choice did he have? He was in Purgatory, waiting for Leonora to be brought to him, and the sharing of his methods had been part of the bargain which would bring her to these shores. He was in Limbo. A wholly unwanted memory of Dante's couplets chimed in his head. He recalled that, in *Il Purgatorio*, his namesake had been killed by a French King. Corradino, the doomed Prince of Sicily, was executed by Charles of Anjou following an unsuccessful coup. *That* Corradino's father, King Manfred, had been murdered too.

But as he turned and met Jacques' warm brown eyes – eager and shining, reflecting Corradino's own love of his trade – he felt comforted and set aside such gloomy thoughts. He had no son to pass his skills to, and perhaps

never would, so this was his chance to share in his knowledge and enjoy teaching if he might.

*There is Leonora of course, but no woman has ever been a glass-
blower, nor ever will.*

All he hoped for his daughter was that she would be happy,
marry well, and enjoy the family life that had been wrested
from him.

'So,' he said to Jacques, with a firmness that belied his
doubts, 'we begin.'

He took up the largest blowpipe, and reached into the
fire for the molten *cristallo*. As he felt the heat blast his face
he thought again of the words of Dante, but this time his
favourite couplet: '*Even so rained down the everlasting heat,
And, as steel kindles tinder, kindled the sands.*' Corradino was
kindling the sands now, coaxing crystalline beauty from a
quintessence of dust. He took such a large amount of
gather on the end of his pipe that he had to constantly
turn the rod as he blew the parison.

Jacques looked confused, and tentatively questioned his
master. '*Maître*, I thought we were to make a mirror, not
to blow glass?'

Corradino slid his eyes sideways as he blew. There was
merriment there.

When the parison was blown Corradino spun the bubble
on the end of the pipe and transferred it to his *pontello*.
He then took the parison to the water tank and let it rest

there, floating like a buoy. As it cooled he took a sharp blade and cut swiftly down the length of the bubble so the sides of the cylinder relaxed flat onto the surface of the water tank, and the amber glass cooled on the surface to a flat clear pane.

'So . . .' breathed Jacques into a reverent silence, '. . . that is how it is done.'

Corradino squatted and squinted with a practised eye down the surface of the tank. He nodded. 'Yes. That is how. 'Twas but an accident when I discovered it, but it is the only way to make a pane of such a size, with the same thickness throughout.'

'And the water?'

'Water, when stilled, is completely flat, wherever it lies on the earth. It is the original mirror – nature's mirror. Even if its tank or vessel is tilted, it will always find its true level. I just hope that the French waters of your pestilent river will make as fine a glass as the sweet *acqua* of Venice's lagoon. Now, we must dress the new-born.' He lifted the cooled pane tenderly and laid it on the surface of the neighbouring vat, which housed a molten silver compound so bright it resembled a mirror itself. 'This is mercury and silver sulfate,' said Corradino, 'but only on the surface. Here too there is water underneath.'

'Why, *Maître?*'

'Because these silvering compounds are very costly. Even for your King it would be too lavish to fill a whole tank with them. But there is sufficient on the surface to cover the glass with the correct thin skin to produce a reflection. You must always take care that you cover the entire surface of the tank, lest there are empty patches which will leave the glass clear. And take care of the mercury – it is an evil compound, and one that enters the skin of a man with ease. Many of our trade have died from its arts – I know of one such very close to me.' He smiled at his black jest as he recalled how he had imitated a mercury poisoning – blackening his own tongue with charcoal and letting the spittle run from his mouth on his 'deathbed'. But when he recalled how the sight of him must have greeted Giacomo he ceased to smile.

He turned back to Jacques. 'Just take care to let as little of the mixture touch you as you can. Here;' he demonstrated, using two small wads of leather to lift out the huge silvered pane. 'The silvering dries very quickly – see? It has almost parched in the heat of the furnace.'

Jacques looked on in awe as the compounds dried, and as they did, his blurred image resolved into a pin-sharp, bright perfection.

'Now, you see that the edges are rough, where I cut the parison? We score down the edges using the same knife and a metal rule,' Corradino suited the action to the words. 'It's only necessary to break the very surface of the silvering, because, as you see, the glass will snap off cleanly along the line you have made. Here there are many metal rules provided for us, for as you know, the crowning panes of our mirrors in the *palazzo* are to be curved, and for those you will need one of these.' Corradino held up a flexible length of metal, which he curved into shape. As Jacques nodded he turned back to the mirrored pane where it lay on the cutting saddle. 'At the last, we take a chamois leather,' he did so, 'dip it in alum, and polish the surface to both protect and brighten the pane. See?'

Jacques had thought the mirror could not be any brighter, but now the glass seemed to sing. His wonder and admiration showed in his face, and Corradino could see that his apprentice was full of questions. '*Maître*, how are mirrors made by others?'

'There have always been mirrors. The Arab infidels used to polish their shields in order to see their images. But in other nations they attempt to roll out the glass thinly from one piece, as if making a pie. The results are passable but it is impossible to make a very large pane this way – the glass cools and hardens, and is lumpy and uneven. But with breath you can make a parison as large as your winds will allow, and when you treat the glass as a cylinder its dimensions open out to more than double the shape you have made. 'Tis simple mathematicks.' He shrugged to deflect the admiration he saw in Jacques' eyes. But he saw something else too – he saw the boy's hands twitch towards the fire just as his own had done.

I know I have babbled aplenty – that I speak more words when talking of my work than at any other time. Those that know me may think me as dumb as an oyster. Let them but speak to me of the glass, they will hear what a prattling parrot I am become. Enough.

He uttered the words he thought he would never say. 'Now you try.'

CHAPTER 27

A Champion

Signor Aldo Savini, curator of rare books at the Libreria Sansoviniana in San Marco, was slightly surprised when asked by a blonde beauty to help her lift down the guild records of the glass and mirror makers of the seventeenth century. But she must be a registered reader. He checked her newly laminated card – she was clearly a Venetian from her name. He shrugged, and handed her a pair of thin cotton gloves from a dispenser. 'You must wear these, *Signorina*. These volumes are very old and fragile. Also you must use the bookstand provided, to minimize damage to the spine, and only turn the pages by the laminated marker. Don't touch the paper itself.'

La Signorina nodded seriously throughout his instruction. Her eyes were green but had silver shards in the centre, the colour of the olive leaves on the farm where Aldo Savini grew up. The librarian suddenly felt his heart quicken and pushed his glasses up his nose, as he always did when flustered. Aldo Savini was not yet forty, and beneath his sweater-vest and tie beat a romantic heart. As he helped the *Signorina* lift down the ancient volumes for the relevant date, her gold hair brushed his arm and he could smell her coconut shampoo mingled with the old leather and vellum of the books. As she smiled and thanked him, Aldo Savini thought he would kill dragons for Signorina Manin.

Aldo Savini saw '*la Principessa*' as he had secretly dubbed her, many times over the next few months. Always she had some peculiar request, which stimulated him as a librarian almost as much as her appearance stimulated him as a man. Guild records, inventories, wills, records of birth and death, letters, bills of works, he had found all these for her. Her questions, posed in perfect Veneziano, intrigued him too. They always revolved around the same man, Corrado Manin. Even Aldo Savini, in his cloistered life, had heard of the man. *La Principessa* hounded him with questions as she had soon found out that Aldo had trained in Paleography at the University of Bologna, and could read the cramped ancient writing where her reading failed her. Do these documents mention Corrado Manin? This mirror that the *Contessa* Dandolo left to the Frari church, was it a Manin? This bill of works for the Palazzo Bruni, does it mention the Manin candlebra? What year was the *palazzo* built? This ship's register, does the entry say Manin, or Marin? These records of death that cite poisoning, does this symbol mean mercury, or some other compound? Aldo Savini became fascinated by the quest, as he was fascinated by her. Apparently she had some help from Ca' Foscari, as she used to shuttle back and forth from the library to the university for advice, and arrive back with a crop of new leads. He divined soon that her helper was Ermanno Padovani, an eminent scholar who had many volumes in this very library. Some Sundays the *Principessa* did not come at all, and Aldo knew that she continued her search elsewhere, the *Professore* having given her, it seemed, fairly comprehensive access to the deepest and most precious sequestered archives of the city.

In his romantic mind, Aldo Savini became a knight championing the cause of the blonde *Principessa*. He saw himself facing the black knight, Ermanno Padovani, in the lists of bibliographical knowledge. He was determined to provide her with some sort of breakthrough, before the *Professore*, so he would be her hero.

Over the coming months of deepest winter, Aldo Savini's chivalric fantasy took a fresh turn. Because it soon became clear that the *Principessa* was pregnant. He saw her belly swell, her angel face take on a rounded, cherubic aspect. Once he saw her, lost in a ship's register, with her hair swept to one side of her swan's neck, writing in a notebook that was balanced on her belly. His heart nearly failed. He, Aldo Savini, would protect her from her foul seducer, whomever he might be. He would help her finish her quest. He must think hard for that breakthrough. And then one day, the breakthrough came.

For many weeks now, Aldo had realized that certain French elements were creeping into the search. Questions about shipping, about the Palace of Versailles, about glass trade to Paris, about the court of Louis XIV the Sun King. Then it struck him – if the *Principessa* was interested in any of the courts of Europe in the seventeenth century, there was one ubiquitous character who would always be able to help her, a personage who hailed from this very city.

The Venetian Ambassador.

La Principessa had been very excited when he showed her the document. After reading it three times, she dragged the volume of letters over to his desk with a speed that made him fear for her condition, which was now very advanced. She badgered him about making a copy, till at last he took the letter in question to the private inner sanctum where the specialized scanners and printers lay dormant. Squat and expensive, these machines could copy even the most delicate parchment with the use of infra-red laser technology. Not for these documents the exposure to the harsh bands of light of the office photocopier, thought Aldo Savini tenderly. He took the pages back to the *Principessa*, who waited at his desk. She grasped the pages to her belly, face-up as if she did not want the child to read the contents from within her. She looked agitated, but not particularly happy. Still, ever good mannered, she gave him one of her peerless smiles.

'Thank you, Signor Savini,' she said.

He pushed his glasses up his nose, gathering courage, but she had already turned before he had uttered the name 'Aldo.'

She had not heard him – she was walking away through the bookstacks, her mind already elsewhere. And in the grand chivalric tradition to which Aldo Savini was so attached, he never saw her again.

CHAPTER 28

The Ambassador

When Jules Hardouin-Mansart, chief architect of the Palace of Versailles, showed Corradino the plans for what he called the '*Salon des Glaces*' even Corradino had a moment of thinking that it could not be done. There were to be twenty-one huge mirrors, each with twenty-one panes. Each pane was to be exquisite, flat, true and with a crystal-clear reflection. There was to be no bevel at the edge, so that the glass would appear as one piece, with no interruptions to the reflected image. Moreover, each glass was to reflect exactly the window opposite it, so exterior light and interior light were partnered, to create, as Hardouin-Mansart said, the lightest room in the world. There was also to be fantastic series of frescoes on the ceiling, depicting the King's life and the glories of France. These were to be painted by Royal Painter Charles Le Brun and his apprentices.

Le Brun himself was a constant presence at the site,

relentlessly questioning Corradino about the direction of light, the angle of reflection, and the implications for his painting. Slowly, Le Brun's wondrous panels came to life – high above, gesso doves fluttered in the stratosphere, and bare-breasted beauties reclined on fat clouds while they watched the golden triumphal chariots of the King. Corradino recognized a kindred talent, but felt the weight of the task presented to him. His glass must reflect these glories.

Even the designer of the great gardens, André Le Nôtre, visited the hall to inspect how his artistry would be reflected in the mirrored wall.

Despite his reservations, however, Corradino found that all help was there at his disposal – conferences with carpenters and masons, the assistance of the latest measuring equipment, mathematicians from Paris. The *fornace* – purpose built in the kitchen gardens of the palace – was well equipped, and Jacques Chauvire worked hard and progressed well. As Corradino taught Jacques his secret method the boy blossomed, and together master and apprentice began to make larger and larger panes. Corradino gradually had to remelt less of Jacques' work, and by the end of Corradino's first month in Paris Jacques had made his first passable square mirror pane.

At night Corradino went back to his well furnished house in the nearby village of Trianon. With six chambers, a maid and a small vegetable garden, it afforded greater luxury than he had known since leaving the Palazzo Manin.

He began to relax – to feel, for the first time in years, that he was not being watched. Sometimes, in the dying sunlight when he stood at the end of his garden watching the enormous palace grow, with a goblet of fine French wine in his hand, thinking of Leonora, he was almost happy.

This new sense of ease was destined to be short-lived.

On the momentous day that the first silvered panes were set in place in the Hall of Mirrors, Corradino stood, arms akimbo, supervising the work as the last glass was set in place. Quite a gaggle had formed to watch the work, including Hardouin-Mansart and Le Nôtre. Privileged company indeed, and at length they were rewarded as the mirror was complete and the crowd stood back in awe. A hush descended as the men surveyed their handiwork – the mirror arched above them, high and clear, gilded struts crossing the panes like light caged with gold. As well as their own reflections, the assembly saw the half-completed gardens, and the half-filled lakes stretching out into the distance, as far as the eye could see, in an optical miracle of design. The thing was truly a marvel, and all assembled could see what wonders they could expect when the hall was complete. No one moved, unable to tear their eyes away. Talk, once hushed, died into silence. But not just through admiration, or respect for the craftsmanship they all witnessed. They were silent for the presence of royalty. The King had entered the room.

Louis strode toward the mirror, and those gathered bowed to the floor instantly. Corradino bent low, his heart thudding.

Will this capricious King approve of my work?

Soon he had greater anxiety to reckon with – his lowered eyes raked the royal slippers, then moved to the pair of shoes next to them – *Bauta* slippers with red laces, sold only on the Rialto.

Venetian shoes.

Corradino's hair crisped on his scalp. He dared not raise his eyes, but as the crowd around him straightened up he contrived to shuffle to the back of the throng, as Hardouin-Mansart and Le Nôtre moved forward to be presented. The King was speaking. Blood thrummed in Corradino's ears so loudly that he could not, at once, hear what was said.

'So Ambassador, *pas mal, hein?* Perhaps even you will be forced to admit that my little *château*, when complete, will rival your crumbling *palazzi*?'

The Ambassador bowed politely, but Corradino could see that his eyes were hooded, and their gaze cool and guarded. He thought he knew the man slightly, a member of the Venetian Guilini family, attaché to the *Arsenale* years ago when Corradino's father was trading with the Baltic.

A taciturn, but highly intelligent youth he had been then. He must have risen through the influence of his family to this exalted state, but looked as if his intellect merited the position. Dressed in the finest Venetian velvets and satins with hair and beard trimmed and oiled, the Ambassador looked not like a dandy but a self possessed, confident, and highly dangerous man.

The King spotted Hardouin-Mansart and Le Nôtre at the front of the throng. He beckoned with a fat beringed hand and the pair bowed low as the King began desultory introductions. 'This is Hardouin-Mansart, my palace architect. And that's Le Nôtre who's doing the gardens. It goes well?' He waved away their answers. 'Yes, yes, but this mirror is better than both your efforts, no? I imagine you two are jealous? Going to get one of your masons to drop a brick on it, Jules?' The King laughed at his own sally as the court joined in. Then, as Corradino began to relax, Louis uttered a question which froze his blood. 'Where's my *Maître des Glaces*? Can't have you two taking all the bouquets . . .' His eyes raked the crowd, found Corradino's. Corradino's heart thumped so he thought he would expire. A smile flitted over the King's features like a summer cloud. 'There's the fellow.'

I am undone – my life is ended.

But the fat hand beckoned Jacques Chauvire. Guillaume Seve, passed over for the job, gave Jacques an officious little shove, and the boy stumbled forward awkwardly, twisting his leather cap in his hand.

Baldasar Guilini regarded Jacques balefully from under an arched eyebrow. He made a circuit of the boy on his Venetian heels, looking him up and down. Then he walked to the mirror, freeing his hand, finger by finger, from his chamois glove. He reached out his index finger and touched the cool, flat glass, leaving a smoky print. Corradino, despite himself, winced as if a seducer had laid a finger on his daughter.

Baldasar turned back to Jacques.

'Something wrong, Ambassador?' asked Louis, who seemed to be suppressing the mirth of a private jest.

The Ambassador visibly recollected himself. 'Forgive me, Majesty, I was thinking that this man – Chauvire, is it – is very young to create such mastery.'

Jacques shifted his weight, as Louis replied, 'Perhaps it is hard to accept that France has at last attained the quality of glasswork that the Venetians have enjoyed these past many years.'

Baldasar looked from the mirror to Jacques and back again. 'How many panes in this mirror, *Maître*?' he gave the title a gentle, ironic stress.

Jacques, properly, looked to the King, who nodded that he may answer. 'Twenty-one, *Gracieux Monsieur*.'

'And how many years have you been on this earth?'

'Twenty-one, *Gracieux Monsieur*.'

'How fitting. There is a pleasing symmetry about that,

don't you find? Indeed, it is a work of passing beauty for
one of such *tender* years. It has clarity, lucidity; one might
almost say a *Venetian* quality about it.' His eyes raked the
crowd and Corradino shifted, dropping his eyes, obscured
behind one of the burlier masons.

'I congratulate you, Majesty.' The Ambassador bowed
once again, but his eyes were thoughtful behind his dip-
lomatic visage.

'Well, well.' The King waved away the compliment modestly as if he had crafted the mirror himself. He moved
off down the hall, with Ambassador and coterie in tow.
Then, briefly, the Royal head turned. Quick as a flash,
Louis' eyes found Corradino. One eye closed for an instant.
Then the King turned back and continued on, the whole
incredible incident taking no more than an instant, and
the court not even faltering in its progress. Corradino, as
he allowed himself to breathe again, tried to comprehend
what he had just seen.

The King had *winked* at him.

*It is a game to him. A piece of amusement. The fact that my life
is forfeit if I am discovered, that whole pantomime with Jacques,
it is all a game; a piece of Royal folly to pass the hours.*

Sweating, glass-limbed, he put a hand to his thudding heart,
as if to keep that organ from leaping from his chest. Guilini
had not seen him, would not even know him if he had,

as Corradino had been but eight years old when he met the adolescent Guilini at the *Arsenale* on business with his father. But was Louis capricious enough to reveal the true identity of his *Maître des Glaces* over brandy after the Ambassadorial dinner? No, reasoned Corradino, the King's national pride, already fully displayed, would dictate that the credit for the Hall of Mirrors would be attributed to French craftsmen, now and for all time in the future. Then, how long would an Ambassador stay? Not more than a week, two weeks? Best to lie low till he heard Guilini had gone. Shaken, Corradino returned to the *fornace*, waving away Jacques' agonized apologies that he had been given credit for Corradino's work. I must talk to Duparcmieur, thought Corradino. I must bring Leonora to me.

But Corradino had forgotten one thing in his reasoning. The mirror itself had betrayed him. In the moment when Louis had looked back, Baldasar Guilini, quick as a cat, had seen the exchange in the mirrored panes. Corradino had been right, Guilini had not recognized him yet. But he knew him for an Italian, and it was but a short step from thence to know him for a Venetian.

That night, after the Ambassadorial dinner in his honour, and the brandy over which Louis told him nothing, Baldasar Guilini returned to his quarters in the *Palais Royal*. He refused the attentions of the courtesan he had brought from Venice, and instead, sat down at his ornate gilded writing desk.

Alone, with the heavy drapes closed, in the warm perfumed closeness of his elaborate chambers, he took up his quill and began to write a letter. At length he sanded the parchment, folded it twice, and heated a stick of red wax at his candle. He pressed the molten wax to the paper, where it lay like a gout of blood. He turned his signet ring and with the ease of long practice impressed the wax clearly with its design – the winged lion of San Marco. He turned the parchment and wrote the direction on the face for Louis' messenger, who waited outside his door.

It was to His Excellency the Doge of Venice.

CHAPTER 29

Before Dawn

Leonora walked all the way home from San Marco. The photocopy of the Ambassador's letter was in her bag, and she felt its presence burning through the canvas. It was early evening, and the streets were deserted. She knew why – it was the eve of *Carnevale*, and all the citizens of Venice were getting ready – putting the finishing touches to their costumes, grabbing much needed sleep before the nights of revelry to come. Tomorrow the tourists would be back in full force and the city would wake from her winter sleep. The shuttered and cold city known only to her residents, would resume her bloom – the princess, once kissed, would slough off her hundred years sleep and blossom for her suitors once more.

And yet the darkest hour comes just before dawn. Leonora's walk home was beset by dreaded shadows once more – not just the spirit of Roberto this time (had he left Venice? Or was he still here?) but also the malign presence of the Ambassador whose words she had just read. Words that condemned Corradino. These twin presences stalked her home. The night froze with the water underfoot and in the air, her breath smoked. She tried to hurry, but the burden of her baby sat hard upon her hips and her pelvis ached. Eight months of growth and icy pavings did not allow a speedy progress. The palaces and houses shunned her with their blank frontages. All was green and grey where once it had been gold and amber. She remembered something that Alessandro had said; that in Venice the moonlight was green because the light reflected from the canal. It was so tonight, but the greenish tint was ghostly, ghastly: it turned living flesh to the hue of the dead. The canal itself was a trough of cold green glass. The city had cooled and hardened. There is no sanctuary here, the houses said. You are no longer one of our own. Even the statue of Daniele Manin, turned by twilight to a greenish ghoul, accused her from his plinth. His copper embodiment proof of his own loyalty; he questioned hers. Her bright windows were a lighthouse beacon to guide her to safe mooring.

Lighted? Someone is there? Alessandro?

Her heart beat hard and painfully as she fitted her key in the lock – but it was not he but his cousin. Marta was seated at the table, *Il Gazzettino* spread in front of her. She looked up and smiled as Leonora entered, pink-cheeked with cold and expectation.

'*Fa freddo, vero?*'

Leonora nodded, shedding gloves and scarves. 'Freezing.'

Rent day. I had forgotten. Thank God I got the rest of my month's wages from Adelino. Christ knows what will happen next month though. I couldn't bear to lose this place too.

As she crossed the kitchen to get the money from inside her Moroccan tagine dish (a hiding place which would be immediately obvious to even the most amateur burglar) she heard Marta tactfully fold the offending paper away. She paid over her month in advance and offered Marta a glass of wine. Her landlady seemed to hesitate.

'I'm not sure … I … actually, yes, please.'

Leonora opened a bottle of Valpolicella and ran the tap for herself. As the water rushed over her hand, running to bone-chilling coldness, she considered her friend from the corner of her eye. The cousin of the man she loved. They really shared nothing in the physiognomy of the face – there were no resemblances to catch at her heart. And yet today she divined something of him in Marta – The familiar hesitation, distance, discomfort. She filled her glass with water and brought the two drinks to the table.

What is she hiding?

Leonora sat and the silence persisted. Then, as if making

up her mind, Marta spoke at last. 'Is Alessandro coming here tonight?'

Leonora looked up from her glass, surprise registering. Throughout her pregnancy, she had not seen as much of him as she would have liked, but they had had enough shared time to foster the notion that they were a couple. When they were together he was the model boyfriend and expectant father – talking to the growing bump, imagining the future child and helping her make the inevitable and exciting changes to the flat. But the notion of cohabitation had become a bone of contention – for some reason he studiously avoided the issue. The flat evolved slowly to accommodate the baby, but in all the plans he never mentioned making a space for himself. Major festivals were spent together, and Alessandro had suggested that he come tonight and that they go to the *Carnevale* together. So Leonora answered his cousin, 'He's coming here after work.'

Marta nodded. She hesitated, took a deep breath, and twitched the paper towards her again. 'I didn't realize that he still saw Vittoria. I just saw them in the Do Mori on my way here.'

Leonora registered her tone before she realized what Marta was saying. She had heard that studied nonchalance once before in her life. She realized when and where and was suddenly as cold as she had been outside.

Jane. In Hampstead. The friend who told me about Stephen.

In her cold horror she grasped at the name Marta had spoken. 'Vittoria?'

Marta sighed. 'Vittoria Minotto. She and Sandro used to live together, then she got promoted away from Venice. But now she's back. But you know that of course. You ... met her.'

Yes; she took away my livelihood. And now Sandro too?

Marta looked bewildered. 'You mean he didn't tell you?'

'No. Yes. I mean – he told me about a journalist he had been seeing, but I never thought ... I never put the two together.'

Stupid, stupid.

Marta frowned. 'But surely, after the article?'

Leonora shook her head. 'He was away when it all happened. Doing his detective's course. I'm not sure how much he knows about it.' Her head was spinning. That woman, that sexy, vicious female, had been *his*? And with *her* he had consented to live, when *she*, the mother of his child, was to cope alone? Involuntarily she put a hand on her bump in what had become an accustomed gesture.

Marta took it for distress. 'Are you going to be alright?'

Leonora forced a smile. She suddenly wanted Marta to go. She needed to think. She knew what it must have cost

Marta to warn her – the Venetians were, like most Italians, extremely loyal to their families. Leonora chatted with forced cheerfulness for what seemed an eternity but must only have been moments. At last Marta got up for her coat. She turned as she reached the door.

'It's nothing,' she said haltingly. 'It's very civilized to be on good terms with your ex. Sandro never did like bad blood or ill will. He likes things to be easy.'

Easy.

So now, at last, she knew the source of the distance. He had lived with Vittoria and been hurt. She had left him. And now she was back, what?

Where do I fit in?

She stayed for long moments at the table, nursing her glass of water, looking at the door through which Marta had left, through which Alessandro was shortly to come. She considered, as the shock drained away and anger replaced it, how she would confront him.

No. That's not the way. Not again.

With Stephen she had faced him out with what she knew, and he had left. This time she would learn the lessons of history. She had to assume Alessandro's innocence as the alternative was too horrible to contemplate – to be alone in a city which now felt alien to her, with a child and no job.

No. I will wait, and hope, and give him the benefit of the doubt.

She knew she was a coward. When he came in from the winter night she embraced him warmly. They ate dinner and talked animatedly of the child and the *Carnevale* to come. He seemed excited about something, hyper. Her heart chilled as she thought that Vittoria was the reason. In denial she took him to her bed and pleased him as much as she could. Only afterwards did she ask him one question, hating herself.

'Marta was here tonight. You just missed her. I thought you were going to be here by seven. What happened?'

His voice was thick with sleep. 'I had to work late. That art theft at the Ca' D'Oro. It's dragging on for ever.'

You've been caught in a lie. Proof.

She turned uncomfortably, her bump ungainly, and shoved at the pillows. She did not want him to see the tears that ran into the linen. The child kicked her, reacting to her movement, and she cupped its form, crying for them both. She felt a touch to her back.

Alessandro murmured 'I love you.'

He has never once said that before. And now it's too late.

CHAPTER 30

Carnevale

Carnevale. The Doge's Palace, that great confection, is *en fête*. The delicate, blanched façade hides the dark and ermetic chambers within. The edifice itself wears a mask. Costumed characters, garish and bright, tangle round the pillars of the white loggia like a gaudy ribbon. Above their heads, like a grey tooth in a peerless smile, sit the two discoloured pillars that stand out from their fellows. Legend has it that these two columns are permanently stained with the blood of the criminals that were hung and quartered there. The revellers do not think of this. They laugh and squawk like parrots at a bagpiper. Venice *La Serenissima* is, today, far from serene. Here a moon capers with a princess, there a *Pierrot* converses with an elephant. Today, a cat can look at a King.

By the bridge of the Riva degli Schiavoni, a man and a woman hail a gondola. The man is dressed as Sandro Botticelli, with a close cap on his curling hair, and

289

Renaissance robes. The woman seems as if she has stepped from his work, so closely does she resemble *La Primavera*. Her gilded hair is twisted about her cherub's face, and gold filaments snatch at the sun. Her hooded green eyes are the colour of a wine bottle, the pupils distended with promise. Her sprigged white dress catches in the wind and her escort hands her into the rocking boat with care – for she is heavily pregnant.

Leonora settled back in the cushions. She had decided that *La Primavera* was the obvious choice for her *Carnevale* costume; as Spring herself was pregnant with the coming Summer, Leonora could find comfort in the flowing robes. The dress was loose and airy, the cushions soft under her back. Her glass heart sat in the notch of her throat; its cool round weight a constant reassurance that she needed more than she knew. Her child squirmed beneath the ceinture of her dress, and its father's hand clasped hers. She looked replete; the oft-used term 'blooming' could have been coined for her. Outwardly, she was as serene as the glassy lagoon under the winter sun. But beneath her surface there was darkness and turmoil in the depths. Two evils, from the past and present, were the tides that tugged at her innards. She doubted the fidelity of the man whose hand she held. And between her filling breasts lay the scratchy secret of the Ambassador's letter. She recalled her dream of the sunlit day when the three of them rode the gondola. Well, here they were – the child unborn but inside her belly. For the baby's sake she wanted resolution – of her quest and her relationship too. The past, as was fitting, should be dealt with first. She began to talk. She told Alessandro everything. Of Corradino. Of Roberto. Of the revelations in *Il Gazzettino*. She watched him carefully when she mentioned Vittoria, but he showed no surprise, no shifty glances or shamefaced blushes. He merely frowned.

Vittoria can wait. For now I want his opinion as a professional.

She went on to speak of Padovani, of her researches in the Sansoviniana. Leonora freed the much-read letter, and handed it to Alessandro. The shadow of the Bridge of Sighs dipped them in darkness and with a quizzical arch of the brow, he began to read, waiting only for the shadow of the bridge to pass.

CHAPTER 31

The Piombi

Giacomo walked over the Bridge of Sighs with the shuffling steps of terror. Through the fine lattice of the windows he looked what may be his last on the Riva degli Schiavoni, where *Carnevale* was in full swing. The passage was small and airless after the massive rooms in which he had been questioned with their magnificence of frescoed gilt. He knew that this was no mere accident but design. The condemned man leaving light and space and warmth to enter the crushing damp darkness of that most dreaded place – the Piombi prison. Named for the leads that slated the roofs, he knew as well as every citizen of Venice that no one left the fabled prison alive.

The perspiration of fear sat between the old man's shoulder blades. His terror had begun last night when they had taken him, and washed over him in waves all day as he had been questioned, relentlessly, by the same dark, masked figure. He looked through the last window with something akin to

love for his lost city. But he did not sigh. Instead, a thin
stream of urine trickled down his leg to the stone floor.
The guard behind him cursed, and dropped a rag which he
scuffed along with his boot, erasing the trail. The old ones
always lost control at this point – they knew their days were
numbered. Even a young man could quickly get lung fever
from the damp of the Piombi, or be driven mad by the
dark. For the old, it was assured. He gave Giacomo a vicious
shove through the yawning mouth of the prison portal, and
as he entered the dark a trick of memory recalled to Giacomo,
word for word, the letter that they had read to him, the
letter that had brought him here.

*Most esteemed and excellent Doge, Duke of the Republic of
Venice, Seneschal of the Three Islands and Emperor of
Constantinople,*

*Lately summering, at your Excellency's pleasure, at the court
of His Majesty Louis XIV of France, I have today made an
unsettling discovery which may pertain to the security of one of
our trading monopolies. This discovery touches on the mirror work
which His Majesty has commissioned for the decoration of his
new palace here at Versailles, where I am newly quartered.*

*I will tax your Excellency's patience no longer but say, in brief,
that it is my belief that a citizen of our own fair Republic is
assisting the French with their labours. Excellency, I must write
that I believe the traitor to be one of our own Murano glassmakers
(so fine is the work) who is even now unburdening the secrets of
our Guilds to the foreign craftsmen.*

I have had sight of the man whom I believe to be a Venetian. He is of his middle years, dark, well-favoured, and of youthful appearance. I will endeavour to discover his name, but casual enquiry reveals he may be under some kind of Royal protection, as well a craftsman of his status may be.

Excellency, if your humble servant may be so bold, I urge you to make such necessary enquiries of the Murano community, of any absence among their number – even a death.

For my own part I will take further steps to bring the identity of this man into the light.

Make haste, Excellency, I beg of you, else our monopoly is lost.

Your servant,

Baldasar Guilini, Venetian Ambassador to the Court of France.

CHAPTER 32

The Lost Heart

The letter fluttered in Alessandro's fingers. The breeze stirred their costumes as they stood, on the Riva bridge, facing the Bridge of Sighs, their gondola ride over. The sun was hot at their backs, and Leonora turned to warm the baby. She was silent – she did not want to say it. Alessandro spoke first. 'It's him.'

It was still a shock to hear it like that.

'It has to be – the age, description, everything. And the date – it's written just a few months after Corradino's "death".'

Leonora nodded. 'I know.'

She turned back to lean on the parapet with him.

'I have to go to France.'

'Yes.'

'I have to find out for sure. *Professore* Padovani has some contacts at the Sorbonne. They'll have more records there.'

Alessandro nodded. 'Next year, when the baby can travel, we'll all go. I can take leave, and ...'

'I have to go *now*.'

Alessandro shut his eyes. When he opened them his voice was level.

'Leonora, you are eight months pregnant. You cannot possibly travel now. You can't fly, for one thing.'

'I can go by train – or by boat like Corradino.'

'*Fuck* Corradino!' The explosion shocked them both. The silence that followed seemed to still the very revelers themselves. Alessandro tempered his voice. 'Any journey at this stage will put you under enormous stress. And what if you go into labour on the train? Or in France? Our baby should be born here, in Venice, as *I* was and as *you* were. Not in some hospital in Paris. I won't allow it.'

'You won't *allow* it?' Leonora was stung – she knew he spoke the truth, that she was losing the battle, but she perversely resented Alessandro's propriatorial tone.

'You're carrying *my* child.'

'Then act like it!' Leonora clutched at the glass heart and lost her head. All her resolutions, to be measured and dispassionate, faded away as her rage boiled. 'Why don't you commit to me? Why can't you be in my life all the time, instead of coming and going like the tide? Is it because of Vittoria?'

'*What?*'

'Yes, you think I don't know, but your own cousin told

me what you wouldn't. You're still seeing her aren't you? Last night, in fact, when you were "working late"?'

Her voice had risen, and passers by were looking on with curiosity at this piece of street theatre. Alessandro drew her below the loggia and forced her to sit on one of the cool marble benches.

'Sit down. You're getting far too agitated for someone of your condition.'

'I like your sudden concern.'

His voice was measured. 'Leonora, whether you know it or not, you and this child are the most important people in my life.'

'And Vittoria?' she spat. The woman that tied me in knots, and rubbished me in public for all to read? Why are you still seeing her if you are so loyal?'

'*Listen.*' He sighed. 'It's true I asked to see her. *Wait*,' as Leonora cried out. 'I knew all about Corradino, and the article. *You* didn't tell me, couldn't share your inner life with me. You let me think that you were looking for your father, but I knew of the real object of your interest. I went to see Roberto after Vittoria's article, to see if I could find out the truth with my new "official" status.' He sketched inverted commas in the air. 'But it seems he has emigrated, to France of all places, taking his secrets with him. That only left Vittoria.' He turned to look at Leonora full in the face. 'Last night was the one and only time that I've seen her. I asked her to show me Roberto's "Primary Source" – the proof that Corradino was a traitor. For old time's sake, she agreed.'

Leonora's mouth was dry. 'What was it?'

'A letter. The last letter written by his ancestor Giacomo del Piero, as he was dying in the *Piombi*.'

They both turned as one to look through the loggia arches at the dark barred windows of the watery prison. Alessandro went on. 'I didn't tell you any of this because the letter is pretty conclusive. He denounces Corradino as a traitor.'

Leonora tried to order her thoughts. 'Then why did Roberto not simply have the contents of the letter published?'

'Because the end of the letter shows Giacomo in a pretty bad light. He reveals the existence of Corradino's daughter, and her whereabouts.'

'The *Pietà*.'

'Yes. I imagine Roberto was as precious about his ancestor's reputation as you are about yours. Denouncing an apprentice who has betrayed you is one thing, but condemning an innocent orphan girl to death is quite another.'

'But she didn't die. She survived, and married, and lived happily ever after.'

'Well, Roberto must not have known that. And anyway, it's the denunciation itself which makes Giacomo look so bad.'

Leonora nodded. 'Why didn't you tell me you were looking into all this for me? Why have you been so distant?'

'How could I be intimate with you when you weren't honest with me? You held Corradino to yourself, even when the ad campaigns and the article made him so public. You thought that because I was away from Venice I wouldn't know. You thought that somehow I would like you less if you were the descendant of a traitor rather than the *maestro* you had boasted of. How could I tell you that someone that mattered so much to you mattered nothing to me? It's *you* I love and you have to find yourself first, before I can find you.' He turned back to the canal. 'And now, you are putting your obsession with a distant ancestor above the wellbeing of your own child. You're crazy. You should be thinking of *him.*'

'I'm *doing* this for him! I have to know before he is born! That's why I have to go to France. Don't you see? If Giacomo revealed Leonora's existence to The Ten *and yet she lived* then Corradino must have saved her somehow. I have to *know.*' Leonora clutched her glass heart for reassurance.

Alessandro caught the gesture and turned on her. 'Why? So you can boast about him at dinner parties? Is your own life not enough? Do you need Corradino to define you? Why can you not simply say, I'm Leonora, I am a glass-blower?'

'But I'm not! I'm not any more! That's why I have to clear his name. My job depends on his reputation. If he is redeemed then the Manin line will sell again and my family's profession is mine again.'

'Why must you rely on Corradino, and that stupid talisman you wear? Why can't you rely on *me*?'

Before Leonora could stop him he snatched the heart from her throat and threw it into the canal. It flew as far as the Bridge of Sighs, winking once as it disappeared into the arching shadow. They only heard, but did not see, the brief splash as the heart disappeared.

They both froze in shock at what had happened. At how much they could hurt one another. The glass heart, gone, meant they had reached a place from which there was no return. In this new insane universe where the centuries had telescoped, Alessandro faced the truth.

Corradino had become his rival.

Eyes shining with tears, Alessandro left her, pushing through the crowd and stumbling towards the Arsenale.

Leonora tried to call out, to tell him that he was right, as she knew he was. That she would not go to France. But she could make no sound. She tried to move but her feet were lead. Only when his black curls had completely disappeared from sight did she realize what was happening, as a band of pain wound tight around her belly, strong enough to make her gasp and clasp the balustrade. Concerned hands fluttered at her back, bystanders stopped to ask if she was alright. But she was not alright.

I am in labour.

CHAPTER 33

The Phantom

Giacomo didn't know how long he had been in the cell. From the length of his whiskers he knew it was many days, perhaps weeks. Weeks of silence. He heard only the rasp of his own breath and the hacking of his new cough. He could not see the walls that held him, but by the touch of their cool slime he knew he was in one of the cells that lay below the water level of the canal. His fear was as cold as the stone.

The silence was complete – so quiet he fancied he was alone in the prison. But he knew this was not the case, that only the thickness of the walls kept the cries of others from him. He thought he would have preferred to hear them. Anything but this solitary dark.

The smell of his own waste was everywhere. For the first days he had confined his excretions to the corners of the cell, finding the conjunction of two walls with his searching hands. Soon he had ceased to bother, and the stench was such that he prayed for his breath to stop.

For the first hours of his incarceration he felt the tingle of horrid expectation bump his flesh. Every moment he expected the door to open and the terrible dark phantom to enter, to ask more questions. They had read him the Ambassador's letter. They thought someone from Murano was helping the French King with his palace. The questions were relentless. Did anyone regularly send letters from the *fornace*? Had anyone been absent from the *fornace*? Ill? Dead? He had cried when he had told them of Corradino's death, as he missed the boy terribly – whether alive or dead, he was no longer with Giacomo day by day. Separation was death too.

They paid his grief no heed. What had Corradino died of? When was this? Then hours in an ante-room while they questioned someone else. From the snatches that Giacomo heard he divined that it was a doctor. The questioning was hard to hear through the oaken doors. But the screams were easy to hear. At the end of the interview the *medico* was taken away, pleading and broken. For the first time that day, Giacomo began to fear for his life as he was led back in to the vast chamber to face the spectre in the black mask. In his fancy he thought it was the same man that had come, years ago, for Corradino at the *fornace*. When he had saved the boy's life. But he knew it could not be. The figure stalked his fitful sleep – as potent as Death itself. But as the time wore on and he waited he knew what they were doing. Dread was their weapon. They wanted to drive him mad.

He fought it. God knows he did. But his fanciful mind in his ailing flesh peopled his cell with figures from his past. The whore he had tumbled in Cannaregio as a young man. She had brought his babe to him – called him Roberto after Giacomo's father, in an attempt to appeal to his instincts. But Giacomo had gone back to the glass, and Roberto and she had gone to Vicenza. Now she sat, with accusing eyes, holding the babe up to him. He looked inside the swaddle and saw the gaping maw of a child's skull, crawling with maggots. Giacomo's screams were muffled by the damp.

Sometimes Corradino himself visited, and mocked the old man with a secret that he would not tell. Giacomo rolled himself into a ball, hugging his own wasted flesh, forehead pressed to the slick wall, so he would not see the shades that loomed from the dark. But in his lucid moments, when his mind was well, he knew his body was sick. His coughs had become agonizing paroxysms that burned his chest, and in the last few fits he had tasted the metallic tang of blood in his mouth. He wished for a glass dagger – one of Corradino's would be best – to end his life.

Days later, he knew not when, a freezing voice spoke to him.

'You suffer greatly.' It was a statement, not a question.

Giacomo turned from the wall that had become his friend. The cell was lit by a single, blessed candle. But Giacomo's relief at the light was short lived. For in the corner, deep in shadow, he saw the spectre of his nightmares. By now, he was used to the ghosts. Even this one would go if he hugged his wall.

He made as if to turn back.

'Heed me, for I am real. I am not one of your imaginings. I can be merciful. I can bring you food, water; even set you free if you tell me what I want to know.'

Giacomo could not speak for some moments, his voice weak from the coughs and screams.

The figure took his hesitation for defiance. Had he but known it, Giacomo would have told him anything, everything, if only he could.

'Do you know why no man ever escapes from here?'

Giacomo knew very well. He desperately tried to say yes, for he did not want to hear it again, not here.

'Because if a guard ever lets a prisoner escape, that guard must finish the prisoner's sentence.'

At last Giacomo could croak. 'I know.'

The faceless figure inclined its cowled head. 'Then you see, I am your only hope.'

Hope. Hope from the Devil.

'We went to Sant'Ariano. To your friend's grave. Do you know what we found?'

Silence.

'We found loose earth and torn sackcloth. Your friend has gone.'

The clouds parted for Giacomo, as realization dawned. *Non omnis moriar.* Corradino did *not* altogether die. He felt like singing. His secret hope since he had read the Latin words had come to pass. His son *was* alive. The note which he had kept *was* an assurance, an instruction that he should not grieve. Praise God. Giacomo felt warm for the first time in months. But the voice went on:

'That night a ship was chartered from Mestre to Marseilles. Two men boarded from a fishing bark which was found with earth in the bottom. Your friend Corrado Manin has gone to France. He is the one we seek.'

A fast as joy and relief came, they left again. Giacomo felt the bile rise as he knew what had been done to him, to Murano, to the art of glass and mirror-making to which he had devoted his life. His dry eyes sprang fresh tears in the dark, but they were not the cold tears of grief but the hot tears of anger. *I shall not altogether die.* No, but you have killed me, and our trade too. Corradino, my son, how could you? You have given our secrets away. *Non omnis moriar.*

The words were echoed in the hideous voice. '*Non omnis moriar.*'

Giacomo's blood froze. They had been to his house. Of course they had. They had the note.

'I see these words have some significance. We found his letter to you.'

Giacomo cursed himself. Sentiment had made him keep

the note – the last thing that Corradino wrote, or so he thought. This note, which meant his own death, was a keepsake from a man who had betrayed him. If Giacomo had known what was planned, he would have killed Corradino himself. The irony was exquisite.

'You helped him.' Again, a statement.

'No!'

'You knew what he planned. He wrote you the note.'

'No, I swear it.' A scream at the last.

'You will die here.'

They left him then. The light, the phantom and the guard outside. As the footsteps receded, Giacomo began to scream. The pain in his chest and throat were nothing. The betrayal hurt the most.

Wordless, nameless hours later. His hours were filled with Corradino, laughing at him, taking his expertise and charity, and yes, love, for years and now making the best glass of his life for the French. The palaces in Giacomo's head were made of walls of crystal. The chairs, tables and food were glass. Corradino sat at the table which groaned with glass food. He ate his fill of the glass delicacies till the blood ran from his mouth, laughing all the time with a glass King. He must be stopped.

Giacomo felt death approach him. And Death came. Again with a guard and a candle.

The door was opened and the phantom entered. 'Well? Are you ready?'

Giacomo's voice was weak, but just audible.

'If I tell you, will you give me materials to write to my son Roberto?'

It was like bargaining with the Devil and it took the last of Giacomo's courage. The terrible shade inclined its cowled head. 'I will send you a scribe if you tell me what I need. And I will send you all comforts for your last hours. Now, hurry. Your life is ebbing away.'

'My son ... he is in Vicenza. He bears the del Piero name. I wish him ... I want him to know, and his sons to know, that Corradino finished me, and that he, not I, was the traitor.'

'It shall be accomplished. Now, what do you have to tell me?'

'Corradino, he ... has a daughter.'

CHAPTER 34

The Mask Falls

The *Salon de Thé* in Petit Trianon reminded Corradino very much of the Cantina Do Mori and as he entered the café for his assignation he missed Venice like a blow to the belly. As he sought the privacy of the backroom as instructed in Duparcmieur's note he passed the patrons who had borrowed the latest eastern fashions for their dress – the Byzantine look was the latest in style, and the gaudy velvets made these genteel Parisians resemble Venetians. The enclosed and exclusive rear area of the café was highly decorated with frescoes and mirrors.

The French, it seems, steal all of their ideas from Venice. Even me they stole.

As he sat and waited he began to wonder anew why Duparcmieur had chosen to meet here, in a mirror image of their first interview. Duparcmieur had been in the habit of coming to Corradino's house, or talking to him in the Palace itself. It was no secret to his colleagues that Duparcmieur was his protector, and that through him, Corradino had a loftier patron; the King himself.

Perhaps there were some delicate negotiations to conduct which demanded a convivial atmosphere. After all it was close on a year since Corradino had come to France, and they were nearing the appointed time for Leonora to come to him. Corradino set his jaw. He would not budge in the matter of Leonora. Every day he thought of her and how it would be when they were together at last – holding her sweet face in his hands, playing in the palace gardens as he worked, or touching their fingers together in their special way – this time without the grille of the Pietà in between. Unconsciously, Corradino spread out his hand in a star of longing – he could almost feel her little pads pressed to his hard, printless fingertips.

I hope she has not forgotten. I cannot wait.

He felt a back settle against his – the bones of a spine behind the nap of fine velvet.

Duparcmieur.

'Why here?' asked Corradino.
'Why not?'
The voice was not French. Not Duparcmieur. But the

perfect, aristocratic patois of the Veneto. As he had done a year before at the Cantina Do Mori, Corradino glanced into the mirror at his side. His guts shrivelled within him.

'I apologize for this unconventional meeting,' said Ambassador Baldasar Guilini smoothly. 'However, as we have met before, I thought such *convivial* surroundings would not offend you. Do you recall our meeting?'

Corradino swallowed. His thoughts flapped like moths in a bottle. He must not give himself away.

'At the Palace, Excellency?'

'Yes, then. But before, a long time before. At the *Arsenale*. You came with your father – he was ratifying a trading treaty with the Dardanelles. Saffron, was it? Or Salt? Forgive me, I forget the particulars of the case. But I remember your father – a noble fellow, Corrado Manin. You resemble him physically, which is your good fortune.' The Ambassador shifted. 'Your ill fortune, of course, is that you resemble him also in your propensity for treachery to the Republic.'

Corradino's frozen heart plummeted. He knew that it was over.

I am unmasked. I am dead. Should I run?

Corradino cast swift glances left and right at the laughing patrons. Any one of them could be assassins, agents of The Ten. It was no good.

As if echoing his resignation, the Ambassador continued. 'It's too late for you, of course. But if you make certain amends, you may be able to save your daughter.'

Fear clutched Corradino's throat with a strangling grip.

How could they know? Dear God, please, not *Leonora.*

'What do you mean?' he choked, in a last desperate parry. 'What daughter?'

'Signor Manin, please. The one in the Pietà of course. Leonora. The issue of your little *amour* with her mother Angelina dei Vescovi. We knew of the affair, of course. But not of the child. I expect old Prince Nunzio was ashamed of the matter, as well he might be. No, we are obliged to your mentor Giacomo del Piero for that information. It's too late for him as well, of course.' Baldasar Guilini sniffed fastidiously, as if he smelled rotten carrion.

Corradino felt his blood turn to water. Giacomo dead! And turned traitor on him, in a reflection of his own sin! He glimpsed down the pit of horrors that must have forced Giacomo to such a pass, and fought to restrain his terror. He must save Leonora, at any cost. 'What must I do?' It was a whisper.

'There is but one thing you can do to secure her safety. If you do this, she will be unharmed and may live out her days in peace in the Pietà or in marriage.'

'What? Dear God, what, anything.'

'We are aware, of course, that you have passed on

somewhat of your *specialist* knowledge to an apprentice. He, of course, will be taken care of.'

Jesu, not Jacques too. He was young; at least Giacomo had been old. A sorry pair of men, at either end of life's journey, who shared a name, a way with the glass, and a friendship for me – the man who has murdered them both.

'What must I do?' Now, almost a scream. Corradino looked savagely in the mirror, tired of the charade.

The Ambassador steepled his hands before his face and blinked his hooded eyes. 'You must go back.'

CHAPTER 35

Pity

Alessandro had no clear plan. He walked down the Riva degli Schiavoni in a daze, through the colourful crowds. He did not know if he was angry or sad or sorry or all these things. He didn't know whether to go back to Leonora or just see her back at her flat later. He didn't know whether to go back at all.

He needed peace to soothe his aching head. As he stumbled along in the direction of the Arsenale a dark door welcomed him. He fell through it.

Dark, peace and cool respite from the sun. A church. He was alone at last save for a single sacristan lighting candles for mass in the Lady chapel. A smell of incense that recalled the childhood masses at which he served as an altar boy. Alessandro had not been one for church since. But as he sank into the cool wooden pew he realized he had been to *this* church before. For over his head, looming from the dark, was an exquisite chandelier. A veritable cathedral of spider-spun silk, which he remembered from times past.

The Pietà.

Alessandro smiled at the irony. He had come here to escape Corradino, and yet his work was all around. And yet, Alessandro too had history here – for it was here that he had first seen Leonora. In that moment he knew he would go back, knew he couldn't be without her. She was stubborn and wrongheaded, but he loved her. Baby or no baby, he would go back.

A baby. Corradino had had a child too. Another Leonora. With a jolt, Alessandro recalled what his Leonora had said: 'But she didn't die ... she lived happily ever after.' The fairytale phrase revolved in his head, to be joined by another.

Once upon a time Corradino's daughter had lived *here*.

All at once, like a revelation, Alessandro saw how it had been. He saw in his mind the literal, pictorial definition of the Pietà, seen a thousand times repeated as a favoured motif of the Renaissance artists. The embodiment of pity; the Virgin Mary cradling the dead, crucified Jesus. But what Alessandro saw now in his mind's eye was the inversion of this trope. He and his unborn baby, and Corradino holding his daughter in his arms. *His* baby. Alessandro rose like one who had witnessed a miracle. Corradino could not leave his child behind for ever any more than Alessandro could. Leonora was right — he *must* have saved her. He would cross oceans, weather storms, fight dragons for the flesh of his flesh, blood of his blood. Corradino may have been an artist and a genius but he was still a man, and they shared this common bond. Just men after all. Alessandro moved through the pews on respectful feet and approached the sacristan who was lighting the flames, and as he asked what he had to ask he felt the first flicker of humanity, the first warmth of fellowship, for Corradino Manin.

CHAPTER 36

Mercury

Jacques waited for Corradino in the secret furnace room at Versailles. He was not concerned by his master's lateness, although it was, 'tis true, the first time he had been there before Corradino. Jacques knew his master had the most exalted of protectors – perhaps some business with the King kept him?

As he waited he raddled the coals, and polished some of the tools, idly twitching things into their proper places, anxious to begin the work of the day. At the last he crossed to the silvering vat, which he half filled with water from a pail. Then he reached for the flask of liquid mercury and poured the compound gingerly onto the surface where it spread like oil. Jacques was careful not to pour too quickly, for then the element could break into globules which spoiled the perfect sheet of silver. As he set the flask back down on the bench a perfectly round drop of the liquid jumped onto his index finger. From habit borne of spills when cooking his meagre supper he almost carried the finger to his mouth, then he remembered Corradino's warning that the mere taste of mercury could mean death. He wiped the digit carefully on his jerkin till all traces were gone. Then he was drawn, inexorably, back to the tank as the liquid settled and stilled into a mirrored sheet. He was so busy watching his undulating reflection that he did not turn to heed the key in the lock. He knew, in any case, that it was his master that entered as none but the two of them had the key.

Jacques was still watching his own image so closely that he did not see the gloved hand which caught the back of his neck and pushed his face into the silver poison.

CHAPTER 37

The Labours of Spring

It was not the first time that the Ospedale Civili Riuniti di Venezia had admitted a woman in labour who was wearing *Carnevale* costume. This was Venice, after all. How could it be otherwise? And yet a significant crowd formed and even the most hardened obstetricians were moved by the sight of *La Primavera* herself twisting in the agony of her burden. The sprigged dress was soaked with birthing waters and clung to her legs.

In the delivery room decisions were made quickly. It had taken a long while for the *Signorina* to get here, as she was unaccompanied, and despite the fact that this was her first baby the birth was well advanced. It was already too late for an epidural, and moreover, the baby was breech. The nuns attempted to offer comfort and relief, but, despite the pain of her labour, Leonora was sensible of the fact that she was alone, here in the very hospital where she herself was born, and the baby was coming. Every couple of minutes a toothsome steel trap closed on her belly and back, and she cried out for Alessandro. She was haunted by Professore Padovani's story of another Leonora's mother.

Angelina dei Vescovi, who died in childbirth . . . died in childbirth.

She felt the same pains as that long-dead beauty. The pain made them sisters over the span of centuries. At last she lost consciousness, albeit briefly, and the nuns thanked Jesus for the brief respite in what would surely be a long night. The obstetrician, a man of many years of experience whose ideas weren't working, noticed that even in her unconscious state *La Primavera* clutched at her throat, as if searching for a trinket that wasn't there.

CHAPTER 38

The Watcher in the Shadows

As Corradino Manin looked on the lights of San Marco for the last time, Venice from the lagoon seemed to him a golden constellation in the dark blue velvet dusk. How many of those windowpanes, that adorned his city like costly gems, had he made with his own hands? Now they were stars lit to guide him at the end of the journey of his life. Guide him home at last.

As the boat drew into San Zaccaria he thought not – for once – of how he would interpret the vista in glass with a *pulegoso* of leaf gold and hot lapis, but instead that he would never see this beloved sight again. He stood in the prow of the boat, a brine-flecked figurehead, and looked left to Santa Maria della Salute, straining to see the white-domed bulk looming in its newness from the dark. The foundations of the great church had been laid in 1631, the year of Corradino's birth, to thank the Virgin for delivering the city from the Plague. His childhood and adulthood had kept pace with the growing edifice. Now it was complete, in 1681, the year of his death. He had never seen its full splendour in daylight, and now never would. He heard a *traghetto* man mournfully calling for passenger trade as he traversed the Canal Grande. His black boat recalled a funeral gondola. Corradino shivered.

He considered whether he should remove his white *bauta* mask as soon as his feet touched the shore; a poetic moment – a grand gesture on his return to the *Serenissima*.

No, there is one more thing I must do before they find me.

He closed his black cloak over his shoulders against the darkling mists and made his way across the Piazzetta under cover of his tricorn and *bauta*. The traditional *tabarro* costume, black from head to foot save the white mask, should make him anonymous enough to buy the time he needed. The *bauta* itself, a spectral slab of a mask shaped like a gravedigger's shovel, had the short nose and long chin which would eerily alter his voice if he should speak. Little wonder, he thought, that the mask borrowed its name from the '*baubau*', the 'bad beast' which parents invoked to terrify their errant children.

From habit borne of superstition Corradino moved swiftly through the two columns of San Marco and the San Teodoro that rose, white and symmetrical, into the dark. The Saint and the chimera that topped their pediments were lost in the blackness. It was bad luck to linger there, as criminals were executed between the pillars – hung from above or buried alive below. Corradino made the sign of the cross, caught himself, and smiled. What more bad luck could befall him? And yet his step still quickened.

There is one misfortune that could yet undo me: to be prevented from completing my final task.

As he entered the Piazza San Marco he noted that all that was familiar and beloved had taken on an evil and threatening cast. In the bright moon the shadow of the Campanile was a dark knife slashing across the square. Roosting pigeons flew like malevolent phantoms in his face. Regiments of dark arches had the square surrounded – who lurked in their shadows? The great doors of the Basilica were open; Corradino saw the gleam of candles from the golden belly of the church. He was briefly cheered – an island of brightness in this threatening landscape.

Perhaps it is not too late to enter this house of God, throw myself on the mercy of the priests and seek sanctuary?

But those who sought him also paid for this jewelled shrine that housed the bones of Venice's shrivelled Saint, and tiled the walls with the priceless glittering mosaics that now sent the candlelight out into the night. There could be no sanctuary within for Corradino. No mercy.

Past the Basilica then and under the arch of the Torre dell'Orologio he hurried, allowing himself one more glance at the face of the huge clock, where tonight it seemed the fantastical beasts of the zodiac revolved in a more solemn measure. A dance of death. Thereafter Corradino tortured himself no more with final glances, but fixed his eyes on the paving underfoot. Even this gave him no respite, for all he could think of was the beautiful *tessere* glasswork he used to make; fusing hot nuggets of irregular glass together, all shapes and hues, before blowing the whole into a wondrous vessel delicate and colourful as a butterfly's wing.

I know I will never touch the glass again.

As he entered the Merceria dell'Orologio the market traders were packing away their pitches for the night. Corradino passed a glass-seller, with his wares ranked jewel-like on his stall. In his mind's eye the goblets and trinkets began to glow rosily and their shapes began to shift – he could almost feel the heat of the furnace again, and smell the sulphur and silica. Since childhood such sights and smells had always reassured him. Now the memory seemed a premonition of hellfires. For was hell not where traitors were placed? The Florentine, Dante, was clear on the subject. Would Corradino – like Brutus and Cassius and Judas – be devoured by Lucifer, the Devil's tears mingling with his blood as he was ripped asunder? Or perhaps, like the traitors that had betrayed their families, he would be encased for all eternity in '. . . *un lago che per gelo avea di vetro e non d'acqua sembiante* . . . a lake that, frozen fast, had lost the look of water and seemed glass.' Corradino recalled the words of the poet and almost smiled. Yes, a fitting punishment – glass had been his life, why not his death also?

Not if I do this last thing. Not if I am granted absolution.

With a new urgency he doubled back as he had planned and took the narrow bridges and winding alleys or *calles* that led back to the Riva degli Schiavoni. Here and there shrines were set into the corners of the houses – well-tended flames burned and illumined the face of the Virgin.

I dare not look in her eyes, not yet.

At last the lights of the Orphanage at the Ospedale della Pietà drew near and as he saw the candlelight warmth he heard too the music of the viols.

Perhaps it is she that plays – I wish it were so – but I will never know.

He passed the grille without a glance inside and banged on the door. As the maid approached with a candle he did not wait for her inquisition before hissing: 'Padre Tommaso – *subito!*' He knew the maid – a surly, taciturn wench who delighted in being obstructive, but tonight his voice carried such urgency that even she turned at once and soon the priest came.

'*Signore?*'

Corradino opened his cloak and found the leather gourd of French gold. Into the bag he tucked the vellum note-book, so she would know how it had been and one day, perhaps, forgive him. He took a swift glance around the dim alley – no, no-one could have drawn close enough to see him.

They must not know she has the book.

In a voice too low for any but the priest to hear he said: '*Padre*, I give you this money for the care of the orphans of the Pietà.' The mask changed Corradino's voice as he had intended. The priest made as if to take the bag with the usual formula of thanks, but Corradino held it back until the father was forced to meet his eyes. Father Tommaso alone must know him for who he was. 'For the orphans,' said Corradino again, with emphasis.

Recognition reached the priest at last. He turned over the hand that held the bag and looked closely at the fin-gertips – smooth with no prints. He began to speak but the eyes in the mask flashed a warning. Changing his mind the father said, 'I will make sure they receive it,' and then, as if he knew; 'may God bless you.' A warm hand and a cold one clasped for an instant and the door was closed.

Corradino continued on, he knew not where, until he

was well away from the Orphanage.

Then, finally, he removed his mask.

Shall I walk on till they find me? How will it be done?

At once, he knew where he should go. The night darkened as he passed through the streets, the canals whispering goodbye as they splashed the *calli*, and now at last Corradino could hear footsteps behind keeping pace. At last he reached the Calle della Morta – the street of death – and stopped. The footsteps stopped too. Corradino faced the water and, without turning, said, 'Will Leonora be safe?'

The pause seemed interminable – splash, splash – then a voice as dry as dust replied.

'Yes. You have the word of The Ten.'

Corradino breathed relief and waited for the final act.

As the knife entered his back he felt the pain a moment after the recognition had already made him smile. The subtlety, the clarity with which the blade insinuated itself between his ribs could only mean one thing. He started to laugh. Here was the poetry, the irony he had searched for on the dock. What an idiot, romanticizing himself, supposing himself a hero in the drama and pathos of his final sacrifice. All the time it was *they* who had planned the final act with such a sense of theatre, of what was fitting, an amusing *Carnevale* exit. A Venetian exit. They had used a glass dagger – Murano glass.

Most likely one of my own making.

He laughed harder with the last of his breath. He felt the assassin's final twist of the blade to snap handle from haft, felt his skin close behind the blade to leave no more than an innocent graze at the point of entry. Corradino pitched forward into the water and just before he broke the surface he met his own eyes in his reflection for the first and last time in his life. He saw a fool laughing at his own death. As he submerged in the freezing depths, the water closed behind his body to leave no more than an innocent graze at the point of entry.

From the shadows of the Calle della Morte, Salvatore Navarro – the new foreman of the *fornace* on Murano – watched, terrified. He had been given this time and place by an agent of The Ten and been told to attend on pain of death. Coming so lately upon the death in the Piombi of his predecessor Giacomo del Piero, he had dared not refuse. As he watched the demise of the great Corradino Manin, a man he had looked up to since his days as a *garzon*, he knew he was here as a witness. That he was expected to go back to Murano and tell all that he had seen.

And that he, and all other glassblowers through him, were being given a warning.

CHAPTER 39

The Notebook

Alessandro followed the sacristan as they wound upward in a small spiral staircase leading from the vestry of the Pietà.

'It's not a library as such, mostly old music books and some records,' the sacristan continued, his words punctuated by the whispering of his flowing robes. 'Once, of course, we had a very significant collection of Vivaldi's handwritten scores. After his popularity revived in the nineteen-thirties we had our book collection properly stored at the correct temperature and insured. That collection is in a museum in Vienna where he died. Are you a student of Vivaldi?' The sacristan did not seem to need an answer but launched into his well rehearsed guidebook version of the red priest's life. Alessandro climbed higher and fought to remain polite. At other times he would have been deeply interested in the history, today he was fired with a quite indecent urge to push past the kind old man and rush ahead into the library. Each turn of the stair seemed the thread of a screw that wound Alessandro's impatience ever tighter. At last they reached an ancient door and Alessandro fidgeted whilst the sacristan went through what seemed like dozens of keys. At last the right one fitted. Turned.

The small room was barely lit by one arched window. Golden motes of dust danced in its light. The draught of the opening door caused the dead-leaf rustle of pages which whispered that no one had read these volumes for years. From floor to ceiling they were piled, not shelved; the dusty bookstacks of Prospero. Alessandro forgot the cant of his guide as he looked around. It would not take long to find what he sought, if it was here, if it existed. He turned decisively.

'*Padre*. I am most grateful for your guidance. Could I beg you to excuse me while I take a little look around here? I'm sure you have other things to do. I'll be most careful, I promise.'

The sacristan set back a little, but then his eyes crinkled. They held the exquisite trust of a man of God, one that believes the world holds no ill. He patted Alessandro's arm. 'A private matter. I see. I'll be downstairs.'

Alessandro flashed his most charming of smiles as the robe whispered from the room.

Then he turned to his task.

There were perhaps a thousand volumes here. Not many.

But if what he sought was here, it would betray itself by its size. He anticipated his search would take a few hours. But after perusing only two floor-to-ceiling stack's worth of books, finding only leather bound music scores and hymnbooks, he saw it. Wedged between the horizontal stacks was a small vellum volume, bound in fine calfskin, the best Venetian workmanship. As he had guessed, the size told the secret.

A book of days. A notebook. A diary.

Alessandro sank to the floor and the velvet of his costume rose around him. He could have been a man from another age as he sat in the pool of cloth, in this ancient chamber, the light from the window turning him back to a painting. His hands shook as he realized this was it – the notebook whose existence he had assumed but not been certain. Surely this was the grail at the end of Leonora's quest? But as he turned the fine pages, wondering at the crabbed script, the detailed drawings, the scrawled measurements and mathematics, a new notion held him. What if this book confirmed her fears?

And so it was. Alessandro's fingertips were suddenly soaked, and the thin vellum began to bubble beneath their wetness till he hurriedly wiped his hands on his robe. For here it was, proof – irrevocable and incontrovertible. The last pages were measurements and drawings that pertained to the Hall of Mirrors at Versailles. Alessandro sat back as the enormity engulfed him. In a legacy of treachery, that room had once housed Vittorio Orlando, Prime Minister of Italy. Had Orlando and the other signatories – Woodrow Wilson, Lloyd George, Georges Clemenceau – looked into Corradino's glass as they had cut the heart and soul out of Germany in that 'Treaty' of 1919, and set in train the inevitable grinding machine which led to the Second World War? Ill deeds bred ill deeds, never more so than here. Alessandro could have wept. He had solved the mystery, but brought the answer Leonora dreaded.

Leonora.

His eye caught her name on the page – the last pair of pages in the book. Here the writing was different – scrawled, passionate, not exact and mathematical, and here and there was a splash of brine or tears. So Alessandro sat and read the letter Corradino had written to his daughter, which could have been written to Leonora, *his* Leonora, herself.

CHAPTER 40

The Ruby

Someone was screaming and crying. Twisting in blood and mess on the sheets. It sounded like Leonora's own voice.

How many hours have I been this way?

Concerned nuns and a doctor in blue scrubs collected at her stirrupped feet. Monitoring belts bound her heaving belly. A machine chattered at her side with a needle spiking over reams of graph paper in improbable peaks. The pain darkened her eyes and she called again for Alessandro, as she had done at every labouring of her body. At last, miraculously, he answered. Not as an ephemeral pain-filled daydream – for she had relived their time together to get her through this – but as a strong presence, here by her bed, his firm dry hand holding her damp one tight. She clasped his fingers, hard enough to bruise bone. The fog cleared and she saw him clearly then, raining kisses on her hand

and forehead. He held something in his hand – a book. He whispered something in her ear – through the thrum of blood in her head as she pushed again, she heard:

'He came back! Corradino came back!'

The pain abated. She knew its dark ways now – there was time enough for her to say what she had to before it came again.

'I don't care. Don't leave me.'

She heard him say, 'never again,' before the pain made her insensible. She was not aware that, as she laboured, he slipped onto her third finger a ring with a ruby red as the banked fires of a furnace. He had been carrying the little box around with him all day – he had meant to propose at the Çarnevale, and that had been the reason for his excitement of last night. This was not as he had planned it. This way she knew nothing of the question that had been asked of her. He could have waited for tomorrow, for hearts and flowers, and the bending of one knee. But he wanted her to have the ring now.

In case tomorrow was too late.

CHAPTER 41

The Letter (part 1)

Leonora was still. Alessandro, his eyes still wet, still held her hand. The hand that wore his ring. Her suffering was over.

And the prize? He slept too, in a clear plastic box next to the bed. A small, perfect bundle with a face crumpled from his ordeal, but to Alessandro the most beautiful thing in the world beside Leonora. He would battle tigers for him. His son. He should be in a casket of gold, not this incongruous tupperware.

Alessandro had been there just in time for the birth. The events of last night were as a dream to him — returning in triumph to an empty house, fearing that Leonora had gone away, then spying the winking red light of the answer phone. The message from the hospital. The mad dash to get here, fearing he knew not what.

She stirred. Her eyes opened and the bloom returned to her cheeks, Spring no more, but full blown Summer, rich, abundant and with a healthy son. He thanked God for the first time since he was a child.

He kissed her gently as she smiled, and the baby, as if sensing his mother's wakefulness, woke too. They smiled at each other as the boy opened his eyes, their dynamic for ever changed from two to three. A triangle now. Alessandro tenderly picked up his son and held him to his chest. Tiny, heavy and real. He moved to the door.

'Where are you going?' A new mother's anxiety.

'My son and I are going for a walk,' his heart thrilled at the words. 'You should rest. But before you do, read that.' He nodded to the vellum notebook where it lay on the coverlet.

'On the final page is a letter for you.'

'For *me*?' But Alessandro had left the room with their son. Their son. She barely had the patience to read, so cocooned was she in her new happiness. But her name on the parchment caught her eye.

Leonora mia,

I will not see you again. Mid-way through the journey of my life, I took the wrong path, the right way being lost. I have sinned against the State, and now I must be punished. Moreover, two fine men, Giacomo del Piero and Jacques Chauvire, died because of what I did. But I want you to think kindly of me if you can. Do you remember when I came to see you last, and we said farewell, and I gave you your heart of glass? I went to France and gave away the secrets of that glass. But now I will make amends. Now I am coming back home, to Venice, so you will be safe and the glass will be safe. And you will be safe, I have been promised. I will walk back through Venice once more, and leave this book for you. By the time I reach the other side of the city, I know they will find me and finish me. Keep your glass heart close, and think of me. I want you to think of the way we touched our hands together that last day, do you remember? Our special way? Every finger and the thumb? If you should read this, remember that Leonora, remember me that way, on that day. And Leonora, my own Leonora, remember how much your father loved you, loves you still.

Tears dropped on the coverlet and soaked the hospital gown they had given her, when they had taken Spring's raiment away. She cried at last for Corradino, but also for Giacomo, for her mother, for her father and for Stephen. They were her past. But by the time her future came back into the room, she was smiling and ready to hold her son. The notebook was tucked away, tidied carefully onto the night stand, ready to return home to the Pietà and the kindly sacristan who had understood why Alessandro needed to take it away.

CHAPTER 42

The Letter (part 2)

Padre Tommaso climbed the stair to the girls tiring chamber, expecting to find the bride-to-be surrounded by her contemporaries, all twittering over her dress and hair. Instead, his heart failed him as he beheld the girl that had become as a daughter to him, the girl that had been like his own since the defection of her father, the girl that had been the delight of his old age. She was alone, kneeling in the sun of the dorter window, her bright head bent.

She was at prayer.

He knew as he watched that the trinket she held at her throat as she prayed was no cross but the heart of glass that her father had given her the day before he had disappeared for ever. Then Corradino was in her thoughts today. It was natural, he supposed, that an orphan should think of her dead parents on her wedding day. It made it easier to tell her what he had to. He waited with his head bowed while she finished her intercessions and chose his words.

She smiled up at him. '*Padre*? Are they ready for me?'

'Yes, child. But before we go, may I speak with you a little?'

A slight frown crossed her perfect features and then cleared. 'Of course.'

The *Padre* lowered himself slowly onto a faldstool, as his bones were no longer young. He gazed at this peerless beauty and tried to remember her as Corradino would have seen her last – without the silver brocade gown, the ringleted hair set with moonstones, and all the trappings of a woman who was shortly to marry into one of the most powerful families in Northern Italy. 'Leonora, are you happy in this match? Is Signor Visconti-Manin truly the choice of your heart? Your head is not turned by his riches? I know his gold must be tempting to one orphaned such as yourself . . .'

'No, *Padre*,' Leonora interrupted with a rush, 'I truly love him. His riches mean nothing to me. Do not forget that when he first came to Venice he was merely a younger son, and he came as a student of history, anxious to find the Venetian branch of his family. Only now after the death of his brother and father, has he assumed the riches that were never his before. I love him – I loved him long before his inheritance. He is kind and good and loving. He wishes to settle here in Venice and bring up his children in the Manin name. I hope . . . you will still be my confessor.'

'*Cara mia*, of course I will. These old eyes would miss you too much, else.' The priest sighed and smiled, his mind at rest. Corradino would be glad that his daughter was to be happily matched. Now he must come to the burden of his visit. 'Leonora, do you remember your father?'

'Of course I remember him. Very fondly, for all that he left me never to return.' She clasped the glass heart. 'He gave me this, and I have worn it always as he said. Why do you speak of him now? No man ever heard from him again.'

Padre Tommaso clasped his hands. 'That is not entirely true. He returned here, just once, and gave me something for you.'

The girl stood, straight as a willow wand, her green eyes wide. 'He came back? When? Is he still alive?'

'Leonora. No. This was many years ago, you were still a child. Only now that you are a woman, might you be able to understand.'

'Understand what? What did he leave for me?'

'He left enough gold for your education, and a handsome dowry. And . . . this.' The gnarled old hand proffered the vellum notebook. 'Your father was a genius. But he was not without sin. Great sin. Read this, and form your own mind. But do not neglect to read the final pages. I will leave you for a moment.'

Padre Tommaso retired into the next chamber, and once there he prayed too. Leonora took so long that he was afraid for the patience of the congregation downstairs in the church. He was also afraid he had taken the wrong course in showing her the book. But at last the door opened and she came out. Tears had turned her eyes to glass.

'My child!' The *Padre* was distraught. 'I was wrong to have shown you.'

Leonora fell into his arms and clasped his frail body tightly. 'Oh, no, Father, no. You were right. Don't you see? Now I can forgive him.'

As Padre Tommaso led Leonora Manin down the aisle of Santa Maria della Pietà, the place that had been her home for one and twenty years, the orphaned girls sang with especial beauty. It seemed to the priest that today they attained divinity in their music, but perhaps it was the more earthly longing – that they too might one day make a match like this – that gave wings to their song. Lorenzo Visconti-Manin stood at the altar in magnificent cloth of gold, and Padre Tommaso felt a misgiving at the man's grandeur until the groom turned to see his bride and his eyes were also wet with tears. As the priest surrendered Leonora to her husband, the couple did not join hands as was customary. With a shared smile and in a practised ritual that Padre Tommaso did not understand, they reached out their right hands and, starlike, placed fingertip to fingertip, thumb to thumb.

CHAPTER 43

At the Do Mori

When Salvatore Navarro went to the Cantina Do Mori
to receive a commission, and the voice of the one that
greeted him was French and not Venetian, he was not
surprised. Only very, very frightened. He was not surprised
because They had warned him that this may come to pass.
All he could think of was Corradino Manin's body, falling
forward into the chilled waters of the canal, a glass blade
in his back and his robes darkening as they accepted the
water and dragged him down to Hell. Salvatore left at
once, without even listening to the Frenchman's proposals.
He knocked over a table in his haste to be away, as if every
instant he spent in the man's company implicated him
further as a traitor.

Salvatore gulped the twilight air and raced down the
Calle dei Mori to the canalside. He waited, dreading
following footsteps until with relief he heard the familiar
mournful cry; '*gondola gondola gondola,*' and hailed the

gondolier. It was not until he had settled back into the velvet cushions, and directed the boatman to the Doge's palace, that he began to shake.

Still inside the Do Mori, Duparcmieur shrugged and took another leisurely sip of his wine. Salvatore could not be persuaded, and Duparcmieur had lost Corradino in a spectacular fashion, but someone soon would be persuaded by the King's gold. He glanced at his goblet and calculated – yes – he had time to finish his wine and still be safely away before Salvatore denounced him to The Ten, and they came looking. He drank deeply. Really, the wine was excellent here.

CHAPTER 44

Leonora's Heart

The birth had been difficult, so the hospital kept Leonora for another day. Never an easy patient, she was anxious to go home and was delighted to be discharged. The three of them took a boat from the hospital as she was still feeling weak, and she looked at the palaces and bridges and gloried in the city. With an open heart she loved Venice again and the city loved her back. She belonged. She had done something as fundamental as giving birth here. She had given *La Serenissima* another son. And as for Corradino – he was forgiven by her and the city too. Carnevale was here, winter was gone. She longed to see her flat again. Better still was the clutter that greeted her as she opened the door – all of Alessandro's things were stacked in the hall. He had moved in overnight. She caught sight of the ruby on her hand as she opened the door and thought of the moment of quiet in the hospital yesterday when he had asked her properly and she had said yes. Alessandro followed her up the stairs with their precious cargo in a carry-cradle which he placed tenderly beside her bed. Their bed. The Madonna of the Sacred Heart smiled benignly down on the three of them from her frame. The heart she held glowed in her hands and Leonora understood her at last. The heart was the Virgin's Son.

In the crazy first weeks of constant feeding and broken sleep Alessandro was home on paternity leave, so he was there when they received an unexpected visitor. Adelino crept quietly into the flat behind a barrage of flowers, kissed mother and father on both cheeks and waggled his fingers at the son. The baby was lying on a sheepskin in the living room, captivated as his mother and grandmother had been by the reflected crystal filigree of the water shimmering on the ceiling. He captured one of Adelino's gnarled digits and seemed happy to hold on.

'He is very strong,' Adelino pronounced, 'very good for his future profession.' Adelino ballooned his cheeks as if blowing a parison, and popped them to amuse the child. He sat on the proffered chair which Alessandro politely vacated to perch on the bed. 'Now; I bring two gifts,' said the old man, 'one for the mother and one for the son. The father I have brought nothing for, but it seems he has everything he wants already. Now, ladies first.' He produced a folded newspaper from his pocket and handed it to Leonora. She received it with the shock of memory which reminded her of darker times.

Il Gazzettino.

She looked at Alessandro in time to see a smile of complicity pass between the two men. 'Go on,' said her fiancé. 'Read it.'

She opened the folds to read the headline. 'MAESTRO AND MARTYR. Corrado Manin returned to certain death for the love of his secret daughter. Read the astonishing true story of self-sacrifice of one of our city's greatest sons.' Her eyes moved down to the byline. 'An exclusive by Vittoria Minotto.'

Leonora raised a brow. 'Vittoria?'

Alessandro smiled. 'I sent her Corradino's notebook. With the sacristan's permission of course. It's safe back in the Pietà now. I wanted it to be a surprise for you.'

'It certainly is. She changed her tune!'

Alessandro sat down beside his son and tickled the baby's belly. 'Not really. If you'd had the misfortune to know her as long as I have you'd realize that the only thing that matters to Vittoria is an exclusive. She's not a bad person, but she will shift sides with ease to get the best story. That's why we would never have worked. Her job was always much more important than people.'

Adelino had the grace to look sheepish at the mention of work. 'Speaking of jobs, we'd ... *I'd* like you back, as soon as your family can spare you.'

Leonora looked down for a moment, remembering her ignominious departure.

'We *need* you back. *All* of us; the *maestri* too. We're going to be pretty busy. That edition only came out this morning and we've already had hundreds of enquiries about the Manin line. The public is a funny beast – they think Corradino is a hero. We're thinking of going national with the ad campaign. Chiara and Semi are very excited.'

Leonora started to laugh. 'I bet they are.' But she began to remember other things, the smell of the *forno*, the hot glass growing beneath her breath, taking shape in her hands. She had loved it, but she did not want to give in at once. 'How do I know you want me back to be a glassblower, and not just to be some figurehead for your world domination?'

'Ah, you must let me come to my second gift,' said Adelino, patting all his pockets in a mock pantomime which elicited a reluctant smile from Leonora. Then, from the last pocket, he pulled, in the manner of a magician revealing a string of handkerchiefs, a length of familiar blue ribbon. Transfixed, Leonora's jaw dropped as the glass heart popped out of Adelino's pocket. Perfect as ever, imprisoning light in its core. Leonora looked at Alessandro, who shook his head, equally amazed.

'But how did you ... when did you ...'

'How did you fish it out of the canal?' They spoke together in a rush.

Adelino drew his white brows together. 'What do you mean?'

Alessandro told the tale, by now ashamed of his part in

it. 'So you see, the heart is ... was ... somewhere under the Bridge of Sighs. I'm just surprised that it was found.'

Adelino smiled. 'No, no. This is not Corradino's heart. That one has found its rest, and just as well. Leave it for the city and the sea to claim.'

As it claimed Corradino. Yes, it was a fitting end.

'This,' Adelino waved the heart, which winked in the sun, 'is one of the ones *you* made at the *fornace*, Leonora. *This* is why I want you back. You must be a better glassblower than you think to mistake your workmanship for your ancestor's.' He smiled expansively, including them all in this new word.

Leonora examined the heart and could not see the flaws she had imagined before. 'Very well,' she said. 'I'll be back. But not yet. I have my son to take care of at the moment. Give me a few months. You can use all the ad material in the meantime.' She smiled. 'But I'm sure you would anyway.' Adelino's grin, the grin of a merchant, a pirate, a buccaneer, had returned.

She looked down at the heart where it shone in her hand. 'I'll keep it close as you asked,' she said quietly, a whisper to a long-dead man who had loved his child too. She made as if to tie the heart round her neck, in its old place, but Adelino stopped her.

'Hey, hey, what are you doing? It's not for you!' The familiar twinkle was back.

'It's not?'

'No, it's for Corradino,' said Adelino, pointing to the baby.

Leonora and Alessandro exchanged a look. Started to smile.

'Here, Corradino,' Leonora dangled the heart over the sheepskin rug, 'how do you like your birthright?'

One tiny hand reached up for the bright glass, closed over it, and didn't let go.

THE END

Acknowledgements

Writing a book is a solitary experience, but I was lucky enough to have someone along for the journey. So most of all I'd like to thank my husband Sacha Bennett for being my editor, muse, psychiatrist, nanny, chef and printer; in short, my everything.

Once the book was finished I had lots of help from some fantastic people: thanks to my brilliant agent Teresa Chris for her constant faith in me, and to Simon Petherick, Tamsin Griffiths and the team at Beautiful Books for getting behind the novel in such a big way. Thanks to friend and writer Helene Wiggin for her encouragement and advice, and to Nigel Bliss for going to the right wedding! Thanks also to my Dad Adelin Fiorato for knowing his way round Dante, and to my Mum Barbara Fiorato for correcting my French.

If this book has a message I guess it is that family are everything. So thank you to Conrad and Ruby for letting mummy write, and for teaching me that when you have a child it's like letting your heart walk around outside of your body.

Last but not least, thank you to the Glassblowers of Murano, who work miracles every day.

Reading
Group
Gold

THE GLASSBLOWER OF MURANO

by Marina Fiorato

About the Author

- A Conversation with Marina Fiorato

Behind the Novel

- "The History of Murano"
  An Original Essay by the Author

Keep on Reading

- Recommended Reading
- Reading Group Questions

A Reading Group Gold Selection

For more reading group suggestions
visit www.readinggroupgold.com.

ST. MARTIN'S GRIFFIN

 *A Conversation with Marina Fiorato*

Could you tell us a little bit about your personal and professional background, and when it was you decided to lead a literary life?

I was born and educated in the north of England and at university I studied history. I then rebelled against my parents' academic background by going to art school and entering the film and music business! I began by generating onscreen graphics and I was lucky enough to work on films like *Tomb Raider* with Angelina Jolie and *Proof of Life* with Russell Crowe. I shifted into rock music and worked with U2 and the Rolling Stones and Aerosmith, but when I became pregnant with my first child I took maternity leave. It was then that my old life found me again, and it was after I had my son that I had the idea for the story for *Glassblower.* I wrote the book while I was on leave and never returned to my job. I think I had been trying to be something I was not, and then, when I had a child of my own, ideas of heritage and my Venetian origins became enormously important. My old interests had found me with a vengeance—it was like being tapped on the shoulder by my past.

> *"My old interests had found me with a vengeance—it was like being tapped on the shoulder by my past."*

Is there a book or author that inspired you to become a writer?

I grew up reading Pamela Kaufman's books about Alix of Wanthwaite and her wonderful earthy writing and sense of period really inspired me—she invokes the sounds, sights, and even smells of the past so well! In more recent writing I love the prose of Thomas Harris. In the Florentine section of *Hannibal* I think he really manages to evoke the beauty but also the brutality of Italy at the same time. It's a modern tale but so Renaissance in spirit.

*You studied history at Oxford University and the
University of Venice, where you specialized in the study
of Shakespeare's plays as an historical source. How has
your education influenced your writing?*

I studied a lot of Shakespeare in school and was
inspired by both the language and the sheer drama
of his storytelling. I'm like a magpie when I write; I
steal shiny bits of the work of my betters and weave
them into my own prose! There is so much Shakespeare
in *The Glassblower of Murano,* from pieces of plot to
direct quotes. I was particularly inspired in this case by
The Merchant of Venice, which is one of the plays I
studied in detail for my master's degree, but I also
lifted a plotline from *Romeo and Juliet.* There's even a
quote from *The Tempest* in there somewhere. At least
I steal from the best!

*Do you scrupulously adhere to historical facts in your
novels, or do you take liberties if the story can benefit
from the change?*

I do try, as far as possible, to be reasonably accurate—
I think because of my training in historical research that
any blatant inaccuracies would really jar. If push came
to shove, though, I would sacrifice total accuracy for the
cause of the story. It's not my job as a novelist to create
a piece of historical documentation. What I'd like to
think is that my books might serve to interest people in
a certain period or character, and serve as a jumping-off
point for them to then go away and research their interests from proper historical sources. My historical hero,
Corradino Manin, is fictional so I wasn't bound by the
constraints of writing about a real person; that gave me
a certain amount of freedom. The context, though, the
world in which he lives, does have to be accurate. There
are real historical figures in the book, like Louis XIV,
but as they tend to be marginal there is not the
obligation to feverishly research them.

*About the
Author*

Are there any parallels between you and Leonora? Can you tell us a bit about your own travels in Venice and experiences with glassblowing?

There are a number of parallels between myself and Leonora, mostly to do with our heritage. Like her, I have a Venetian family. I was actually lucky enough to study at the University of Venice for six months and I lived on the Lido, taking the *vaporetto* into Ca' Foscari every day, which was wonderful. While there I remember taking a tourist trip to Murano, where I saw a glassblower make a tiny, perfect crystal horse in about sixty seconds. I remember that it seemed like a miracle, and the episode stayed with me; in fact it's included in the book when Giacomo makes a glass horse for the young Corradino. I returned to Venice years later to get married, in a little church on the Grand Canal. The whole wedding party was in eighteenth-century dress, which was fabulous, and we took boats out to the islands for the reception. It was unforgettable.

You've mentioned that one of your favorite blown-glass windows in Venice is at Ca' Foscari, a palace on the waterfront of the Grand Canal. What do you see when you look at that window, in particular, and all blown glass, in general? What is it about Venice, blown glass, and the process of glassblowing that you hoped to reveal to your readers?

There are hundreds of beautiful windows on the Grand Canal, but Ca' Foscari has a special resonance for me because of studying there. Originally a palace, Ca' Foscari is now used as a university and stands in a particularly beautiful bend of the canal; what fascinates me is that the window itself is as beautiful as what you can see through it. I like the way that these windows also tell the story of Venice's history—they are a wonderful hybrid of western and eastern design and exemplify Venice's identity, a republic standing astride two empires.

> *"I love the way glass is such a shifting entity. In many ways it has as many faces as Venice itself."*

Blown glass fascinates me because, like most great
crafts, it's incredibly difficult to achieve a good result. I
used the word *miraculous* in the book and I think it's
deserved. I love the way glass is such a shifting entity.
In many ways it has as many faces as Venice itself, and I
think that nature of changeability, of having many faces,
is what I wanted to reveal about the city. Glass begins
life as a powder which becomes liquid, then solid;
there's only a very short window to work with glass
before it hardens, and it takes a true artist to do it.
Incredible, too, that such beauty comes from humble
sand—true artistry from a quintessence of dust.

Venice is so unchanging; it's essentially the same place
architecturally as it was in the seventeenth century. There
are few places in the world about which one can say this,
because most cities have changed to accommodate roads
and sprawling suburbs. But because Venice as a "character" was the same then as now, I thought it would be
really interesting to take a look at ideas of heritage and
continuity of a particular Venetian family, with a peculiar
creative genius. I was inter-
ested in whether or not a
skill like glassblowing is
passed down in the same
way that, say, facial characteristics are. Is glassblowing
in the Venetian DNA? Are
these skills built into the
Venetian genome, and how
much does the city itself
create artists by a kind of
osmosis which has nothing
to do with the century they
are in? These are the kinds
of questions which interested me.

Geoff Budd

Marina's wedding kiss

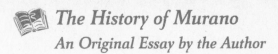

The History of Murano
An Original Essay by the Author

When writing the historical strand of *The Glassblower of Murano* it was important to me to get some sense of the significance of glass in Venice at the end of the seventeenth century. And when you visit, the evidence is before your eyes; the city seems to be almost made of glass. As well as boasting the most beautiful windows in the world, exquisite chandeliers hang from the frescoed ceilings of every palazzo, the basilica is clothed in jewel-like mosaics comprised of nuggets of glass covered in lapis and gold; and at the other end of the scale the streets in the Merceria dell'Orologio behind San Marco are crowded with bijoux little shops crammed with glass fancies, beads, and bonbons.

"Murano is the glass heart of Venice."

But it is Murano, one of the trio of islands set far into the Venetian lagoon, which is and was the glass heart of Venice. In 1291, an edict of the Great Council, Venice's ruling body, decreed that all glass furnaces should be moved to the island after a series of serious fires which threatened the city. In the Renaissance period, glass was a priceless monopoly for the Republic of Venice, and at the heart of their mystery was the closely guarded secret of how to make mirrors. The manufacture of mirrors of reasonable size and reflectivity was deeply problematic until the glassblowers of Murano stumbled across the optimum method through an accident of glassblowing. Thereafter they began to make mirrors brighter, clearer, and larger than any in the world. Venetian mirrors quickly became the Republic's most valuable commodity, more precious than saffron; more costly than gold.

The Council of Ten, the vicious ruling junta of Venice's Great Council, quickly realized the value of the glassblowers of Murano, and threatened them with death if they ever divulged their methods. Often, the glassblowers' entire families were kept as hostages by the state. Venetian law was very clear on the matter:

If any worker or artist should transport his talents to

another country, and if he does not obey the order to return, all of his closest relatives will be put in prison.

Incredibly, despite such threats, some of the glassblowers of Murano did betray their secrets and their city. In the 1680s, Louis XIV, the Sun King, was in the throes of his Grand Design: the Palace of Versailles, for which he planned to construct a great chamber made entirely out of mirrors, and needed assistance from the best of the best. Thus, many of Murano's glassblowers were secretly transported to Paris. Recruited by Pierre de Bonzi, the French Ambassador to Venice, they were tempted by tales of foreign lands, exotic women, and great riches. By the autumn of 1665, twenty Murano fugitives had been spirited away to Paris where they began work upon the task of making the dream of a king a reality.

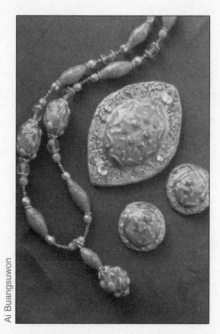

Fiorato beads. Image courtesy of Ann Mitchell and Karen Mitchell of AnKara Designs, www.ankaradesigns.com.

Behind the Novel

As we now know, the Hall of Mirrors in Versailles was built and remains for all to see—a cathedral of glass that is undeniably one of the modern wonders of the architectural world. Not only does the work mitigate the treachery of those brave souls from Murano, it is also a tribute to the craftsmen of France, who would someday become the forerunners for the genius of Baccarat and Lalique.

On a more personal note, I made a discovery of my own while researching the history of glassmaking in Murano: I was delighted to discover that *Fiorato,* my Venetian family name (which means "floral"), is also the name for a type of Murano glass. Fiorato glass features tiny glass flowers enameled and fused into beads. Fiorato beads are tiny, but they are beautiful. It felt great to be, in some small way, part of such a wonderful tradition.

"It's great to be, in some small way, part of such a wonderful tradition."

A portion of the essay originally appeared in *Italian* magazine (© 2008). Reprinted with permission from the author.

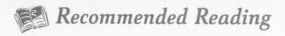 *Recommended Reading*

The Count of Monte Cristo
by Alexandre Dumas

A wonderful epic tale of a man who comes back
from the "dead." A direct influence on my
historical plotline.

The Comfort of Strangers
by Ian McEwan

An extremely dark take of Venice, in contrast
to the way in which the city is usually portrayed in
literature. McEwan creates a wonderful sense of
unease throughout. Here, the city is dangerous;
it can kill, and it does.

*Keep on
Reading*

Brideshead Revisited
by Evelyn Waugh

One of my favorite novels. Tucked in the central
section is one of the most golden, languid portraits
of Venice ever written. Entirely seductive, the city
here is the polar opposite of the one in
The Comfort of Strangers.

Hannibal
by Thomas Harris

Another one of my favorites. Not a Venetian
setting but half of the novel is set in Florence and
it's a wonderful portrait of a city which has never
left the beautiful, brutal Renaissance. Everything is
here; the art, the corruption of those in power, and,
of course, the bloodletting.

Through a Glass, Darkly
by Donna Leon

Donna Leon knows Venice so well that every detail places you in the city. I'm a big fan of her Guido Brunetti detective novels, but this is my favorite; a great tale of murder set in the glass factories of Murano.

Death in Venice
by Thomas Mann

Another wonderful portrait of Venice, this time seen from the Lido (where I used to live). In this novella the city is sick; death stalks Venice in the shape of a mysterious disease, in a marked contrast to the youthful perfection of the Adonis of the Hotel des Bains.

The Merchant of Venice
by William Shakespeare

Not a novel, I know, but a wonderful play and a direct influence on my book. *The Merchant of Venice*, as the name suggests, is proof positive that trade was the lifeblood of the city in Shakespeare's day. Interesting too, that *every* section of society engaged in trade, even the nobility; in other Renaissance kingdoms, nobles thought trade was a dirty word.

 *Reading Group Questions*

1. Glass and Venice are both metaphors for change in the novel. How do they mirror the changing reflections of the characters? In particular, discuss this facet of the novel in relation to the roles of Leonora and Corradino.

2. Marina Fiorato uses imagery of glass: its beauty yet changeability; its strength yet fragility, throughout her novel. How does this portray an unfamiliar, dark, and sinister side to the most romantic European city?

3. Do you think Corradino Manin did the right thing by his "betrayal"?

4. Discuss the narrative structure of *The Glassblower of Murano*. In what ways do the two intertwined strands of the novel, the story set in the Renaissance and Leonora's modern-day narrative, shape the story?

5. Marina Fiorato says in her acknowledgments that having a child is like letting your heart walk around outside your body. Discuss the various relationships between parent and child in the story. How do they vary, and in what ways are they similar? What do you think is signified by Leonora's gift of the glass heart pendant to her child?

6. How important was it for Leonora to leave everything behind and move to Venice, and what do her discoveries teach her about family?

7. Think about the male-dominated *fornace* on Murano. Leonora has an uncertain relationship with the *maestros* in the factory because she is a woman in what remains a man's world. How do you think this relationship affects her view of her own femininity?

8. Is it acceptable—because of the importance of glassblowing to Venetian heritage—for Leonora to be treated as an outsider by the *maestros*?

*Keep on
Reading*

9. The story of *The Glassblower of Murano* is centered around Corradino's secret and Leonora's search for the truth. Discuss the various elements of mystery in these pages. What types of narrative devices does Marina Fiorato use to keep the reader guessing?

10. Few places are as romanticized, celebrated, and praised as Venice. Have you traveled to Venice? If so, do you agree with the portrayal of Venice in the story? If not, how did reading this book confirm or deny your preconceived notions of one of the world's most famous places?

Visit www.stmartins.com/MarinaFiorato
for a sneak preview of Marina Fiorato's next book

The Botticelli Secret

Available in Spring 2010

*I*n the heart of fifteenth-century Florence, part-time model and full-time prostitute Luciana Vetra is asked by one of her most exalted clients to pose for the central figure of Flora in Sandro Botticelli's *Primavera*. During her time in Botticelli's studio, Luciana makes a startling discovery: a dark secret may be hidden among the brushstrokes of Botticelli's most famous painting. Luciana enlists the help of the one man who has never desired her beauty—novice librarian Brother Guido of Santa Croce—to learn the truth. Monk and courtesan soon find themselves in mortal danger as they are pursued through nine cities of Renaissance Italy in an attempt to decode the painting's secrets, and soon realize that the *Primavera*'s hidden message reveals a political conspiracy that reaches all the way up to Lorenzo de Medici.

W9-CEE-877

OFFICIAL GUIDE to
BOTTLES
Old & New

by

HAL L. COHEN

Author of

OFFICIAL GUIDE TO
POPULAR ANTIQUES & CURIOS

OFFICIAL GUIDE TO
PAPER AMERICANA

OFFICIAL GUIDE TO
COMIC BOOKS

OFFICIAL GUIDE TO
SILVER & SILVERPLATE

OFFICIAL GUIDE TO
COLLECTIBLE PLATES

ISBN 0-87637-330-9

Library of Congress Catalog No. 73-93246

*House of
Collectibles*
INCORPORATED

Printed in the United States of America

Any book as complex, and comprehensive as this one, requires the help, and cooperation of many individuals, and companies. If anyone is not included it is through oversight, not intention.

With much thanks and appreciation to the following for help in obtaining pictures and information:

Mr. Hans Schonewald, American Beverage Brokers; Mr. Nicoló Luxardo, Girolamo Luxardo Company; Mr. Brian C. Abbott, Jules Wile Sons & Company; Mr. John McKey II, The Carter's Ink Company; Mr. James Samuelson, Barton Brands Inc.; Mrs. Frances Shoemaker, Heinz U.S.A.; Mr. J.M. Starke, McCormick Distilling Company; Mr. John Edwards, Publisher; Mrs. Ellen Ladner, Mr. Martin Lewin, James Beam Distilling Company; Dr. Larry Freeman, Antiques Book Club; Mr. Charles B. Gardner, New London Conn.; Mr. Lynn R. Stuart; Mr. Bud Hastin; Mrs. Marion Mann, Avon Products, Inc.; Mr. David H. Lowenstein, Ms. Sue Wilson, Mr. Even G. Kulsveen, Lionstone Distilleries Ltd.; Mr. Charles W. Wagner, Wheaton/nuline Company; Mr. Eugene R. Weill, Jr., "21" Brands, Inc.; Mr. Richard E. Martin, Famous Firsts Ltd.; Mr. H. Silverman, S. Kostman, T. O'Shea, G. Walsh, J. Tremont, K. Axel, Marvin Frank Advertising & Ezra Brooks Distilling; Mr. J.C. Malin, Mr. Fruend, William Grant & Sons Inc.; Mr. Howard Nutt, Austin Nichols Company; Mr. William C. Handlan, Jack Daniels Distillery; Mr. Howard Lesser, Old Charter-Dant Distillers; Mr. R.O. Parrish, Stitzel-Weller Distillers, Mr. Ted Gustenhoven, Mr. Joel Cohen, I.W. Harper-Dickel Distillers, Mr. Sy Feit, Frankfort Distillers; Numano International Inc., Ms. Debbie Master, Jim Beam; Mr. Tony Palmisano, Ms. Maxine DeVoney, Mr. H. Cutler, Marvin H. Frank Co., Somerset Importers, Ltd., Mr. Ed Johnson, Holly City Bottle; etc.

Special thanks to Mr. Julius Kessler of A. & J. Kessler Liquors, and Mr. Morris Lourie, of Lourie Liquors Inc., for use of their store inventory, and private collections of collectable bottles to list and illustrate, Luxardo, Bischoff, Garnier, Beam, Bardi, Bols, Brizard, Barsottini, etc.

Also to Jeff Neff, for illustrations of Beam, Garnier, and Bischoff Bottles, and to Ken Sheller for illustrations of Bitters Bottles, and Milk Bottles, and Coca-Cola Bottles, and to Bill Jenkins and his crew for helping put it all together.

Acknowledgements 3
Bottle Clubs .... 6 –10
National Bottle Clubs 6
Ezra Brooks Bottle Clubs 10
Newspapers and Magazines 11
Bibliography –– Other Bottle Books .... 12 – 14
How to find and Collect New Bottles .... 15 – 16
New Bottle Pricing 17
Average Buying Price & Retail Price 17
Where to Buy & Sell Bottles .... 15 – 16
Bottle Grading––New Bottles 18
Bottle Grading––Old Bottles..19
What To Look For––Old Bottles .... 19 – 20
Mold Marks   19

PART 1/NEW BOTTLES

AVON BOTTLES.................................... 22 – 76
Avon Introduction 22

JIM BEAM BOTTLES .... 77 – 153
Jim Beam Introduction 77
Customer Specialties .... 78 – 85
Centennial Series .... 86 – 89
Glass Specialties.. 90 – 94
Trophy Series .... 95 – 106
Political Series ....107 – 108
State Series...109 – 114
Executive Series ....115 – 117
Regal China ....118 – 153

EZRA BROOKS BOTTLES............................ 154 – 225
Ezra Brooks Introduction..154

BALLANTINE BOTTLES 226
BARDI-BARSOTTINI-BRALATTA-BEEFEATER 227
BOLS-BORGHINI-BRIZARD 228

BISCHOFF BOTTLES.................................. 229 – 236
Bischoff Introduction..229

JOSEPH E. SEAGRAM & SONS INC., BOTTLES 237

TABLE OF CONTENTS   5

BOTTLES BEAUTIFUL — FAMOUS FIRSTS . . . . *238 – 244*
J.W. DANT BOTTLES . . . . *245 – 248*
GARNIER BOTTLES . . . . *249 – 265*
GARNIER MINIATURES *265*
HOLLY CITY BOTTLES . . . . *266 – 267*
JAPANESE BOTTLES . . . . *268 – 269*
KENTUCKY GENTLEMEN *270*
LIONSTONE BOTTLES . . . . · . . . *271 – 281*
Lionstone Introduction *271*

LUXARDO BOTTLES . . . . *282 – 291*
Luxardo Introduction *282*
GRENADIER BOTTLES *292*
McCORMICK BOTTLES, Old Blue Ribbon Bottles . . . . *293 – 295*
OLD FITZGERALD — STITZEL/WELLER . . . . *296 – 306*
MISCELLANEOUS BOTTLES . . . . *307 – 308*
    I.W. Harper - Nichols - Southern Comfort
    Old Hickory - Double Springs - Old Taylor
    Dickel - Old Blue Ribbon
WHEATON/NULINE . . . . *309 – 313*

PART II/OLD BOTTLES

BITTERS BOTTLES . . . . *315 – 355*
Bitters Introduction *315*
BARBER BOTTLES *356*
COCA-COLA BOTTLES . . . . *357 – 359*
HISTORICAL & POLITICAL FLASKS . . . . *360 – 368*
INK BOTTLES . . . . *369 – 376*
MILK BOTTLES . . . . *377 – 386*
WHISKEY & BAR BOTTLES . . . . *387 – 397*
WHISKEY BOTTLES—I.W. HARPER—JACK DANIELS *388*

COLOR PAGES

AVON, GARNIER, WHEATON/NULINE, EZRA BROOKS,
LIONSTONE, FAMOUS FIRSTS - BOTTLES BEAUTIFUL . . . . . *97 – 104*

ANTIQUE FLASKS & BITTERS, JIM BEAM, J.W. DANT,
NEW COLLECTIBLE BOTTLES, LUXARDO, ANTIQUE
BOTTLES OF ALL TYPES . . . . *297 – 304*

• NATIONAL BOTTLE CLUBS •

ANTIQUE BOTTLE COLLECTORS ASSOCIATION
P.O. Box 467
Sacramento, California 95802

NATIONAL EZRA BROOKS BOTTLE CLUB
420 West First Street
Kewanee, Illinois 61443

NATIONAL JIM BEAM BOTTLE & SPECIALTIES CLUB
490 El Camino Road
Belmont, California 94002

• STATE BOTTLE CLUBS •

All Bottle Clubs welcome visitors, inquiries,
and new members.

A.B.C. OF COLORADO
Box 63
Denver, Colorado

A.B.C. OF JACKSONVILLE
P.O. Box 1767
Jacksonville, Fla. 32201

A.B.C. OF ORANGE COUNTY
223 E. Ponona
Santa Ana, California 92707

A.B.C.A. OF FRESNO
Steve Kincade
P.O. Box 1932
Fresno, California 93718

A.B.C.A. OF FLORIDA
4324 S. W. 13th St.
Miami, Fla. 33801

A.B.C.A. OF RENO-SPARKS
P.O. Box 6145
Reno, Nevada 89503

ALABAMA BOTTLE COLLECTOR'S SOCIETY
1768 Hanover Circle
Birmingham, Alabama

ALAMO CHAPTER A.B.C.A.
c/o Robert Duff
701 Castano Avenue
San Antonio, Texas 78209

AMETHYST BOTTLE CLUB
3245 Military Avenue
Los Angeles, California

ANCHORAGE BEAM CLUB
5401 Chera Avenue
Anchorage, Alaska 99504

ANTIQUE BOTTLE & GLASS COLLECTORS
311 Avenue East
Snohomish, Washington 98290

ANTIQUE QUESTERS
172 Conners Avenue
Chico, California 95926

ARIZONA TERRITORY A.B.C.
P.O. Box 1221
Tucson, Arizona 85715

AVON COLLECTORS CLUB
P.O. Box 1406
Mesa, Arizona 86201

APOLLO BEACH A.B.C.A.
P.O. Box 3354
Apollo Beach, Florida 33570

AVON BOTTLE & SPECIALTIES COLLECTORS
Southern California Division
9233 Mills Avenue
Montclair, California 91763

AMERICAN ASSOCIATION OF PERFUME COLLECTORS
P.O. Box 55074
Houston, Texas 77055

BEAM CLUB OF SOUTHERN CALIFORNIA
114 Coronado Terrace
Los Angeles, California 90026

ARNFALT COLLECTORS BEAM CLUB
Tony Arnfalt
New Richland, Minnesota 56072

All Bottle Clubs welcome visitors, inquiries
and new members.

• STATE BOTTLE CLUBS •

**CAPITOL BOTTLE
COLLECTORS**
Route 7 Box 44596
Olympia, Washington 98501

**CATSKILL MOUNTAIN
JIM BEAM BOTTLE CLUB**
c/o William Gibbs
Six Gardner Avenue
Middletown, New York 10940

CONN. SPEC. BOTTLE CLUB
1135 Barnum Ave.
Bridgeport, Conn. 06610

**CENTRAL SOUTH
OREGON A. B. C.**
708 South F. Street
Lakeview, Oregon 97630

DECANTER CLUB
Two Spring Street
Potsdam, New York 13676

DIXIE BEAM BOTTLE CLUB
C.B. Carter
Forest Hill Ave.
Clarksville, Virginia 23927

**EMMETT HISTORICAL
BOTTLE ASSOCIATION**
108 Grove Street
Petoskey, Michigan 49770

**EVERGREEN STATE BEAM
BOTTLE & SPECIALTIES CLUB**
P.O. Box 99244
Seattle, Washington 98199

**BOTTLE COLLECTORS
ASSOCIATION OF FLORIDA**
14301 S.W. 8th Avenue
Miami, Florida

**CHEROKEE STRIP
EZRA BROOKS CLUB**
P.O. Box 631
Arkansas City, Kansas 67005

CALIFORNIA LIONSTONE CLUB
212 So. El Molino St.
Alhambra, Calif. 91801

CHEYENNE A.B.C.
4417 E. 8th St.
Cheyenne, Wyom. 82001

**DES MOINES JIM BEAM &
SPECIALTY CLUB**
Edward Van Dyke
2417 48th Street
Des Moines. Iowa 50310

EAGLE VALLEY GOPHERS
805 Winnie Lane
Carson City, Nev. 89415

**EMERALD EMPIRE
BOTTLE CLUB**
Rattlesnake Creek Road
Dexter, Oregon 97431

**EZRA BROOKS
SPECIALTIES CLUB**
636 W. Ivy Street
Glendale, California 91204

CAVE CITY A.B.C.
Route 1, Box 155
Carlsbad, New Mexico 88220

**CENTRAL & MIDWESTERN STATES
BEAM & SPECIALTIES CLUB**
c/o Elmer Collins
44 S. Westmore
Lombard, Illinois 60148

CENTRAL OHIO BOTTLE CLUB
P.O. Box 19864
Columbus, Ohio 43219

DANT "AMERICANA"
J.W. Dant Distillers Co.
1290 Ave. of the Americas
New York, New York 10019

DIRIGO BOTTLE COLLECTOR'S CLUB
c/o 59 Fruit St.
Bangor, Maine 04401

**EASTERN MONROE COUNTRY
BOTTLE CLUB**
c/o Bethlehem Lutheran Church
1767 Plank Road
Webster, New York

DOVER FOXCROFT BOTTLE CLUB
c/o Wayne Champion
50 Church Street
Dover Foxcroft, Maine 04426

**EMPIRE STATE BOTTLE
& SPECIALTY CLUB**
William Bateman
East Main Street
Milford, New York 13807

BOTTLE CLUBS

All Bottle Clubs welcome visitors, inquiries
and new members.

• STATE BOTTLE CLUBS •

**ENDLESS MOUNTAIN
ANTIQUE BOTTLE CLUB**
P.O. Box 373
Eirie, Penn. 16512

FINGER LAKES B.C.A.
4742 Sweeney Road, R.D. 4
Cortland, New York 13045

**EVERGREEN STATE BEAM
BOTTLE CLUB**
1540 Maple Lane
Kent, Washington 98031

FRONTIER COLLECTORS
504 N.W. Bailey
Pendleton, Oregon 97801

**GREEN MOUNTAIN
BOTTLE CLUB**
c/o Fred Brown
P.O. Box 269
Bradford, Vermont 05033

GOLD DIGGERS A.B.C.
P.O. Box 56
Gold Hill, Ore. 97525

"HIGH-COUNTRY" A.B.C.
311 14th St.
Alamosa, Colorado

ILLINOIS BOTTLE CLUB
416 East Webster
Griggsville, Illinois 62340

JIM BEAM BOTTLE CLUB
c/o Al Cembura
139 Arlington
Berkeley, California

**J.V. GUNN MIDWEST
EZRA BROOKS LIMITED
BOTTLE CLUB**
Box 29198
Lincoln, Nebraska 68529

**EZRA BROOKS BOTTLE
& SPECIALTIES CLUB**
420 N. First Street
Kewanee, Illinois 61443

FIRST CHICAGO BOTTLE CLUB
P.O. Box 254
Palatine, Ill. 60067

FORT WAYNE BOTTLE CLUB
Thurman Fuhrman
5622 Arbor Avenue
Fort Wayne, Indiana

GEORGIA BOTTLE CLUB
Tom Zachary
2996 Pangborn Road
Decatur, Georgia 30033

**THE GENESEE VALLEY BOTTLE
COLLECTORS ASSN.**
P.O. Box 9660
Rochester, NY. 14604

THE HEART OF ILLINOIS A.B.C.
2010 Bloonington Rd.
East Peoria, Illinois 61611

**HUNTSVILLE HISTORICAL
BOTTLE CLUB**
113 Monto Sono Blvd. S.E.
Huntsville, Alabama

IOWA ANTIQUE BOTTLEERS
1506 Albia Road
Ottumwa, Iowa 52501

JERSEY DIGGERS BOTTLE CLUB
Belleplain Road
Leesburg, New Jersey 08327

JOLIET BOTTLE CLUB
c/o C. W. Sieber
12 E. Kenmore Avenue
Joliet, Illinois 60431

FALLON BOTTLE CLUB
Tolas Place
Fallon, Nevada

FIGURAL BOTTLE ASSOCIATION
The Bottle Stopper
Eagle, Wisconsin 53119

**FLINT HILLS BEAM &
SPECIALTY CLUB**
201 W. Pine
El Dorado, Kansas 67042

FRIENDLY JIM'S BEAM CLUB
James Bradley, Sr.
508 Benjamin Franklin H.W. East
Douglassville,Pennsylvania 19518

GRANITE STATE BOTTLE CLUB
c/o Alfred Davis
116 Academy Street
Laconia, New Hampshire 03246

HELLGATE A.B.C.
P.O. Box 411
Missoula, Montana 59801

HISTORICAL BOTTLE DIGGERS
Route 3, Box 204
Broadway, Virginia 22815

INTERNATIONAL DECANTERS CLUB
Opal Redman
101 E. Third Street
Dayton, Ohio 45402

JIM BEAM COLLECTORS
107 Mohawk Drive
Barrackville,West Virginia 26559

JIM BEAM COLLECTORS CLUB
10 Lunt Road
Folmouth, Maine 04105

All Bottle Clubs welcome visitors, inquiries,
and new members.

• STATE BOTTLE CLUBS •

KCYE CITY BOTTLE CLUB
Route 1, Box 155
Carlsbad, New Mexico

KELLY CLUB
Mary Kelly
147 North Brainard Avenue
La Grange, Illinois 60525

**KIM CLUB FOR
BOTTLE COLLECTORS**
22000 Shaker Boulevard
Shaker Heights, Ohio 44122

**LIONSTONE WESTERN
FIGURAL CLUB**
P.O. Box 2275
Colorado Springs, Colo.80901

LITTLE ROCK A.B.C.
P.O. Box 5003
Little Rock, Ark, 72205

MEMPHIS A.B.C.
1070 Terry Circle
Memphis, Tennessee 38107

MIDDLE TENNESSEE B.C.C.
2804 Belmont, Apt. 1
Nashville, Tennessee 37212

**MILK BOTTLES ONLY
ORGANIZATION (MOO)**
Box 5456
Newport News, Virginia 23605

MILWAUKEE JIM BEAM & A.B.C.
Box 56
6361 South 27th
Frankland, Wisconsin 53132

**MINNESOTA FIRST
ANTIQUE BOTTLE CLUB**
5001 Queen Ave. No.
Mound, Minn. 55430

MINERAL COUNTY, A.B.C.
Box 237
Hawthorne, Nevada

LARKIN BOTTLE CLUB
Clarence Larkin
107 W. Grimes
Red Oak, Iowa 51566

**NATIONAL EARLY
AMERICAN GLASS CLUB**
31 Norwood Street
Sharon, Massachusetts

NORTH JERSEY A.B.C.A.
P.O. Box 617
Westwood, New Jersey 07675

NORTHERN NEW YORK B.C.A.
Box 257
Adams Center, New York 13606

**NEBRASKA ANTIQUE BOTTLE
& COLLECTORS CLUB**
1718 South 8th
Omaha, Nebraska 68108

NUTMEG STATE BEAM CLUB
Roy Schmidt
25 Meadowood Drive
Middletown, Connecticut 06457

NEW ENGLAND BOTTLE CLUB
Box 472
Henniker, New Hampshire 03242

OHIO BOTTLE CLUB
P.O. Box 585
Barberton, Ohio 44203

PINETREE BOTTLE CLUB
c/o Gene Swiger
79 School Street
South Portland, Maine 04100

PAUL BUNYAN BOTTLE CLUB
c/o Mrs. Francis Kearns
237 14th Street
Bangor, Maine 04401

**SEA WAY VALLEY BEAM &
DECANTER CLUB**
RFD #2c c/o Dick Cook
Potsdam, New York 13676

RICHMOND AREA B.C.A.
5901 Wonderland Lane
Mechanicsville, Va. 23111

ST. LOUIS ANTIQUE BOTTLE ASSN.
c/o J. Messler
32 W. Jackson
St. Louis, Miss. 63119

POCATELLO A.B.C.A.
Route 2
Inkon, Idaho 83245

SOUTHEASTERN A.B.C.
2996 Pangborn Road
Decatur, Georgia 30033

TULSA OKLAHOMA BOTTLE CLUB
5752 E. 25th Place
Tulsa, Oklahoma 74114

UTAH BOTTLE CLUB
P.O. Box 15
Ogden, Utah 84402

YANKEE BOTTLE CLUB
c/o Kay Fox
Page Street
Keene, New Hampshire 03431

EZRA BROOKS BOTTLE CLUBS

**KENTUCKY BLUEGRASS EZRA
BROOKS BOTTLE CLUB**
6202 Tabor Drive
Louisville, Kentucky 40218
Pres. Mr. Donald R. Ballard

**OHIO EZRA BROOKS
BOTTLE CLUB**
8741 Kirtland-Chardon Road
Kirtland, Ohio 44094
Pres., Mr. Edward Bauman

**ST. LOUIS EZRA BROOKS
CERAMICS CLUB**
42 Webster Acres
Webster Groves, Missouri 63199
Pres., Mr. Edward J. Boyd

**MISSION TRAILS EZRA BROOKS
BTL. & SPECS. CLUB**
4923 Bel Canto Drive
San Jose, Calf. 95124
Pres., Mr. Grant Blackledge

**NEW JERSEY EZRA BROOKS
BOTTLE CLUB**
South Main Street
Cedarville, New Jersey
Pres., Mr. Edward Bradford

**WICHITA EZRA BROOKS BTL. &
SPECS. CLUB**
8045 Peachtree Street
Wichita, Kansas 67207
Pres., Mr. Larry Carter

**THE CHINOOK EZRA BROOKS
BOTTLE CLUB**
223 Kelso Drive
Kelso, Washington 98626
Pres., Mrs. Mildred Ceglowski

**THE NUTMEG STATE
EB BOTTLE CLUB**
191 W. Main Street
Meriden, Connecticut 06450
Pres., Dr. Erwin Chambers

**FLINT EAGLES EZRA
BROOKS BOTTLE CLUB**
1117 W. Remington Avenue
Flint, Michigan 48507
Pres., Mr. R. W. Christenson

**GOLDEN BEAR EZRA
BROOKS BOTTLE CLUB**
8808 Capricorn Way
San Diego, Calf. 92126
Pres., Mr. Jack Coffin

**THE CHEROKEE STRIP EB
BOTTLE & SPECS. CLUB**
P.O. Box 631
Arkansa City, Kansas 67005
Pres., Mr. Jack Dempsey

**CHICAGO EZRA BROOKS
BTL. & SPECS. CLUB**
3635 West 82nd Street
Chicago, Illinois 60652
Pres., Mr. William Driscoll

**INDIANA EZRA BROOKS
BOTTLE CLUB**
P.O. Box 24344
Indianapolis, Indiana 46224
Pres., Mr. John D. Finch

**NATIONAL EZRA BROOKS
BOTTLE & SPECS. CLUB**
420 West 1st Street
Kewanee, Illinois 61443
Pres., Mr. Jack H. Fuller

**GREATER GREENSBORO
MOOSE EB BOTTLE CLUB**
217 S. Elm Street
Greensboro, N.C. 27401
Pres., Mr. Ralph B. Jenkins

**BLUE AND GRAY EZRA
BROOKS BOTTLE CLUB**
2106 Sunnybrook Drive
Frederick, Maryland 21201
Pres., Mr. Frank R. Joy

**"ORIGINAL SIPPIN" EZRA
BROOKS BOTTLE CLUB**
5823 Bartmus
Commerce, Calf. 90040
Pres., Mr. Barney Leto

**HAWAII BOTTLE
COLLECTORS CLUB**
Box 8618
Honolulu, Hawaii 96815
Pres., Mrs. Alberdene Little

**"CAJUN COUNTRY COUSINS" EZRA
BROOKS BOTTLE & SPECS. CLUB**
1000 Chevis St.
Abbeville, Louisiana 70510
Pres., Mr. Raywood Maihes

**WILD & WONDERFUL WEST VIRGINIA
EZRA BROOKS BOTTLE & SPECS. CLUB**
1929 Pennsylvania Court
Weirton, W. Va. 26062
Pres., Mr. George Monezis

**COLORADO MILE–HIGH EZRA
BROOKS BOTTLE CLUB**
7401 Decatur Street
Westminster, Colorado 80030
Pres., Mr. Gil Nation

**EAST COAST EZRA
BROOKS BOTTLE CLUB**
2815 Fiddlers Green
Lancaster, Pennsylvania 17601
Pres., Mr. James Quinn

**KACHINA EZRA BROOKS
BOTTLE CLUB**
3818 W. Cactus Wren Drive
Phoenix, Arizona 85021
Pres., Mr. Robert B. Robinson

**GOLDEN GATE EZRA BROOKS
BOTTLE & SPECS. CLUB**
715 Capra Drive
Vallejo, Calif. 94590
Pres., Mr. George Saroff

STEEL CITY EB BOTTLE CLUB
R.R. No. 2 P.O. Box 32-A
Valparaiso, Indiana 46383
Pres., Mrs. Willabelle Spurling

**HOLLY WOOD STARS – EZRA
BROOKS BOTTLE CLUB**
2200 North Beachwood Drive
Hollywood, Calif. 90028
Pres., Mr. Clyde Thebaut

**MT. RAINIER EZRA
BROOKS BOTTLE CLUB**
P.O. Box 1201
Lynwood, Washington 98178
Pres., Mr. Richard Tucker

**WEST COAST FLORIDA EZRA
BROOKS BOTTLE CLUB**
1360 Harbor Drive
Sarasota, Florida 33579
Pres., Mr. Charles Twain

The following publications are very interesting and helpful to collectors, dealers, and anyone interested in bottles.

•

All publications listed are available by mail, either individual issues, or b, subscription. All these listed are excellent sources to buy, sell, or trade bottles of all types.

Many publications offer a free sample trial issue, write and inquire.

• NEWSPAPERS •

ANTIQUE MONTHLY
P.O. Drawer 440
Tuscaloosa, Alabama 35401

ANTIQUE NEWS
Box B
Marietta, Pennsylvania 17547

ANTIQUE TRADER
Box 1050
Dubuque, Iowa 52001

COLLECTOR'S NEWS
Box 156
Grundy Center, Iowa 50638

COLLECTOR'S WEEKLY
Box 1119
Kermit, Texas 79745

TRI-STATE TRADER
P.O. Box 90-DM
Knightstown,
Indiana 46148

• MAGAZINES •

ANTIQUES JOURNAL
P.O. Box 1046
Dubuque, Iowa 52001

NATIONAL ANTIQUES REVIEW
P.O. Box 619
Portland, Maine 04104

DOWN EAST GLASSMAN
P.O. Box 203
West Hartford,
Connecticut 06107

RELICS
P.O. Box 3668
1012 Edgecliff Terrace
Austin, Texas 78704

SPINNING WHEEL
Everybodys Press, Inc.
Hanover, Pennsylvania 17331

WESTERN COLLECTOR
P.O. Box 9166
San Francisco,
California 94129

OLD BOTTLE MAGAZINE
P.O. Box 243
Bend, Oregon 97701

PICTORIAL BOTTLE REVIEW
B & K Enterprises, Inc.
P.O. Box 42558
Los Angeles, California 90050

EASTERN ANTIQUITY
1 Dogwood Drive
Washington,
New Jersey 07882

WESTERN ANTIQUE MART
P.O. Box 2171
Eugene, Oregon 97402

HOBBIES
Lightner Publishing Corp.
1006 South Michigan Avenue
Chicago, Illinois 60605

NATIONAL BOTTLE GAZETTE
P.O. Box 1011
Kermit, Tx. 79745

BOTTLE NEWS
P.O. Box 1000
Kermit, Tx. 79745

THE BOTTLE TRADER
P.O. Box 69
Gas City, Indiana 46933

BOTTLES & RELICS
P.O. Box 654
Conroe, Tx. 77301

The books listed below are recommended for anyone interested in a special-ized aspect of bottle collecting, or a particular type of collectable bottle. They can be obtained by mail from the following Antique Book Distributors, or direct from the authors or publishers.

• ANTIQUE BOOK DISTRIBUTORS •

HOTCHKISS HOUSE
89 Sagamore Drive
Rochester, New York 14617

ANTIQUE PUBLICATIONS
Emmitsburg, Maryland 21727

OLD TIME BOTTLE PUBLISHING CO.
611 Lancaster Drive N.E.
Salem, Oregon 97301

**MID-AMERICA
BOOK COMPANY**
Main Street
Leon, Iowa 50144

OLE EMPTY BOTTLE HOUSE
Box 136
Amador City,
California 95601

• BOTTLE BOOKS •

GENERAL INTEREST

Adams, John P. **BOTTLE COLLECTING IN NEW ENGLAND.** New Hampshire Publishing Company, Somersworth, New Hampshire 03878, 1969. $3.95.

Blumenstein, Lynn. **BOTTLE RUSH U.S.A.** Salem, Oregon: Old Time Bottle Publishing Company. 1966. $4.25.

OLD TIME BOTTLES FOUND IN GHOST TOWNS. Privately printed, 1966. $2.50.

"REDIGGING THE WEST" FOR OLD TIME BOTTLES. Privately printed, 1966. $4.25.

Freeman, Dr. Larry. **GRAND OLD AMERICAN BOTTLES.** Watkins Glen, New York: Century House, 1964. $25.00.

Illinois Glass Company. **OLD BOTTLE LIST BONANZA, ILLUSTRATED CATALOGUE & PRICE LIST.** Watkins Glen, New York: Century House, Americana Publishers.

Kendrick, Grace. **THE ANTIQUE BOTTLE COLLECTOR.** Pyramid Books, NY, 1971. $2.95

"THE MOUTH-BLOWN BOTTLE." Privately printed, 1968. $6.95.

PRICE SUPPLEMENT TO THE ANTIQUE BOTTLE COLLECTOR. Privately printed, 1965. $1.50.

Munsey, Cecil. **THE ILLUSTRATED GUIDE TO COLLECTING BOTTLES.** New York: Haw-thorn Books, Inc., 1970. $9.95.

BOTTLE COLLECTING MANUAL WITH PRICES for above—John Hotchkiss, Hotchkiss House, 89 Sagamore Drive, Rochester, N.Y. 14617.

• GENERAL INTEREST •

McKearin, George L. and Helen. **AMERICAN GLASS.** New York: Crown Publishers, Inc., 1959. $14.95.

Wood, Serry. **THE OLD APOTHECARY SHOP.** Watkins Glen, New York: Century House, 1956. $2.00.

• CONTEMPORARY BOTTLES •

Pictorial Bottle Review. **COLLECTORS EDITION PRESENTS BEAMS, AVONS, EZRA BROOKS, LUXARDOS, GARNIERS, FANCY AND FIGURAL BOTTLES.** B & K Enterprises, P.O. Box 42558, Los Angeles, California 90050, 1969.

• AVON BOTTLES •

Stuart, Lynn R. **STUART'S BOOK ON AVON COLLECTABLES.** Privately printed, 1973. $4.50 . (Order from author, P.O. Box 862, Gilbert, Arizona 85234.) Also 1970, 1971, 1972.

Stuart, Lynn R. **COLLECTOR'S GUIDE TO AVON GLASS FIGURAL BOTTLES,** 1974. $2.50 . (Order from author P.O. Box 862, Gilbert, Arizona 85234.) Also: 1972

Hastin, Bud. **AVON BOTTLE ENCYCLOPEDIA.** Privately printed, 1972. $9.95. (Order from author, Box 9868, Kansas City, Missouri 64134.)

Western Collector. **AVON-2: A WESTERN COLLECTOR HANDBOOK & PRICE GUIDE.** 1971. $4.95. (Order from Western Collector Books, 511 Harrison Street, San Francisco, California 94105.)

• JIM BEAM BOTTLES •

Cembura, Al, and Avery, Constance. **JIM BEAM BOTTLES, 1973-74 IDENTIFICATION AND PRICE GUIDE.** Privately printed, $7.95. (Order from Al Cembura, 139 Arlington Avenue, Berkeley, California 94707.) Also: 1967, 1968, 1969, 1970, 1971, 1972.

• BISCHOFF BOTTLES •

Avery, Constance and Leslie, and Cembura, Al. **BISCHOFF BOTTLES, IDENTIFICATION AND PRICE GUIDE.** Privately printed, $4.75. (Order from Al Cembura, 139 Arlington Avenue, Berkeley, California 94707.)

• EZRA BROOKS •

Western Collector. **WESTERN COLLECTOR'S HANDBOOK AND PRICE GUIDE TO EZRA BROOKS DECANTERS.** San Francisco, California: Western World Publishers, $4.95. (Order from Western Collector Books, 511 Harrison Street, San Francisco, California 94105.)

B & K Enterprises. **EZRA BROOKS BOTTLES, IDENTIFICATION & PRICE GUIDE.** (Order from B & K, P.O. Box 42558, Los Angeles, Calif. 90050.)

• GARNIER BOTTLES •

Avery, Constance, and Cembura, Al. **GARNIER BOTTLES.** Privately printed. $4.95. (Order from Al Cembura, 139 Arlington Avenue, Berkeley, California 94707.)

• LUXARDO BOTTLES •

Avery, Constance, and Cembura, Al. **LUXARDO BOTTLES: IDENTIFICATION AND PRICE GUIDE.** Privately printed. $4.75. (Order from Al Cembura, 139 Arlington Avenue, Berkeley, California 94707.)

• BITTERS BOTTLES •

Watson, Richard. **BITTERS BOTTLES.** New York: Thomas Nelson & Sons, 1965. $10.00.

SUPPLEMENT TO BITTERS BOTTLES. Camden, New Jersey: Thomas Nelson & Sons, 1968. $6.50.

Umberger, Art & Jewel. **IT'S A BITTERS!—BITTERS PRICE GUIDE Vol. 1 & 2.** $4.25 each (Order from Corker Book Co., 819 W. Wilson Tyler, Texas.)

• FLASKS •

Edwards, John. **COLLECTOR'S PRICE GUIDE TO HISTORICAL BOTTLES & FLASKS.** John Edwards, Publisher: 61 Winton Place, Stratford, Conn. 06497. $6.00.

EARLY AMERICAN BOTTLES & FLASKS—REVISED. Stratford, Connecticut, 1969. $15.00. (Order from J. Edmund Edwards, 61 Winton Place, Stratford, Conn. 06497.)

• INKWELLS •

Nelson, Lavinia, and Hurley, Martha. **OLD INKS.** Privately printed, 1967. $5.00. (Order from "Old Inks," 22 Bryant Road, Nashua, New Hampshire.)

Covill, William, E. Jr.,**INK BOTTLES & INKWELLS,,** Taunton Mass. William E. Sullwold, Publishing, 1971. $17.50

• MILK •

Taylor, Gordon A. **MILK BOTTLE MANUAL, 1971.** $3.95. (Order from Old Time Bottle Publishing Co., Salem Oregon.)

• SODA AND MINERAL WATER •

Fountain, John C., and Colcleaser, Donald. **DICTIONARY OF SODA & MINERAL WATER BOTTLES.** Amador City, California: "Ole Empty Bottle House Publishing Company," 1968. P.O. Box 136 $3.75.

• WHISKEY AND BEER •

Fountain, John C., and Colcleaser, Donald. **DICTIONARY OF SPIRITS AND WHISKEY BOTTLES.** Amador City, California: "Ole Empty Bottle House Publishing Company," 1969. P.O. Box 136 $3.75.

• FOREIGN COLLECTABLES •

Foreign distillers such as Luxardo, Garnier, Bischoff, Bols, Brizzard, etc. had been packaging their products in "collectable" decanters and bottles, for many years. Many of these pre-1960's bottles are listed in this book, and many are quite scarce and valuable.

• THE U.S. BOTTLE BOOM •

In the United States, the success of the first "gift" decanter produced by the James B. Beam Distilling Company, in the early 1950's, generated a line of Beam collectable bottles. Soon other American distillers, packagers, and importers jumped on the bandwagon. The flood of collectable bottles continues to this day, with new companys entering the field, and issuing bottles on every conceivable theme.

• BOTTLE CLUBS & PUBLICATIONS AND "THE MARKET" •

The establishment of Bottle Clubs (1950's & 1960's), and publications devoted to Bottle collecting as a hobby, was another large factor in the growth and interest in bottle collecting. This increased public interest led to the creation of a "market", where collectors and others, could buy, sell, or trade, and dealers who specialized in bottles could fill the needs of all.

• THE BEGINNING COLLECTOR •

Obviously the best place for a beginning collector to start would be the local "Bottle Club". There one can get help, advice, and information. Clubs are listed on pages 6 - 10 If there is no club in your town or city, write to the National Club, and they will send a list of the nearest clubs.

• WHERE TO BUY BOTTLES •

"Antique" and hobby newspapers, and magazines, have many ads and notices from Bottle dealers, collectors, and clubs offering bottles of all types for sale. A list of these publications is on page 11. Many of them will ship bottles direct, and guarantee safe delivery, or refund.

Most of the bottles listed in "BOTTLES-NEW", are available in liquor stores, package stores, drug stores that sell liquor, etc., or wherever bottled liquor is sold. If a liquor dealer does not have the type of bottle you want, he can order it from his supplier, or it could be ordered direct from the company that produces the liquor and the bottle.

• TYPES OF NEW COLLECTABLE BOTTLES •

Contemporary bottles are made to appeal to the collector. They are usually made of ceramic, and generally are figural, historical, or commemorative in theme. Color is used lavishly on these ceramic bottles. A small percentage are made of glass, and these are usually embossed colored glass.

Sizes are: pints, 1/5ths, quarts, 1/2 gallons, and gallons. Many of these bottles are also produced in miniature.

• RARITY & SUPPLY •

Many of the imported and domestic bottles produced before the surge of popularity of bottle collecting, are very valuable today, due to the limited amount of these bottles produced, and the high loss rate of breakable bottles.

• SCARCITY & VALUE •

To assure scarcity today, manufacturers announce limited production, and destroy the original molds from which the bottles are made. Supply, to a great extent determines the value of contemporary bottles. Nevertheless collectors demand based on factors other than scarcity, can cause large price fluctuations. Two differently designed bottles issued by a company at the same time, and in the same quantities, may vary considerably in retail price. These factors can be; uniqueness of design, error in lettering, production or color, scarcity due to breakage or recall of a bottle for legal reasons.

• PRICING AND CONDITION •

The prices listed herein are approximate current **RETAIL** prices for original bottles in **Mint Condition,** complete with Handles, Stoppers, Labels, and Accessories when issued as a part of the bottle. **Mint Condition** means: about as issued—no cracks, chips, repairs, with color clear and clean.

• WHERE TO SELL BOTTLES •

The "Antique" and hobby newspapers, and magazines have many ads, and notices from bottle dealers, collectors and clubs. These are excellent sources for the sale of bottles. A list of clubs is on pages 6-10, newspapers & magazines on page 11.

• ANTIQUE DEALERS & FLEA MARKETS •

Antique dealers also buy desirable bottles. To find your local dealer, check your phone book under "ANTIQUES" and "ANTIQUES DEALERS". If there are none near you, visit an antiques show, flea market, auction, garage sale, or bottle club meeting or convention. There you will find many dealers, collectors, and hobbyists at one time, eager to buy, sell, or trade.

• RETAIL PRICE •

The RETAIL PRICE is the amount you would have to pay an authorized dealer for a particular bottle or decanter. The retail prices in this book have been compiled from dealers, auction lists, catalogs, antique magazines, and newspapers, and other authoritative publications. Retail prices are affected by a wide variety of factors including source, type of bottle, desirability and condition. Combined with this is the fact that many bottles are deliberately produced for special situations, in limited quantities without reissues. Given the above variables in the market, these prices may jump abruptly at any time.

• AVERAGE BUYING PRICE •

The AVERAGE BUYING PRICE (A.B.P.) is the amount an authorized dealer *will pay you* for a particular bottle or decanter. Once an item is purchased from a dealer it disappears into a private home or collection and is permanently removed from the active market. Consequently, because of this scarcity, dealers welcome people with genuine and desirable bottles and decanters to sell. We have given A.B.P.s for a few categories. However, where it has not been included in a category, a good "rule of thumb" would be to calculate the Average Buying Price as 50-35% of the retail price. As with the retail price, the A.B.P. is contingent upon scarcity, condition, source and desirability.

• INVENTORY CHECK LIST •

Appearing beside all listings is a check box. This will enable you to keep an accurate record of items which you own, or would like to own as well as their condition. You may show the condition of an object by placing one of the following symbols in the check box.

◩"As found"   ◪"Good"   ⊟"Fine"   ⊠"Excellent or Mint"

To the left of the check box, a simple cross will serve to remind you of an article that you would like to acquire, while a check mark will mean you already own it.   ✕ ☐"Want"   ✓ ☐"Have"

• REPRODUCTIONS & FAKES •

Some of the rarest and most valuable of the contemporary bottles have been illegally reproduced, and this practice will probably continue as long as people buy bottles. Antique & Historical flasks are also reproduced.

• HOW TO GUARD AGAINST BUYING REPRODUCTIONS •

The best protection against acquiring a reproduction while paying for the original is to *buy only from a reputable dealer.* He will have had many years of experience in the field, or in his specialty, and will be able to differentiate between the two.

BOTTLE GRADING
• NEW BOTTLES OR DECANTERS—ALL TYPES •

Most bottles listed in this book are priced for Mint Condition. In order for the buyer, or seller to properly evaluate a given bottle it is necessary to define what MINT CONDITION actually means. In order to give a proper frame of reference, other grades and classifications should also be explained. Many bottles are bought and sold in conditions other than Mint, and prices should be scaled down accordingly. We have listed here price reductions for lesser conditions.

<u>MINT—M—</u> Empty bottle, complete with like new intact labels. Color bright and clean, no chips, or scrapes, or wear. Tax stamp like new, but cut. Box in like new condition. All stoppers, handles, spouts like new.

<u>EXTRA FINE—EF—</u> Bottle complete with labels, stamps, etc. All color clean and clear, slight wear on labels and tax strip, Gold or Silver embellishments perfect. Stoppers, handles, spouts in fine condition. Box or container missing. **WORTH 10% LESS THAN LISTED RETAIL PRICE.**

<u>FINE—F—</u> Bottle shows slight wear, but color is clear and bright overall. Tax stamp complete but worn. Labels could be missing. Gold or Silver embellishments perfect. Stoppers, handles, spouts complete and undamaged. No box or container. **WORTH 15% LESS THAN LISTED RETAIL PRICE.**

<u>VERY GOOD—VG—</u> Bottle shows some wear, Gold or Silver slightly worn. Labels missing, Tax stamp missing. Stoppers, handles, spouts complete. No box or container. **WORTH 25% LESS THAN LISTED RETAIL PRICE.**

<u>GOOD—G—</u> Bottle shows wear, complete but color faded, Gold or Silver shows wear. Labels and Tax stamp missing. Stoppers, handles, spouts complete. No box or container. **WORTH 40% LESS THAN LISTED RETAIL PRICE.**

<u>FAIR—FR—</u> Color worn and Gold or Silver faded. Labels and Tax stamp missing. Stoppers, handles, spouts complete but worn. An undesirable category. No box or container. **WORTH 50% TO 75% LESS THAN LISTED RETAIL PRICE.**

The following is a list of descriptions of many of the important features of Old Bottles listed in this book on pages 315 to 397. In general these characteristics apply to all Old Bottles,

APPLIED LIP—On older bottles (pre-1880), after removal from the blow-pipe, the neck applied, therefore the seams ended below the top of the lip. pipe, the neck and lip were applied, therefore the seams ended below the top of the lip. This helps distinguish Old Bottles from New —if the seams end below the top of the lip it is usually a hand-blown applied top, if they run to the very top of the lip, the bottle was probably machine-made.

BLOB TOP—A large thick blob of glass was placed around the lip of Soda or Mineral Water bottles, the wire that held the stopper was seated below the blob, and anchored the wire when the stopper was closed, to prevent carbinktion from escaping.

BLOB SEALS—A popular way of identifying an unembossed bottle, was to apply a molten coin-shaped blob of glass to the shoulder of the bottle, into which a seal with the logo, or name of the distiller, date, or product name was impressed.

IMPERFECTIONS—Bubbles of all sizes and shapes, bent shapes and necks, imperfect seams, errors in spelling, and embossing, increase rather than decrease the value of Old Bottle, providing these imperfections were formed as a part of the natural production of the bottle. The more imperfections, the greater the value.

KICKUP BOTTOM—An indented bottom of any bottle is known as a "Kick-up". This can vary from deep indentions, to a very slight impression. Wine bottles as a group, are usually indented.

THREE PIECE MOLD—There are 2 main types:

a.) **THREE PIECE DIP MOLD**—In which the bottom part of the bottle mold was one piece, and the top, from the shoulder up, was 2 separate pieces. Mold seams appear circling the bottle at the shoulder, and on each side of the neck.

b.) **FULL HEIGHT 3 PIECE MOLD**—The entire bottle was formed in the mold, and the 2 seams run the height of the bottle to below the lip on both sides.

TURN MOLD BOTTLES—A bottle which was turned in forming, in a mold containing a special solvent. The action of turning, and the solvent, erased all seams and mold marks, and imparted a high luster to the finished bottle. As a group, most old Wine Bottles were made this way.

WHITTLE MOLD, or "WHITTLE MARKS"—Many mold used in the 1800's, and earlier, were carved of wood. Bottles formed in these molds have genuine "Whittle Marks". The same effect was also caused by forming hot glass in early morning cold molds, this combination caused "goose pimples" on the surface of these bottles. As the mold warmed the later bottles were smooth. "Whittle Mold," and "Whittle Mark" bottles are in demand, and command higher prices.

PONTIL MARKS—To remove the newly blown bottle from the blowpipe, an iron rod with a small amount of molten glass was applied to the bottom of the bottle, after the neck and lip were finished. A sharp tap removed the bottle from the pontil, leaving a jagged glass scar. This Pontil Scar" can be either round-solid, or ring-shape. On better bottles, the jagged edges were ground down.

ROUND BOTTOMS—Many soda bottles containing carbonated beverages were made of heavy glass, designed in the shape of a torpedo. This enabled the bottle to lie on its side, keeping the liquid in contact with the cork, and preventing the cork from drying, and popping out of the bottle.

SHEARED LIP—In the early years of bottle making, after the bottle was blown, a pair of scissors-like shears clipped the hot glass from the blowpipe. Frequently no top was applied, and sometimes a slight flange was created. The Sheared Top is a usual feature of Old Patriotic Flasks.

SNAP—A more effective way of detaching the blown bottle from the blowpipe was the "Snap". This device, which made it's appearance in the 1860's, was used to grip the blown bottle in a spring cradle in which a cup held the bottom of the bottle. The bottles, held in a Snap during manufacture, have no pontil scars, or marks, but may have grip marks on the side.

LADY'S LEG—Called by the manufacturers "long bulbous neck". The shape of the neck earned this type of bottle its nickname.

PUMPKIN SEED—A small round flat flask, often found in western areas. Generally made of clear glass, the shape resembled nothing more than the seed of the grown pumpkin. These bottles are also known as "Mickies", Saddle Flasks", or "Two-Bit Ponies".

OPALIZATION—This is the frosty bottle or variated color bottle, sometimes found, that have been buried in the earth, or in mud or silt, and minerals in these substances have interacted with the glass of the bottle to create these effects. Many collectors have a high value on bottles of this type. BEWARE: Many of these effects are included in reproductions.

BOTTLES – New

PART 1/NEW BOTTLES

AVON BOTTLES. . . . . *22 – 76*
Avon Introduction *22*
JIM BEAM BOTTLES . . . . *77 – 153*
Jim Beam Introduction *77*
Customer Specialties . . . . *78 – 85*
Centennial Series . . . . *86 – 89*
Glass Specialties . . . . *90 – 94*
Trophy Series . . . .*95 – 106*
Political Series . . . . *107 – 108*
State Series . . . . *109 – 114*
Executive Series . . . . *115 – 117*
Regal China . . . . *118 – 153*
EZRA BROOKS BOTTLES . . . . *154 – 225*
Ezra Brooks Introduction *154*
BALLANTINE BOTTLES *226*
BARDI-BARSOTTINI-BRALATTA-BEEFEATER *227*
BOLS-BORGHINI-BRIZARD *228*
BISCHOFF BOTTLES . . . . *229 – 236*
Bischoff Introduction *229*
FRANKFORT DISTILLERS BOTTLES *237*
BOTTLES BEAUTIFUL — FAMOUS FIRSTS . . . . *238 – 244*
J.W. DANT BOTTLES . . . . *245 – 248*
GARNIER BOTTLES . . . . *249 – 265*
GARNIER MINIATURES *265*
HOLLY CITY BOTTLES . . . . *266 – 267*
JAPANESE BOTTLES . . . . *268 – 269*
KENTUCKY GENTLEMAN *270*
LIONSTONE BOTTLES . . . . *271 – 281*
Lionstone Introduction *271*

LUXARDO BOTTLES . . . . *282 – 299*
Luxardo Introduction *282*
GRENADIER BOTTLES *300*
McCORMICK BOTTLES *Old Blue Ribbon Bottles* . . . . *301 – 303*
OLD FITZGERALD — STITZEL/WELLER . . . . *304 – 306*
MISCELLANEOUS BOTTLES . . . . *307 – 308*
 I.W. Harper-Nichols-Southern Comfort
Old Hickory-Double Springs-Old Taylor
Dickel-Old Blue Ribbon
WHEATON/NULINE . . . . *309 – 313*

AVON BOTTLES

Among the most recent collectables are the popular assortment of Avon Bottles. Originally containing perfumes, powders and toiletries of Avon Products, Inc., these bottles are produced in an assortment of unique shapes, sizes and colors. The Avon section contains some of the most sought-after examples of this contemporary art form. Prices will vary according to the rarity and condition of the item, while color variations are quite common owing to manufacturing techniques.

• THE START OF AVON COLLECTING •

In 1965, Avon introduced a men's after shave in an attractive Stein decanter and a men's cologne in an amber Boot. It was at this point that collectors began acquiring Avon bottles, realizing the intrinsic beauty and future worth of these items. Today, Avon collecting is still gaining in popularity, promising to be one of the most important collectables.

• THE CALIFORNIA PERFUME COMPANY •

The original company that later became Avon, was founded by Mr. D.H. McConnell, and was known as the California Perfume Company. The original building and door-to-door sales by a staff of ladies, was in New York City. This company issued many beauty products in attractive packages and containers. The first appearance of the name Avon was in January of 1929. Between 1933 and 1939 some items carried both the CPC and Avon names. After 1939 the CPC was dropped entirely. It is impossible to date CPC items accurately because so many of the bottle designs were used over the entire period, and held many different preparations.

Pricing these rare and valuable items is difficult, since they are extremely scarce, therefore all listed Retail Prices should be considered an approximation only. All CPC items in the section are indicated with an asterisk.

• ACKNOWLEDGEMENT •

The listing, information, and pictures used in this section of Avon collectables, are with the kind permission of Mr. Lynn R. Stuart.

Mr. Stuart's books on Avon Collectables are the best source of information, pictures, and pricing on this fascinating hobby and are recommended without reservation.

STUART'S BOOK ON AVON COLLECTABLES, 1973 $4.50 (Also available 1970-1971 & 1972)
COLLECTOR'S GUIDE TO AVON GLASS FIGURALS, 1972 $2.75 (1974 Supplement $2.50)

SEE BIBLIOGRAPHY   PAGE 13 FOR ADDITIONAL AVON BOOKS.

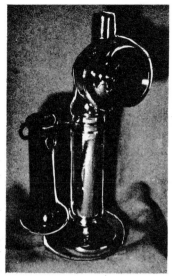

'69 Avon Calling
$7.50 — $10.00

Ariel Sachet
Jardin D'Amour Sachet
$55.00 — $65.00

American Ideal Soap†
$75.00 — $85.00

**All Prices are for Empty Bottles in Mint Condition,
With Handles, Spouts & Stoppers.**

AVON BOTTLES

Prices are for Empty Bottles in Mint Condition with Tops, Holders, Handles & Labels

$80.00 — $140.00

$8.00 — $10.00

American Beauty
Fragrance
8 oz. Jar

'71 Aladdin's Lamp

$110.00 — $135.00

American Ideal

Item, Date, Description	A	Retail
☐ Abraham Lincoln Decanter, 1971		5.00
☐ After Bath Refreshers, 1964	EACH	5.00
☐ After Shave, 1951		8.00
☐ After Shave, 1957		5.00
☐ After Shave, 4-A, 1964		27.50
☐ After Shave Samples	EACH	5.00
☐ After Shave Soother, 1968		2.50
☐ After Shower, 1959		55.00
☐ After Shower, black, 1959		10.00
☐ Aladdin's Lamp, 1971		8.00 — 10.00
☐ All-Purpose Bottle, 1937		20.00 — 25.00
☐ Alpine Flask, 1966		35.00 — 50.00
☐ Amber (Honey Amber) Candleholder, 1965		14.00
* ☐ American Beauty Fragrance Jars, Footed, CPC†		80.00 — 140.00
☐ American Eagle, 1971		5.00 — 6.00
☐ American Ideal Perfume, 1 oz. & 2 oz. CPC†		110.00 — 135.00

† **CPC—California Perfume Company**
* **6 oz. Jar — Flat Bottom — $45.00**

Item, Date, Description   **Retail**

☐ American Ideal Talc, 3-1/2 CPC† ....120.00 — 140.00

☐ Angel, 1968 Golden Angel.. 5.00

☐ Angler, 1970.. 6.00

☐ Apothecary Jar, 1965 .... 15.00

☐ Ariel Perfume, CPC†...100.00 — 120.00

   Verna Fleur, Ariel, 391; or Gardenia, Ariel, Bolero Perfume in Gold Box

☐ Ariel Toilet Water, 202, CPC† .... 80.00 — 120.00

☐ Atomizer Set, CPC† White Rose......................................180.00 — 220.00

☐ Attention Set, 1947.. 130.00

☐ Avon Blossoms, 1950 — 4 Bottles.................................... 70.00

☐ Avon Calling, 1969 Telephone .... 7.50 — 10.00

☐ Avon Hair Lotion, 1957.. 10.00

☐ Avon Mug, 1970 "Freddy the Frog" 4.50

☐ Avonshire Blue, 1971 .... 6.50

☐ Avon Open, 1972.. 6.50

B

☐ Baa-Baa Black Sheep, 1952 2 Bottle Set 60.00

☐ Baby Set, CPC† Powder & Toilet Water................225.00 — 275.00

☐ Ballad Perfume, 1940 .... 125.00

☐ Bandoline Hair Dressing, CPC†.................................40.00 — 50.00

☐ Bath Seasons, 1967 .... 2.50 — 4.50

☐ Bath Seasons, 1968 .... 2.00 — 4.00

☐ Bath Seasons, 1969 Salt Shaker.............................2.50 — 4.50

☐ Bath Urn, 1963 Cruet with Handle.........................8.50 — 12.50

☐ Bath Urn, 1967 Glass Decanter w/Handle ....6.50 — 8.50

☐ Bath Urn, 1971..2.50 — 4.50

**All Prices are for Empty Bottles in Mint Condition,
With Handles, Spouts & Stoppers.**

† **CPC—California Perfume Company**

$40.00 — $50.00

Bandoline Hair
Dressing
& Wave Lotion

$225.00 -- $275.00

$5.00 — $6.00

'69 Bird of Paradise
Cologne

Baby Set Powder-
Soap 2 oz. Violet
Toilet Water

$80.00 — $120.00

Ariel Toilet Water

Gold Box Verna Fleur,
Ariel, 391 Perfume, or
Gardenia, Ariel, Bolero Perfume
$80.00 — $120.00

Prices are for Empty Bottles in Mint
Condition with Tops, Holders, Handles & Labels

'70 Cologne Mist

Bird of Paradise

Bleach Cream
2 oz. Jar

Item, Date, Description	Retail
☐ Bay Rum, 1964 Square Shaped Bottle	10.00
☐ Bay Rum Jug, 1962 with Handle	5.00 — 10.00
☐ Bay Rum Keg, 1965 Keg Shaped	15.00
☐ Beauty Basket, 1947 2 Bottles	65.00

BIRD OF PARADISE LABEL (1969-70)

☐ '69 Emollient Oil	5.00
☐ '69 Cologne	5.00
☐ '70 Cream Sachet Jar	3.00
☐ '70 Cologne Mist	6.00
☐ Bird of Paradise Cologne 1970 Bird Shape Bottle.*	6.00 — 8.00
☐ Bleach Cream, CPC† 2 oz. Jar	55.00 — 65.00
☐ Blue Blazer, 1965 Deluxe Set, Boxed & Full	45.00 — 55.00
☐ Blue Lotus, 1967 Tall Bottle	4.00
☐ Boot, 1965 Boot-Shaped Bottle - Silver Top**	6.50 — 8.50

† **CPC—California Perfume Company**   *Illustrated in color on cover
**Gold Top — $4.00 — $6.00

AVON BOTTLES

Prices are for Empty Bottles in Mint
Condition with Tops, Holders, Handles & Labels

Item, Date, Description	Retail
☐ Boots and Saddle, 1968 2 Bottles	6.50 — 12.50
☐ Boxing Gloves, 1960 Plastic Bottles	20.00 — 24.00
☐ Bravo, 1969 Faceted Bottle	2.50

BRIGHT NIGHT LABEL (1954-59)

☐ '54 Cologne	15.00 — 28.50
☐ '54 Toilet Water	12.00 — 18.00
☐ '54 1/2 oz. Perfume *	80.00 — 90.00
☐ '54 Powder Sachet	7.50 — 12.50

BROCADE LABEL (1967-69)

☐ '67 Cologne	3.00 — 4.00
☐ '68 Cologne-Silk	3.50 — 4.50
☐ '69 1/2 oz. Cologne	2.50 — 3.50
☐ Bubble Bath, 1952	12.00 — 16.00
☐ Bucking Bronco, 1971 Cowboy on Horse	5.00 — 7.00
☐ Bud Vase, 1968 To A Wild Rose	5.00 — 7.50
☐ Buffalo Nickel, 1971 Indian Head Nickel Shaped Bottle	5.00 — 6.50

$60.00 — $80.00 $5.00 — $6.50

'54 Bright Night
Toilet Water
$12.00 — $18.00

'54 1/2 oz.
Bright Night Perfume

'68 Cologne Silk

Bright Night
'54 Cologne **$15.00 — $28.50**

*Glass Stopper — Tag Label
$60.00 — $80.00

$4.50 — $6.50

1963
Cologne

$8.50 — $10.00

'70 Capitol

$4.50 — $6.50

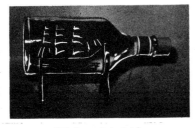

'70 Captain's Pride

Item, Date, Description	Retail

BUTTONS 'N' BOWS LABEL, 1960-62

☐ 1963 Cologne with Bow on Neck	8.50 — 10.00
☐ 1960 Cologne Mist	5.50 — 7.50
☐ 1962 Bubble Bath	5.50 — 7.50
☐ 1962 Cream Lotion	5.50 — 7.50

C

☐ Capitol, 1970 Bottle in the shape of the Capitol Building	4.50 — 6.50
☐ Captain's Choice, 1964 Green After Shave Bottle	7.50 — 9.50
☐ Captain's Pride, 1970 "Ship in Bottle" on stand	4.50 — 6.50
☐ Car Award Pitcher & Glasses	12.00
☐ 1971 Car Pitcher w/Handle	5.00
☐ 1971 Car Glasses set of 8	10.00
☐ Casey's Lantern, 1966 Green After Shave Bottle	14.50 — 19.50
☐ Casey's Lantern, 1966 Bottle in Shape of Railroad Lantern	18.00 — 22.00

*CANADIAN BLACK CAP – $10.00 — $12.00

AVON BOTTLES

Prices are for Empty Bottles in Mint
Condition with Tops, Holders, Handles & Labels

Item, Date, Description   **Retail**

COTILLION LABEL (1940-69)

☐ Cotillion Deluxe, 1953 3 Bottle Set Boxed .... 60.00 — 80.00
☐ Cotillion Duo, 1964 2 Bottle Set Box.. 16.00 — 20.00
☐ Cotillion Enchantment Set, 1953 2 Bottle Set Boxed .... 30.00 — 40.00
☐ Cotillion Powder Sachet, CPC† .... 18.00 — 20.00

☐ Country Gardens, 1971 Jar w/Ribbon.. 6.50
☐ Courting Lamp, 1970 Miniature Oil Lamp Bottle.......................... 7.50 — 9.50
☐ Courtship Perfume, 1940.. 80.00 — 100.00
☐ Covered Wagon, 1970 Wagon Shaped Bottle................................ 3.50 — 5.50
☐ Crabapple Blossom Perfume, CPC†
    Bottle Only... 80.00 — 100.00
    Bottle & Original Box... 120.00 — 150.00

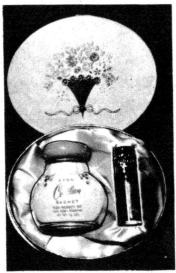

'53 ENCHANTMENT
$30.00 — $40.00

**EACH
$30.00 — $40.00**

Sachets in Gardenia,
Violet, White Lilac
American Ideal,
White Rose,
Heliotrope &
Carnation

'70 Courting
Lamp
$7.50 — $9.50

'40 Courtship
Perfume   '69 Classics
(Set of Four)

Retail

CHARISMA LABEL 1968/69

- [ ] '68 Cologne Mist .... 3.50 — 5.50
- [ ] '68 Cologne .... 3.50 — 5.50
- [ ] '68 Cream Sachet .... 2.00 — 3.00
- [ ] '69 Cologne Silk .... 3.50 — 4.50

- [ ] Charlie Brown, 1968 Plastic Bottle .... 4.50 — 6.00
- [ ] Charlie Brown, 1971 Comb & Brush .... 3.50 — 4.50
- [ ] Christmas Cologne, 1969 Bottle in Shape of Christmas Tree Decoration   6.00
- [ ] Christmas Tree, 1968 Cone Shaped Tree .... 4.50 — 6.50
- [ ] Circle of Pearls, 1957 Set 65.00
- [ ] Classics, 1969 4 Book-Shaped Bottles .... 14.50 — 18.50
- [ ] *Close Harmony, 1963 Barber Bottle — Milk Glass .... 24.00 — 26.00
- [ ] Cologne Classic, 1967 Swirl Bottle .... 4.50 — 6.50
- [ ] Cologne Gems, 1967 .... 5.50 — 7.50
- [ ] Cologne Elegante, 1971 Bud Vase 8 Rose .... 6.50 — 8.50
- [ ] Cologne Mist, 1963 ....   2.50
- [ ] Cologne Mist, 1966 Ribbed Bottle — Gold Cap .... 3.50 — 4.50
- [ ] Cologne Mist, 1968 Ribbed Bottle 3.50
- [ ] Cologne Mist, 1969 — Gold Cap .... 4.00 — 6.00
- [ ] Cologne Silk, 1967 .... 3.50 — 5.50
- [ ] Cornucopia, 1971 "Horn of Plenty" Shaped Bottle — Milk Glass ... 5.50 — 7.50

*Without Tip—$20.00

AVON BOTTLES

**Prices are for Empty Bottles in Mint
Condition with Tops, Holders, Handles & Labels**

Daisies
Won't
Tell

'57 Cream
Lotion

$7.00 —
$9.00

'57 Cologne

Item, Date, Description	Retail
☐ Cranberry Glass Candleholder, '65	9.50 — 12.50
☐ Cranberry Shaker, 1969 w/Ribbon	3.50 — 5.50
☐ Crimson Carnation, 1940 w/Box	45.00 — 55.00
☐ Crystal Chandelier, 1969	6.00 — 8.00
☐ Crystal Cologne, 1966	5.00 — 7.00
☐ Crystal Cologne Mist, 1971	3.50 — 6.50
☐ Crystal Glory, 1961	6.50 — 12.50
☐ Crystallite, 1970 "Waffle" Pattern Bottle	4.00 — 6.50
☐ Cupid's Bow, 1953 4 Small Bottle Set	47.50 — 52.50

D

DAISIES WON'T TELL LABEL 1957-62

☐ '57 Cologne w/white cap	7.00 — 9.00
☐ '57 Cream Lotion w/white cap	7.00 — 9.00
☐ '58 Spray Cologne w/white cap	7.00 — 9.00
☐ '58 Field of Daisies Set	18.50 — 26.00
☐ '62 Cologne	7.50 — 9.50

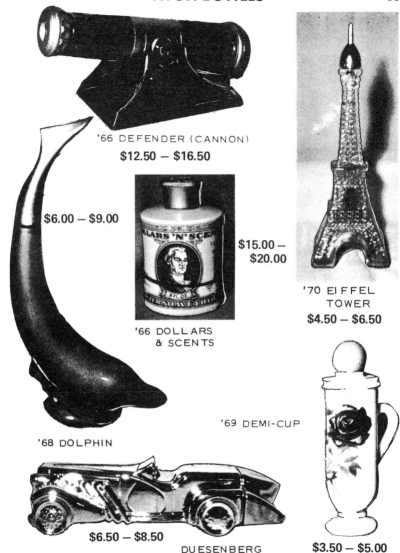

'66 DEFENDER (CANNON)
$12.50 — $16.50

$6.00 — $9.00

$15.00 — $20.00

'66 DOLLARS
& SCENTS

'70 EIFFEL
TOWER
$4.50 — $6.50

'69 DEMI-CUP

'68 DOLPHIN

$6.50 — $8.50

DUESENBERG

$3.50 — $5.00

Prices are for Empty Bottles in Mint
Condition with Tops, Holders, Handles & Labels

Item, Date, Description	Retail
☐ Danish Modern Candleholder, 1970	4.00 — 6.00
☐ Daylight Shaving Time, 1968 Bottle in Form of Pocket Watch	4.00 — 7.00
☐ Decanter, 1966 w/Handle & Top	5.50 — 7.50
☐ Decisions, 1965	20.00 — 25.00
☐ Decisions, foreign	12.50 — 18.50
☐ Defender, 1966 Cannon Bottle	12.50 — 16.50
☐ Deluxe Set, 1962 2 Bottles	16.00 — 22.00
☐ Demi-Cup, 1968 w/Handle, Milk Glass	3.50 — 5.00
☐ Demi-Cup, 1969 Rose Design, Milk Glass	3.50 — 5.00
☐ Deodorant, 1963	4.00 — 6.00
☐ Dew-Kiss, 1960	6.50 — 8.50
☐ Dew-Kiss, 1967	1.50 — 2.50
☐ Dollars 'n' Scents, 1966 Bottle in Shape of Roll of Dollar Bills	15.00 — 25.00
☐ Dolphin, 1968 Bottle in Shape of Dolphin Fish	6.50 — 8.50
☐ Dramatic Moments, 1958 2 Piece Set w/Box	25.00
☐ Duesenberg, 1970 Car shaped Bottle, silver coated	6.00 — 9.00
☐ Duette, 1963 2 Bottle Set	10.00 — 12.00
☐ Dune Buggy, 1971 Car Shaped Bottle	3.50 — 5.50

E

☐ Eau de Cologne, foreign	2.50 — 3.50
☐ Eau de Quinine, 1912, 8 oz. Bottle CPC† Hair Tonic	110.00 — 130.00
☐ Eiffel Tower, 1970 Bottle Shaped like Parisian Eiffel Tower	4.50 — 6.50
☐ Electric Charger, 1970 Black Glass Car Shaped Bottle	6.50 — 8.00
☐ Electric Shave, 1966 Ribbed Bottle	2.00 — 4.00

† **CPC—California Perfume Company**

'57 ½ OZ. $85
PERFUME
$65.00 — $85.00

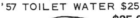

'57 TOILET WATER $25
$25.00 — $35.00

'57 COLOGNE $25
$12.00 — $20.00

'57 POWDER $15
SACHET
$15.00 — $20.00

'57 SPARKLING BURGANDY SET $65
$50.00 — $70.00

Item, Date, Description

Retail

•ELEGANTE LABEL—1957

☐ '57 Cologne, Swirl Bottle w/Ribbon..**12.00 — 20.00**

☐ '57 Toilet Water, Swirl Bottle w/Ribbon....................................**25.00 — 30.00**

☐ '57 1/2 oz. Perfume Bottle Swirl w/ Ribbon.............................**65.00 — 85.00**

☐ '57 1002. Powder Sachet Swirl Bottle.......................................**15.00 — 20.00**

☐ '57 Sparkling Burgundy Set 4 Piece & Box..............................**50.00 — 70.00**

•Items Complete with Box Worth $15.00 more

Item, Date, Description	Retail
☐ Embossed Carriage, 1961 8 oz. Gold Cap	20.00 — 25.00
☐ Emerald Bud Vase, 1971	4.50 — 6.50
☐ Enchanted Tree, 1969	7.50
☐ Excalibur, 1969	3.50 — 6.50
☐ Eye and Throat Oil, 1965	2.00 — 3.00

—F—

☐ Face Lotion, CPC†	100.00 — 125.00
☐ Fair Lady, 1940 4 Bottle Set	70.00 — 85.00
☐ Fair Lady, 1949 Boxed Set	60.00 — 75.00
☐ Fan-shaped Cologne, 1958 1/2 oz. Bottle	7.50 — 10.00
☐ Fashion Figurine, 1971 Old Time Costume Bottle	5.50 — 7.50

$20.00 — $25.00 $100.00 — $125.00

$5.50 — $7.50

'61 Embossed
Carriage

$3.50 — $6.50

'69 Excalibur

Face Lotion

'71 Fashion
Figurine

† **CPC—California Perfume Company**

Item, Date, Description   **Retail**

☐ Fielder's Choice, 1971 Baseball & Glove Bottle.............................3.00 — 5.00

☐ Field Flowers, Umbrella, 1971 ....5.00 — 6.50

☐ First Christmas Candleholder, '67...12.50 — 15.00

☐ First Class Male, 1970 Mailbox Shaped Bottle ....3.50 — 5.50

☐ First Down, 1965 Football Shape Bottle......................................4.00 — 6.00

☐ First Down, 1970 Football Shaped Bottle on stand......................3.00 — 5.00

☐ First Edition, 1967 Book Shaped Bottle......................................4.50 — 7.50

☐ First Edition Gift Set, 1965...22.50 — 25.00

☐ First Volunteer, 1971 Ole Time Fire Engine Bottle........................6.00 — 8.00

☐ Flamingo, 1971 Bird Shaped Bottle...4.50 — 7.50

☐ Flower Belle, 1969 ....3.00 — 4.50

☐ Flowertime Set, 1949 2 Bottles Boxed....................................40.00 — 50.00

☐ Flowertime Talc, 1949...17.50 — 20.00

☐ Flying Ace, 1969 "Snoopy" Bottle...2.00 — 3.00

☐ Forever Spring, 1950 Perfume, Glass Perfume ....55.00 — 65.00

☐ Fox Hunt, 1966 ....15.00 — 17.50

☐ Fragrance Bell, 1968 Bell Shaped Bottle w/Handle......................4.00 — 6.00

☐ Fragrance Belle, 1965 Bell Shaped Bottle..................................8.50 — 12.50

☐ Fragrance Chest, 1966 4 Bottle Set with Box ....27.50 — 40.00

☐ Fragrance Fling, 1968 1/2 oz. Cologne ....4.50 — 7.50

☐ Fragrance Gold & Tray, 1964 3 Bottle Set ....12.50 — 14.50

☐ Fragrance Hours, 1971 Grandfather Clock Bottle ....4.50 — 6.50

☐ Fragrance Rainbow, 1953 4 Bottles, Ribbons, White Tops, Boxed 50.00

☐ Fragrance Rainbow, 1954 4 Bottles, White Tops, Flower Tops...50.00 — 60.00

☐ Fragrance Splendor, 1971 Elaborate glass Floral Stopper ....6.00 — 8.00

☐ Fragrance Tie-Ins, 1953 4 Bottles Boxed..................................40.00 — 50.00

**All Prices are for Empty Bottles in Mint Condition,
Complete with Handles, Spouts & Stoppers.**

38

AVON BOTTLES

'51 Toilet
Water

'70
First Down

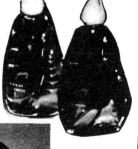

$3.50 —
$5.00

$3.50 —
$5.00

'70 First Class
Male

$4.50 — $7.50

'71 Flamingo
$12.50 — $15.00

$4.00 — $6.00

'68
Fragrance
Bell

'65 Fragrance
Belle

'69 Futura

$45.00 — $55.00

'69 Fragrance
Touch

'64 French Perfume

Item, Date, Description	Retail
☐ Fragrance Touch, 1969 Hand Shaped Bottle	**4.50 — 7.50**
☐ French Perfume, 1964 Glass Bottle, Elaborate Stopper w/Box	**45.00 — 55.00**
☐ French Telephone, 1971 Antique French Phone Bottle	**15.00 — 20.00**
☐ Frosted Candleholder, 1967 w/Gold Band	**10.00 — 12.50**
☐ Futura, 1969 Abstract Shape Bottle	**12.50 — 15.00**

—G—

☐ Gardenia Perfume, 1940 Gold Cap w/Box	**60.00 — 75.00**
☐ Gardenia Sachet, CPC†	**60.00 — 85.00**
☐ Garden of Love Perfume, 1940 Plastic Handle	**15.00 — 20.00**
☐ Gavel, 1967 Gavel Shaped Bottle Glass Top w/Tag	**12.00 — 14.00**
☐ Gems in Crystal, 1957 4 Bottle Set with Tags	**60.00 — 80.00**
☐ General 4-4-0, 1971 Antique Locomotive Bottle	**8.00 — 10.00**
☐ Gentlemen's Selection, 1970	**1.50 — 2.50**

† **CPC—California Perfume Company**

Item, Date, Description   **Retail**

☐ George Washington Decanter, 1970 Gold Eagle Cap ....3.50 — 5.50

☐ Gift Cologne, 1959 "Topaze" Gold Cap ....4.00 — 6.00

☐ Gift Cologne, 1969 Gold Cap..4.50 —6.50

☐ Gift Fancy, 1962 Gold Cap & Tassel ....3.50 — 4.50

☐ Gift Lotion, 1963 w/Dispenser..12.50 — 15.00

☐ Gift Magic, 1959 Small Bottle...3.50 — 5.00

☐ Gold Box, CPC+ 3 Perfume Bottles with Gold Box ....80.00 — 100.00

☐ Gold Box, 1948 3 Bottles Gold Tops with Box ....60.00 — 80.00

$60.00 — $75.00 $15.00 — $20.00

'40 Gardenia
Perfume

'40 Garden of
Love Perfume

$3.50 — $5.50

'70 George
Washington
Decanter

'71 General 4 — 4 — 0
$8.00 — $10.00

$35.00 — $40.00

'58 Happy
Hours

'51 Golden Promise Set
$50.00 — $60.00

$10.00 — $25.00

$12.00 — $14.00

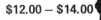

'67 Gavel

Here's My Heart
'58 Cologne

Item, Date, Description	Retail
☐ Gold Cadillac, 1969 Car Shaped Bottle, Gold Colored......................**5.50 — 8.50**
☐ Golden Jewel, 1963 Gold Top..**30.00 — 35.00**
☐ Golden Moments, 1971 Antique Watch Bottle, and Chain...........**12.00 — 15.00**
☐ Golden Promise Deluxe, 1949 4 Piece Set in Box.....................**80.00 — 90.00**
☐ Golden Promise Set, 1951 2 Piece Set in Box...........................**50.00 — 60.00**
☐ Greek Island Magic, 1969 Statue of Greek Goddess Bottle..............**6.50 — 8.50**
☐ Greek Warrior, 1967 Blue & Silver Warrior Head Bottle:............**10.00 — 12.50**

'69 Gold Cadillac

$5.50 — $8.50

All prices

for Mint Condition

'69 Greek
Island Magic

$6.50 — $8.50

—H—

| ☐ Hair Lotion, 1957 "Avon" Label...**8.00 — 10.00** |
| ☐ Hand Lotion, 1957 "Avon" Label with Dispenser ....**10.00 — 12.00** |
| ☐ Happy Hours, 1958 3 Bottle Set...**35.00 — 40.00** |

$42.50 — $48.50

4 oz. Headache Cologne
This Bottle Used for
Numerous Other Items

$150.00 — $160.00

48 1/2 oz.
Perfume

$35.00 — $40.00
'58 Sweethearts

'57 Cologne
Mist
$15.00 — $20.00

'58 Powder
Sachet

$7.00 — $10.00

Item, Description, Date   Retail

☐ Happy Time, 1951 3 Piece Set..**45.00 — 55.00**
☐ Harmless Colors, CPC† 8-1 oz. Assorted Color Bottles Set.....**250.00 — 300.00**
☐ Hawaiian White Ginger, 1965...**2.50 — 3.50**
☐ Hawaiian White Ginger, 1967 "Hourglass" Shape.........................**1.50 — 2.50**
☐ Hawaiian White Ginger Cologne Mist, 1971................................**3.00 — 5.00**
☐ Headache Cologne, CPC† Ribbed Bottle....................................**42.50 — 48.50**
☐ Heartfelt, 1964 2 Piece Set Boxed... **30.00**
☐ Heliotrope Powder Sachet, CPC†..**75.00 — 100.00**

HERE'S MY HEART LABEL — 1948-1969

☐ '48 1/2 oz. Perfume Bottle with Box....................................**150.00 — 160.00**
☐ '58 "Heart" Shape Glass Bottle—White Top — Cologne ....**10.00 — 12.50**
☐ '57 "Heart" Shape Cologne Mist...**15.00 — 20.00**
☐ '58 Powder Sachet, White Top...**7.00 — 10.00**
☐ '58 Sweethearts 2 piece set Boxed...**35.00 — 40.00**
☐ '64 Perfume Oil Bottle, White Top...**12.00 — 14.00**
☐ '69 1/2 oz. Cologne Bottle..**2.00 — 3.00**

☐ Honey Bun, 1964 2 Piece Set Boxed.......................................**25.00 — 30.00**
☐ Honeysuckle, 1966...**3.00 — 4.00**
☐ House of Charm, 1952 4 Bottle Set, "House" Box ....**90.00 — 100.00**

— I —

☐ Icicle, 1967 "Icicle" Shape, Gold Top...**4.00 — 5.00**
☐ Indian Head Penny, 1970 Penny Shape Bottle, Copper color, Black Top   **6.00**
☐ Inkwell, 1969 Antique Ink Bottle & Quill Pen ....**7.50 — 8.50**
☐ Island Lime, 1966 "Straw" wrapped Bottle....................................**4.50 — 6.50**
☐ It's A Blast, 1970 Brass Horn Shape Bottle with "Bulb" Top ....**4.50 — 6.50**

† **CPC — California Perfume Company**

'66 Island Lime
$4.50 — $6.50

'69 Ink Well
$4.50 — $8.50

$4.50 — $6.50

'70 It's A
Blast

$120.00 — $140.00

'54 Jardin D'Amour
Perfume

Item, Description, Date   **Retail**

—J—

- [ ] Jardin d'Amour Perfume, 1954 Perfume Bottle in Blue & Gold Bucket   **140.00**
- [ ] Jardin d'Amour Sachet, CPC† "Ariel" Label.............................**50.00 — 60.00**
- [ ] Jasmine Bath Salts, 1946 Black Top.....................................**20.00 — 25.00**
- [ ] Just Two, 1965 Tall Faceted Bottles Pointed Tops ....**45.00 — 65.00**

—K—

- [ ] Keynote, 1967 Glass Key Plastic Top ....**8.50 — 12.50**
- [ ] King Pin, 1969 Bowling Pin Bottle Milk Glass...........................**3.00 — 5.00**
- [ ] Koffee Klatch, 1971 "Coffee Pot" Bottle, with Handle.................**6.00 — 8.00**

—L—

- [ ] Lady Slipper, 1970 Slipper Bottle with Bow ....**7.50 — 9.50**
- [ ] Lavender Fragrance Jar, CPC† 8 oz. Jar...............................**150.00 — 180.00**
- [ ] Lavender Powder Sachet, 1965 ....**4.50 — 6.50**
- [ ] Lavender Sachet, 1962 .... **12.00**
- [ ] Legendary Hero, 1968 Frosted Glass Warrior Head.......................**4.50 — 6.50**
- [ ] Leisure Hours, 1970 "Antique" Mantel Clock Bottle Gold Top ....**5.50 — 7.50**
- [ ] Liberty Bell, 1971 "Bell" Shape Bottle, "Wood" Top.....................**4.50 — 6.50**
- [ ] Liberty Dollar, 1970 Silver Dollar Bottle, Eagle Top.......................**4.00 — 6.00**
- [ ] Lights and Shadows, 1969 2 Bottles.....................................**6.00 — 8.00**
- [ ] Lilac Vegetal Toilet Water, CPC† ....**60.00 — 80.00**
- [ ] Lily of the Valley Perfume, CPC† 7 Dram & Flaconette..**160.00 — 180.00**
- [ ] Linus, 1968 Plastic Bottle Comic *..**3.00 — 4.00**
- [ ] Little Champ, 1967 ....**4.00 — 5.00**
- [ ] Little Doll, 1954 Set Cologne, Lotion Pomade.............................**4.00 — 5.00**
- [ ] Little Folks Gift Set, CPC 1936, 4 small bottles in Fancy Box..**110.00 — 140.00**

*1970 Full figure — same

† **CPC—California Perfume Company**

'69 King Pin
$3.00 — $5.00

'70 Leisure Hours
$5.50 — $7.50

'65 Just Two
SET: $45.00 — $65.00

'70 Lady Slipper
(Bow) Perfume
$7.50 — $9.50

'68 Legendary
Hero
$4.50 — $6.50

'68 Linus
$3.00 — $4.00

$110.00 − $140.00

$4.00 − $5.00

'70 Looking Glass

Little Folks Gift Set
Perfume in Ariel, Gardenia
Bolero & Trailing Arbutus

$8.50 − $9.50

'67 Mallard Duck

Item, Description, Date	Retail
☐ L'Odeur de Violette, CPC 1/2 oz., 1 oz., 2 oz., 4 oz.	130.00 − 160.00
☐ Lollypop Boot, 1967 Glass Boot with Tassel	5.00 − 7.00
☐ Looking Glass, 1970 Hand Mirror Bottle	4.00 − 5.00
☐ Lotion Lovely, 1964 Round Glass Top	6.00 − 9.00
☐ Lotus Cream, CPC† Round Top with Ribbon	180.00 − 230.00
☐ Love Bird, 1969 Bird Shape Bottle	5.50 − 8.50
☐ Lovely Touch Decanter, 1971 Waffle Pattern, Dispenser Top	5.00 − 7.00

† **CPC—California Perfume Company**

AVON BOTTLES

$3.50 — $5.50

$4.50 — $6.00

'68 Lucy

'50 Luscious Perfume

Miss Lolypop

'36 Lucy
Hays Perfume
$40.00 — $50.00

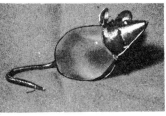
'70 Perfume Petite
(Mouse)
$5.00 — $7.00

'69 Minuette
Cologne
$2.50 — $3.50

Item, Description, Date	Retail
☐ Lucy, 1968 "Peanuts" Comic Character, Plastic	3.50 — 5.50
☐ Lucy Hays Perfume, 1936 Small Bottle	40.00 — 50.00
☐ Luscious Perfume, 1950 Small Bottle & Case	12.00 — 14.00

—M—

☐ Mallard, 1967 Duck-Shape Bottle, Gold Head	8.50 — 9.50
☐ Man's World, 1969 World Globe Bottle on Stand	7.00 — 8.50
☐ Milkglass Candleholder, 1964 with Cover	10.00 — 15.00
☐ Milkglass Candleholder, 1966 Gold Band, No Cover	6.50 — 12.00
☐ Ming Cat, 1971 Milkglass Cat Bottle with Ribbon	6.50 — 8.00
☐ Minuette Cologne, 1969 Small Bottle, Round Top	2.50 — 3.50
☐ Miss Lollypop, 1967 "Cute Head" Bottle with Hat	4.50 — 6.00
☐ Mouse, 1970 Petite Mouse Bottle, Gold Head & Tail	5.00 — 7.00

Item, Description, Date   Retail

—N—

☐ Narcissus Perfume, CPC 7 Dram Perfume & Flaconette ....**150.00 — 175.00**
☐ Natoma Rose Perfume, CPC† Round Top with Ribbon & Box .**100.00 — 150.00**

NEARNESS LABEL 1955-59

☐ '55 Cologne, Round Bottle, Pointed Top .... **20.00 — 22.00**
☐ '55 1/2 oz. Perfume Bottle in Shell with Pearl * **65.00**
☐ '56 Toilet Water, Round Bottle, Pointed Top ....**15.00 — 17.00**
☐ '56 Body Powder, Round Bottle, Round Top ....**20.00 — 22.50**

'69 Man's World

'55 1/2 oz.
Perfume

'55 Cologne

'56 Body Powder

'70 Liberty
Dollar

† **CPC—California Perfume Company**
*Circle of Pearls set — **$65.00 — $75.00**

$4.50 – $7.50

'70 Nesting Dove

$5.00 – $8.00

'63 Powder Sachet

'64 Perfume Oil
$5.00 – $8.00

'63 COLOGNE MIST
$4.50 – $6.50

Old Barrel
$12.00 – $16.00

Item, Description, Date   **Retail**

☐ Nesting Dove, 1970 Milk Glass with Bird Top...............................**4.50 – 7.50**

–O–

OCCUR LABEL 1963-69

☐ '63 Cologne Mist, Gold Top ....**4.50 – 6.50**
☐ '63 Powder Sachet, Black Top ....**5.00 – 8.00**
☐ '64 Perfume Oil, Small Bottle, Gold Top......................................**5.00 – 8.00**
☐ '69 1/2 oz. Cologne, Gold Top..**2.00 – 3.00**

☐ Old Barrel, Foreign Barrel Shape with Staves ....**12.00 – 16.00**
☐ One I Love, 1957 3 Bottle Set **35.00**

Item, Description, Date   **Retail**

☐ One, Two, Lace My Shoe, 1968 ....**5.00 — 7.00**
☐ Opening Play, 1968 Football Helmet Bottle ....**5.00 — 7.00**
☐ Original Set, 1965 2 Bottle Set - Black Labels **25.00**
☐ Ornaments, 1967 Xmas Ball Bottle..**5.00 — 6.50**

—P—

☐ Packard Roadster, 1970 Antique Car Shaped Bottle ....**5.00 — 7.50**
☐ Parlor Lamp, 1971 Oil Lamp Bottle..**6.50 — 8.50**
☐ Peanuts Mugs, 1969 Charlie Brown, Snoopy, Lucy......................**3.00 — 5.00**
☐ Perfection Coloring Set, CPC† 4-1 oz. Bottles, 1-2 oz. Bottle Boxed........ **210.00**
☐ Perfection Flavoring Extract, CPC† 5 Bottle Set - Boxed ......**180.00 — 210.00**
☐ Perfume, 1/2 oz., 1969 Ribbed Bottle & Stopper ....**12.00 — 15.00**
☐ Perfume Petite (snail), 1968, Snail shaped Bottle, Gold Head........ **6.50 — 9.50**

$6.50 — $8.50

$180.00 — $210.00

$5.00 — $7.00

Perfection Coloring Set
4-1 oz. Bottles,
1-2 oz. Bottle

'71 Parlor
Lamp

'68 Opening
Play

† **CPC—California Perfume Company**

Item, Description, Date	Retail

☐ Perfume Oil, 1965 Round Bottle...6.50 — 8.50

PERSIAN WOOD LABEL—1956-63

☐ '56 Cologne Mist...8.50 — 12.50

☐ '59 Cologne—Gold Top ....8.50 — 12.50

☐ '59 Toilet Water—Gold Top ....9.00 — 13.00

☐ '63 Perfume Oil—Gold Top ....6.50 — 8.50

☐ Petal of Beauty, 1945 2 Piece Set in Original Box..................90.00 — 120.00

☐ Petal of Beauty, 1952 2 Piece Set in Original Box.................... 30.00 — 35.00

☐ Pipe Dream, 1957 "Carved" Glass pipe in Holder.....................12.50 — 14.50

PERSIAN WOOD

'59 Cologne

$8.50 — $12.50

'56 Cologne Mist
$8.50 — $12.50

'59 Toilet
Water
$9.00 — $13.00

**All Prices are for Empty Bottles in Mint Condition,
With Handles, Spouts & Stoppers.**

Item, Description, Date   Retail

☐ Pipe Full Decanter, 1971 Briar Pipe Shape Bottle.................................. **5.00**

☐ Pony Decanter, 1968 Horse Head Shaped Bottle with Mouth Ring . **4.00 — 6.00**

☐ Pony Express, 1971 Horse & Rider Bottle on Base.....................**5.00 — 7.00**

☐ Pony Post, 1966 Horse Head Hitching Post Bottle......................**4.50 — 7.50**

☐ Pot-Belly Stove, 1970 Stove Bottle on Base...................................**3.50 — 5.50**

☐ Precious Pear, 1953 2 Small Bottles in Gold "Pear & Leaf" Box........... **160.00**

☐ Pretty Peach, 1964 Cologne "Peach" Top ....**4.50 — 6.50**

☐ Pretty Peach Soda, 1964 "Ice Cream Soda" Bottle.....................**8.00 — 10.00**

☐ Purse Petite, 1971 Small Glass Purse with Chain ....**3.50 — 4.50**

☐ Pyramid, 1969 Pyramid Shaped Bottle, Pointed Top...................**9.00 — 12.50**

—Q—

QUAINTANCE LABEL—1949

☐ '49 3 Dram Perfume in Box ....**110.00 — 120.00**

☐ '49 Cologne Bottle "Rose" Top..**20.00 — 25.00**

☐ '49 1/2 oz. Perfume, Small Bottle..**30.00 — 35.00**

☐ '49 Powder Sachet Bottle..**9.50 — 13.50**

☐ '49 Harmony 2 Piece Set with Box ....**50.00 — 60.00**

$30.00 — $35.00

$9.00 — $12.50

49 1/2 oz.
Perfume

'69 Pyramid of
Fragrance

**$130.00 —
$160.00**

'53 Precious
Pear

$4.50 — $6.00

'68 Pony
Decanter

$4.50 — $7.50

'66 Pony Post

'49 Perfume Quaintance

$110.00 — $120.00

—R—

☐ Raindrops, 1954 3 Piece Set ....**60.00 — 80.00**

RAPTURE LABEL—1964

☐ '64 Perfume Oil Bottle...**6.00 — 8.00**

☐ '64 Cologne Bottle...**2.00 — 3.00**

☐ '69 1/2 oz. Cologne Bottle..**1.50 — 2.50**

☐ Rapture Rhapsody, 1964 Set with Tray ....**25.00 — 30.00**

Item, Description, Date	Retail

☐ Regence Label, 1966 - 69 Colognes, oil, sachets....................**2.50 — 5.50**
☐ Renaissance Perfume, 1966 1/2 oz. Bottle ....**15.00 — 25.00**
☐ Ribbed Warrior, 1971 Glass Trojan Warrior Head, Gold Top...........**3.50 — 5.50**
☐ Riviera Cologne, 1968 Gold Top, Base & Design on Bottle.............**4.50 — 6.50**
☐ Rocker Perfume, 1960..**4.00 — 6.00**
☐ Rosebud Vase, 1962 Tall Glass Bottle, Glass Stopper .*...............**4.00 — 6.00**

All Prices are for Empty Bottles in Mint Condition, With Handles, Spouts & Stoppers.

Rapture

$65.00 — $80.00

'64 Cologne

'54 Raindrops
Young Hearts

*'71 Emerald Bud Vase — $5.00
*'70 Ruby Vase — $5.00

'69 1/2 oz.
Cologne

'65 Royal Orb

AVON BOTTLES

$4.00 — $6.00

$25.00 — $30.00

$4.50 — $6.50

'48 Rose Fragrance

'62 Rose Bud
Vase

'70 Sea Horse

'71 Side Wheeler

$4.00 — $6.00

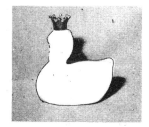

'71 Royal Swan

$3.50 — $4.50

COURTESY: *STUARTS BOOK ON AVON COLLECTABLES—1972*

Item, Description, Date	Retail
☐ Rose Fragrance, 1948 Glass Perfume Bottle & Top	**25.00 — 30.00**
☐ Rose Geranium Bath Oil, 1957	**20.00 — 25.00**
☐ Rose Perfume, CPC+ 7 Dram Perfume & Flaconette	**130.00 — 160.00**
☐ Rosewater, CPC+ Round Bottle, Glass Top	**90.00 — 120.00**
☐ Royal Orb, 1965 Round Bottle with "Orb" Top	**25.00**
☐ Royal Swan, 1971 Swan Shaped Bottle, Crown Top	**3.50 — 4.50**
☐ Royal Vase, 1970 Vase Shaped Bottle	**5.00.**
☐ Ruby Vase, 1970 Ruby-Red, Vase Shaped Bottle	**4.50 — 6.50**

—S—

☐ Saddle Kit, 1970 3 Piece Set "Cowskin" Box	**14.00 — 18.00**
☐ Savory Coloring, CPC+ 4 oz. Bottle	**40.00 — 60.00**
☐ Schroeder Bubble Bath, 1970 Comic Character with "Piano" Box	**3.50 — 4.50**
☐*Scimitar, 1968 Gold & Red "Arabic Sword" Shaped Bottle	**14.50 — 18.50**
☐ Sea Horse, 1970 Sea Horse Shaped Bottle, Gold Top	**4.50 — 6.50**
☐ Sea Maiden, 1971 "Mermaid" Shaped Bottle, Gold Top	**6.00 — 7.50**
☐ Sea Treasure, 1971 Sea Shell Shaped Bottle, Gold Top	**5.00 — 8.00**
☐ Secret Tower, 1969 Red Pointed Top	**3.50 — 4.50**
☐ Shampoo, CPC+ Square Bottle 6 oz.	**100.00 — 120.00**
☐ Side Wheeler, 1971 Paddle-Wheel Boat Shaped Bottle	**4.00 — 6.00**
☐ Sitting Pretty, 1971, Rattan Chair with Cat, Bottle	**5.50 — 7.50**

† **CPC—California Perfume Company**   **$14.50 — $18.50**   '68 Scimitar

*Without Box—$5.00 Less

Item, Description, Date	Retail

SKIN-SO-SOFT LABEL 1962-69

- ☐ '62 Glass Bottle .... 10.00 — 12.00
- ☐ '64 Ribbed Bottle, Gold Top 14.00
- ☐ '65 Urn Bottle, Gold Top .... 10.00 — 12.00
- ☐ '69 Round Bottle, Pointed Glass Top .... 3.00 — 4.00
- ☐ '70 Tall Ribbed Bottle, Pointed Gold Top .... 2.00 — 3.00

$3.00 — $4.00

'69
Skin-So-Soft

'62 Skin-So-Soft
(Glass)

$10.00 — $12.00

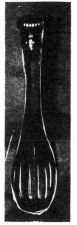

'64
Skin-So-Soft
$12.00 — $14.00

'65
Skin-So-Soft
Urn

$10.00 — $12.00

'70
Skin-So-Soft
$2.00 — $3.00

A.B.P. — 40% - 60%
of Retail Price

Item, Description, Date	Retail

☐ Small World, 1970 Splashu & Heidi..................................**4.00 — 5.00**
☐ Small World, 1971 Gigi with Beret Top...........................**4.50 — 5.50**
☐ Smart Move, 1971 Gold Horse-Head, Chess Piece Bottle.............**4.00 — 5.00**
☐ Snoopy, 1970...**1.50 — 2.50**
☐ Snoopy Decanter, 1969 Milk Glass Bottle, Comic Character..........**5.00 — 6.00**

SOMEWHERE LABEL — 1961-69

☐ '61 1 oz. Perfume Bottle in Box Rhinestone Bottom ....**75.00 — 80.00**
☐ '61 Cologne Mist Bottle, Pink Plastic..............................**7.00 — 8.00**
☐ '61 Cologne Bottle Glass ....**7.00 — 8.00**
☐ '64 Perfume Oil, Glass...**10.00 — 12.00**
☐ '66 Cologne, Glass Bottle, Gold Top ....**3.50 — 4.50**
☐ '66 Perfume Oil Bottle, Gold Top ....**10.00 — 12.00**

☐ Song Bird, 1971 Bird-Shaped Bottle, Gold Base ....**4.00 — 5.00**
☐ Sparkler, 1968 Xmas Bulb Bottle ....**5.00 — 6.00**
☐ Sparkling Burgundy Set, 1957 ....**70.00**
☐ Spicy Cologne Plus, 1965 Square Bottle **15.00**
☐ Spicy After Shave, 1967 Round Glass Bottle ....**1.50 — 2.50**
☐ Spirit of St. Louis, 1970 "Lindbergh's Plane" Bottle, Silvered ......**8.00 — 9.00**
☐ Sports Rally, 1965 Glass Bottle ....**6.00 — 8.00**
☐ Spray Boot, 1966 Boot-Shaped Bottle................................**4.00 — 5.00**
☐ Spring Goddess, 1957 3 Piece Set ....**40.00 — 50.00**
☐ Stage Coach, 1970 Coach-Shaped Glass Bottle........................**6.00 — 7.00**
☐ Stamp, 1970 Hand Stamp Bottle......................................**5.00 — 6.00**
☐ Stanley Steamer, 1971 "Old-Time" Car Shaped Glass Bottle...........**5.00 — 6.00**

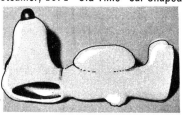

$3.00 — $4.00

Snoopy Soap Dish — 1968

'61 1 oz.
Perfume
$70.00 — $80.00

'61 Cologne
Mist
$7.00 — $8.00

'61 Cologne
$7.00 — $8.00

'64 Perfume
Oil
$10.00 — $12.00

'66 Cologne
$3.50 — $4.00

'66
Perfume
Oil

$10.00 — $12.00

SOMEWHERE LABEL — 1961 - 69

COURTESY: *STUARTS BOOK ON AVON COLLECTABLES—1972*

AVON BOTTLES

Prices are for Empty Bottles in Mint
Condition with Tops, Holders, Handles & Labels

'70 Spirit of St. Louis
$8.00 — $9.00

'70 Stamp

$5.00 — $6.00

'70 Stage Coach

$6.00 — $7.00

'71 Stanley Steamer

$5.00 — $6.00

Item, Description, Date	Retail
☐ Station Wagon, 1971 "Old-Time Wagon Shaped Bottle	6.00 — 7.00
☐ Stein, 8 oz., 1965 Silver Bottle with Handle	7.00 — 9.00
☐ Stein, 6 oz., 1968 Silver Bottle with Handle	5.50 — 7.00
☐ Sterling Six, 1968 Classic Car Shaped Bottle	8.00 — 9.00

Item, Description, Date	Retail

- [ ] Straight Eight, 1969 Classic Racing Car Shaped Glass Bottle .... **7.50 — 8.00**
- [ ] Sunny Hours, 1953 2 Piece Set in "Parasol" Holder **75.00**
- [ ] Super Cycle, 1971 Motorcycle Shaped Bottle .... **6.00 — 7.00**
- [ ] Sweet as Honey, 1951 4 Bottles in "Beehive" Box .... **100.00 — 120.00**
- [ ] Sweet Pea Perfume, CPC† Flaconette & 7 Dram Perfume Bottle **175.00**
- [ ] Swinger, 1969 Golf Bag & Clubs Bottle .... **6.00 — 8.00**

'71 Station Wagon **$6.00 — $7.00**

'69 Straight Eight **$7.50 — $8.50**

'65 Stein (8 oz.)
$7.00 — $9.00

$6.00 —$7.00

'71 Super Cycle

† **CPC—California Perfume Company**

AVON BOTTLES

$70.00 — $80.00 $16.00 — $18.00 $16.00 — $18.00

'50 3 Dram
Perfume

'50 Cologne

'50 Toilet
Water

Item, Description, Date   **Retail**

—T—

TAI WINDS LABEL — 1971
- ☐ 5 oz. Cologne Bottle ....5.00 — 6.00
- ☐ 5 oz. After Shave Bottle...4.00 — 5.00
- ☐ Boxed Gift Set ....8.00 — 10.00

TO A WILD ROSE LABEL — 1950-1969
- ☐ '50 3 Dram Perfume Bottle...70.00 — 80.00
- ☐ '50 Cologne Bottle..16.00 — 18.00
- ☐ '50 Toilet Water Bottle..16.00 — 18.00
- ☐ '53 Bath Oil Bottle...16.00 — 18.00
- ☐ '50 Petals of Beauty ....40.00 — 50.00

**All Prices are for Empty Bottles in Mint Condition,
With Handles, Spouts & Stoppers.**

TOPAZE LABEL—1959 - 69

$6.00 — $8.00

'59 Topaze **$125.00 —**
Perfume **$150.00**

'59 Cologne

'59 1 oz.
Perfume

$125.00 —
$150.00

'59 Cologne
$10.00 — $12.00

'61 Bath Oil
$10.00 — $12.00

'59 Gift Cologne

$25.00 — $30.00

TOPAZE LABEL — 1959-60

- ☐ '59 1 oz. Perfume, Square "Diamond" Top ....**125.00 — 150.00**
- ☐ '59 Cologne, Square Bottle, Gold Top ....**6.00 — 8.00**
- ☐ '59 Cologne, Tall Bottle, White Neck Glass "Diamond" Top..........**10.00 — 12.00**
- ☐ '59 Cologne & Gift Box ....**25.00 — 30.00**
- ☐ '61 Bath Oil, Tall Bottle, White Neck Glass "Diamond" Top ....**10.00 — 12.00**

- ☐ Topaze Perfume, 1959 Square Bottle, Glass "Diamond" Top in Gift Box   **30.00**
- ☐ Touring T, 1969 Antique Model "T" Car Glass Bottle..................**8.00 — 10.00**
- ☐ Town Pump, 1968 Old Pump Bottle ....**4.00 — 6.00**
- ☐ Trailing Arbutus Perfume, CPC† Round Top, Floral Label & Gift Box **130.00**
- ☐ Trailing Arbutus Set, CPC† 3 Piece Set, 4 oz. Toilet Water, Sachet, Talc,
  Gift Boxed ....**275.00 — 325.00**
- ☐ Trailing Arbutus Toilet Water, CPC† 2 oz. Square Bottle, Gold Top **40.00**
- ☐ Treasure Turtle, 1971 Glass Turtle Bottle, Gold Head ....**4.00 — 5.00**
- ☐ Tribute, 1963 Aftershave Cologne... **4.00 — 6.00**
- ☐ Trilogy, 1957 3 Milk Glass Bottles, Round Tops in Box.............**35.00 — 45.00**
- ☐ Trilogy, 1969 3, 1-1/2 oz. Cologne Glass Bottle in Box.............**10.00 — 12.00**
- ☐ Twenty Dollar Gold Piece, 1971 Gold Color Liberty Head, Bottle,
  Eagle Cap...**4.50 — 6.50**
- ☐ Twenty Paces, 1967 Matched Set, Dueling Pistol Bottles, Boxed **30.00**

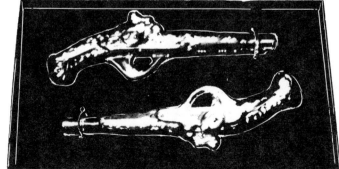

'67 Twenty
Paces

† **CPC — California Perfume Company**   **$25.00 — $30.00**

Avon Trio
Trailing Arbutus Toilet Water;
Daphne Talc, Ariel Sachet
$130.00 — $160.00 set

CPC Perfumes
Trailing Arbutus
Natoma Rose
Crab Apple Blossom

$130.00 — $160.00 each

$3.50 — $5.50

'65 Cologne
Mist

Mizer Set Perfume Extract
1 oz. All Fragrances
White Rose
$180.00 — $220.00

'65
Perfume
Oil

$8.00 — $10.00

'68 Cream
Sachet

'69 1/2 oz.
Cologne

$2.00 — $3.00

—U—

Item, Description, Date	Retail
☐ Ultra-Sheer, 1966 Gold Top	3.00 — 4.00

UNFORGETTABLE LABEL—1965-66

☐ '65 Cologne Mist Bottle, Plastic Gold Top	3.50 — 5.50
☐ '65 Cologne Bottle, Glass, Gold Top	2.50 — 3.50
☐ '65 Perfume Oil Bottle, Gold Top	8.00 — 10.00
☐ '69 1/2 oz. Cologne, Small Bottle	2.00 — 3.00
☐ Beauty Dust, 1965	5.00 — 7.00

71 Victorian Pitcher
and Bowl

$8.00 — $10.00

Item, Date, Description	Retail

—V—

☐ Valet Set, 1949 2 Piece with Box .... 35.00 — 40.00
☐ Vernafleur Perfume, CPC† 1 oz. Bottle, Glass Stopper .... 80.00 — 100.00
☐ Vernafleur Toilet Water, CPC in Original Box .... 100.00 — 125.00

☐ Vernafleur Perfume, CPC† 1 oz. Bottle, Glass Stopper .... 80.00 — 100.00
    In Original Box .... 100.00 — 125.00
☐ Vernafleur Toilet, Water, CPC 2 oz. Ribbed Glass Bottle, Metal Cap 80.00
☐ Viking Horn, 1966 Horn Shaped Bottle, Gold Top & Tip .... 10.00 — 12.50
☐ Victorian Pitcher & Bowl, 1971 Milk Glass Antique Handled Pitcher &
    Bowl Bottle .... 8.00 — 10.00
☐ Violet Perfume, CPC† 1 oz. Perfume Bottle with "Crown" Glass Stopper
    & Ribbon 95.00
☐ Violet Toilet Water, CPC Foral Label, 2 oz. Bottle with Metal Cap 125.00
☐ Volkswagen, 1970 Black "Bug" Shaped Bottle * .... 3.50 — 4.50

† **CPC—California Perfume Company**
*Red — 1972   **$3.50 — $4.50**

Item, Date, Description   Retail

—W—

☐ Wassail Bowl Candleholder, 1969..**6.00 — 8.00**
☐ Weather or Not, 1969 Barometer Shaped Bottle Gold Eagle Top.....**5.00 — 7.00**
☐ Western Choice, 1967 Steer Horns, Gold Tips ....**15.00 — 20.00**
☐ Western Saddle, 1971 "Saddle" Bottle on Fence...........................**7.50 — 8.50**
☐ White Lilac Perfume, CPC† 1 oz. Bottle "Crown" Glass Stopper Ribbon
    on Neck...**100.00 — 130.00**
☐ White Rose Perfume, CPC† Atomizer Set, 1 oz. Bottle in Black Box........ **200.00**
☐ White Rose Toilet Water, CPC† 2 oz. Square Bottle, Round Top...**30.00 — 40.00**
☐ Wild Country, 1968 Round Bottle, Gold Top.................................**3.50 — 4.50**
☐ Wild Rose Set, 1951 Body Powder & Cologne, Boxed...............**20.00 — 30.00**
☐ Windjammer, 1968 Glass Bottle, White Sailing Ship Label, Ring Top...... **4.50**
☐ Wine Server, foreign Wine Bottle in Serving Basket...................**18.00 — 22.00**
☐ Wise Choice, 1969 Owl Bottle Gold Head....................................**6.00 — 8.00**

**All Prices are for
Empty Bottles in Mint Condition,
With Handles,
Spouts & Stoppers.**

Wine Server

$15.00 — $20.00   **$18.00 — $22.00**

'67 Western Choice

† **CPC—California Perfume Company**

$20.00 — $25.00

$18.00 — $20.00

'54 Cologne

'53 Bubble Bath

Item, Date, Description   **Retail**

WISHING LABEL — 1963-65

- [ ] '63 Cream Lotion, Milk Glass ....**2.50 — 3.00**
- [ ] '63 Cologne Bottle, White Top ....**8.00 — 10.00**
- [ ] '63 Perfume Oil Bottle, White Top..**8.00 — 10.00**
- [ ] '65 Cologne Mist, White Bottle & Top ....**5.00 — 6.00**

- [ ] World's Greatest Dad, 1971 Loving Cup Bottle.............................**2.00 — 3.00**

—Y—

YOUNG HEARTS LABEL — 1951-54

- [ ] '54 "Little Doll" Set, 4 Pieces, Blue Doll Handbag.....................**50.00 — 60.00**
- [ ] '54 "Honey Bun" 2 Piece Set..**20.00 — 25.00**
- [ ] '53 "Rain Drops", 3 Piece Set, Red Umbrella Bag.....................**70.00 — 80.00**
- [ ] '54 "Kiddie Cologne", 2 oz. Bottle, White Dog Head ....**18.00 — 20.00**
- [ ] '53 "When The Cat's Away" 4 oz. Bottle, Cat Head Cap.............**20.00 — 25.00**
- [ ] '54 Young Hearts Set, Cologne, Bubble Bath, Talc ....**40.00 — 50.00**
- [ ] '51 Young Hearts Set, "Happy Time", Talc..........................**40.00 — 50.00**

AVON BOTTLES

'63
Cologne
$8.00 — $10.00

69 Wise Choice
$6.00 — $8.00

'51
Young Hearts
Set
$40.00 — $50.00

'51 Powder
Sachet

$40.00 — $50.00

'51 Happy Time

Item, Date, Description	A	Retail
☐ Amber Cruet with Stopper — 1973		**6.00 — 8.00**
☐ American Schooner, 1972		**7.00**
☐ Andy Capp, foreign bottle		**25.00**
☐ Armoire, Milk Glass 1972		**6.00**
☐ Atlantic 4-4-2 Locomotive		**12.00**
☐ "At Point"-Setter Dog — 1973		**6.00**
☐ Auto Lantern — 1973		**15.00**
☐ Avon Calling (1906) Antique phone — 1973		**12.00**
☐ Avon Open, 1972		**27.00**
☐ Avonshire Blue Decanter — 1973		**7.00 — 9.00**

B

☐ Bath Treasure — Glass Snail		**8.50**
☐ Beautiful Awakening Alarm Clock 1973		**7.50**
☐ Big Game Rhino, 1972		**6.00**
☐ Big Mack - Mack Truck — 1973		**7.50**
☐ Big Whistle, 1972		**5.00**
☐ Blue Volkswagen Decanter '73		**5.00**
☐ Bon Bon — French poodle — 1973		**5.00**
☐ Bon Bon (poodle) dark glass, 1972		**3.50**
☐ Bottled by Avon Seltzer Bottle 1973		**5.00**
☐ Breath Fresh Decanter, 1972		**3.50**
☐ Bulldog Pipe, milk glass bowl — 1972		**6.00**
☐ Butterfly, clear glass wings - 1972		**5.00**

C

☐ Camper, Camper Truck — 1972		**10.00**
☐ Canada Goose - on base — 1973		**9.00**
☐ Candlestick Cologne, 1972		**7.50**
☐ Charlie Brown — Plastic 1971		**5.00**
☐ Chimney lamp — Milk glass shade — 1973		**8.00**
☐ Classic Beauty Cream Lotion, 1972		**5.00**
☐ Classic Lion -Crouching — 1973		**8.50**
☐ Collectors Pipe - Glass bowl - 1973		**5.00**
☐ Cologne Elegante - Atomizer — 1973		**9.00**
☐ Cologne Royale, 1972 - Glass Crown		**3.50**
☐ Compote, 1972		**6.50**
☐ Country Charm - Butter Churn - 1973		**5.00**
☐ Country Kitchen - Milk glass Chicken — 1973		**7.50**
☐ Country Store Antique Coffee Mill		**8.50**

AVON 1972-1973

Item, Date, Description	Retail
☐ Country Store Mineral Spring — 1973	8.50
☐ Country Vendor - Antique Peddlers Truck — 1973	8.00
☐ Courting Carriage - Clear glass - old time carriage — 1973	5.00
☐ Creamy Decanter - Flower vase decor — 1973	6.00

D

☐ Dachsund, long glass "hot dog", 1973	5.00
☐ Decorator Cologne Mist, 1972	73.00
☐ Deep Woods, 1972	31.55
☐ Deep Woods, Tree stump , 1973	5.00
☐ Double Dip, 1968, plastic, ice cream sundae	5.00
☐ Dutch Girl, In costume holding flowers, 1973	7.50
☐ Dutch Pipe, stenciled bowl, 1973	10.00

E

☐ Elizabethan Fashion Figurine, milk glass, 1972	6.50

F

☐ Fashion Boot Pin Cushion, milk glass plush top, 1972	6.50
☐ Flower Basket Soap Dish with handle, 1972	6.50
☐ Flower Maiden, holding flow basket, milk glass, 1973	7.50

G

☐ Golden Thimble, 1972, antique design	5.00
☐ Gone fishing, plastic fisherman glass boat, 1973	8.50
☐ Grecian Pitcher, 1972, classic head in milk glass.	6.50

H

☐ Harvester, glass tractor, 1973	6.50
☐ Haynes - Apperson, antique open car glass, 1973	6.50
☐ Hidden Treasure, 1972	6.50
☐ Hobnail Bell, with gold handle, 1973	6.00
☐ Hobnail Pitcher, antique milk glass design, 1972	8.50
☐ Hunter's Stein, 1972	7.50

I

☐ Indian Chieftain, head with feathers, 1972	3.50

J

☐ Jaguar, Sports car, glass, 1973	7.00

Item, Date, Description	K	Retail

K

- ☐ Kanga Winks, plastic duck, 1972 .... **5.00**
- ☐ King Chesspiece, gold cap, 1972 .... **5.00**
- ☐ Kitten Little, milk glass cat, 1972 .... **5.00**
- ☐ Kitten Petite, playing with ball, 1973 .... **5.00**

L

- ☐ Little Dutch Kettle, with gold cover & handle, 1972 .... **7.50**
- ☐ Little Girl Blue, old time costume, 1972 .... **5.00**

M

- ☐ Maxwell '23, antique touring car, 1972 .... **7.50**
- ☐ Mini-Bike, glass motor bike, 1972 .... **7.50**
- ☐ Model A, Ford car with rumble seat, 1972 .... **6.00**

N

- ☐ Nile Blue Bath Urn, classic shape w/handle, 1972 .... **8.50**

O

- ☐ Old Faithful, St. Bernard dog w/barrel, 1972 .... **8.00**

P

- ☐ Period Piece Decanter, 1972 .... **8.00**
- ☐ Pheasant, Bird bottle, 1972 .... **8.00**
- ☐ Piano, Old-time upright, 1972 .... **5.00**
- ☐ Piglet Petite with gold cap nose, 1972 .... **7.00**
- ☐ Pineapple Petite, glass body, gold cap, 1972 .... **3.50**
- ☐ Puffer Chugger, Toy train set (3), 1972 .... **8.00**

R

- ☐ Randy Pandy, Top soap holder, 1972 .... **3.50**
- ☐ Remember When Radio, 1930's radio, 1972 .... **5.00**
- ☐ Reo Depot Wagon, 1910 car, 1972 .... **7.50**
- ☐ Roaring Twenties Figurine, milk glass in fur coat, 1972 .... **7.00**
- ☐ Rolls.Royce, Silver Cloud-1920's, 1972 .... **10.00**
- ☐ Royal Apple, with gold leaves, 1972 .... **6.00**
- ☐ Royal Coach, milk glass, 1972 .... **8.00**

Item, Date, Description	S	Retail

☐ School Desk, Old-time desk, 1972 ....**7.00**
☐ Sea Garden Bud Vase, 1972 ....**8.50**
☐ Sea Horse, glass miniature, 1973 ....**5.00**
☐ Sea Trophy, leaping sailfish, 1972 ....**7.00**
☐ Secretaire, cabinet, 1972 ....**7.50**
☐ Small Wonder, glass snail, 1972 ....**6.00**
☐ Snowman, glass w/gold top hat, 1973 ....**7.50**
☐ Sonnet, 3 piece set, 1972 ....**20.00**
☐ Super Shaver, double edge razor, glass handle, gold head, 1973 ....**5.00**
☐ Sure Winner, supercharged race car, 1972 ....**7.50**
☐ Sure Winner, baseball decanter, 1973 ....**4.50**
☐ Suzette, French poodle, milk glass, 1973 ....**4.50**

T

☐ Tiffany Lamp, antique shade & stand, 1972..................**10.00**

V

☐ Victorian Figurine, with feathered bonnet, milk glass, 1972 ......**6.00**
☐ Victorian Manor, gingerbread house with gables, milk glass, 1972 ..**7.00**
☐ Victorian Wash stand, milk glass cabinet, bowl & pitcher, 1973 ....**6.50**
☐ Volkswagon (red), famous "Bug" in glass, 1972...............**5.00**

W

☐ Western Boot, glass with spurs **6.00**

The history of the James B. Beam Distilling Company goes back to the late 1700's. Jacob Beam founded his distillery in Kentucky in 1788, his great-grandson, Colonel James B. Beam is the one who's name the distillery now bears.

• THE BEAM COLLECTABLES •

These bottles originally were started by the James B. Beam Distilling Company to package their excellent Beam Bourbon Whiskey in a special Christmas decanter for gift giving in 1953. The fabulous success of this first issue led to the many series and varieties of "Beam" bottles.

• THE EXECUTIVE SERIES •

To commemorate the 160th Anniversary of the Company in 1953, Beam issued the first of the Executive Series. These 22 Karat gold decorated bottles are issued each year.

• REGAL CHINA-CUSTOMER-POLITICAL-CENTENNIAL •

The year 1955 also saw the issuance of the first Regal China Specialty the Ivory Ash Tray bottle. In 1956 the Customer Specialty Series began with a bottle for Foremost Liquor Stores of Chicago, and the Political Series with the donkey and Elephant bottles. The State Series began with Alaska and Hawaii being honored, in 1958, others soon followed.
The first Centennial Series bottle was the Santa Fe issued in 1960.

• PRODUCTION OF BEAMS •

Over 350 bottles have been issued since 1953, and more are issued each year on a variety of each series. The ceramic bottles are much more popular with collectors than the glass bottles. The ceramic bottles are made by the Regal China plant in Illinois, the glass bottles are produced by the Wheaton Glass Company of Millville, New Jersey.

Most Regal China bottles are figural-shaped in the form of a state, an animal, bird or fish, or a person. They are colorfully decorated, and embossed, and often embellished with gold.

• PRICING & CONDITION •

Prices quoted are for bottles in Mint Condition, complete with stoppers, labels, handles, with no cracks or flaws, and clear bright color. Fakes have been made of the most valuable.

*A.B.P.—Average Buying Price: This is the approximate price a dealer would pay you for a wanted bottle in Mint condition.

ACKNOWLEDGEMENT: Mr. Martin Lewin, Executive Vice President, & Mrs. Ellen Ladner. JAMES B. BEAM DISTILLING CO., Chicago, Ill. 60611., Ms. Debbie Master.

PICTURES COURTESY OF: Mr. Martin Lewin, A. J. Kessler Liquors, Lourie Liquor Company.

1. ☐*FIRST NATIONAL BANK OF CHICAGO—1964

Issued to commemorate the 100th anniversary of the First National Bank of Chicago, about 130 were issued, 117 were given as mementos to the bank directors, none for public distribution. This is the most valuable Beam bottle known. Sky blue color, circular shape, gold embossed design around banner lettered "THE FIRST NATIONAL BANK OF CHICAGO". Center oval with ornate bank logo "1st," and "100th Anniversary" in gold. Gold embossed "1st" on the stopper.

Bottom marked "CREATION OF JAMES B. BEAM DISTILLING CO.—GENUINE REGAL CHINA".

Reverse: Round paper label inscribed "BEAM CONGRATULATES THE FIRST NATIONAL BANK OF CHICAGO—100th ANNIVERSARY. 100 YEARS OF SUCCESSFUL BANKING". .... **Retail** $2700.00 — $3500.00

All Prices are for Empty Bottles in Mint Condition, With Handles, Spouts & Stoppers.

1.

$2700.00 — $3500.00

*Beware of reproductions

$350.00 — $450.00

$250.00 — $300.00

9.

10.

$20.00 — $30.00

8.

$150.00 — $200.00

5.

Item, Date, Description	Retail

2. ☐ **FOREMOST—BLACK & GOLD—1956**
Pylon shaped decanter with a deep black body embossed with gold nuggets. The square white stopper doubles as a jigger. This is the first Beam bottle issued for a liquor retailer. Foremost Liquor Stores of Chicago, many others have followed. Regal China. **130.00 — 140.00**

3. ☐ **FOREMOST—GREY & GOLD—1956**
Same as above. Tapered decanter with gray body and gold nuggets. Both decanters are 15-1/2" high and are Regal China... **130.00 — 140.00**

4. ☐ **FOREMOST—SPECKLED BEAUTY—1956**
The most valuable of the "Foremost" bottles. Also known as the "Pink Speckled Beauty," was created in the shape of a Chinese vase and spattered in various colors of pink, gold, black and gray. The spattered colors may vary from bottle to bottle since it was hand applied. Regal China, Height 14-1/2".......... **325.00 — 375.00**

A.B.P. — Average Buying Price 40% to 60% of Retail.

Item, Date, Description   Retail

5. ☐ **YELLOW KATZ**—1967
   The emblem of the Katz Department Stores (Missouri),
   a green-eyed meowing cat, is the head (and stopper)
   of this bottle. The pylon shaped, orange color body
   has a curved tail. The "Katz" commemorates the 50th
   birthday of the store. .... **20.00 — 30.00**

6. ☐ **BLACK KATZ**—1968
   Same Kitty different color: black cat, green eyes, red
   tongue, white base. Both Katz are Regal China. Height
   14-1/2". .... **5.95 — 12.95**

*7. ☐ **BROADMOOR HOTEL**—1968
   To celebrate the 50th Anniversary of this famous
   hotel in Colorado Springs, Colorado, Beam issued
   this bottle replica complete with details of windows,
   doors, roof tiles and tower capped with a "roof"
   stopper. The base bears the legend "1918—THE
   BROADMOOR—1968" in white ovals on a black
   background. .... **5.00 — 8.50**

• **HAROLDS CLUB BOTTLES** •

8. ☐ **HAROLDS CLUB (MAN-IN-A-BARREL)**—1957/58
   This was the first in a series made for the famous
   Harolds Club in Reno Nevada. The man-in-a-barrel
   was an advertising logo used by the club. In 1957,
   Jim Beam issued a bottle using the figure of "Percy"
   in-a-barrel with "HAROLDS CLUB" embossed on the
   front. "Percy" has a top hat, a monocle, a mus-
   tache, a white collar and a bright red tie, and spats.
   He stands on a base of "Bad News" dice cubes.
   Regal China. Height, 14-1/2". .... **350.00 — 450.00**

9. ☐ **HAROLDS CLUB (MAN-IN-A-BARREL—2)**—1958
   Twin brother of "Percy" No. 1. No mustache, "HAR-
   OLDS CLUB" inscribed on base of the bottle. Regal
   China 14-1/2" high. .... **250.00 — 300.00**

*Also a Regal China bottle

Item, Date, Description   **Retail**

10. ☐ **HAROLDS CLUB—NEVADA (GREY)—1963**
"HAROLDS CLUB OF RENO" inscribed on base of
the bottle created for the "Nevada Centennial—1864-
1964" as a State bottle. Embossed picture of miner
and mule on the "HAROLDS" side, crossed shovel
and pick are on stopper. Embossed lettering on base
is grey-toned and not bold. This is a rare and valuable
bottle.. **150.00 — 200.00**

11. ☐ **HAROLDS CLUB—NEVADA (SILVER)—1964**
Same as above. Base lettering now reads "HAROLDS
CLUB RENO," the letters are bolder and are bright
silver... **165.00 — 225.00**

12. ☐ **HAROLDS CLUB—VIP EXECUTIVE—1967**
An "Alladins Lamp" shaped decanter. "HAROLDS
CLUB RENO" embossed gold label on bottle. Overall gold & green color on bottle. Limited quantity
issued. Regal China. 12-1/2" high.............................. **45.00 — 70.00**

13. ☐ **HAROLDS CLUB—VIP EXECUTIVE—1968**
An overall "bubble" pattern in cobalt blue with silver
trim and handle distinguishes this bottle. "HAROLDS
CLUB RENO" in silver, on an embossed oval emblem,
is in the center of the bottle. Regal China. Height
12-3/4"... **40.00 — 60.00**

14. ☐ **HAROLDS CLUB—VIP EXECUTIVE—1969**
An oval shaped decanter with an overall motif of roses.
"HAROLDS CLUB RENO" is embossed in gold on the
yellow-toned bottle. The bottle was used as a Christmas gift to the Casino's executives. Regal China,
12-1/2" high... **80.00 — 100.00**

**All Prices are for Empty Bottles in Mint Condition,
Complete with Handles, Spouts & Stoppers.**

6.

$5.95
— $12.95

$65.00
—$110.00

15.

$15.00 —
$22.50

16.　17.

Item, Date, Description

Retail

15. ☐ **HAROLDS CLUB—PINWHEEL—1965**
A round bottle supporting a design of a spinning
pinwheel of gold and blue, with gold dots on the
edge. "HAROLDS CLUB RENO" embossed in gold in
the center, "FOR FUN" on the stopper. Regal China
10-1/2" high.. **65.00 — 110.00**

16. ☐ **HAROLDS CLUB—BLUE SLOT MACHINE—1967**
A blue-toned "One Armed Bandit" with 2 gold bells
showing in the window, and a gold colored handle,
the money slot is the stopper. "HAROLDS CLUB
RENO" and a large "H" on a pinwheel emblem are
on the front. Regal China, 10-3/8" high...................... **15.00 — 22.50**

17. ☐ **HAROLDS CLUB—GRAY SLOT MACHINE—1968**
Same as above but with an overall grey tone. Regal
China, 10-3/8" high.. **5.00 — 8.50**

18. ☐ **HAROLDS CLUB—SILVER OPAL—1957**
Issued to commemorate the 25th Anniversary of
Harolds Club, bright silver color with a "snowflake"
design center and a red label. Glass, 11-1/8" high. **18.50 — 24.50**

Retail

19. ☐ **HAROLDS CLUB—COVERED WAGON—1969/70**
A Canestoga wagon with "HAROLDS CLUB" embossed on the side pulled by a galloping ox, driven by a cowboy. The bottle is "arch" shaped, framing Nevada's mountains and the wagon. Regal China, 10" high.   **4.50 — 9.50**

• RENO, NEVADA BOTTLES •

20. ☐ **CAL-NEVA—1969**
This is a standard square-bottle, green toned with "RENO 100 YEARS" deeply embossed and "CAL-NEVA, CASINO • HOTEL, RENO • LAKE TAHOE" in the oval shaped emblem. Regal China, 9-1/2" high.   **4.50 — 12.50**

21. ☐ **HORSESHOE CLUB—1969**
Same as above with "RENO'S HORSESHOE CLUB" and a horseshoe in yellow & black on the emblem.   **8.50 — 16.00**

22. ☐ **PRIMA-DONNA—1969**
Same as "CAL-NEVA" with "PRIMA-DONNA CASINO" and show girls on the emblem....................................   **8.50 — 16.00**

23. ☐ **GOLDEN GATE—1969**
This almond-shaped bottle has "LAS VEGAS" embossed in bright gold in a banner on the front. Mountains, a helicopter, a golfer, and a gambling montage, with "GOLDEN GATE CASINO" in gold on a shield are featured. Regal China, 12-1/2" high......................   **50.00 — 75.00**

24. ☐ **GOLDEN NUGGET—1969**
Same as above "GOLDEN NUGGET" in gold on shield in front. Regal China, 12-1/2" high. ....   **50.00 — 75.00**

25. ☐ **HARRAH'S CLUB NEVADA—GRAY—1963**
This is the same round bottle used for the Nevada Centennial and Harolds Club with the miner, and mule and lettered "NEVADA CENTENNIAL". The base has "HARRAH'S RENO AND LAKE TAHOE" embossed on the gray-tone base. Regal China, 11-1/2" high...   **400.00 — 500.00**

A.B.P. — Average Buying Price - 40% to 60% of Retail.

Item, Date, Description	Retail

26. ☐ **HARRAH'S CLUB NEVADA—SILVER—1963**
Same as above, Nevada Centennial bottle, "HARRAH'S RENO AND LAKE TAHOE" embossed on base in silver. Regal China, 11-1/2" high.............................. **800.00 — 900.00**

• **LIQUOR STORE SPECIALS** •

27. ☐ **ARMANETTI AWARD WINNER—1969/70**
A pale blue bottle in the shape of the number "1", to honor Armanetti Inc. of Chicago as "LIQUOR RETAILER OF THE YEAR" in 1969. In a shield, gold & blue lettering proclaims "ARMANETTI LIQUORS 1969 AWARD WINNER". Heavily embossed gold scrolls decorate the bottle. .... **8.50 — 14.50**

28. ☐ **ARMANETTI VASE—1968/69**
Yellow toned decanter embossed with many flowers and a large letter "A" for Armanetti. .... **7.50 — 12.50**

29. ☐ **ZIMMERMAN BLUE BEAUTY—1969/70**
The name "ZIMMERMAN'S LIQUORS" is embossed in bright gold on a sky blue bottle decorated with flowers and scrolls. Reverse has Chicago skyline embossed on blue toned bottle. Arrow with "ZIMMERMAN'S" points to store. Regal China, 10" high. .... **15.00 — 25.00**

30. ☐ **ZIMMERMAN CHERUBS PINK & LAVENDER—1968/69**
Winged cherubs and leaves and vines are embossed over the surface of these slender round bottles. They were issued for the Zimmerman Liquor Stores of Chicago. Regal China, 11-1/2" high. .... **5.00 — 8.50**

31. ☐ **ZIMMERMAN—TWO HANDLED JUG—1965**
Shaped and colored like an avocado, this dark green bottle has embossed grapes and grape leaves on the front; and two side handles. Regal China, 10-1/4" high. **110.00 — 130.00**

32. ☐ **ZIMMERMAN—GLASS—1969**
A white outline of the Chicago skyline with "ZIMMERMAN'S" store on front of this glass bottle. White stopper has "MAX ZIMMERMAN'S" portrait. Glass, 11-1/4" high. .... **7.50 — 12.50**

34.
$4.50
—$7.50

23.
$50.00 — $75.00

31.
$110.00 —
$130.00

Item, Date, Description	Retail

33. ☐ **ZIMMERMAN'S—THE PEDDLER—1971**
A bottle-statue of Max Zimmerman himself, "The Peddler" with his "ZIMMERMAN'S COLLECTOR'S CART", and a display of "Beam" bottles. Dressed in cowboy boots and Stetson hat. "Max the Hat" is col-orjd bright blue, his hat and boots are dark brown. Regal China, 12" high.. **15.00 — 22.50**

34. ☐ **RICHARD'S—NEW MEXICO—1967**
Created for Richard's Distributing Company of Al-buquerque, New Mexico. Lettered "NEW MEXICO" and "RICHARD SAYS DISCOVER NEW MEXICO", in blue. Embossed scene of Taos Pueblo. Picture of "Richard" on stopper and front. Regal China, 11" high. **4.50 — 7.50**

35. ☐ **MARINA CITY—1962**
Commemorating Modern Apt. complex in Chicago. Light blue with Marina City in gold on the sides. Regal China. Height, 10-3/4".................................... **30.00 — 42.50**

JIM BEAM BOTTLES—CENTENNIAL SERIES

**All Prices are for Empty Bottles in Mint Condition,
Complete with Handles, Spouts & Stoppers.**

Item, Date, Description	Retail

1. ☐ **ALASKA PURCHASE—1966**
Blue and gold bottle with star-shaped stopper. Mt. McKinley pictured with State flag on top. Regal China. Height, 10".. **14.50 — 22.50**

2. ☐ **CHEYENNE WYOMING—1967**
Circular decanter in shape of a wheel. Spokes separate scenes of Cheyenne history. Regal China............ **6.50 — 12.50**

3. ☐ **CIVIL WAR NORTH—1961***
Blue and grey bottle depicting Civil War battle scenes. Stopper has Lee's face on one side, Grant's on the other. Regal China. Height, 10-3/4"........................... **each**
30.00 — 40.00

4. ☐ **CIVIL WAR SOUTH—1961 ***
One side portrays the meeting of Lee and Jackson at Chancellorville. On the other side a meeting of southern Generals. Regal China. Height, 10-3/4". .... **each**
35.00 — 45.00
*When sold as a pair . . . .**80.00 — 90.00**

1.   2.   3.

$14.50 — $22.50 $6.50 — $12.50 $30.00 — $40.00

Item, Date, Description	Retail

5. ☐ SANTA FE—1960
Governor's Palace blue-tone sky, date 1610-1960 (350th Anniversary). Navaho woman with Indian basket on reverse. Gold lettering. Height 10", Regal China. .... **200.00 — 300.00**

6. ☐ ANTIOCH—1967
The Regal China Company is located in Antioch, Illinois. This decanter commemorates the Diamond Jubilee of Regal. Large Indian head ("Sequoit") on one side. Blue and Gold diamond on reverse.
Regal China. .... **5.50 — 10.50**
With arrow package .... **7.00 — 12.50**

7. ☐ SAN DIEGO—1968
Issued by the Beam Company for the 200th Anniversary of its founding in 1769. Honoring Junipero Serra, Franciscan missionary. Serra and Conquistador embossed on gold front. Height 10", Regal China. **7.50 — 12.50**

5. $200.00 — $300.00

7. $7.50 — $12.50

6. 5.50 — 10.50

Item, Date, Description   Retail

8. ☐ **LARAMIE—1968**
   "CENTENNIAL JUBILEE LARAMIE WYO. 1868-1968",
   embossed around cowboy on bucking bronco.
   Locomotive of 1860's on reverse.............................   **4.50 — 8.50**

$4.50 —
$8.50

8.

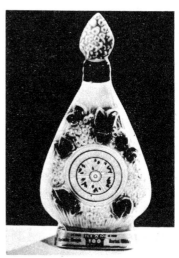

13.

$6.50 — $9.50

9. ☐ **RENO—1968/69**
   "100 YEARS—RENO" embossed over skyline of
   downtown Reno. "THE BIGGEST LITTLE CITY IN THE
   WORLD" lettered over skyline. Reverse "RENO 100
   YEARS" and scenes of Reno. Regal China.
   Height, 9-1/4". ....   **4.50 — 9.50**

10. ☐ **ST. LOUIS ARCH—1964**
    The silhouette of St. Louis with the Mississippi flow-
    ing past. The famous stainless steel arch frames the
    bottle. "ST. LOUIS, GATEWAY TO THE WEST" and
    "200 YEARS" embossed in gold. The ferry boat
    "ADMIRAL" is on the back. Regal China, height 11".   **17.50 — 27.50**

Item, Date, Description	Retail

11. ☐ **ST. LOUIS ARCH**—re-issue 1967
Same as above. .... **15.00 — 22.50**

12. ☐ **BASEBALL**—1969/70
To commemorate the 100th Anniversary of the professional sport, this baseball shaped bottle was issued. "PROFESSIONAL BASEBALL'S 100th ANNIVERSARY—1869-1969" in gold & black on the front. Decal of player in action on top. Reverse has story of growth of baseball. .... **3.50 — 7.50**

13. ☐ **LOMBARD**—1969/70
A pear-shaped decanter, embossed with lilacs and leaves around a circular motto "VILLAGE OF LOMBARD, ILLINOIS—1869 CENTENNIAL 1969", lilac shaped stopper. Reverse has an embossed outline map of Illinois. Colors are lavender and green. .... **6.50 — 9.50**

• GLASS BOTTLES •

14. ☐ **PORTOLA TREK**—1969
This gold glass bottle has a painting of "THE PORTOLA TREK" reproduction in full color on the front. This bottle was issued to celebrate the 200th Anniversary of San Diego, and is a companion to the Regal China bottle. .... **3.50 — 6.50**

15. ☐ **POWELL EXPEDITION**—1969
Another gold glass bottle with a full color painting depicting John Wesley Powell's survey of the Colorado River and his traversing the Grand Canyon. .... **7.00 — 10.00**

A.B.P. — Average Buying Price - 40% to 60% of Retail Price Listed.

JIM BEAM—GLASS SPECIALTIES

**All Prices are for Empty Bottles in Mint Condition,
Complete with Handles, Spouts & Stoppers.**

Item, Date, Description   Retail

1. ☐ **COFFEE WARMERS—1954**
   Four types are known in Red, Black, Gold and White
   necks, plastic cord over cork. The Corning Glass Company made the Pyrex bottles. Round stoppers are
   made of wood. Pyrex Glass, 9" high............................   7.50 — 9.50

2. ☐ **COFFEE WARMERS—1956**
   Two types with metal necks and handles, black and gold
   stripes on one, gold neck with black handle on the
   the other. White Star design on sides of Pyrex glass
   on both. Round black plastic tops. Some have holder
   type candle warmers. Pyrex Glass, 10" high..............   3.50 — 6.50

$7.50 — $9.50   1.

3.

$3.50 — $6.50

$6.50 — $9.50

All Prices are for Empty Bottles in Mint Condition, Complete with Handles, Spouts & Stoppers.

Item, Date, Description	Retail

3. ☐ **CLEAR CRYSTAL BOURBON—1967**
Patterned embossed glass bottle with "swirl" stopper. Starburst design on base of the bottle. Clear Glass, 11-1/2" high. .... **6.50 — 9.50**

4. ☐ **CLEAR CRYSTAL VODKA—1967**
Same as above... **6.50 — 9.50**

5. ☐ **EMERALD CRYSTAL BOURBON—1968**
Emerald Green bottle, patterned embossed glass. Flat stopper, "swirl" embossed. Green Glass, 11-1/2" high. .... **3.50 — 6.50**

6. ☐ **OPALINE CRYSTAL—1969**
Milk glass bottle same pattern and embossing, and stopper. Milk Glass, 11-1/2" high. .... **3.50 — 6.50**

7. ☐ **RUBY CRYSTAL—1967**
Amethyst colored, patterned embossed bottle. "Swirl glass stopper. When bottle is filled with bourbon it's ruby red. Sunburst pattern on bottom. Amethyst Glass, 11-1/2" high... **6.00 — 9.00**

8. ☐ **CLEAR CRYSTAL SCOTCH—1966**
The original patterned embossed bottle. Glass stopper ("DOORKNOB") Bottom is unpatterned and has number and date of issue. Clear Glass, 11-1/2" high. **6.00 — 9.00**

9. ☐ **ROYAL EMPEROR—1958**
Made in the Shape of a Classic Greek urn. Warrior figure with spear and helmet and fret design in white on purple-black glass. White glass stopper. Glass, 14" high... **4.50 — 6.50**

10. ☐ **OLYMPIAN—1960**
Another Greek urn decanter. Chariot horses, and warriors design in white on light blue bottle. White glass stopper, embossed base. Glass, 14" high. **5.00 — 7.50**

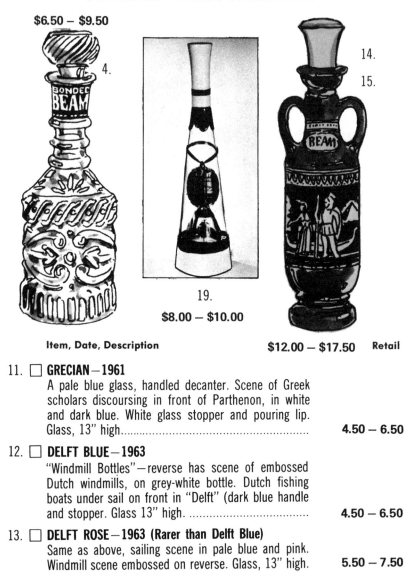

$6.50 – $9.50

4.

14.

15.

19.

$8.00 – $10.00

$12.00 – $17.50   Retail

Item, Date, Description

11. ☐ **GRECIAN—1961**
A pale blue glass, handled decanter. Scene of Greek scholars discoursing in front of Parthenon, in white and dark blue. White glass stopper and pouring lip. Glass, 13" high..   **4.50 – 6.50**

12. ☐ **DELFT BLUE—1963**
"Windmill Bottles"—reverse has scene of embossed Dutch windmills, on grey-white bottle. Dutch fishing boats under sail on front in "Delft" (dark blue handle and stopper. Glass 13" high. ....   **4.50 – 6.50**

13. ☐ **DELFT ROSE—1963 (Rarer than Delft Blue)**
Same as above, sailing scene in pale blue and pink. Windmill scene embossed on reverse. Glass, 13" high.   **5.50 – 7.50**

**All Prices are for Empty Bottles in Mint Condition,
Complete with Handles, Spouts & Stoppers.**

Item, Date, Description	Retail

14. ☐ **CLEOPATRA YELLOW—1962**
Black purple, 2 handled, amphora-decanter. Yellow figures of Mark Anthony in armor, & Cleopatra beside the Nile, Pyramid and Sphinx background. Egyptian border design circles bottle, white stopper. Rarer than Cleopatra Rust. Glass, 13-1/4" high. .... **12.50 — 17.50**

15. ☐ **CLEOPATRA RUST—1962**
Same as Cleo Yellow. Scene with Mark Anthony and Cleopatra in white on rust-red background. .... **4.50 — 7.50**

16. ☐ **MARK ANTHONY—1962**
Same as Cleo bottles, amphora-decanter, 2 handles, white stopper. Mark Anthony alone before Nile scene, white on rust background. Bottle color is black-purple. Glass, 13-1/4" high...................................... **12.00 — 20.00**

17. ☐ **ROYAL OPAL—1957**
A round, handled bottle, of Opal glass. Embossed geometric design on one side. White glass stopper. Bottle made by Wheaton Glass of Millville, New Jersey. Same bottle was used for Harolds Club, 25th Anniversary in silver. Glass, 10-3/4" high.................. **12.00**

18. ☐ **ROYAL CRYSTAL—1959**
Starburst design embossed on both sides on this clear flint glass decanter. Gold label on neck and flat black stopper. Starburst theme appears on label and stopper. Glass, 11-1/2" high............................... **7.00 — 10.00**

19. ☐ **TALL DANCING SCOT—1964/70**
A small Scotsman encased in a glass bubble in the base dances to the music of the base. A tall pylon shaped glass bottle with a tall stopper. No dates on these bottles. Glass, 17" high. .... **8.00 — 10.00**

A.B.P. — Average Buying Price - 40% to 60% of Listed Retail Price.

Item, Date, Description   **Retail**

20. ☐ **SHORT DANCING SCOT—1963**
A short barrel-shaped bottle with the dancing Scot, and music box in the base. Square shaped stopper, a rare bottle. Glass, 11" high.................................... **32.50 — 42.50**

21. ☐ **CAMEO BLUE—1965**
Also known as the "Shepherd Bottle." Scenes of of shepherd and dog in white, on the sky blue, square-shaped bottle. White glass stopper. Glass, 12-3/4" high. .... **4.50 — 6.50**

22. ☐ **SMOKED CRYSTAL—1964**
Dark greenish in tone, and resembling a "Genie's" magic bottle, this tall bottle has a bulbous embossed base, and a slender tapering shape, topped by an em-bossed glass stopper. Glass, 14" high. .... **6.50 — 9.50**

23. ☐ **DUCKS & GEESE—1955**
A scene of wild ducks and geese flying up from marshes in white is featured on this clear glass decanter. A round, tall bottle with a large base and slender tapering neck. Tall gold stopper sits in a flared top glass, 13-1/2" high. .... **7.50 — 10.00**

5.

$3.50 — $6.50

**All Prices are for Empty Bottles in Mint Condition,
Complete with Handles, Spouts & Stoppers.**

Item, Date, Description	Retail

1. ☐ **CATS—1967**
Trio of three cats, Siamese, Burmese, and Tabby. Colors: Grey-blue eyes, dark brown & white—yellow eyes, and white with tan—blue eyes. Regal China, 11-1/2" high. .... **10.00 — 15.00**

2. ☐ **DOE—1963**
Pure white neck markings, natural brown body. "Rocky" base. Regal China. Height, 13-1/2".............. **35.00 — 45.00**

3. ☐ **DOE—RE-ISSUED—1967**
As above... **30.00 — 40.00**

4. ☐ **DOG—1959**
Long-eared Setter Dog, soft brown eyes, black and white coat. Regal China. Height, 15-1/4"................... **55.00 — 75.00**

5. ☐ **DUCK—1957**
Green-headed Mallard, bright yellow bill, brown breast, back wings. Regal China. Height, 14-1/4"....... **30.00 — 50.00**

6. ☐ **EAGLE—1966**
White head, golden beak, deep rich brown plumage, yellow claws on "tree trunk" base. Regal China. Height, 12-1/2". .... **15.00 — 20.00**

7. ☐ **FISH—1957**
Sky blue Sailfish, pink underside, black dorsal fin and side markings on "ocean waves" base. Regal China. Height, 14"... **30.00 — 50.00**

8. ☐ **FOX—1965**
Bushy-tailed Fox with white pants, dark green coat, and scarlet cravat. Regal China. Height, 12-1/4"......... **40.00 — 60.00**

9. ☐ **FOX—RE-ISSUED—1967**
As above... **32.50 — 42.50**

JIM BEAM BOTTLES—TROPHY SERIES

6.
$15.00 — $20.00

1.
$10.00 — $15.00

8.
$40.00 —
$60.00

20.
$180.00 -
$220.00

Item, Description, Date	Retail
10. ☐ **HORSE (BLACK)**—1962 Black Horse with white nose blaze, white hooves, and black tail. Regal China. Height, 13-1/2".	25.00 — 30.00
11. ☐ **HORSE (BLACK)**—1962—RE-ISSUED—1967 As above.	22.50 — 27.50

For Complete Listing & Pricing
See "AVON BOTTLES" Section

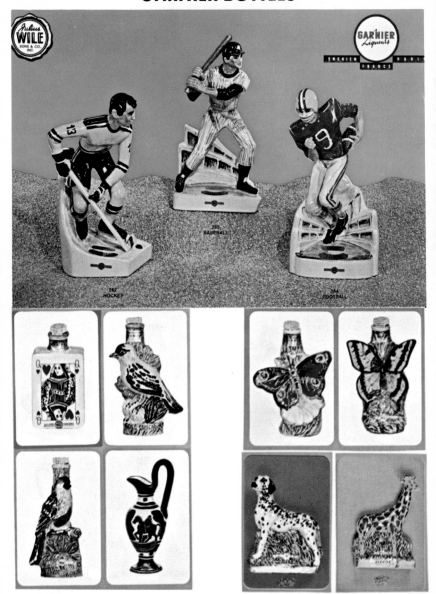

For Complete Listing & Pricing See "GARNIER BOTTLES"

PRESIDENTAL CAMPAIGN SERIES

1 – MC GOVERN & SHRIVER
    (REVERSE)
2 – MC GOVERN & SHRIVER
3 – MC GOVERN & EAGLETON
    (REVERSE)
4 – NIXON & AGNEW
5 – MC GOVERN & EAGLETON

Listing & Prices:
WHEATON - NULINE
SECTION

COLLECTORS' BOTTLES

1 – SKYLAB 1
2 – APOLLO 17
3 – SKYLAB 2
4 – CLARK GABLE
5 – ALEXANDER
    GRAHAM
    BELL
6 – MARK TWAIN
7 – W.C. FIELDS
8 – LYNDON B.
    JOHNSON
9 – HARRY S.
    TRUMAN
10 – HERBERT
    HOOVER
11 – CHRISTMAS 1973

Courtesy:
WHEATON - NULINE,
Millville, N.J.

PANDA

KACHINA DANCER

CLOWN TRAMP

NAMU KILLER WHALE

SKI BOOT

HIGH WHEELER

BULL ELK

TOTEM POLE

BOWLING A STRIKE   U.S.C TROJANS   BUCKING BRONCO

BURMESE ELEPHANT   VERMONT SKIING

MR.
PENGUIN

V.F.W.
75th
ANNIVERSERY

"FIREWATER"
JUG

LIONSTONE BOTTLES

ROSES ON
PARADE

COWGIRL

PEREGRINE
FALCON

Listing & Prices See "LIONSTONE BOTTLES"

THE
PERFESSOR

DANCE
HALL
GIRL

INDIAN
MOTHER
&
PAPOOSE

SCREECH
OWLS

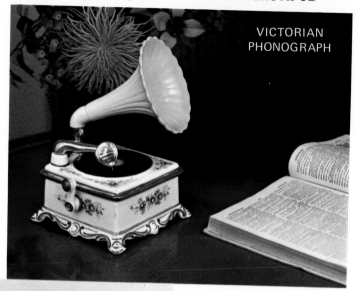

VICTORIAN
PHONOGRAPH

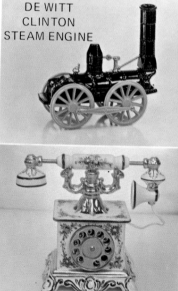

DE WITT
CLINTON
STEAM ENGINE

LOMBARDY SCALES

FRENCH TELEPHONE

For Listing & Pricing See
"FAMOUS FIRSTS" Section

Item, Description, Date   **Retail**

12. ☐ **HORSE (BROWN)** — 1962
Brown Horse with white blaze on nose, black hooves and tail. Regal China. Height, 13-1/2".......................... **22.50 — 28.50**

13. ☐ **HORSE (BROWN)** — 1962 — **RE-ISSUED** — 1967
As above... **18.50 — 24.50**

14. ☐ **HORSE (GREY)** — 1962
Grey Mustang with grey flowing mane and tail. Regal China. Height, 13-1/2". .... **20.00 — 25.00**

15. ☐ **HORSE (GREY)** — 1962 — **RE-ISSUED** — 1967
As above... **18.50 — 24.50**

16. ☐ **JACKALOPE** — 1971
The fabulous Wyoming Jackalope; a rare cross twixt Jackrabbit and Antelope. With the body and ears of the Western Jackrabbit and head and antlers of an Antelope. Golden brown body on "prairie grass" base. Regal China, 14" high..................................... **15.00 — 20.00**

17. ☐ **PHEASANT** — 1960
Ring-necked Pheasant with red-circled eyes, green and blue head, and soft brown plumage perched on a "fence" base. Regal China. Height, 13"........................ **18.00 — 24.00**

18. ☐ **PHEASANT** — 1961
Re-issued also: '63, '66, '67, '68. As above. .... **14.50 — 20.00**

19. ☐ **POODLE** — **GREY & WHITE** — 1970
Both poodles sit up with one paw on a ball. The grey has a green banded ball embossed "PENNY," the white has a blue banded ball. Black eyes, and nose and a gold collar on each. Regal China, 12" high. **16.00 — 22.00**
PAIR

20. ☐ **RAM** — 1958
Stylized Ram in soft tans and browns. Calendar mounted on green base, and a round metal thermometer in the curve of the horn. Regal China. Height, 12-1/2" (without thermometer worth less) .... **180.00 — 220.00**

JIM BEAM BOTTLES—TROPHY SERIES

THE BIRD SERIES (LOCKHART DESIGN)

18.

$14.50 — $20.00

22.

$40.00
—$50.00

24.

$5.50 — $9.50

Item, Description, Date	Retail

21. ☐ **BLUE JAY**—1969
Tones of sky blue on the birds body with black & white markings. Black claws grip "oak tree stump" with acorns & leaves embossed.............................. 5.50 — 9.50

22. ☐ **CARDINAL**—1968 (KENTUCKY CARDINAL)
A bright red bird with a black mask, tail, and markings. Perched on a dark "tree stump" base................. 40.00 — 50.00

23. ☐ **ROBIN**—1969
An Olive grey bird with a soft red breast, dark toned head and tail. The Robin has a yellow beak and stands on a "tree trunk" with an embossed branch and leaves. Regal China, 13-1/2" high....................................... 5.50 — 9.50

24. ☐ **WOODPECKER**—1969
Bright glazed red head, white breast and markings, black beak and dark wings and tail. "Woody" grips a "tree trunk" base. Regal China, 13-1/2" high. .... 5.50 — 9.50

**All Prices are for Empty Bottles in Mint Condition,
Complete with Handles, Spouts & Stoppers.**

Item, Date, Description   Retail

1. ☐ **DONKEY & ELEPHANT BOXERS—1964 ***
The G.O.P. elephant has blue trunks with red stripes,
white shirt and black top hat with stars on the band.
His gloves are brown.
   The donkey has red trunks with a blue stripe, and
black shoes and top hat. The hat band is white with
red and blue stars..   **32.50 — 40.00
PAIR**

2. ☐ **DONKEY & ELEPHANT CLOWNS—1968 †**
Both are dressed in polka dot clown costumes.
Elephant has red ruffs and cuffs, with blue dots.
Donkey has blue with red dots. Yellow styrofoam
straw hat, and clown shoes on both elephant and
donkey. Their heads are the stoppers. Regal China,
12" high..   **16.00 — 20.00
PAIR**

3. ☐ **DONKEY & ELEPHANT CAMPAIGNERS—1960**
Elephant is dressed in a brown coat, blue vest with
a gold chain, he carries a placard stating "REPUBLI-
CANS—1960" and the State where the bottle is sold.
Donkey is dressed in black coat, tan vest and grey
pants. His placard reads "DEMOCRATS—1960" and
State where sold. Regal China, 12" high.....................   **32.50 — 40.00
PAIR**

4. ☐ **DONKEY & ELEPHANT ASH TRAYS—1956**
They were made to be used as either ash trays w/
coaster, or book ends. The stylized Elephant and
Donkey heads are in lustrous grey china. The "Beam"
label fits the round coaster section of the bottle.
Regal China, 10" high...   **32.50 — 40.00
PAIR**

***EACH — $16.00 — $20.00
+EACH — $ 8.00 — $10.00**

PRICES
ARE
RETAIL

PAIR
$32.50 — $40.00

EACH
$16.00 — $20.00

1.

PAIR
$16.00 — $20.00

EACH
$8.00 — $10.00

2.

A.B.P. — Average Buying Price 40% — 60% of Retail Price.

All prices shown are approximate for Mint Condition

Item, Description, Date   **Retail**

1. ☐ **ALASKA — 1958**
   Star-shaped bottle in turquoise blue and gold. Symbols of Alaskan industry in corners of star, gold "49" in center. Regal China. Height, 9-1/2"................$ **75.00 — 90.00**

2. ☐ **ALASKA — 1964-65, re-issued.**
   As above..   **65.00 — 80.00**

3. ☐ **ARIZONA — 1968/69**
   Embossed scene of Canyon, river, and cactus in blue, yellow and brown, "THE GRAND CANYON STATE". "ARIZONA" in gold. Map embossed on stopper. Reverse has scenes of Arizona life. Regal China, 12" high..   **4.00 — 6.00**

4. ☐ **COLORADO — 1959**
   Light turquoise showing pioneers crossing the rugged mountains with snow capped peaks in background. "COLORADO" and "1859-1959" in gold. Bottle has a leather thong. Regal China. Height, 10-3/4"................   **45.00 — 60.00**

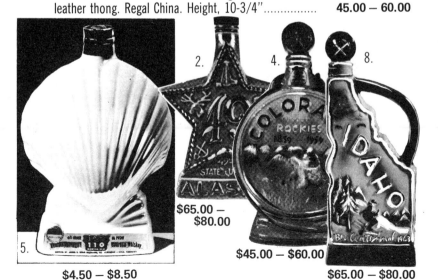

2.

4.

8.

$65.00 — $80.00

5.

$45.00 — $60.00

$4.50 — $8.50

$65.00 — $80.00

Item, Description, Date	Retail

5. ☐ **FLORIDA SHELL—1968/69**
Shell-shaped bottles made in 2 colors, mother of pearl, and iridescent bronze, for a shimmering luminescent effect. Reverse has map of Florida, and "SEA SHELL HEADQUARTERS OF THE WORLD." Regal China, 9-3/4" high. .... **4.50 — 8.50**

6. ☐ **HAWAII—1959-60**
Tribute to 50th State. Panorama of Hawaiian scenes; palm trees, the blue pacific, outriggers, and surfboarders. Gold "50" in star. Regal China.
Height, 8-1/2" .... **55.00 — 70.00**

7. ☐ **HAWAII—Re-issued—1967**
As above. .... **42.50 — 60.00**

8. ☐ **IDAHO—1963**
Bottle in the shape of a State of Idaho. Skiier on slope on one side and farmer on other side. Pick & shovel on stopper. Regal China. Height, 12-1/4"..................... **65.00 — 80.00**

9. ☐ **KANSAS—1960-61**
Round, yellow-toned bottle shows harvesting of wheat on one side, and "KANSAS 1861-1961 CENTENNIAL" embossed in gold. On the other side, symbols of the modern age with aircraft, factories, oil wells, and dairies. Leather thong. Regal China. Height, 11-3/4". **60.00 — 75.00**

10. ☐ **KENTUCKY BLACK HEAD & BROWN HEAD—1967 ***
The stopper is a horse's head, some are made in brown, some black. State map on bottle shows products of Kentucky. Tobacco, distilling, farming, coal, oil, and industries. Regal China, 11-1/2 high.
BLACK HEAD... **10.00 — 18.00**
BROWN HEAD... **10.00 — 20.00**

White Head — $16.00 — $24.00

All prices shown are for Mint Condition

Item, Date, Description	Retail

11. ☐ **MONTANA—1964**
Tribute to gold miners. Names of "ALDER GULCH." LAST CHANCE GULCH, BANNACK" and "MONTANA 1864 GOLDEN YEARS CENTENNIAL 1964" are embossed on bottle. Regal China. Height, 11-1/2"............ **85.00 — 120.00**

12. ☐ **NEBRASKA—1967**
Round bottle bears the words, "WHERE THE WEST BEGINS" with a picture of a covered wagon drawn by oxen. Regal china, 12-1/4" high. .... **10.00 — 14.50**

13. ☐ **NEVADA—1964**
Circular silver and grey bottle, with silver "NEVADA", bearing outline of State with embossed mountain peaks, forests, and a factory. Reverse is a miner & donkey. Regal china. Height, 11-1/2". Same bottle used by Harolds Club & Harrah's .... **55.00 — 70.00**

$16.00 — $24.00

10.

11.

12.

$85.00 — $120.00

$10.00 — $14.50

14. ☐ **NEW JERSEY GREY—1963-64**
    Grey map of State filled with embossed colorful
    fruits, vegetables, and flowers, set on pyramid shaped
    bottle. "NEW JERSEY—THE GARDEN STATE, FARM
    & INDUSTRY" in gold. Regal china. Height, 13-1/2".   **65.00 — 80.00**

15. ☐ **NEW JERSEY—YELLOW—1963-64**
    Same as above, yellow toned map of New Jersey......... **55.00 — 70.00**

16. ☐ **NEW HAMPSHIRE—1967-68**
    Blue-tone bottle in the shape of the state. Decal of
    state motto, seal, flower and bird. Stopper in the shape
    of "The Old Man of the Mountain". Regal China,
    13-1/2" high. .... **7.50 — 10.50**

17. ☐ **NORTH DAKOTA—1964**
    Embossed memorial picture of a pioneer family in
    NORTH DAKOTA—75" embossed in gold in banner.
    Yellows, greens and browns. Regal china. Height, 11-3/4 " **95.00 — 120.00**
    "NORTH DAKOTA—75" embossed in gold in banner.

13.

14.
15.

16.

$55.00 — $70.00 $65.00 — $80.00

$7.50 — $10.50

$8.50 – $12.50 $12.50 – $16.50

24.

20.

Item, Description & Date	Retail

18. ☐ **OHIO—1966**

Bottle in shape of State. One side bears State seal, other side has pictures of State industries. Regal china. Height, 10"... **12.00 — 16.00**

19. ☐ **OREGON—1959**

Green-tone bottle to honor Centennial of the state. Depicting famous scenery on both sides. Two beavers on bottle neck. Regal china. Height, 8-3/4"................. **40.00 — 50.00**

20. ☐ **PENNSYLVANIA—1967**

Keystone-shaped bottle in blue tones. Decal of state seal "HISTORIC PENNSYLVANIA—THE KEYSTONE STATE" on front. Reverse: scenes of history and industry. Keystone stopper with gold "1776". Regal china. 11-1/2" high.. **8.50 — 12.50**

A.B.P. — Average Buying Price · 40% to 60% of Retail.

Item, Description, Date	Retail

21. ☐ **WEST VIRGINIA — 1963**
Waterfall scene in blue and green with gold embossed "BLACKWATER FALLS — WEST VIRGINIA — 1863 CENTENNIAL 1963" surrounded by scrolled "picture frame" bottle. Reverse: State bird-red cardinal and gold "35" in a star. Bear's head and maple leaf on each side of stopper.. **120.00 — 140.00**

22. ☐ **SOUTH DAKOTA — MOUNT RUSHMORE — 1969-70**
The faces of Washington, Jefferson, T. Roosevelt, and Lincoln are shown in relief in white with blue sky and green forest. This landmark is called the Mount Rushmore National Memorial. Reverse: Scroll with information about Memorial. Regal china. 10-1/2" high. **4.50 — 6.50**

23. ☐ **WYOMING — 1965**
An embossed bucking bronco with a cowboy "Hangin' On" with mountains in the background, and "WYOMING — THE EQUALITY STATE" in gold on tones of blue & tan. A rectangle shape on a pyramid, with a gold buffalo on the stopper. Reverse: State bird, flower, and Old Faithful. Regal china. 12" high............. **65.00 — 80.00**

24. ☐ **ILLINOIS — 1968**
The log cabin birth place of "Abe Lincoln" embossed on front, oak tree, and banner with 21 stars (21st state) and "Land of Lincoln". Made to honor the Sesquicentennial 1818-1968 of Illinois, home of the James B. Beam Distilling Company. Regal China, 12-3/4" high. .... **12.50 — 16.50**

25. ☐ **SOUTH CAROLINA — 1970**... **6.50 — 9.50**

26. ☐ **MAINE — 1970** .... **6.50 — 9.50**

27. ☐ **HAWAII — 1971** .... **8.50 — 12.50**

*See Regal China Specialties for Michigan & Delaware State Bottles.

All prices shown are for Mint Condition

Item, Date, Description   **Retail**

1. ☐ **BLUE CHERUB—1960**
   Blue and white decanter with heavily embossed fig-
   ures of Cherubs with bow & arrows gold details.
   Scrolls and chain holding Beam Label around neck.
   Regal China. Height, 12-1/2"..................................... **130.00 — 160.00**

2. ☐ **FLOWER BASKET—1961**
   Blue Basket filled with embossed pastel flowers and
   green leaves resting on gold base, gold details and
   stopper. Regal China. Height, 12-1/4"........................ **70.00 — 100.00**

3. ☐ **GOLDEN CHALICE—1961**
   Chalice with grey-blue body, gold accents. Band of
   embossed pastel flowers on the neck. Gold scrolled
   neck and base. Regal China. Height, 12-1/4".............. **70.00 — 100.00**

4. ☐ **GREY CHERUB—1958**
   Checkered design, bordered with scroll work, accent-
   ed with 22 karat gold. 3 embossed cherubs on neck.
   Regal China. Height, 12".. **200.00 — 250.00**

1.

$130.00 — $160.00·

2.

$35.00 —
$45.00

$70.00 — $100.00

5.

Item, Date, Description	Retail

5. ☐ MAJESTIC—1966
Royal blue decanter with handle, on a base of golden leaves. Gold scrolled stopper, and lip. Regal China. Height, 14-1/2".. **35.00 — 45.00**

6. ☐ MARBLED FANTASY—1965
Decanter on a blue marbled base, set in a cup of gold with a heavy gold ring around the center. Gold lip and handle, blue & gold stopper. Regal China. Height, 15"... **70.00 — 90.00**

7. ☐ ROYAL DI MONTE—1957
Mottled design, black and white bottle. Hand painted with 22 karat gold and bordered in gold. Gold & black stopper. Regal China. Height, 15-1/2"........................ **80.00 — 110.00**

8. ☐ ROYAL GOLD DIAMOND—1964
Diamond-shaped decanter set on a flaring base, all in mottled gold. Gold chain holds label. Regal China. Height, 12"... **50.00 — 65.00**

$70.00 — $90.00 $80.00 — $110.00 $50.00 — $65.00

6.   7.   8.

$60.00 — $80.00

$70.00 — $90.00

$125.00 — $150.00

Item, Description, Date	Retail

9. ☐ **ROYAL GOLD ROUND**—1956
Mottled with 22 karat gold, in classic round shape with graceful pouring spout, and curved handle. Gold neck chain holds label. Regal China. Height, 12".. **125.00 — 150.00**

10. ☐ **ROYAL PORCELAIN**—1955
Gleaming black decanter, tapered with a large flared pouring lip, white stopper, gold cord & tassel. Regal China. Height, 14-1/2".. **250.00 — 300.00**

11. ☐ **ROYAL ROSE**—1963
Decanter, gold embossed with hand painted roses on a background of soft blue, gold spout, stopper base & handle. Regal China. Height, 17"...................... **60.00 — 80.00**

12. ☐ **TAVERN SCENE**—1959
Two "beer stein" tavern scenes are embossed on sides, framed in wide gold band on this round decanter. Regal China. Height, 11-1/2"............................ **70.00 — 90.00**

**All Prices are for Empty Bottles in Mint Condition,
Complete with Handles, Spouts & Stoppers.**

Item, Description, Date	Retail

1. ☐ **IVORY ASH TRAY—1955**
Designed for a dual purpose, as a bottle, and as an ash tray. Bottle lies flat with cigarette grooves and round coaster seat. Ivory color. Regal China, 12-3/4" high.. **22.00 — 28.50**

2. ☐ **MUSICIANS ON A WINE CASK—1964**
"Old time" tavern scene: musicians, guitar and accordian, embossed on cask-shaped embossed bottle. Wooden barrel effect, and "wood" base. Grey china color. Regal China, 9-3/4" high. .... **7.00 — 10.00**

3. ☐ **NEW YORK WORLD'S FAIR—1964**
The emblem of the N.Y. World's Fair of 1964—the Unisphere forms the shape of this bottle. Blue tone oceans, grey continents crossed by space flight routes. Emblem embossed in gold "1964 WORLD'S FAIR—1965". Stopper has Unisphere. Regal China, 11-1/2" high. .... **15.00 — 20.00**

4. ☐ **SEATTLE WORLD'S FAIR—1962**
"The Space Needle" as this bottle is known embossed in gold on one side, "CENTURY 21" on the other. Pylon shaped with color scenes of fruit, airplanes over mountains, salmon, etc. Stopper is the Fair's revolving restaurant. Regal China, 13-1/2" high. **18.00 — 24.50**

5. ☐ **GREEN CHINA JUG—1965**
Deep mottled green china jug, with embossed "PUSSY WILLOW" branches and buds on side. Solid handle. Regal China, 12-1/2" high. .... **7.50 — 12.50**

A.B.P. — Average Buying Price - 40% to 60% of Retail Price.

$4.50 — $8.50

$7.50 — $12.50

$3.50 — $4.50
Retail

Item, Date, Description

6. ☐ **REDWOOD** — 1967
Pyramid shaped bottle Coast Redwoods embossed on front in tones of brown and green. "REDWOOD EMPIRE OF CALIFORNIA" lettered below tree. Reverse: scenes of Redwood country. Regal China, 12-3/4" high.. **7.50 — 12.50**

7. ☐ **YOSEMITE** — 1967
Oval shaped bottle with scenes from the Park, and trees, embossed on the front. "YOSEMITE CALIFORNIA" lettered on front. Gold pine tree on stopper. **4.50 — 8.50**

8. ☐ **BLUE DAISY** — 1967
Also known as "ZIMMERMAN BLUE DAISY". Light blue with embossed daisies and leaves around bottle. Background resembles flower basket. .... **4.50 — 8.50**

9. ☐ **GREY SLOT MACHINE** — 1968-69 *
The famous "HAROLDS CLUB SLOT MACHINE" in tones of grey and tan. Gold pinwheel and black "H" on front. Regal China, 10" high. .... **3.50 — 7.50**

*Blue Slot Machine—$15.00 — $20.00

Item, Date, Description	Retail

10. ☐ PONY EXPRESS

Clearly embossed figure of horse and Pony Express Rider with "SACRAMENTO, CALIF.—OCTOBER 1861" and "ST. JOSEPH, MO.—APRIL 1860" and stars around figure. Reverse: Map of the Pony Express route. Yellow & brown tones. .... **3.50 — 7.50**

11. ☐ CABLE CAR—1968/69

A grey-green bottle in the form of a San Francisco Cable Car, complete with doors, windows and wheels. A gold label with "Van Ness Ave., CALIFORNIA & MARKET STREETS" in black on one end, "POWELL & MASON STREETS" on the side. The stopper is the side. The stopper is the front light. Regal China, 4-1/2" high, 7" long.. **4.50 — 8.50**

12. ☐ ANTIQUE TRADER—1968/69

The widely read ANTIQUE TRADER weekly newspaper of the trade, forms this bottle with the front page clearly shown in black and red, along side the "1968 NATIONAL DIRECTORY OF ANTIQUE DEALERS" both are on a black base. Regal China, 10-1/2" high. **4.50 — 8.50**

$3.50 — $7.50

10.

11.

$4.50 — $8.50

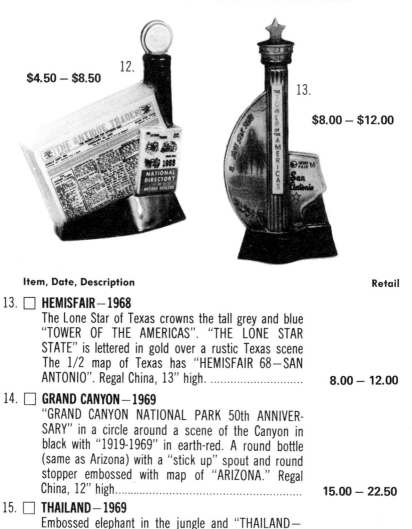

12.

$4.50 — $8.50

13.

$8.00 — $12.00

Item, Date, Description	Retail

13. ☐ HEMISFAIR—1968
The Lone Star of Texas crowns the tall grey and blue "TOWER OF THE AMERICAS". "THE LONE STAR STATE" is lettered in gold over a rustic Texas scene The 1/2 map of Texas has "HEMISFAIR 68—SAN ANTONIO". Regal China, 13" high. .... **8.00 — 12.00**

14. ☐ GRAND CANYON—1969
"GRAND CANYON NATIONAL PARK 50th ANNIVERSARY" in a circle around a scene of the Canyon in black with "1919-1969" in earth-red. A round bottle (same as Arizona) with a "stick up" spout and round stopper embossed with map of "ARIZONA." Regal China, 12" high.. **15.00 — 22.50**

15. ☐ THAILAND—1969
Embossed elephant in the jungle and "THAILAND— A NATION OF WONDERS" on the front. Reverse: A map of Thailand and a dancer. Regal China, 12-1/2" high.. **3.50 — 6.50**

Item, Date, Description	Retail

16. ☐ **RUIDOSO DOWNS**—1968-69 *
A round decanter with a unique "horsehead" stopper. Embossed silver horseshoe, branding iron and cowboy hat, "RUIDOSO DOWNS—NEW MEXICO, WORLD'S RICHEST HORSE RACE" on front. Reverse: Red, white and blue emblem. The bottle is known in "Pointed & Flat Ears." Regal China, 12-3/4" high.................. **25.00 — 35.00**

17. ☐ **LAS VEGAS**—1969
This bottle was also used for CUSTOMER SPECIALS— CASINO SERIES. "Almond" shaped with gold embossed "LAS VEGAS" in a banner, and scenes of Nevada, and a gambling montage. Reverse: Hoover Dam and Lake Mead. Regal China, 12-1/2" high............................... **4.00 — 6.00**

18. ☐ **CHURCHILL DOWNS—RED ROSES**—1969-70
"CHURCHILL DOWNS—HOME OF THE 95th KENTUCKY DERBY" is embossed in gold on the front, around the main paddock building. The shell-shaped bottle comes with both red roses framing the scene. Reverse: "ARISTEDES", 1st Derby winner in 1875, on a decal. Regal China, 10-3/4" high. .... **7.50 — 9.50**

19. ☐ **CHURCHILL DOWNS—PINK ROSES**—1969-70
Same as above, pink embossed roses......................... **4.50 — 8.50**

20. ☐ **BELL SCOTCH**—1970
Tan center, gold base, brown top with coat-of-arms of Arthur Bell & Sons on front. Bottle is in the shape of a large hand-bell. Regal China, 10-1/2" high........... **8.50 — 12.50**

21. ☐ **DEL WEBB MINT**—1970 †
A large gold "400" and "DEL WEBB'S LAS VEGAS," embossed under crossed checkered flags. Stopper is gold dune buggy. Checkered flags on edge of bottle. "MINT" on front for the Vegas Hotel that originally had the bottle. Regal China, 13" high................. **10.00 — 20.00**

*Flat Ears—$3.50 — $8.50
+Motorcycle Stopper—$10.00 — $20.00

**Prices are for Empty Bottles in Mint
Condition with Tops, Holders, Handles & Labels**

PRICES ARE
RETAIL

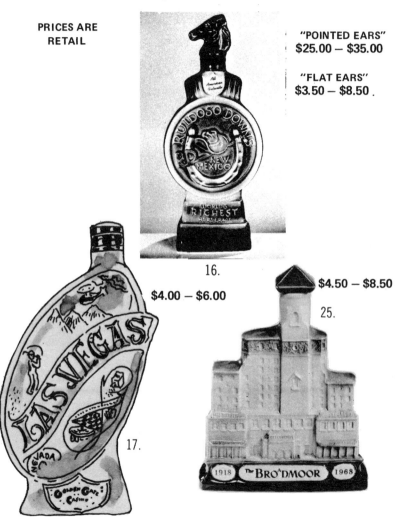

"POINTED EARS"
$25.00 — $35.00

"FLAT EARS"
$3.50 — $8.50

16.

$4.00 — $6.00

$4.50 — $8.50

25.

17.

Item, Date, Description	Retail

22. ☐ **SUBMARINE REDFIN—1970**
Embossed submarine on ocean-blue background. MANITOWOC SUBMARINE MEMORIAL ASSOCIATION" in black. Round stopper, with map of Wisconsin. Regal China, 11-1/2" high...................................... **3.50 — 6.50**

23. ☐ ***HOFFMAN—1969-70**
The bottle is in the shape of "HARRY HOFFMAN LIQUOR STORE" with the Rocky Mountains in the background. Beam bottles, and "SKI COUNTRY— USA" are in the windows. Reverse: embossed mountain & ski slopes with skier. Regal China, 9" high. **3.50 — 6.50**

24. ☐ **PONDEROSA—1969**
The home of the Cartwrights of "Bonanza" TV fame. A replica of the Ponderosa Ranch log cabin in brown tones. Reverse: Lake Tahoe. Bottles with green lined box are worth more. Regal China, 7-1/2" high, 10" wide.. **6.50 — 12.50**

25. ☐ ***BROADMOOR HOTEL—1968**
To celebrate the 50th Anniversary of this famous hotel in Colorado Springs, Colorado, Beam issued this bottle replica complete with details of windows, doors, roof tiles and tower capped with a "roof" stopper. The base bears the legend "1918—THE BROADMOOR—1968" in white ovals on a black background... **4.50 — 8.50**

26. ☐ **NEW HAMPSHIRE EAGLE BOTTLE—1971**
Under the New Hampshire banner on this beautiful Regal China bottle, a solid gold eagle against a blue field stands as a proud reminder of the original symbol, a great, carved wooden bird, which was placed atop the New Hampshire State House when it was built in 1818. On the back of the bottle, beneath the slogan "Granite State," a decal recounts the history of the first New Hampshire Eagle, Height, 12-1/2" **40.00 — 60.00**

* This bottle is also classified as a CUSTOMER SPECIALTY".

JIM BEAM BOTTLES
REGAL CHINA SPECIALTIES

27.

$10.00 — $15.00

29.

28.

125

$8.50 — $12.50

16.

Item, Description, Date	Retail

27. ☐ V.F.W. BOTTLE—1971
A handsome Regal China creation designed to commemorate the 50th anniversary of the Department of Indiana V.F.W. This proclamation is made on the neck of the bottle, in a plaque in the shape of the state of Indiana, over a striking reproduction of the medal insignia of the V.F.W. Height, 9-3/4". .... **7.50 — 12.50**

28. ☐ JACKALOPE BOTTLE—1971
The fabulous Wyoming Jackalope; a rare cross twixt Jackrabbit and Antelope. The whimsical Regal China sculpture features the body and ears of the Western Jackrabbit and the head and antlers of an Antelope. Height, 14"... **8.50 — 12.50**

29. ☐ BEAM'S NATIONAL ASSOCIATION CONVENTION BOTTLE—1971
Created to commemorate the occasion of the 1st National Convention of the National Association of Jim Beam Bottle and Specialty Clubs hosted by the Rocky Mountain Club, Denver, Colorado, June, 1971. Height, 11"... **10.00 — 15.00**

Item, Description, Date   Retail

30. ☐ **HANSEL AND GRETEL BOTTLE**—1971
The forlorn, lost waifs from the Brothers Grimm's
beloved fable "Hansel and Gretel" are depicted on the
front of this charming and beautiful Regal China bottle. Above them, the words "GERMANY...LAND OF
HANSEL AND GRETEL" stand out in gold.
Height, 10-1/4"..   **8.50 — 10.50**

31. ☐ **KAISER INTERNATIONAL OPEN BOTTLE**—1971
This handsome Regal China creation commemorates
the Fifth Annual Kaiser International Open Golf Tournament to be played this year at Silverado in California's beautiful Napa Valley. The stopper is a "golf
ball' decorated with the Kaiser International Open
logo suspended over a red tee. The logo is repeated,
in gold against a blue field, in the center of the front
panel and is surrounded by a ring of decorated golf
balls. Listed on the back are the particulars of the
tournament. Height, 11-1/4"...................................   **7.50 — 9.50**

32. ☐ **MINT 400**-1971
The annual Del Webb Mint 400 is commemorated
this year by a striking Regal China sculpture which
captures the feeling of the desert, surrounded by
mountains, beneath a blue Las Vegas sky—Home of
one of the racing world's most grueling off-road
events. The bottle's most prominent feature is the
gold-painted motorcycle racer on the stopper. Black
and white checkered flags are crossed on the front
above large gold letters. Black and white checks
edge the sides. A decal on the reverse details infor-
mation about the race. Height, 8-1/4"......................   **10.00 — 20.00**

33. ☐ **SAHARA INVITATIONAL BOTTLE**—1971
Introduced in honor of the Del Webb 1971 Sahara
Invitational Pro-Am Golf Tournament. The prom-
inant feature of this Regal China bottle is a large "Del
Webb Pro-Am 1971" golf ball atop a red tee on the
face. Listed on the back are the winners of this annual
contest from 1958 through 1970. Height, 12"............   **8.50 — 12.50**

30.

$8.50 — $10.50

$7.50 — $9.50

31.

32.

$8.50 — $12.50

33.

34. $10.00 — $20.00

PRICES
ARE RETAIL

$8.50 — $10.50

Item, Description, Date	Retail

34. ☐ WISCONSIN MUSKIE BOTTLE—1971
This striking Regal China sculpture pays tribute to the state fish of Wisconsin, as the mighty Muskellunge dances on his powerful tail in a burst of gold flecked blue water. Height 14".. **8.50 — 10.50**

35. ☐ GREAT CHICAGO FIRE BOTTLE—1971
This historical decanter was created to commemorate the great Chicago fire of 1871, and to salute Mercy Hospital which rendered service to the fire victims. This first hospital of Chicago was started in 1852 by the Sisters of Mercy. The new Mercy Hospital and Medical Center, opened in 1968, is depicted on the reverse side. The front of the bottle shows towering flames engulfing Chicago's waterfront as it appeared on the evening of October 8. 1871. The look of actual flames has been realistically captured in this Regal China masterpiece. Height, 7-1/2"..................... **20.00 — 25.00**

36. ☐ FANTASIA BOTTLE—1971
This tall, delicately hand crafted Regal China decanter is embellished with 22 karat gold and comes packaged in a handsome midnight blue and gold presentation case lined with red velvet. Height, 16-3/4". **15.00 — 20.00**

37. ☐ HAWAIIAN OPEN BOTTLE—1972
Cleverly decorated to simulate a pineapple with the famous "Friendly Skies" logo in gold, this genuine Regal China Bottle honors the 1972 Hawaiian Open Golf Tournament. The reverse side commemorates United Air Lines' 25th year (1972) of air service to Hawaii. The stopper is designed to look like pineapple leaves. Height, 10".. **9.50 — 12.50**

All Prices are for Empty Bottles in Mint Condition, Complete with Handles, Spouts & Stoppers.

$20.00 – $25.00

$15.00 – $20.00

PRICES
ARE
RETAIL

35.

36.

$9.50 – $12.50

38.

$12.50 – $17.50

37.

Item, Description, Date   Retail

38. ☐ **BING'S 31ST CLAM BAKE BOTTLE—1972**
An inspired Regal China Bottle heavily decorated in gold. The front features a full 3-dimensional reproduction of the famous Pebble Beach, California wind-swept tree overlooking the Pacific Ocean. The back commemorates the 31st Bing Crosby National Pro-Amateur Golf Tournament at the World Famous Pebble Beach course, January, 1972. The stopper is the official seal of the Tourney. Height, 10-3/4".   **12.50 — 17.50**

39. ☐ **DELAWARE BLUE HEN BOTTLE—1972**
This diamond shaped bottle, fashioned of genuine hand crafted Regal China commemorates the state of Delaware, "The first state of the Union." The front of the bottle depicts the act of ratification of the Federal Constitution on December 7, 1787. The back shows the Delaware State House, a state map and the famous Twin Bridges..   **8.50 — 12.50**

40. ☐ **MICHIGAN BOTTLE—1972**
The map of the "Great Lakes State" adorns the front of this striking commemorative Regal China bottle. The state flower and the major cities are shown along with an inset plaque of an antique automobile, one of Michigan's traditional symbols. A capsule description of the state, a drawing of the magnificent Mackinac Bridge and the state motto of the "Wolverine State" appear on a scroll on the back. The stopper depicts an antique wooden wheel on one side and a modern automobile wheel on the other. Height, 11-7/8".   **8.00 — 12.00**

41. ☐ **KENTUCKY DERBY BOTTLE—1972**
Designed to commemorate the 98th "Run For The Roses" at Churchill Downs, showing Canonero II, 1971 winner, garlanded with the traditional American Beauty Roses. The reverse side depicts famous Churchill Downs Clubhouse in relief and etched in gold. The stopper is a replica of an American Beauty Rose. Height, 11"..   **15.00 — 20.00**

INDIANAPOLIS
SESQUECENTENNIAL

$40.00 — $60.00

42.

LONDON BRIDGE 1971
$5.50 — $8.50

$8.50 — $12.50

**STATE
BOTTLES**

40.

PRICES ARE
RETAIL

$8.00 — $12.00

$8.50 — $12.50

39.

Item, Description, Date   Retail

42. ☐ **TWIN BRIDGES BOTTLE—1971**
Designed to commemorate the largest twin bridge
complex of its kind in the world. The twin bridges
connect Delaware and New Jersey and serve as major
links between key East Coast cities. Handsomely
accented in gold and bearing the sheild of the Twin
Bridges Beam Bottle and Specialty Club, this Regal
China bottle portrays the twin spans on the front and
provides a descriptive story on the back. The stopper
is a replica of the bridge toll house. Height, 10-1/2".   **40.00 — 60.00**

43. ☐ **ZIMMERMAN'S THE PEDDLER BOTTLE—1971**
This unulsual bottle in genuine Regal China was made
in honor of Zimmerman's, the world's largest liquor
store, in Chicago, Illinois. Max Zimmerman, "The
Peddler" himself, who specializes in personal service
and works the counters of the store himself, is famous
for his Stetson hat and cowboy boots. He is affec-
tionately known in the trade as "Max the Hat." Zimmerman's has always been active in merchandising
Beam's collectors' bottles. Height 12".......................   **17.50 — 22.50**

44. ☐ **JIM BEAM ELECTION BOTTLES—1972**
"Pick the winning team." The Democratic donkey and
the G.O.P.'s elephant are depicted in football costumes
atop genuine Regal China footballs in this 1972
version of Beam's famous election bottle series.   **PAIR**
Each is 9-1/2" high..   **25.00 — 30.00**

44. $25.00 —
                                                         $30.00

PRICES ARE RETAIL

JOHN HENRY—1972
$50.00 — $70.00

MILWAUKEE CLUB
1972 ... $40.00 — $60.00

**UNCLE SAM
NATIONAL FOX
1971** ....
$14.50 — $18.50

**ZIMMERMAN
PEDDLER**
1971 ... $17.50 — $22.50

PGA—1971 .... $3.50 — $7.50

PRICES ARE RETAIL

TEXAS RABBIT—1971 ......

$7.50 — $10.50

FIJI ISLAND INDEPENDENCE
$7.50 — $10.50

HYATT HOUSE—1972
$22.50 — $32.50

KENTUCKY DERBY—1972
$15.00 — $20.00

**Prices are for Empty Bottles in Mint
Condition with Tops, Holders, Handles & Labels**

PRICES ARE RETAIL

**GENERAL STARK
1972** .... $18.50 — $22.50

**NEW HAMPSHIRE
EAGLE** $40.00 — $60.00

**BING CROSBY 30th
1971** ...... $3.50 — $6.50

<u>A.B.P.</u>
A DEALERS OFFER OF
40% TO 60% OF RETAIL PRICE
WOULD BE QUITE FAIR.

Retail

45. ☐ **BEAM NATIONAL CONVENTION '72**
This beautiful Regal China creation honors the second annual conventional of the National Association of Jim Beam Bottle and Specialty Clubs, held June 19 through 25 in Anaheim, California. Features as a stopper the national symbol of the Beam Bottle Clubs. Height: 13 inches. . . . .   **16.00 — 20.00**

46. ☐ **TIFFINY POODLE — 1973**
Genuine Regal China bottle created in honor of Tiffiny, the poodle mascot of the National Association of the Jim Beam Bottle & Specialties Clubs. Mr. and Mrs. Milton Campbell, officers of the National Association, are the proud owners of the mascot. . . . .   **10.00 — 15.00**

47. ☐ **RENEE THE FOX — 1974**
This interesting Regal China bottle represents the companion for the International Association of Jim Beam bottle and specialty group's mascot. Renee the Fox is the life long companion of Rennie the Fox. . . . .   **12.00 — 16.00**

48. ☐ **CHERRY HILLS COUNTRY CLUB**   Retail

A very handsome genuine Regal China bottle, commemorating the 50th anniversary of the famous Cherry Hills Country Club. Located in Denver, Colorado, Cherry Hills has hosted some of the top professional golf tournaments. The front of the bottle illustrates the many activities available at Cherry Hills, while the name of the club circles the bottle in luxurious 22 carat gold. . . . . **8.00 — 12.00**

49. ☐ **BING CROSBY NATIONAL PRO-AM — 1973**

The fourth in its series honoring the Bing Crosby Gold Tournament, Genuine Regal China Bottle in luxurious fired 22 carat gold with a white stopper, featuring replicas of the famous Crosby hat, pipe and golf club. . . . . **15.00 — 20.00**

50. ☐ **14TH ANNUAL DESERT CLASSIC — 1973**

The first Genuine Regal China Bottle created in honor of the Bob Hope Desert Classic, an annual charity fund raising golf tournament. A profile of Bob Hope is shown on the front side, with a golf ball and tee perched at the tip of his nose. . . . . **16.00 — 20.00**

51. ☐ **BOB HOPE DESERT CLASSIC — 1974**

Retail

This Regal China creation honors the famous Bob Hope Desert Classic. Bob Hope silhouette and the sport of golf that he is so well known is a color feature of the bottle. .... **15.00 — 20.00**

52. ☐ **U.S. OPEN — 1972**

Whimsically depicts Uncle Sam's traditional hat holding a full set of golf clubs. This charming Regal China creation honors the U.S. Open Golf Tourney at the famous Pebble Beach course in California. Height - 10½ inches. .... **12.00 — 16.00**

53. ☐ **HAWAIIAN OPEN — 1973**

The second bottle created in honor of the United Hawaiian Open Golf Classic. Of genuine Regal China designed in the shape of a golf ball featuring a pineapple and airplane on the front. .... **10.00 — 15.00**

Retail

54. ☐ **HAWAIIAN OPEN — 1974**
Genuine Regal China Bottle commemorating the
famous 1974 Hawaiian Open Golf Classic. . . . .   **8.50 — 12.50**

55. ☐ **FIESTA BOWL —1973**
The second bottle created for the Fiesta Bowl. This
bottle is made of genuine Regal China, featuring a
football player on the front side. . . . .   **12.00 — 18.00**

56.   57.   58.

Retail

56. ☐ **NEBRASKA FOOTBALL — 1972**
    This strikingly handsome genuine Regal China
    creation commemorates the University of
    Nebraska's national championship football team of
    1970-1971 season. The stopper features an exact
    likeness of Bob Devaney, the "Cornhuskers" head
    coach. Height - 8¾ inches. . . . .   **8.50 — 12.50**

57. ☐ **FOOTBALL HALL OF FAME — 1972**
    This bottle is a reproduction of the striking new
    Professional Football Hall of Fame building,
    executed in genuine Regal China. The stopper is in
    the shape of half a football. Height - 9¾ inches. . . . **12.00 — 16.00**

58. ☐ **SMITH'S NORTH SHORE CLUB –1972**
    Commemorating Smith's North Shore Club, at
    Crystal Bay, Lake Tahoe. This striking genuine
    Regal China bottle features theanchor, symbol of
    the club and is topped by a giant golden golf ball.
    Height: 12 inches. . . . . **22.50 — 27.50**

59. **60.** **61.**

Retail

59. ☐ FRESH WATER FISHING HALL OF FAME — 1973

Created in honor of the National Fresh Water Fishing Hall of Fame, located in Hayward, Wisconsin, scheduled for completion in 1974. A genuine Regal China creation designed after the Largemouth Bass. Its stopper features the Official Seal of the Hall of Fame. .... **8.50 — 12.50**

60. ☐ BOYS TOWN OF ITALY — 1973

A handsome genuine Regal China bottle created in honor of the Boys Town of Italy. This home for Italian orphans began after World War II. The bottle features a map of Italy, showing the various provinces of that country. .... **8.00 — 12.00**

61. ☐ GERMANY BOTTLE — WEISBADEN 1973

This bottle, of genuine Regal China, depicts a map of the famous Rhine wine-growing regions of Germany. Special attention is given to the heart of this wine country at Wiesbaden. .... **8.00 — 12.00**

62.   **63.**   **64.**

Retail

62. ☐ **PONDEROSA RANCH TOURIST — 1972**
Commemorating the one millionth tourist to the
Ponderosa Ranch. This horseshoe shaped bottle of
genuine Regal China features the Ponderosa Pine
and "P" symbol that have made the ranch famous.
The stopper is a traditional ten gallon hat, made
famous by Dan Blocker. Height: 11 inches. . . . . .   **16.00 — 20.00**

63. ☐ **ST. LOUIS STATUE — 1972**
This handsome Regal China bottle features the
famous statue of St. Louis on horseback atop its
pedestal base. The entire statue is fired gold. The
back bears the inscription, Greater St. Louis Area
Beam and Specialties Club. Height: 13¼ inches. . .   **20.00 — 25.00**

64. ☐ **PEARL HARBOR MEMORIAL — 1972**
Honoring the Pearl Harbor Survivors Association,
this handsome genuine Regal China bottle is
emblazoned with the motto: "REMEMBER PEARL
HARBOR — KEEP AMERICA ALERT". The
stopper features the official seal of the armed
services that were present December 7, 1941 —
Army, Navy, Marine Corps., and Coast Guard. The
stopper is set off by an American eagle. 11½ inches
tall . . . .   **12.00 — 16.00**

65. ☐ **AHEPA 50TH ANNIVERSARY — 1972**   Retail

This striking Regal China bottle was designed in honor of AHEPA'S (AMERICAN HELLENIC EDUCATIONAL PROGRESSIVE ASSOCIATION) 50th anniversary. The Order's anniversary logo is reproduced on the front. Current officers listed on the back. The "Greek Key" design appears on both the bottle itself and on the stopper which is a hollow vase. The bottle's neck is a traditional Greek column. Height: 12 inches. . . . .   **12.00 — 16.00**

66. ☐ **PERMIAN BASIN OIL SHOW — 1972**

This dramatic genuine Regal China bottle is fashioned after an oil derrick and its attendant buildings. Commemorates the Permian Basin Oil Show in Odessa, Texas, October 18 through 21, 1972. The building is inscribed: The E.E. "Pop" Harrison No. 1 well. The back of the "flag" says "The oil industry provides energy, enterprise, employment for the nation". The stopper is fashioned in the shape of the logo for the Oil Field Workers Show with their motto' "let's go." Height: 13 inches. . . . .   **8.50 — 13.50**

67. ☐ **SEAFAIR TROPHY RACE — 1972**

This dramatic genuine Regal China creation commemorates the Seattle Seafair Trophy Race, August 6, 1972 and features an unlimited hydroplane at speed with picturesque Mt. Ranier in the background. Height: 11½ inches. . . . .   **9.50 — 13.50**

68.   **69.**   **70.**

68. ☐ **PORTLAND ROSE FESTIVAL — 1972**   Retail

To commemorate the 64th Portland Oregon Rose Festival which began in 1889. The Regal China bottle is encompassed in a garland of red roses which is commemorative of the oldest and largest rose show in America. On the reverse side there is a brief description of the festival with the very poignant line, "For You A Rose In Portland Grows." Height: 10¼ inches. . . . .   **8.50 — 12.50**

69. ☐ **MINT '400' — 1973**

Commemorating the 1973 running of the famous Del Webb Desert Rallye, the Mint '400'. An exciting bottle created in 22 carat gold with a gold racing helmet as its stopper. . . . .   **7.00 — 9.00**

70. ☐ **ROCKY MARCIANO —1973**

A handsome Genuine Regal China Bottle in honor of Rocky Marciano, the world's only undefeated boxing champion. The bottle takes the shape of a rock, with a likeness of Rocky Marciano on the front. The back of the bottle features Marciano's complete professional record of 49 fights, all victories, 43 knockouts and 6 decisions. . . . .   **8.50 — 12.50**

71.   **72.**   **73.**

Retail

71. ☐ **FIESTA BOWL — 1973**
The second bottle created for the Fiesta Bowl. This
bottle is made of genuine Regal China, featuring a
football player on the front side. . . . .   **12.00 — 16.00**

72. ☐ **AKRON RUBBER CAPITAL — 1973**
A unique Regal China Creation honoring Akron,
Ohio, The Rubber producing Capital of the World.
This creation is in the shape of an automobile tire,
and features a Mag Wheel . . . in the center of the
wheel bears the inscription —— Rubber Capital Jim
Beam Bottle Club. . . . .   **8.50 — 12.50**

73. ☐ **SHRINER'S TEMPLE '72**
This beautiful Regal China bottle features the
traditional symbols of Moila Temple —— the
scimitar, star and crescent, the fez and the
pyramid; and the stopper is the head of a Sphinx.
This bottle is unique in that it features three
simulated precious stones, two of them in the
handle of the sword and the third is the center
point of the star. Height - 11½ inches. . . . .   **27.50 — 32.50**

74.

75.

74. ☐ **CLINT EASTWOOD – 1973**
A handsome genuine Regal China bottle, commemorating the Clint Eastwood Invitational Celebrity Tennis Tournament held in Pebble Beach. The bottle features two tennis rackets across the front, while the stopper features an exact likeness of Clint Eastwood. Two ribbons adorn the front of the bottle; one with stars on a field of blue; the other in red with the name of the tournament emblazoned in 22 carat gold. . . . .   **6.50 – 8.50**

75. ☐ **BEAM'S KING KAMEHAMEHA –1972**
A replica of the famous King Kamehameha statue, this genuine Regal China Bottle has been designed to commemorate the 100th Anniversary of the celebration of King Kamehameha Day. A hero of the Hawaiian people, King Kamehameha is credited for uniting the Hawaiian Islands. . . . .   **12.50 – 16.50**

76.   77.   78.

Retail

76. ☐ **KOALA BEAR — 1973**

The Koala Bear, the native animal of Australia. A genuine Regal China creation. The bottle features two Koala Bears on a tree stump, the top of the stump is its pourer, with the name Australia across the front of the bottle.................... **10.00 — 15.00**

77. ☐ **EMMETT KELLY –1973**

A delightful Genuine Regal China creation. An exact likeness of the original Emmett Kelly, as sad-faced Willie the Clown, who has captivated and won the hearts of millions of friends over the years from the Big Top to television.............. **9.00 — 12.00**

78. ☐ **PIED PIPER OF HAMELIN — 1974**

This charming bottle of genuine Regal China was especially produced for the United States Armed Forces in Europe as a commemorative of the famous German Legend, the PIED PIPER OF HAMELIN........................... **9.00 — 12.00**

79.   **80.**   **81.**

Retail

79. ☐ **PHI SIGMA KAPPA — 1973
(CENTENNIAL SERIES)**
A regal China Creation commemorating the 100th Anniversary of this National Fraternity . . . . A Fraternity dedicated to the Promotion of Brotherhood, the Stimulation of Scholarship, and the Development of Character. The Fraternity insignia is in silver on a magenta background outlined in white and lavendar. . . . .   **6.50 — 9.50**

80. ☐ **HANNAH DUSTON — 1973**
A beautiful Regal China creation designed after the granite monument erected in her memory on Contoocook Island, in the Merrimack River north of Concord. This was where in 1697 Hannah Duston, her nurse and a young boy made their famous frantic escape from Indians, who held them captive for two weeks. . . . .   **17.00 — 22.00**

81. ☐ **RALPH CENTENNIAL — 1973**
Made of genuine Regal China, this bottle was designed to commemorate the 100th anniversary of the Ralphs Grocery Company in California. The bottle depicts two sides of a coin struck especially for the occasion and an early version of a Ralphs delivery wagon. . . . .   **15.00 — 20.00**

82.

83.

84.

Retail

82. ☐ **FOOTBALL HALL OF FAME BOTTLE — 1972**
This bottle is a reproduction of the striking new
Professional Football Hall of Fame building,
executed in genuine Regal China. The stopper is in
the shape of half a football. 9¾ inches tall. . . . . . .   **9.00 — 12.00**

83. ☐ **BEAM'S I.B.A. — 1973**
A commemorative Regal China bottle honoring the
International Bartenders' Association on the first
International Cocktail Competition in the United
States. . . . .   **12.00 — 16.00**

84. ☐ **VOLKSWAGEN COMMEMORATIVE BOTTLE**
Commemorating the Volkswagen Beetle . . . the
largest selling single production model vehicle in
automotive history. Handcrafted of genuine Regal
China, this unique and exciting bottle will long
remain a memento for bottle collectors the world
over. . . . .   **25.00 — 30.00**

85.

86.

Retail

85. ☐ **CALIFORNIA RETAIL LIQUOR DEALERS ASSOCIATION – 1973**
Made of genuine Regal China, this bottle was designed to commemorate the 20th anniversary of the California Retail Liquor Dealers Association. The bottle depicts the emblem of the association showing a liquor store superimposed on the State of California. . . . .   8.50 – 12.50

86. ☐ **NATIONAL TOBACCO FESTIVAL – 1973**
Regal China bottle commemorating the twenty-fifth anniversary of the National Tobacco Festival. The festival was held in Richmond, Virginia on October 6 through the 13th. On the base of this special bottle, historic data of the growth and development of the tobacco industry is featured . . . the unique closure is the bust of an American Indian. . . . .   9.50 – 12.50

87. ☐ **AMERICAN SAMOA – 1973**
The enchantment of one of America's outside territorial possessions is captured in this genuine Regal China Bottle. The Seal of Samoa signifies friendship, the whip and staff signify authority and power held by the great chiefs. . . . .   9.50 – 12.50

88. **89.** **90.**

Retail

88. ☐ **TRUTH OR CONSEQUENCES FIESTA — 1974**
A ruggedly handsome Regal China bottle in honor of Ralph Edwards' famous Radio and television show and the city of Truth or Consequences, New Mexico. . . . .   **6.50 — 8.50**

89. ☐ **MINNESOTA VIKING — 1973**
A strikingly handsome Regal China creation designed after the famous Viking statue in Alexandria, Minnesota, known as the "Largest Viking in the World." The bottle features a helmet as its stopper. The back depicts a replica of the Kensington Runestone. . . . .   **6.50 — 8.50**

90. ☐ **WASHINGTON — THE EVERGREEN STATE — 1974**
A unique Regal China creation, honoring the state of Washington - The Evergreen State. Contoured to the shape of the state of Washington, this bottle features a dimensional carving of an evergreen on the front. . . . .   **8.50 — 12.50**

91.

92.

Retail

91. ☐ **NEW MEXICO STATEHOOD — 1972**
Commemorating New Mexico's 60 years of statehood. This dramatic genuine Regal China Bottle has been designed to represent the historical Indian Ceremonial Wedding Vase, used through the centuries by the New Mexico Indians in tribal wedding ceremonies.   **8.50 — 12.50**

92. ☐ **OHIO — 1973**
A handsome bottle made of genuine Regal China, created in honor of the 120th Ohio State Fair. . . .   **12.50 — 16.50**

93.

94.

Retail

93. ☐ **BEAM'S EXECUTIVE — 1972**
This elegantly handcrafted REGAL CHINA BOTTLE is heavily embellished with fired 22 carat gold and features a bouquet of tiny flowers about its mid-section. Each bottle comes in its own handsome dark red presentation case lined with velvet. . . . .   **15.00 — 20.00**

94. ☐ **BEAM'S EXECUTIVE — 1973**
An elegantly handcrafted genuine Regal China, heavily embellished with 22 carat gold and features a floral design on the front. Each bottle comes in its own handsome presentation case lined with velvet. . . . .   **15.00 — 20.00**

One of the most collectable, and original line of contemporary bottles are the products of the Ezra Brooks Distilling Company. Originally known as "The Smallest Distillery in Kentucky", this dynamic organization went into collectable bottle production in a big way after the phenomenal success of their 1968 "FLINTLOCK DUELING PISTOL." This first of the Ezra Brooks-Heritage China ceramic decanters, was so enthusiastically received by collectors, and the general public, it inspired the line of Ezra Brooks Heritage China decanters.

In 1966 Ezra Brooks Distilling merged with "21" Brands Inc. This event also contributed to the emergence of Ezra Brooks in the forefront of collectable bottle producers. The knowledgeable and far-sighted management followed up the success of "DUELING PISTOL" with the "CLASSIC GUN SET", in 1969—4 famous American pistols, reproduced in 3 sculptured dimensions on rectangular, rugged glass bottles.

An interesting sidelight to the production of the "FLINTLOCK DUELING PISTOL", is the Japanese version. Produced in Japan, these ceramic bottles were discovered to be leakers. Most were destroyed at the distillery, but a quantity did get into the collecting market. Because of scarcity these bottles range in price from $50.00-$75.00. They can be identified by the wooden support rack, the clarity of detail, and the "made in Japan" on the handle.

• THE GOLDEN ROOSTER •

Probably the most famous Ezra Brooks bottle is the "GOLDEN ROOSTER", an exact reproduction of the solid 18K gold rooster belonging to the NUGGET CASINO of Reno, Nevada. This bottle was made with the provision that it only be sold at the Nugget in Sparks (East Reno). Only 6,000 were produced and they quickly sold out. Since the Ezra Brooks policy, as stated by the President Mr. Herbert Silverman[*], is never to reissue a bottle once the normal marketing is completed, the demand by collectors has escalated the resale price of the empty bottle to a range of $100.00-$150.00.

• ACKNOWLEDGMENTS •

Thanks and appreciation to Mr. Skip Kostman, Senior Vice President, Marvin H. Frank & Company—Advertising, Chicago, Illinois, for his help and cooperation.

Also to the members of the Exra Brooks "team" — Mr. Herb Silverman[*], President, Mr. Tom O'Shea. Vice President, Mr. Glenn Walsh, Assistant to the President, Mr. Harold Roman, President — Heritage China Co., Ms. Maxine DeVoney, Mr. Howard Cutler.

PICTURES COURTESY OF: *MARVIN H. FRANK INC., Chicago, Ill.*

*Deceased

$15.00 — $30.00

$10.00 — $15.00

2.

A.B.P.
A DEALERS OFFER OF
40% — 60% OF QUOTED
RETAIL PRICE WOULD BE
QUITE FAIR.

EZRA BROOKS BOTTLES

A.B.P. — A DEALERS OFFER OF 40% — 60% OF
QUOTED RETAIL PRICE WOULD BE QUITE FAIR

Item, Date, Description	Retail

1. ☐ **AMERICAN LEGION.** Distinguished embossed star emblem born out of WWI struggle. Combination blue and gold. On blue base. 1971 .... **$15.00 — $30.00**

2. ☐ **ANTIQUE PHONOGRAPH.** Edison's early contribution to home entertainment. White, black, "Morning Glory" horn, red. Richly detailed in 24k. gold. 1970 .... **$10.00 — $15.00**

3. ☐ **ARIZONA.** Man with burro in search of "Lost Dutchman Mine", golden brown mesa, green cactus, with 22k. gold base, "ARIZONA" imprinted. Released 1969. **$10.00 — $15.00**

Prices are for Empty Bottles in Mint
Condition with Tops, Holders, Handles & Labels

$10.00 — $15.00

3.

$25.00 —
$35.00

4.

Item, Date, Description	Retail

4. ☐ **BIG BERTHA.** Nugget Cashino's very-own elephant with a raised trunk, gray, red, white and black, yellow & gold trim. "Blanket," and stand. .... **$25.00 — $35.00**

5. ☐ **BIG DADDY.** Salute to South Florida's "STATE" liquor chain, and "Big Daddy's" lounges. White, green, red. 1969 Release. .... **$12.50 — $17.50**

**Prices are for Empty Bottles in Mint
Condition with Tops, Holders, Handles & Labels**

5.

$12.50 — $17.50

8.

$17.50 — $22.50

Item, Date, Description   **Retail**

6. ☐ **BORDERTOWN".** Borderline Club where California and
Nevada meet for a drink. Brown, red, white. Club
Building with Vulture on roof stopper, and outhouse.   **$22.50 – $27.50**

7. ☐ **BUCKET OF BLOOD.** Fabled Virginia City, Nevada
saloon. Bucket shape bottle. Brown, red with gold
lettering on reverse side. Released 1970......................   **$25.00 – $35.00**

8. ☐ **BULLDOG.** Mighty canine mascot and football symbol.
Red, white. 1972...   **$17.50 – $22.50**

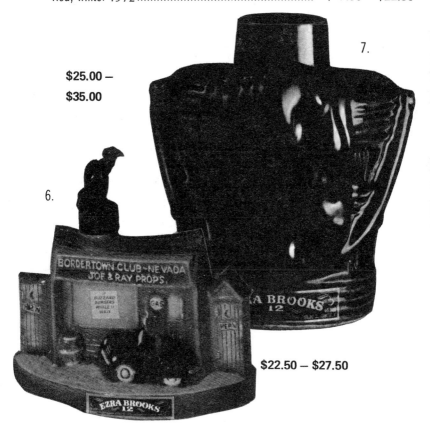

$25.00 –
$35.00

6.

7.

$22.50 – $27.50

9.

$4.00 —
$8.00

Item, Description, Date	Retail

9. ☐ **CABLE CARS.** San Francisco's great trolly-car ride in Bottle form. Made in 3 different colors: green, gray and blue, with red, black, gold trim. Open Cable Car with passengers clinging to sides. Released 1968 .... **$4.00 – $8.00**

10. ☐ **CALIFORNIA QUAIL.** Widely admired game bird shape bottle. Crested head stopper. Unglazed finish. Green, brown, white, black, gray.1970 .... **$6.50 – $12.50**

11. ☐ **CHEYENNE.** Honoring the Wild West and her "Cheyenne Frontier Days." Sheriff and outlaw shoot-out over mirrored bar. Brown tone with multicolor............. **$5.00 – $10.00**

12. ☐ **CHURCHILL.** Commemorating "Iron Curtain" speech at Westminster College, Churchill at lectern with hand raised in "V" sign. Fulton, Mo. Gold color—1970. **$5.00 – $10.00**

13. ☐ **CIGAR STORE INDIAN.** Tobacconist's sidewalk statue bottle form. The original Wooden Indian first appeared in 1770. Dark Carmel—1968. .... **$10.00 – $15.00**

$6.50 — $12.50

10.

All Prices are for Mint Condition

11.

$5.00 — $10.00

EZRA BROOKS BOTTLES

12.

$10.00 —
$15.00

13.

$5.00 —
$10.00

14.

SET $18.50 — $22.50

$8.50 —
$12.50

16.

Item, Description, Date	Retail

14. ☐ **CLASSIC FIREARMS.** 4 Bottle embossed gun set consisting of: Derringer, Colt .45, Peacemaker, Over & Under Flintlock, Pepper box. Green, blue, violet, red—1969.. **$18.50 — $22.50**

15. ☐ **CLOWN.** The big top's venerable funny men with bowl hat, concertina and flop shoes. Multi-colored. **$8.50 — $12.50**

16. ☐ **CONQUISTADORS.** Tribute to a great drum & bugle corps. Silver colored Trumpet attached to drum. **$15.00 — $20.00**

17. ☐ **COURT JESTER.** A common sight in the throne rooms of Europe. Yellow and Blue suit, pointed cap............... **$17.50 — $22.50**

EZRA BROOKS BOTTLES

15.

$17.50 — $22.50

17.

$8.50 — $12.50

18.

$10.00 – $15.00

19.

$7.50 – $13.50

Item, Description, Date	Retail

18. ☐ **DEAD WAGON.** To carry gunfight losers to Boot Hill, old-time hearse with Tombstones on side. Vulture adornment on stopper. White, with Black details— 1970.. **$10.00 – $15.00**

19. ☐ **DELTA BELLE.** Proud paddlewheeler on the New Orleans to Louisville passage steamboat shape with embossed details. White, brown, red with 22k gold trim—1969... **$7.50 – $13.50**

Item, Description, Date

20. ☐ **DISTILLERY—CLUB BOTTLE.** Reproduction of the Ezra Brooks Distillery in Kentucky, complete with smokestack. Beige, black, brown with 22k. gold roofs. **$25.00 — $35.00**

21. ☐ **DUESENBERG.** Jaunty vintage convertible. Famous SJ model reproduction complete with superchargers & white sidewalls. Blue & gold, or solid gold color. **$8.50 — $12.50**

$25.00 — $35.00 20.

$8.50 — $12.50 21.

Item, Description, Date   **Retail**

22. ☐ **ENGLISH SETTER—BIRD DOG.** Happy hunting dog retrieving red pheasant. White flecked with black, yellow base. 1971 .... **$6.50 — $12.50**

All Prices are for Empty Bottles in Mint Condition, Complete with Handles, Spouts & Stoppers.

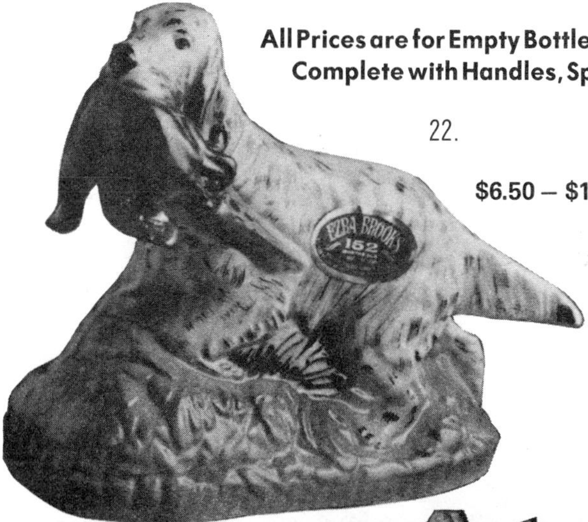

22.

$6.50 — $12.50

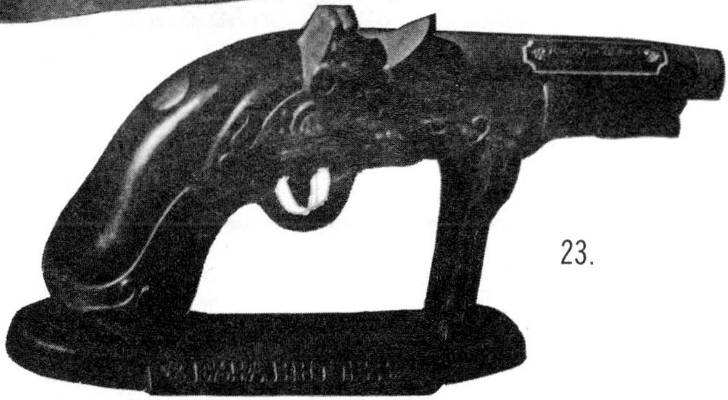

**JAPAN
$50.00
HERITAGE
$10.00 —
$15.00**

23.

23. ☐ **FLINTLOCK.** Dueling pistol rich in detail. Japanese version has wooden rack, "Made in Japan" on handle. Heritage-china gun has plastic rack, less detail. Gunmetal gray & brown, silver & gold trim. 1968 .... **(JAPANESE)
(HERITAGE)

PRICES
LISTED ABOVE**

Item, Description, Date   Retail

24. ☐ **FOREMOST ASTRONAUT.** Tribute to major liquor
supermart, foremost liquor store. Smiling "Mr. Bottle-
Face" clinging to space rocket on white base. .... **$8.50 — $15.00**

25. ☐ **FRESNO DECANTER.** Map of famed California grape
center. Stopper & inscription gold finish. Blue, white. **$6.50 — $12.50**

24.
$8.50 — $15.00

25.
$6.50 — $12.50

Item, Description, Date   **Retail**

26. ☐ **GAMECOCK.** All feathers and fury against rival birds. Red with yellow base. 1970 .... **$10.00 – $15.00**

27. ☐ **GO BIG RED #1 & #2.** Football shaped bottle with white bands and laces on base embossed, "GO BIG RED." Brown, white, gold detail. Released 1970.   **PRICE SAME AS BELOW**

26.

$10.00 – $15.00

All prices for Mint Condition

27.

No. 1. $25.00 – $30.00
No. 2. $15.00 – $25.00

<u>A.B.P.</u>
A DEALERS OFFER OF 40% – 60% OF QUOTED RETAIL PRICE WOULD BE QUITE FAIR.

$25.00 — $35.00

30.

28.

$7.50 — $12.50

Item, Description, Date	Retail

28. ☐ **GOLD PROSPECTOR.** Rugged miner with white beard panning for gold. Black, pink and gold trim. Released 1970... $7.50 — $12.50

Item, Description, Date   **Retail**

29. ☐ **GOLDEN ANTIQUE CANNON.** Symbol of Spanish power. Embossed details on barrel, wheels and carriage. Dark brown, with lavish 22k. gold trim. 1969.... **$5.00 — $10.00**

30. ☐ **GOLDEN EAGLE.** Majestic bird possessing great stamina and strength. Rich plummage, sitting on a branch. Gold color. 1971.. **$25.00 — $35.00**

31. ☐ **GOLDEN GRIZZLY BEAR.** Tremendous size, unmatched power. A Bear shape bottle, on haunches. Brown with gold highlights. 1970... **$5.00 — $8.00**

32. ☐ **GOLDEN HORSESHOE.** Salute to Reno's Horseshoe Club. Goodluck symbol of horseshoe. 24k. gold covered, on a blue base. 1970.................................. **$65.00 — $100.00**

33. ☐ **GOLDEN ROOSTER.** A replica of the famous solid gold Rooster on display at "Nugget Casino" in Reno, Nevada. Crowing Rooster in 22k. gold on black base. **$85.00 — $150.00**

34. ☐ **GRANDFATHER CLOCK.** Popularized by Henry Clay Work's endearing song of 1880. Replica of one in Ford Theatre where Lincoln was shot. Brown with gold highlights, much embossed detail. 1969 .... **$6.50 — $12.50**

35. ☐ **GREAT STONE FACE—OLD MAN OF THE MOUNTAIN** Famous profile found in mountain of New Hampshire. Stopper has seal of New Hampshire. 1970.................. **$15.00 — $30.00**

36. ☐ **HAMBLETONIAN.** Harness Racer honors the N.Y. town and race track that sired harness racing, trotting, horse pulling driver and sulky. Green, brown, white, yellow, blue, gold base. 1971..................................... **$10.00 — $15.00**

All Prices are for Empty Bottles in Mint Condition, Complete with Handles, Spouts & Stoppers.

37.

$12.00 — $15.00

33.

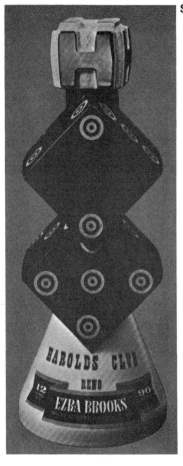

$85.00 — $150.00

**All Prices are for Mint Condition,
Complete with Handles, Spouts & Stoppers.**

$5.00 — $10.00

29.

36.

$10.00 — $15.00

EZRA BROOKS BOTTLES

$5.00 — $8.00 $15.00 — $30.00

35.

31.

**Prices are for Empty Bottles in Mint
Condition with Tops, Holders, Handles & Labels**

32.

$65.00 — $100.00

$6.50 — $12.50

34.

Item, Description, Date	Retail

37. ☐ **HAROLD'S CLUB DICE.** Lucky 7 dice combination topped with H-cube stopper, on round white base. Red and white with gold trim. 1968 .... **$12.00 — $15.00**

38. ☐ **HEREFORD.** Best beef on the hoof in bottle form. Brown, white face. 1972 .... **$12.50 — $17.50**

39. ☐ **HOPI INDIAN.** "KACHINA DOLL". Creative tribe doing ritual song-and-dance. White, red ornamental trim. **$65.00 — $130.00**

40. ☐ **HISTORICAL FLASKS.** Unique series of whiskey flasks based on patriotic American symbols and events. Green, amber, blue and amethyst........................SET **$8.00 — $16.00**

43. $12.50
— $17.50

"KEYSTONE KOPS"
HOLLYWOOD BOTTLE
$25.00 — $35.00

*ERROR BOTTLE
VERY RARE

BLACK FACE
COPS
$400.00 — $500.00

$8.00 — $16.00

Item, Description, Date	Retail

41. ☐ **INDIAN HUNTER.** Traditional buffalo hunt. Indian on horseback shooting buffalo with bow & arrow. Horse white, buffalo brown, yellow base. 1970...................... **$12.50 — $26.50**

42. ☐ **INDIAN CEREMONIAL.** Colorful tribal dancer from New Mexico Reservation. Multi-colored, gold trim. **$22.50 — $35.00**

43. ☐ **INDIANAPOLIS 500.** Sleek, dual-exhaust racer commemorating this famous Speedway and Race. White, blue, black, silver trim. 1970.................................... **$12.50 — $17.50**

44. ☐ **IRON HORSE LOCOMOTIVE.** Replica of old-time locomotive, complete with funnel, cow-catcher and oil burning headlamp. Black and red with 22k. gold trim. **$12.50 — $17.50**

41. $12.50 — $26.50

**Prices are for Empty Bottles in Mint
Condition with Tops, Holders, Handles & Labels**

$22.50 — $35.00

42.

$12.50 — $17.50

44.

Item, Description, Date   **Retail**

45. ☐ **JACK O' DIAMONDS.** The symbol of good luck, a
bottle in the shape of the "Jack" right off the card.
A Royal Flush decorates the front. White, Red, Blue
& Black. 1969.. **$9.50 — $13.50**

46. ☐ **JAY HAWK.** Funny bird with a large head perched on
a "tree trunk" base. Symbol of Kansas during and
after Civil War. Yellow, red, blue & brown. 1969 .... **$10.00 — $15.00**

**All Prices are for Empty Bottles in Mint Condition,
With Handles, Spouts & Stoppers.**

45.

46.

$9.50 —
$13.50

$10.00 —
$15.00

PAIR $20.00 – $30.00

47.

48.

$15.00 – $22.50

Item, Description, Date   **Retail**

47. ☐ **KATZ CATS.** Seal point and blue point. Siamese cats
are symbolic of Katz Drug Company of Kansas City,   **PAIR**
Kansas. Grey and blue, tan and brown. 1969.............. **$20.00 – $30.00**

48. ☐ **KATZ CATS PHILHARMONIC.** Commemorating its 27th
Annual star night, devoted to classical and pop music.
Black tuxedo, brown face. 1970................................. **$15.00 – $22.50**

Item, Description, Date   Retail

49. ☐ **KING OF CLUBS.** Figure of card symbol. Sword and
orb symbolize wisdom and justice. Royal Flush in
Clubs on front. Yellow, red, blue, black and white
with gold trim. 1969 .... **$10.00 — $15.00**

50. ☐ **KING SALMON.** State of Washington's Chinook that
instinctively battles its way upstream to spawn. Bot-
tle in shape of leaping salmon. Natural red. 1971 .... **$50.00 — $100.00**

51. ☐ **LIBERTY BELL.** It rang in U.S. Independence in 1776.
Replica of the famous bells complete with "wooden"
support. Dark copper color, embossed details. 1970 ... **$12.50 — $22.50**
                                                (without crack) **50.00**

52. ☐ **LITTLE GIANT.** Replica of the first horse-drawn steam
engine to arrive at the Chicago fire in 1871. Red,
black with gold trim. 1971... **$8.50 - $12.50**

53. ☐ **MAINE LOBSTER.** Delectable denizen of the deep.
Bottle in Lobster shape, complete with claws. Pink-
ish-red color. Bottle is sold only in Maine, home of
fine Lobsters. 1970 .... **$22.50 — $34.50**

53.

$22.50 — $34.50

**All Prices are for Mint Condition,
Complete with Handles, Spouts & Stoppers.**

All Prices are for Empty Bottles in Mint Condition, With Handles, Spouts & Stoppers.

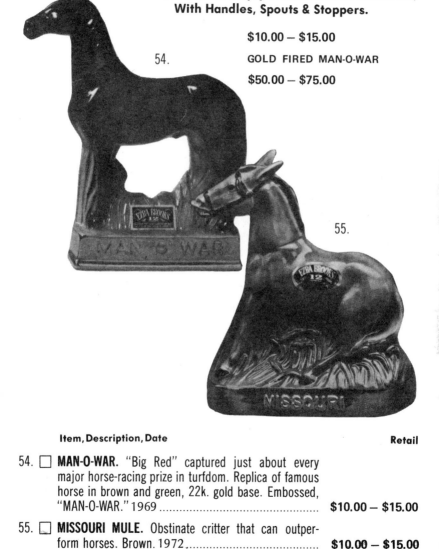

$10.00 — $15.00

GOLD FIRED MAN-O-WAR

$50.00 — $75.00

54.

55.

Item, Description, Date	Retail

54. ☐ **MAN-O-WAR.** "Big Red" captured just about every major horse-racing prize in turfdom. Replica of famous horse in brown and green, 22k. gold base. Embossed, "MAN-O-WAR." 1969 .... **$10.00 — $15.00**

55. ☐ **MISSOURI MULE.** Obstinate critter that can outperform horses. Brown. 1972 .... **$10.00 — $15.00**

EZRA BROOKS BOTTLES

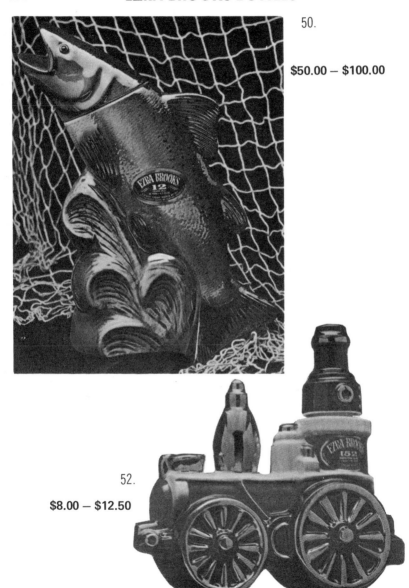

50.

$50.00 — $100.00

52.

$8.00 — $12.50

49.

$10.00 — $15.00

51.

$12.50 — $22.50
WITHOUT CRACK
$60.00

**All Prices are for Mint Condition,
Complete with Handles, Spouts & Stoppers.**

EZRA BROOKS BOTTLES

$15.00 —
$25.00

57.

56.

$15.00 — $25.00

Item, Description, Date   **Retail**

56. ☐ **MR. FOREMOST.** An authentic reproduction of the famous Bottle-shaped symbol of Foremost Liquor stores, "Mr. Foremost," known for good wines and spirits. Red, white and black. 1969............................ **$15.00 — $25.00**

57. ☐ **MR. MERCHANT.** JUMPING MAN, Whimsical, checkered-vest caricature of amiable shopkeeper, leaping into the air, arms outstretched. Yellow, black. 1970.... **$15.00 — $25.00**

58. ☐ **MOTORCYCLE.** Motorcycle rider & machine. Rider dressed in Blue pants, red jacket, w/stars 'n stripes helmet. Motorcycle Black with red tank on silver base. **$7.50 — $12.50**

59. ☐ **MOUNTAINEER.** Hearty breed from the hills of West Va. Rock-rugged mountaineers. Figure dressed in buckskin, holding rifle. "MOUNTAINEERS ARE ALWAYS FREE" embossed on base. Bottle is hand-trimmed in platinum. One of the most valuable Ezra Brooks figural bottles. 1971... **$90.00 — $150.00**

60. ☐ **NEW HAMPSHIRE STATE HOUSE.** 150-year old State House. Embossed doors, windows, steps. Eagle topped stopper. Gray building with gold. 1970........................ ***$18.50 — $22.50**

61. ☐ **NUGGET CLASSIC.** Replica of golf pin presented to golf tournament participants. Finished in 22k. gold. **$17.50 — $35.00**

65.

*GOLD FIRED STATE HOUSE — $50.00

$17.50 — $35.00   61.

$90.00 — $150.00
59.

58.

$7.50 — $12.50

62.

$18.50 — $22.50   GOLD FIRED — $50.00   60. $12.50 — $17.50

Item, Description, Date   **Retail**

62. ☐ **OIL GUSHER.** A gushing salute to America's wild-catters and their rigs. Bottle in shape of oil drilling rig. All silver, jet black stopper in shape of gushing oil.   **$12.50 — $17.50**

**Prices are for Empty Bottles in Mint
Condition with Tops, Holders, Handles & Labels**

Item, Description, Date	Retail

63. ☐ **OLD CAPITAL.** Bottle in shape of Iowa's seat of government when corn State was still frontier territory. Embossed windows, doors, pillars. "OLD CAPITOL, /IOWA 1840-1857" on base. Reddish color with gold dome stopper.1971................................... **$32.50 — $37.50**

64. ☐ **OLD WATER TOWER.** Famous landmark. Survived the Chicago fire of 1871. Embossed details, towers, doors, stones, windows. Grey & Brown, Gold base.1969...... **$12.50 — $17.50**

65. ☐ **ONTARIO, 500.** California 500 is a speedway classic with an "Indy" style racing oval. Red, white, blue and black with silver trim. 1970.................................... **$6.00 — $12.50**

66. ☐ **OVERLAND EXPRESS.** Leavenworth to Denver in 10 days for $125, on the original of this stagecoach bottle. Brown.1969 .... **$10.00 — $15.00**

66. $10.00 — $15.00

$32.50 –
$37.50

63.

64.

All prices shown are for Mint Condition

$12.50 – $17.50

<u>A.B.P.</u>
A DEALERS OFFER OF
40% TO 60% OF QUOTED
RETAIL PRICE WOULD BE
VERY FAIR.

Item, Description, Date	$40.00 — $95.00 Retail
67. ☐ **PHOENIX BIRD.** Famous mythical bird reborn from its own ashes honoring Arizona. Blue bird with outstretched wings arising from Gold flames. 1971..........	**$40.00 — $95.00**
68. ☐ **PIANO.** An "Old Time" piano player and his upright piano. Player wears blue pants, striped shirt, red bow tie, black derby, and yellow vest. Piano is brown with gold trim.1970..	**$10.00 — $15.00**
69. ☐ **PIRATE.** A swashbuckling sailor with beard and eye-patch and "Hook" hand, who flew the Jolly Roger (skull & crossbones) o'er the 7-seas. Black hat & jacket & boots, yellow striped shirt, pistol, sword & treasure chest on Gold Base.1971.........................	**$8.50 — $12.50**

$10.00 — $15.00

69.

68.

$8.50 — $12.50

**All Prices are for Empty Bottles in Mint Condition,
With Handles, Spouts & Stoppers.**

Item, Description, Date	Retail

70. ☐ **PORTLAND HEAD LIGHTHOUSE.** It's guided ships safely into Maine Harbor since 1791. White, red trim, gold "Light" stopper. "MAINE" embossed on rock base. 1971 .... **$20.00 — $30.00**

71. ☐ **POT-BELLIED STOVE.** "Old-Time" round coal burning stove with ornate legs and "Fire" in the grate. Black and red. 1968 .... **$7.50 — $12.50**

$7.50 —
$12.50

71.

$20.00 —
$30.00

70.

72. ☐ **QUEEN OF HEARTS.** Nevada claims her as a symbol of good luck. Playing card symbol with Royal Flush in Hearts on front of bottle. 1969 .... **$6.50 — $12.50**

73. ☐ **RAZORBACK HOG.** Left behind by DeSoto in 1542, later to become fitting Arkansas' emblem. Bright red Hog with white tusks and hooves running on green grass. 1970 .... **$8.50 — $12.50**

74. ☐ **RENO ARCH.** Honoring the "biggest little city in the world", Reno, Nevada. Arch shape with "RENO" embossed on yellow. Front of bottle multi-color decal of: dice, rabbits foot, roulette wheel, slot machine, etc. White and yellow, purple stopper. 1968 ...... **$7.50 — $20.00**

75. ☐ **SAILFISH.** Leaping deep water Sailfish with swordlike nose and large spread fin. Blue-green luminous tones on green "waves" base. 1971 .... **$10.00 — $15.00**

76. ☐ **SEA CAPTAIN.** Salty old seadog, white hair and beard, in blue "captains" jacket with gold buttons and sleeve stripes, white cap, gold band. Holding pipe, on "wooden" stanchion base. 1971 .... **$12.50 — $17.50**

77. ☐ **SENATOR.** Cigar-chomping, whistle-stopping State Senator, stumping on a platform of pure nostalgia. Black "western" hat and swallow-tail coat, red vest, string tie, gold, black red, white. 1971 .... **$15.00 — $20.00**

78. ☐ **1804 SILVER DOLLAR.** Commemorates the famous and very valuable "1804 Silver Dollar". Embossed replica of the Liberty Head dollar. Platinum covered round dollar shaped bottle on black base. Made with black and white bottoms. 1970 .... **$12.50 — $17.50**

79. ☐ **SILVER SPUR.** Cowboy-boot shaped bottle with silver spur buckled on. "SILVER SPUR—CARSON CITY NEVADA" embossed on side of boot. Brown boot with platinum trim. 1971 .... **$20.00 — $30.00**

72.

$6.50 — $12.50

$10.00 — $15.00

75.

$7.50 − $20.00

74.

$12.50 − $17.50
WHITE BASE
WORTH LESS

78.

73.

$8.50 –
$12.50

$20.00 – $30.00

79.

$12.50 – $17.50   76.

Item, Description, Date   **Retail**

80. ☐ **SIMBA.** The King of Beasts, the African Lion, crouched on a rock about to spring on his prey. Beautifully detailed Lion is reddish-brown color. Head of Lion is stopper. "Rock" base is dark gray. 1971............... **$6.00 — $12.00**

81. ☐ **SLOT-MACHINE.** A tribute to the "Slots" of Las Vegas, Nevada. A replica of the original nickel "LIBERTY BELL" slot machine invented by Charles Fey in 1895. The original is in Reno's Liberty Belle Saloon. Top window shows 2 horseshoes and a bell, bottom panel shows prizes. Grey body with Gold trim. 1971.... **$20.00 — $30.00**

82. ☐ **SPRINT CAR RACER.** A decanter replica of the race car sponsored by Ezra Brooks. Supercharged racer with black Firestone racing tires, and silver and blue trim. Goggled driver in white and red jump suit at wheel. Cream colored car with silver & blue trim. **$10.00 — $15.00**

83. ☐ **STOCK MARKET TICKER.** A unique replica of a ticker tape machine. Gold colored machanism with white market tape under plastic dome. Black base with embossed plaque "STOCK MARKET QUOTATIONS". 1970 **$7.50 — $12.50**

84. ☐ **JOHN L. SULLIVAN.** "The Great John L." mustached, last of the bare nuckle fighters, in fighting stance. Red tights, gold belt cord, white gym shirt. John stands on a Gold base. 1970 .... **$12.50 — $17.50**

85. ☐ **PATTON TANK.** Reproduction of a U.S. Army tank. Turret top with cannon is the stopper. Embossed details on tracks, tools, etc. Camouflage green and brown. 1972... **$15.00 — $20.00**

**Prices are for Empty Bottles in Mint
Condition with Tops, Holders, Handles & Labels**

EZRA BROOKS BOTTLES

$10.00 — $15.00

82.

83.

84.

$7.50 —
$12.50

$12.50 —
$17.50

$6.50 – $12.50

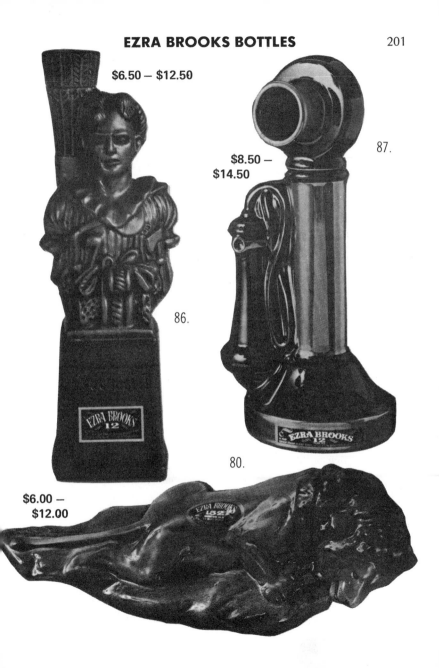

$8.50 –
$14.50

87.

86.

80.

$6.00 –
$12.00

85. $15.00 — $20.00

Item, Description, Date	Retail

86. ☐ **TECUMSEH.** The symbol known as "The God of 25" (passing grade at Annapolis). The figure head of the U.S.S. Delaware, this decanter is an embossed replica of the statue at Annapolis. Feathers in quiver form stopper. Gold figure on brown "wood" base 1969 $6.50 — $12.50

87. ☐ **TELEPHONE.** A replica of the "old-time" upright handset telephone. 24Kt. Gold body, mouth piece, and base trim, black receiver, wires, base and head. Mouthpiece and head form the stopper. 1971 .... $8.50 — $14.50

**All Prices are for Mint Condition,
Complete with Handles, Spouts & Stoppers.**

88.

$15.00 – $32.50

Item, Description, Date	Retail

88. ☐ **TEXAS LONGHORN.** Model of the famous beef, symbolic of the great football teams of Texas. Realistic longhorn on tall green Texas "grass" base. Long-horned head is stopper. Reddish-brown body, white horns and mask, gold trimmed base. 1971 .... **$15.00 – $32.50**

89. ☐ **TOM TURKEY.** Replica of the American White Feathered Turkey. Tail spread, red head and wattles, yellow feet and beak. On a brown "tree trunk" base. **$20.00 – $30.00**

90. ☐ **TRACTOR.** A model of the 1917 Fordson made by Henry Ford. Embossed details of engine and hood seat and steering wheel. Red tractor wheels, grey body with silver trim. 1971 .... **$12.50 – $17.50**

91. ☐ **TROUT & FLY.** The Rainbow Trout leaping and fighting the McGinty Fly. A luminescent replica of this angler's dream on a blue "water" base, complete with scales, fins and flashing tail. 1970 .... **$8.00 – $12.50**

89.

$20.00 —
$30.00

90.

$12.50 — $17.50

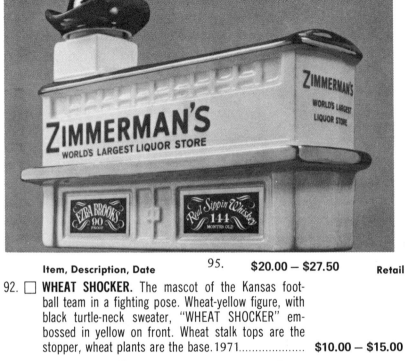

| Item, Description, Date | 95. | $20.00 – $27.50 | Retail |

92. ☐ **WHEAT SHOCKER.** The mascot of the Kansas football team in a fighting pose. Wheat-yellow figure, with black turtle-neck sweater, "WHEAT SHOCKER" embossed in yellow on front. Wheat stalk tops are the stopper, wheat plants are the base. 1971 .... **$10.00 – $15.00**

93. ☐ **WHISKEY FLASKS.** Reproductions of collectable American patriotic whiskey flasks of the 1800's, Old Ironsides, Miss Liberty, American Eagle, Civil War Commemorative. Embossed designs in gold, on blue, amber green and red. 1970 .... **$2.50 – $5.00**

94. ☐ **WICHITA CENTENNIAL.** Replica of the Witchita's center of culture and commerce, Century II, the round building with the square base. Blue roof with gold airliner on top symbol of "Air Capital of the World." Blue, brown, black and gold. 1970 .... **$12.50 – $22.50**

$8.00 − $12.50

91.

94. $12.50 − $22.50

Item, Description, Date	Retail

95. ☐ **ZIMMERMAN'S HAT.** A salute to "Zimmerman's— WORLD'S LARGEST LIQUOR STORE." A replica of the store, embossed windows, doors, and roof. The "Zimmerman Hat" caps the store and is the bottle stopper. Red, white, brown and gold. 1968 .... **$20.00 − $27.50**

**All Prices are for Mint Condition,
Complete with Handles, Spouts & Stoppers.**

96.   **97.**

Item, Date, Description	Retail

96. ☐ **AMERICAN LEGION.** Ezra Brooks salutes the American Legion, its Illinois Department, the Land of Lincoln and the city of Chicago, host of the Legion's 54th National Convention. — 1972 . . . . . . **18.00 — 30.00**

97. ☐ **AMERICAN LEGION.** Hawaii, our fiftieth state, hosted the American Legion's 1973 annual convention. It was the largest airlift of a mass group ever to hit the islands. Over 15,000 Legionnaires visited the beautiful city of Honolulu to celebrate the Legion's fifty-fourth anniversary. — 1973 . . . . . **22.00 — 32.00**

99.

98.

Item, Date, Description	Retail

98. ☐ **BASEBALL HALL OF FAME.** Ezra Brooks is proud to salute the past, present, and future of baseball. And especially the Baseball Hall of Fame in Cooperstown, New York. It is there that one can truly understand the heritage that baseball has produced. Baseball fans everywhere will enjoy this genuine Heritage China ceramic of a familar slugger of years gone by. — 1973 . . . .   **12.00 — 18.00**

99. ☐ **BIGHORN RAM.** Bighorns still scramble up and down the Rockies from Alaska to Mexico, choosing the highest, most rugged peaks. High-spirited, fearless, free and independent, the bighorn ram has massive, curled horns. Today, most bighorn rams live in mountain sanctuaries where they are seldom seen by man. — 1973 . . . .   **10.00 — 15.00**

100.   **101.**

Item, Date, Description	Retail

100. ☐ **BUSY BEAVER.** This genuine Heritage China ceramic is a salute to the beaver, truly one of nature's wonders. Beavers are best known for their constant working. It's always work with a purpose, however. Once a family of beavers finds a likely sight for a "lodge" or home, they dam up the stream to form a pond. .... **10.00 — 15.00**

101. ☐ **BULL MOOSE.** The Alaskan moose may weigh as much as 1,800 pounds and stand over 7 feet high at the shoulder. The entire antler may span over 75 inches and weigh up to 60 pounds. — 1973 .... **12.00 — 18.00**

102.

103.

Item, Date, Description	Retail

102. ☐ **CHAROLAIS BEEF.** The Charolais have played an important role in raising the standards of quality in today's cattle, and it is for this reason they are honored each year at the largest livestock show in the world — the Houston Fat Stock Show and Exposition. — 1973 .... **15.00 — 20.00**

103. ☐ **CLUB BOTTLE.** The third commemorative Ezra Brooks Collector Club bottle is created in the shape of America. From the East Coast to the West—and at all points in between—you'll find Ezra Brooks Collectors join the ranks. Each gold star on the new club bottle represents the location of an Ezra Brooks Collectors Club. — 1973 .... **20.00 — 35.00**

104. ☐ **CLYDESDALE HORSE.** The Clydesdale is noted for his high action, both walking and trotting. He stands 16 hands or higher and averages 1700 pounds. In the early days of distilling, Clydesdales carted the bottles of whiskey from the distillery to towns all across America. — 1973 .... **12.00 — 18.00**

**All Prices are for Empty Bottles in Mint Condition.
Complete with Handles, Spouts & Stoppers.**

105.

106.

Item, Date, Description	Retail

105. □ **ELEPHANT.** There are three distinct species of elephants — one Asiatic, two African.. African elephants are the ones more often seen in jungle movies because of their impressively larger ears and tusks. An African's tusks can weigh close to 300 pounds and extend over 11 feet in length. — 1973 .. **12.00 — 18.00**

106. □ **ELK.** While the elk herd is still relatively scarce in the United States, the elk name flourishes as a symbol for many worthwhile organizations, especially those whose primary object is the practice of benevolence and charity in its broadest sense. Ezra Brooks salutes these organizations with this genuine Heritage China Ceramic bottle. — 1973 .... **12.00 — 18.00**

| Item, Date, Description | Retail |

107. ☐ **FLORIDA 'GATORS'.** To adversaries, the Florida
Gators football team sometimes appear to be a lot
like their namesakes, the Florida alligator — so
strong you wish you could ,walk the other way,
tough skinned, able to tear apart anything within
reach, up to 500 pounds and 12 feet long. Both
kinds of Gators have only one enemy: human
leather-hunters. — 1973 .... **15.00 — 20.00**

108. ☐ **GREATER GREENSBORO OPEN**   The Greater
Greensboro Open is more than just doglegs and
putting greens. It is a community working together,
people from all walks of life, both athletes and
businessmen. To commemorate this event, Ezra
Brooks has designed this genuine Heritage Ceramic
bottle. — 1972 .... **30.00 — 45.00**

109.

110.

Item, Date, Description	Retail

109. ☐ **HOPI KACHINA.** The oldest still-occupied village in the United States is a Hopi village, settled about 1125 A.D. And until the white man came, the Hopi culture was more advanced than any other that ever existed north of Mexico. Ezra Brooks salutes the century-old Hopi Kachina tradition with this genuine Heritage China ceramic reproduction of a Hummingbird Kachina Doll. — 1972 . . . . **35.00 — 45.00**

110. ☐ **IDAHO — SKI THE POTATO.** Ezra Brooks salutes the beautiful state of Idaho, its incomparable ski resorts and famous Idaho potatoes, with this genuine Heritage China Ceramic bottle. — 1973 . . . . **12.50 — 17.50**

**All prices are for Empty Bottles in Mint Condition.
Complete with Handles, Spouts & Stoppers.**

112.

111.

Item, Date, Description	Retail

111. ☐ **KILLER WHALE.** Although they're so often found just off the Washington coast, they cruise throughout all the seas of the world, all year long. Their travels take them as far as the polar ice caps. Killer Whales talk to each other by clicking underwater. This clicking also serves as the whale's "radar" since he can judge distance by the echo. — 1972 . . . . **15.00 — 20.00**

112. ☐ **MR. MAINE POTATO.** From early beginnings the people of Maine have built the small potato into a giant industry. Today potatoes are the number one agricultural crop in the state. Over thirty-six billion pounds are grown every year. — 1973 . . . . **12.50 — 17.50**

113.

114.

Item, Date, Description	Retail

113. ☐ **NEBRASKA — GO BIG RED!** The stands rock with the familiar cry, "Go Big Red! Go Big Red!" Big Red's football team is on the field, and the stadium's overflow crowd belongs to them. Ezra Brooks salutes Nebraska's Big Red and their loyal boosters with this genuine Heritage China reproduction of a game ball and fan. Trimmed in genuine 24 karat gold, this Ezra Brooks tribute to 1971's National Collegiate Football Champion is truly a collector's item — 1972 . . . . **15.00 — 20.00**

114. ☐ **PENNY FARTHINGTON HIGHWHEELER.** Bicycles have become the newest and most convenient means of commuting in the big cities. Bicycling has even grown to the point where bicycle makers are now offering more specialized bikes for any personal transportation need one might have. Ezra Brooks salutes the millions of cyclists everywhere, and the new cycling boom with this genuine Heritage China ceramic of the Penny Farthington bicycle. — 1973 . . . . **8.00 — 12.00**

Item, Date, Description	Retail

115. ☐ **PANDA — GIANT.** The United States saw its first Giant Panda in 1936, when Su-Lin was captured and brought here by explorer, Ruth Harkness. Today, the two Giant Panda gifts from China are the prime attractions at the National Zoo in Washington, D.C. Ezra Brooks Giant Panda ceramic bottle commemorates this gift. — 1972 . . . . **10.00 — 15.00**

116. ☐ **PENGUIN.** There are 16 species of penguins. The most common is the Emperor Penguin of the Antarctic. Others are found throughout the southern hemisphere in New Zealand, Australia, South Africa and southern South America. At sea penguins travel in flocks and on land live in huge colonies. Ezra Brooks salutes the penguin with a genuine Heritage China ceramic figural bottle. — 1972 . . . . . **8.00 — 12.50**

117.

118.

Item, Date, Description

Retail

117. ☐ **PHOENIX JAYCEES.** One of the finest rodeos is sponsored by the Phoenix Junior Chamber of Commerce. 1972 is the 50th anniversary of the Phoenix Jaycees and their 43rd year as sponsor of the rodeo. Ezra Brooks is proud to honor the Phoenix Jaycees and the Rodeo of Rodeos with this Heritage China reproduction of a silver saddle – 1973 . . . . **10.00 – 15.00**

118. ☐ **SKI BOOT.** With over 4,500,000 skiers in the U.S. alone, skiing isn't merely just a sport; it's big business as well. There are more than 800 ski areas in America and this figure is on the constant increase. Ezra Brooks salutes the exciting sport of skiing with this genuine Heritage Ceramic Ski Boot. – 1972 . . . . **7.50 – 12.50**

**All Prices are for Empty Bottles in Mint Condition.
Complete with Handles, Spouts & Stoppers.**

120.

119.

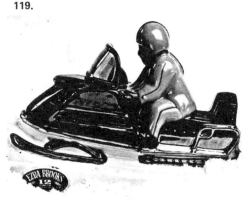

Item, Date, Description

119. ☐ **SNOWMOBILES.** There are already 1,000,000 snowmobiles in operation throughout the U.S., not to mention such countries as Denmark and Germany. The snowmobile is used for many things other than merely having a good time. It has already replaced the dog sled as the chief means of transportation in Alaska and Canada. And the users of these "northern camels" cover the entire spectrum of occupations. – 1972 . . . .

Retail

8.50 – 12.50

120. ☐ **SENATORS OF THE U.S.** Times have changed. Jets have replaced trains and television debates have all but done away with whistle stop speeches. But senators still respond to their constituencies with the same candor and concern as they did in days gone by. Ezra Brooks honors the Senators of the United States of America with this genuine Heritage Ceramic "Old Time" courtly Senator. – 1972 . . . . .

15.00 – 20.00

121.

Item, Date, Description   **Retail**

121. ☐ **TIGER ON STADIUM.** The tiger is one of nature's
most impressive creations. Adult males sometimes
reach a length of ten feet and can weigh over four
hundred pounds. Its graceful movement, muscular
form, and distinctive markings add to its reputation
as one of the most prized members of the entire
animal kingdom. Many college teams that have
chosen him for their mascot. The roar of the crowds
"Go Tiger" cheers on the college playing fields act
as an impressive testimonial to the spirit and
enthusiasm of those individuals who call themselves
"Tigers". — 1973 . . . .   **10.00 — 12.00**

122. ☐ **TENNIS PLAYER.** Today, over nine million
Americans are enjoying tennis, exceeding golfers by
over a million. And more than 50 million are playing
in other countries. The United States sports more
than 100,000 tennis courts, with new ones being
built at the rate of 7,000 a year. The original grass
surgace courts have been joined by materials like
clay, asphalt and concrete. Ezra Brooks salutes
tennis, and tennis' lovers everywhere, with this
genuine Heritage China ceramic "Tennis Player"
bottle. — 1972 . . . .   **10.00 — 15.00**

123.

124.

Item, Date, Description   **Retail**

123. ☐   **TOTEM POLE.** The kind of totem poles we're accustomed to seeing in books and. movies probably didn't come into being before the 1790's. Ezra Brooks commemorates the totem art of the American Indian with this genuine Heritage China reproduction of an ornate, intricately designed Indian totem pole. — 1972 . . . .   **12.50 — 17.50**

124. ☐   **TOTEM POLE.** The Indians of North America have a proud history. And in many instances, that history is beautifully portrayed in totem pole art. It is a truly remarkable art form that will enrich the world for generations to come. Ezra Brooks commemorates the totem pole art of the North American Indian with this genuine Heritage China reproduction of an ornate, intricately designed Indian totem pole. — 1973 . . . .   **12.50 — 17.50**

126.

125. ☐ **TRAIL BIKE RIDER.** Ezra Brooks salutes the trail bike riders of America with this genuine Heritage China Ceramic bottle. Depicting the supreme uphill climb, it symbolizes the courage, and love of adventure of trail riders everywhere. — 1972 ...... **10.00 — 15.00**

126. ☐ **TEN PINS — BOWLING.** In Colonial days Massachusetts and Connecticut banned "bowling at nine pins" along with dice and cards. But bowlers avoided the law by simply adding a 10th pin. Thus 10 pin bowling was born. Today the sport of bowling is enjoyed by more than 30,000,000 Americans. — 1973 .... **8.50 — 12.50**

All Prices are for Empty Bottles in Mint Condition.
Complete with Handles, Spouts & Stoppers.

127.

128.

Item, Date, Description	Retail

127. ☐ **TROJANS — U.S.C. FOOTBALL.** In the last dozen years alone, the Trojans have given U.S.C. seven Pacific-Eight Conference titles, six Rose Bowl teams, 23 All-Americans, two Heisman Trophy winners (Mike Garrett and O.J. Simpson), three undefeated seasons, and three national championships. — 1973 . **20.00 — 30.00**

128. ☐ **VIRGINIA —RED CARDINAL.** A glorious bird, the Cardinal represents this illustrious state. (From early settlement days to the present, memorable Virginia has filled history books with prominent dates.) It's mild climate; wide, sandy beaches; historic monuments and national and state parks and forests have helped make Virginia the great state it is today. — 1973 .... **13.50 — 18.50**

129.

130.

Item, Date, Description	Retail

129. ☐ **WEST VIRGINIA —MOUNTAIN LADY.** The West Virginian mountain lady has always pulled her load and then some. She still is the lifeblood of the state of West Virginia, whether she is raising a family, teaching school, or tending patients in a hospital. The mountain lady remains an inspiration to American womanhood. — 1972 .... **25.00 — 35.00**

130. ☐ **VERMONT SKIER.** The smooth hills of Vermont boasted America's first ski-tow, in 1934. The ski-tow revolutionized the sport all across the country. Each year when the green mountains of Vermont turn frosty white, and New England's winter athletes take to the slopes, the people of Vermont remember that historic event. — 1972 .... **12.00 — 20.00**

131.

132.

131. ☐ **V.F.W. — VETERANS OF FOREIGN WARS.** The V.F.W. holds its National Convention each year in an American city. Ezra Brooks salutes the Veterans of Foreign Wars of the United States and the 1.8 million fighting men of five wars who wear the Cross of Malta emblem linked by bonds of comradeship that only shared overseas military service can forge. — 1973 .... **8.50 — 12.50**

132. ☐ **WESTERN RODEOS.** To celebrate the end of the round-up the cowboys would hold competitions. These contests became so popular, people came from miles around to watch the cowboys. And from these traditional get-togethers evolved today's rodeo. Today rodeos are not only for fun and amusement, they're big business. The Rodeo Cowboys Association sanctions over 500 rodeos each year which attract more than 10 million spectators. Ezra Brooks salutes the rodeo, from its early pioneers to its professional circuit riders, with this genuine Heritage China bottle. — 1973 .... **12.50 — 18.50**

EZRA BROOKS BOTTLES

133.

134.

Item, Date, Description	Retail

133. ☐ **SEALION —GOLD.** Having few natural enemies, though always on the lookout for sharks, California Sealions are some of the most playful animals in the world. Ezra Brooks commemorates the great State of California and her world-famous marine showmen, with the California Sealion ceramic bottle, hand detailed in 24 carat gold. — 1972 ..... **12.50 — 17.50**

134. ☐ **SYRACUSE –NEW YORK.** Today Syracuse boasts a population of over 200,000 and is the fourth largest city in New York. As in its earliest days, it's still an industrial city. Ezra Brooks salutes the great city of Syracuse, its past and its present. — 1973 ... **10.00 — 15.00**

Name of Bottle	Retail
1. ☐ BALLANTINE, DUCK	8.00 – 12.00
2. ☐ BALLANTINE, FISHERMAN	12.00 – 16.00
3. ☐ BALLANTINE, SEATED FISHERMAN	12.50 – 17.50
4. ☐ BALLANTINE, GOLF BAG	8.00 – 12.00
5. ☐ BALLANTINE, SILVER KNIGHT	16.00 – 20.00
6. ☐ BALLANTINE, SCOTTISH KNIGHT	8.00 – 12.00
7. ☐ BALLANTINE, MALLARD DUCK	8.00 – 12.00
8. ☐ BALLANTINE, OLD CROW CHESSMAN	8.00 – 12.00
9. ☐ BALLANTINE, ZEBRA	10.00 – 15.00

Pictures Courtesy: "21" BRANDS, Inc., NYC

BARDI–BARSOTTINI–BRALATTA BOTTLES

2.

11.

6.

18.

Bottle		Retail

• BARDI BOTTLES •

1. ☐ **MANDOLIN,** Ceramic, Height, 12-1/2"..........................	15.00 – 20.00
2. ☐ **SANTA CLAUS,** Ceramic, red-white-blk..........................	24.00 – 27.50
3. ☐ **ALASKAN TOTEM POLE,** Ceramic, Height, 11-1/2"......	28.00 – 32.00

• BARSOTTINI BOTTLES •

4. ☐ **TIVOLI CLOCK,** Ceramic, Height, 15".*	24.00 – 27.50
5. ☐ **PISA'S LEANING TOWER,** Grey & white	7.50 – 12.00
6. ☐ **ALPINE PIPE,** Ceramic, Height, 10"..........................	10.00 – 14.00
7. ☐ **PARIS ARC de TRIOMPHE,** Height, 7-1/2"...................	12.50 – 17.00
8. ☐ **FLORENTINE STEEPLE,** Grey & white......................	10.00 – 12.00
9. ☐ **EIFFEL TQWER,** Grey & white, Height, 15"...................	10.00 – 14.00
10. ☐ **ROMAN COLISEUM,** Ceramic...................................	10.00 – 12.00
11. ☐ **CLOWNS,** Ceramic, Height, 12" each	4.50 – 6.00
12. ☐ **ANTIQUE AUTOMOBILE,** Ceramic, coupe...................	6.00 – 8.00
13. ☐ **ANTIQUE AUTOMOBILE,** Open car..........................	4.50 – 6.00
14. ☐ **MONASTERY CASK,** Ceramic, Height, 12"....................	15.00 – 20.00
15. ☐ **FLORENTINE CANNON,**Length, 15"	18.50 – 20.00

• BRALATTA BOTTLES •

16. ☐ **MASKS,** Black with yellow & white trim	6.50 – 10.00
17. ☐ **MASKS,** Height, 10"..	18.50 – 21.95
18. ☐ **BEEFEATER,** Ceramic, red & black, Height, 21"	15.00 – 20.00

*Clock with cherub 32.00 – 36.00

BOLS—BORGHINI—BRIZARD BOTTLES

Bottle	• BOLS (DUTCH) BOTTLES •	Retail
1. ☐ **PEWTER**, Height, 5", circa 1969		12.50 — 15.00
2. ☐ **PEWTER**, Height, 8", circa 1969		15.00 — 20.00
3. ☐ **DELFT-TYPE**, Blue & white, Height, 8"		10.00 — 12.00
4. ☐ **DELFT-TYPE**, Blue & white, Height, 11"		12.50 — 15.00
5. ☐ **DELFT-TYPE**, Blue & white, Height, 5-1/4"		8.00 — 10.00
6. ☐ **DELFT-TYPE**, Blue & white, Height, 5" (On tray)		8.50 — 10.00
7. ☐ **DELFT-TYPE**, Blue & white, Height, 3-1/2" (On tray)		6.00 — 8.00

• BORGHINI BOTTLES •

8. ☐ **FEMALE HEAD**, Ceramic, Height 9-1/2"		15.00 — 25.00
9. ☐ **CATS**, Black with red ties, Height, 6"		12.00 — 15.00
10. ☐ **CATS**, Black with red ties, Height, 12"		15.00 — 25.00
11. ☐ **PENGUIN**, Black & white, Height, 6"		8.00 — 12.00
12. ☐ **PENGUIN**, Black & white, Height, 12", 1969		15.00 — 25.00

• MARIE BRIZARD •

13. ☐ **LADY IN ERMINE CAPE**, Height, 7"		12.50 — 15.00
14. ☐ **KIOSK**, Colorful Parisian signpost, Height, 11-1/2"		17.50 — 20.00
15. ☐ **CASTLE** Ceramic chessmen, dark brown		7.50 — 9.50
16. ☐ **KNIGHT** Ceramic chessmen, dark brown		8.00 — 12.00
17. ☐ **BISHOP** Ceramic chessmen, dark brown		7.00 — 9.00
18. ☐ **PAWN** Ceramic chessmen, dark brown		7.50 — 9.50

The Bischoff bottles are an unusual and beautiful line of imported bottles, produced by the foremost glass, pottery, and porcelain companies of Czechoslovakia (Bohemia), Murano (Italy), Austria, & Germany, many containing the world famed Bischoff Liquers.

• KORD BOHEMIAN DECANTERS •

These hand-blown, hand-painted glass bottles were originally created in Czechoslovakia by the Kord Company, based on a long tradition of Bohemian cut, engraved, etched, and flashed glass. These hand-crafted bottles were imported to the U.S. by Imported Brands, Inc., in limited quantities, starting in 1948. Typical Bohemian themes were used to decorate the bottles. Complete bottles with stoppers and labels are very difficult to find today.

Cut glass and Ruby-etched decanters were imported in the early 1950's, these are traditional forms of Bohemian glass. The cut glass are of lead crystal and are hand cut, the Ruby-etched are done in the typical two layer manner with the outside ruby glass etched through to show the clear glass underneath. The designs are quite elaborate, with leaping deer, castles scrolls, foliage, wild birds, grapes, lattice-work, etc. The overall color can be amber, or topaz, but Ruby is the most common.

On some bottles the under layer of glass is opaque, therefore showing the cut design very clearly. Some of these etched decanters were made in Austria, and should have labels to that effect.

Most of these decanters came packaged with matching sets of glasses.

The Double Dolphin, Hunter & Lady, Horse's Head, are also Czech made of thick, hand-blown glass, and are not as rare as the Ruby-etched since they are still imported. They only have value if complete with stoppers.

• VENETIAN GLASS FIGURALS •

The famous glass artisan island of Murano, near the city of Venice, is the birthplace of the Bischoff Venetian Glass Figurals. All these glass figurals were created for use in containing the Bischoff Liquers, and are quite unique in design and color. These limited edition figurals are made by the world famous Seguso Glass Company of Murano, Italy, on the themes of birds, fish, and animals.

ACKNOWLEDGEMENTS: *IMPORTED BRANDS, INC., Brooklyn, N.Y.*
A. & J. KESSLER LIQUORS, NYC, LOURIE LIQUOR INC., NYC.

PICTURES COURTESY OF: *A. & J. KESSLER LIQUORS, 23 East 28th Street, NYC*
LOURIE LIQUOR INC., 871 9th Ave., NYC.

Special thanks to Mr. Julius Kessler, and Mr. Morris Lourie
for permission to use bottles from their private collections. Illustrations: Jeff Neff

BISCHOFF BOTTLES
(CZECH) BOHEMIAN GLASS—KORD DECANTERS

All Prices are for Mint Condition,
Complete with Handles, Spouts & Stoppers.

Retail

1. ☐ **OLD COACH BOTTLE**—1948
   Old time coach and white horses hand-painted on a hand-blown Bohemian glass bottle pale amber color. Round ground glass stopper. Bottle and stopper are both numbered. 10" high.. **45.00 — 55.00**

2. ☐ **OLD SLEIGH BOTTLE**—1949
   Hand painted, signed, Czech winter old-time sleigh scene. Driver sits on lead horse and blows trumpet, passengers on top of coach are pouring drinks. Glass decanter has fine white trace lines. Glass stopper is known clear and painted. 10" high............. **40.00 — 45.00**

AVERAGE BUYING PRICE: 40% — 60% of Retail Price

(CZECH) BOHEMIAN GLASS—KORD DECANTERS

All Prices are for Mint Condition, Complete with Handles, Spouts & Stoppers.

Retail

3. ☐ **DANCING—COUNTRY SCENE—1950**
Clear glass hand-blown decanter with hand-painted and signed colorful scene of peasant boy & girl doing a country dance beside a tree, Bohemian village background. Spider bold white lines painted on bottle and stopper. 12-1/4" high............................ **40.00 — 50.00**

4. ☐ **DANCING—PEASANT SCENE—1950**
Colorful peasants in costume, dancing to music of bag-pipes, hand painted and signed. The decanter is of pale amber glass fine black lines painted on bottle. Stopper is ground to fit and fine line painted, 12" high.. **40.00 — 50.00**

5. ☐ **ANISETTE—1948/51**
Clear glass bottle with 2 handles and a ground glass stopper. Clear glass ribbing on sides of bottle, 11" high.. **RARE**

6. ☐ **BOHEMIAN RUBY ETCHED—1949/51**
Etched design in typical Bohemian style, castle, birds, deer and scrolls and curlecues in clear glass, ruby-red color "flashed" on bottle, except for etching and cut neck. Ground glass, etched stoppers on this tall, round, decanter, 15-1/2" high tapered neck. **40.00 — 50.00**

7. ☐ **FLYING GEESE PITCHER—1957**
Clear crystal, handled pitcher. Hand-painted and signed colorful scene of wild geese flying over Czech marshes. Gold painted neck, pouring lip, and stopper, 9-1/2" high. .... **30.00 — 40.00**

BISCHOFF BOTTLES
(CZECH) BOHEMIAN GLASS—KORD DECANTERS

All Prices are for Mint Condition,
Complete with Handles, Spouts & Stoppers.

Retail

8. ☐ **FLYING GEESE PITCHER**—1952
Same as above, but with green glass handle and stopper. This pitcher has a glass base. .... **26.00 — 28.50**

9. ☐ **CUT GLASS DECANTER (BLACKBERRY)**—1951
A geometric design hand-cut over-all on this lead glass decanter. The stopper is hand cut and ground to fit the bottle, 10-1/2" high.................................... **45.00**

10. ☐ **CZECH HUNTER**—1958
Round thick clear glass body with green collar and green glass buttons and heavy round glass base. The stopper-head is of glass with a jaunty green "Bohemian" hat with feather crowning pop-eyes white mustache and red button nose, 8-1/2" high.............. **18.00 — 20.00**

11. ☐ **CZECH HUNTER'S LADY**—1958
"Mae West" shaped decanter of "cracked" clear glass. Green collar at neck of bottle with amber glass stopper-head. Brown hair, glasses and yellow earrings make up the lady's head. She's taller than the Hunter, 10" high.. **18.00 — 20.00**

12. ☐ **HORSE HEAD**—1947-69
Pale amber colored bottle in the shape of a horses head. Embossed details of horses features are impressed on this hand-blown bottle. Round pouring spout on top, 8" high.. **15.00 — 20.00**

13. ☐ **DOUBLE-DOLPHIN**—1949-69
Fish-shaped twin bottles joined at the "bellies." They are made of hand-blown clear glass and have fins and "fish tail" ground glass stoppers, each has fish eyes and mouth.. **16.00 — 18.00**

A.B.P. — 40% — 60% of Retail

BISCHOFF BOTTLES

(CZECH) BOHEMIAN GLASS—KORD DECANTERS

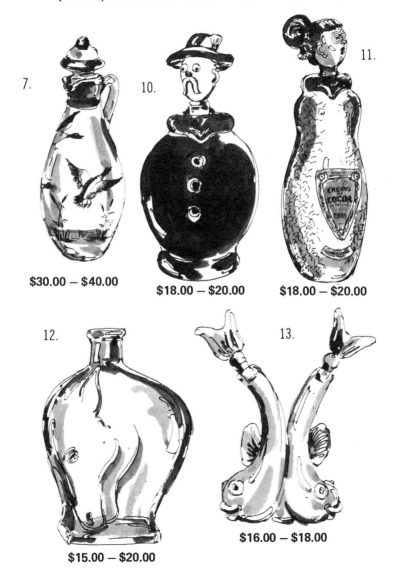

7.

$30.00 — $40.00

10.

$18.00 — $20.00

11.

$18.00 — $20.00

12.

$15.00 — $20.00

13.

$16.00 — $18.00

BISCHOFF BOTTLES
(CZECH) BOHEMIAN GLASS—KORD DECANTERS

All Prices are for Mint Condition,
Complete with Handles, Spouts & Stoppers.

14. ☐ **WILD GEESE—RUBY GLASS—1952**   Retail
Etched design of wild geese rising above the marshes.
A tall round decanter with tapering, etched neck, and
etched hand-ground stopper. Ruby-red color "flashed"
on bottle, 15-1/2" high... **25.00 — 30.00**

15. ☐ **WILD GEESE—AMBER GLASS—1952**
Same as above, except bottle is a "flashed" yellow-
amber color... **25.00 — 30.00**
Matching glasses were made for both the Ruby &
Amber.

16. ☐ **JUNGLE PARROT—RUBY GLASS—1952**
Profusely hand-etched jungle scene with parrot,
monkeys, insects, flowers, and leaves, cut through
the ruby "flashed" body. A Tall round decanter with
tapering etched neck, 15-1/2" high. .... **35.00 — 40.00**

26.

$15.00 — $20.00

22.

$50.00 — $60.00

25.

$38.50 — $42.50

(CZECH) BOHEMIAN GLASS—KORD DECANTERS

17. ☐ **JUNGLE PARROT—AMBER GLASS—1952**   **Retail**
Same as above, except bottle is "flashed" a yellow-amber color.. **35.00 — 40.00**

18. ☐ **AMBER FLOWERS—1952**
A two-toned glass decanter. Amber flowers, stems and leaves on a Pale Amber background. The long tapering neck is etched in panels and circles. The stopper is dark amber and hand-ground to fit, 15-1/2" high.. **32.50 — 37.50**

19. ☐ **AMBER LEAVES—1952**
Multi-tone bottle with dark amber leaves, and flowers, on pale amber etched background. Stopper neck and base are cut in circles and panels. Round bottle with long neck, 13-1/2" high. .... **32.50 — 37.50**

20. ☐ **CORONET CRYSTAL—1952**
A broad band of flowers leaves, and scrolls, circle this multi-toned bottle. The designs are cut in dark amber glass revealing the opaque pale amber background. Stopper neck and base are cut in circles and panels. A round tall bottle 14" high.................... **35.00 — 42.50**

• VENETIAN GLASS FIGURAL •

21. ☐ **BLACK CAT—1969**
Glass black cat, with curled tail, 12" long.............. **30.00 — 32.00**

22. ☐ **DOG—ALABASTER—1969**
Seated alabaster glass dog, 13" high. .... **15.00 — 20.00**

23. ☐ **DOG—DACHSHUND—1966**
Alabaster long dog with brown tones, 19" long........... **38.00 — 42.50**

24. ☐ **DUCK—1964**
Alabaster glass tinted pink & green, long neck, upraised wings, 11" long... **40.00 — 50.00**

25. ☐ **FISH—MULTICOLOR—1964**
Round fat fish, alabaster glass. Green, rose, yellow. **50.00 — 60.00**

26. ☐ **FISH—RUBY—1969**
Long, flat, ruby glass fish, 12" long........................ **15.00 — 20.00**

A.B.P. — 40% to 60% OF RETAIL

CERAMIC DECANTERS & FIGURALS

Many of the most interesting, attractive and valuable Bischoff bottles are made of ceramic, stoneware or pottery. They have a "rougher" surface appearance than the glass or porcelain bottles. Values quoted are for complete bottles with handles, spouts and stoppers in mint condition.

	Bottle name & date	Retail
1. ☐	AFRICAN HEAD — 1962	18.00 — 22.00
2. ☐	BELL HOUSE — 1960	30.00 — 34.00
3. ☐	BELL TOWER — 1960	30.00 — 34.00
4. ☐	BOY (CHINESE) FIGURAL — 1962	32.00 — 40.00
5. ☐	BOY (SPANISH) FIGURAL — 1961	32.00 — 40.00
6. ☐	CLOWN WITH BLACK HAIR — 1963	40.00 — 45.00
7. ☐	CLOWN WITH RED HAIR — 1963	40.00 — 45.00
8. ☐	DEER FIGURAL — 1969	20.00 — 24.00
9. ☐	EGYPTIAN DANCING FIGURAL — 1961	20.00 — 24.00
10. ☐	EGYPTIAN PITCHER 2 MUSICIANS — 1969	18.00 — 22.00
11. ☐	EGYPTIAN PITCHER 3 MUSICIANS — 1959	26.00 — 32.00
12. ☐	FLORAL CANTEEN — 1969	20.00 — 26.00
13. ☐	FRUIT CANTEEN — 1969	18.50 — 22.50
14. ☐	GIRL IN CHINESE COSTUME — 1962	38.00 — 42.00
15. ☐	GIRL IN SPANISH COSTUME — 1961	32.00 — 40.00
16. ☐	GREEK VASE DECANTER — 1969	10.00 — 15.00
17. ☐	MASK — GRAY FACE — 1963	20.00 — 24.00
18. ☐	OIL & VINEGAR CRUETS BLACK & WHITE — 1959	22.50 — 26.00
19. ☐	VASE — BLACK & GOLD — 1959	36.00 — 42.00
20. ☐	WATCHTOWER — 1960	10.00 — 15.00

13.

$18.50 — $22.50

8.

$20.00 — $24.00

$10.00 — $15.00

16.

$10.00 — $15.00

3.

1.

$8.50 — $12.50

5.

4.

$8.50 — $12.50

$10.00 — $12.50

Retail

1. ☐ **GEORGE WASHINGTON**
American Patriot Series of ceramic statuettes, white.   **10.00 — 15.00**

2. ☐ **HENRY McKENNA**
Early American 1/2 gallon ceramic jug of natural-
colored stoneware...   **5.00 — 7.50**

3. ☐ **PILGRIM'S FLASK, SABRA LIQUEUR**
The story of the Pilgrim's Flask is told on the scroll
in the gift presentation box. ....   **8.50 — 12.50**

4. ☐ **THE GOLFER**
Ceramic figurine...   **8.50 — 12.50**

5. ☐ **ZODIAC SERIES**
Ceramic decanters. Six bottles, bearing the repre-
sentations of two of the twelve signs of the Zodiac .   **10.00 — 12.50**

Pictures Courtesy of: JOSEPH E. SEAGRAM & SONS, INC.
Acknowledgements: MR. SY FEIT, AD DIRECTOR

BOTTLES BEAUTIFUL—FAMOUS FIRSTS
All prices are for Mint Condition

• BOTTLES BEAUTIFUL •

Item, Description, Date	Retail
1. ☐ **THE FRENCH TELEPHONE,** 1969	28.00 — 35.00
2. ☐ **VICTORIAN PHONOGRAPH,** Height, 10"	25.00 — 32.00
3. ☐ **NAPOLEON,** Height, 17-1/4"	20.00 — 28.00
4. ☐ **GARIBALDI,** Height, 17-1/2"	20.00 — 28.00
5. ☐ **BERSAGLIERI,** Height, 17"	20.00 — 28.00
6. ☐ **CENTURION,** Height, 18-1/4"	20.00 — 28.00
7. ☐ **RICARDO THE ROOSTER,** Height, 15"	20.00 — 28.00
8. ☐ **FILOMENA THE HEN,** Height, 12-1/2"	20.00 — 28.00
9. ☐ **OLD COFFEE MILL,** orange, 13" high.	30.00 — 40.00
10. ☐ **LOMBARDY SCALES,** 13" high.	25.00 — 32.00
11. ☐ **GARIBALDI'S SEWING MACHINE,** 10" high	25.00 — 32.00
12. ☐ **HURDY GURDY** with monkey, 13" high	25.00 — 32.00
13. ☐ ***BUTTERFLY GOLD,** 10-1/2" high, wings 14-1/2"	25.00 — 32.00

• FAMOUS FIRSTS •

Item, Description, Date	Retail
14. ☐ **THE SPIRIT OF ST. LOUIS** Length, 15-1/4"	38.00 — 50.00
15. ☐ **DEWITT CLINTON LOCOMOTIVE,** Length, 13-1/2"	30.00 — 45.00
16. ☐ **MARMON WASP,** Length 13-1/3"	30.00 — 40.00
17. ☐ **RENAULT GRAND PRIX,** 1906, Length, 15-1/4"	30.00 — 45.00
18. ☐ **AMERICA,** Yacht, Length, 14"	30.00 — 40.00
19. ☐ **ROBERT E. LEE,** Steamboat, Length, 17"	35.00 — 50.00
20. ☐ **FIRST BALLOON,** Height, 13"	35.00 — 50.00
21. ☐ **THE NATIONAL,** 1912 Racing Car	30.00 — 45.00
22. ☐ **THE WINNIE MAE,** Airplane, 7-1/4" long.*	10.00 — 15.00
23. ☐ **FORMULA I LOTUS,** Racing Car, 12" long	30.00 — 40.00
24. ☐ **GOLDEN WASP,** 1/2 pint, 8" long	25.00 — 30.00
25. ☐ **INDY '71 FORMULA,** Racer, 12" long	25.00 — 30.00

*Medium, 15½" - 19.00 — 24.00
*Large, 22" -   40.00 — 50.00

3.

4.

5.

6. 2.

15.

17.

16.

18.

14.

COURTESY: *MR. RICHARD E. MAGID, BOTTLES BEAUTIFUL*

21.

12.

20.

19.

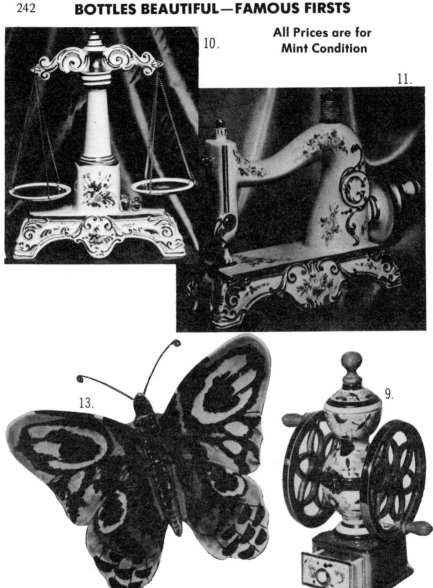

10.

**All Prices are for
Mint Condition**

11.

13.

9.

COURTESY: *MR. RICHARD E. MAGID, BOTTLES BEAUTIFUL*

BOTTLES BEAUTIFUL—FAMOUS FIRSTS

All prices are for Mint Condition
1972-1973-1974-ISSUES

Bottle, date, size	Retail
* 1. ☐ SAN FRANCISCO CABLE CAR, 1973, Length, 14".	38.00 — 50.00
2. ☐ THE ROULETTE WHEEL, 1972, Diameter, 11"....	30.00 — 40.00
3. ☐ "HE & SHE SPORTSTERS" — TENNIS PLAYER, 1973, 12" high	30.00 — 40.00
4. ☐ "HE & SHE SPORTSTERS" — THE SKIERS, 1973, 12" high	30.00 — 40.00
5. ☐ "HE & SHE SPORTSTERS" — THE GOLFERS, 1973, 12" high	30.00 — 40.00
6. ☐ THE ALPINE BELL, 1972, 11" high	12.00 — 18.00
7. ☐ ST. PAUL BELL, 1972 11" high	12.00 — 18.00
8. ☐ DON SYMPATICO "LITTLE MONK" 1972, 12" high	15.00 — 20.00
9. ☐ DOG — "BENNIE BOW—WOW", 1974, 18" high ...	20.00 — 28.00
10. ☐ CAT — "MINNIE MEOW", 1974, 18" high	20.00 — 28.00

*MINIATURE CABLE CAR, 6½" - 12.00 — 17.00

$12.00 — $18.00

6.

$30.00 — $40.00

2.

13.

8.

7.

The beautiful bottles of the J.W. Dant Distilling Company of Louisville, Kentucky, are on American subjects, and "Americana". As one of the oldest distilleries (1863), this subject matter is ideal for their contemporary bottles.

Most are conventionally shaped bottles with historical scenes applied in full color. The reverse of all rectangular bottles is an embossed American Eagle and shield with stars. On some "BOSTON TEA PARTY" bottles, an error appears, the eagle faces his own left instead of right.

All Dant bottles are produced on a limited basis, and no reissues will be made, therefore insuring future value to consumers and collectors.

ACKNOWLEDGEMENTS: *Mr. Howard Lesser, Advertising Mgr.,*
OLD CHARTER—DANT DISTILLERS COMPANY,

	Name of Bottle	Retail
1. ☐	ALAMO	3.50 — 6.50
2. ☐	AMERICAN LEGION	8.50 — 10.00
3. ☐	BOBWHITE	3.00 — 5.50
4. ☐	BOEING 747	7.50 — 12.50
5. ☐	BOSTON TEA PARTY	4.50 — 6.50
6. ☐	BOURBON	2.50 — 3.50
7. ☐	CALIFORNIA QUAIL	3.00 — 5.00
8. ☐	CHUKAR PARTRIDGE	3.00 — 5.00
9. ☐	CONSTITUTION & GUERRIERE	3.50 — 6.50
10. ☐	DUEL BETWEEN BURR & HAMILTON	3.50 — 6.50
11. ☐	EAGLE	1.50 — 3.50
12. ☐	FORT SILL CENTENNIAL, 1969	10.00 — 15.00
13. ☐	INDIANAPOLIS 500	5.00 — 9.00
14. ☐	MOUNTAIN QUAIL	3.50 — 6.50
15. ☐	MT. RUSHMORE	10.00 — 15.00
16. ☐	PATRICK HENRY	4.50 — 7.00
17. ☐	PAUL BUNYAN	4.50 — 7.00
18. ☐	PRAIRIE CHICKEN	3.00 — 5.95
19. ☐	REVERSE EAGLE	4.50 — 6.50

J.W. DANT BOTTLES

$4.50 — $7.00

17.

25.

16.

9.

10.

5.

19.

1.

"AMERICANA SERIES"
$3.50 — $7.00

4.

15.

$10.00 — $15.00

$7.50 — $12.50

"GAME BIRD"

AVERAGE RETAIL
$4.00 — $7.00

Prices are for Empty Bottles in Mint
Condition with Tops, Holders,
Handles & Labels

$10.00 — $15.00

	Name of Bottle	Retail
20. ☐	RING-NECKED PHEASANT	4.50 — 6.50
21. ☐	RUFFED GROUSE	4.50 — 6.50
22. ☐	SAN DIEGO	3.00 — 5.00
23. ☐	SPEEDWAY 500	4.50 — 6.95
24. ☐	TEA PARTY, WHITE	2.00 — 3.00
25. ☐	WASHINGTON CROSSING DELAWARE	4.00 — 8.00
26. ☐	WOODCOCK	4.50 — 6.95
27. ☐	WRONG WAY CHARLIE	40.00

5.

12.

15.

PICTURES COURTESY OF: *OLD CHARTER—DANT DISTILLERS COMPANY.*

**Prices are for Empty Bottles in Mint
Condition with Tops, Holders, Handles & Labels**

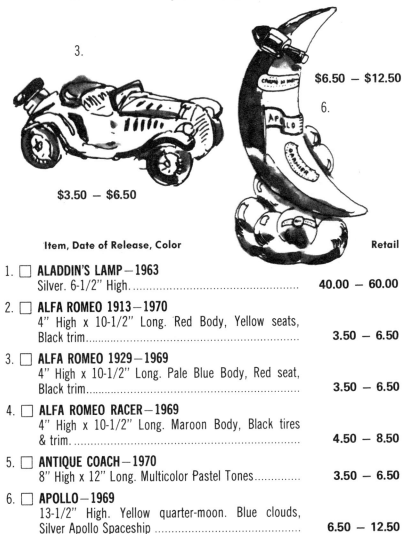

3.

$6.50 — $12.50

6.

$3.50 — $6.50

Item, Date of Release, Color	Retail
1. ☐ **ALADDIN'S LAMP** — 1963 Silver. 6-1/2" High.	**40.00 — 60.00**
2. ☐ **ALFA ROMEO 1913** — 1970 4" High x 10-1/2" Long. Red Body, Yellow seats, Black trim..	**3.50 — 6.50**
3. ☐ **ALFA ROMEO 1929** — 1969 4" High x 10-1/2" Long. Pale Blue Body, Red seat, Black trim..	**3.50 — 6.50**
4. ☐ **ALFA ROMEO RACER** — 1969 4" High x 10-1/2" Long. Maroon Body, Black tires & trim.	**4.50 — 8.50**
5. ☐ **ANTIQUE COACH** — 1970 8" High x 12" Long. Multicolor Pastel Tones.............	**3.50 — 6.50**
6. ☐ **APOLLO** — 1969 13-1/2" High. Yellow quarter-moon. Blue clouds, Silver Apollo Spaceship	**6.50 — 12.50**

GARNIER BOTTLES

Prices are for Empty Bottles in Mint Condition with Tops, Holders, Handles & Labels

Item, Date of Release, Color	Retail

7. ☐ **AZTEC VASE** — 1965
11-3/4" High. "Stone" Tan, Multicolor Aztec design   **10.00 — 15.00**

8. ☐ **BABY FOOT-SOCCER SHOE** — 1963 *
3-3/4" High x 8-1/2" Long. Black with White trim.   **6.50 — 12.50**

9. ☐ **BABY TRIO** — 1963
6-1/4" High. Clear Glass, Gold Base............   **6.50 — 12.50**

10. ☐ **BACCHUS — FIGURAL** — 1967
13" High. Purple, Brown, Flesh Tones. ....   **16.00 — 18.50**

11. ☐ **BALTIMORE ORIOLE** — 1970
Approx. 11" High. Multicolor, Green, Yellow, Blue   **6.50 — 12.50**

12. ☐ **BANDIT-FIGURAL** — 1958
11-1/2" High. Pin Ball Shape, Multicolor..............   **25.00 — 35.00**

13. ☐ **BEDROOM CANDLESTICK** — 1967
11-1/2" High. White with Hand Painted Flowers..........   **16.00 — 18.50**

14. ☐ **BELLOWS** — 1969
4" High. 14-1/2" Long. Gold & Red............   **16.00 — 18.50**

15. ☐ **BIRD ASHTRAY** — 1958
3" High. Clear Glass, Gold Stopper............   **6.50 — 8.50**

16. ☐ **BURMESE MAN VASE** — 1965
12" High. "Stone" Gray, Multicolor Eastern Design.   **15.00 — 20.00**

17. ☐ **BLUEBIRD** — 1970
Approx. 11" hivh. 2 Blue Birds, Multicolor Green,
Brown & Yellow. ....   **4.50 — 8.50**

18. ☐ **BOUQUET** — 1966
10-1/4" High. White Basket, Multicolor Flowers...........   **16.50 — 20.00**

19. ☐ **BULL (& MATADOR) — ANIMAL FIGURAL** — 1963
12-1/2" High x 12-1/2" Wide. A "Rocking" Bottle
Bronze & Gold. ....   **10.00 — 15.00**

    ***1962 Soccer Shoe — Large**   **30.00 — 45.00**

**Prices are for Empty Bottles in Mint
Condition with Tops, Holders, Handles & Labels**

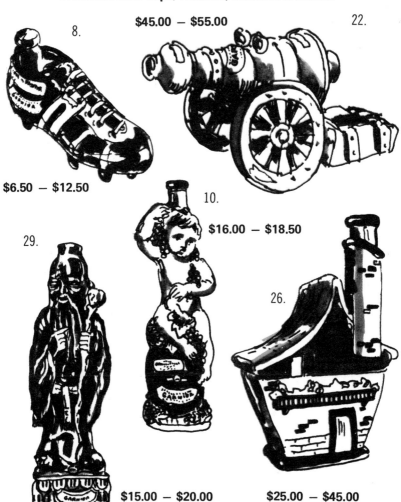

8.

$45.00 — $55.00

22.

$6.50 — $12.50

29.

10.

$16.00 — $18.50

26.

$15.00 — $20.00

$25.00 — $45.00

GARNIER BOTTLES

Prices are for Empty Bottles in Mint
Condition with Tops, Holders, Handles & Labels

Item, Date of Release, Color   **Retail**

20. ☐ **CANDLESTICK — 1955**
10-3/4" High. Yellow Candle, Brown Holder w/Gold Ring.. **32.50 — 42.50**

21. ☐ **CANDLESTICK GLASS — 1965**
10" High. Ornate leaves & fluting............................... **15.00 — 18.50**

22. ☐ **CANNON — 1964**
7-1/2" High x 13-1/2" Long. With Wheels & Carriage. Mottled Yellow-Brown... **45.00 — 55.00**

23. ☐ **CARDINAL STATE BIRD — ILLINOIS — 1969**
11-1/2" High. Bright Red Bird, Green & Brown "Tree"   **6.50 — 12.50**

24. ☐ **CAT, BLACK — 1962**
11-1/2" High. Black cat with Green eyes..................... **8.50 — 14.50**

25. ☐ **CAT, GREY — 1962**
11-1/2" High. Greyish-white cat with Yellow eyes. ...... **8.50 — 14.50**

26. ☐ **CHALET — 1955**
9" High. White, red, green & blue............................... **25.00 — 45.00**

27. ☐ **CHIMNEY — 1956**
9-3/4" High. Red bricks & fire, white mantel with picture... **45.00 — 55.00**

28. ☐ **CHINESE DOG — 1965**
11" High. Foo Dogs, carved, embossed. Ivory white on dark blue base.. **20.00 — 25.00**

29. ☐ **CHINESE STATUETTE, MAN — 1970**
12" High. Yellow robe, dark skin, blue base. .... **15.00 — 20.00**

30. ☐ **CHINESE STATUETTE, WOMAN — 1970**
12" High. Ebony skin tones, Lavender robe, Blue base. **15.00 — 20.00**

31. ☐ **CHRISTMAS TREE — 1956**
11-1/2" High. Dark green tree, Gold decorated, white candles, red flame... **50.00 — 65.00**

Prices are for Empty Bottles in Mint
Condition with Tops, Holders, Handles & Labels

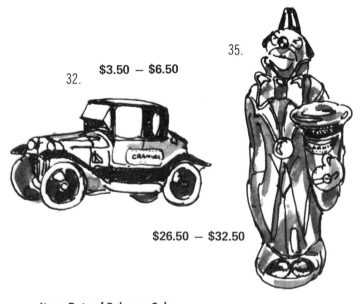

35.

32. $3.50 — $6.50

$26.50 — $32.50

Item, Date of Release, Color	Retail

32. ☐ CITROEN, 1922—1970
4" High x 10-1/2" Long. Yellow Body, Black Trim
Wheels... **3.50 — 6.50**

33. ☐ CLASSIC ASHTRAY—1958
2-1/2" Long. Clear Glass, round with pouring spout. **5.00 — 7.50**

34. ☐ CLOCK—1958
9" High. Clear Glass, round on black base. Working
clock in center... **22.50 — 28.50**

35. ☐ CLOWN HOLDING TUBA—1955
12-3/4" High. Green clown with gold trim................... **26.50 — 32.50**

36. ☐ COFFEE MILL—1966
White with blue flowers.. **22.50 — 27.50**

GARNIER BOTTLES

**Prices are for Empty Bottles in Mint
Condition with Tops, Holders, Handles & Labels**

Item, Date of Release, Color   **Retail**

37. ☐ **COLUMBINE FIGURAL**—1968 *
13" High. Female partner to Harlequin. Green and
blue, black hair & mask.. **16.50 — 20.00**

38. ☐ **DRUNKARD**—**DRUNK ON LAMPOST**
14-3/4" High. Figure in Top Hat & Tails holding
"wavy" lampost. Black, red, blue & white.................. **6.50 — 12.50**

39. ☐ **DUCKLING FIGURAL**—1956
Yellow ducking, white basket & red flowers, pink hat. **26.50 — 32.50**

40. ☐ **DUO**—1954
7-1/4" High. 2 Clear Glass bottles stacked, 2 pouring
spouts.. **22.50 — 26.50**

41. ☐ **EGG FIGURAL**—1956
8-3/4" High. White egg shape house, pink, red, green. **55.00 — 70.00**

42. ☐ **EIFFEL TOWER**—1951 **
13-1/2" High. Ivory with Yellow Tones....................... **20.00 — 28.50**

43. ☐ **ELEPHANT FIGURAL**—1961
6-3/4" High. Black with Ivory white tusks.................. **22.50 — 30.00**

44. ☐ **EMPIRE VASE**—1962
11-1/2" High. Green & white, gold design & trim. **15.00 — 22.50**

45. ☐ **FIAT 500, 1913**—1970
4" High x 10-3/4" Long. Yellow body, red Hub caps,
black trim.. **10.00 — 15.00**

46. ☐ **FIAT NEUVO, 1913**—1970
4" High x 10-3/4" Long. Open top. Blue body &
Hub caps, yellow & black trim................................... **3.50 — 6.50**

47. ☐ **FLASK GARNIER**—1958
3" High. Clear Glass, embossed cherries.................... **12.50 — 17.50**

48. ☐ **FLYING HORSE PEGASUS**—1958
12" High. Black Horse. Gold mane & tail, red "marble"
candle holder.. **40.00 — 55.00**

*HARLEQUIN — 16.50 — 20.00 **EIFFEL TOWER 12½" — 16.50 — 20.00

**Prices are for Empty Bottles in Mint
Condition with Tops, Holders, Handles & Labels**

$22.50 — $26.50

$6.50 — $12.50

38.

40.

42.

$20.00 — $28.50

48.

$40.00 — $55.00

45.

$10.00 — $15.00

Prices are for Empty Bottles in Mint
Condition with Tops, Holders, Handles & Labels

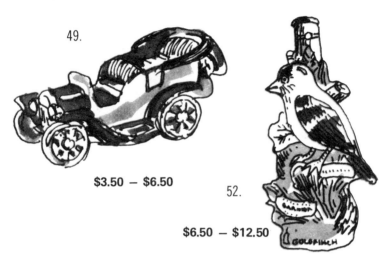

49.

$3.50 — $6.50

52.

$6.50 — $12.50

Item, Date of Release, Color	Retail

49. ☐ **FORD, 1913—1970**
4" High x 10-3/4". Green open body & wheels, black trim.. 3.50 — 6.50

50. ☐ **FOUNTAIN—1964**
12-1/2" High. Brown with Gold Lion Head spout & embossing. .... 20.00 — 26.50

51. ☐ **GIRAFFE—1961**
18" High. Yellow "marble", modern Animal figure. 25.00 — 32.50

52. ☐ **GOLDFINCH—1970**
12" High. Yellow Bird, black wings & tail, green & brown leaves & limbs. .... 6.50 — 12.50

53. ☐ **GOOSE—1955**
9-1/4" High. White with gold decoration. Modern swirl shaped goose... 16.50 — 22.50

GARNIER BOTTLES

$30.00 — $45.00 $50.00 — $60.00

54.   58.

55.

| Item, Date of Release, Color | $22.50 — $27.50 | Retail |

54. ☐ *GRENADIER — 1949
   13-3/4" High. Light Blue Soldier with sword in uniform of 1800's.. **30.00 — 45.00**

55. ☐ HARLEQUIN WITH MANDOLIN — 1958
   14-1/2" High. Seated comedy figure, mandolin & mask, white with multicolored circles, black buttons & shoes... **50.00 — 60.00**

56. ☐ HARLEQUIN STANDING — 1968
   13-1/4" High. Columbine's mate. Brown costume, blue cape, black cap & shoes. .... **16.50 — 20.00**

57. ☐ HORSE PISTOL — 1964
   18" Long. Embossed brown antique pistol, gold details   **12.50 — 16.50**

58. ☐ HUNTING VASE — 1964
   12-1/4" High. Tan & gold with embossed hunting scene... **22.50 — 27.50**

   *Faceless Figures.

GARNIER BOTTLES

Prices are for Empty Bottles in Mint
Condition with Tops, Holders, Handles & Labels

Item, Date of Release, Color	Retail

59. ☐ *HUSSAR — 1949
13-3/4" High. French Cavalry Soldier of 1800's holding sword. Maroon color.. **35.00 — 50.00**

60. ☐ INDIAN — 1958
11-3/4" High. "Big Chief" with Headress bowling pin shape. Bright Indian design colors............................ **12.50 — 18.50**

61. ☐ JOCKEY — 1961
12-1/2" High x 12" Wide. Bronzed gold horse & & jockey "rocking" bottle. .... **12.50 — 18.50**

62. ☐ LANCER — 1949
13" High. Light green soldier holding drum................. **25.00 — 40.00**

63. ☐ LOCOMOTIVE — 1969
9" Long. Tan, old fashioned Locomotive.................... **6.50 — 12.00**

64. ☐ LOG — ROUND — 1958
10" High. Brown & Tan "Log" shape, silver handle & spout.. **12.50 — 20.00**

65. ☐ LOON — 1970
11" High. Sitting Bird, white, brown, tan, blue base. **3.50 — 6.50**

66. ☐ MAHARAJAH — 1958
11-3/4" High. White and gold, Indian ruler with Turban.. **60.00 — 70.00**

67. ☐ M.G. 1933 — 1970
4" High. 11" Long. Green body, orange trim, white wheels.. **3.50 — 6.50**

68. ☐ MOCKINGBIRD — 1970
11" High. Black & White Bird on "tree" stump. .... **6.50 — 12.00**

69. ☐ MONTMARTRE JUG — 1960
11" High. Colorful Parisian Bohemian scene, green handle.. **18.50 — 22.50**

*Faceless Figures.

**Prices are for Empty Bottles in Mint
Condition with Tops, Holders, Handles & Labels**

66.

$60.00 — $70.00

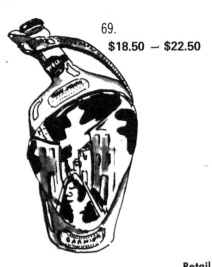

69.
$18.50 — $22.50

Item, Date of Release, Color	Retail

70. ☐ **MONUMENTS—1966**
13" High. A cluster of Parisian Monuments, Eiffel
Tower spout, multicolor... **16.50 — 20.00**

71. ☐ **NAPOLEON ON HORSEBACK—1969**
12" High. Rearing white horse, Napoleon in red cloak,
black hat and uniform.. **20.00 — 24.50**

72. ☐ **NATURE GIRL—1959**
13" High. Native girl under palm tree. Black with
bronze.. **16.50 — 20.00**

73. ☐ **PAINTING—1961**
12" High. Multicolor painting of girl, in tan "wood"
frame.. **28.50 — 32.00**

74. ☐ **PACKARD, 1930—1970**
4" High x 10" Long. Orange body cream roof &
wheels, black trim.. **3.50 — 6.50**

GARNIER BOTTLES

**Prices are for Empty Bottles in Mint
Condition with Tops, Holders, Handles & Labels**

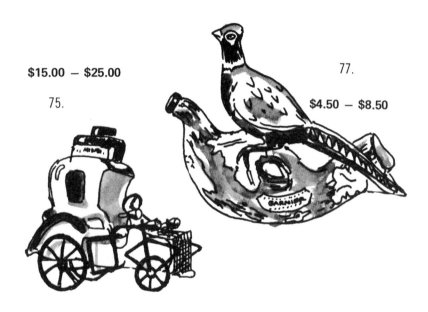

$15.00 — $25.00

75.

77.

$4.50 — $8.50

Item, Date of Release, Color	Retail

75. ☐ **PARIS TAXI** — 1960
   9" High, 10-1/2" Long. "Old-Time" cab, yellow
   body, red windows & headlights, black wire frame. **15.00 — 25.00**

76. ☐ **PARTRIDGE** — 1961
   10" High. Multicolor game bird, on "leaf" base........... **4.50 — 10.00**

77. ☐ **PHEASANT** — 1969
   12" High. Multicolor game bird on "rocking" tree
   trunk base. .... **4.50 — 8.50**

78. ☐ **PIGEON** — CLEAR GLASS — 1958
   8" High. Bird-shape bottle, gold stopper..................... **22.50 — 28.50**

GARNIER BOTTLES

POLICEMEN—
ALL NATIONS—
1970, 12" High

$6.50 — $10.00
EACH

Item, Date of Release, Color	Retail

79. ☐ **BAHAMAS**
Black policeman, white jacket, hat, black pants, red
stripe, gold details. .... **6.50 — 10.00**

80. ☐ **CANADA**
"Mountie" in red jacket, black jodphur, brown boots. **6.50 — 10.00**

81. ☐ **INDIA**
Turbaned figure. White jacket, blue kilts, red sash. **6.50 — 10.00**

82. ☐ **LONDON—"BOBBY"**
Dark blue uniform, silver helmet shield....................... **6.50 — 10.00**

83. ☐ **PARIS**
French policeman in black, white gloves, hat and
harness... **6.50 — 10.00**

84. ☐ **NEW YORK**
Dark blue uniform with gold shield & buttons............. **6.50 — 10.00**

**Prices are for Empty Bottles in Mint
Condition with Tops, Holders, Handles & Labels**

Item, Date of Release, Color	Retail

85. ☐ **PONY—1961**
8-3/4" High. "Modern" shaped horse, "wood" grain
tan.. **22.50 — 28.50**

86. ☐ **POODLE—1954 (BLACK & WHITE)**
8-1/2" High. "Begging" Poodles in white or black
with red trim.. **18.50 — 22.50**

87. ☐ **RENAULT, 1911—1969**
4" High x 10-3/4" Long. Green body & hood, red
hubs, black trim.. **4.50 — 10.00**

88. ☐ **ROAD RUNNER—1969**
12" High. Multicolor bird, green "cactus" pouring
spout... **8.50 — 14.50**

89. ☐ **ROBIN—1970**
12" High. Multicolor bird on "tree" stump with leaves. **4.50 — 8.50**

90. ☐ **ROCKET—1958**
10-3/4" High. "Rocket" shape bottle, wire holder,
yellow nose. .... **12.50 — 16.50**

91. ☐ **ROLLS ROYCE 1908—1970**
4" High x 10-1/2" Long. Open touring car in yellow,
red seats & hubs, black trim....................................... **4.50 — 10.00**

92. ☐ **ROOSTER—1952 (BLACK & MAROON)**
12" High. "Crowing" rooster with handle, black or
maroon with gold trim.. **22.50 — 27.50**

93. ☐ **SAINT TROPEZ JUG—1961**
Colorful French Riviera scene, tan jug, black handle. **9.50 — 16.50**

94. ☐ **SCARECROW—1960**
12" High. Yellow "straw" body & hat, green jacket,
red stripe face & tie, bird on shoulder. .... **13.50 — 22.50**

GARNIER BOTTLES

**Prices are for Empty Bottles
in Mint Condition with Tops,
Holders, Handles & Labels**

86.

$18.50 — $22.50

95.

$16.50 — $22.50

98.

$85.00 — $95.00

Item, Date of Release, Color	Retail
95. ☐ **SHERIFF—1958** 12" High. Two guns, badge & cowboy hat. "Pin-ball shape. White & gold.	**16.50 — 22.50**
96. ☐ **SNAIL—1950** 6-1/2" High. 10" Wide. White & brown with spiral shell.	**28.50 — 36.50**
97. ☐ **SOCCER SHOE—1962** 10" Long. Black shoe, white laces.	**30.00 — 45.00**
98. ☐ **S.S. FRANCE—LARGE—1962** 5" High, 19" Long. Commemorative model of ocean liner. Black Hull, Blue-green decks, red & black stacks, with gold labels	**85.00 — 95.00**

GARNIER BOTTLES

Prices are for Empty Bottles in Mint
Condition with Tops, Holders, Handles & Labels

Item, Date of Release, Color	Retail

99. ☐ **S.S. FRANCE—SMALL—1962**
4-1/2" High, 14" Long. Same as above. .... **60.00 — 75.00**

100. ☐ **S.S. QUEEN MARY—1970**
4" High, 16" Long. Black hull, green-blue decks,
blue "water", 3 red & black stacks............................ **10.00 — 20.00**

101. ☐ **STANLEY STEAMER 1907—1970**
4" High, 10-1/2" Long. Open blue car yellow &
black trim... **3.50 — 6.50**

*102. ☐ **TEAPOT—1961**
8-1/2" High. Yellow & black striped body, black
handle & spout.. **18.50 — 22.50**

103. ☐ **TROUT—1967**
11" High. Gray-blue speckled leaping Trout, "water"
base. .... **12.50 — 20.00**

104. ☐ **VALLEY QUAIL—1969**
11" High. Black marked bird on "wood" base............. **5.00 — 12.50**

105. ☐ **VIOLIN—1966**
14" High. White violin, hand painted flowers and
details... **12.50 — 18.50**

106. ☐ **WATCH-ANTIQUE—1966**
10" High. Antique pocket watch tan & gold................. **22.50 — 25.00**

107. ☐ **WATER PITCHER—1965**
14" High, glass body, silver base, handle and top. **12.50 — 18.50**

108. ☐ **WATERING CAN—1958**
7" High. Hand painted design, handle & pouring spout. **20.00 — 25.00**

109. ☐ **YOUNG DEER VASE—1964**
12" High. Embossed figures. Tan color....................... **22.50 — 25.00**

*TEAPOT, 1935:   **15.00 — 20.00**

MINIATURES 1973/74

For color illustrations see GARNIER BOTTLES

A new line of Garnier Fancy miniatures, featuring a colorful variety of safari animals, dogs, European houses, Tropical fishes, Butterflies, etc., was introduced in 1972 in the United States by Julius Wile & Sons & Co.,Inc.

Produced by Garnier Liqueurs of Enghien, France, these miniature bottles are enjoying increased popularity as collector's items throughout the world. The collectors of miniature have a choice of the regular replicas of the Garnier bottles, plus fancy ceramic, porcelain, and glass figurals. The early surge in miniature collecting in the 1930's peaked again in the late 1960's and is still going strong today.

Bottle   **Retail**

DOGS — 1972

1. ☐ COLLIE, DASCHUND, TOY POODLE, GERMAN SHEPHERD, COCKER SPANIEL, DALMATIAN .... EACH 4.50 — 5.00

SAFARI ANIMALS — 1973

2. ☐ LION, ELEPHANT, PANDA, TIGER, GIRAFFE, ZEBRA .... EACH 3.50 — 5.00

EUROPEAN HOUSES

3. ☐ FRANCE, HOLLAND, ITALY, ENGLAND, SWITZERLAND, SPAIN .... EACH 4.50 — 5.50

PLAYING CARDS

4. ☐ JACK OF CLUBS, JACK OF HEARTS, QUEEN OF CLUBS, QUEEN OF HEARTS, KING OF CLUBS, KING OF HEARTS, EACH .... 4.50 — 6.00

SPORT FIGURES

5. ☐ HOCKEY PLAYER, BASEBALL PLAYER, FOOTBALL PLAYER EACH .... 4.50 — 6.00

TROPICAL FISH — 1974

6. ☐ GOLDFISH, GUPPY, GRAMMY, ANGELFISH, BUTTERFLY FISH, ZEBRA SAILFIN .... EACH 3.50 — 5.00

COURTESY: Julius Wile Sons & Co., Inc.

HOLLY CITY BOTTLES

Courtesy: Mr. Ed Johnson

CLEVENGER HANDMADE COMMEMORATIVE DECANTERS

Authentic American Handmade mouth blown commemorative decanters. For over 50 years Clevenger Brothers master glass blowers have devoted themselves to the preservation of this fast disappearing art. They have even retained the original formulas enabeling them to produce the same blue, green, amethyst and amber colors so much admired in the glass first made by Casper Wistar in Allowaystown, New Jersey.

Clevenger Brothers decanters are painstakingly made ONE AT A TIME by skilled craftsmen useing the same tools and methods as were used generations ago. All Clevenger decanters produced for Holly City Bottle are embossed with "CB" (Clevenger Brothers), Holly Leaves, and are dated.

DECANTERS MADE FOR HOLLY CITY BOTTLE BY CLEVENGER

	Bottle, Quantity, Color	Retail
1. ☐	Watergate (First run 500 bottles, amethyst)	50.00 − 75.00
2. ☐	Watergate (Second run 500 bottle, blue, 2 stars added)	15.00 − 25.00
3. ☐	Watergate (Third run 1,000 bottles, topaz 3 stars & 3 birds added)	8.00 − 15.00
4. ☐	Israel's 25th Anniversary (First run 500 bottles, honey)	8.00 − 15.00
5. ☐	John F. Kennedy "Rocking Chair" Memorial (First run 1,000 bottles, blue)	15.00 − 25.00
6. ☐	Senator Sam Ervin/Senator Howard Baker (First run 500 bottles, topaz)	15.00 − 25.00
7. ☐	The Jersey Devil (First run 1,000 bottles, green - numbered)	8.00 − 15.00
8. ☐	1973 Christmas "St. Nick" (First run 200 bottles, amber)	15.00 − 25.00
9. ☐	Delaware BiCentennial (First run 1,000 bottles, light amethyst)	8.00 − 15.00
10. ☐	Pennsylavania BiCentennial (First run 1,000 bottles, green)	8.00 − 15.00

HOLLY CITY BOTTLES

PRICES QUOTED ARE FOR
MINT CONDITION

6a.

6b.

7.

SENATOR ERVIN

SENATOR BAKER

9a.

9b.

FRONT

BACK

8.

4.

10.

JAPANESE BOTTLES

• HOUSE OF KOSHU BOTTLES •

Bottle	Retail
1. ☐ **DAUGHTER**	**13.50 — 15.50**
2. ☐ **FAITHFUL RETAINER**	**19.50 — 23.00**
3. ☐ **"KIKU" GEISHA,** Blue, 13-1/4" high	**30.00 — 35.00**
4. ☐ **"YURI" GEISHA,** Pink, Red Sash, 13-1/4" high	**30.00 — 35.00**
5. ☐ **GOLDEN PAGODA**	**7.00 — 12.00**
6. ☐ **RED LION MAN.***	**12.00 — 20.00**
7. ☐ **MAIDEN**	**8.50 — 12.50**
8. ☐ **NOH MASK**	**15.00 — 17.00**
9. ☐ **OKAME MASK**	**15.00 — 17.00**
10. ☐ **GOLDEN PAGODA**	**6.00 — 10.00**
11. ☐ **WHITE PAGODA**	**7.50 — 12.00**
12. ☐ **PLAYBOY**	**9.50 — 12.00**
13. ☐ **PRINCESS**	**9.50 — 12.00**
14. ☐ **SAKE GOD,** Colorful robe, Porcelain 10" high	**6.00 — 9.00**
15. ☐ **SAKE GOD,** White, Bone China, 10" high	**6.00 — 9.00**
*WHITE LION MAN	**12.00 — 20.00**

• KIKUKAWA BOTTLES •

16. ☐ **HOKUSAI,** Round flask, porcelain, multicolor	**7.50 — 9.50**
17. ☐ **TOYOKUNI,** Round flask, porcelain, Kabuki actor	**8.50 — 12.00**
18. ☐ **HARUNOBO,** Round flask, Geishas	**8.50 — 12.00**
19. ☐ **UTAMARO,** Oval flask, porcelain, multicolor	**9.50 — 13.50**

• KAMOTSURU BOTTLES •

20. ☐ **DAOKOKU,** God of wealth	**14.50 — 18.50**
21. ☐ **EBISU,** God of fisherman	**14.50 — 18.50**
22. ☐ **HOTEI,** God of wealth	**14.50 — 18.50**
23. ☐ **GODDESS** of art	**10.00 — 13.50**

Pictures Courtesy: Numano International Inc.

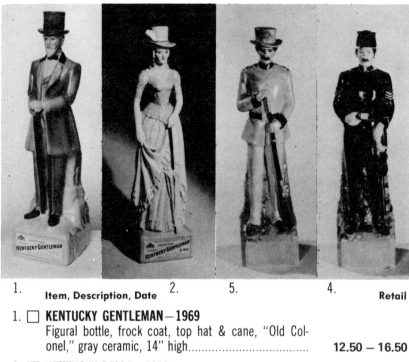

1.　　　　　　　　　　2.　　　5.　　　　　　4.

	Item, Description, Date	**Retail**

1. ☐ **KENTUCKY GENTLEMAN—1969**
Figural bottle, frock coat, top hat & cane, "Old Colonel," gray ceramic, 14" high .... **12.50 — 16.50**

2. ☐ **KENTUCKY BELLE—1969**
Long bustle skirt, feathered hat, parasol, pink, 13-3/4" high .... **12.50 — 16.50**

3. ☐ **FRONTIERS MAN—1969**
Coonskin cap, fringed buckskin, powder horn and long rifle, tan, 14" high .... **12.00 — 16.50**

4. ☐ **UNION ARMY SARGEANT**
In dress blue uniform, with sword 14" high. .... **9.95 — 12.50**

5. ☐ **CONFEDERATE INFANTRY**
In gray uniform, holding rifle 13-1/2" high. .... **9.95 — 12.50**

6. ☐ **REVOLUTIONARY WAR OFFICER**
In dress uniform, and boots, holding sword, 14" high. **9.95 — 12.50**

The motto of Lionstone Distilleries, Ltd., should most certainly be, "Go West young man, go West!", for the majority of their beautiful and unique collectable figure bottles depict the fascinating and legendary characters of the Old West. Although a comparative newcomer to the ranks of collectable bottle producers, Lionstone Distilleries items quickly become among the most sought after, and admired, by the bottle collecting fraternity, and the general public.

THE WESTERN FIGURALS

The Western figurals, such as: Jesse James, Sod-Buster, Mountain Man, Proud Indian, Wells Fargo Man, Cowboy, Gold Panner, Highway Robber, Chinese Laundryman, Gentleman Gambler, etc., are distinguished by a remarkable clarity of detail in costume, character accessories, and color.

Each bottle is a miniature piece of sculpture that exactly captures the expression of these storied Western characters. The female Western personalities are not neglected, with Annie Oakley (complete with gun & medals), The Madam, Camp Follower, etc., all are represented in original costumes, and poses. The bottles for 1973/74 continue with Buffalo Hunter, Calamity Jane, Judge Roy Bean, Blacksmith, etc.

MINT BAR SET & SHOOTOUT

The 'Piece de resistance in Lionstone bottles is the Mint Bar Set, which is composed of 3 separate Western Bar scenes, featuring Cowboys, Dance Hall Girl, Travelin' Man, and Bartender, all framed in hand-carved border. Two varieties are known — with nude in the bar painting, and without nude.

The latest Lionstone Western bottle (not yet available) is the fantastic "Shootout At OK Corral", featuring Wyatt Earp, Doc Holliday, and the Clanton Gang — 9 Gunfighters, 2 horses. Three bottles, together recreating the famous gunfight of October 26, 1881. This will probably become one of the most valuable collectable bottles ever produced.

Lionstone's other bottles on American Game Birds, and Racing Cars, are also done with great fidelity in color and form. New series on SPORTS, CIRCUS PEOPLE, TROPICAL BIRDS, ORIENTAL WORKERS, continue the great Lionstone traditional of beauty, accuracy, and collectibility in bottles.

ACKNOWLEDGEMENTS

With thanks and appreciation for advice, and cooperation to Mr. David H. Lowenstein, President, Lionstone DISTILLERIES' LTD., Denver, Colorado and Ms. Sue Wilson.

LIONSTONE BOTTLES

$18.00 — $22.00   2. $18.00 — $24.50   3. $18.00 — $24.00

8.

All prices are for Mint Condition

Name of Bottle	Retail
1. ☐ AL UNSER #1	18.00 — 22.00
2. ☐ ANNIE CHRISTMAS	18.00 — 22.00
3. ☐ ANNIE OAKLEY	18.00 — 24.00
4. ☐ BARTENDER	28.00 — 36.00
5. ☐ BELLY ROBBER	18.00 — 22.00
6. ☐ CASUAL INDIAN	12.00 — 20.00
7. ☐ CAVALRY SCOUT	10.00 — 18.00
8. ☐ COUNTRY DOCTOR	18.00 — 24.50
9. ☐ CAMP COOK	20.00 — 30.00
10. ☐ COWBOY	10.00 — 18.00

LIONSTONE BOTTLES

$20.00 — $30.00

9. **$28.00 — $36.00**

4.

$22.50 — $32.50

18.

28.

31.

$25.00 — $35.00

$28.00 — $32.50

LIONSTONE BOTTLES

All prices are for Mint Condition

Name of Bottle	Retail
11. ☐ CAMP FOLLOWER	18.50 — 22.00
12. ☐ CHINESE LAUNDRYMAN	14.50 — 22.00
13. ☐ CIRCUIT JUDGE	20.00 — 26.00
14. ☐ CHERRY VALLEY CLUB	32.00 — 35.00
15. ☐ FRONTIERSMAN	22.50 — 29.00
16. ☐ GAMBELS QUAIL	15.00 — 22.50
17. ☐ GENTLEMAN GAMBLER	10.50 — 15.00
18. ☐ GOLD PANNER	22.50 — 32.50
19. ☐ HIGHWAY ROBBER	12.50 — 25.00
20. ☐ JESSE JAMES	14.50 — 22.00
21. ☐ JOHNNY LIGHTNING	12.00 — 20.00
22. ☐ MINIATURES, WESTERN. Set of six	70.00 — 80.00
23. ☐ MINT BAR SCENE. With Frame.*	300.00 — 400.00
24. ☐ MINT BAR SCENE. With Nude & Frame.*	400.00 — 500.00
25. ☐ MOUNTAIN MAN	26.50 — 32.00
26. ☐ PROUD INDIAN	12.50 — 20.00
27. ☐ RAILROAD ENGINEER	16.50 — 22.00
28. ☐ RENEGADE TRADER	25.00 — 35.00
29. ☐ RIVERBOAT CAPTAIN	14.50 — 22.00
30. ☐ ROADRUNNER	35.00 — 45.00
31. ☐ SHEEPHERDER	28.00 — 32.50
32. ☐ SHERIFF	4.50 — 12.00
33. ☐ SOD BUSTER	18.50 — 22.00
34. ☐ STP TURBOCAR	10.00 — 15.00
35. ☐ STP TURBOCAR. Gold & Platinum, pair	60.00 — 75.00
36. ☐ SQUAWMAN	18.50 — 25.00
37. ☐ STAGECOACH DRIVER	22.00 — 29.00
38. ☐ TELEGRAPHER	22.00 — 24.00

*Individual Bar Scene No. 1,2,3,4 — 85.00 - 120.00 Each

LIONSTONE BOTTLES

$14.50 – $22.00

12.

$15.00 – $22.50

$18.50 – $22.00

16.

11.

33.

15.

20.

$18.50 – $22.00

$22.50 – $29.00

$14.50 – $22.00

LIONSTONE BOTTLES

34.

$10.00 — $15.00

$18.00 — $22.00

1.

23.

$300.00 — $400.00

$400.00 — $500.00
(with nude)

MINT BAR SET — 4 Individual Scene Bottles, Framed.

1972–73–74

All Prices are for Mint Condition

Retail

1. ☐ Annie Christmas .... 20.00 – 24.00
2. ☐ Blacksmith .... 20.00 – 22.50
3. ☐ Buffalo Hunter (see cover) .... 24.50 – 28.50
4. ☐ Clamity Jane .... 32.00 – 36.00
5. ☐ Judge Roy Bean .... 28.00 – 32.00
6. ☐ Lonely Luke .... 32.00 – 36.00
7. ☐ Lucky Buck .... 22.00 – 26.00
8. ☐ Molly Brown .... 24.50 – 28.50
9. ☐ Tinker .... 28.00 – 32.00
10. ☐ Tribal Chief .... 30.00 – 34.00
11. ☐ Woodhawk .... 18.00 – 28.00

3.

$24.50 – $28.50

8.

$24.50 – $28.50

LIONSTONE BOTTLES
72 – 73 – 74

ORIENTAL WORKER SERIES:

Name of Bottle	Retail
12. ☐ Basket Weaver	32.50 – 35.00
13. ☐ Egg Merchant	32.50 – 35.00
14. ☐ Gardner	32.50 – 35.00
15. ☐ Sculptor	32.50 – 35.00
16. ☐ Tea Vendor	30.50 – 32.00
17. ☐ Timekeeper	30.50 – 32.00

SPORTS SERIES:

18. ☐ Baseball	COMPLETE SET
19. ☐ Basketball	$180.00 – $220.00
20. ☐ Boxing	
21. ☐ Football	EACH
22. ☐ Hockey	$24.50 – $30.00

TROPICAL BIRD SERIES:
(Miniatures)

23. ☐ Blue Crowned Chlorophonia	COMPLETE SET
24. ☐ Emerald Toucanet	$60.00 – $70.00
25. ☐ Northern Royal Flycatcher	
26. ☐ Painted Bunting	EACH
27. ☐ Scarlet Macaw	$10.00 – $15.00
28. ☐ Yellow Headed Amazon	

CIRCUS SERIES:
(Miniatures)

29. ☐ Burmese Lady	
30. ☐ The Barker	
31. ☐ Fat Lady	COMPLETE SET
32. ☐ Fire Eater	$80.00 – $100.00
33. ☐ Giant with Midget	
34. ☐ Snake Charmer	EACH
35. ☐ Strong Man	$10.00 – $15.00
36. ☐ Sword Swallower	
37. ☐ Tattooed Lady	

72 – 73 – 74

BIRD SERIES:

	Name of Bottle	Retail
38. ☐	Bluebird – Wisconsin	35.00 – 40.00
39. ☐	Bluejay	35.00 – 40.00
40. ☐	Peregrine Falcon	25.00 – 30.00
41. ☐	Meadowlark	18.50 – 22.00
42. ☐	Swallow	20.00 – 24.50
43. ☐	Screech Owl	22.50 – 26.00

OTHER LIONSTONE BOTTLES:

		Retail
44. ☐	The Bucaneer	30.00 – 36.00
45. ☐	The Cowgirl	24.50 – 30.00
46. ☐	Dance Hall Girl	28.00 – 32.00
47. ☐	Fire Fighter No. 2	25.00 – 30.00
48. ☐	Indian Mother & Papoose	24.50 – 30.00
49. ☐	Peregrine Falcon	25.00 – 30.00
50. ☐	Screech Owls	22.50 – 27.50
51. ☐	Roses on Parade	40.00 – 50.00
52. ☐	Unser–Olsonite Eagle	30.00 – 38.00
53. ☐	The "Perfesser"	24.50 – 30.00

45. $24.50 – $30.00   **46.** $28.00 – $32.00

LIONSTONE BOTTLES
72 – 73 – 74

48.

$24.50 — $30.00

49.

$25.00 — $30.00

A.B.P.
40%—60%
of Retail Price

72 – 73 – 74

50.　　　　$22.50 — $27.50

51.　　$40.00 — $50.00

53.　$24.50 — $30.00

52.　　$30.00 — $38.00

LUXARDO BOTTLES

Luxardo or "Ardo" decanters are made in Italy, and are included in many of the finest bottle collections in the world. These distinctive, colorful glass and Majolica (pottery) containers are exported to over 50 countries around the world including the United States.

Many of the Luxardo bottles, both glass and Majolica, are figural, using animals, birds, fish, and classic and popular figures. The first of the Majolica amphoras· were imported into the U. S. in 1930. Most of the Majolica decanters and bottles are resuable as vases, jars, lampbases, or ash trays.

• THE NEW DESIGNS •

Between three and six new designs are selected every January for that year's production. The most popular, such as the *Cellini* bottle first created in the early 1950s still continues to be used—it is an outstanding example of the Luxardo line. Sometimes however, a design is dropped after only one year's use, one example is the *Chess Set* of 1959. Too difficult and too costly to produce, it was dropped from the line.

• ZARA DECANTERS & MURANO GLASS •

Collectors are unaware of the names given to most of the Luxardo decanters or when they were made or imported. Early collectors often removed the paper labels which prevents proper identification.

The Zara decanters created before World War II are extremely rare and are expected to increase in value and become a greater challenge to collectors. The "First Born" of the Murano Venetian glass, if ever located, will command a still higher price and the Naponelli "signed" decanters will increase in price as time passes considering the limited number that were imported.

• VALUE OF LUXARDO BOTTLES & DECANTERS •

Collectors will find many of these bottles for sale at flea markets giving the knowledgeable collector an unusual opportunity to find real buys at low low prices. An added value to all Luxardo decanters should be stressed: they are all hand made and hand decorated, no two are alike, and it is probable that bottles in mint condition bearing their labels will bring the highest prices. All prices listed are for empty bottles, in fine to mint condition.

• WHERE TO GET LUXARDO BOTTLES •

Many fine liquor stores throughout the country stock Luxardo bottles containing the excellent liquers and wines made by the GIROLAMO LUXARDO Co. of Torreglia, Italy. If not available, the dealer can order from the importer: Hans Schonewald, American Beverage Brokers, 420 Market St., S. F. Calif.,94111.

ACKNOWLEDGEMENTS: *Mr. Nicoló Luxardo, GIROLAMO LUXARDO CO. Torreglia-Padova, Italy. Mr. Hans Schonewald, AMERICAN BEVERAGE BROKERS.*
PICTURES: *Mr. Nicoló Luxardo, Mr. Hans Schonewald. A. & J. Kessler Liquors*

**Prices are for Empty Bottles in Mint
Condition with Tops, Holders, Handles & Labels**

Item, Description, Date	Retail
1. ☐ **ALABASTER FISH—FIGURAL—1960**	**35.00 — 37.50**
2. ☐ **ALABASTER GOOSE—FIGURAL—1960**	**32.50 — 35.50**
3. ☐ **AMPULLA—FLASK—1959**	**35.00 — 37.00**
4. ☐ **BLUE FIAMMETTA—Decanter—1957**	**17.50 — 22.00**
5. ☐ **CANDLESTICK—ALABASTER—1961**	**25.00 — 30.00**
6. ☐ **CELLINI VASE—1958** Glass & Silver Decanter	**22.50 — 27.00**
7. ☐ **CELLINI VASE—1957** Glass & Silver Handled Decanter. With Serpent Handle—1958, as above.	**32.00 — 35.00**
8. ☐ **COCKTAIL SHAKER—1957** Glass & Silver Decanter	**17.50 — 22.50**
9. ☐ **CURVA VASO VASE—1961** Green, Green & White, Ruby Red.	**25.00 — 28.00**
10. ☐ **DOGAL SILVER & GREEN DECANTER—1952-55** Hand painted Gondola	**22.50 — 24.50**
11. ☐ **DOGAL SILVER SMOKE DECANTER—1952-55** Hand painted Gondola	**20.00 — 24.00**
12. ☐ **DOGAL SILVER SMOKE DECANTER—1953-54** Hand painted Gondola	**18.50 — 22.50**
13. ☐ **DOGAL SILVER RUBY—1952-54** Hand painted Gondola	**22.50 — 26.00**
14. ☐ **DOGAL SILVER GREEN DECANTER—1956** Hand painted Gondola	**20.00 — 24.00**
15. ☐ **DOGAL SILVER SMOKE DECANTER—1956** Hand painted silver Clouds & Gondola.	**18.50 — 22.50**

LUXARDO BOTTLES—VENETIAN GLASS

1.

$35.00 – $37.50

23.

$35.00 – $37.50

$22.50 – $27.50

6.

19.

$32.50 – $35.00

RED & GOLD

26.

BLACK: $175.00 – $250.00

$12.50 – $14.50

**Prices are for Empty Bottles in Mint
Condition with Tops, Holders, Handles & Labels**

Item, Description, Date	Retail
16. ☐ **DOGAL SILVER SMOKE DECANTER — 1957** Hand painted Gondola, buildings, flowers, neck bands.	18.50 — 22.50
17. ☐ **DOGAL SILVER RUBY DECANTER — 1956** Hand painted Venetian scene & flowers......................	22.50 — 24.00
18. ☐ **DOLPHIN FIGURAL — 1959** Yellow, Green, Blue..	85.00 — 110.00
19. ☐ **"DOUGHNUT" BOTTLE — CLOCK BOTTLE — 1962** Working clock in Doughnut shape bottle....................	12.50 — 14.50
20. ☐ **DUCK-GREEN GLASS FIGURAL — 1960** Green & Amber Duck Clear Glass Base......................	32.50 — 35.00
21. ☐ **FISH — GREEN & GOLD GLASS FIGURAL — 1960** Green & Silver & Gold, Clear Glass Base....................	28.50 — 30.00
22. ☐ **FISH — RUBY MURANO GLASS FIGURAL — 1961** Ruby red tones of glass...	34.00 — 38.00
23. ☐ **PUPPY — MURANO GLASS FIGURAL — 1960** Amber Glass, Crystal Base.......................................	35.00 — 37.50
24. ☐ **PUPPY — CUCCIOLO GLASS FIGURAL — 1961** Amber & Green glass...	26.00 — 30.00
25. ☐ **PENGUIN — MURANO GLASS FIGURAL — 1968** Black & White penguin, crystal base...........................	36.00 — 38.00
26. ☐ **PHEASANT — RED & GOLD FIGURAL — 1960** Red & Gold glass bird on crystal base.	32.50 — 35.00
27. ☐ **PHEASANT — MURANO GLASS FIGURAL — 1960 *** Red & clear glass on a crystal base...........................	30.00 — 32.00
28. ☐ **SILVER BROWN DECANTER — 1952-55** Hand painted silver flowers and leaves......................	22.50 — 25.00
*BLACK PHEASANT **RARE**	175.00 — 250.00

LUXARDO BOTTLES
VENETIAN GLASS

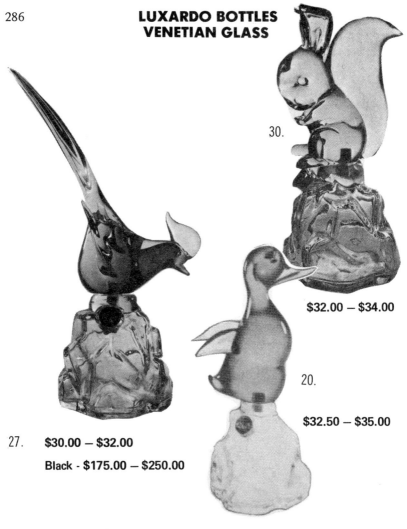

30.

$32.00 — $34.00

20.

$32.50 — $35.00

27.   **$30.00 — $32.00**

Black - $175.00 — $250.00

29. ☐ **SILVER BLUE DECANTER**—1952-54
Hand painted silver flowers and leaves...................... **22.50 — 25.00**

30. ☐ **SQUIRREL GLASS FIGURAL**—1968
Amethyst colored squirrel on crystal base................... **32.00 — 34.00**

Item, Description, Date	Retail
1. ☐ **APOTHECARY JAR**—1960 Hand painted multicolor, green & black......................	**12.50 — 15.00**
2. ☐ **AUTUMN LEAVES DECANTER**—1952 Hand painted, 2 handles...	**30.00 — 35.00**
3. ☐ **APPLE FIGURAL**—1960 * Yellow apple, green leaves......................................	**15.00 — 17.50**
4. ☐ **ASSYRIAN ASHTRAY DECANTER**—1961 Grey, tan, and black...	**22.50 — 25.00**
5. ☐ **AUTUMN WINE PITCHER**—1958 Hand painted country scene, handled pitcher.	**30.00 — 35.00**
6. ☐ **BABYLON DECANTER**—1960 Dark green & gold..	**18.00 — 22.00**
7. ☐ **BABY AMPHORAS**—1956 Six hand painted miniature bottles set, vari-colored.....	**15.00 — 20.00**
8. ☐ **BAROQUE GOLD RUBY AMPHORA**—1955 Ruby red & gold. Gold handles..................................	**50.00 — 60.00**
9. ☐ **BAROQUE GOLD TURQUOISE PITCHER**—1956 Turquoise bottle with gold handle and trim.................	**24.00 — 28.00**
10. ☐ **BAROQUE GOLD RUBY AMPHORA**—1957 2 Gold handles and gold trim on Ruby red bottle.	**25.00 — 30.00**
11. ☐ **BLACK & GREEN AMPULLA**—1958 2 handles, painted forest scene...............................	**30.00 — 34.00**
12. ☐ **BIZANTINA**—1959 Gold embossed design white body...........................	**28.50 — 32.50**
13. ☐ **BLUE & GOLD AMPHORA**—1968 Blue and gold with pastoral scene in white oval.	**16.50 — 20.00**
14. ☐ **BROCCA (PITCHER)**—1958 White background pitcher with handle multicolor flowers, green leaves..	**26.00 — 30.00**
*GRAPES, PEAR FIGURAL	**15.00 — 17.50**

288

LUXARDO BOTTLES—MAJOLICA

**Prices are for Empty Bottles in Mint
Condition with Tops, Holders,
Handles & Labels**

37.

50C.

38.

1.

13.

48.

18.

44.

51.

Item, Description, Date	Retail

15. ☐ **BUDDHA GODDESS FIGURAL—1961**
Goddess head in green-gray stone. .... **20.00 — 26.00**

16. ☐ **BURMA ASH TRAY—SPECIALTY—1960**
Embossed white dancing figure, dark green background   **30.00 — 32.50**

17. ☐ **BURMA PITCHER—SPECIALTY—1960**
Green & gold, white embossed dancing figure.............. **24.00 — 26.00**

18. ☐ **CALYPSO GIRL—FIGURAL—1962**
Black West Indian girl, flower headress in bright
colors. .... **17.50 — 20.00**

19. ☐ **CERAMIC BARREL—1960**
Barrel shape, barrel color, painted flowers, embossed
scroll with cameo head. .:.. **13.00 — 15.00**

20. ☐ **CLASSICAL FRAGMENT—SPECIALTY—1961**
Embossed Classic Roman female figure and ˈvase. **22.50 — 25.00**

21. ☐ **COFFEE CARAFE—SPECIALTY—1962**
"Old-time" coffee pot, with handle and spout, white
with blue flowers.. **15.00 — 17.50**

22. ☐ **CHERRY BASKET—FIGURAL—1960**
White basket, red cherries... **35.00 — 37.50**

23. ☐ **DERUTA CAMEO AMPHORA—1959**
Colorful floral scrolls and cameo head on eggshell
white 2 handled vase.. **45.00 — 50.00**

24. ☐ **DERUTA AMPHORA—1956**
Colorful floral design on white 2 handled decanter. **35.00 — 40.00**

25. ☐ **DIANA—DECANTER—1956**
White figure of Diana with deer on black sungle handled
decanter.. **30.00 — 35.00**

26. ☐ **DRAGON PITCHER—1958**
One handle, white pitcher, colorful dragon and scroll
work. .... **32.50 — 35.00**

27. ☐ **DRAGON AMPHORA**—1953
    2 handled white decanter with colorful dragon and
    flowers.. **34.50 — 38.00**

28. ☐ **DERUTA PITCHER**—1953
    Multicolor flowers on white single-handled pitcher. **40.00 — 48.00**

29. ☐ **EGYPTIAN—SPECIALTY**—1959
    2 handle amphora, Egyptian design on tan & gold
    background. .... **17.50 — 19.50**

30. ☐ **EUGANEAN BRONZE**—1952-55

30. ☐ **EUGANEAN BRONZE**—1952-55................................ **35.00 — 40.00**

31. ☐ **EUGANEAN COPPER**—1952-55................................ **35.00 — 40.00**

32. ☐ **ETRUSCA DECANTER**—1959
    Single handle black Greek design on tan background. **22.50 — 25.00**

33. ☐ **EAGLE, ONYX**—1970................................... **40.00 — 50.00**

34. ☐ **FAENZA DECANTER**—1956
    Colorful country scene on white single handle decanter **32.50 — 38.00**

35. ☐ **FLORENTINE MAJOLICA**—1956
    Round handled decanter, painted Italian scene. .... **25.00 — 30.00**

36. ☐ **FIGHTING COCKS**—1962
    Combination decanter & ashtray, black & red fighting birds **27.50**

37. ☐ **GONDOLA**—1959
    Highly glazed "abstract" gondola & gondolier in black,
    orange, and yellow. Stopper on upper prow, 12-1/4"high **30.00 — 35.00**

38. ☐ **GONDOLA MINIATURE**-1959
    Same as above, 4-1/2" high..................................... **6.00 — 8.00**

39. ☐ **GONDOLA**—1960
    Same as 1959, Stopper moved from prow to stern **16.00 — 18.00**
    ☐ Miniature—1960 .... **5.00 — 6.00**

40. ☐ **GAMBIA**—1961
    Black princess, kneeling holding tray, gold trim,
    10-3/4" high... **15.00 — 20.00**

41. ☐ **GOLDEN FAKIR**—1961
    Seated snake charmer, with flute and snakes, gold **42.00 — 45.00**

42. ☐ **MAYAN—1960**
A Mayan temple God head mask, brown, yellow,
black, white, 11" high.. **27.50 — 32.50**

43. ☐ **MOSAIC ASHTRAY—1959**
Combination decanter ashtray, mosaic pattern of
rearing horse, black, yellow, green, 11-1/2" high. **24.00 — 28.00**

44. ☐ **NUBIAN**
Kneeling black figure, gold dress & headress, 9-1/2" **15.00 — 20.00**
☐ Miniature, as above, 4-3/4" high. .... **4.50 — 5.50**

45. ☐ **OPAL MAJOLICA—1957**
Two gold handles, translucent opal top, pink base,
also used as lamp base, 10" high............................ **40.00 — 50.00**

46. ☐ **PRIMAVERA AMPHORA—1958**
2 handled vase shape, with floral design in yellow,
green, and blue, 9-3/4" high.................................... **30.00 — 40.00**

47. ☐ **SIR LANCELOT—1962**
Figure of English knight in full armor with embossed
shield, tan-gray with gold, 12" high........................... **42.50 — 50.00**

48. ☐ **SUDAN—1960**
Two handle classic vase, incused figures, African
motif in browns, blue, yellow & gray, 13-1/2" high **20.00 — 22.50**

49. ☐ **SPRINGBOK AMPHORA—1952**
Vase with handle, leaping African deer, with floral
and lattice background, black, white, brown, 9-3/4" high **40.00 — 45.00**

50. ☐ **TOWER OF FRUIT—MAJOLICAS**
 a. ☐ **TORRE BIANCA—1962**
White and grey tower of fruit, 10-1/4" high .... **18.50 — 22.50**
 b. ☐ **TORRE ROSA—1962**
Rose tinted tower of fruit, 10-1/4" high...................... **22.50 — 27.50**
 c. ☐ **TORRE TINTA—1962**
Multicolor tower of fruit, natural shades..................... **16.00 — 18.00**
 d. ☐ **TOWER OF FRUIT—1968**
Various fruits in natural colors, 22-1/4" high. .... **14.50 — 17.50**

51. ☐ **TOWER OF FLOWERS—1968**
Heaping flower basket in natural colors, 22-1/4" high.. **14.50 — 17.50**

Prices are for Empty Bottles

in Mint Condition

1.

11.

1. ☐ NAPOLEON.............45.00 — 65.00
2. ☐ MARSHAL LASSAL...   34.95
3. ☐ MARSHAL NEY........18.00 — 21.95
4. ☐ MARSHAL EUGENE...18.00 — 21.95
5. ☐ MARSHAL LANNES...18.00 — 21.95
6. ☐ MARSHAL MURAT ...18.00 — 21.95

7. ☐ 2nd MARYLAND.............. 29.95
8. ☐ CONTINENTAL MARINES.... 20.00
9. ☐ BAYLORS 3rd................... 20.00
10. ☐ 3rd NEW YORK 20.00
11 ☐ 1st PENNSYLVANIA 20.00
12. ☐ 18th CONTINENTAL......... 20.00

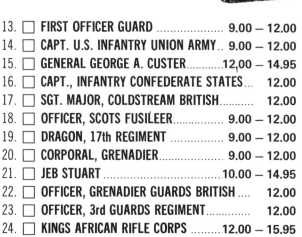

24.

13. ☐ FIRST OFFICER GUARD .... 9.00 — 12.00
14. ☐ CAPT. U.S. INFANTRY UNION ARMY.. 9.00 — 12.00
15. ☐ GENERAL GEORGE A. CUSTER...........12,00 — 14.95
16. ☐ CAPT., INFANTRY CONFEDERATE STATES... 12.00
17. ☐ SGT. MAJOR, COLDSTREAM BRITISH.......... 12.00
18. ☐ OFFICER, SCOTS FUSILEER................ 9.00 — 12.00
19. ☐ DRAGON, 17th REGIMENT .... 9.00 — 12.00
20. ☐ CORPORAL, GRENADIER................... 9.00 — 12.00
21. ☐ JEB STUART ....10.00 — 14.95
22. ☐ OFFICER, GRENADIER GUARDS BRITISH 12.00
23. ☐ OFFICER, 3rd GUARDS REGIMENT............. 12.00
24. ☐ KINGS AFRICAN RIFLE CORPS ....12.00 — 15.95
25. ☐ KINGS AFRICAN RARE QUART SIZE...12.00 — 25.00

McCORMICK BOTTLES

O.B.R. BOTTLES (OLD BLUE RIBBON)

1. ☐ BLUE BIRD .... 12.00 — 16.50
2. ☐ K.C. ROYALS... 15.00 — 20.00
3. ☐ AIR RACE DECANTER (PYLON) .... 8.50 — 12.50
4. ☐ JUPITER '60 MAIL CAR... 10.00 — 14.00
5. ☐ JUPITER 60 PASSENGER CAR................................. 12.50 — 16.50
6. ☐ JUPITER 60 WOOD TENDER.................................... 22.00 — 30.00
7. ☐ JUPITER 60 LOCOMOTIVE...................................... 22.00 — 30.00

O.B.R. TRANSPORTATION SERIES

8. ☐ RIVER QUEEN * .... 10.00 — 15.00
9. ☐ BALLOON .... 6.50 — 9.50
10. ☐ PRAIRIE SCHOONER.. 7.50 — 12.95
11. ☐ 5TH AVE. BUS.. 10.50 — 14.95

O.B.R. HOCKEY SERIES

12. ☐ NEW YORK RANGERS.. 15.00 — 17.95
13. ☐ MINNESOTA NORTH STARS .... 15.00 — 17.95
14. ☐ DETROIT RED WINGS.. 15.00 — 17.95
15. ☐ BOSTON BRUINS... 15.00 — 17.95
16. ☐ CHICAGO BLACK HAWKS .... 15.00 — 17.95
17. ☐ ST. LOUIS BLUES .... 15.00 — 17.95

*RIVER QUEEN — GOLD
$15.00 — $20.00

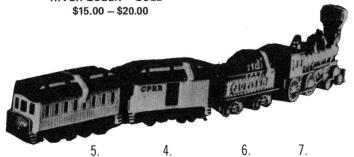

5.   4.   6.   7.

$8.50 — $12.50

3.

$15.00 — $20.00   2.

KANSAS CITY CHIEFS—1971
COMMEMORATIVE BOTTLE 15.00 — 25.00

7.

MISSOURI SESQUICENTENNIAL—1970
COMMEMORATIVE DECANTER   **$25.00 — $35.00**

Courtesy: McCORMICK DISTILLING CO., Weston, Missouri

1972–74

Bottle	Retail

1. ☐ "PIRATES" – 6 DIFFERENT TYPES & COSTUMES
   EACH .... 10.00 – 14.00
2. ☐ ROBERT E. LEE .... 25.00 – 35.00
3. ☐ YACHT "AMERICA" .... 25.00 – 35.00
4. ☐ "PLATTE VALLEY" POTTERY JUG .... 7.50 – 10.00
5. ☐ AGING BARREL WITH SPIGOT .... 6.00 – 9.00
6. ☐ WESTERN GUNFIGHTERS WYATT EARP, JESSE JAMES,
   DOC HOLIDAY, BILLY THE KID, BAT MASTERSON,
   BLACK BART, WILD BILL HICKOCK, CALAMITY JANE,
   MEXICAN GUN FIGHTER .... EA. 21.50 – 26.50

O.B.R. (OLD BLUE RIBBON) BOTTLES

7. ☐ PIERCE–ARROW .... 13.50 – 18.50
8. ☐ CABOOSE MKT .... 11.50 – 15.00
9. ☐ "TITANIC" OCEAN LINER .... 26.50 – 30.00
10. ☐ "SANTA MARIA" COLUMBUS SHIP .... 12.50 – 16.50

5.

$6.00 – $9.00

4.

AGED IN THE HILLS

PLATTE VALLEY

STRAIGHT
CORN WHISKEY

$7.50 – $10.00

Courtesy: STITZEL—WELLER, Louisville, Kentucky

Bottle, Description, Date	**Retail**

1. ☐ **JEWEL DECANTER**—1951-52
   Flint glass, beveled neck. .... **8.50 — 15.00**

2. ☐ **GOLD WEB DECANTER**—1953
   Flint glass, gold web and frame fused onto decanter. **18.00 — 22.50**

3. ☐ **GOLD COASTER DECANTER**—1954
   Flint glass decanter, gold metal coaster..................... **14.50 — 18.00**

4. ☐ **HILLBILLY BOTTLE**—PINT—1954
   "Hillbilly" on Barrel with Rifle, in brown, tan, black
   & green, 9-1/8" high... **30.00 — 45.00**

5. ☐ **HILLBILLY BOTTLE**—QUART—1954
   Same as above, 11-3/8" high.................................. **35.00 — 45.00**

6. ☐ **HILLBILLY BOTTLE**—GALLON—1954
   Same as above, gallon size Very Rare...................... **200.00**

7. ☐ **CANDLELITE DECANTER**—1955
   Removable gold candle holder mounted on flint glass. **20.00 — 30.00**

8. ☐ **OLD CABIN STILL DECANTER**—1958
   Gold letters "OLD CABIN STILL" infused on Flint
   glass bottle, solid faceted stopper. .... **15.00 — 25.00**

9. ☐ **WELLER MASTER PIECE**—1963
   White porcelain apothecary bottle, rebus design,
   gold bands, 10-5/8" high...................................... **35.00 — 50.00**

10. ☐ **POINTING SETTER DECANTER**
    Dog on point, brown, tan & white, glass, 12" high. **14.50 — 16.50**

11. ☐ **BROWSING DEER DECANTER**—1967
    Deer and woods scene, brown, tan, and white, amber
    stopper. .... **6.50 — 9.00**

12. ☐ **LEPRECHAUN BOTTLE**—1968
    Porcelain bottle, gold band, green shamrocks, Irish
    verse, 10-1/8" high.. **20.00 — 30.00**

13. ☐ **QUAIL ON THE WING DECANTER**—1968
    Round glass bottle, 3 color design, 12" high.............. **6.00 — 8.50**

EAGLE & MASONIC FLASK

Listing & Prices:
"OLD FLASKS"
&
"BITTERS
BOTTLES"

BROWN'S
INDIAN HERB
BITTERS

CORNOCUPIA
& FRUIT
BASKET
FLASK

Index of American Design
National Gallery of Art
Washington, D.C.

JIM BEAM BOTTLES

For Listing & Pricing See:
"JIM BEAM BOTTLES"

MT. RUSHMORE
PRESIDENTS

BOEING 747

AMERICAN
LEGION

For Listing & Pricing See "J.W. DANT" Section

NEW COLLECTIBLE BOTTLES

GEORGE
DICKEL
POWDER
HORN

OLD CABIN STILL

WINGS
ACROSS THE
CONTINENT

For Listing & Pricing See:
"OLD CABIN STILL" &
"MISCELLANEOUS BOTTLES"

NEW COLLECTIBLE BOTTLES

OLD FITZGERALD
SONGS OF IRELAND

McCORMICK - MISSOURI
State-shaped Bottle

JACK DANIELS - OLD NO. 7
Reproduction of Antique Bar Bottle

Courtesy: **GIROLAMO LUXARDO CO.**
Torreglia, Italy

For Listing & Pricing See:
"LUXARDO BOTTLES"

For Listing & Pricing See: "OLD WHISKEY BOTTLES"

Bottle, Description, Date	Retail

14. ☐ **HILLBILLY—1969**
Same bottle as 1954 "HILLBILLY" more detail and
color, 11-1/2" high .... **8.50 — 12.50**

15. ☐ **SONS OF ERIN—PORCELAIN—1969**........................ **10.00 — 20.00**

16. ☐ **MEMPHIS COMMEMORATIVE—PORCELAIN—1969**...... **15.00 — 30.00**

17. ☐ **COLONIAL DECANTER—GLASS—1969** .... **6.00 — 8.50**

18. ☐ **MAN O'WAR DECANTER—GLASS—1969** .... **6.50 — 9.00**

19. ☐ **LEAPING TROUT DECANTER—1969** .... **6.50 — 9.00**

20. ☐ **SOUTH CAROLINA TRICENTENNIAL—1970** .... **12.50 — 16.50**

21. ☐ **CALIFORNIA BICENTENNIAL—1970**........................... **10.00 — 12.50**

22. ☐ **AMERICA'S CUP COMMEMORATIVE—1970**.................. **20.00 — 25.00**

23. ☐ **LSU ALUMNI DECANTER—1970**............................... **12.00 — 15.00**

24. ☐ **OHIO STATE CENTENNIAL—1970**............................. **15.00 — 18.00**

25. ☐ **PILGRIM LANDING COMMEMORATIVE—1970**............. **10.00 — 12.50**

26. ☐ **RIP VAN WINKLE FIGURINE—1971**
Famous Catskill character with blunderbuss and elf,
multicolor, 9-1/4" high.. **15.00 — 25.00**

Bottle, Description, Date   **Retail**

27. ☐ "REBEL YELL RIDER"-FIGURINE-1970
Confederate cavalryman bottle in 6 colors,
sold only in the South, 9¾" high .... 10.00 — 15.00
28. ☐ "BLARNEY CASTLE"-PORCELAIN-1970 .... 12.00 — 16.50
29. ☐ "WINGS ACROSS THE CONTINENT"-PORCELAIN
Duck finial-1972 .... 10.00 — 13.50
30. ☐ "SONGS OF IRELAND"-PORCELAIN-1972 .... 8.50 — 12.00
31. ☐ "GOLDEN BOUGH" DECANTER-GLASS-1971 ..... 4.50 — 6.00

28.

13.

11.

26.

19.

Retail

1. ☐ **DICKEL POWDER HORN**
Amber glass, holder and handle,15" high ... **9.50** 13" high   **4.00 – 6.00**

2. ☐ **DOUBLE SPRINGS – CERAMIC BOTTLES**
Boy Peasant, 13-1/4" High, Girl Peasant, 13" High,
Owl, 10-1/2" high ....   **10.00 – 15.00**

3. ☐ **ANDREW JACKSON – OLD HICKORY**
White ceramic figural of General Jackson, 11" high......   **25.00 – 35.00**

4. ☐ **SOUTHERN COMFORT – ROBERT E. LEE**
Ceramic figure , with BOOTS & SWORD, 11" high........   **16.50 – 22.00**

5. ☐ **OLD TAYLOR CASTLE – 1966**
Embossed ceramic castle, grey & white.....................   **5.00 – 7.50**

6. ☐ **OLD BLUE RIBBON – RIVERQUEEN – 1968**
Steamboat shape ceramic bottle, 10" high.................   **8.00 – 12.00**

7. ☐ **WILD TURKEY – AUSTIN NICHOLS**
Ceramic Wild Turkey , multicolor, limited edition, 14" high   **25.00 – 75.00**

• I.W. HARPER •

1. ☐ **I.W. HARPER, MAN, BLUE** ....   **9.50 – 15.00**

2. ☐ **I.W. HARPER, MAN, GRAY** ....   **15.00 – 20.00**

3. ☐ **I.W. HARPER, MÁN, WHITE** ....   **50.00 – 65.00**

Courtesy: I.W. HARPER – DICKEL DISTILLERS – AUSTIN NICHOLS INC.

Name of Bottle	Retail

1. □ AUSTIN NICHOLS — WILD TURKEY BOTTLES
   WILD TURKEY NO. 1 . . . . 60.00 — 75.00
   WILD TURKEY NO. 2 . . . . 30.00 — 40.00
   WILD TURKEY NO. 3 . . . . 25.00 — 35.00
   WILD TURKEY NO. 4 (Turkey with little Turkey at feet) 24.95 — 30.00
2. □ BLACK & WHITE SCOTTIES (Black and White Scotch) . . 19.95 — 28.00
3. □ DOUBLE SPRINGS BOTTLES
   CADILLAC — 1913 AUTOMOBILE . . . . 14.00 — 25.00
   MERCER AUTOMOBILE . . . . 14.00 — 25.00
   STANLEY STEAMER — 1911 AUTOMOBILE . . . . 16.50 — 24.00
   STUTZ BEARCAT — 1919 AUTOMOBILE . . . . 18.00 — 26.00
   MODEL T FORD AUTOMOBILE . . . . 18.00 — 26.00
   MILWAUKEE BUCK . . . . 10.00 — 14.50
   GEORGIA BULLDOG . . . . 12.50 — 15.50
   W.C. FIELDS — FIGURAL . . . . 18.50 — 22.50
4. □ IRISH MIST — SOLDIER, Green, red, black & white . . . . 10.00 — 15.00
5. □ OLD MR. BOSTON — BUST, Gold on Porcelain . . . . 4.50 — 6.50
6. □ OLD CROW — FIGURAL, Black crow bird . . . . 50.00 — 60.00
7. □ GRANT — "DRUMMOND" HIGHLANDER, Scot figure . 15.00 — 20.00
8. □ GRANT — "LAMMOND" CLANSWOMAN, Scot figure . . 15.00 — 20.00
9. □ DICKEL GOLF CLUB, Large size . . . . 4.50 — 6.50

THE PRESIDENTIAL SERIES

1. ☐ **ANDREW JACKSON** GREEN – 1971 .... **8.00 – 10.00**
2. ☐ **THOMAS JEFFERSON** RUBY – 1970 .... **5.00 – 7.50**
3. ☐ **THEODORE ROOSEVELT** BLUE – 1970 .... **7.50 – 15.00**
4. ☐ **GEORGE WASHINGTON** FROSTY FLINT – 1969 .... **6.50 – 12.50**
5. ☐ **WOODROW WILSON** BLUE – 1969 .... **7.50 – 15.00**
6. ☐ **GENERAL EISENHOWER** (Special Memorial Issue)........ **12.50 – 20.00**
7. ☐ **ABRAHAM LINCOLN** TOPAZ – 1968 .... **6.00 – 12.50**
8. ☐ **PRESIDENT EISENHOWER** GREEN – 1969 .... **12.50 – 24.00**
9. ☐ **FRANKLIN D. ROOSEVELT** GREEN – 1967 .... **10.00 – 22.50**
10. ☐ **JOHN F. KENNEDY** BLUE – 1967* .... **30.00 – 60.00**
11. ☐ **PRESIDENT GRANT** TOPAZ – 1972 .... **3.50 – 6.50**

*VERY RARE–HAS BEEN "QUOTED" AS HIGH AS $100.00

WHEATON/NULINE DECANTERS

Name of Bottle   **Retail**

CAMPAIGN SERIES

12. ☐ **1968 NIXON-AGNEW** TOPAZ .... 12.00 — 16.00
13. ☐ **1969 HUMPHREY-MUSKIE** GREEN .... 12.00 — 16.00

GREAT AMERICAN SERIES

14. ☐ **PAUL REVERE** BLUE — 1971 .... 5.00 — 8.00
15. ☐ **CHARLES EVANS HUGHES** BLUE — 1971 .... 4.50 — 7.50
16. ☐ **HELEN KELLER** FROSTY FLINT — 1970 .... 5.00 — 7.50
17. ☐ **JOHN PAUL JONES** GREEN — 1970 .... 5.00 — 8.00
18. ☐ **REV. BILLY GRAHAM** GREEN — 1970 .... 6.00 — 12.00
19. ☐ **BENJAMIN FRANKLIN** AQUA — 1970 .... 9.00 — 16.00
20. ☐ **BETSY ROSS** RUBY — 1969 .... 6.00 — 12.00
21. ☐ **WILL ROGERS** TOPAZ — 1969 .... 5.00 — 10.00
22. ☐ **ROBERT E. LEE** GREEN — 1969 .... 5.00 — 9.50
23. ☐ **THOMAS EDISON** BLUE — 1969 .... 3.50 — 4.50
24. ☐ **CHARLES LINDBERGH** BLUE — 1968 .... 4.50 — 8.50
25. ☐ **DOUGLAS MACARTHUR** AMETHYST — 1968 .... 4.50 — 8.50
26. ☐ **MARTIN LUTHER KING** AMBER — 1968 .... 12.50 — 20.00
27. ☐ **ROBERT KENNEDY** GREEN — 1967 .... 8.00 — 12.50
28. ☐ **HUMPHREY BOGART** (Star Decanter) GREEN — 1971 . 4.50 — 8.00
29. ☐ **JEAN HARLOW** (Star Decanter) TOPAZ — 1972 .... 3.50 — 6.00

GREAT AMERICAN SERIES

14.

$5.00 — $8.00

15.

$4.50 — $7.50

16.

$5.00 — $7.50

17.

$5.00 — $8.00

19.

$9.00 — $16.00

29.

$3.50 — $6.00

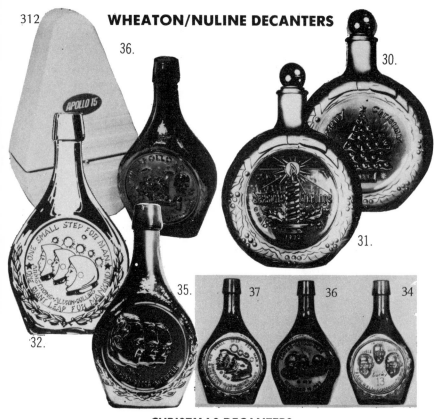

WHEATON/NULINE DECANTERS

CHRISTMAS DECANTERS

30. ☐ **MERRY CHRISTMAS** — 1971 GREEN	....	**6.00 — 8.00**
31. ☐ **SEASONS GREETINGS** — 1972 TOPAZ	....	**4.50 — 6.00**

ASTRONAUT SERIES

32. ☐ **APOLLO 11** BLUE — 1969	....	**20.00 — 40.00**
33. ☐ **APOLLO 12** RUBY — 1969	....	**30.00 — 50.00**
34. ☐ **APOLLO 13** BURLEY — 1970	....	**10.00 — 14.00**
35. ☐ **APOLLO 14** AQUA — 1971	....	**6.00 — 8.00**
36. ☐ **APOLLO 15** GREEN — 1971	....	**3.50 — 6.00**
37. ☐ **APOLLO 16** IRIDESCENT FLINT — 1972	....	**3.00 — 6.00**

THE PRESIDENTIAL SERIES

Bottle	Retail
1. ☐ LYNDON B. JOHNSON—BURLEY—1973	6.00 – 8.00
2. ☐ HARRY S. TRUMAN—RUBY—1973	6.00 – 8.00
3. ☐ MINI PRESIDENTIAL SET 1,2,3	12.50 – 15.00

GREAT AMERICAN SERIES

4. ☐ GENERAL GEORGE S. PATTON—AQUA—1973	5.00 – 7.50
5. ☐ MARK TWAIN—AMETHYST—1973	5.00 – 7.50
6. ☐ ALEXANDER GRAHAM BELL—1973	5.00 – 7.50

CHRISTMAS DECANTERS

7. ☐ CHRISTMAS HOLLY—RUBY—1973	6.00 – 8.00

ASTRONAUT SERIES

8. ☐ APOLLO 17—AMETHYST—1973	20.00 – 30.00
9. ☐ SKYLAB I—BLUE—1973	6.00 – 8.00
10. ☐ SKYLAB II—1973	6.00 – 8.00

STAR SERIES

11. ☐ W.C. FIELDS—AQUA—1973	10.00 – 15.00

PRESIDENTIAL CAMPAIGN SERIES

12. ☐ McGOVERN & SHRIVER—AMETHYST—1972 Reverse Facing Donkey Tail	Pair 50.00 – 100.00
13. ☐ McGOVERN & EAGLETON—TOPAZ—1972	5.00 – 7.50
14. ☐ McGOVERN & SHRIVER—TOPAZ—1972	5.00 – 7.50
15. ☐ NIXON & AGNEW	5.00 – 7.50

BOTTLES – Old

As a group OLD BOTTLES & FLASKS & BITTERS BOTTLES are rising in value far more rapidly than any other category of collectibles bottles. Many examples of rare types are in the $500.00 – $1,000.00 plateau, and even the more common bottles, have increased in value at auctions, and in dealers shops and advertisements.

The first OLD BOTTLE to realize the astounding sum of over $10,000.00 was the VERY RARE - TIPPACANOE NORTH BEND CABIN BOTTLE in olive green. This unique piece was sold at auction in 1974 in New Hampshire for the sum of $10,100.00.

BOTTLE GRADING

• OLD BOTTLES AND FLASKS •

Old bottles, decanters, and flasks listed in this book are priced for Mint Condition. In general the same grading standards apply as for New Bottles, as listed above, with certain differences:

To be considered Mint, an Old Bottle should be intact, with no chips, cracks, or major flaws. "Whittle marks", pontil marks, mold marks, and seams, should be clearly defined if they are a part of the bottle. Handles, and stoppers should be complete (particularly on decanters) and original. Color should be clear and clean.

Labels on Old Bottles should be intact, no rips tears, or repairs, clean and bright. Label may show wear, and slight discoloration, or yellowing, and still be considered Mint.

•

PART II/OLD BOTTLES

BITTERS BOTTLES . . . . *315 – 355*
Bitters Introduction *315*
BARBER BOTTLES *356*
COCA-COLA BOTTLES . . . . *357 – 359*
HISTORICAL & POLITICAL FLASKS . . . . *360 – 365*
INK BOTTLES . . . . *366 – 376*
MILK BOTTLES . . . . *377 – 386*
WHISKEY & BAR BOTTLES . . . . *387 – 397*
WHISKEY BOTTLES – I.W. HARPER – JACK DANIELS *388*

BEWARE: Reproductions are made of many of the most valuable OLD BOTTLES, FLASKS, & BITTERS. The best protection is to buy only from reputable dealers.

The vast majority of Bitters Bottles listed in this section where produced in the years 1860—1905. Due to a number of reasons, Bitters proliferated in this period. The pressure of anti-drinking associations opposing the consumption of whiskey, gin, and rum, and the Revenue Tax Act of 1862 which taxed these beverages much higher than proprietary medicines, led to the increase in production and consumption of Bitters.

• ALCOHOL CONTENT •

An examination of the alcohol content of popular Bitters of this period shows that most of them ranged from 15% to 60%, although the producers and sellers of Bitters emphasized the "medicinal" properties of their beverages, and most of those that consumed bitters did it with this thought in mind.

• BOTTLE SHAPES •

The Bitters bottles were made in an enormous variety of sizes and shapes. Round, square, rectangular, figural, barrel-shape, gin-shape, twelve-sided, flask-shape etc., more than a thousand varieties have been located, and new ones are constantly being discovered. Many rare ones are being reproduced.

The most common type is the figural bottle: Indians, drums, ear of corn, fish, soldiers, cannons, lighthouse, pigs, drums, etc, are some of the forms found, cabin-shapes were also quite common.

• EMBOSSING-LABELS-COLORS •

Bitters bottles were generally embossed with identifying lettering and designs. A number are made with paper labels, and some were made with either embossing, or paper labels. The embossed glass bitters are the more valuable.

Colors: Amber and it's various shades, ranging from pale golden yellow to dark amber-brown, are the most common. Aqua (light blue), is the next most popular shade, clear glass and green of all shades are also found. Deep blue, amethyst, milk glass, and puce are very rare.

• SUPPLY & VALUE •

Certain bottles of limited supply have developed a following that has escalated their cost out of proportion to others that are perhaps more deserving from a standpoint of design, shape and history.

Here again we find that as in most other antique collecting, everything else being equal, an American bottle will command a premium price over bottles made elsewhere. Bitters bottles seem well entrenched as one of the solid pillars under the whole bottle collecting field. They should continue to merit interest and acquisition by all serious bottle collectors.

BEWARE OF REPRODUCTIONS.

Illustrations: Ken Sheller

BITTERS BOTTLES

All prices are for Very Fine to Mint Condition

2.

3.

Item, Description, Date	Retail

1. ☐ **ABBOTT'S BITTERS (C.W. ABBOTT & CO. BALTIMORE)**
   Round bottle, amber, machine made............................ 10.00 — 15.00
   Miniature, pewter stopper. .... 8.00 — 12.00

2. ☐ **WILLIAM ALLEN'S CONGRESS BITTERS**
   Rectangular bottle, deep green, clear, light amber,
   10" high... 90.00 — 120.00

3. ☐ **AFRICAN STOMACH BITTERS**
   Round bottle, amber, 9-3/4" high.............................. 45.00 — 65.00

4. ☐ **AMAZON BITTERS**
   Square bottle, amber, 9" High. .... 55.00 — 70.00

5. ☐ **AMERICAN STOMACH BITTERS** *
   Oval bottle, clear glass 9" high. .... 20.00 — 30.00

6. ☐ **AROMATIC ORANGE STOMACH BITTERS**
   Square bottle, amber... 120.00 — 150.00

   *Square bottle, amber   65.00 — 75.00

BITTERS BOTTLES

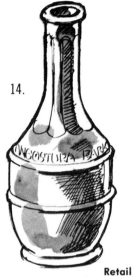

8.

12.

14.

Item, Description, Date	Retail
7. ☐ **ATWELL'S WILD CHERRY BITTERS** Oval bottle, aqua, 8" high.	**22.00 – 26.00**
8. ☐ **ATWOODS QUININE TONIC BOTTLES** Rectangular bottle, aqua 8-1/2" high.	**35.00 – 45.00**
9. ☐ **ATWOOD'S BITTERS—VEGETABLE JAUNDICE** Round bottle, aqua, Moses F. Atwood.	**6.50 – 10.00**
10. ☐ **ATWOOD'S BITTERS—VEGETABLE JAUNDICE** Rectangular bottle, aqua, 6-3/4" high.	**40.00 – 50.00**
11. ☐ **ATWOOD'S GENUINE BITTERS** Round bottle, aqua, 6-1/2" high.	**15.00 – 30.00**
12. ☐ **ATWOOD'S JAUNDICE BITTERS** 12-sided bottle, aqua, "Moses Atwood", 6-1/4" high.	**5.00 – 8.50**
13. ☐ **ATWOOD'S JAUNDICE BITTERS** 12-sided bottle, "FORMERLY MADE BY MOSES AT-WOOD", aqua, 6" high.	**4.00 – 7.50**

14. ☐ **ANGOSTURA BARK BITTERS**
Figural bottle, "EAGLE LIQUOR DISTILLERIES"
Amber, 7" high... **45.00 — 55.00**

15. ☐ **BERRY'S VEGETABLE BITTERS**
Square bottle with label, amber, 9-1/2" high............... **32.50**

16. ☐ **BAKER'S ORANGE GROVE BITTERS** *
Square bottle. Amber, ruby, 9-1/2" high..................... **125.00 — 150.00**

17. ☐ **BEGG'S DANDELION BITTERS**
Rectangular bottle, clear, 8" high.............................. **50.00 — 65.00**

18. ☐ **BEGG'S DANDELION BITTERS**
Square bottle, amber, 9-1/4" high. .... **50.00 — 65.00**

19. ☐ **BILLING'S MANDRAKE TONIC BITTERS**
Rectangular bottle, aqua, 8" high.............................. **10.00 — 20.00**

20. ☐ **DR. BAXTER'S MANDRAKE BITTERS**
12-sided, amber, "LORD BROS."............................... **15.00 — 20.00**
As above, clear... **6.00 — 12.00**

21. ☐ **BIG BILL BEST BITTERS**
Square bottle tapered, amber, 12" high Embossed ..... **130.00 — 150.00**

16.

17

*Other "BAKER'S ORANGE GROVE"   **90.00 — 150.00**

26.

27.

**All Prices are for Original Bottles
in Very Fine to Mint Condition**

30.

Item, Description, Date	Retail

22. ☐ **DR. BELL'S BLOOD PURIFYING BITTERS**
Rectangular bottle, amber, 9-7/8" high...................... **120.00 — 150.00**

23. ☐ **BENGAL BITTERS**
Square bottle, amber, 8-7/8" high. .... **50.00 — 70.00**

24. ☐ **BOKER'S STOMACH BITTERS**
Round bottle, paper label, amber, 12-1/2" high........... **30.00 — 40.00**

25. ☐ **BENDER'S BITTERS**
Rectangular bottle, aqua, 10-1/2" high...................... **65.00 — 80.00**

26. ☐ **BOURBON WHISKEY BITTERS** *
Barrel shape bottle, amber, 9" high. .... **160.00 — 200.00**

27. ☐ **BERSHIRE BITTERS — PIG †**
Pig shape Figural bottle "AMANN & CO.", amber,
10" long.. **200.00 — 280.00**

28. ☐ **BROWN'S CELEBRATED INDIAN HERB BITTERS** **
Indian maiden Figural, amber, 12-1/2" high. .... **350.00 — 450.00**

*Also in Green & Puce **Black Very Rare $450.00 — $600.00
†Large - Olive amber $1500.00

Item, Description, Date	Retail

29. ☐ **BROWN'S IRON BITTERS**
Square bottle, amber, 8-1/2" high. .... **20.00 — 30.00**

30. ☐ **BROWN'S AROMATIC BITTERS**
Oval bottle, aqua, 8-1/2" high................................... **60.00 — 75.00**

31. ☐ **BURDOCK BLOOD BITTERS**
Rectangular bottle, clear, 8-3/4" high........................ **16.50 — 20.00**

32. ☐ **BURDOCK BLOOD BITTERS**
Square bottle, machine made, aqua. .... **6.00 — 15.00**

32a.☐ **BURNNETT'S COCAINE (MEDICAL)**
Rectangular bottle, light green, 6-3/4" high................. **35.00 — 50.00**

33. ☐ **CALIFORNIA FIG BITTERS**
Square bottle, "CALIFORNIA EXTRACT OF FIG CO.",
Amber, 9-5/8" high... **60.00 — 70.00**

34. ☐ **CALIFORNIA WINE BITTERS**
Round bottle "M. KELLER, LOS ANGELES", pale
green, 12-3/8" high. .... **50.00 — 65.00**

35. ☐ **CALDWELL'S HERB BITTERS ***
Multi-sided bottle, "GREAT TONIC" amber,
12-5/8" high. .... **150.00 — 175.00**

36. ☐ **DR. CALLENDER & SONS LIVER BITTERS**
Square bottle "CELEBRATED LIVER BITTERS", light
amber, 9-5/8" high...

37. ☐ **CARACAS BITTERS**
Round bottle, pale green, 12-3/8" high....................... **40.00 — 50.00**

38. ☐ **CANTON BITTERS**
Round bottle, Lady's Leg neck, amber, 12-1/8" high. **160.00 — 180.00**

39. ☐ **CARTER'S LIVER BITTERS**
Oval bottle, with label, amber 8-5/8" high................... **85.00 — 110.00**

40. ☐ **CELEBRATED BERLIN STOMACH BITTERS**
Square bottle, light green, 9-1/2" high. .... **75.00 — 100.00**

*Caldwell's "Iron Bitters" RARE   **180.00 — 220.00**

All Prices are for Original Bottles
in Very Fine to Mint Condition

32A.

28.

35.

38.

39.

REPRODUCTIONS ARE MADE

Item, Description, Date	Retail

41. ☐ **E.R. CLARKE'S SARSAPARILLA BITTERS**
Rectangular bottle, aqua, 7-7/8" high.......................... **70.00 — 90.00**

42. ☐ **CLARK'S GIANT BITTERS**
Rectangular bottle, "PHILADA-PA." aqua, 6-3/4" high. **35.00 — 55.00**

43. ☐ **CLARKE'S COMPOUND MANDRAKE BITTERS**
Oval bottle, aqua, 7-5/8" high................................... **40.00 — 65.00**

44. ☐ **CLAYTON & RUSSELL'S BITTERS**
Square bottle, "CELEBRATED STOMACH BITTERS"
label, amber, 8-7/8" high. .... **22.00 — 30.00**

45. ☐ **CARMELITER KIDNEY & LIVER BITTERS**
Square bottle, "CARMELITER STOMACH BITTERS
CO.—NEW YORK", amber, 10-5/8" high..................... **35.00 — 45.00**

46. ☐ **COCAMOKE BITTERS**
Square bottle, amber, 9" high. .... **45.00 — 65.00**

47. ☐ **COMPOUND HEPATICA BITTERS**
Oval bottle, "H.F. SHAW M.D." Aqua, 8-3/8" high. **75.00 — 90.00**

Item, Description, Date	Retail

48. ☐ CLIMAX BITTERS
Square bottle, "SAN FRANCISCO—CAL.", amber,
9-1/2" high. .... **60.00 — 75.00**

49. ☐ CONSTITUTION BITTERS
Rectangular bottle, " SEWARD & BENTLEY", Olive
green, 9-1/2" high. .... **100.00 — 130.00**

50. ☐ DAMIANA BITTERS
Round bottle, "BAJA CALIFORNIA", Aqua,
11-5/8" high. .... **45.00 — 55.00**

51. ☐ DAMIANA BITTERS
Round bottle, "LEWIS HESS MFG". .... **40.00 — 50.00**

52. ☐ DANDELION XXX BITTERS
Rectangular bottle, clear, 7-3/4" high........................ **50.00 — 65.00**

53. ☐ DEMUTH'S STOMACH BITTERS
Square bottle, amber, 9-5/8" high. .... **35.00 — 50.00**

54. ☐ DEVIL—CERT STOMACH BITTERS
Round bottle, clear, 8" high...................................... **55.00 — 70.00**

55.

55

**with
paper
label**

56.

Item, Description, Date	Retail

55. ☐ **DE WITTS STOMACH BITTERS**
Flask bottle, "CHICAGO", amber, 7-7/8" high............. **45.00 — 60.00**

56. ☐ **DOYLE'S HOP BITTERS**
Square bottle, "1872", light amber, 9-1/2" high. .... **24.00 — 30.00**

57. ☐ **DIMMITT'S 50CTS BITTERS**
Flask bottle, "SAINT LOUIS", amber 6-1/2" high. **75.00 — 85.00**

57a. ☐ **S.T. DRAKES PLANTATION X BITTERS**
Square, "log cabin" shape, 10" high many variations
known, amber...................... **40.00 — 85.00**
Citron yellow, olive green, dark green........................ **85.00 — 150.00**

58. ☐ **EAGLE AROMATIC BITTERS**
Round bottle, "EAGLE LIQUOR DISTILLERIES", yel-
low amber, 6-3/4" high... **20.00 — 30.00**

59. ☐ **EAGLE LIQUOR DISTILLERIES ANGOSTURA BARK
BITTERS**
Figural bottle
Round bottle, amber, 7-1/8" high.............................. **70.00 — 90.00**

60. ☐ **EAST INDIA ROOT BITTERS**
Gin shaped bottle "BOSTON MASS", amber,
9-5/8" high. .... **120.00 — 150.00**

All prices shown are approximate for Mint Condition

Item, Description, Date   Retail

61. ☐ **ELECTRIC BITTERS**
Square bottle, "H.E. BUCKLEN & CO., CHICAGO,
ILL." amber, 9" high.. **20.00 — 35.00**

62. ☐ **"ELECTRIC" BRAND BITTERS**
Square bottle, "H.E. BUCKLEN & CO. CHICAGO, ILL.",
amber, 8-3/4" high.. **15.00 — 25.00**

63. ☐ **DR. E.P. EASTMAN'S YELLOW DOCK**
Rectangular bottle, "LYNN MASS." aqua, 7-3/4" high.   **40.00 — 60.00**

64. ☐ **SIR EDGAR'S ENGLISH LIFE BITTERS**
Square bottle, "C.E. GRAVES—PROPRIETOR", amber,
9" high. .... **80.00 — 95.00**

57.

57A.

62.

63.

BITTERS BOTTLES

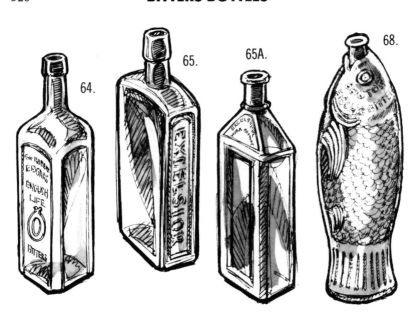

Item, Description, Date	Retail

65. ☐ **EXCELSIOR BITTERS**
Rectangular bottle, amber 9-3/8" high. .... **95.00 — 115.00**

65a. ☐ **EXCELSIOR HERB BITTERS**
Rectangular, roofed shoulder, amber, 10" high. .... **120.00 — 140.00**

66a. ☐ **FAVORITE BITTERS**
Round barrel shape, "POWELL & STUTENROTH",
amber, 9-1/4" high. .... **130.00 — 160.00**

66. ☐ **EMERSON EXCELSIOR BOTANIC BITTERS***
Rectangular bottle, "E.H. BURNS—AUGUSTA-MAINE"
amber, 9" high. .... **8.50 — 16.00**

67. ☐ **DR. M. M. FENNERS CAPITOL BITTERS**
Rectangular bottle, "FREDONIA—N.Y.", aqua,
10-1/2" high. .... **35.00 — 45.00**

*Sun Colored $50.00 — $60.00

Item, Description, Date   **Retail**

68. ☐ **DR. FISCH'S BITTERS** *
Figural fish shape bottle, "W.H. WARE", yellow amber,
and brown amber, 11-5/8" high.................................. **160.00 — 185.00**

69. ☐ **THE FISH BITTERS** **
Figural fish shape bottle, "W.H. WARE, PATENTED
1866", yellow amber & dark amber, 11-5/8" high. **160.00 — 190.00**

70. ☐ **FERRO QUINA STOMACH BITTERS**
Square bottle, "BLOOD MAKER", ladies leg neck,
amber 9" high. .... **85.00 — 100.00**

71. ☐ **DR. FLINT'S QUAKER BITTERS**
Rectangular bottle, "PROVIDENCE — R.I.", aqua,
9-5/8" high. .... **20.00 — 35.00**

71a.☐ **FOWLER'S STOMACH BITTERS**
Square, light amber, "STOMACH BITTERS," 10" high. **180.00 — 200.00**

*Amber   **100.00 — 130.00**

Clear - Very Rare   **450.00 — 600.00

66A.   70.   71A.

Item, Description, Date

72. ☐ **DR. GILMORES LAXATIVE—KIDNEY & LIVER BITTERS**
Oval bottle, amber, 10-3/8" high.............................. 80.00 — 90.00

72a. ☐ **DR. GODDIN'S BITTERS**
Square, aqua, "GENTIAN BITTERS", 10" high............. **160.00 — 180.00**

72b. ☐ **GOLDEN BITTERS**
Rectangular, aqua, "GEO. C. HUBBEL & CO.",
10-1/4" high. .... **75.00 — 95.00**

73. ☐ **GOLDEN SEAL BITTERS**
Square bottle, amber, 9" high. .... 82.50 — 100.00

74. ☐ **GERMAN BALSAM BITTERS**
Square bottle, "W.M. WATSON & CO.", milk glass,
9" high. 85.00

74a. ☐ **GERMAN HOP BITTERS**
Square, amber, "READING MICH." 9-1/2" high. .... 35.00 — 65.00

74b. ☐ **GERMAN TONIC BITTERS**
Square, aqua, "BOGGS, COTMAN & CO." 9-3/4" high.. 120.00

74A. 74B. 72A.

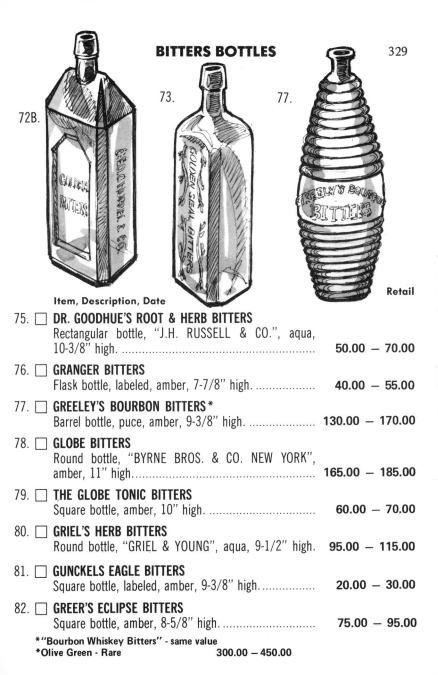

72B.

73.

77.

Retail

Item, Description, Date

75. ☐ **DR. GOODHUE'S ROOT & HERB BITTERS**
Rectangular bottle, "J.H. RUSSELL & CO.", aqua,
10-3/8" high. .... **50.00 — 70.00**

76. ☐ **GRANGER BITTERS**
Flask bottle, labeled, amber, 7-7/8" high. .... **40.00 — 55.00**

77. ☐ **GREELEY'S BOURBON BITTERS** *
Barrel bottle, puce, amber, 9-3/8" high. .... **130.00 — 170.00**

78. ☐ **GLOBE BITTERS**
Round bottle, "BYRNE BROS. & CO. NEW YORK",
amber, 11" high. .... **165.00 — 185.00**

79. ☐ **THE GLOBE TONIC BITTERS**
Square bottle, amber, 10" high. .... **60.00 — 70.00**

80. ☐ **GRIEL'S HERB BITTERS**
Round bottle, "GRIEL & YOUNG", aqua, 9-1/2" high. **95.00 — 115.00**

81. ☐ **GUNCKELS EAGLE BITTERS**
Square bottle, labeled, amber, 9-3/8" high. .... **20.00 — 30.00**

82. ☐ **GREER'S ECLIPSE BITTERS**
Square bottle, amber, 8-5/8" high. .... **75.00 — 95.00**

*"Bourbon Whiskey Bitters" - same value
*Olive Green - Rare   **300.00 — 450.00**

Item, Description, Date	Retail

83. ☐ **GOLD LION BITTERS**
Round bottle, Labeled, clear 6" high............................. **20.00 — 30.00**

84. ☐ **HAGAN'S BITTERS**
Multi-sided bottle, amber, 9-5/8" high. .... **100.00 — 120.00**

85. ☐ **HALL'S BITTERS**
Barrel-shape bottle, pale amber, dark amber,
9-1/2" high. .... **75.00 — 100.00**

86. ☐ **HALL'S BITTERS**
Barrel-shape bottle, "NEW HAVEN", amber, 9-3/8" high. **105.00 — 125.00**

87. ☐ **HARTWIG'S CELEBRATED ALPINE BITTERS ***
Square bottle, "ST. JOSEPH MISSOURI", golden am-
ber, 9-3/8" high.. **100.00 — 120.00**

87a.☐ **HART'S STAR BITTERS**
Oval, clear glass, "PHILADELPHIA, PA." 9" high......... **70.00 — 90.00**

88. ☐ **HAVIS IRON BITTERS**
Square bottle, "WILLIAMSBURG KY" amber, 8" high. **65.00 — 85.00**

85.

87 A.

*European "Hartwig's"   **65.00 — 105.00**

All prices shown are approximate for Mint Condition

Item, Description, Date	Retail

89. ☐ **HENDERSON'S CAROLINA BITTERS**
Square bottle, amber, 9-5/8" high. .... **65.00 — 85.00**

90. ☐ **DR. HARTERS WILD CHERRY BITTERS**
Rectangular bottle, "ST. LOUIS", amber, 8" high. **30.00 — 40.00**

91. ☐ **DR. HARTER'S WILD CHERRY BITTERS**
Rectangular, "DAYTON, O.", amber, 8" high. .... **40.00 — 50.00**

92. ☐ **DR. HARTER'S WILD CHERRY BITTERS**
Pint size, same as above, 4-3/4" high. .... **25.00 — 35.00**

93. ☐ **HERKULES BITTER**
Figural-ball shape bottle, "1 QUART," Labeled, deep
green, 7-3/4" high. .... **65.00 — 85.00**

94. ☐ **DR. R.F. HIBBARD'S WILD CHERRY BITTERS**
Round bottle, "C.N. CRITTENTON," aqua, 8" high. **80.00 — 95.00**

95. ☐ **HILL'S MOUNTAIN BITTERS**
Rectangular bottle, "INDIANA DRUG SPECIALTY
COMPANY", amber, 7-3/4" high................................. **35.00**

96. ☐ **DR. J. HOSTETTER'S STOMACH BITTERS ***
Square Bottle 9" High
Dark green, Olive Green, Crude .... **85.00 — 120.00**
Amber, "L & W" on base..................................... **15.00 — 20.00**
Black with bubbles... **80.00 — 120.00**
Amber—18" FLUID OZ."—8-3/4" high...................... **12.00 — 14.00**
Misspelled "STOMACHIC", 8-3/4" high...................... **16.00 — 20.00**
Machine made, amber or green, brown .... **7.50 — 12.00**

97. ☐ **DR. HOFFLAND'S GERMAN BITTERS**
Rectangular bottle, "LIVER COMPLAINT", aqua,
8" high. .... **35.00 — 45.00**

98. ☐ **DR. HOOFLAND'S GERMAN BITTERS**
Rectangular bottle, aqua, pint 4" high........................ **25.00 — 35.00**

*"S. McKee & Co." on base   **7.00 — 15.00**

90.

99.

93.

102A.

102B.

102C.

Item, Description, Date   **Retail**

99. ☐ **HOPS & MALT BITTERS**
Square bottle, yellow amber, amber, 9-5/8" high......... **60.00 — 75.00**

100. ☐ **HYGEIA BITTERS**
Square bottle, "FOX & CO.", amber, 9" high................ **50.00 — 65.00**

101. ☐ **HOP & IRON BITTERS**
Square bottle, "UTICA N.Y." amber, 8-5/8" high. **35.00 — 50.00**

102. ☐ **HILL'S HOREHOUND BITTERS**
Round bottle, labeled, "IRISH MOSS" 6-1/2" high....... **7.50 — 12.00**

102a.☐ **HORSE SHOE BITTERS**
Horseshoe shape, amber, "COLLINSVILLE ILLS."........ **180.00 — 240.00**

102b.☐ **H.P. HERB WILD CHERRY BITTERS**
Square, cabin shape, brown & gold amber, 10" high. **120.00 — 145.00**

102c.☐ **ISAACSON SEIXAS & CO. BITTERS**
Square, light amber, "66 & 68 COMMON ST."
10-3/8" high. .... **160.00 — 180.00**

104.

107.

108A.

BITTERS BOTTLES

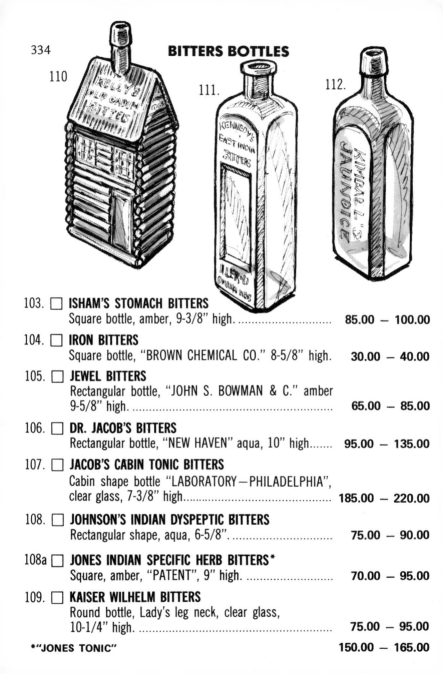

110

111.

112.

103. ☐ **ISHAM'S STOMACH BITTERS**
Square bottle, amber, 9-3/8" high. .... **85.00 — 100.00**

104. ☐ **IRON BITTERS**
Square bottle, "BROWN CHEMICAL CO." 8-5/8" high. **30.00 — 40.00**

105. ☐ **JEWEL BITTERS**
Rectangular bottle, "JOHN S. BOWMAN & C." amber
9-5/8" high. .... **65.00 — 85.00**

106. ☐ **DR. JACOB'S BITTERS**
Rectangular bottle, "NEW HAVEN" aqua, 10" high....... **95.00 — 135.00**

107. ☐ **JACOB'S CABIN TONIC BITTERS**
Cabin shape bottle "LABORATORY—PHILADELPHIA",
clear glass, 7-3/8" high... **185.00 — 220.00**

108. ☐ **JOHNSON'S INDIAN DYSPEPTIC BITTERS**
Rectangular shape, aqua, 6-5/8". .... **75.00 — 90.00**

108a ☐ **JONES INDIAN SPECIFIC HERB BITTERS***
Square, amber, "PATENT", 9" high. .... **70.00 — 95.00**

109. ☐ **KAISER WILHELM BITTERS**
Round bottle, Lady's leg neck, clear glass,
10-1/4" high. .... **75.00 — 95.00**

*"JONES TONIC" **150.00 — 165.00**

BITTERS BOTTLES

Item, Description, Date   **Retail**

110. ☐ **KELLY'S OLD CABIN BITTERS** *
Cabin-shape bottle, "PAT. 1863", deep amber, light
amber, 9-1/8" high...RARE **475.00 — 650.00**

As above "1870", amber............................... RARE **250.00 — 300.00**

111. ☐ **KENNEDY'S EAST INDIA BITTERS**
Square bottle, clear glass, 9" high............................. **35.00 — 50.00**

112. ☐ **KIMBALL'S JAUNDICE BITTERS**
Rectangular bottle, amber-green, 7-1/8" high. .... **150.00 — 175.00**

113. ☐ **KING SOLOMON BITTERS**
Rectangular bottle, amber, 8-1/2" high...................... **75.00 — 95.00**

114. ☐ **LOWELL'S INVIGORATING BITTERS**
Square bottle, "BOSTON-MASS." aqua, 8-1/4" high. **35.00 — 60.00**

115. ☐ **LACOUR'S BITTERS**
Round bottle, amber, 9-1/8" high.............................. **50.00 — 65.00**

As above, light apple green............................. RARE **450.00 — 475.00**

As above, yellow green.........................VERY RARE **475.00 — 525.00**

*Green Very Rare   **1200.00**

115.   116.   117

with
paper
label

BITTERS BOTTLES

336

120C.

120A.

120B.

117A.

116. ☐ LADY'S LEG BITTERS *
Round bottle, "REEDS", amber, 8-1/4" high.............. **65.00**

117. ☐ LASH'S KIDNEY & LIVER BITTERS
Square bottle, "CATHARTIC—BLOOD PURIFIER", amber, 9-1/8" high.. **20.00 — 35.00**
Many varieties of "LASH'S BITTERS" known, in amber, clear, amethyst, labeled, etc...................................... **15.00 — 30.00**

117a.☐ LASH'S BITTERS CO.—VARIANTS
Round, cylindrical, "NEW YORK, CHICAGO, SAN FRAN- CISCO", clear, aqua, amber, 10-1/2" to 11-1/2". **25.00 — 50.00**

118. ☐ LINCOLN BITTERS
Rectangular bottle, labeled, clear glass, 9-3/8" high. **40.00**

119. ☐ LIPPMAN'S GREAT GERMAN BITTERS
Square bottle, "SAVANNAH GEORGIA", amber, 10" high... **65.00 — 90.00**

120. ☐ LITTHAUER STOMACH BITTERS
Gin shape bottle, milk glass, 9-1/4" high. .... **100.00 — 125.00**

120a.☐ DR. LOEW'S CELEBRATED STOMACH BITTERS
Square, deep green, 9-1/2" high. .... **130.00 — 160.00**

120b.☐ LOHENGRIN BITTERS
Square-gin shape, milk glass, 9-1/2" high................... **175.00 — 200.00**

*Olive Green, Red, Amber, Coppertone   **SAME PRICE**

Item, Description, Date	Retail

120c. ☐ **DR. LOVE GOODS FAMILY BITTERS**
Square, cabin shape, amber, 10-1/2" high. .... **250.00 — 375.00**

121. ☐ **MACK'S SARSPARILLA BITTERS**
Rectangular bottle, "SAN FRANCISCO", amber,
9-1/4" high. .... **90.00 — 110.00**

122. ☐ **MALARION BITTERS**
Square bottle, "ST. LOUIS, MO.", amber, 9-1/2" high. **75.00**

122a. ☐ **MCKEEVER'S ARMY BITTERS**
Round, drum shape, amber 10-1/2" high. .... **850.00 — 1200.00**

123. ☐ **McNEIL'S INDIAN VEGETABLE BITTERS**
Oval bottle, labeled, aqua, 6-3/4" high. **28.50**

124. ☐ **MISHLER'S HERB BITTERS**
Square bottle, "DR. HARTMAN & CO." yellow-amber. **35.00 — 50.00**

124a. ☐ **MORNING STAR BITTERS ***
Triangular, amber, "INCEPTUM 5869", 13" high. .... **180.00 — 200.00**

124b. ☐ **MOULTONS OLOROSO BITTERS**
Round, aqua, ribbed bottle, 11-1/2" high. .... **115.00 — 125.00**

125. ☐ **MURRAY'S PURIFYING BITTERS**
Rectangular bottle, labeled, aqua, 8" high. .... **20.00 — 30.00**

126. ☐ **NATIONAL BITTERS**
Figural-corn shaped bottle, "1867", amber,
12-1/2" long. .... **185.00 — 250.00**
as above, olive-yellow .... **360.00 — 475.00**

127. ☐ **NIGHTCAP BITTERS**
Multi-side bottle, "SCHMIDLAPP & CO.", clear glass,
9-3/8" high. .... **60.00 — 80.00**

128. ☐ **NORTHCRAFTS BOTANIC BITTERS**
Square bottle, labeled, machine made, amber,
9-1/4" high. .... **8.50 — 12.50**

129. ☐ **O'LEARY'S 20th CENTURY BITTERS**
Square bottle, amber, 8-1/2" high. .... **75.00 — 95.00**

*With Iron Pontil   **Rare**   **220.00 — 250.00**

BITTERS BOTTLES

All Prices are for Original Bottles in Mint Condition

Item, Description, Date	Retail
130. ☐ **OLD CABIN BITTERS** Cabin-shape bottle, "PATENTED 1863", amber, 9" high.	**130.00 — 160.00**
140. ☐ **OLD HOMESTEAD WILD CHERRY BITTERS *** Cabin-shape bottle, golden amber, 10" high.	**100.00 — 140.00**
*Old Homestead - Citrine Color — Very Rare	**600.00 — 750.00**

**ALL PRICES SHOWN ARE APPROXIMATE FOR VERY FINE
TO MINT CONDITION**

Item, Description, Date	Retail

141. ☐ OLD SACHEM BITTERS & WIGWAM TONIC
Barrel-shape bottle, amber, 9-3/8" high. .... 85.00 — 110.00

As above, red amber .... 130.00 — 160.00
As above, yellow.. 130.00 — 160.00
As above, emerald green .... 140.00 — 165.00
As above, aqua... 90.00 — 115.00

142. ☐ OLD DR. SOLOMON'S INDIAN WINE BITTERS
Rectangular bottle, aqua, 8-1/2" high......................... 45.00 — 65.00

143. ☐ ORANGE BITTERS
Round bottle, labeled, machine made, pale green,
11-3/4" high. .... 15.00 — 30.00

144. ☐ OXYGENATED BITTERS
Rectangular bottle, "FOR DYSPEPSIA", aqua, 8" high. 40.00 — 60.00

145. ☐ ORRURO BITTERS
Round bottle, dark green, machine made, 11-1/8" high 12.00 — 18.00

146. ☐ ORIGINAL POCAHONTAS BITTERS
Barrel-shape bottle, "FERGUSON" 9-1/2" high.............. 95.00 — 115.00

147. ☐ DR. PALMERS TONIC BITTERS
Square bottle, labeled, aqua, 8-3/4" high.................... 7.50 — 15.00

148. ☐ PAINE'S CELERY COMPOUND BITTERS
Rectangular bottle, amber, 8" high............................. 6.50 — 12.00

As above, clear glass. .... 7.50 — 15.00

149. ☐ PATENTED BITTERS
Square bottle, "CHICAGO", amber, 9-1/4" high........... 60.00 — 75.00

150. ☐ PAWNEE BITTERS
Rectangular bottle, "INDIAN MEDICINE CO.", aqua,
8-5/8" high. .... 100.00 — 120.00

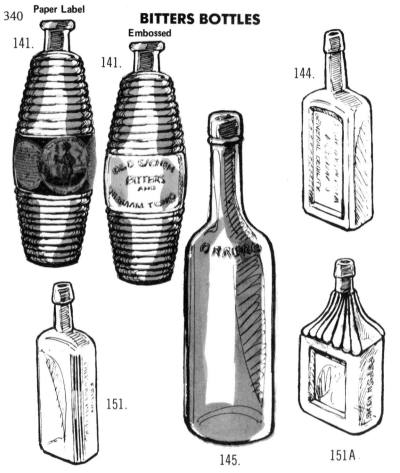

Paper Label

BITTERS BOTTLES

Embossed

141.

141.

144.

151.

145.

151A.

Item, Description, Date	Retail

151. ☐ **PEPSIN CALISAYA BITTERS**
Square bottle, "DR. RUSSEL" pale green, 4-3/8" high. **20.00 – 30.00**
As above, emerald green. 8" high .... **30.00 – 60.00**

151a.☐ **PEPSIN BITTERS (DAVIS)**
Rectangular, yellow-green, "CHICAGO, U.S.A.",
8-1/2" high. .... **160.00 – 175.00**

Item, Description, Date	Retail

152. ☐ **PENN'S FOR THE LIVER BITTERS**
Square bottle, amber, 8-1/2" high. .... **50.00 — 60.00**

153. ☐ **PERUVIAN BITTERS**
Square bottle, amber, 9-1/4" high. .... **25.00 — 35.00**

154. ☐ **PHOENIX BITTERS ***
Rectangular bottle, "NEW YORK" dark green,
5-3/8" high. .... **130.00 — 140.00**

154a. ☐ **DR. PETZOLDS GENUINE GERMAN BITTERS**
Oval, log cabin, amber, 10-1/4" high. .... **125.00 — 150.00**

155. ☐ **DR. PORTER STOMACH BITTERS**
Rectangular bottle, labeled, clear glass, 5-1/2" high. **10.00 — 20.00**

153.

154 A.

156A.*

156.

with paper label

*Aqua — various sizes 25.00 — 50.00

BITTERS BOTTLES

158 A.

157

163A.

161.

with paper label

Item, Description, Date	Retail

156. ☐ **PRICKLY ASH BITTERS**
Square bottle, amber, 9-3/4" high. .... 25.00 — 45.00

As above, machine made.. 7.50 — 15.00

157. ☐ **POND'S BITTERS**
Square bottle, "UNEXCELLED LAXATIVE", clear glass,
9-7/8" high. .... 30.00 — 45.00

158. ☐ **DR. GEORGE PIERCE'S INDIAN RESTORATIVE BITTERS** *
Rectangular bottle, "LOWELL, MASS.", aqua,
7-1/2" high. .... 35.00 — 45.00

158a. ☐ **PRUNE STOMACH & LIVER BITTERS**
Square, amber, 9" high... 70.00 — 85.00

159. ☐ **RED CLOUD BITTERS**
Square bottle "TAYLOR & WRIGHT," green, 9-1/2" high 95.00 — 120.00

160. ☐ **REX KIDNEY & LIVER BITTERS**
Square bottle, "LAXATIVE & BLOOD PURIFIER",
red-amber, 10" high. .... 45.00 — 60.00

*With label or Pontil 45.00 — 55.00

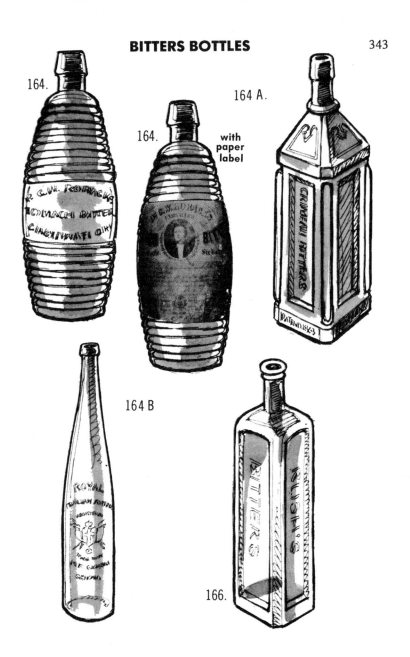

164.

164.

**with
paper
label**

164 A.

164 B

166.

Item, Description, Date	Retail

161. ☐ **W.L. RICHARDSON'S BITTERS**
Rectangular bottle, "MASS." aqua, 7" high.................. **45.00 — 60.00**

162. ☐ **RED JACKET BITTERS**
Square bottle, "BENNET & PIETERS", amber,
9-1/2" high. .... **50.00 — 65.00**

163. ☐ **RED JACKET BITTERS**
Rectangular bottle, "MONHEIMER & CO.", amber,
8-1/2" high. .... **45.00 — 60.00**

163a.☐ **REED'S BITTERS**
Round, ladies leg neck, 12-1/2" high......................... **225.00 — 275.00**

164. ☐ **DR. C.W. ROBACK'S STOMACH BITTERS**
Barrel-shape bottle, "CINCINNATI, O.", brown,
9-1/2" high. .... **120.00 — 180.00**

164a.☐ **ROMAINES CRIMEAN BITTERS**
Square, amber, "PATEND 1863", 10" high.................. **95.00 — 120.00**

164b.☐ **ROYAL ITALIAN BITTERS**
Round, tall, red amber, 13-1/2" high. .... **75.00 — 85.00**

165. ☐ **ROYAL PEPSIN STOMACH BITTERS**
Rectangular bottle, amber, 9" high............................ **65.00 — 85.00**

166. ☐ **RUSH'S BITTERS**
Square bottle, "A.H. FLANDERS, M.D. N.Y.", aqua,
pint size... **10.00 — 20.00**
As above, amber, 9" high. .... **30.00 — 40.00**

167. ☐ **RUSS' ST. DOMINGO BITTERS**
Square bottle, NEW YORK", amber, 10" high............... **55.00 — 65.00**

168. ☐ **ROSSWINKLE'S CROWN BITTERS**
Square bottle, amber, 8-3/4" high. .... **70.00 — 80.00**

168a.☐ **SAZERAC AROMATIC BITTERS**
Round, ladies leg neck, milk white, cobalt blue,
12" high... **250.00 — 350.00**

Item, Description, Date	Retail

169. ☐ **SANBORN'S LAXATIVE BITTERS**
Rectangular bottle, labeled, clear glass, 10" high.........   **20.00 — 30.00**

169a ☐ **SANDORN'S KIDNEY & LIVER VEGETABLE BITTERS**
Rectangular, amber, 10" high. ....   **85.00 — 120.00**

170. ☐ **SAN GENTO BITTERS**
Square bottle, "DR. F.A. MITCHELL'S" amber,
8-3/4" high. ....   **65.00 — 75.00**

168 A.

165.

169 A.

Prices quoted are for original bottles.

Item, Description, Date   **Retail**

180. ☐ **SARASINA STOMACH BITTERS**
Square bottle, amber, 9-1/4" high. .... **85.00 — 125.00**

181. ☐ **SAZERAC AROMATIC BITTERS**
Round bottle, "PHP & CO.", milk white, lady's leg
neck, 12" high. .... **Rare** **275.00 — 380.00**

As above, amber, 6" high. .... **325.00 — 400.00**

182. ☐ **GENERAL SCOTT'S ARTILLERY BITTERS**
Figural-cannon shape bottle, "NEW YORK", amber,
13" long. .... **850.00 — 1250.00**

182a.☐ **SEAWORTH BITTERS COMPANY**
Round, light house shape, light gold amber, "CAPE
MAY", 11-1/2" high. .... **62.50 — 70.00**

182.

182 A.

183 A.

VERY RARE

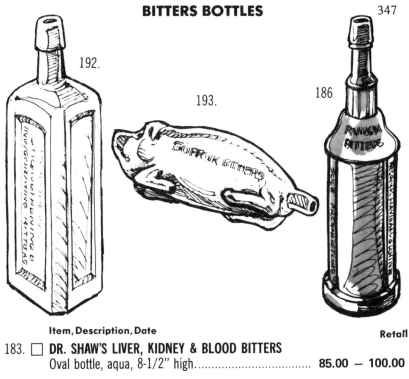

192.

193.

186

Item, Description, Date	Retail

183. ☐ **DR. SHAW'S LIVER, KIDNEY & BLOOD BITTERS**
Oval bottle, aqua, 8-1/2" high.................................. **85.00 — 100.00**

183a. ☐ **SIMON'S CENTENNIAL BITTERS**
Figural, bust shape, aqua, amber, clear, 10-1/4" high. **50.00**

184. ☐ **DR. SKINNER'S CELEBRATED 25¢ BITTERS**
Rectangular bottle, "SO. READING, MASS." aqua.
9-1/2" high. ....**100.00 — 120.00**

185. ☐ **DR. SKINNER'S SHERRY WINE BITTERS**
Rectangular bottle, "SO. READING MASS." aqua,
8-1/2" high. .... **95.00 — 115.00**

186. ☐ **S.C. SMITH'S DRUID BITTERS**
Barrel shape bottle, brown, 9-1/2" high.....................**250.00 — 280.00**

186a. ☐ **SOL FRANCKS PANACEA BITTERS**
Round, light house, amber, 10" high. .... **95.00 — 110.00**

BITTERS BOTTLES

All prices shown are for Mint Condition

Item, Description, Date	Retail

187. ☐ **SOMER'S STOMACH BITTERS**
Square shape bottle, amber, 9-1/2" high. .... **65.00 — 80.00**

188. ☐ **STEKETEE'S BLOOD PURIFYING BITTERS**
Square bottle, amber, 6-1/4" high. .... **55.00 — 70.00**

189. ☐ **DR. STOEVER'S BITTERS**
Square, "KRYER & CO.", amber, 9" high...................... **75.00 — 95.00**

190. ☐ **SUMTER BITTERS**
Square bottle "CHARLESTON, S.C.", light amber,
9-1/2" high. .... **75.00 — 95.00**

191. ☐ **SUN KIDNEY & LIVER BITTERS**
Square bottle, "VEGETABLE LAXATIVE", amber 9-1/2"
high, machine made. .... **42.50 — 60.00**

192. ☐ **SOLOMON'S STRENGTHENING & INVIGORATING BITTERS**
Square bottle, "SAVANNAH-GEORGIA," cobalt blue,
9-3/4" high. .... **180.00 — 220.00**

193. ☐ **SUFFOLK BITTERS** *
Figural-pig shape bottle, "PHILBROQK & TUCKER",
yellow amber, 9-3/4" long....................................... **425.00 — 475.00**

194. ☐ **THORN'S HOP & BURDOCK TONIC BITTERS**
Square bottle, "BRATTLEBORO, VT.", amber; 8" high. **27.50**

195. ☐ **TIP-TOP BITTERS**
Multi-sided bottle, labeled, amber, 8-1/2" high. **27.50**

195a. ☐ **TONOLA BITTERS**
Square, aqua, "PHILADELPHIA", 8" high. .... **40.00 — 60.00**

196. ☐ **TUFTS TONIC BITTERS**
Rectangular bottle, labeled, aqua, 9" high................... **15.00**

196a. ☐ **TURNER'S BITTERS**
Rectangular, clear glass, 8" high. .... **50.00 — 65.00**

*Amber pig RARE **275.00 — 325.00**

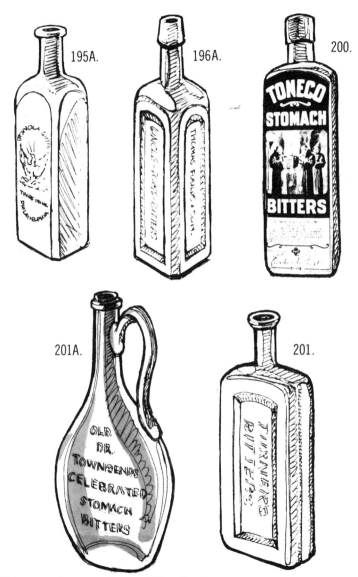

195A.

196A.

200.

201A.

201.

Prices are for very fine to Mint Condition

BITTERS BOTTLES

201B.

202A.

202B.

197. ☐ **TURNER BROTHERS BITTERS**
Barrel shape bottle, labeled, amber, 9-3/8" high......... **130.00 — 180.00**

198. ☐ **TIPPECANOE BITTERS**
Round bottle, log and canoe shape, olive, amber,
8-1/2" high. .... **65.00 — 85.00**

199. ☐ **TYLER'S STANDARD AMERICAN BITTERS**
Square bottle, amber, 9" high. .... **75.00 — 95.00**

200. ☐ **TONECO STOMACH BITTERS**
Square bottle, "APPETIZER & TONIC" clear glass........ **30.00 — 45.00**

201. ☐ **UNCLE TOM'S BITTERS**
Square bottle, "THOMAS FOULD'S & SON", pale
amber, 10" high.. **75.00 — 95.00**

201a.☐ **OLD DR. TOWNSENDS CELEBRATED STOMACH BITTERS**
Handled jug, light amber, 8-3/4" high........................ **100.00 — 130.00**

201b.☐ **TRAVELLERS BITTERS**
Oval, amber, 10-1/2" high 1834/1870 Embossed ....**850.00 — 1200.00**

VERY RARE

All prices shown are for Original Bottles

Item, Description, Date	Retail

202. ☐ **UNDERBERG-ALBRECHT**
Round bottle, labeled, red-amber, lady's leg neck, 12" high.. **40.00 — 60.00**

202a. ☐ **U.S. GOLD BITTERS**
Square, aqua, "U.S. 1877", 10" high. .... **180.00 — 200.00**

202b ☐ **USQEBAUGH BITTERS**
Square-tapered aqua, 10-1/2" high............................ **150.00 — 180.00**

203. ☐ **ALEX VON HUMBOLDT'S STOMACH BITTERS**
Square bottle, pale amber, 10" high.......................... **65.00 — 85.00**

204. ☐ **PETER VIERLING'S BLOOD PURIFYING BITTERS**
Square bottle, amber, 10" high. .... **60.00 — 82.50**

205. ☐ **VERMO STOMACH BITTERS**
Square bottle, "TONIC & APPETIZER", Clear glass, 9-1/2" high. .... **22.50 — 30.00**

205.

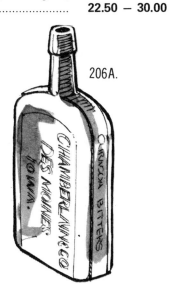

206A.

209.

206B.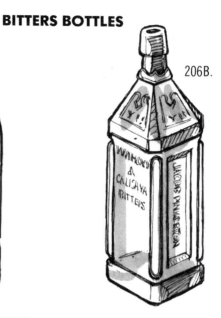

206. ☐ **VICTORIA TONIC BITTERS**
Square bottle, "MEMPHIS TENN", pale amber,
9-1/2" high. .... **80.00 — 95.00**

206a. ☐ **DR. VON HOPF'S CURACOA BITTERS**
Rectangular, amber, "CHAMBERLAIN & CO.",
7-7/8" high. .... **25.00 — 40.00**

206b. ☐ **WAHOO & CALISAYA BITTERS**
Square, amber, "JACOB PINKERTON," 10" high.......... **55.00**

207. ☐ **WALLACE'S TONIC STOMACH BITTERS**
Square bottle, amber, 9" high. .... **110.00 — 140.00**

208. ☐ **WARD'S EXCELSIOR BITTERS**
Rectangular bottle, "C.H. WARD & CO.", clear glass,
8" high. .... **40.00 — 60.00**

209. ☐ **WARNER'S SAFE TONIC BITTERS***
Oval bottle, labeled, "ROCHESTER—N.Y.", amber,
7¼" high, embossed.. **250.00 — 325.00**

*9—5/8" High **60.00 — 80.00**

Item, Description, Date	Retail
210. ☐ **WARNER'S KIDNEY & LIVER CURE** Oval bottle, labeled, amber.	**22.50 — 32.50**
210a.☐ **.I.N.C. BITTERS** Round, barrel-shape, amber, 10-1/2" high.	**120.00**
210b.☐ **WEST INDIA STOMACH BITTERS** Square, amber, "ST. LOUIS MO." 10" high.................	**45.00 — 70.00**
210c ☐ **WHEELER'S BERLIN BITTERS** Hexagonal, olive green "BALTIMORE" 9-1/2" high.......	**145.00 — 175.00**
211. ☐ **WHITE'S STOMACH BITTERS** Square bottle, amber, 9-3/8" high.	**60.00 — 75.00**
212. ☐ **WILD CHERRY & BLOOD ROOT JAUNDICE BITTERS** Round bottle, labeled, aqua, 9-1/2" high.	**8.50 — 15.00**
213. ☐ **N. WOOD'S BILOUS BITTERS** Rectangular bottle labeled, aqua, 6" high.	**12.00 — 17.50**

210 C.

210 A.

210.

210 A.

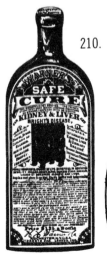

Item, Description, Date	Retail

213a. ☐ **DR. WILSON'S HERBINE BITTERS**
Oval, aqua, 6" high.. 30.00 — 40.00

214. ☐ **WILDERS STOMACH BITTERS**
Square Cabin shape bottle, "WHOLESALE DRUGGISTS"
clear glass.. 110.00 — 140.00

214a. ☐ **DR. WONSER'S U.S.A. INDIAN ROOT BITTERS**
Round, amber, 10-1/2" high. .... 95.00 — 120.00

214b. ☐ **WOODCOCK PEPSIN BITTERS**
Rectangular, Smoky amber, 8" high. .... 75.00 — 95.00

215. ☐ **WOODS TONIC WINE BITTERS**
Square bottle, "CINCINNATI OHIO", aqua, 9-3/4" high. 80.00 — 100.00

213 A.

214 A.

214 B.

216.

217.

218.

Item, Description, Date

216. ☐ **YERBA BUENA BITTERS***
Flask bottle, "S.F. CAL", amber, 8-3/8" high. .... **60.00 — 75.00**

217. ☐ **ZOELLER'S STOMACH BITTERS**
Rectangular bottle, amber, 9-1/2" high...................... **62.50 — 87.50**

218. ☐ **ZINGARI BITTERS**
Round bottle, lady's leg neck, amber, 11-1/4" high. **150.00 — 180.00**

*Other "Yerba Buena" Bottles   SAME VALUE
Dark amber, pint bottle   100.00 — 125.00

All prices are for Original Bottles in Very Fine to Mint Condition.

Bottles were used in the trade for containing tonic and shampoo. They were made from a variety of transparent, translucent and opaque glasses.

GLASS SQUIRT TOPS FOR BARBERS' BOTTLES.

MILK GLASS

HOBNAIL

ROUND BASE   AMBER GLASS

All prices are for Original Bottles in Fine Condition With Stoppers & Tops

Item, Description, Date	Retail
☐ **AMBERGLASS**	22.50 — 30.00
☐ **AMETHYST**	25.00 — 35.00
☐ **AMETHYST.** Enamel, blown and shaped	24.50 — 32.00
☐ **BOHEMIAN GLASS.** Hand-painted floral exterior	50.00 — 80.00
☐ **CLEAR.** Blue base, ribbed sides	15.00 — 30.00
☐ **COBALT.** Dark blue, heavy enamel. Pair	50.00 — 70.00
☐ **CRANBERRY.** Matched pair	60.00 — 85.00
☐ **CRANBERRY.** Portrait of woman on exterior	35.00 — 65.00
☐ **CUT GLASS.** Cover of sterling	60.00 — 100.00
☐ **END-OF-DAY.** (Spatter-ware)	35.00 — 65.00
HOBNAIL	
☐ **AMBERGLASS**	30.00 — 53.00
☐ **DARK BLUE**	32.00 — 55.00
☐ **OPALESCENT**	45.00 — 70.00
☐ **HONEY-COLORED AMBERGLASS**	40.00 — 65.00
MILKGLASS	
☐ **HEXAGONAL BASE**	12.50 — 20.00
☐ **ROUNDED BASE**	16.00 — 24.00
☐ **STRAIGHT-FORMED NECK**	10.00 — 20.00
☐ **SAPPHIRE BLUE.** Thumbprint pattern	40.00 — 65.00
☐ **STRIPED.** Opalescent color	45.00 — 55.00
☐ **TIFFANY GLASS TYPE**	110.00 — 125.00

*Beware of reproductions

COCA-COLA BOTTLES

The "Coca-Cola" trademark, one of the best known symbols in the world, began at a soda fountain in Jacobs' Pharmacy in Atlanta Georgia in 1886. When the fountain beverage was originally bottled it was in a round embossed bottle with a Hutchinson stopper, (#1). The bottle was a returnable "deposit" bottle.

The search for an original bottle to package the popular drink led to the "Hobble Skirt" (#2), design in 1915, by Alex Samuelson of the Root Glass Co. The inspiration was the skirts worn by women in pre-World War I America. The modification of this design was the production model for the millions of Coca-Cola bottles distributed and sold throughout the world.

Through the years there have been many modifications and revisions of this basic design. Many independent bottlers through the years produced, and used local bottles of different design and embossing, these are also classified as "Coca-Cola" collectables.

All prices are for bottles in Mint Condition, with no chips, cracks, or flaws .

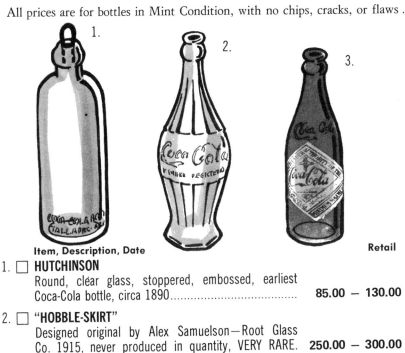

Item, Description, Date	Retail
1. ☐ **HUTCHINSON** Round, cléar glass, stoppered, embossed, earliest Coca-Cola bottle, circa 1890	**85.00 — 130.00**
2. ☐ **"HOBBLE-SKIRT"** Designed original by Alex Samuelson—Root Glass Co. 1915, never produced in quantity, VERY RARE.	**250.00 — 300.00**

ILLUSTRATIONS: *Ken Sheller*

4.

5.

6.

Item, Description, Date   **Retail**

3. ☐ **PAPER LABEL**
Applied glass top, embossed, clear glass, round
straight shape, 1915.. **12.50 — 17.50**

4. ☐ **COCA COLA BOTTLING WORKS — PHOENIX, ARIZ.**
Round, light green, embossed, 8" high, circa 1905. **12.50 — 17.50**

5. ☐ **"HOBBLE-SKIRT" COCA-COLA BOTTLE**
Production model, embossed "BOTTLE PAT'D 1916".

6. ☐ **COCA-COLA SODA**
Embossed, panels and stars, clean glass, 1920's. **8.50 — 15.00**

7. ☐ **"COCA-COLA BOTTLING CO., CHARLESTON S.C."**
Clear, round, embossed... **5.00 — 8.50**

8. ☐ **PAPER LABEL**
Round, embossed "COCA-COLA" on side, clear,
circa 1900..**Rare** **25.00 — 40.00**

9. ☐ **"BEST BYA DAM SITE"**
Embossed made by "COCA COLA BOTTLING CO.
PRODUCTS LAS VEGAS NEV.", light green, 7-3/4"
high, 1936.:...**Rare** **40.00 — 60.00**

All Prices are for Original Bottles in Mint Condition

8.

9.

10.

11.

Reproductions are made of the most valuable bottles

Item, Description, Date	Retail
10. ☐ **COCA COLA, "HOBBLE-SKIRT"** Clear, embossed "DEC. 25, 1923."	**6.00 — 9.50**
11. ☐ **FOUNTAIN SYRUP BOTTLE** Round, clear, cork closure, applied label, 1920.	**25.00 — 35.00**
12. ☐ **COCA COLA PRESENTATION** Commemorative bottle, flasked gold, applied label 1950-1960..	**100.00 — 150.00**

HISTORICAL FLASKS

• THINGS THAT A COLLECTOR SHOULD KNOW •

A scarred base or a sheared mouth is a sure sign that the flask or bottle was made previous to 1850, the scar or pontil being caused by the breaking of the glass from the iron rod which held the flask while being finished. Some time between the years 1850 and 1860 a snap was used which held the flask while finishing, doing away with the rough place or pontil, but leaving a round hollow depression in the base. About the same time a ring or collar was added to the neck or mouth, this process doing away with the sissors which were used to shear the neck while the glass was still pliable.

• HISTORY OF FLASK MAKING •

In 1813 there were several manufacturers of glass in Pittsburgh, Pennsylvania, and in 1815, at Keene, New Hampshire. About 1765 William Henry Stiegel started to manufacture glass at Mannheim, Lancaster County, Pennsylvania. In the very short time in which he made glass he made some interesting and beautiful pieces in wonderful colors, using the various shades of blue, and amethyst, and green. All these are much sought after by the collectors of old glass, a great many pieces being found in Ohio and Indiana, no doubt having been brought there by the Quakers and Mennonites from Pennsylvania in ox carts. Coming farther west to Zanesville, Ohio, we find that glass was manufactured there as early as 1815, and in Covington, Kentucky, in 1848. At Louisville, Kentucky, about 1850 or earlier, we find that many of the so-called violin flasks and the eagle flask were made.

• PRICING & VALUES • *

There is no standard or fixed price for any bottle; the supply and demand is generally responsible for prices, but not always, for sometimes there is a collector who is willing to pay a fancy price for a certain flask.

In giving the values for the bottles pictured in this book the compilers have endeavored to give a fair and impartial price, we show a price range. The price you will get for a particular bottle can vary according to such factors as the number of bottles produced, condition of your bottle, demand, prevalent economic conditions, etc.

• ACKNOWLEDGEMENT •

The Introduction, listings, and illustrations, in this section are taken from: COLLECTOR'S PRICE GUIDE TO HISTORICAL BOTTLES & FLASKS," compiled by Charles B. Gardner & J. Edmund Edwards, and used with the kind permission of the Publisher, Mr. John Edwards. For those interested in this subject we recommend the book without reservation. It is available from JOHN EDWARDS PUBLISHER, 61 Winton Place. Stratford, Conn. 06497 at a cost of $6.00.

*Accurate reproductions are made of the most valuable bottles.
  Buy only from reputable dealers and auctioneers.

All Prices are for Original Bottles in Mint Condition

Item, Description, Date	Retail

1. ☐ **WASHINGTON AND EAGLE FLASK**
Pint size, aquamarine. Bust of Washington, branch on sides. Reverse: Eagle facing right, arrows olive branch, rays, 13 stars overhead. Philadelphia about 1836. .... **250.00 — 350.00**

2. ☐ **WASHINGTON AND EAGLE FLASK**
Pint size, aquamarine. Bust of Washington, "GENERAL WASHINGTON" above, "ADAMS AND JEFFERSON, JULY 4th, A.D. 1776," on the edge. Reverse: Eagle facing to the right, rays and "E PLURIBUS UNUM" above. Kensington Glass Works, Philadelphia, about 1835. .... **125.00 — 175.00**

3. ☐ **WASHINGTON AND TAYLOR FLASK**
Quart, size, aquamarine. Bust of Washington facing right. Above, "BRIDGETOWN, NEW JERSEY." Reverse: Bust of Taylor, facing to the right. In circle over head "BRIDGETOWN, NEW JERSEY." Cohansey Glass Manufacturing Company, Bridgeport, New Jersey, about 1840. .... **110.00 — 150.00**

*4. ☐ **WASHINGTON AND EAGLE FLASK**
Quart size, aquamarine. Bust of Washington facing to the left. Reverse: A large eagle facing to the right, 7 stars above and 5 stars below. Bridgetown, New Jersey, about 1840. .... **85.00 — 130.00**

5. ☐ **WASHINGTON AND JACKSON FLASK
Pint size, olive amber. Bust of Washington in uniform, facing to the left, "WASHINGTON" above. Reverse: Jackson in uniform, facing to the left, "JACKSON" above. Baltimore, Maryland, about 1832. .... **150.00 — 190.00**

6. ☐ **BYRON AND SCOTT FLASK**
Half pint flask, light amber. Draped bust of Lord Byron, facing to the right. Reverse: Draped bust of Sir Walter Scott, facing to the left. Coventry Glass Works, at Coventry, Connecticut, 1830. .... **145.00 — 185.00**

*Green-$175.00-$195.00, Amethyst-$360.00-$420.00
**All Varieties-same approximate value.

OLD FLASKS

All Prices are for Original Bottles in Mint Condition

Beware-Reproductions are made of many of the most valuable old flasks. Buy only from reputable dealers and auctioneers.

Item, Description, Date	Retail

7. ☐ **RINGOLD AND TAYLOR FLASK** *

Pint size, aquamarine. Bust of Ringold facing right, "MAJOR" above, and "RINGOLD" at the bottom. Reverse: Bust of Taylor, at the bottom, "ROUGH AND READY." Baltimore Glass Works, at Baltimore, Maryland, about 1848. .... 90.00 — 140.00

8. ☐ **LOG CABIN FLASK**

Pint size, aquamarine. Log Cabin, rail fence, and 13 stars above. Reverse: Barrel with the Words "HARD CIDER" above, plow and flag with pole. Maker unknown, date about 1840. .... 800.00 — 1200.00

9. ☐ **EAGLE AND AGRICULTURE FLASK**

Pint size, sea green. Large eagle with shield, arrows and olive branch, resting on oval panel, "GLASS," "WIHMSENS" above. Reverse: Sheaf of grain, rake, fork, cycle, scythe and plow. Above, "AGRICULTURE." Maker unknown, Ohio, about 1830............................... 325.00 — 450.00

10. ☐ **CANNON FLASK** **

Pint size, purple tint. Cannon and balls lengthwise of Pint size, purple tint. Cannon and balls lengthwise of flask. "GENERAL TAYLOR NEVER SURRENDERS." Reverse: Small bunches of grapes. "A LITTLE MORE GRAPE CAPTAIN BRAGG." Bridgetown, New Jersey, about 1848.. 245.00 — 280.00

11. ☐ **JACKSON AND EAGLE FLASK**

Quart Size, Aquamarine. Bust of Jackson facing front. "ROUGH AND READY" overhead, eight-pointed star underneath. Reverse: Spread eagle on arrows, head left, shield on breast. 13 stars "MASTERSON" above. Maker unknown, about 1840........................... 325.00 — 450.00

*Smoky Aqua, Pint Open Pontil   130.00 — 160.00
**Orange Amber, Pint, — Rare Open Pontil   350.00 — 400.00

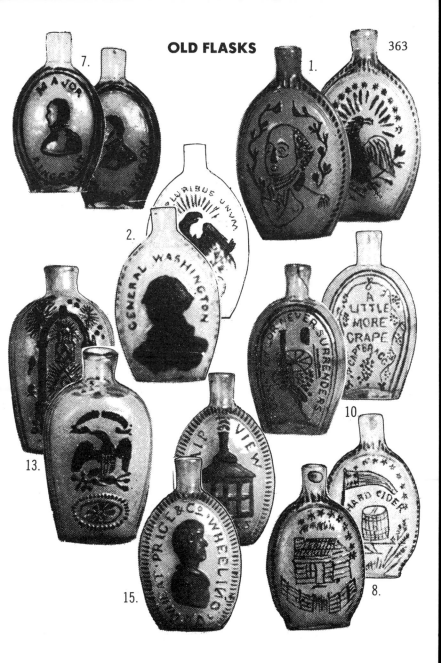

All Prices are for Original Bottles in Mint Condition

Item, Description, Date	Retail

12. ☐ **SHIP AND MASONIC FLASKS** *
Pint size, Aquamarine. Full rigged ship, "FRANKLIN" underneath. Around the edge "KENSINGTON GLASS WORKS, PHILADELPHIA." Reverse: Masonic arch sheaf of grain, pitchfork, rake, shovel, ax and scythe. Curled ornaments below. Around the sides "FREE TRADE AND SAILORS RIGHTS." Kensington Glass Works, Philadelphia, Pa., 1835.................................. **225.00 – 275.00**

13. ☐ **EAGLE AND MASONIC FLASK** **
Quart size, Sea Green. Eagle facing left, ribbon in back. Beaded oval panel below. Reverse: Masonic arch containing sunburst, square, compasses, and triangle letter "G" underneath. Numerous emblems outside. New Granite Glass Company, at Stoddard, N.H., 1840. **300.00 – 500.00**

14. ☐ **FRANKLIN AND T.W. DYOTT FLASK**
Pint size, Aquamarine. Bust of Franklin, over head "BENJAMIN FRANKLIN." On the edge "KENSINGTON GLASS WORKS, PHILADELPHIA." Reverse: Bust of T.W. Dyott. In circle overhead "T.W. DYOTT, M.D." On the edge: "WHERE LIBERTY DWELLS THERE IS MY COUNTRY." Kensington Glass Works, Philadelphia, Pa., 1834.. **160.00 – 200.00**

15. ☐ **WHEELING, VA., FLASK**
Pint size, a Beautiful Green. Unknown bust facing to the right, "WHEAT PRICE & CO., WHEELING, VA." in circle around head. Reverse: Picture of glass works in center. "FAIRVIEW" above, below "WORKS." Corrugated edge, central rib, sheared mouth, scarred base. Made by Wheat, Price and Company at Wheeling, Va., about 1845... **280.00 – 400.00**

16. ☐ Same as No. 22, except with a different bust. .... **280.00 – 400.00**

*Other "Ship" Flasks 60.00 – 100.00 Sloop & Baltimore Monument 850.00
**Eagle & Masonic, ½ pint & pint Aqua, Amber, Blue 120.00 – 300.00

OLD FLASKS

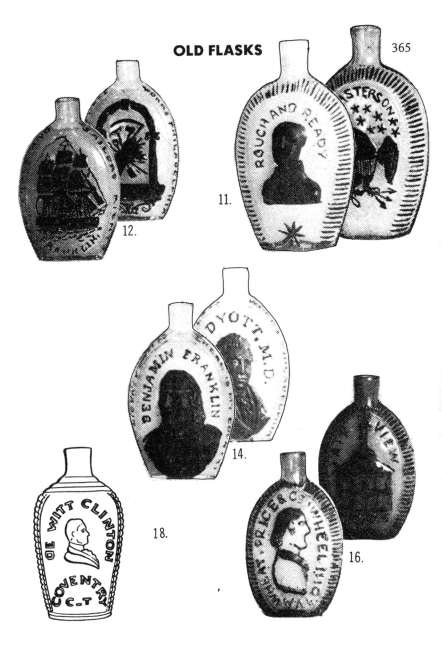

365

11.

12.

14.

18.

16.

Item, Description, Date   Retail

17. ☐ **LAFAYETTE AND EAGLE FLASK***
Pint size, Aquamarine. Bust of LaFayette facing front, "GENERAL LAFAYETTE." Around bust, "REPUBLICAN GRATITUDE" around edge. Reverse: Spread eagle with rays "E PLURIBUS UNUM" above. Shield on breast, below beaded oval with "T.W.D." On edge "KENSINGTON GLASS WORKS, PHILADELPHIA." Kensington Glass Works at Philadelphia, Pa., 1825...........

Also in Green Less Value

150.00 — 180.00

18. ☐ **LAFAYETTE AND DEWITT CLINTON FLASK**
Pint size, Olive Amber. Bust of LaFayette facing right. "LAFAYETTE" overhead, letters "T.S." below. Renverse: Bust of DeWitt Clinton, facing right, "DEWITT CLINTON" around bust, letter "D" in DeWitt being reversed. Below "COVENTRY" and "C. T." Thomas Stebbins at Coventry, Conn., about 1828. ....

Also in ½ Pint Same Value

375.00 — 475.00

19. ☐ **RAILROAD AND EAGLE FLASK****
Half-pint size, Dark Amber. Horse and loaded four-wheeled cart on rails, lengthwise of flask. Above, "RAILROAD", below "LOWELL." Reverse: Eagle with arrows and olive branch, lengthwise of flask, 13 stars surrounding the eagle. Lowell, Mass., about 1829.......

Also in Olive Green Same Value

160.00 — 280.00

20. ☐ **RAILROAD FLASK**
Pint size, Yellow Amber. Horse and loaded cart lengthwise, "SUCCESS TO THE RAILROAD" in circle around horse and cart. Reverse: A large spread eagle lengthwise, with arrows and olive branch, 17 stars surrounding the eagle. Maker unknown, about 1830........

Also in Olive Green Same Value

200.00 — 250.00

21. ☐ **EAGLE AND MASONIC FLASK**
Pint size, Sea Green. Large eagle rays over head, arrows and olive branch on a beaded panel, "OHIO" in panel. Below, "J. SHEPARD & CO." Above eagle, "ZANESVILLE." Reverse: Masonic arch and pavement. Inside of arch a sheaf of grain, shovel, rake, ax and scythe. Ornaments under arch. J. Shepard and Company, Zanesville, Ohio, about 1835. ....

175.00 — 225.00

*Other "Lafayette" Flasks ½ pint & pint   100.00 — 300.00
**Other Railroad Flasks, Aqua, Green, Puce, Clear 200.00 — 400.00

All Prices are for Original Bottles in Mint Condition

Item, Description, Date	Retail
22. ☐ **Same as above, only in golden brown**	210.00 — 260.00
23. ☐ **Same as above, only in olive green**	200.00 — 240.00

24. ☐ **EAGLE AND GRAPE FLASK**
Quart size, Aquamarine. A large eagle facing left, 13
stars above. Reverse: A large bunch of grapes. Four
ribs on each side of central rib, scarred base, sheared
mouth. Coffin & Hay at Hammonton, N.J., about 1838. 60.00 — 120.00

25. ☐ **STAG AND TREE FLASK**
Half-pint size, Aquamarine. Stag facing right, "GOOD"
"GAME" on side under head. Reverse: A large
weeping willow tree. Coffin & Hay at Hammonton,
N.J., about 1838... 140.00 — 180.00

OLD FLASKS

All Prices are for Original Bottles
in Mint Condition

21.

22.

24.

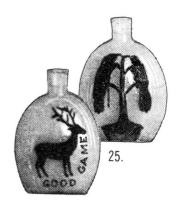

25.

**Reproductions
are made of many
OLD FLASKS.**

Ink was originally imported into America from England in ceramic jugs and in bulk, then diluted and used in ink wells.

• MASTER INKS & INK BOTTLES •

The Maynard & Noyes Company of Boston manufactured the first ink in America in 1816, many other companies soon followed. To ship, and contain their products, Master Inks, and Ink Bottles evolved. Master Inks were storage bottles made in pint and quart sizes, from which the Ink Bottles were filled.

• THE GLASS INK BOTTLE •

Ink bottles (and inkwells), were the glass containers placed on desks, and had to be both practical and attractive. Over a thousand types and varieties are known, in many different shapes influenced by the need to have a non-tippable bottle, into which a quill pen was dipped. These early bottles were hand-blown, and most have pontil marks on the bottom.

With the advent of the fountain pen around 1900, a standard square bottle evolved. Many of the early fountain pen bottles are also collectable, particularly the novelty bottle, or unusual shapes.

ACKNOWLEDGEMENTS: *Mr. John McKey II, Advertising Manager,*
THE CARTERS INK COMPANY

PICTURES COURTESY OF: *THE CARTER'S INK COMPANY,*
Cambridge, Mass. 02142

Item, Description, Date

1. ☐ **ALLINGS** *
   Clear glass, circa 1870 .... **12.50 — 20.00**

   As above, green glass .... **30.00 — 50.00**

2. ☐ **ARNOLD, P & J**
   Collared with pour-lip, brown, 9-1/4" high. .... **8.50 — 12.50**

3. ☐ **BOAT SHAPE**
   Aqua, 2-1/2" long .... **14.00 — 18.00**

4. ☐ **"BANKER'S WRITING INK"—BILLING & CO.**
   Aqua, 2" high .... **3.50 — 7.50**

5. ☐ **BOAT SHAPE**
   Clear glass, 2-1/2" long .... **14.00 — 18.00**

6. ☐ **BONNEY, W.E.** **
   Aqua, 3" high .... **12.00 — 16.00**

*Blue/Green — Rare 65.00 — 95.00
**Aqua, Barrel Shape, Pontil — Rare 50.00 — 75.00

Item, Description, Date	Retail

7. ☐ **BIXBY** *
Aqua, quart size, with spout. .... **16.00 — 20.00**

8. ☐ **BROOKS, D.B. & CO.**
Amber, 2"1 x 1-2-1/2"..................................... **20.00 — 24.00**

9. ☐ **CARTER'S**
Clear glass, 2 ounce, cork stopper Cone w/Label ..... **2.50 — 5.00**

10. ☐ **CARTER'S** No. 3
Cobalt-blue, circa 1920, embossed 6-1/8" high......... **35.00 — 55.00**

11.

12.

11. ☐ **CARTER'S — "THE CATHEDRAL"**
Cathedral shaped and embossed bottle, Blue-Black
ink "RYTO" paper label, quart size, cobalt................... **45.00 — 65.00**

As above, 3 pint size, with Label.............................. **35.00 — 50.00**
As above, 2 pint size, with Label.............................. **30.00 — 40.00**

12. ☐ **"CARTER'S — SCHOOLHOUSE"**
Aqua, with Label .... **7.50 — 12.50**

13. ☐ **CARTER'S**
Cone shaped, cobalt.. **15.00**

*CONE SHAPE, AMBER, GREEN **6.50 — 10.00**
*MUSHROOM SHAPE, AQUA **45.00 — 65.00**

INK BOTTLES

17.

18.

19.

ROUND SHAPE

CONE SHAPE

21.

20.

ROUND BASE

Item, Description, Date	Retail

14. ☐ **CARTER'S**
Cone shaped, green.. **7.50 — 12.50**

15. ☐ **CARTER'S**
Cone shaped, 1897 emerald green "Made in U.S.A.". **18.50 — 24.00**
As above, aqua 5″ high .... **4.50 — 7.50**

16. ☐ **CARTER'S**
Round base bottle, green... **5.00 — 8.00**

17. ☐ **CARTER'S "VIOLET INK"**
Round, 1882, paper label "B & S STATIONERS".......... **6.50 — 10.00**

18. ☐ **CARTER'S "COMBINED WRITING & COPYING"**
Round, paper label, 1896... **8.00 — 12.50**

19. ☐ **CARTER'S "BLACK LETTER INK"**
Round, flat bottle, paper label, 1897 , amber, green... **8.00 — 12.50**

20. ☐ **CARTER'S "VIOLET INK"**
Paper label, cone shaped, 1899 .... **6.50 — 12.00**

21. ☐ **CARTER'S "NEW CARMINE WRITING FLUID"**
Paper label, round bottle, 1906............................... **6.50 — 12.00**

Item, Description, Date	Retail

22. ☐ **CARTER'S "BLACK LETTER INK"**
Paper label, cone shape bottle Cobalt Blue............... **17.50 — 25.00**

23. ☐ **CARTER'S "VERMILLION INK"**
Paper label, square bottle, 1911................................. **4.50 — 6.50**

24. ☐ **CARTER'S "HOUSEHOLD INK-RED"**
Paper label, square bottle, 1911.............................,.... **6.50 — 8.50**

25. ☐ **CARTER'S "KOAL BLACK INK"**
Paper label, square bottle, 1916................................. **2.50 — 5.00**

26. ☐ **CARTER'S "FOR FOUNTAIN PENS"**
Paper label, square bottle, 1932............................... **2.00 — 4.00**

27. ☐ **CARTER'S "MR. & MRS. CARTER"**
Figural shaped bottles, round base, 3-5/8" high,
figures in color Made in Germany .... **PAIR** **85.00 — 120.00**

28. ☐ **CAW'S "NEW YORK"**
Embossed in circle, aqua or clear. 2¾" high.............. **8.50 — 14.50**

29. ☐ **CONE SHAPE** *
Blown in the mold, aqua, clear, approx. 2-3/4" high. **2.50 — 5.00**
As above, cobalt blue... **17.50 — 25.00**

30. ☐ **CONE SHAPE**
Blue, cobalt blue, brown, emerald, amber.................. **150.00 — 325.00**

31. ☐ **"COVENTRY"**
Blown 3 mold, olive amber, rough pontil, circa 1840. **95.00 — 130.00**

32. ☐ **CROSS PEN CO.**
Aqua, 2-3/4" high . 12 panels "CPC"........................ **18.50 — 26.50**

33. ☐ **DIAMOND INK CO.— "MILWAUKEE"**
Embossed in ring square, clear, 1-5/8" high............... **5.00 — 10.00**

34. ☐ **DIAMOND INK CO**
Amethyst. 2¼" square.. **3.50 — 6.50**

***UMBRELLA, 8-SIDED, PANELLED, AQUA, AMBER
GREEN, 2¼" to 2¾" RARE**   **30.00 — 90.00**

All Prices are for Original Bottles in Mint Condition

25.

23.

26.

24.

22.

29.

27.

INK BOTTLES

Item, Description, Date   Retail

35. ☐ **EARLE'S INK CO.**
Pouring lip, tan, 6-1/8" high..................................... **12.00 — 16.00**

36. ☐ **EDISON INK CO.**
Clear 2-7/8" high.. **4.50 — 8.50**

37. ☐ **FARLEY P. CO.**
Sheared top, dark green, 2" high Umbrella................ **60.00 — 85.00**

38. ☐ **FARLEY'S (STODDARD)**
8 sided, amber 3" high, Open pontil .... **285.00 — 325.00**

39. ☐ **GREENWOOD'S**
Sheared top, clear 1-1/2" high................................. **6.00 — 10.00**

40. ☐ **HALEY INK CO.**
Clear glass, 2-5/8" high round shape .... **12.00 — 18.00**

41. ☐ **HARRISON'S COLUMBIAN INK***
Sheared top, aqua glass, 1-1/2" high , 8 sided.......... **50.00 — 90.00**

42. ☐ **HIGGINS "CHARLES M. HIGGINS & CO."**
Master ink, aqua .... **10.00 — 15.00**

43. ☐ **HIGGINS INKS, "BROOKLYN N.Y."**
Round bottle, amethyst 2" high................................ **3.50 — 6.00**

44. ☐ **HOOKER'S**
Sheared top, aqua, 2" high with penholders .... **40.00 — 60.00**

45. ☐ **HUNT PEN CO. "SPEEDBALL, U.S.A."**
Round bottle, paper label, clear................................ **.50 — 1.00**

46. ☐ **J. & I. E. M. (MOORE TURTLE) ****
Amber glass... **75.00 — 100.00**

47. ☐ **JOHNSON INK CO.**
Sheared top, dark green, 5-7/8" hih. .... **25.00 — 40.00**

48. ☐ **KIDDER F.**
Light green, round bottle with lip 2-1/2" high............. **26,50 — 30.00**

*EMBOSSED 8-SIDED, OPEN PONTIL, GREEN, COBALT BLUE, SAPPHIRE BLUE
AQUA — 10.00 — 15.00   **— 75.00 — 100.00
  COBALT BLUE — 325.00 — 400.00

CONE SHAPE

30.

SQUARE SHAPE

33.

49.

Item, Description, Date	Retail

49. ☐ **KELLER INK "DETROIT"**
Square bottle, screw-on top, amethyst, 2" high........... 25.00 — 35.00

50. ☐ **KELLER**
Round bottle, amethyst, 2-1/2" high........................... 2.50 — 5.00

51. ☐ **L.E. WATERMAN CO.**
Machine made clear glass, with label. .... 4.50 — 6.50

52. ☐ **MAYNARD'S writing ink (MAYNARD & NOYES)**
Sheared top, dark green, amber case, 2" high............. 45.00 — 80.00

53. ☐ **MOORE & SON 1885**
Sheared top, aqua, 1-7/8" high Squat cylinder .... 7.50 — 10.00

54. ☐ **MOSES BRICKETT (BRICKETT & THAYER)**
Olive green, 4-1/2" high................................. RARE 150.00 — 180.00

55. ☐ **MILLE FIORI GLASS**
Paperweight base of bottle...................................... 60.00 — 80.00

56. ☐ **MAYNARD & NOYES, "BOSTON"**
Rough pontil with label , Aqua, Olive Green.............. 60.00 — 90.00

57. ☐ **NATIONAL SURETY INK**
Clear glass, 9" high... 12.00

58. ☐ **OLIVER TYPEWRITER**
Round bottle, clear glass, 2" high............................. 5.50 — 7.50

Item, Description, Date	Retail
*59. ☐ **OPDYKE** Barrel shape, 4 rings around barrel, clear glass, 2" high.	13.50 — 17.00
60. ☐ **PREMIUM, "PREMIUM BLACK"** Paper label, octagon shape, aqua	15.00 — 20.00
61. ☐ **"PENN. MFG. WORKS PHILADELPHIA"** Embossed, eight flat sides, white glass (milk glass)	12.50 — 16.00
62. ☐ **PARKER** Cobalt glass, 2-1/2 high, Diamond shape, embossed	7.50 — 12.00
63. ☐ **PENNELL, J.W.** Aqua, 2" high	20.00 — 25.00
64. ☐ **READ'S** Aqua-blue glass, 2" high	30.00 — 32.50
65. ☐ **ROUND INK BOTTLES** Light blue, clear glass, cobalt blue, 2-1/2" to 3" As above, 9-1/2" high, pouring spout	3.00 — 6.00 8.00 — 15.00
66. ☐ **S.S. STAFFORD'S Quart bottle, master pouring, with spout, aqua, cobalt blue	14.50 — 20.00
67. ☐ **SANFORD'S INK** Round bottle, clear glass, crown top, 2-1/2" high.	7.00 — 15.00
68. ☐ **SANFORD'S INKS & LIBRARY PASTE** Pint size, oval base, amber, crown top, 7-3/8" high.	5.00 — 8.50
69. ☐ **SIGNET INK "PERMANENT WRITING FLUID— LE PAGES"** Paper label, round bottle, cobalt blue	13.50 — 20.00
70. ☐ **SQUARE INK BOTTLES** Amethyst, aqua, cobalt blue, 2-1/2" high.	2.50 — 6.50

*Aqua, embossed - 50.00 — 60.00
**Other S.S. STAFFORD'S - 7.50 — 18.00, Teal Green - 35.00 — 45.00

Milk bottles were first made in the late 1800's in the U. S., largely as a health measure during the time milk was delivered and dipped from a large community can. The "Father of the Milk Bottle" is considered to be Dr. Harvey D. Thatcher. Thatcher was a druggist from Potsdam, New York, who in 1883, invented and produced the first true milk bottle, "THE MILK PROTECTOR", a round glass bottle embossed with a cow being milked by a farmer. The bottle closed with a Lightning fastener.

• EARLY MILKS •

"THE GLASS MILK JAR" made by the Whitney Glass Works in 1888, the F. K. Ward "MILK PRESERVING JAR", and the products of the A. G. Smalley, company were some of the other products of the period. The round bottle was the most popular milk bottle shape until the 1940 introduction of the square bottle for shipping and storage of milk.

• THE CREAM TOP •

The Cream Top bottle was popular in the 1930's, and resulted in the production of some interesting variations. Homogenized milk did away with the need for these bottles.

• EMBOSSING •

Embossing was the most available and economical way of placing lettering or designs on milk bottles. Since the cost was low, most dairies had personalized milk bottles, creating the enormous variety of designs and types that can be found today.

• MILK BOTTLES AS COLLECTABLES •

Interest in this container is relatively recent, but growing rapidly. The most difficult to locate are the early ones before the waxed tagboard disc was pressed into the top to form a seal. 1900 might be considered an approximate dividing line for the new type still used today.

Interest in the newer bottles is likely to grow with the continual replacement of home deliveries and the glass bottle by the paper container used in the super-market. In fact it will not be long before some of these paper containers may be added to some collections. The early ones may not be easy to come by because they were disposable.

SIZES & COLORS: Milk bottles were made in a large variety of sizes, from miniature promotion bottles to one gallon. The most popular sizes are ½ pint, and quart. The great majority of milk bottles are of clear glass, some are of amber, and a few of amethyst, this color occurs when the clear glass bottle is exposed to the ultra-violet rays of the sun.

MILK BOTTLES

All prices are for Mint Condition

Item, Description, Date	Retail

1. ☐ *ABSOLUTELY PURE MILK
   Thatcher Milk Protector bottle, 1884 Quart, Rare .... **50.00 — 65.00**

2. ☐ **A.G.S. & CO. (A.G. SMALLEY & CO.), 1898**
   Handle & top. clamp top, metal bands .... **45.00 — 60.00**

3. ☐ **AMERICAN DAIRY CO.**
   1930's, round bottle, embossed, quart..................... **2.50 — 3.50**

4. ☐ As above, 1/4 pint... **4.50 — 6.50**

5. ☐ **ARDEN**
   1930, round bottle, embossed................................. **3.50 — 5.00**

6. ☐ **ARDEN**
   Applied label.. **2.50 — 3.50**

7. ☐ **BABY FACE (FIGURAL)****
   Embossed baby face on cream top SUNSHINE
   DAIRY, square bottle ½ pt., pt., quart .... **3.50 — 6.00**

8. ☐ **BIRCH CREEK DAIRY**
   1930's, Applied label, pint .... **2.50 — 3.50**

9. ☐ **BORDEN CONDENSED MILK**
   Tin Top, circa 1900, ribbed & embossed. .... **10.00 — 15.00**

10. ☐ **BORDENS**
    Round, quart, "Cream Top" applied label.................. **3.50 — 4.50**
    a. ☐ Half pint, round, ribbed, embossed......................... **2.50 — 3.50**
    b. ☐ 1940's, quart, square, amber "BORDEN'S & ELSIE",
    Applied label... **3.50 — 4.50**
    c. ☐ Half pint, round, applied label. .... **1.50 — 2.00**

11. ☐ **BRIGHTON PLACE DAIRY "ROCHESTER, N.Y."**
    Quart, round bottle, embossed, circa 1934, green
    glass. Rare .... **40.00 — 50.00**

12. ☐ **BROOKFIELD (DOUBLE BABYFACE)****
    Embossed on cream top, square bottle...................... **4.50 — 6.50**

*Reproductions made "CROWNFORD CHINA CO." 1965

"BABYFACE" Single, & Double, other companies ½ pt., pt., quart. **2.50 — 5.50

MILK BOTTLES

All prices are for Mint Condition

Item, Description, Date	Retail
13. ☐ **CALIFORNIA DAIRIES**	
Half pint, round, embossed......................................	**2.50 — 3.50**
14. ☐ **CALISTOGA CREAMERY**	
Quart, round, embossed, neck ribs............................	**3.00 — 5.00**
15. ☐ **CANYON CREEK DAIRY**	
Quart, round, applied label, "PASTURIZED"...............	**2.50 — 3.50**
16. ☐ **CAPITOL CITY CO. CREAMERY**	
Quart, round, embossed "CO-OPERATIVE".................	**2.50 — 3.50**
17. ☐ **CARNATION**	
Quart, round, embossed "CARNATION".....................	**2.00 — 4.00**
18. ☐ **CLOVERDALE**	
Round, quart, applied label..	**2.00 — 4.00**
19. ☐ **CLOVERLEAF DAIRY**	
Round, quart, embossed with 4 leaf clover................	**3.50 — 5.00**
20. ☐ **CLOVERLEAF HARRIS DAIRY**	
Round, embossed, cream separator top.	**5.00 — 7.50**
21. ☐ **COOS BAY MILK ASSOCIATION**	
Round, half pint, embossed, "ribbed" neck...............	**3.00 — 5.00**
22. ☐ **CRYSTAL CREAMERY CO.**	
Round, 12 oz. embossed...	**4.50 — 6.50**
23. ☐ **CRYSTAL MILK JAR**	
Round, tin top, embossed, "WT & CO." (WHITALL TATUM & CO.) circa 1880's RARE.	**100.00 — 125.00**
24. ☐ **DARIGOLD***	
Square, quart, applied label	**2.00 — 3.50**
25. ☐ **DAIRY, INC.**	
1/2 pint, round, embossed, amethyst.........................	**3.50 — 5.50**
26. ☐ **DAIRYLAND**	
Quart, round, embossed with cow.	**5.00 — 7.00**

*DAIRYLEE "BABYFACE"   **6.00 — 8.00**

Item, Description, Date	Retail
27. ☐ **DAIRYLAND (CANADIAN)** Square quart, applied label.	**2.50 — 4.50**
28. ☐ **DAMASCUS** Round, quart, embossed.	**3.00 — 5.00**
29. ☐ **DAMASCUS CREAMERY** Pint, round, embossed amethyst.	**3.50 — 6.00**
30. ☐ **E.L. RIKERS DAIRY** Round, quart, embossed "BATH"	**2.50 — 4.00**
31. ☐ **EMPIRE DAIRY** 1/2 Pint, round, embossed, circa 1920	**4.50 — 6.00**
32. ☐ **EUGENE STORE BOTTLE** Round, pint, embossed "10¢ STORE BOTTLE"	**2.50 — 4.00**
33. ☐ **FAIRMONT** Round, pint, embossed "FAIRMONT"	**2.50 — 4.00**
34. ☐ **FAIRVIEW DAIRY** Square, 1/2 pint, applied label	**1.50 — 2.50**
35. ☐ **FAIRVIEW FARMS** Square, quart, amber with white lettering.	**6.50 — 8.00**
36. ☐ **F.K. WARDS MILK JAR** Round bottle, tin top, embossed "MILK PRESERVING JAR", etc. circa 1890-92, VERY RARE	**150.00 — 175.00**
37. ☐ **FLUSHING DAIRY** Round, pint, embossed, cow.	**6.50 — 8.00**
38. ☐ **GRANDVIEW DAIRY** Round, quart, embossed, "BROOKLYN, N.Y.".	**2.50 — 4.00**
39. ☐ **GRAYS HARBOR PRODUCTS** Round, quart, embossed.	**2.50 — 4.00**
40. ☐ **HAMPDEN "J.H. SAVERY CREAM"** 1/2 pint, tin top, embossed, circa 1900. **Rare**	**35.00 — 50.00**
41. ☐ **HAZELWOOD** Round, "ribbed" 1/2 pint, yellow tint.	**2.50 — 3.50**

MILK BOTTLES

All prices are for Mint Condition

Item, Description, Date	Retail
42. ☐ **H.I. ARNOLD FARM DAIRY** Round 1/2 pint, embossed.	**2.75 — 3.50**
43. ☐ **HI GRADE** Round, quart, embossed..	**2.00 — 4.00**
44. ☐ **JACOBSEN DAIRY** Round, quart, embossed..	**2.50 — 4.00**
45. ☐ **JESSEN CREAMERY** Round, quart, embossed..	**2.00 — 3.50**
46. ☐ **JOHN DRAVES** Round, tin top, embossed, "UNION HILL, N.Y." circa 1890..**Very Rare**	**75.00 — 90.00**
47. ☐ **JUNIPER VALLEY DAIRY CO.** Round, quart, embossed..	**3.00 — 5.00**
48. ☐ **LANGS CREAMER, INC.** Round, quart, bulbous "Cream Top", embossed.	**5.50 — 7.00**
49. ☐ **LECOMPTE MILK CO.** Round, pint, applied label.	**2.00 — 3.00**
50. ☐ **L. TAYLOR** Round, quart, embossed..	**2.50 — 4.00**
51. ☐ **MAYFLOWER MILK** Square, quart, applied label......................................	**2.00 — 3.00**
52. ☐ **McCANN & CO.** Round, embossed, "FRESH BUTTERMILK", red, amber circa 1890's..**Very Rare**	**45.00 — 60.00**
53. ☐ **MEADOW BROOK DAIRY** Round, quart.	**2.50 — 4.00**
54. ☐ **MEDOWSWEET DAIRIES** Round, quart, embossed..	**2.50 — 4.00**

MILK BOTTLES
All Prices are for Mint Condition,

55. ☐ **MEADOWVIEW DAIRY**
Square, quart, embossed.. **4.50 — 6.00**

56. ☐ **MILK FOR HEALTH**
Square, quart, amber.. **5.00 — 7.00**

57. ☐ **MILK FOR INFANTS**
Round, tin top, embossed, circa 1890. .... Very Rare **35.00 — 45.00**

58. ☐ **MODERN DAIRY ***
Round, quart, cream top—"COP THE CREAM"............ **7.50 — 9.50**

59. ☐ **MOODY MILK**
1/2 pint, embossed.. **2.50 — 3.50**

60. ☐ **NORTHLAND MILK**
Round, quart, "Cream Top", applied label.................. **4.50 — 6.50**

61. ☐ **NPM**
Round, quart, embossed.. **3.50 — 5.00**

62. ☐ **O.K. DAIRY CO.**
Round, quart, embossed, neck studs........................ **5.00 — 7.00**

63. ☐ **ONE QUART**
Round, quart, embossed.. **2.50 — 4.00**

64. ☐ **OUR OWN DAIRIES, INC.**
Round, 1/2 pint, embossed... **6.50 — 8.00**

65. ☐ **PEOPLES DAIRY**
Round, quart, applied label amber, 1934 Rare............. **35.00 — 45.00**

66. ☐ **PICKNEY BRO. DAIRY**
Round, pint, embossed, amethyst............................. **3.50 — 5.00**

67. ☐ **PIONEER UNITED DAIRY**
Round, quart, embossed.. **3.00 — 4.50**

68. ☐ **PURE MILK NATURE FOOD**
Pint, round... **2.75 — 4.00**

69. ☐ **PURITY DAIRY CO.**
Round, quart, embossed.. **3.25 — 4.50**

*"COP THE CREAM" other companies - same value.

MILK BOTTLES

All prices are for Mint Condition

385

74.

75.

80.

79.

70.

66.

82.

Item, Description, Date	Retail

70. ☐ **QUEENS FARMS INC.**
Round, quart, embossed................................. **3.50 — 5.00**

71. ☐ **RACY CREAM CO.**
Round "bowling pin," 1 pint, embossed.............. **4.50 — 6.50**

72. ☐ **RIVIERA DAIRY**
Round, quart "Cream Top" baby face, applied label .... **4.50 — 6.50**

73. ☐ **R. TAYLOR & BRO.**
Round, quart, embossed with cow...................... **4.50 — 6.50**

74. ☐ **SALEM SANITARY MILK CO.**
Round, quart, embossed................................ **3.00 — 4.00**

75. ☐ **SALEM STORE BOTTLE**
Round, quart, embossed................................ **1.75 — 2.50**

76. ☐ **SHADY LAWN**
Round, quart, embossed................................ **1.50 — 2.50**

77. ☐ **SNIDER DAIRY & CO.**
Round, pint, embossed................................. **1.00 — 2.00**

78. ☐ **STANDARD DAIRY**
Square, quart, applied label.......................... **1.50 — 2.50**

79. ☐ **STONES DAIRY**
Round, quart, applied label, embossed neck............. **2.50 — 3.50**

80. ☐ **SUNNY BROOK DAIRY**
Square, quart, amber, white label..................... **2.50 — 4.00**

81. ☐ **THATCHERS DAIRY**
Round, quart, tin top embossed with cow, 1884......... **25.00 — 40.00**

82. ☐ **THE THATCHER MILK PROTECTOR***
Round, embossed with "ABSOLUTELY PURE MILK"
& cow being milked, 1884, VERY RARE.................... **150.00 — 200.00**

83. ☐ **TO BE WASHED AND RETURNED**
Embossed, round. pint. .... **1.50 — 2.50**

84. ☐ **TURNER CENTRE CREAMERY**
Round, embossed, machine made, circa 1903,
VERY RARE... **125.00 — 150.00**

*The first true production milk bottle.

Historical and pictoral flasks (see pages 360 - 368), were the forerunners of the collectable Old Whiskey Bottles.

• THE BININGER BOTTLES •

The earliest bottles made specifically for whiskey, where the "BININGER BOTTLES" used in the Bininger grocery stores in New York from 1830 to 1880. These bottles came in a large variety of shapes and colors. All original Biningers' are quite valuable.

• WHISKEY BOTTLES 1860-1880 •

The most common glass bottle of the years 1860-1880, was the cylindrical fifth of a gallon. They usually featured heavy embossing of the makers, or distributors name, and design embellishments. Original bottles of this period are quite scarce.

• WHISKEY BOTTLES 1880-1920 •

The use of embossing plate molds, and improvement of glass-blowing techniques, from 1880 on, saw a tremendous upsurge in bottle production of the embossed round 1/5th. The 1/2 pint, pint oval (pumpkinseed), and rectangular flasks were also produced in large quantities. The bottles of this period are the most available Whiskeys, and many are still low in price, although rising steadily.

Colors of Whiskeys: Usually clear glass, and Amber in various shades. Green glass was fairly common, while cobalt-blue is the rarest and most valuable.

BAR BOTTLES

The distillers who shipped whiskey in bulk in barrels or demijohns, gave quart or 1/5th size cylindrical clear glass bottles to bar or tavern owners to help dispense their whiskey.

These "BAR BOTTLES" were usually embellished with enameled, lettered names of the whiskey, or the company that produced it. Competition among distillers for display and attraction, resulted in elaborate lettering, gilding, molding, and hand painting.

Distillers also offered Bar Bottles with the name of the bar, or hotel inscribed. Recessed color lithographed labels covered with a glass panel are also a very valuable and desirable form of Bar Bottle.

Bar bottles generally were of clear glass and used cork stoppers.

PICTURES COURTESY OF: *Mr. Charles B. Gardner, New London, Conn., JACK DANIELS DISTILLERY, Lynchburg, Tenn.*

ACKNOWLEDGEMENTS: *Mr. William C. Handlan, JACK DANIEL DISTILLERY,*

OLD WHISKEY BOTTLES *

All Prices are for Original Bottles in Mint Condition

• I.W. HARPER •

	Name of Bottle	Retail
1. ☐	**AMBER**	15.00 — 20.00
2. ☐	**CERAMIC, 1913, NAUTICAL**	30.00 — 40.00
3. ☐	**CIRCA 1910** Clear glass, bar bottle, "PURE OLD I.W. HARPER"	25.00 — 35.00
4. ☐	**G.A.R., 1895,** Flask with metal top "G.A.R." label.	80.00 — 100.00
5. ☐	**MEDAL, POTTERY, TAN**	30.00 — 40.00
6. ☐	**WICKER COVER, AMBER GLASS**	8.50 — 16.50

• JACK DANIELS •

	Name of Bottle	Retail
7. ☐	**HIP FLASK, SILVER TOP,** Pumpkin Seed Shape	26.50 — 30.00
8. ☐	**JUG, LYNCHBURG, TENNESSEE** "Old Time"	28.00 — 32.00
9. ☐	**JUG, OLD, NO. 7**	50.00 — 60.00
10. ☐	**OLD LINCOLN COUNTY, LABEL** Round Bottle	22.00
11. ☐	**GOLD MEDAL, NO. 7, NEW** Black Label, Square	18.00 — 22.00
12. ☐	**GOLD MEDAL, NO. 7, OLD** Clear Glass, Embossed	60.00 — 75.00
13. ☐	**GOLD MEDAL OLD NO. 7, 19TH—CENTURY**	120.00 — 150.00
14. ☐	**OLD TIME DISTILLERY** No. 7, Embossed, Clear	18.00 — 25.00
15. ☐	**TENNESSEE WHISKEY** Gallon, Embossed, Clear	20.00 — 27.50
16. ☐	**S.W.T. & C.D. GUNTER** No. 7, Clear, Pint	14.50 — 18.50

*See color picture section.

All Prices are for Original Bottles in Mint Condition

Item, Description, Date		Retail

1. ☐ **BOTTLE, PROHIBITION—1920's**
Whiskey, amber. screw top, Pint .... **10.00 — 12.50**

2. ☐ **BOTTLE, PROHIBITION—1920's**
Whiskey, amber, H. 8in. Embossed spider web .... **10.00 — 12.50**

3. ☐ **BOTTLE, WHISKEY**
clear, Circa 1880. Enamelled lettering .... **17.50 — 22.50**

4. ☐ **BOTTLE, WHISKEY**
clear, Circa 1900. "LINCOLN CLUB" lettered .... **18.00 — 24.50**

5. ☐ **BOTTLE, WHISKEY**
Olive-green, H. 9in., Circa 1820. Open pontil **95.00**

*6. ☐ **BOTTLE, WHISKEY**
Amber, "STAR WHISKEY", pint pontil ....**190.00 — 220.00**

7. ☐ **BOTTLE, SPIRITS**
Light amber, green handle. "Ambrosial", Open Pontil....**175.00 — 200.00**

8. ☐ **A.M. BININGER & CO.**
Amber whiskey bottle, circa 1860. round, embossed **425.00**

9. ☐ **"BININGER'S"
Amber, square whiskey bottle. quart, pontil .... **50.00 — 65.00**

10. ☐ **"BININGER'S"
Barrel shape whiskey bottle. amber, pontil RARE ....**160.00 — 190.00**

11. ☐ **"BININGER'S"
Barrel, qt. whiskey bottle. Amber, w/label RARE ....**180.00 — 220.00**

12. ☐ **"BININGER'S"
Barrel, 3/4 qt. whiskey bottle.....................................**130.00 — 150.00**

13. ☐ **"BININGER'S"
Amber, round whiskey bottle. Embossed ....**190.00 — 230.00**

14. ☐ **"BININGER'S"—19 BROAD ST., NEW YORK**
Amber, cannon whiskey bottle circa 1860, 12" in. high **375.00 — 425.00**

*"STAR WHISKEY", Handled, open pontil, pour spout, amber, RARE **550.00**
**"OLD KENTUCKY BOURBON"

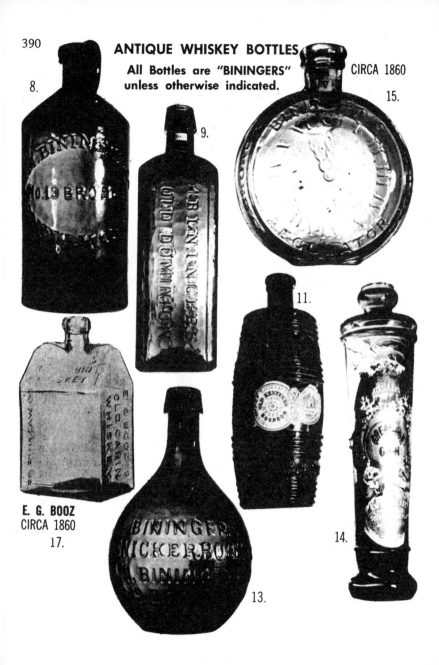

390

ANTIQUE WHISKEY BOTTLES
All Bottles are "BININGERS" unless otherwise indicated.

CIRCA 1860

8.

9.

15.

11.

E. G. BOOZ
CIRCA 1860
17.

14.

13.

OLD WHISKEY BOTTLES

15. ☐ **"BININGER'S"—19 BROAD ST., NEW YORK**
Clock, Circa 1860 whiskey bottle, dark amber............ **400.00 — 450.00**

16. ☐ **"BININGER'S"**
Amber, Circa 1865 whiskey bottle............................. **225.00 — 300.00**

*17. ☐ **E.G. BOOZ'S**
Circa 1860 whiskey bottle. **350.00**

18. ☐ **E.G. BOOZ**
Square, amber, "FED. LAW FORBIDS"........................ **8.00**

19. ☐ **E.G. BOOZ'S**
Milk glass whiskey bottle... **30.00**

20. ☐ **CROWN DISTILLERS**
Round, amber, quart, 11" high.................................. **30.00 — 40.00**

21. ☐ **CUTTER & MARTIN**
Round, amber... **15.00 — 20.00**

22. ☐ **"CASPER'S WHISKEY"**
Circa 1895 whiskey bottle, cobalt blue, embossed....... **165.00 — 200.00**

23. ☐ **CARTAN & McCARTHY**
San Francisco. Whittled, yellowish-green ₁amber,
glopped top. .... **70.00 — 80.00**

24. ☐ **COLUMBIAN**
Kentucky Bourbon. Very dark amber with picture of
explorer... **165.00**

25. ☐ **CRESCENT BOTTLE**
No Embossing except crescent. Three-piece whittle-
mold liquor bottle. Deep green................................. **25.00 — 35.00**

26. ☐ **J.H. CUTTER**
Bottled by "A.P. HOTALING & CO." Old looking,
yellowish-green amber, whittled effect, glopped´top,
concave bottom. .... **50.00 — 75.00**

*NOTE: **E.G. BOOZ "OLD CABIN WHISKEY"**, 8-1/2" High, amber, shaped like an
old log cabin—ORIGINAL..**450.00 — 600.00**
REPRODUCTIONS—Period missing after "WHISKEY",
Early Reproductions...**35.00 — 50.00**
Recent Reproductions ....**12.00 — 18.00**

OLD WHISKEY BOTTLES

All Prices are for Original Bottles in Mint Condition

Item, Description, Date	Retail

27. ☐ **J.F. CUTTER**
Extra trademark shield, "OLD BOURBON." Very crude
glopped top, yellowish-green tinted amber.................. **60.00 — 80.00**

28. ☐ **J.H. CUTTER**
"OLD BOURBON, A.P. HOTALING, SOLE AGENTS".
Crown on neck, gold amber, whittled, concave bottom,
glopped top. .... **170.00 — 200.00**

29. ☐ **J.F. CUTTER**
Trademark, "E. MARTIN CO., SAN FRAN., CALIF."
Light golden amber, very weak strike, deep whittle
effect... **150.00 — 172.50**

30. ☐ **CIRCULAR-SIDED BOTTLE**
Heavy floral embossing around rim, sides and base.
Contained Bullseye Whiskey. No other identification .... **35.00 — 40.00**

31. ☐ **COBLENTZ & LEVY**
Amethyst bottle with long neck. Inscribed with name
and address of Oregon distillers, 11-1/2" high. .... **15.00 — 20.00**

32. ☐ **COMMODORES ROYAL O.K. KENTUCKY BOURBON**
Narrow neck with crest and crown on front................. **15.00 — 17.50**

33. ☐ **DEWARS**
Round amber, "PROPERTY OF DEWAR", 12" high....... **5.00 — 8.50**

34. ☐ **DUFFY MALT WHISKEY CO.**
Round amber quart.. **6.50 — 12.00**

35. ☐ **EAR OF CORN**
Amber whiskey bottle.. **70.00 — 85.00**

36. ☐ **EARLY TIMES**
Prohibition whiskey bottle, flask shape...................... **50.00 — 65.00**

37. ☐ **GOLDEN WEDDING**
Carnival glass, "FEDERAL LAW PROHIBITS"................ **12.50 — 15.00**

38. ☐ **GOLD DUCT**
Kentucky Bourbon bottle, clear or amethyst................ **125.00**

OLD WHISKEY BOTTLES
All Prices are for Original Bottles in Mint Condition

Item, Description, Date	Retail

39. ☐ **GAMBRINUS BREWING CO.**
Amber color with tapering neck. Trademark in center of circle.. **7.00 — 9.50**

40. ☐ **KING GEORGE IV. ENGLISH WHISKEY**
Olive color. Inscribed: "PROPRIETORS. THE DISTILLERS COMPANY LTD.".. **17.50 — 20.00**

41. ☐ **G.O. BLAKE'S**
Rye & Bourbon bottle, clear glass. Blown-in-mold. **25.00 — 30.00**

42. ☐ **G.O. BLAKE'S**
Rye & Bourbon bottle, barrel shape............................ **6.00 — 8.00**

43. ☐ **GOLD THIMBLE**
Very dark amber pinch bottle. Scotch whiskey distilled in Glasgow. Inscribed "SCOTCH WHISKEY, BLOCH BROS. GLASGOW". Pointed top....................... **20.00 — 25.00**

44. ☐ **GOLDEN WEDDING**
Iridescent glass whiskey bottle .... **30.00 — 40.00**

45. ☐ **GUNDLACH**
Bundschu Wine Co. Bacchus Brand. Figure of Bacchus raising glass.. **30.00 — 40.00**

46. ☐ **HARPER, I.W.**
Round, wicker covered, handle, whiskey bottle........... **15.00 — 17.50**

47. ☐ **HARRIS, ADOLPH**
Flask, amber, 10oz.. **4.00 — 7.00**

48. ☐ **JACK DANIELS**
Circa 1900 whiskey bottle, clear .... **15.00 — 20.00**

49. ☐ **JACK DANIELS**
Circa 1910 bar, bottle, clear.................................... **20.00 — 25.00**

50. ☐ **JACK DANIELS**
Circa 1910, whiskey bottle, clear.............................. **18.50 — 22.50**

51. ☐ **J.W. FRIEDENWALD & CO.**
Whiskey bottle. **65.00**

A.B.P. — 35% to 50% of Retail

	Item Description, Date	Retail
52. ☐	**JESSE MOORE & CO.** "OLD BOURBON", Whiskey bottle, amber..................	**22.00 — 30.00**
53. ☐	**JESSE MOORE & CO.** "RYE", whiskey bottle, amber....................................	**22.00 — 30.00**
54. ☐	**JOHN & JAMES BUCHANAN'S** "WHITE LABEL" whiskey bottle, 3 part mold, dark green...	**7.50 — 10.00**
55. ☐	**KENTUCKY DEW BOURBON** Oval whiskey bottle, aqua, quart................................	**5.00 — 7.50**
56. ☐	**KEYSTONE MALT** Oval whiskey bottle, amber, Phil., Pa.........................	**12.50 — 18.00**
57. ☐	**KELLERSTRAUS DISTILLING CO.** St. Louis, whiskey bottle, amethyst color.	**18.00 — 22.00**
58. ☐	**KELLERSTRAUS** Washington, D.C. quart, whiskey bottle, clear glass.....	**16.50 — 20.00**

OLD WHISKEY BOTTLES

All Prices are for Original Bottles in Mint Condition

Item, Description, Date	Retail

59. ☐ LOUIS TAUSSIC & CO.
Amethyst whiskey bottle with screw threads inside
neck. Anagram inside circle. San Francisco.................. **25.00 — 40.00**

60. ☐ MT. VERNON
Round whiskey bottle, amber, "RE-USE PROHIBITED" **6.50 — 10.00**

61. ☐ MAIL BOX RYE
Figural Whiskey bottle, quart, clear glass. .... **95.00 — 120.00**

62. ☐ MOUNT VERNON
"PURE RYE", whiskey bottle, Circa 1890's, amber ...... **12.00 — 20.00**

63. ☐ OLD PIONEER
Whiskey pinch bottle with heavy indentations on sides
and square neck. Name inscribed across front. . . . . **15.00 — 22.50**

64. ☐ OLD BUSHMILL
Whiskey bottle, "ESTABLISHED 1784"........................ **25.00 — 30.00**

65. ☐ OLD BUSHMILL'S DISTILLERY
Whiskey bottle, "1784" quart.................................... **12.00 — 17.50**

66. ☐ OLD C.H. MOORE
"BOURBON & RYE", whiskey bottle, amber................. **20.00 — 24.00**

67. ☐ OREGON IMPORTING
Whiskey bottle, "PORTLAND ORE.", dark amber. .... **25.00 — 35.00**

68. ☐ OLD BELLE
Whiskey bottle, milk glass, 7" high, Circa 1910 .... **130.00 — 165.00**

69. ☐ OLD BELLE
Whiskey bottle, milk glass, 8-1/4" high, Circa 1910..... **120.00 — 150.00**

70. ☐ OLD GUCKENHEIMER
Round whiskey bottle, Circa 1890, paper label, amber. **30.00 — 45.00**

All Prices are for Original Bottles in Mint Condition

Item, Description, Date	Retail
71. ☐ **OLD TIMES WHISKEY** Round Whiskey bottle, "FIRST PRIZE WORLD'S FAIR 1893", clear glass	8.50 — 12.50
72. ☐ **OLD TIMES WHISKEY** Squat bottle with thatched wicker case. Inscribed: "FIRST PRIZE WORLD'S FAIR 1893"	35.00 — 50.00
73. ☐ **OLD KENTUCKY VALLEY** Square whiskey bottle, amber, paper label	30.00 — 45.00
74. ☐ **PAUL JONES** 4-1/2" in. high, whiskey bottle, amber	10.00 — 15.00
75. ☐ **PAUL JONES** 9-1/2 in. high, whiskey bottle, amber	12.50 — 15.00
76. ☐ **PAUL JONES** Round whiskey bottle, amber blob seal	14.00 — 16.50
77. ☐ **PAUL JONES** Whiskey bottle, red amber	12.00 — 16.00
78. ☐ **PEPPER DISTILLERY** Hand made sour mash. Pepper & Co., amber, whiskey bottle	50.00 — 60.00
79. ☐ **PIG WHISKEY BOTTLE*** Figural pig-shape bottle, "DRINK WHISKEY FROM THIS HOG", clear glass	55.00 — 65.00
80. ☐ **QUAKER MAID** Whiskey bottle, amber	18.50 — 26.00
81. ☐ **YE OLD MOSSROOF BOURBON** Top of bottle embossed in shape of roof. Inscribed: "RS Roehling I Schutz Inc. Chicago". Dark amber.	12.50 — 20.00

*Other Pig figural bottles, amber, milk glass, etc.   22.50 — 35.00

OTHER COLLECTOR SERIES BOOKS

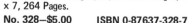

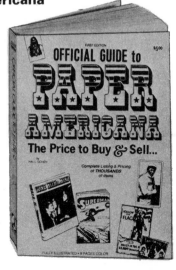

OTHER COLLECTOR SERIES BOOKS

Official Black Book of U.S. Coins

by I. Cohen, M. Dinkin, R. Morton

Contains latest dealer buying and selling prices of all U.S. Coins, Gold, Silver, Commemoratives and Proof Sets from 1793 to date, a handy check list, and photos of all types of U.S. Coins. Also Included: Introduction to Coins, History of U.S. Coins, How Coins are Minted, Where to Buy and Sell, Chart of Gold and Silver Values, comprehensive easy-to-follow Grading Section, and Mintages of all U.S. Coins. All in a handy, easy to use book. More up-to-date and accurate than any book of this type. A must for both the experienced collector and novice.

New Section on Colonial Coins from 1616 to 1796. History of Colonial Coins, up-to-date prices, grading. All coins fully illustrated.

192 Pages——Pocket Size
No. 220—$1.25   ISBN 0-87637-220-5

Official Guide to U.S. Paper Money

by Ted Kemm

This book contains latest dealer buying and selling prices of U.S. Paper Money of all denominations, Federal Reserve Notes, Silver Certificates, Gold Certificates, and Legal Tender Notes from 1861 to date, are included along with photos of each, dates, signatures, and seals. A handy check list enables you to record the note you have, and provides an inventory control. Also information on Collecting, Grading, History of Paper Money, Printing & Engraving, Where to Sell, Rareties and Fabulous Finds, and new sections on Fractional Currency, Mules & Blocks. New Section of Freaks and Errors with descriptions, up-to-date prices, Fully Illustrated. 192 Pages——Pocket Size.

No. 223—$1.25   ISBN 0-87637-223-X

Official Guide to Coin Collecting

Written by Brad Mills one of the foremost authorities and columnists in the field of numismatics. A comprehensive and thoughtful analysis of all aspects of collecting. Commencing with "Basic Approach" and concluding with "Numismatics Today" the 25 chapters cover such topics as Rare Versus Common Coins. Buying & Selling, Grading, Cleaning, Investment, Dealing, Developing a Balanced Coin Collection, Mint Errors, Medals and Tokens, Foreign Coins, Paper Money, Hoarding, Speculative Buying, Gold & Silver, and much more. Fully illustrated with many charts and prices. 192 pages Hardbound. Size: 5-3/8" X 7-7/8"

No. 238 — $2.95   ISBN 0-87637-238-8